D1266313

A Guest for the Night

A Guest for the Night

S. Y. AGNON

Translated from the Hebrew by Misha Louvish

SCHOCKEN BOOKS · NEW YORK

A Guest for the Night

CHAPTER ONE

I Came to My Home Town

On the eve of the Day of Atonement, in the afternoon, I changed from the express to the local train that runs to my home town. The Jews who had traveled with me got out and went their way, while Gentile townsfolk, men and women, made their way in. The wheels rolled sluggishly between hills and mountains, valleys and gorges; at every station the train stopped and lingered, let out people and baggage, and started up again. After two hours, signs of Szibucz sprouted from both sides of the road. I put my hand to my heart. My hand throbbed against my heart, just as my heart throbbed under my hand. The townsfolk put out their pipes and shoved them into their leggings, got up to collect their baggage, and sat down again; the women elbowed their way to the window, crying 'Rubberovitch,' and laughed. The train whistled and puffed, whistled again, then sprawled to rest opposite the station.

Along came the dispatcher called 'Rubberovitch'; his left arm had been lost in the war; the new one they gave him was made of rubber. He stood erect, waving the flag in his hand, and called: 'Szibucz!' It was many years since I had heard the name of Szibucz coming from the lips of a man of my town. Only he who is born there and bred there and lives there knows how to pronounce every single letter of that name. After Rubberovitch had got the name of Szibucz out of his mouth, he licked his mustache as if he had been munching sweetmeats, carefully scrutinized the passengers stepping down, stroked his rubber arm, and made ready to send off the train.

I picked up my two valises and walked to the back of the station yard, looking for a carriage to take me into town. The yard lay in the sun; the smell of pitch and steam mingled with that of grass and plants, the odor of railway stations in small towns. I looked this way and that, but found no carriage. This is the eve of the Day of Atonement, I said to myself, time already for the Afternoon Service, so the coachmen are not going out on the road; if you want to get to town you will have to use your feet.

It takes an ordinary man a half hour to walk to the center of town; carrying baggage, it takes a quarter of an hour more. I took an hour and a half: every house, every ruin, every heap of rubbish caught my eye and held me.

Of the large houses of two, three, or four storeys, nothing was left except the site. Even the King's Well, from which Sobieski, King of Poland, had drunk when he returned victorious from war, had its steps broken, its commemorative tablet cracked; the golden letters of his name were faded, and sprouted mosses red as blood, as if the Angel of Death had wiped his knife on them. There were no boys and girls standing on streetcorners, there was no singing, no laughter; and the well spouted water, pouring it into the street, as water is poured in the neighborhood of the dying. Every place was changed— even the spaces between the houses. Nothing was as I had seen it when I was little, nor as it had been shown to me in a dream shortly before my return. But the odor of Szibucz had not yet evaporated—the odor of millet boiled in honey, which never leaves the town from the day after Passover until the end of November, when the snow falls, covering all.

The streets stood empty, and the market too. The town was already resting from its everyday labors, and the shops were locked; surely at that moment the men were reciting the Afternoon Service and the women preparing the final meal before the fast. Except for the noise of the ground echoing my footsteps, there was no sound.

I paid no attention to the echo from the ground, and walked on, wondering where I could put down my baggage and find lodging. Looking up, I saw a group of men standing around. I went up to them and asked, 'Where can I find a hotel here?' They looked at my two bags and the clothes I was wearing, and did not answer. I asked again, 'What hotel can I stay in here?' One of them spat out a shred of tobacco from his lips, rubbed his neck a little, stared at me and said:

'D'you think there are so many hotels here that you can choose
the one you want? Of all the places in town, only two are left.'
Another said to him: 'In any case, the divorcee's is not the
right place for this gentleman.' 'Why?' 'D'you hear?' said the
second to his fellows. 'He asks why. All right, if he wants
to go there, no one will stop him.' He folded his arms and
turned his head away from me, as if to say: From now on I
wash my hands of you.

Another spoke up. 'I'll explain. When this poor woman
came back after the war, she found nothing but the house her
father had left. So she set to work and made it into a hotel,
for her and her four daughters to earn a living. But when business got worse, she stopped being too careful about her guests,
and the house became a rendezvous for sinners. Reb Hayim's
wife she was—and he such a scholar, a good man, fit to be the
rabbi of the town—and now what has become of her!' 'And
where is Reb Hayim?' I asked. 'Where's Reb Hayim? He's
a prisoner of the Russians. They took him and carried him
away to the other end of Russia, and we don't know whether
he's alive or dead, for we've heard nothing from him all these
years, except for the time when he sent his wife a bill of
divorce, so that she wouldn't remain tied all her life to a
missing man.'

I picked up my two bags and asked, 'So where *can* one
stay?' 'Where? Daniel Bach will show you. He's going home
and he lives next door.'

While he was still speaking, a man came up and said,
'You mentioned my name, so here I am. Come with me, sir,
and I will show you your hotel.'

Daniel Bach was tall and lean, his head small, his hair
chestnut, and his beard short, not pointed, not blunt; a kind
of smile hung on his lips, spreading into his sunken cheeks;
and his right leg was wooden. I walked along keeping pace, so
as not to distress him by too long steps. Daniel Bach noticed
this. 'If you are worrying about me, sir,' he said, 'you
needn't, because I walk like any other man. In fact, this man-
made leg is better than the other, which is the work of God.
It doesn't have to worry about rheumatism, and beats the
other for walking.' 'Does it come from the war?' I asked.

'Oh no,' said he, 'but the rheumatism in the other I got from the war.' Then I said, 'If that's the case, then permit me to ask, sir, were you injured in the pogroms?' He smiled and replied: 'From the pogroms I came out sound in body. And the hooligans should thank their stars they got out of my hands alive. So where did I get this leg? From the same source as all the other troubles; from things Jews have to do for a living. Hatach, "the cutter," the angel in charge of livelihoods, did not find me right with two legs, so he cut one off and made me stand on the other. How did it happen? But you have reached your hotel, and I my house, and you have to hurry for the final meal. I wish you a full atonement.' I took his hand and said to him, 'The same to you, sir.' Bach smiled and said: 'If you mean me, it's a wasted greeting, for I don't believe the Day of Atonement has any power to make things better or make them worse.' Said I, 'If it does not atone for those that do not repent, it atones for those that do.' 'I'm a skeptic,' he replied, 'I don't believe in the power of repentance.' 'Repentance and the Day of Atonement atone for half,' said I, 'and the troubles of the rest of the year for the other half.' 'I've already told you I'm a skeptic,' retorted Daniel Bach, 'and I don't believe the Almighty cares about the welfare of His creatures. But why should I be clever with you at dusk on the eve of the Holy Day? I wish you a full atonement.'

CHAPTER TWO

The Eve of the Day of Atonement

The people of the hotel received me as an untimely guest, for they had already finished the Closing Meal and were about to go to synagogue, and they were afraid I might detain them. 'Don't worry,' I told them, 'I won't trouble you much, all I ask is a place to sleep.' The innkeeper looked outside, and looked at me. Then he looked at the food left over from the meal, and looked at me again. I saw that he was considering whether it was still light enough to eat before the beginning of the fast at sunset. I too considered whether it was permissible for me to eat, for we are enjoined to add to the sacred at the expense of the secular, and to begin the fast before dark. I said to him, 'There is no time to sit down to a meal,' opened my bag, took out my festival prayer book and my prayer shawl, and went to the Great Synagogue.

In my childhood I thought that there was no bigger building in the world than the Great Synagogue, but now its area had dwindled and its height shrunk, for to eyes that have seen temples and mansions the synagogue appears even smaller than it is.

There was not a man I knew in the synagogue. Most of the worshippers were recent arrivals, who occupied the honorable places by the eastern wall and left the others empty. Some of them had risen and were walking about, either to show their proprietorship or because they did not feel comfortable in their places. The radiance that is wont to shine on the heads of the sacred congregation on the Eve of Atonement did not shine on their heads, and their prayer shawls shed no light. In the past, when everyone would come to pray and each would bring a candle, in addition to those that burned in the candelabra, the synagogue was brightly lit, but now that the candelabra had been plundered in the war and not all came to pray, the candles were few and the light was scanty. In the past, when the prayer shawls were adorned with collars of silver, the light used to gleam from them upon the heads of the worshippers, but now that the adornments had been carried off the light was diminished.

The cantor did not draw out the prayers—or perhaps he did, but that was my first prayer in my home town, and it was Atonement Eve, when the whole world stands in prayer, so I wanted to draw out the prayers even more and it seemed to me as if the cantor were cutting them shorter all the time. After he had ended the service, all the worshippers surrounded the Ark and recited the mourners' Kaddish. There was not a man there who did not say Kaddish.

After the service they did not recite psalms, nor did they chant the Song of Unity or the Song of Glory, but locked the synagogue and went home.

I walked to the river and stood there on the bridge, just as my father, of blessed memory, used to do on Atonement Eves; he used to stand on the bridge over the river because the odor of the water mitigates thirst and leads men to repentance; for as this water, which now meets your eye, was not here before this moment and will not be here afterwards, so this day, which was given us to repent of our sins, was not yet in the world before and will never be in the world again, and if you do not use it for repentance you have wasted it.

The water comes and the water goes; as it comes, so it goes, and an odor of purity rises from it. It seems as if nothing has changed since the day I stood here with Father, of blessed memory, and nothing will change here until the end of all the generations. Along came a group of boys and girls with cigarettes in their mouths. No doubt they had come from the feast they had held that night, as they do every year on Atonement Eve, to show that they are not in awe of the Day of Atonement. The stars were fixed in the firmament and their light gleamed on the river; the lights of the cigarettes moved among them. At the same time my shadow fell on the bridge and lay flat before the young people. Sometimes it mingled with their shadows and sometimes it was alone, quivering all the time as if it felt the trampling feet of the passers-by. I turned my eyes away and looked up at the sky, to see if that hand had appeared of which the children tell: they say that on Atonement Eve a little cloud, like a hand, rises in the firmament, for at that time the Almighty stretches out His hand to receive the repentant.

A young woman passed by and lit a cigarette. A young man passed by and said, 'Look out or you'll burn your mustache!'

Startled, she dropped the cigarette from her mouth. The young man bent down and picked it up. Before he could put it in his mouth or the girl's, another came up, snatched the cigarette from his hand, took the girl by the arm, and disappeared with her.

The bridge began to empty of passers-by. Some of them went to the town and some turned toward the wood behind the slaughterhouse on the bank of the Stripa beside the oaks.

I looked down at the river again. A fine odor rose from the water. I breathed in deeply and savored the air.

The well in the old market at the center of town could be heard again. Some little distance away was the gurgling of the King's Well, and the water of the Stripa also added its voice—not the water I had seen at first, for that had already gone, but fresh water, which had taken its place. The moon shone from the river and the stars began to dwindle. I said to myself: The time has come for sleep.

I went back to my hotel and found it closed. I was sorry I had not taken a key with me, for I had promised the people that I would not trouble them much, and now I had to rouse them from their sleep. Had I known that the *klois* still existed I should have gone there, for there the people would be awake all night singing hymns and psalms, and some would be studying all night long the talmudic tractates of *Yoma*, treating of the Day of Atonement itself, and *Keritot*, which deals with grave offenses.

I put out my hand to the door, as one puts out his hand when he does not expect it to open, but as I touched it the door opened. My host knew that his guest was outside, and he had not locked the door in his face.

I entered on tiptoe so as not to disturb the sleepers. If I had not worn my boots when I went out, they would not have heard my footsteps. But the streets of the town are dirty and I am fastidious, so I wore my boots, and when I came in they sensed my entrance and turned in their sleep.

A memorial light burned on the table in the middle of the dining room, and a prayer shawl and a prayer book lay there. The smell of warm povidl, which had been put away in the oven, sweetened the air of the house. For many years I had not felt its taste or come across its smell—that smell of ripe plums in the oven, which brings back the memory of days gone by, when Mother, may she rest in peace, would spread the sweet povidl on my bread. But this was not the time to think of such things, although the Torah has not forbidden the enjoyment of odors on the Day of Atonement. My host came out of his room and showed me my bed, leav-

ing the door open so that I could undress in the candlelight.
I closed the door behind him and went to bed.

The memorial candle shone into my room. Or perhaps it
did not, and it only seemed to me that it shone. I said to myself: This night I shall know no sleep. Rubberovitch's hand or
Bach's foot will come to terrify me. But as soon as I lay down
on my bed, sleep overcame me, and I slept. And it is almost
certain that I did not dream.

CHAPTER THREE

Between the Services

An hour and a half had passed since dawn. The morning dew
still lingered; an air of purity mantled the town and its ruins,
the spirit that rests on the houses of Israel on the morning of
the Holy Day. I walked slowly, saying to myself: I need not
hurry; no doubt the people have not risen too early, lest sleep
overtake them during the service. But as soon as I entered the
synagogue I saw that the Morning Service was over; they were
taking the Scrolls out of the Ark to read the Torah before the
Additional Festival Service.

Neither the Scroll the cantor was holding nor the Scroll
from which the final portion was to be read was adorned with
crown or other embellishment, for the precious sacred orna-
ments, the glory of the Torah, made of pure silver by skilled
craftsmen, had been taken by the government during the war
to buy guns and ammunition, and the Torah was left without
its adornments. The Trees of Life, the staves on which the
Scroll is rolled, protruded sadly, their faded color wringing
one's heart. See how humble is the King who is the King of
Kings, the Holy One, blessed be He, who said, 'Mine is the
silver and mine is the gold,' but has not left Himself even an
ounce of silver to adorn His Torah.

May God not think me sinful if I say that most of those
summoned to the rostrum for the reading of the Torah were
not of the kind that deserve this honor on the Days of Awe.

Why should these men have been honored on the Holy Day? Surely it is fitting to give great honor to the Almighty by summoning for the reading God-fearing men and such as study His Torah. Had they bought the honor with generous donations? Not so. On the contrary, their pledges were scanty, and I felt certain they did not esteem the honor.

I am not one of those who compare the present to days gone by, but when I see the petty standing in the place of the great, and the poor in deeds in the place of men of great achievement, I grieve over this generation, whose eyes have not seen Israel's greatness, who believe that Israel never had any greatness at all.

An old man, one of the last of the Great Synagogue's elders, chanted the portion aloud, with the proper intonation and with tears in his voice. It seemed as if he were weeping not only over the death of Aaron's sons but over the members of his own generation who had passed away. Since I had not yet recited the Morning Service I went to the old Beit Midrash to pray.

The old Beit Midrash was totally changed. The bookcases, once full, had disappeared, and nothing was left but six or seven shelves. Some of the long, heavy benches, on which the elders once sat, were empty, and others were occupied by men who saw no difference between one place and another. On the seat of the learned sage, presiding judge of the religious court, sat Elimelech Kaiser, one of the group I had met yesterday in the street; it was he who had mocked at me when I inquired about a hotel. One day, perhaps, the town will produce great scholars and restore the glory of the Torah, but the books that were lost will never be restored. Five thousand books we had in our old Beit Midrash—or perhaps only four thousand or even three thousand, but more than there were in all the other houses of study in the town and its surroundings.

The ceiling and the walls were altered, too. That ceiling, once black with soot, was now covered with whitewash, and those walls, which were worn and rubbed, were covered with plaster. I do not say that the black was more beautiful than the white, or the worn surface more pleasing than the plaster, but that soot had come from the smoke of our fathers' candles, which lighted the Torah for their study, and those walls, so long as they were worn, showed the mark of every man who had sat there. And if we felt ourselves lowly in comparison with those who had worn those walls smooth, we were important because we lived in their generation. Now the plastered walls looked as if no one had ever sat there.

The Beit Midrash was almost empty. I doubt whether there was twice the quorum of ten, and most of them worshipped without a prayer shawl. And this on the Day of Atonement, on which we worship all day wrapped in our prayer shawls. I remembered a story of how the dead came to the synagogue on the Eve of Atonement and it became very crowded; so the congregation took off their shawls and the dead went away. Thereupon it was made a custom to pray on the Eve of Atonement without a tallit. But that happened in another town and the custom was applied there at night, when the wearing of the tallit with its fringes is not obligatory; so why were they now praying without it? An old man stood before the pulpit chanting the prayers melodiously. From the way he stood it could be seen that he was a humble man, and if he had a home it was no doubt empty. Every single word he uttered showed his heart was crushed and broken. If it pleases the King of Kings, the Holy One, blessed be He, to make use of broken vessels, this vessel was suited for His use.

After the memorial prayer, some of the congregation sat down to rest. I sat among them and asked why they were praying without the tallit. 'We have not managed to buy new ones,' said one with a sigh. 'And where are the old ones?' I asked. 'Where are they? D'you think I know? Either gone up to heaven in flames or made into sheets for whores.' 'Some have been stolen and some burned,' added another. 'When were they burned and when were they stolen?' I asked. They all sighed and said, 'In the last pogrom, when the Gentiles surrounded the town and plundered us.'

Another continued: 'After the war was over and we had returned home, the pogroms came. Anyone who survived them sound in body found himself naked and barefoot. Not even a small prayer shawl was left us.' I sighed for the men of our town, who had been stricken by the judgment of God, and I looked straight ahead, like a man who has escaped sorrow himself and now takes on the sorrow of his brethren. Elimelech Kaiser misunderstood, and thought that I was disturbed because they were praying without being covered with the tallit. He stretched out one leg in front and one leg behind and looked at me sidewise, saying, 'D'you think the Almighty won't accept our prayers like this? If so, let Him ask the Gentiles to pray to Him. Now that He has given them our prayer shawls, all they have to do is to put them on and pray.' Anger and hatred flashed from his greenish-yellow eyes, which gleamed like the shell of a tortoise lying in the sun. I thought his comrades would rebuke him; not only did they not rebuke him, they liked what he said. So I left them and went over to the window.

This was one of the two windows of our old Beit Midrash that faced the hillside. When I was a boy I used to stand there at one of the tall desks studying and writing poetry. Often I would look out of that window and, as it were, try to teach the Almighty what He should do with me in the future. What a pity I did not allow my blessed Creator to do His will, for my teachings were not successful.

A wonderful light shone from the Beit Midrash upon the hillside and from the hillside upon the Beit Midrash, a light such as you have never seen in your lives, one light made up of many luminosities. Nowhere else in the world will you find such a place. I stood there and said to myself: I will not move from here until it be His will to take my soul from me. And even though I had thought of my death I was not sad. Perhaps my face was not joyful, but my heart was glad. And I am almost certain that not for years had I had this feeling: my heart was joyful but my face did not share its joy.

The elder knocked on the table and called out, 'Additional Service!' So they put back the Scrolls in the Ark and the cantor took his place before the pulpit. He bowed low, laid his head on the prayer book, and said the prayer that begins, 'Here I am, poor in deeds!' Then he recited the short Kaddish, but he mingled with the tune some of the themes of the mourners' Kaddish. Again I stared at the hill facing our

Beit Midrash and said to myself: From this side you can be
sure that they will not come to kill you. That is why our forefathers used to build their Beit Midrash next to a hill, for if
the murderers came to kill them they would take shelter there,
so that the hill might defend them on the one side and the
authorities on the other. Until a man's last day comes, he has
no better place than this.

CHAPTER FOUR

The Key

Between the Additional and the Afternoon Service, the people
came back and sat down to rest. I went over and sat down
among them.

One of them spoke up: 'Reb Shlomo took longer over the
Additional today than ever before.' 'If he takes as long over
the Closing Service, we won't eat before midnight,' replied
another. Said a third, 'Perhaps you have a pound of meat and
half a liter of wine waiting for you at home, that you are so
worried the prayer might take too long? You'll be lucky if you
have enough food for a tooth and a half.'

I broke into their conversation and said, referring to our
old Beit Midrash, 'A fine place you have.' One of them sighed
and said, 'Fine or not so fine, in any case we are leaving town
immediately after the Holy Day.' 'What do you mean, "leaving town"?' I asked. 'Leaving town means that we are going
away from the town,' he replied. 'Some are going to America
and some to other countries where even Adam never set foot.'
'And where no one is sure he will be allowed to enter,' added
the other. 'How can you leave what is certain and go to seek
what is in doubt?' said I. Said he, 'Some things are certain,
and not in any doubt; for instance, that we, who suffered
from the pogroms, certainly cannot live here.' 'I heard there
were massacres here three or four years ago and the newspapers reported them,' I said with a sigh. 'Yes, my dear
friend,' said he, 'there were massacres here—four years ago,

three years ago, a year ago, and three months ago. But the newspapers reported only the first massacres, which were a novelty, when my Gentile neighbor and I were brothers in distress and stood together as one man in battle; but when we came out alive from the war and went home, he found his fields and gardens still there, while I found nothing, and in the end he raised his hand to kill me. Then, when the massacres were repeated a second and a third time, they were no longer a novelty, and the newspapers no longer reported them. And they were right not to report them. Was it really necessary to make all the Jews depressed, or to let the Gentiles far away hear about them and learn from their brothers? As I always say, ever since they gave publicity to what happened at Kishinev, there has been no period without its pogroms. Now I don't say that Esau, the wicked one, hates blood, for Esau's hands are hot, and when he is enraged he takes an axe and kills. But to go out in gangs and kill—that they learned from the newspapers. And once they had learned, it became a habit. As for help in money and clothes, by the time one town sends help to another, it is overtaken by the pogroms and needs help itself. Now you know, sir, why we are leaving this place. We are leaving the place because He whose place is on high has left us, though He has not left us any peace.'

'Can you leave like this a place where you and your fathers lived?' said I. 'We never thought it was an easy thing,' he replied, 'but a man wants to live and not to die.' I spread out my hands toward the walls of the Beit Midrash and said, 'Will you leave this place where your fathers prayed?' 'Perhaps you would like to settle down here, sir,' said Elimelech Kaiser, 'and pray in the same place as your fathers? These tourists stay in fine great cities, and travel about all over the world, and they tell us to stay here where we are, where our fathers prayed, so that we should have the privilege of dying as holy martyrs and win the world's praises by showing what fine people the Jews are, who willingly accept suffering and die for the glory of God. Esau butchers us because it's the way of the powerful to raise his hand against the weak, and they come along and tell us that the Holy One, blessed be

He, wants to purify Israel. Isn't that so, sir? And another thing they ask of us, that we should make all our days either the Day of Atonement or the Fast of Av or Sabbath, to show that this people cleaves to its God and mourns for Jerusalem. But people's simple needs for the Sabbath, and a morsel of bread after the fast, don't interest them. You've heard the people talking; don't you know they've been standing in prayer since last night? Do you think any of us knows what he'll break his fast with?'

No man should be judged by what he says in distress. It was obvious that he too was one of those who did not know with what they would break their fast. He took my hand and said, 'Perhaps you would like to know the story of one man— for instance, that old man who led the prayers? I'll tell you. There are places in the Land of Israel they call kvutzot. Young lads and girls work there and live as laborers. His son Yeruham lived in a kvutza called Ramat Rahel. He wrote to his father: Come and stay with us, like other old men, my comrades' parents. But before the old man could make the journey, an Arab attacked his son and killed him. Now he has no son and no place to live.'

'Slander, Elimelech,' broke in one man, 'slander! Didn't Yeruham's comrades write to Reb Shlomo that he should come to them and they would give him a home and his keep as if his son were alive?' 'And if they wrote, what about it?' retorted Elimelech. 'Don't you know that he doesn't want to go? He doesn't want them to have to keep him; he has pity on them, because they have to keep the orphan Yeruham left behind him, and they themselves can hardly make a living. The Almighty knows what He is doing, but in this we are entitled to have our doubts about His ways. For what difference would it have made to Him if Yeruham had lived? Didn't he fully obey the commandment to honor one's father? Isn't that so, Reb Shlomo?'

Reb Shlomo raised his head from his prayer book, wiped both eyes with the corner of his prayer shawl, and said, 'There was not a festival when I didn't receive money from him, besides what he used to send me at other times.' As he was speaking, he fumbled in his prayer book and said, 'I will show you something interesting.' He took out a letter from the book and smoothed out the envelope. I looked at it without seeing anything interesting. The old man noticed and pointed to the stamps, saying, 'They're from the Land of Israel, with Hebrew letters on them!' And Reb Shlomo continued, 'When I received the first letter I put it in the prayer book next to the blessing "Who buildeth Jerusalem," and today I placed it in the festival book at the prayer "And because of our sins we were exiled from our Land," so as to bring to the Almighty's attention the merits of the Land for which my son gave his life.'

One man asked Reb Shlomo, 'And where did you put the letter from his comrades?' 'That was a good question,' said Reb Shlomo. 'I put it next to the prayer "Give honor, O Lord, to Thy people," to show the Almighty that the sons of Israel deserve that He should do them honor. It is written, "The Lord shall reign . . . before his elders in glory," and so sons who pay honor to the aged deserve that the Holy One, blessed be He, should pay honor to them.'

I gazed at that old man, whose face was marked with love of God, love of his fellow men, humility and lowliness of spirit, and I said, 'When our righteous Messiah comes and sees Reb Shlomo, he will greet him with great joy.' Said Elimelech Kaiser, 'It is clear that all the gentleman looks forward to is the joy of the Messiah. Perhaps he will live in our town until the Messiah comes, and see his joy.' I nodded my head and was silent.

The man pointed to me and said, 'He nods his head but says nothing; his head speaks and his lips are silent.' I laid my hand on my heart. 'My head and my heart are the same,' I replied, 'but I have not yet shaped the words with my mouth.'

'Perhaps you are waiting for permission,' said Elimelech Kaiser mockingly. 'Look, we'll give it to you. And if you like we'll hand you over the key and you can be master of the whole Beit Midrash.' Another spoke up: 'We're leaving and we don't need the key. We'll give you the key and it won't lie about in the muck. Elder, give him the key and let him take care of it.' The elder saw my hand stretched out to receive it. He rose, mounted the platform, went up to the lectern, and put his hand into the drawer. He took out a large brass key with iron wards, came down, and, standing on the lowest step of the platform, held out the key to me. This was the great key with which I used to open our old Beit Midrash when I was a boy to study the Torah, early and late. For many years I had not seen it even in a dream, and suddenly it was being presented to me outright, in public, in the Beit Midrash, on the Day of Atonement. I took the key in my hand and put it away in my pocket.

Some of the people who had not taken part in our conversation came up and looked at me. I wanted to say something to them, but the words did not take shape in my mouth.

I raised my eyes and looked at the people in the Beit Midrash to see if perhaps they would change their minds and take the key. I put my hand in my pocket and was ready to give it back even before they asked for it, but no man stretched out his hand, for they were moving next day and leaving this place, and what did it matter to them whether the key lay in the drawer of the lectern or in the pocket of this visitor? At that moment I was overcome by a deep sadness. I began to feel sorry that I was sad. And because I was sorry that I was sad, my sadness was redoubled.

At that moment they opened the sacred Ark and took out a Torah Scroll for the Afternoon Service reading. With one hand I embraced the Scroll and with the other held on to the key of our old Beit Midrash, where I had studied the Torah and spent the days of my youth. And I did not yet know that I was destined to make it my accustomed place. But let us not anticipate.

CHAPTER FIVE

The Closing Service

The sun stood in the treetops, close to setting. The walls of
the Beit Midrash darkened, and the few candles dimly lit its
duskiness. People who had not been in synagogue all day
came in and stood there sadly, their eyes twitching as they
looked at the cantor, who lifted up his voice and chanted the
first psalm of the Closing Service. The whole day long they
had sat at home as if ashamed, but now that the sun was
setting and the hour had arrived when the judgment is sealed,
they rose and went to the Beit Midrash. Perhaps they had no
intention to pray, because they did not believe in the power
of prayer and did not expect any reward, but the hour overcame their reason.

The cantor bowed low, bent all his body, like a sinner
who is lowly in his own eyes, and chanted the Kaddish, leaving out not a single note of the traditional melody. It was not
like the Kaddish before the Additional Service, in which he
had intertwined the melody the mourners use. The cantor set
aside the death of his son in respect for the greatness of his
Father in heaven. In the end his voice was drowned by the
Amen of the congregation; at last the voices of the congregation died out, and finally the entire Beit Midrash was silent.
The silence did not last long; sighs that did not make up any
speech or any language began to rise. Only He who knows
all secrets understood this language.

After I had finished the silent prayer, I saw Daniel Bach
standing bowed in front of the table at the southern end, beside the door, with a book in his hand. He was standing in
the same position as the cantor—but the cantor stood on both
his feet, while one of Daniel Bach's legs was made of wood.
I put out of my mind the bitter words he had spoken to me
yesterday at dusk on the eve of the Day of Atonement, so

17

that his sins should not be brought up against him at the time when the judgment was being sealed.

The congregation took more time over this prayer than over any prayer of the whole day. Even those who had just come drew closer to their neighbors and looked into their prayer books, and a kind of murmur rose from their throats. When they came to the shorter confession, some of them beat their breasts as is the custom: 'We have been guilty, we have dealt treacherously.' The Beit Midrash grew darker, but the memorial candles somewhat lit up the darkness. After the whole of the congregation had finished the silent prayer, the cantor mounted the steps of the sanctuary, opened the doors of the Holy Ark, came down, and took up his place in front of the lectern. He waited a moment and began in a loud voice, 'Blessed art Thou, O Lord. . . .' The candles were almost burned out, and the cantor chanted rapidly, 'Have mercy on Thy creatures . . .'; then he raised his voice and said, 'Open us Thy gate, the day is ending,' and then, 'Many are the needs of Thy people.' The walls of the Beit Midrash grew dark and the facing hillside added its share of darkness.

The worshippers drew nearer to the cantor and surrounded the reading desk with their prayer books to catch a little of the light from the candle that burned there. Perhaps the light sensed their presence and perhaps not, but in any case it leaped up toward them. The cantor clapped both his hands in joy and read, 'Israel is delivered by the Lord with an eternal deliverance'; clapped once again, and said, 'Even today they will be delivered by the word of Thy mouth, O Dweller on high.' A sound of weeping rose from the darkness, like the voices of a crowd supporting the cantor in his prayer. The doors of the Ark stood open, like a heavenly ear attentive to Israel's prayer. From the table in the south beside the door there was a dull sound, like wood striking on wood. Daniel Bach had changed his position. Again the same sound was heard, as of wood striking on wood. It seemed that his foot could find no rest. The cantor took a watch out of his pocket, looked at it, and began to shorten the chants, for the sake of the old men who had not the strength to remain on their feet on account of the fast. When he came to the verse 'Every city is builded in its place and the City of God is degraded to the depths of hell,' he wept for a long time. And for as long as he wept at this line, so long did he raise his voice in joy at the line 'We are Thy people.' After the ram's horn had been blown to mark the end of the fast, all those who had come for the Closing Service went away, except for Daniel Bach, who remained in the Beit Midrash.

The cantor lowered the prayer shawl from his head to his shoulders and read the weekday Evening Service before the lectern, as the year of mourning for his son had not yet elapsed. As for his leading the prayer on the Day of Atonement, though a mourner does not lead the prayers on a holy day, the Day of Atonement is different from other holy days, for the cantor is the emissary of the congregation, like the High Priest, who offers up the sacrifice even immediately after a bereavement.

After the mourners' Kaddish, the congregation wished each other a good and blessed year. That troublesome fellow, Elimelech Kaiser, came up and greeted me. 'I believe I have not yet offered you my good wishes,' he said, and put out his hand. I returned his greeting and reminded him of the matter of the key I had received through him. 'I was joking,' said he, stammering, 'and I ask you to forgive me.' 'On the contrary,' said I, 'it is a precious gift that I have received through you.' Said he, 'You are laughing at me, sir, so now we have nothing against each other.'

Daniel Bach went up to the cantor and said, 'A happy new year, Father, a happy new year. Come home with me and have a meal.' Reb Shlomo replied, '*Nu, nu,*' and it was not clear from his voice whether he was agreeing or not. Daniel Bach looked at him and said, 'Father, please come. Sara Pearl will warm you up a glass of milk. Warm milk is good for the throat after the fast. Aren't you hoarse, Father?' 'What are you thinking of, son, to say I am hoarse,' said Reb Shlomo. 'If we had been given two Days of Atonement, I would have recited all the prayers over again.' 'A glass of warm milk with a little honey in it is good after the fast,' repeated Daniel. 'Come, Father, the child wants to hear the Havdala at the end of the Holy Day.' 'We must recite the sanctification for the new moon first,' said Reb Shlomo. 'Well,' said Daniel, 'we'll wait for you to come, Father.' 'How well this one knows how to ask!' said Reb Shlomo. 'If you had asked your Father in heaven like that you would have been saved. You were here during the Closing Service. I heard the sound of your foot. It made me very sad. It is high time you were saved.'

Reb Shlomo went out to the yard of the Beit Midrash to sanctify the new moon, and Daniel Bach went after him. A fine moon stood in the sky, shining on the upper and the lower worlds. I stood and waited for the congregation to finish the sanctification of the moon and go home, for I held the key to the Beit Midrash, and someone might have left something there and come back to fetch it. When they had all gone, I locked up the Beit Midrash.

And still Daniel stood waiting for his father. After Reb Shlomo had shaken the skirts of his coat, as is the custom after the sanctification, Daniel whispered to him, 'Come, Father, come.' 'I am coming, I am coming,' said Reb Shlomo, nodding his head. Daniel bowed his head and said, 'Yes, yes, Father.' So he took his arm and they went. Said Reb Shlomo, 'I cannot run like you.' 'You can't run,' said Daniel, 'I'll shorten my steps.'

As he was going he said to me, 'We are going the same road, aren't we? Won't you go with us?' So I went with them, although I knew the way myself.

CHAPTER SIX

Within and Without

Before the month of Tishri was out, the people of the Beit Midrash had gone off on their separate ways, except for Reb Shlomo the cantor, who delayed his going up to the Land of Israel. Szibucz did not notice its loss. In these days, the towns of Poland are used to shedding their inhabitants by stealth, a few today and a few tomorrow, and one group does not grieve for the other; nor, of course, does one group envy the other. These are days when it is bad for Jews who stay at home and bad for those who go elsewhere. In the past, when a man changed his place he changed his luck; now, wherever a Jew goes, his bad luck goes with him. Nevertheless, you find some consolation in moving, because you move yourself from the realm of 'certainly' to the realm of 'perhaps.' Everywhere else, if you have a choice between 'certainly' and 'perhaps,' 'certainly' is better; but here 'perhaps' is better than 'certainly.' For you are certain that the place where you live is hard; perhaps your salvation will come from somewhere else. And why do they travel in the winter, as if the cold days were good for traveling? Surely the summer is best. But summer is better for the rich, and winter is better for the poor, for in winter most of the ships leave empty and lower their fares. If I returned to the Land of Israel now, my voyage would cost me less. For the time being it is not my intention to return, but since we were talking of ships I remembered my own ship.

One day my host said to me, 'I have heard that you want to stay with us. If so, we shall treat you as a permanent guest and reduce your bill. Or perhaps you would like to rent a house for yourself. There are many houses standing empty, but you will not find a good one. We have one room where all the fine folk who come here like to stay. If you wish, we shall clear it for you.' 'I don't want to change either my lodging or my room,' I replied, 'but I am afraid that if you see I am satisfied with everything you will think little of me.' Said the hotelkeeper, 'Because a man is satisfied with me, should I think little of him?' Said I, 'Let us ask the mistress of the house; perhaps I am too much trouble for her. I am not finicky about food, but you know I don't eat meat. It may be difficult to cook special dishes for me.' 'Who eats meat here?' said the mistress of the house. 'All six days of the week no one has a taste of meat. And for the Sabbath I can cook you special dishes. During the war we learned to cook without meat; only in wartime we cooked without meat or anything else, and the food had no flavor or anything; but since the war I have learned to make the food tasty even without meat.

There was a doctor here who didn't eat any flesh foods, and he taught me to make all kinds of dishes with vegetables, and I haven't forgotten his teaching yet.'

It is not quite proper for a man to sing his own praises, but in general I am happy with my lot. I have a room in the hotel, with a bed, a table and a chair, a lamp and a wardrobe. As for food, the hotelkeeper's wife makes me a good meal every day. Since I am not ungrateful, I sing her praises to her face, and when she hears them she makes her cooking tastier and tastier.

This is the food she prepares for me. In the morning a cup of coffee, with a layer of cream covering it like the lid of a pot, and a hot dish of beans made like a kind of porridge, or potatoes with cheese, or chopped cabbage, or cabbage leaves filled with rice or groats, sometimes with raisins or mushrooms—all made with butter. On Sabbath eves: pancakes filled with buckwheat, or cheese with raisins and cinnamon, baked in the morning and eaten hot. The midday meal is fuller than the breakfast, for it includes soup and vegetables. The evening meal is less, but there is always something new. For Sabbath she cooks fish, boiled or stuffed, or pickled or marinated, besides other good things. And it goes without saying that there is no Sabbath without a pudding. She is helped by Krolka, one of those few still left of the Swabians who were brought to Galicia by the Emperor Joseph, and who speaks German mingled with Yiddish. So I sit in the hotel, sometimes in my room and sometimes in the dining room, which they usually call the salon. As the guests are few and the work is not heavy, the host is almost idle. His face is straight and his forehead narrow; his hair is black, streaked with grey; and his eyes are half closed, either because he does not expect to see anything new or because he wants to preserve the old sights. He keeps the stem of his pipe in his mouth and his thumb on the bowl. Sometimes he adds more tobacco and sometimes he sucks it empty. He lets fall a word and then is silent, so as to give the guest time to answer, either out of respect for the guest or in order to test his character.

I am this guest. I reply to everything he asks and add

things he did not ask about, and I do not conceal even things about which one is usually silent. Since the people of my town cannot imagine that a man should describe things as they really are, they believe I am a shrewd fellow, who talks much and evades the main point. At first I tried to tell them the truth, but when I found that the true truth deceived them, I left them with the imaginary truth.

In fact, I need not talk much. The innkeeper knows his guests and does not ask to hear more. He sits in his usual way, his lips holding the stem of his pipe and his eyes half closed, for he has given up the idea of seeing anything new and wishes to preserve what he has seen. And his wife is busy all day in the kitchen. Though there are not many guests, she has to cook for them, and of course for herself and her husband and her sons and daughters.

Of her sons and daughters I shall tell elsewhere, or perhaps I shall say nothing of them, for I have nothing to do with them. Just as I have nothing to do with them, so they have nothing to do with me. When the innkeeper's two sons, Dolik and Lolik, realized that I did not come here to do business, they put me out of their minds, and now they pay no attention to me. It is the same with their sister Babtchi, who is occupied half the time in a lawyer's office and half the time with herself. As for Rachel, the innkeeper's youngest daughter, she is no longer a child but not yet a young woman. She is eighteen years old. A twenty-year-old might make advances to her, but not a man who has arrived at years of understanding. So I am free to myself to do whatever I wish. And so I do. Immediately after breakfast I take the large key of the old Beit Midrash, go in, and sit until it is time for the midday meal.

So I sit alone in the old Beit Midrash. The scholars who used to meditate on the Torah have passed away and gone to their eternal home, and the books that were here have disappeared. We had many books in our old Beit Midrash. Some of them I studied, even adding remarks in the margin— I was childish then and thought I had it in my power to add to their wisdom—and some of them I used to weep over, as children do, who try to obtain by weeping what is beyond the reach of reason. Now nothing is left of all the books but one here and another there. Where have they disappeared to, all those books? It is told in the *Book of the Pious* that the souls of the dead have their books; as they studied in their lifetime so they study after they are dead. If so, we may imagine that the sages who have died have taken their books with them, so as to study them after their passing. And they are right, for no one has remained in the Beit Midrash, and there is no one here who needs a book.

Before the few books that have remained shall disappear, I want to examine them. So I take a book and read it to the end. In years gone by I would take one book and lay it down, then take another and lay it down, as if the wisdom of one book were not enough for me. Suddenly I saw that in one book there is enough to sustain ten wise men without exhausting all its wisdom. Even books I knew by heart seemed new to me. Seventy faces has the Torah; whatever the face you turn to it, it turns that face to you.

I sat silent before the book, and the book unsealed its lips and revealed to me things I had never heard before. When I was tired of studying I thought many thoughts, and this is one of them: Many generations ago a wise man wrote a book and he did not know of this man who sits here, but in the end all his words prove to be meant for him.

This too I learned, that time is longer than I thought, and it is divided into many parts; each part stands by itself, and a man can do many things in one period, provided he is sitting alone and no one distracts him from his work. In jest I said: That is why the whole universe was created in one day, because the blessed Creator was alone in His universe.

Now that I have come to understand the nature of time, I divide my time among several things. Until noon I sit in the Beit Midrash and study, and in the afternoon I go out into the forests of my town. At this season the trees have not yet shed their leaves, and the sight rejoices the eye. Some of them are dappled, some shine like copper, and there are other shades of color for which there is no name.

I stand among the trees, rejoicing my eyes with the sight, and say: 'Beautiful, beautiful.' The skies smile at me; they almost seem to say, 'This man knows what is beautiful, and it is fitting that he should see more.' You can see that this is so, for immediately they show me things I have never seen before. I do not know whether new things have been added, or whether this man's power of vision has been doubled.

I am alone in the forest, as I am alone in the Beit Midrash. No one enters the forest, because it belongs to the baron of the town, and although there are no longer any guards, the fear of them remains. Perhaps you have heard the story of the old woman who goes out to the forest to collect twigs, to cook porridge for her grandsons. If so, why do I not meet that old woman? Because her grandsons have grown up and been killed in the war, and she too is dead. Or perhaps she and her grandsons are still alive, but when they want to eat, the grandsons go out and fall on the Jews, and rob and steal and plunder, and bring food to their grandmother too, so that she need not toil in the forest. And where are the couples who used to go out to the forest to reveal their love for one another? Those things that used to be done in private are now done in the open, and there is no need to take the trouble to go to the forest. Or the explanation may be that when love for one's fellow men ceased, so did the loves of youths and maidens. Now a man meets a woman in the market; if he and she desire each other, he brings her into his house, and before their love has entered into their hearts they are tired of each other.

The Almighty puts a blindfold over my eyes, so that I should not see His creatures in their depravity. And when He removes the apron from my eyes they see what not every eye notices. For instance, Ignatz, whose nose has been destroyed in the war, and who has a hole in place of the nose. Ignatz stands in the market, leaning on his stick, his hat in his hand, and calls out to the passers-by: *'Pieniadze!'* which means 'Money!' That is, 'Give me charity!' And since no one pays any attention to him, I pay double attention. First, because of the compassion that is innate in the heart of Israel. And second, because I am idle and have time to put my hand in my pocket and take out a coin, for I have learned that time is long, and sufficient to do many things. When I came across

Ignatz for the second time, he said '*Mu'es,*' which means money in the Holy Tongue. In two or three days he had succeeded in learning how to say money in Hebrew. When I gave him my alms the three holes in his face shone, namely his two eyes and the hole below his eyes where his nose used to be.

Although time is long, it has a limit. When you sit alone by yourself you imagine that time stands still, for between five before the hour and five past the hour you have thought enough to fill a whole universe; when a man accosts you, time jumps and passes by. It happened once that I left the hotel to go to the Beit Midrash and was accosted by Daniel Bach. In no time at all half a day had passed. First I asked how he was, then I asked after his father; and then he asked how I was. In the meantime half a day was gone and the time had come for lunch. So I returned to my hotel as if the key of the old Beit Midrash were of no use at all.

CHAPTER SEVEN

A Parable and Its Meaning

At first I thought that all the disabilities must have come from the war, but Daniel Bach told me that some came from earning a living, as in his case. So long as he was in the line of battle he was sound of limb; when he took up the burden of earning a living he lost his leg.

This is how it happened. After the war he went back to his town, and found his home in ruins, his sawmill a heap of rubble, and his wife and daughters sitting on the rubble lamenting and wishing they had never come back. For when the sword of war rested, the people mistakenly thought the days of the Messiah had come, so Daniel Bach's wife took her daughters and went back to her own town. But they did not know that the Messiah was still dressing his wounds; the world had not yet returned to health, and there was no difference between one place and another except for the tribulations specific to that place. Today Daniel Bach has only one daughter and a sick child that was born after the war. But on the day he came back from the war he had three daughters, one of whom died immediately after his return and another at the beginning of the influenza epidemic; there had also been a son who was buried on the roadside by his mother when she fled before the approaching Russian armies.

So his wife and his daughters sat on the rubble, half-naked, barefoot, and hungry; the town was in ruins and most of the houses were burned down; all trade and barter was at a standstill; his father was wandering at the other end of the country, and they had no idea where he was, until he came back naked, barefoot, and hungry like everyone else. Daniel Bach was even hungrier than everyone else. So long as he had been in the army, the Emperor had provided him with food, and when there was not enough to satisfy, the terror of war had mitigated his hunger; but here a man had nothing else but his hunger. He was hungry when he rose in the morning and hungry when he went to bed; hungry in the day-time and hungry at night; hungry awake and hungry in dreams. Then the charity officials came to the town, gave bread to the hungry, and helped those who wanted to start in trade. He too managed to set up a business, not like the one he had before the war, but a small soap business. Soap was a com-modity much in demand after the war, because everyone felt soiled and wanted to cleanse himself. Even the peasants who had never seen soap in their lives came to buy soap. Daniel Bach's business prospered and he earned a very good living. Once, however, he said to himself: Esau wants to wash his hands of the blood he has shed during the war. Shall I make a profit out of it? So he lowered the price. Once he had lowered the price his profits disappeared. Before very long his stocks were gone and he had no money to buy more. So hunger came back to plague him and his household more than at the beginning, for they had already become used to eating, and now they had nothing to eat. At that time our people were struck by the first pogroms. The charity officials came and gave money to the victims. With the money Daniel Bach went and bought saccharin, which had become a good business in those days, for as a result of the war many had fallen sick

with diabetes and sweetened their food and drink with saccharin. But the trader had to be careful not to be caught with
his goods; saccharin was a state monopoly and the government was on the lookout to prevent any harm to its own
revenue. Anyone who had a head on his shoulders was careful, but the head is far from the feet, especially in the case
of Daniel Bach, who is a tall man, and by the time his feet
managed to hear what his head was thinking, the deed was
already done. Once he jumped onto a train and his right foot
got stuck in the wheels; the train moved off, dragging the
foot with it, and cast it out far from the station. By rights,
he should have been paid for damages, distress, harm, disuse,
and injury, according to law, but they did not pay, and moreover they fined him six hundred zlotys because they found
grains of saccharin in the sock on his foot. And now how
does he make a living and earn his food? He has a stock of
wood in his house for building and heating, and his wife is
a midwife. For the time being no one is building a new house
and no one lights his stove, but when the babies his wife
brings into the world grow up they will build new houses
and light their stoves, so that he will find income flying in
from all sides. But the trouble is that, since they came back
from the war, many Jews have become ascetics, and will
neither marry nor beget children, and were it not for the
uncircumcised the seed of our father Adam would have died
out. And the daughters of the uncircumcised do not resort to
our midwives except in times of danger.

Wherever you cast your eyes you find either suffering or
poverty. But there is one place in the town where you find
no suffering. This is the old Beit Midrash, the key of which
is in my possession. Ever since I noticed this, I have doubled
my stay there. If I was accustomed to sit there in the morning,
I now sit there in the afternoon too. Sometimes I sit and study,
and sometimes I stand by the window and look out at the
facing hill.

Once, the whole of that hill was settled. Porters and
craftsmen used to live there, and they had a fine Beit Midrash,
which the dwellers on the hill built with their own hands by
moonlight, since in the day they were busy with their trades

in the town. And they had a regular teacher who used to teach them the scriptural portion of the week and the *Sayings of the Fathers*. When the war came, the young men fell by the sword and died; the old men died of hunger; and their widows and children were killed in the pogroms. So the community was uprooted; not one stone of their Beit Midrash was left standing on another; and the hill was desolate, and could no longer enlarge the mind. Not so with books. The more you look into them, the more your mind is enlarged and your heart gladdened.

I do not study to enlarge my mind or to become wise and know the works of the Lord. I am like a man who walks by the wayside—the sun beats on his head, the stones bruise his feet, the dust blinds his eyes, and all his body is weary. Then he sees a booth and enters—and the sun no longer beats on his head, nor do the stones bruise his feet or the dust blind his eyes. As he is weary, he wishes to rest, and pays no attention to anything. After he has recovered, he notices the booth and its furnishings. And if he is not ungrateful he gives praise and thanks to Him who made a booth for him and prepared everything in it to supply his needs.

I am that man, and that booth is our old Beit Midrash. I had been walking in the sun among the stones and dust, when suddenly I found myself sitting in the Beit Midrash. And since I am not ungrateful, I give praise and thanks to the Almighty and look upon His furnishings, namely the books that are in the Beit Midrash.

What is written in these books? The Holy One, blessed be He, created the universe according to His will and chose us from all the peoples and gave us His Torah so that we should know how to serve Him. While we are studying His Torah and observing His commandments, not one of the peoples can injure us. When we do not obey His Torah, even the smallest *goy* can injure us. The Torah surrounds those who study it with goodness and virtue and enhances their favor in the eyes of the world. When we turn our eyes away from the Torah, the Torah turns its eyes away from us, and we become the lowest of all the nations. For what reason did the Holy One, blessed be He, choose us and lay upon us the yoke of the Torah and the commandments, for isn't the Torah heavy and difficult to observe? Some solve the problem one way and some another, but I will explain it by a parable. It is like a king's crown, made of gold and precious stones and diamonds. So long as the crown is on the king's head, men know that he is king. When he removes the crown from his head, not all are aware that he is king. Does the king refrain from putting the crown on his head because it is heavy? On the contrary, he puts it on his head and delights in it. The king's reward for the crown being on his head is that everyone exalts and honors him and bows down before him. What good does this do the king? That I do not know. Why? Because I am not a king. But if I am not a king, I am a king's son and I ought to know. But this man has forgotten, he and all Israel his people, that they are sons of kings. The books tell us that this forgetfulness is worse than all other evils—that a king's son should forget he is a king's son.

Rachel, the innkeeper's younger daughter, has also forgotten that she is a daughter of kings, and when I reminded her of this, she laughed at me. This girl, who between yesterday and today stopped being a child and has not yet become a young woman, has dared to rebuke a man who has reached his fortieth year, to say to him, 'What are you talking about? Don't I know that everything you're saying is just a joke?' I do not remember the details—only the general sense of the words.

One night I was sitting with her father and found him distressed. I was about to go, but he stopped me. 'No, no,' he said, 'let us hear your opinion, sir.' The girl raised her eyes and looked at me, or perhaps she just raised her eyes. So I had my say. She made a wry face and said, 'Why should I take on myself the burden of past generations? Let past generations look after themselves and my generation look after itself. Just as the generations before me lived in their own way, so my generation lives in its own way. And as for what you said, that every daughter of Israel should think of herself as a daughter of kings, there's nothing more foolish than that. Today, when the crowns of kings are lying in museums and no one takes pride in them, you come and say:

Every daughter of Israel should think of herself as a daughter of kings.'

I could have questioned what she said, but I answered nothing. Better she should think she had vanquished me. I do not know women, but I know that if a woman has vanquished you, in the end she will come back to your words.

I speak here of Rachel, the innkeeper's younger daughter, although she is not that close to the center of my concerns. The girl does not really hate me, and there is no reason why she should. In her eyes I am like a guest for the night, here today and elsewhere tomorrow.

Rachel is no longer a child, but not yet a young woman. Her neck is slender, her forehead high, and her eyes sad, and a kind of smile rests on her lips. At first sight it seems that there is something impudent about her, but by the way she bends her head it can be seen that she does not think much of herself and is prepared to submit to one greater than herself. And this is surprising, for she has no respect for kings or noblemen, no fear of her father and mother; and it goes without saying that she has no fear of our Father in heaven. So who could this be to whom she is prepared to bow her head? Often she will twitch her shoulders, as if a hand had touched them, and half close her eyes. Not like her father, who wants to preserve what he has already seen, but like one who half closes his eyes to see what is still to happen.

What is this girl waiting for? Surely there is nothing to be expected of this world, and men are not so made as to bring good. I held my tongue and examined my own self. Not that I am better than anyone else, but I am not so made as to bring any harm to that girl. And I am glad I said nothing to her and did not lead her into despair.

I looked at my watch and said, 'Oh, it is already after midnight.' So I went into my room to sleep.

CHAPTER EIGHT

Between Father and Son

One night I found the old cantor, Reb Shlomo Bach, sitting in the hotel, bent over his stick. As I entered he rose, put out his hand, and greeted me. I returned his greeting and said to him, 'You are still here. I thought you had already gone up to the Land of Israel.'

'I am partly here, and partly in the Land of Israel,' replied Reb Shlomo, 'for my late son Yeruham's comrades have already sent me a ticket, and I wanted to see you because I heard that you came from there. Perhaps you will give me some good advice about the journey.'

'Nothing simpler,' said I. 'You go to the railway station and give the clerk money, and he gives you a ticket. You get into the coach and travel to Trieste. There you board a ship and travel five days by sea until you reach Jaffa. Once you have reached Jaffa, you are standing in the Land of Israel.' So long as I was describing his journeyings outside the Land, he did not seem to be listening, but as soon as I mentioned Jaffa, he fixed his eyes on me and repeated my words.

Daniel, his son, came in. 'I am sorry for you, son,' said his father, 'that you did not hear what the gentleman was telling me.' Daniel Bach looked at me, as if wondering what it was this man had said that he should be sorry for not having heard. 'I was telling your father how to go to the Land of Israel,' said I. Daniel brought his feet together and said, 'Yes, yes' (meaning: I knew it was something simple that this man told you). 'Take a piece of paper and write,' said I, 'so that your father can know the order of the journey.'

After he had written down the order of the journey to the Land of Israel, he asked me to explain the route from Jaffa to Ramat Rahel, where his father was going. I said, 'You leave the ship, embark in a boat, and land. If your father finds a young fellow from the kvutza, so much the better; if not, let him book a place in an automobile and travel to

Jerusalem. When he arrives in Jerusalem he takes the bus for Talpiot. When he gets to the end of Talpiot, he will see young men and women setting out for Ramat Rahel; he walks with them until he reaches the place.'

Since I had mentioned Talpiot, I remembered the trouble that had overtaken me there when the Arabs destroyed my house and left me not even a pillow for my head. At that moment I was sad and Reb Shlomo was happy. I was sad because I had left there, and he was happy because he was going there.

I ordered tea and cakes for my guests. Reb Shlomo said the blessing over food, broke off a small piece of the cake and ate it, then said the appropriate blessing over tea and drank. He took out a letter he had received from Ramat Rahel and spread it out before me. Although he knew the letter by heart he read it over again. Then he folded it up, put it in his pocket next to his heart, and said, 'So I am going to the Land of Israel.' Daniel Bach nodded his head and said, 'Yes, Father, you are going to the Land of Israel.' Said Reb Shlomo, 'How pleasant my journey would be if you promised me, my son, that you would follow the right way.' Daniel jumped up from his chair, placed his right hand on his heart, and pointed upward with his left. 'Was it I that made the way crooked?' he cried. 'It was He that made the way crooked.' 'Enough, son, enough,' said his father. 'Whatever the Almighty does He does to test us. If we stand the test, so much the better. If not, He sends a test harder than the first.' Said Daniel, 'Doesn't the Almighty see that we can't stand His first test, that He takes the trouble to subject us to new ones?' 'Evil thoughts are a great stumbling block,' said Reb Shlomo, 'but I am not speaking to you about thoughts. What I ask of you, my son, is that you should obey His laws and observe His commandments; then in the end He will take away your evil thoughts from your heart. We have troubled the gentleman too much; let us say the final grace and go.' Reb Shlomo shook the crumbs from his beard, wiped his mouth, said the grace, and rose.

When he was about to leave he said, 'It is not right to sing a man's praises to his face, but we may sing part of them.

Daniel, my son, was once a good Jew, as strict in his observance of minor duties as of major ones. Isn't that so, son?' 'Just like all the good Jews who obey the commandments without thinking what they are doing,' replied Daniel Bach. 'Who asks you for thoughts!' said Reb Shlomo. 'What does God demand of you, except to fear Him and love Him?' 'In return for my love, He is my adversary,' said Daniel, to the tune of the scriptural chant. A sadness unlike any other appeared on his face.

'Do you remember the episode of the tefillin?' said Reb Shlomo. Daniel Bach's eyes darkened and his forehead wrinkled as he recalled the story. 'The episode of the tefillin is one out of many,' said he, looking at his father. 'It happened only to test you,' said Reb Shlomo. 'There's never a trouble but they explain it as a test,' replied Daniel. Said Reb Shlomo, 'And how else would you fulfill the commandment to love God "with all thy soul," as our sages explain: even if He takes your soul?' 'A man can bind himself on the altar and give up his life for the glory of God,' cried Daniel. 'With his dying breath he can pronounce the confessions of faith, "Hear, O Israel, the Lord is our God, the Lord is One," and prolong the final "One," like the great Rabbi Akiba in his torment, until his soul departs. But to be bound every day, every hour, every moment, on seven altars, to have one limb consumed today and another tomorrow—that is something not every man can stand. I'm only a human being, flesh and blood, and when my flesh rots and my blood stinks, my lips cannot utter the praises of the Almighty. And if I do utter His praises, is it to the glory of God if a lump of rotting flesh or a skinful of stinking blood cries out, "Thou are righteous, no matter what befalls me, and I have been wicked," and even then He does not lift His hand from me and continues to afflict me?' ' "What have you to do with the secrets of the Merciful One?" ' said Reb Shlomo. 'Whatever the trouble that befalls a man, they sweeten it for him with a saying of the sages,' replied Daniel.

Reb Shlomo smoothed his beard with one hand and said, 'On the contrary, my son, let us be grateful to our rabbis for elucidating matters and explaining events; for were it not for them we should have had to wear ourselves out, but now that they have given the explanation for every single thing we can spend our lives in study and good deeds, and no one need waste his time on questionings, but can serve his Creator and obey His commandments. And a man should make a particular effort to obey commandments in which he is weak, like you, my son, with the commandment to put on tefillin.' 'Father,' said his son, 'just as it is right to give an injunction that will be obeyed, so it is right not to give an injunction that will not be obeyed.' 'In what connection?' 'In connection with what you have said,' replied Daniel. 'Meaning?' 'Meaning the matter of putting on tefillin. I give you my solemn word that I shall not put on tefillin.' Said Reb Shlomo, 'How can a man swear not to do a thing that he has been sworn to do ever since Mount Sinai?'

'What are you so excited about?' I asked Daniel Bach. 'Ach, nonsense!' replied Reb Shlomo. 'Something happened to him during the war.' Daniel Bach jumped up from his chair in a rage and shouted, 'Nonsense you call it?' 'What is the story?' I said to him. 'Were you in the war?' he asked. 'I was sick,' I replied, 'and they did not find me fit to fight the Emperor's wars.' 'I went to war from the beginning, and continued fighting until the final defeat,' said Daniel Bach. 'I was a great patriot, like all the other Jews in this country. As the days went on my patriotism grew less, but once you go in you don't get out again. All the time I was in the army I did not eat a forbidden thing and observed all the commandments, and it goes without saying that I was careful to put on tefillin every day.' Reb Shlomo looked at his son with great love, nodding his beard above the stick on which he leaned as he sat, and his warm eyes shone in his face.

Daniel went on: 'So careful was I to put on tefillin every day that if I did not manage to put them on I ate nothing the rest of the day. One night I was lying in the trenches, buried up to the neck and over in soft, rotting earth. The guns fired without stopping; piles of dirt erupted and slid into the trench, and the smell of burnt flesh rose all around me. I felt the fire had caught my flesh and I was being burned to death, and I was almost sure I would not come out alive: I would either be consumed by the fire or buried in the ashes. At

that moment the sun appeared in the sky; the time had come
for the morning prayer. I said to the Angel of Death: Wait
for me until I fulfill the commandment of tefillin. I put out
my hand to seek my tefillin. My hand touched a tefillin strap.
I thought a bullet had struck the bag where the tefillin were
kept and they had been scattered all around. But when I
pulled the strap and touched the tefillin, I was struck by a
stench. I saw that one strap was fastened to the arm of a
dead man, for that trench was a mass grave, and that arm
belonged to a Jewish soldier, who had been blown to pieces
as he stood in prayer adorned with his tefillin.'

Reb Shlomo wiped his eyes with both hands, and the
stick on which he was leaning fell. He choked down his sighs
and looked at his son with great compassion. No doubt he
had heard the story many times before, yet his eyes were
moved and he wanted to weep. Daniel bent down and lifted
the stick, and the old man leaned on it once more. Daniel
tucked in his legs and rubbed his left knee with his right hand,
and a kind of smile hung on his lips, like a child who has
done wrong and then been caught in his naughtiness.

The people of the hotel had gone to sleep; Reb Shlomo,
Daniel his son, and I sat silent. Daniel's smile faded away;
a look of melancholy appeared on his lips, spread, and was
absorbed in his sunken cheeks.

I took Daniel Bach's hand and said to him: 'Let me tell
you a story; I read it in the book *The Rod of Judah*. It tells of
a group of exiles from Spain, who set out to sea. On the way
something went wrong with the ship, and the captain cast
them ashore at a desolate spot where no one lived. Most of
them died of hunger, but the survivors summoned up strength
and set out to look for a place of human habitation. One
woman collapsed by the road and died. The woman's husband
took up their two children in his arms and went on. All three
of them fainted away for hunger. When the man came to
himself he found his two children dead. He stood up and said,
"Lord of the Worlds, Thou dost much to make me abandon
my faith; know that in spite of heaven I am a Jew and a Jew
I shall be, and all that Thou hast brought upon me and may

bring upon me will be of no avail." So he gathered dust and grasses, covered up the boys, and went to seek a place of habitation. The group of Jews had not waited for him, lest they too should die of hunger, for each was engrossed with his suffering and paid no heed to the sufferings of his fellows.'

'And what was the end of that Jew?' 'I do not know.' 'Perhaps the Almighty led him to a Jewish settlement and he married another woman and had sons and daughters.' 'Perhaps.' 'But even if so, I see no recompense in that. Job, who never existed but was only a parable, was consoled for the death of his wife and children, after the Lord has blessed his end more than his beginning; but I doubt whether a living man would accept such consolation.'

Reb Shlomo stroked his beard and said: 'The story is told of a man whose son had become an infidel. He went to the saintly Baal Shem Tov. The Baal Shem Tov told him that he should love his son twice as much as before.' Daniel Bach smiled and said, 'You know, sir, what Father means by telling us the story; he means that he loves me. Pity the Almighty doesn't follow the advice of the Baal Shem Tov.' 'How do you know,' said Reb Shlomo, 'that the Almighty does not do so?' 'Father,' replied Daniel, 'is it possible that after all the troubles you have known you should still say so?' 'Who else should say so,' replied Reb Shlomo, 'one who has known nothing but good all his life and for very happiness does not see the mercies of the blessed Lord? On the contrary, it is fitting for me to say that every hour I see the goodness of the blessed Lord. And I hope I am not sinning before Him by making distinctions between His acts and saying: This is good and this is not good. But I hope that when I have the privilege of living in the Land of Israel the Almighty will open my eyes to see that all His actions are right. And now that we have finished with a good word, let us say good night to the gentleman and go.'

CHAPTER NINE

In Fire and Water

After they had gone, I went to my room and lit a candle, lay down on my bed, and took a book to sweeten my sleep. I had not started to read when I began to think. What did I think of and what did I not think of . . .

There sits that old man, his chin resting on his stick, the wrinkles shining on his face, giving off sparks of light that flow down his beard. Near him sits his son, stroking his leg, sometimes the leg he was created with at his birth and sometimes the leg they grafted onto him later, and you do not know which is dearer to him, the one that was made by the Almighty or the one that was made by man. Says the one-legged man to his father, 'Father, the war of Gog and Magog has already come, but the Messiah, the son of David, has not yet come.' His father replies, 'My son, the war of Gog and Magog exists in every generation, in every era, in every hour, in every single man, inside a man's house, inside his heart, in his heart and the hearts of his children. Be still, my son, be still. Long ago Jeremiah said of the wicked: "Thou art near in their mouth and far from their reins," and the words still cry out from the heart of Israel.' I say to myself: Soon that old man will go up to the Land of Israel. From the material point of view, that is fine; the air of the Land of Israel is healthy, and his son Yeruham's comrades will give him food and lodging, and treat him with respect. But maybe that old man will have more regard for his own honor there and waive the honor due his Father in heaven, for he will see that they neglect some of the commandments, such as the observance of the Sabbath, and keep silent. Or maybe a man shuts his eyes to the evil deeds of his son, but not to the evil deeds of his son's comrades. But then again—his love for others may be as dear to him as his love for his son, like those old men who have suffered many tribulations and have taught themselves to accept everything with love, and not like most young men, who follow after their own hearts, and if they have the opportunity to do a good deed are afraid for their consciences and refrain from doing it. How many compromises does a man make without concern, but when it comes to the observance of the Torah, he is concerned because of his conscience. But why should I interfere with something that I cannot put right? I will close my eyes and sleep.

Before I went to sleep I knew that this night would not pass without dreams. And so it was. I myself opened the door to the Master of Dreams, that he might come and provoke me. But I overcame the Master of Dreams, and left him behind me—whenever I left him—and I arose and embarked in a ship full of Jews, old men and old women, lads and maidens. Never in my life have I seen such beautiful people. I might compare the men with the sun and the women with the moon, but the sun and the moon are covered sometimes and their light cannot be seen, while these people shone without a pause. Once on the Day of Atonement, near the hour of the Afternoon Service, I had seen a marvelous light through the window of the old Beit Midrash and I believed that there could be none to compare with it, but now I suddenly saw a light more marvelous still. Moreover, the light in our Beit Midrash was inanimate, while here the light was alive—or, if you like, eloquent, for every single spark sang. Has light a voice? Can it speak or sing? This is a thing that cannot be explained, and even if I were able to explain it I would not do so—instead I would enjoy the light.

Now, what were these people doing on the sea? The old men and women sat, with their hands on their knees, gazing at the sea, while the lads and maidens danced and sang and danced. And do not be surprised, for that ship was going to the Land of Israel. I too danced, and when I stopped my feet rose up and made me dance again. An old man took hold of me and said, 'We are one short of the minyan for prayer.' I wrapped myself in my tallit, and went with him to the room set aside for prayer. All the congregation were surprised, for it was time for the Evening Service, when the tallit is not worn. The old man went up to the Ark and lit a candle. I went after him to take a prayer book. The candle touched my prayer shawl and the fire caught it. I was confused and jumped into the sea. If I had thrown off my tallit I could have been saved from the flames. But I did not do so; instead I jumped into the sea. Not only was I not saved from the flames, but I was about to drown. I raised my voice and shouted, so that others should hear and shout and come to my aid. But they did not shout; no voice was heard except my own, crying out, 'Comfort the city that is mourning and burned.' I said to myself: Where is the old man? I raised my eyes and saw him leaning on the rail of the ship, not moving or nodding his beard. A man came up, resembling Daniel Bach, but he is missing one leg and this one was missing his two hands. I despaired and resigned myself to the waves of the sea. The sea lifted me gently and carried me to a certain place. I saw a light glimmering and thought: The place is inhabited, and surely the Jews will have mercy on me and bring me to dry land. I raised my eyes to see where the light was coming from. A strong wind came and put out the candle. I saw that it was the same candle I had lit beside my bed. I turned over and closed my eyes. Sleep fell upon me and I slumbered.

After I had eaten breakfast I took the key and went to the Beit Midrash, opened the door, went in and took out a book, and sat down to study. My book gripped me, and I studied with joy.

CHAPTER TEN

I Must Have an Overcoat Made

The coming of the cold days was in the air; its fear touched every living thing. The sun stayed hidden in the clouds, appearing only briefly, and when it did emerge it no longer looked as it had yesterday and the day before. So it was with the people; they went to market with gloomy faces. More than at other times they talked of clothes; everyone needed them, but not everyone could purchase them.

One day, as I rose from the midday meal, the innkeeper came up to me, examined my clothes, and asked if I had no others. His wife heard him and said, 'We have severe frosts in our town, and if you don't get a warm overcoat made you won't be able to stand the cold.' Here she hunched her shoulders and bent her neck like one shivering with cold. Her husband looked at her and twitched his eyes, like someone who wants to say something and has been stopped. He looked again at my clothes and said, 'You ought to have some warm clothing made, sir.'

The innkeeper and his wife are right: I ought to have some warm clothing made, for all I have are summer garments from the Land of Israel, which cover the body but do not warm it, and this cold that's on the way is a severe cold, and lasts six months and more, and never stops, night or day. Even those who are accustomed to it need warm clothes; all the more so I, who am not.

Now this overcoat, how shall I have it made? And even if I have it made, how shall I show myself in it in front of people, when I am ashamed to go out in new clothes? And why am I ashamed? It may be because I do not want to shame those who have no new clothes, or it may be something else that worries me—a new garment marks its wearer, and marks him only because of his dress, as in that story about a man who went to seek a maiden's hand. When this man appeared before the girl's father dressed in new clothes, the father said, 'Since he is completely dressed in new clothes, it seems his old ones are not fit to wear; a man like that is not suitable for my daughter.'

The parable is not quite a close fit, and it would be wrong to put off making the coat because of the story—even so, it is worth remembering. That young man put on new clothes to improve his appearance, but in the end he was sadly disillusioned, because all that people saw in him was his clothes.

I go to the Beit Midrash, but my going gives me no satisfaction. I do not suffer from the cold as yet, but something else troubles me as I go, for I scrutinize the passers-by, looking at them and their clothes. I, who am not accustomed to observe anything outside my own little acre, have become a

noser. And the trouble is that since I pay attention to others
I no longer pay attention to myself.

But since I am looking at the people, I will say something about them. Everyone here wears old clothes. They
are so old that you doubt if they were ever new; in other
words, they were already old when they were bought. And
those they bought them from had also bought the clothes
when they were old. This is particularly noticeable with the
children. There is not a single child whose clothes are not
older than himself.

The cold that was on the way took another course and
flowed to the forests and the rivers, the hills and the valleys,
but its traces and the traces of its traces could be felt in
the town.

Sour and insipid fruit sprout in the marketplace, autumn
fruit without any sap; salt herrings, whole and chopped, give
out a salty and rancid odor; the smell of pickled cabbage, sour
marrows, and the garlic with which the preserves are made,
is wafted from every house. The sweet odor of millet in honey
—the odor that sweetens our town from the day after Passover
until the middle of November—has evaporated.

The sun is hidden in the sky and comes out only at
intervals, and when it does come out it is wrapped in clouds,
like a sick man who is set down in the open for a little while.
A sick man who has been brought outside finds fault with
every place where they set him down; he wraps himself up,
and covers his face, complaining, 'The wind is blowing; it's
cold outside; it's raining.' And when they put him back inside,
he turns his face away and sulks.

Even worse than the sun is the ground. Either it sends
up clouds of dust, or it makes puddles and patches of swamp
and rottenness. Poets are in the habit of comparing the winter
to a dead man and the snow to the graveclothes. Perhaps
there is some resemblance, and perhaps not, but, in any case,
if the snow does not come down and cover up the earth, the
stench will surely bury the town.

The whole town is weary and sad. If a man has a house,
the roof is shaky and the windows broken, and it goes without
saying that he does not have double windows. If he has sons

and daughters, he has not yet had shoes made for their feet, bought potatoes for them, or prepared wood for the fire.

The skies hang sluggishly—skies? or clouds?—dripping, dripping drops like needles that have gone rusty. The town's two wagoners stand in the marketplace clapping their hands to warm themselves a little. Winter is not yet here, but a man's body is already cold. The wagon horses stand with heads bowed, looking at the ground, which yesterday was joyful and today is sad, wondering at their shadows, which lie so cold beneath their feet. Those men whom I found in the Great Synagogue on the eve of Atonement Day walking up and down to show themselves as proprietors now stand at the doors of their shops, how poor, how helpless. From the ninety villages that surround the town, not a man comes to buy anything in the shops—not because the ground is rotting and the villager has become finicky, but because each village has learned to have its own shop. Each farmer sells his crops himself, and has no need of a middleman. And even the Jews who used to live in the village, and through whom the towns-folk used to earn their livelihood, have moved out and now rot in poverty together with their fellows.

There are old men in the town who remember other days, when there was peace in the world, and joy, when a man had his victuals in plenty and his belly carried his legs; for people used to eat much and there was strength in their legs; a man had shoes on his feet, and his body was dressed in fine clothes, and everyone's livelihood came flying straight into his house. And how was that? Immediately after the festival season the landowners used to come into town, with their wives and sons and daughters, their manservants and maid-servants. All the village gentry would set out in dancing carriages harnessed to two or four horses and drive into town with loud and happy cries. They sold their winter crops to the grain merchants, the brandy of their distilleries to the brandy merchants, leased their forests to the timber agents, and all the craftsmen in the town would stand around them and ask, 'Have you any repairs to make in your houses?' And they would go in and buy copper and zinc and lead to repair vats and boilers and kettles. When they had finished their business, they would go to the shopkeeper and buy winter clothing, of wool and leather, long and short, for home and travel, for themselves and their households, and for their mistresses and *their* households. The days gone by were not like these days of ours. In these days, when one of the gentry casts his eye on a woman, he takes her to some such place as the divorcee's inn, and that's the only roof he'll ever provide her with. But in days gone by, the gentry used to build mansions for their mistresses, and provide them with every luxury, with footmen and maids to serve them. As for the clothes the gentry used to have made—five people would get a profit out of every single garment: the seller of the cloth, the seller of the fur, the tailor, the furrier, and the go-between. Or perhaps we should say six, for there is no go-between without another go-between at his heels.

But a simple fur is not enough to warm a man. And if even he who cannot afford to buy a simple skin buys a decent garment, you can be quite sure that he who *can* afford to buy a simple skin also buys many other clothes. You see this street; now it is in ruins and the shops are a heap of rubble. In the past there were two rows of shops here, one on one side and one on the other, and every shop was full of cloths and fabrics, velvet and satin, silk and linen. People used to go in and buy whether they needed to or not. Often the shop was too small to hold all the customers; so the people would go to another street and buy shoes. If those shops were full, they would turn to the grocers', and if they were full, they went to the restaurants. This body of ours has both an inside and an outside; just as you must clothe and shoe it, so must you feed it. So people would eat and drink and make merry, and gladden their servants with gifts of money. And when the servants had money they would also go to the shops to buy clothes and shoes and hats, for they had bodies too; the inner man they would sustain in the restaurants, and the outer man in the shops.

On the Gentile Sabbaths the village teachers would also come into town. These tutors were especially hired for the children of the gentry, each of whom would hire one, provide him with food and drink at his table, and pay him his stipend.

Part the teacher would give to his poor parents and part he would save toward entering the university. When a teacher came into town he would go into the bookseller's and buy two or three books. You must know that before the war the town even had a bookshop, with books for study, and books for teaching, and romances to while away the time. Today they still make books they call romances, just as they still call our town a town. The teacher would take his books, put them under his arm and go into a friend's house. His friend would have a sister—perhaps pretty, perhaps not, but she who has luck needs neither beauty nor cleverness. The girl's mother would come in and see a young man sitting with her son. She would say in surprise, 'Your honor is here? Perhaps you would be good enough to eat with us.' While she is standing and talking, her daughter comes in, dressed like a lady. The mother goes back to her cooking, while the daughter sits down with the teacher. She tells him things she has read in her romance and he tells her things he has read in his romance; so the outcome is a third romance. When dinner is ready, in comes the girl's father, greets the visitor and sits down at the table, with a square skullcap on his head, like a *rabbiner*. That day the girl's mother has cooked many dishes, so they sit a long time over the meal. For the longer the meal, the longer the conversation. A merchant's conversation is always about business, and normally he talks about the transactions in which he has made a profit. But not so in the case of the girl's father, for he tells about his losses, and really great losses he had, yet he talks about them so easily, as if he had taken only a copper out of his pocket. Says the teacher to himself: With this money I could finish my studies, and become a doctor, a lawyer, or a notary. Great is the power of money, for though the teacher is a socialist and criticizes the men of means who make money out of the sweat of the poor, nevertheless he is not hard on his friend's father. And not even that, he even feels honored at sharing the merchant's talk about his business. After all, the teacher eats at the table of his master, who is richer than that merchant. But his master looks at him as if he were not there, while the girl's father is polite to him and talks to him about his business.

As a result, he comes again. Someone approaches him and hints that the girl's father can support him until he finishes his studies, so that he need not waste time in the village. He falls in with the idea, leaves his pupils, and goes to the university, where the girl's father looks after him until he becomes a doctor or a lawyer. His master hires another teacher for his children and the fathers of girls treat him as they did his colleague. And if the girl's father cannot keep his promise, he quickly arranges a wedding before the young man has a chance to withdraw. Once he is married and has produced sons and daughters, he forgets his studies and looks for a living in some other quarter.

This is what happened to the host of my hotel, Mr. Nissan Zommer. In the second year after he left high school, he happened to visit a friend in the town, a hatter's son, whose mother was an excellent cook and his sister a handsome brunette. Now he reads no books and no longer speaks in the language of the romances; but in the past, when he was a village teacher, he was never without some books under his arm, and all his conversation was of romances. It is the same with his wife. She stands between the oven and the stove, and you would never imagine that she once attracted a boy's heart. The burden of earning a living, advancing years, and the experiences of wartime can change anyone, especially one who has gone through all of them and suffered many wounds. Nissan's wounds have healed already, and if he closes his eyes it is not in pain, but he closes his bodily eyes so as to see with the eyes of his spirit the things that have happened to him.

While he was still young he set out to earn his own living; his father was partly a seller of provender and partly an agent, who used to provide tutors for the villagers' sons, and he did not earn enough to keep his family, so Nissan used to teach his wealthy schoolfellows for pay while he was still a student at high school. When he left high school and it became time for him to go to the university, his father found him a place with one of the village gentry. But he suddenly fell in love with a girl and then fell under the yoke of earning a living, for the girl's father was a man of imaginings, and imagined he could keep Nissan until he finished his university studies. But when the father found himself unable to do this, he introduced Nissan to matrimony and business. Nevertheless, this particular occupation, selling hats, is not especially burdensome; you might even call it light and pleasant work. You take a hat, turn it this way and that, put it on the customer's head, stand him in front of the mirror, and look delighted; immediately he sees from your delight that the hat suits him, so he buys it and gives you money. As you do to this one, so you do to everyone else. Thus you see the heads of your townsfolk and know what is going on in each of them.

As time went on and Nissan fathered sons and daughters, he forgot that he had studied Latin and Greek and began to behave like all the other pious Jews. He went to the Beit Midrash to pray, sent his little sons to the religious school, and was not ashamed of his father and mother—unlike the doctors in our town, who are ashamed of their parents. Had he not been caught by the war, he would have stood and sold hats all his life. But war is not light and easy, nor is it pleasant. The head is king of the limbs; you wash it in hot water and rinse it in cold; soap it, and comb it, and crown it with a new hat every year; but suddenly some villain fires a shell and knocks it off. And perhaps we were mistaken when we said that the innkeeper closes his eyes to preserve what he has seen; maybe he closes them so that he should not see what he has seen. Human beings are deceptive; you think you know what they are like, but they are not like that at all.

Sometimes Babtchi brings him a newspaper. If the newspaper is spread out before him with the front page uppermost he reads till he gets to the end of the page, and does not turn it over even if he is in the middle of a story. If the back page is uppermost, he reads it from the top, and even if he is in the middle of a story he does not turn back to find out the beginning. If you think he does that because he is lazy, you are mistaken, for if his pipe goes out he gets up from his chair and goes to the kitchen to get an ember, even if matches are lying before him. But let us leave the innkeeper and go back to the subject with which we started.

CHAPTER ELEVEN

The Tailor and the Shopkeeper

All the winds in the world are blowing and shaking the town; from end to end you can hear the sound of doors banging, windows shattering, tiles dropping. The Stripa rages and screams, the bridge above it groans and roars. The sun has darkened, dust storms rise from earth to heaven. The townsfolk shiver, and it is natural that they should shiver, for their clothes are torn and cannot keep them warm.

I said to myself: These people are accustomed to the cold, but I, who have come from the Land of Israel—where one ray of the sun is stronger than the whole of the sun we see here—I cannot stand the cold, and surely I must make me a coat.

So I made an appointment and went to the tailor's. The tailor knew I was coming to see him—still he did not raise his head from his needle, like a craftsman busy with his work, who must not be idle.

At that, I took a cigarette and lit it, as if I had come for nothing else but to smoke a cigarette.

The tailor put down his needle and said in a singsong, 'The District Governor is friendly to me, and he will not resent it if I put off his work, for I have already made him a number of garments and you, sir, certainly need an overcoat, a fine, warm overcoat.' While speaking, he lifted himself up, skipped peculiarly, then said again in a singsong, 'A fine overcoat.'

The tailor took out a pattern book and began to discuss every single type of garment in extraordinary detail, explaining which coat was handsome and which was handsomer still, as well as the reason why he said the one was handsome and the other more so. Finally he put one leg over the other, bent his left arm, put his head inside it, and looked at me

48

through the wing with great affection. His cinnamon-brown eyes sparkled, and a kind of moisture appeared in them.

For many years he had not had the opportunity of making a new overcoat, but the pattern book he had was new, and there were many marks in it, which the tailor had made with his nails. There are many opinions among tailors; what one finds handsome the other does not, and every tailor changes and mends according to his own opinion.

I looked at the pattern book and could not find the overcoat I wanted. That tailor, on the other hand, guessed at every kind of coat, except the one I was looking for. He stood and looked at me, sometimes with affection and sometimes with great affection, rubbing his hands together. Suddenly he gave his peculiar skip and straightened himself like a stick. I said to him, 'Sit down, and I will tell you something.' So he sat down and fixed his eyes on my mouth.

I said to him, 'When I go to a barber and he does not know me, if he is a clever man he understands by himself what kind of haircut would suit me. If not, he asks me, and I tell him, "I am no expert at this kind of work; do it as you understand." If he is not a fool, he takes trouble with me and gives me a very good haircut, but if he is a fool, he says to himself: I will just pass the scissors over his head and take my money. I look in the mirror and see that he has made me look ugly. I say to myself: It is in the nature of hair to grow again, but this fellow, who has made me look ugly, will not see another penny of my money. So it is with the coat. I cannot imagine what kind of coat suits me and what kind does not; but you are an expert, so take thought and make me a coat that will suit me. And if you think an overcoat is not like a haircut, for a man has his hair done several times a year but he does not have an overcoat made until several years have passed, let me tell you that besides a coat I need other clothes as well.' The tailor looked glad and said, 'Words like these I have never heard in my life.' He closed his eyes, put his left hand on them, and added in a whisper, 'I shall make you a fine overcoat.'

After he had taken my measurements, he said, 'I shall now show you some fine fabrics, none better. Even if you

looked in all the shops you would not find anything like
them. If I say so, you can believe me.' 'I like to buy my
materials from a shop and give the work to a craftsman,' I
said, 'so that each can do his business and earn his money,
the shopkeeper with the materials and the craftsman with his
craft.'

The tailor paid no attention to what I said, took another
skip, and drew out a piece of cloth. Crushing it in his hand
and squeezing the edge into his palm, he said, 'You see, sir,
it's as smooth as before, exactly as it was before; you can't
see even a sign of a crease.' 'Didn't I tell you I want to buy
the cloth from a shopkeeper?' I replied. Said he, 'It wasn't to
have you buy from me that I showed you this; all I ask you
to do is to look at this piece.' 'I have already looked at it,'
said I. 'That was not what I asked you,' said he. 'Examine
the cloth with your hands.' I passed my hands over his cloth
and said, 'Very fine, very fine.' The tailor's face shone with
joy and he said, 'And didn't I tell you this cloth is fine? I am
not pressing you to buy it. All I ask is that you should hear
how it came into my hands.'

This is how that piece of cloth came into the tailor's
hands. The colonel of his battalion used to take every beautiful object that he saw in the possession of the enemy and
send it to his wife. He would pick out messengers and exempt
them from their army duties for a few days to take his booty
back to his wife. 'Once he sent me with all kinds of food and
drink, silver vessels and cloth, and gave me permission to
stay at home for a few days. I said to my comrades, "For a
year or more I have not seen my wife and children, and now
that I am going to visit them I have no presents to bring."
There was a certain soldier there, a Gentile of peasant stock—
I used to write letters for him to his father and mother. It
happened that his mother had sent him a pot of butter that
day. He gave me the butter and said, "Take it, brother, take
it and give it to your wife, to spread on the bread for your
children." When I came to the colonel's wife and brought her
the gifts from her husband, she saw the pot in my hand.
"What is that in your hand?" said she. "A little piece of butter,"
said I, "which I am bringing to my wife to spread on the
bread for our little children." Said she, "Tonight I am making

a banquet for the important people of the town, and I should like to have an extra piece of butter in the house. You take this piece of cloth and give me the butter." I found it hard, for I wanted to please my wife and children. But the lady took the pot from me and gave me the cloth. So I said to myself: So be it.'

Before I left the tailor, I told him to fix a time and keep to his word. I myself do not place a great value on my time, but I value a man's honor, for if he breaks his word his honor is soiled; and even more, he is a craftsman and I have a great respect for the honor of craftsmen, and I do not wish to see them doing wrong. The cloth I found in the shop was not so good as the tailor's, and it cost more, but I did not go to look for other shops, for there would be no end to the matter: however fine the goods, you can always find better. After I had paid for the material, the shopkeeper's wife asked me, 'To which tailor are you giving the cloth to make you a coat?' 'I have just come from Schuster,' I replied. 'A fine tailor you have found!' said the shopkeeper's wife. 'May the Lord not punish me for my words—he's nothing but a puffed-up pauper. All Schuster has to boast of is that he once lived in Germany. Heavens above, who didn't live in Germany? I know people who were in Paris. And if he was in Berlin, what about it? Perhaps Hindenburg commissioned him to make him a tefillin sack? Ha, ha, ha. Let me send for my own tailor and you will see the difference between one tailor and another.' 'I do not want to have him waste his time for nothing,' said I. 'What d'you mean for nothing?' exclaimed the shopkeeper's wife. 'Isn't that what he's there for? Feivel, Feivel,' cried the woman to her husband, 'why don't you say something? Just you listen to what my husband says. Sometimes a man says a thing a thousand women can't say!' Said her husband, 'After all, the gentleman has just come from Schuster, and found him suitable.' 'What d'you mean, found him suitable?' said his wife. 'What does a man know? They tell him that's a tailor, and he believes them. If the world depended only on men, the human race would have died out already. I am surprised they didn't tell you anything in the hotel. Wasn't it Dolik who sent your honor to my shop?' 'Not at all,' I replied, 'it was Schuster who sent me to you.' 'Schuster?

But whenever anyone comes to him he offers them his own cloth.' 'And has he cloth to sell?' 'He had.' 'And now?' 'Now, O sir, he has nothing left. And whatever he has left he needs for himself.' 'Why for himself?' I asked. 'Because he has a sick wife at home. She is sick with asthma, and he puts his cloth under her head, for all the pillows he has are not enough. You should thank the Almighty, sir, that you didn't take his cloth. Surely you haven't come here to take the pillow from under a sick woman's head. I hear that your honor comes from the Land of Israel. It's very hot there. Burns like fire. There's a lad who's come back from there, no doubt you've seen him. He's dark and he has a double forelock. He works at repairing the roads. Now that boy says it's just the same there as here, and the same here as there. In fact, it's hotter there than here, but for most of the day there's a wind blowing that softens the heat a little; and here it's different—when it's hot a man can't stand the heat. But who'd believe him? He's a communist, half a Bolshevik, or perhaps more than half, and that's why they put him out of there, for the Land of Israel was given only for the Zionists. But what do the Zionists get out of it all? They get killed there. One lad from our town was there—really you can't call him a lad, for he got married there. Anyway, that lad I was talking about, Daniel Bach's brother—that's the one-legged fellow who goes about with a wooden leg—was killed there for nothing. He was standing one night on guard and an Arab passed by, so the Arab took it into his head to fire a bullet at him, and he did and killed him. And the English look on and say nothing. And surely the English are not just *goyim* who hate Jews, so why do they say nothing? What do you think, sir, is there any remedy for the Land of Israel? My father, may he rest in peace, used to say that if it was a good thing for us, our Emperor would say to the Turk, "Listen!" and the Turk would immediately give him the whole of the Land of Israel. Since you're in a hurry, sir, I don't want to hold you up, but what I ask you is this: If you have to get a suit made you should know that we have all kinds of fine cloth in our shop.'

Her husband spoke up. 'I used to know his grandfather, may he rest in peace,' said he. 'He held me at my circumci-

sion.' His wife interrupted him. 'So now you've finished singing the praises of his grandfather?' cried she. 'And is that all
his grandfather did for you? Didn't he give you a present at
your wedding, a spicebox of pure silver? Before the Russians
marched in and took it away, it used to stand in our house.'
'Now you've already told about it and didn't let me tell,' replied her husband. 'My husband's a modest man,' said the
shopkeeper's wife, 'and he leaves others to praise him, but I
say if you don't praise yourself, others certainly won't praise
you.' Said the shopkeeper, 'His grandfather, may he rest in
peace, used to send a wedding present to everyone he had held
on his knees at circumcision.' 'To everyone?' said his wife,
clenching her hands together. 'Anyway, the present he gave you
was better than anyone else's, for he gave you a box of pure
silver. Just wait, your honor, and my husband will bring you
your roll of cloth to the tailor.' 'There is no need,' I said. 'If
you don't want to trouble my husband,' said the shopkeeper's
wife, 'here is Ignatz; he will bring it.' 'I want to accustom myself to carry my own cloth,' I replied. 'What d'you mean, you
want to accustom yourself?' said the woman. 'Will you really
carry a parcel in the marketplace?' 'That was what I intended
when I bought cloth to make a coat,' I replied. 'And what difference does it make to me if I carry my coat afterwards, or if
I carry it now?'

CHAPTER TWELVE

On the Way and at the Hotel

When I left the shop, it was still day. Although the time had
come for the sun to disappear, there was no sign of evening.
    The sun stood stuck to the sky, like an inseparable part
of it, and a kind of warmth tempered the air. This air, as well
as the light of the sun, changed the faces of the passers-by,
and they became more pleasant to each other. People I did
not know nodded their heads and greeted me. Along came Ignatz and followed me, wanting to carry my parcel. Shopkeep-

ers looked at me and the parcel in my hand. The shops were many and the customers were few, and anyone who bought something in one shop aroused the resentment of the other shopkeepers. On the way I came across that young man of whom the shopkeeper's wife had spoken. I had seen him many times before, and I was fond of him. I must say he was not dark, but sunburnt, and his forelock was not double; that woman had been chattering nonsense, for what is the meaning of a double forelock? This forelock I'm speaking of gave him a manly look. I do not like men who have nothing on their head but their forelock like the peacock who covers his ugly feet with his beautiful feathers. But it was not so with that young man, Yeruham Freeman; he had something else besides his forelock. You could see that painful things had happened to him and he had pushed them away from his heart, just as he pushes his forelock away from his forehead. His face was lean, like the rest of the people of Szibucz nowadays, and he had a small dimple in his right cheek. People usually call a mark like that a charm spot, and in fact it added charm to his face and contradicted all the indignation in his eyes.

Yeruham was sitting by the roadside near the King's Well, cutting a drain to prevent the water's flooding the road. You find young fellows like him in the Land of Israel in every town and village, and you pay no heed to them. Here in Szibucz he was something new. There sits a Jewish lad outdoors in Szibucz mending the road, and he imagines he is mending the whole world. Between ourselves, this work he is doing is superfluous. You who do not know Szibucz may say: What do you mean by superfluous? After all, the road is in bad repair, so it ought to be mended. But I, who do know Szibucz, say: What is the good of mending one place, when all the other roads are in bad repair, and it seems to me that they can never be mended? But I mention all this only in connection with Yeruham's work. Of Yeruham himself, all that can be said is that he is digging up the dirt and sitting in the mud. When he saw me, he gave me an unfriendly look, and went back to his work as if I were not there. I took no offense, but greeted him, and even put out my hand. He paid no attention and did not return my greeting, or, if he did, he returned it under his breath.

I looked back at Ignatz and saw him talking to Yeruham. I did not like that: first, because he had suddenly left me alone, and second, because my arms were getting tired. I shifted my parcel to my left hand and said to myself: Ignatz has left me only for my own benefit, to tell that young fellow that I am the best of men, that I always give and give generously. I wonder if the lad is not sorry he behaved discourteously to me. I felt sorry for him and decided to give him an opportunity to make it up with me.

In the meantime the day was passing. The sun, which had stood stuck in the sky, as if inseparable from it, had disappeared. Yeruham rose, shook the dirt from his clothes, took up his tools, and went off. So I went to the tailor, left the cloth with him, and returned to my hotel.

In those days the hotel was empty of guests. Apart from myself, there was only an old man who had to make a declaration on oath in court. When he was hungry he would take out a crust from his basket and eat. When they brought him a glass of tea, he would drink hesitantly, for a glass of tea costs a penny, and he did not have a spare penny in his pocket. Before the war he had fields and orchards in the countryside, and a large house in town; he was one of the owners of the Szibucz bank, with a handsome, intelligent wife and successful sons. Then the war came, took away his sons, sent his wife out of her mind, and destroyed his house; others took over his property, and of all his wealth nothing was left but debts. The Lord impoverishes and makes rich, enriches and makes poor.

This is how that man's troubles started. On the day he went off to war his wife went out to the fields to survey her property. She saw that the crops were standing ripe and scorching in the sun, for there was no one to take up the sickle and reap. She was still waiting there when they came and told her that her two sons had fallen in battle. In her grief she pulled off her kerchief and threw it on the ground. So the sun beat down on her head and touched her mind.

There is nothing new or out of the ordinary in this story,

and I tell it only to show how welcome I am to the people of the hotel, which has such poor guests.

Krolka laid the table and brought in supper. I must say to my hostess' credit that the meal was tasty as usual; but to my own discredit I admit that I did not touch it, much to her distress. I noticed that distress and said, 'There is one kind of food that I should like, namely olives.' 'Olives!' said the inn-keeper's wife. 'But they are salty and bitter.' I nodded my head and said, 'Yes, salty and bitter.' 'Look,' said Rachel, 'you say "salty and bitter" and you look as if you were eating something sweet.' 'When I was in Hungary,' said the mistress of the house, 'I was served with olives. I thought they were plums, so I took a handful and ate them. What shall I tell you? They twisted my lips and I wanted to spit out my tongue—they were so salty and bitter.' 'In your mouth they are salty and bitter,' I replied, 'but to me they are sweet. Until I left the Land of Israel I never sat down to a meal without olives. Any meal without olives was not called a meal.' Said Babtchi, 'Every man to his taste. If anyone served me figs, I'd eat them.' Said Dolik, 'I like one of our pears and apples better than all the figs and dates and carobs and all the other kinds of fruit the Zionists boast about.' 'Figs are tasty and fragrant,' said I to Babtchi, 'but they cannot compare with olives. Now let us hear what Mistress Rachel has to say.' Rachel blushed. 'I have never eaten olives,' said she, 'but I can imagine they're fine food.' 'What makes you think they're fine food?' asked Babtchi. 'Look, she is blushing.' Her mother spat and said, 'May all my enemies' faces go green! What made you start on her all of a sudden?' 'What did I say?' said Babtchi. 'I only said she was blushing. And if her face was red, what of it? I think red is just as nice as black, for example.' 'I don't see that I was blushing,' said Rachel. 'And is there any reason why I should blush?' And as she spoke she blushed still more. Babtchi laughed. 'Dolik,' she cried, 'did you hear? She doesn't see she's blushing and she doesn't know the reason. Ladies and gentle-men, perhaps you will explain the reason.' Rachel rose, saying, 'Am I blushing? I'll go and see in the mirror.' Dolik put out his tongue at Babtchi and laughed. The innkeeper looked at his son and daughter, pushed his thumb angrily into the bowl

of his pipe, and asked, 'Where is Lolik?' 'Lolik? He's gone to his lady.' Said I to myself: You did well that night to let Rachel vanquish you. Now, not only does she follow what you say, but she agrees with you even about things of which she knows nothing. I was so puffed up with myself that I forgot what had happened to me with that young fellow, Yeruham Freeman.

CHAPTER THIRTEEN

The Overcoat

Schuster's house is in King's Street behind the well, one of a few scattered houses that have survived the war. It is close to the street and a little below street level, so there is a smell of damp about the place; but at night there is just the smell of damp and by day there is a smell of dust as well. The whole house consists of one square room and is no higher than an ordinary man, for it was built long ago, when people were lowly in their own eyes and content with small houses. High on the wall, near the ceiling, to the right of the door, is a long, narrow window, through which you can see the heads of the passers-by but not their faces, though you can hear their voices and see the dust they raise with their feet. One broken shutter hangs over the window outside, and when the wind passes the shutter knocks on the window and shuts out the light. Apart from the paraphernalia of the tailor's craft, such as a sewing machine, a long table, two irons, a mirror, and a wooden, cloth-covered dummy shaped like a woman without head or feet, on which the clothes are measured, there is not much furniture in the room. And for this reason the plush-covered chair that stands near the fireplace stands out particularly; they brought it from Berlin, where they used to live before they came back to Szibucz.

This chair has had many adventures. During the war some people grew rich and built themselves mansions, which they adorned with antique furniture, like nobles with long pedigrees. They used to go to old peasants in distant villages to

buy old furniture, and pay with good money. In order to have
something to sell, the peasants commissioned the craftsmen in
town to make furniture of the kind that was sought after.
When a rich man came to buy, the peasant would be struck
with amazement and say, 'Mother of God, a piece that my
great-grandfather's great-grandfather in the time of the Great
Prince put aside as unfit for use, and the city folk come and
want to buy it!' It seems reasonable that they would sell such
things cheap, but not at all. First, because professors had already proposed putting them in a museum; and second, how
can a man let out of his house a piece like this which has been
standing there for four hundred years without even asking
once for food or drink? When the rich people heard this they
would give the peasant as much as he wanted; sometimes they
gave him a new piano for a chair like this. When the plague
of inflation came and the rich men lost their property, they
sold their mansions to foreigners. These foreigners did not
have the *Gemüt* of the Germans; they threw all those things
out or sold them for next to nothing, so the tailor was lucky
enough to buy that chair, and the newspapers made the whole
of Germany ring with the story: a chair on which German
princes used to sit, a Polish Jew now sat on. It was a blessed
thing Schuster did not read the papers and did not know that
he had helped to add to the malice of Israel's enemies.

Whenever I come to Schuster, I find his wife sitting on
the chair, with a stool at her feet and two sticks at her side,
one propped against her knee and the other on the floor. She
is not thin like her husband; on the contrary, she is fat and
thick, for most of the time she lies on her bed behind the
curtain that divides the room, or sits on this chair with a long
pipe in her mouth filled with fragrant herbs, smoking to ease
her breathing, for she suffers from asthma. It was because of
this sickness that they left Berlin and came back to Szibucz,
although they made an ample living in Berlin and here they
really don't have enough for a proper meal. And why did they
move? Because the walls of the houses in Berlin reach up to
the sky and block the air one breathes.

At first the tailor used to boast to me that all the nobles
flocked to his door, as they were great connoisseurs and knew

that he was an artist. But as soon as he started to make my coat he forgot the nobles and they forgot him, and not a man turned up to have a patch put on. And this was really a surprise: here was a skillful tailor, expert in making clothes, and he was left to sit in idleness.

Schuster stands bent over the table, arranging the cloth, pursing his lips but leaving them slightly open, as if he meant to whistle, examining the cloth again and cutting it. There is something marvelous about this cloth, which the tailor has cut. Yesterday it was formless; now he has passed the scissors over it, and cut it, and given it a form. The form is still latent, but you can guess that he is making an overcoat. He is a great craftsman, this tailor. You have one advantage over him, because you have the money, but between ourselves, does money do anything? If you put together all your banknotes could you make an overcoat with them? You have another advantage over him: he is dressed in rags, while you cover yourself with a fine, whole overcoat. But this joy the tailor feels when he produces something well made is greater even than the joy of the overcoat's owner.

Let us stay with the tailor a little, so long as he is engaged in making the overcoat. I sit before the tailor's wife and we talk to each other. This woman is sickly and housebound; there is no one at home except her husband, for she buried her sons in Berlin before they came back. Here she has only her husband, and he's no man to talk with, for whenever he opens his mouth he weeps because he has left Berlin, where he lived a decent life and earned a decent livelihood. That is why she likes to talk to me. At first I used to tell the praises of Germany when speaking to her, but when I saw that this disturbed her I started to praise Szibucz. What a fine town it was before the war. What fine people its people were. And even though your parents in Szibucz did not use foreign expressions like *Kindchen*, you saw yourself as a beloved child.

The praise of Szibucz brought back to her her youth, when she was a good-looking young girl and lived with her father and mother on the big hill behind the Beit Midrash, and all the young craftsmen used to run after her, until Schuster came and captured her heart. The sound of his voice misled her and she thought he was thinking of her good, but he was thinking only of his own good, that he should have a good-looking wife. And when she listened to him and married him, he led her on again with the sound of his voice and brought her to Germany, where the houses are high up to the sky, blotting out the sun, and no one eats fruit fresh from the tree. And when a man wants to enjoy himself he goes to the café, where the Germans sit packed together, reading newspapers, playing billiards, and smoking cigars with a smell no one can stand. If a person wants to enjoy himself more, he goes outside the city and travels for hours in long, high railroad carriages. 'Do you think, my friend, that outside their cities you find a grassy spot? Nothing of the kind. For there, too, the houses are high up to the sky. And if you find gardens or trees there, those gardens and trees are not alive, my friend; they are just trickery, like most of the things the Germans do, for they make everything in their factories. Once I saw a cherry tree. I put out my hand and picked a cherry, but as soon as I sank my teeth in it I learned it was made of wax. I say to my husband, "Schuster, isn't there any place here where one can have a good time?" Says he to me: "Sprintze, wait a little and I will bring you to a place where you'll burst your sides laughing." Say I to him: "Let my enemies burst their sides laughing, so long as I can get relief from boredom." So he brings me to one of their theaters. There you see all kinds of Germans, men and women. They look like human beings, but they are dummies and dolls—just like the Germans themselves, for the males are like dummies and the women like dolls. And what annoys you most, my friend, is that all the people who are sitting with you in the theater are laughing or crying, all according to the actions of the dummies or dolls. And here your gall is likely to split. Heaven almighty, do I have to laugh or cry because that German is jumping about and talking nonsense? From their amusements you can tell what the rest is like. But a man has every right to do whatever he likes in his own country, and the Germans are entitled to bore each other to tears. So I say to Schuster, "Schuster, I don't want any of it; d'you hear? I don't want it." Says he to me, "*Kindchen*, what do you mean you don't want it? Should I turn the whole of Germany upside down just because you don't like it?" Say I to him, "Leave Germany just as it is. Neither you nor your friends will make the Germans any different, but I tell you I don't want it, and you've no right to call me *Kindchen*." Says he to me, "What do you want, then, that I should call you a red cow?" For you must know, my friend, that at that time I still had all my hair, and it was red like the red cow in the Bible. And that made the eyes of the German women pop out of their heads, for their hair is the color of dust, and mine was red and shining. In short, I tell him one thing and he tells me another. Suddenly I go cough, cough, cough —suddenly, oh, my friend, I lose my breath, and I can't say a word, only cough, cough, cough! Schuster is beside himself and wants to call a doctor. I say to him, "Never mind the doctors." Says he to me, "Well, then, what shall I do?" I say to him, "What shall you do? Take me back to Szibucz." Schuster gets even more excited and cries, "How can I take you back to Szibucz, for . . . ?" Say I, "Cough, cough, cough, cough!"—not three times but four times. All the same, he ignored what I said and brought a doctor. Says the doctor, "Madam is suffering from asthma." Say I to Schuster, "Now Schuster, you've become wiser, for you've learned a new German word." Says Schuster, "What shall I do?" Say I to him, "And didn't I tell you—cough, cough, cough!—and didn't I tell you I want to go back to Szibucz?" Says he to me, "And didn't I tell you it's impossible? Szibucz is in ruins and most of her people have died, some in the war, some in the plague, and some of other diseases." Say I to him, "But the air of Szibucz is still there. Take me back and let me breathe the air of Szibucz before I choke here." It didn't take long before he was severely punished for not listening to me. For my two children fell sick of typhoid and died. And they shouldn't have died, for they were pure and innocent like angels. And why did they die?—because we lived in a foreign country. If I'd been living in my own town, I'd have stretched myself on the grave of my fathers and shaken heaven and earth with my voice, and the children would have lived. After they died Schuster began to think about what I had said and

prepared to leave. Another reason for leaving was the inflation, but that was not the main reason. The main reason, my
friend, was what I had said earlier. Although that reason, I
mean the inflation, was enough to drive a man out of the
world. Just imagine, my friend, that you have become a mil-
lionaire, a real Rothschild, and with all your millions you
can't buy even half a pound of cherries. Once Schuster worked
a whole week for Pieck & Klottenburg, a shop that sold
clothes; they'd never taken in a Jewish workman, though
most of their customers were Jews, but in those days they
allowed even Jewish tailors to work for them. Schuster worked
all week and got a sackful of millions for his pay. I said to
him, "Schuster, if they hear we have so much money, robbers
will come, God forbid, and kill us." What does he answer? He
doesn't say a word, just puts his hands on his hips and laughs.
I say to him, "Cough, cough, cough! What are you laughing
like that for?" Says he to me, "Here, I'll throw all the money
into the street and the robbers won't have to take the trouble
to come into the house." Say I to him, "Heaven forbid, that
wasn't what I meant." Says he to me, "Before the robbers
come to pick up the millions, a policeman will come and fine
me for throwing this rubbish in the street." Ever hear such
things, my friend? And right he was, all that money wasn't
worth a penny.

'On top of that, Schuster began to get mixed up in politics. I say to him, "What have you to do with politics? If the
Germans are divided among themselves, why should a Jew
stick his nose in? Let them beat each other until they hurt
their hands and stop." And meanwhile, my friend, human
blood is spilled in the streets and I am struck with terror. I
thought those Germans were dummies, but when it comes to
bloodshed they are just like all the Gentiles, and they kill each
other because Hans has a different opinion from Fritz and
Mueller from Schmidt. In short, my friend, it isn't good. And
if they kill each other though they are Gentiles, what will
happen, heaven forbid, when they get to Schuster, and he a
Jew? And meanwhile, my friend—cough, cough, cough!—I get
short of breath, so I can't explain the whole matter to him
properly. But I pay no attention to myself and my sickness,

and tell him all my heart tells me. Says he to me, "Silly dear"—
that's what he says to me, and not in affection, but just "Silly
dear," and perhaps there was even a hint of anger in his voice.
I could have forgiven him for everything, but he went on to
add some more rude expressions, and even called me an owl,
though I don't know why he thought of calling me that. I
wanted to answer him so he should know that there were rude
expressions to fit him too, but at this point I couldn't get a
word out of my mouth; all I could say was "cough, cough,
cough!" And it wasn't only at that moment, but whenever I
wanted to tell him something, that cough, cough, cough came
and closed my mouth, sometimes for a long time and sometimes for a short, for in those days the sickness had spread
right through my body. But since it had spread, Schuster
had to come back here with me. Perhaps you think, my friend,
that I'm telling you something that isn't true; if you do, ask
Schuster. Here he is standing beside you; let him say if I've
been exaggerating.'

Schuster stood by the table doing his work, his head bent
and one shoulder jutting up. Whenever I tried to look at him,
his wife started her talk and prevented me. 'This sickness isn't
like the other diseases, which spoil the blood vessels,' the
woman said, 'but there's a certain evil spirit in the world that
attacks a person who has gone far away from where he was
born; it comes and sits at the entrance to his heart, and there's
no remedy but smoking. It's done this way: they bring herbs
from that person's town, of the kind that grow near the house
he was born in, and put them in a pipe—it makes no difference where the pipe was made—and he smokes it, and the
smoke dulls the brain of the evil spirit and eases the breathing.' She, too, had been greatly relieved. But the relief was
not sufficient until she herself found out the secret. 'And of
course, my friend, knowledge of the disease is half the remedy.'
In fact she was already half healed, for at the beginning she
used to cough, cough, cough three or four at a time, and now
only three, and sometimes even two. 'And you, my friend,'
she said, suddenly changing the subject, 'were in the Land of
Israel and came back here. I'll tell you why you came back:
because you felt a longing to eat the fruit of the trees in our

town. Wait, my friend, wait till summer, when the trees are
covered with fruit, and you stretch out your hand and pick,
today a bunch of cherries and tomorrow an apple or a pear.
That pleasure, my friend, no one fully enjoys except in the
town where he was born. And just then you hear the singing
of a bird that was also born in the same tree, in that same
tree where you are eating the fruit. And the girls in the field
answer the song of the bird. Now, my friend, the cold days are
coming and all the world is cold. But never mind that—if
only the Jewish exile would last no longer than the winter!—
the summer will soon be back again to its nest.'

The Almighty distributes His cold according to a man's
clothes. Once I had covered myself with my overcoat, the
whole world was filled with cold. The overcoat was handsome
and warm, and very well made. I was surprised they didn't
call me the Man with the Coat. That was a fitting name for
me, and I was fitting for it, for I was the only man in the town
with this fine, warm coat. I hold myself straight and have no
fear of the cold. If there is any question of fear, it is the cold
that is afraid of me. If only you could see how it humbles
itself before me, how hard it tries to warm itself in my coat.
But I pretend I do not notice it, and the cold shrinks into
itself, as if it were nothing at all.

The overcoat has somewhat changed the character of
this man. When a poor man comes up to me, I do not put my
hand in my pocket as before to take out a copper; I find it
troublesome to pull up the skirts of my coat and put in my
hand to take out my purse. Since it is troublesome, I turn my
eyes away from the poor man, and I feel angry at the poor,
born to make trouble for people. Since the day I first saw
Ignatz, I have been in the habit of giving to him generously.
But now, when he stands before me and cries 'Mu'es,' I hide
both my eyes from him, and at that moment the Almighty has
only the two eyes of this invalid and the hole in place of his
nose, where a grenade splinter pierced him.

But here let me leave the matter of the overcoat for a
moment, and justify myself for not acting properly toward
Ignatz. Now he is like an innocent lamb, but in the days of
the war he was like a ravenous wolf. Decent people told me

that he used to go from place to place, with friends as empty and nasty as himself, breaking into houses, robbing and plundering, and leaving people with nothing.

Let me come back to the matter of the overcoat. There is another thing about this new overcoat: I feel as if I were wearing a mirror, and when I go out into the marketplace this mirror blinds people's eyes.

I have compared my overcoat to a mirror, and indeed it is like that, for by means of it I can see the people of the town. The whole town is dressed in rags, and through the rags I can see their wearers. So long as a man is dressed in whole garments he is not completely seen, but when his clothes are torn you can immediately see him as he is. It is the way of a garment to deceive, for it covers the body. It is only a man's holes that reveal him. And it is not only his body they reveal, but his soul also. The flesh that peeps out through the holes sometimes looks like a poor man's hand asking for charity, and sometimes like the hand of a poor man who has despaired of charity. And it is not only the owners of the rags I see; I see myself too, whether my heart is good and whether I have compassion for the poor.

There are some holes that do not reveal a man's flesh but only another torn garment, which is in no better shape than the torn garment over it. It is whole in one place and torn in another. Poverty does not fly like a pistol bullet, which scorches the garment right down to the flesh; it twists and turns like a tangle of thorns, winding its way into one place and leaving another alone.

Why do people not repair their clothes? Surely they could use the time it takes them to cover their holes with their hands to pick up a needle and thread and a patch to sew up the holes. But since their hands are occupied in covering their holes they are not free to repair their clothes.

CHAPTER FOURTEEN

Rachel

It is hard to make out my host's character. He sees Dolik and Lolik and Babtchi doing whatever they like and he says nothing, but when he sees his younger daughter going about like a mute lamb, he is angry. Whenever she comes into the room, he immediately puffs at his pipe as if his anger were blowing through him. Is she worse than her brothers and sisters? I am not telling tales or revealing secrets if I say they have no spark of Jewishness in them.

Babtchi, the innkeeper's eldest child, has her hair cut like a boy's, wears a leather jacket, and is never without a cigarette in her mouth. She behaves like the young men, and not like the best but like the worst of them. She was the girl I saw smoking on the eve of the Day of Atonement. Lolik is fat and heavy, his jowls slack and ruddy, hanging down to his chin. His shoulders are thin and round, and his chest bulges upward toward the Napoleonic forelock that hangs over his forehead and shades his eyes, which smile like a country girl's. When you see Babtchi and Lolik, you wonder whether this one is the brother of the other or the other is the sister of this one. Perhaps I have exaggerated slightly, but in the main I have not. Their brother Dolik is no better. He is a mocker and a rude fellow. If he jested at those who are well off I would say he benefits from it and they lose nothing. But he mocks at wretches, who are insulted all their lives, like Hanoch and his wife, and his horse. Hanoch and his wife do not mind, but the horse turns his head aside whenever he sees Dolik and droops his tail dejectedly. There is that pauper in the town, left over from the Austrian armies, Ignatz, who was struck by the judgment of God and had his nose blown off in the war. Once he came to the hotel to beg for charity. Dolik poured him out a glass of brandy. The poor man put out his hand to take it, but Dolik said, 'No, no—only if you drink it

66

with your nose.' And he has no nose, for it was struck by a
grenade splinter, which left him nothing there but a hole.
I said to Dolik, 'How can a man born of a Jewish woman be
so cruel to his brother? He too was created in the image of
God. And if for our many transgressions his image is defaced,
does he deserve to have you jest at him?' Dolik laughed and
said, 'If you like the look of him, send him to the kvutzot as
a model to the girls, so that they should bear children as
handsome as he is.' At that moment I felt like doing to Dolik
what they had done to Ignatz, but I said to myself: One
man's wound is enough for us. Now that I have told you something of the way they behave, is it not surprising that my host
leaves them alone and quarrels only with Rachel?

I have no interest in Rachel's brothers and sister. At first
they sought my company, but when they saw I thought little
of them they left me alone. Still, they are respectful to me,
because I am well dressed, and eat and drink without working, and because I have always lived in big cities. They, too,
once lived in a big city, Vienna, but the Vienna where they
found themselves during the war was no different from Szibucz, while I, on the other hand, have lived in Berlin and
Leipzig, Munich and Wiesbaden, and other great cities. If so,
why did he go to live in the Land of Israel? But before you
ask that, you might as well ask why he came to Szibucz. In
any case, even there, in the Land of Israel, he did not work as
a laborer, not like those they call pioneers, who leave their
homes and wallow in the dust.

I have no interest in Dolik, nor in Lolik, nor in Babtchi—
but with Rachel, my host's younger daughter, I do sometimes
talk. Why should Rachel spend so much time talking to me?
If it is because I smile at her, so does every other guest. And if
it is because her father and mother are fond of me, do children
always follow the affections of their parents? Or perhaps we
do not actually converse with each other, but every word that
comes from Rachel's lips seems to me like a complete conversation. Let me pause a little, to see if I can remember her
words.

This very act of remembering is a thing to wonder at.
Until that child came along all your body was in your own

possession, but when she let fall a word or two they won a place in your heart, so that you gave up part of what was yours and it became hers.

What did Rachel tell and what did she not tell? Some of her words I have told elsewhere, and some are of no importance except for the time when they were spoken. If so, why should they be remembered? For the place where Rachel has deposited her words belongs to Rachel, and she can do as she pleases in her own domain. However, may Rachel be blessed for not having laid claim to all that is mine, so that I can remember some words that were not Rachel's, such as those her mother told me.

Rachel was three years old when the war struck us. A few weeks before, she felt pains in her head and her limbs, and lost all her strength. There was never a smile on her lips, she did not play with her friends, and she had a high fever. It was difficult to know what sickness this was, for she was a baby and you could not tell it from her words. The fever burned in her, and her intestines were upset. But her mother did not pay attention to this, for she thought she had become constipated because she was not eating. As a result of fever, hunger, and lack of appetite, Rachel's weight fell day by day. The face of the little one, which had looked like a red apple, shriveled up like a dried fig. Her skin hung on the bones of her hands and feet like an umbrella case when the umbrella has been taken away and nothing is left but the stick; she was just like a mildewed ear of corn. The fat that rounds out the limbs of healthy children and gives them charm was all gone; her body was enveloped in thin, dry, burning skin that hung slackly on her bones. In the second week of the war the fever went down a little in the morning, but Rachel was still and silent, paying no attention to anything, and lay in her bed immersed in dreams; and when evening fell the fever rose again. After a few days, the fever fell in the evening too, but Rachel was silent, as if she felt nothing, and she asked for neither water nor food. After a month the fever stopped and her digestion began to come back to normal. She ate a little gruel, and you could see the first signs of recovery. Suddenly her temperature rose again and the sickness returned. Her

weight fell until it was down to twenty pounds. 'Nevertheless,'
her mother said, 'we didn't despair. On the contrary, we hoped
she was beginning to recover, for we knew that this disease,
which is called paratyphus, is not generally fatal. But we did
not know then that it was a children's disease, and indeed the
disease passed, thank God, and the children got better. In
fact, they recovered what they had lost by their sickness. And
I need not tell you that God was good to Rachel and adorned
her with every kind of beauty and charm in the world.'

To cut a long story short, Rachel was three years old when
the calamity of the war reached the town and there was a
rumor that the enemy was near. The whole town took to its
heels and fled, some on carts and some on foot, for most of
the horses had already been taken to serve the King, and there
were not enough for all the people. So Rachel's mother took a
large shawl, tied one end to her shoulders and the other to
her waist, and put in the child, wrapped around with cushions
and blankets against the cold. Although the sun was burning
hot, she was afraid Rachel might catch cold. So she set out
with all the other people of the town, with Rachel tied to her
back and the other three children dragging after her, holding
on to her skirts, Dolik on one side and Lolik and Babtchi on the
other, and sometimes the other way around, Lolik and Babtchi
on one side and Dolik on the other. And Rachel peeped out
from among the cushions and blankets, above her mother's
shoulder, not uttering a word, so that you did not notice her
at all. The mother would turn her head and see that Rachel
was sleeping, and then turn to the three children running
about at her feet and changing place all the time, Babtchi and
Lolik here, and Dolik there. So they walked for hours, in a
crowd of exiles, old men and women, pregnant women, in-
valids and children—all the roads were black with them. Now
Dolik and Babtchi and Lolik were little and weak, holding on
to her skirts, and Rachel was fastened to her back, so the
mother walked slowly in order not to make things hard for
them. And she moved slowly for her own sake as well, for it
was very hot at the time, and she was not in the habit of
walking in the heat. Finally she found herself at the end of
the whole caravan, separated from it by a curtain of dust. She

closed her eyes and went on walking in her sleep. And the heat continued to rise; the dust penetrated and covered the sun; the pillows, blankets, and shawls pressed heavy on her body and her body sweated; outside of this, she could feel nothing, not even the child's breathing, not even her voice. The mother thought Rachel was asleep, and she gave thanks to the Almighty for lulling the child to sleep so that it did not feel the trials of the journey. And the mother turned in her daze to the other children and comforted them with loving words. She said to herself: My husband has gone out to war and does not know that the town has been condemned to flee and his wife and children are wandering on the roads. And perhaps even the Almighty does not know; for if He knew, would He hide His eyes from their trouble? At that moment she was seized with despair, and if she had not had compassion for her children she would have wished to die.

As she was walking, she came to a hill. She and her children climbed the hill and then went down the other side. Rachel fell out of the shawl and her mother did not notice, since the pillows and blankets pressed heavily on her back and they weighed more than the child, whose entire weight was only twenty pounds. The children suddenly stopped and sat down. 'Perhaps you want to eat?' she said. 'Perhaps you would like to drink?' She turned her back to take out water and food from her satchel, and saw the pillows and blankets on her back —but no Rachel. For as she had come down the hill the shawl had struck the side of the hill and the knot at her waist had loosened, and Rachel had fallen out. Rachel's mother lifted up her voice and cried aloud, until the sound reached the end of the caravan. People turned around and called after her not to go back, for the sound of the enemy's guns could already be heard. But she ignored them; she handed over her three children to some of the people and started to go back, while the children screamed and wept, 'Mother, Mother, we don't want to stay without Mother.' She ran and ran until she found Rachel lying among thorns, with hornets circling her, ready to sting. She bent down to shield Rachel, picked her up in her arms and ran with her through the fields and forests, hills and valleys (for in her confusion she lost her way), and did not find the people of her town and of her group, or Dolik, Lolik, and Babtchi, for they had already turned and gone in another direction. There she stood, crying, 'My children, my children.' Along came another group of Jewish refugees, so she joined them and walked on with them, holding Rachel fast in her arms, for not every day does a miracle happen. After several days they came to the Hungarian frontier. A widow, a Gentile woman, had pity on them and took her and Rachel into her house. 'All I have in the house is for you, just as for me,' she said. 'It may well be that while you are staying with me my son may be staying with your sister, and in return for my kindness to you she will be kind to my son.'

So she stayed with that widow until her feet, which had been bruised on the roads, were healed and her body was somewhat recovered, and looked after Rachel until she was well again. But since it is not right to accept favors for nothing, she did not stay there long, especially as they had had words, because of the good heart of that Gentile woman, who was sorry for her because she would not taste any cooked food or let the sick child taste soup and meat, for her food, of course, was not prepared according to Jewish law. So Rachel's mother left all the widow's kindness behind and went to the town, where she found work as a maid in a hotel, for which she received her food and lodging. There she stayed until she heard that her children were in Vienna. She took Rachel and went to Vienna, where she found them, one here and one there, clad in rags, hungry and barefoot, their bodies bruised. She gathered them together, took a room, and healed their bodies. Merciful people gave her work to earn her living, and one who took particular trouble was Rabbi Zvi Perez Chajes, of blessed memory, who spent himself completely in the service of the Jews and was like an angel of deliverance to them. She earned her living with her own hands making knapsacks for soldiers, and when she was out of that work she found other employment, to keep herself and her children, and even make enough to send tobacco to her husband, for he could do without anything except smoking. At first, before he went into the army, he did not smoke, but when the war came he could not go on without smoking, for smoking dulls the reason, and distracts a man's mind from his deeds. At last the war ended and some people began to think of going back to their home towns. So the woman took her children and went back to Szibucz. It was not in one day, or two, or three, that they went back; but they wandered for weeks and weeks on the roads, for all the trains were full of returning soldiers, and many who found no room inside the trains climbed up and lay on the roofs. Some were wounded there and others were killed. May the good God have mercy on their bones, scattered along the wayside, and comfort their dear ones.

In short, they came to Szibucz hungry, thirsty, and weary. Now Szibucz itself was in ruins in those days, and people were tired and depressed, restless and homeless, no one knowing where he would lay his head or find his next meal. After several days, Mrs. Zommer's husband returned, melancholy and dejected, and it goes without saying that he came back without a penny, except for an iron amulet the government gave him for standing up like a hero in battle. What should he do? Go back to selling hats? Was there a single man there with a head on his shoulders? Said Mrs. Zommer, 'People come to tour the town and see the ruins, and they need bed and board. I will open a hotel, and whatever I have left over from the guests I will give my husband and children.' So she set to with great vigor and opened a hotel. After some time the rest of the people came back to Szibucz and the town returned to life, and charity officials, commercial travelers, and others began to arrive. 'So by God's mercy,' she said, 'we managed to keep alive, sometimes in pain and sometimes in pleasure, whatever seemed fitting to the Almighty, more than we deserve according to our deeds.'

I sit in the hotel, sometimes in pain and sometimes in pleasure, whatever seems fitting to the Almighty. Even in this hotel, where I am a guest for the night, there are things that give pleasure to the beholder. Rachel, the innkeeper's younger daughter, sits and sews, passes the thread through the hole of the needle, or takes the tip of it between her lips, and I watch her as she works as if she were doing my eyes a kindness. And since I am not ungrateful I tell her things to sweeten her work.

What did I tell her and what did I not tell her. If I were telling Rachel this story at this very moment, I should tell her the story of a king's daughter, seventeen or eighteen years old and upright as a young pioneer girl on the day she comes to the Land of Israel. The first time I saw the king's daughter my heart stood still and I wanted to weep at how the Almighty had scattered His grace over the daughters of the nations. Or perhaps this grace came to her from the kings of the House of David, for she was of their seed. For when the Queen of Sheba visited Solomon he satisfied all her desires, whatsoever she asked, and there were born to her the kings of Ethiopia. I raised my hat and greeted her. She nodded her head by way of acknowledgment, and the white of her eyes gleamed like mother-of-pearl. Mother-of-pearl of the kind I found on an autumn day on the Jaffa seashore. That was when little Ruhama was still present. You have heard of Ya'el Hayot, but you have not yet heard the name of Ruhama. But I tell you that this Ruhama was worth more than Ya'el Hayot. If so, you may ask, why did I leave Ruhama and run after Ya'el Hayot? Because at that time my mind was not yet mature, and I behaved like the young men who run away from what is right for them and run after what is not right for them. But it is not only young men who do this; every man does so, and even inanimate things. Perhaps you will say: But is it possible for an inanimate thing to run away, since it is fastened to its roots? But I tell you: I myself have seen it, for when I was a boy in the Beit Midrash, the Beit Midrash ran away from me, and when I went up to the Land of Israel, the Land ran away from me.

Now I will tell you something of the hair of the king's daughter. Her hair was black and shining. Rachel's hair also was black and shining, but the other's hair was more beautiful than Rachel's—not the hair itself, which was very much like Rachel's, but the way she wore it; for it was long, not trimmed, and it hung in braids behind her. And it is almost certain that it was not prickly—unlike hair cut short, which has a way of pricking.

Rachel fingered her hair, looked up at me, and said, 'My hair isn't prickly either, though it is cut short.' 'Perhaps it isn't prickly,' said I, 'and perhaps it is; but even if it isn't prickly actually, it does prick my thought. And this, Rachel, is particularly hard to take. Besides, there is something missing of your hair, and perhaps the part that was cut off is the essential part. To complete my description I must add about that daughter of kings that her clothes were beautiful and very well fitted. She wore a woman's gown, not a half-masculine garment, and her shoes were neither broad nor heavy. Now, Rachel, let us leave this princess, whom I have seen only twice, that time I spoke of and a second time. She was attended by two girls, as well as the chief vizier of her father the king. You will understand yourself that I greeted her the second time. I am a faithful soul, and if I do a good thing once I go on with it. So, since I greeted her the first time, I greeted her again the second. How surprised that vizier was. If he had been a wise man he would not have been surprised, for she was a king's daughter, and even though they had taken the kingdom from her father, the kingdom still existed. I have already told you, Rachel: Woe to him who forgets that he is a king's son. And since she did not forget that she was a king's daughter, I did not forget either.'

Rachel is a modern girl and is not interested in legends about the sons and daughters of kings. What she wants to hear is stories about girls like herself, such as the stories of Ya'el Hayot and little Ruhama.

But for a man who has reached my years, it is not fitting to repeat tales of youth, so I told her the story of Tirza and Akavia. I said to Rachel, 'This is a thing worth hearing. There was a certain man called Akavia Mazal and he was as old as Tirza's father, and Akavia Mazal did not think of Tirza even in a dream. But Tirza went and hung on Akavia's neck. Isn't this a miracle! In your opinion it is a simple matter, an everyday affair, and if it didn't happen today it may happen tomorrow. Blessed be this hour when you have said so!'

And since I hold dear all good things I wanted to fix the time when Rachel's words were said. So I took out my watch and looked at it. 'Why did you look at your watch?' said Rachel. Said I, 'It is already midnight. What are you thinking about, Rachel?' Rachel looked at me and said, 'I'm not thinking about anything.' 'If you like,' I said, 'I will tell you what you were thinking about.' 'I was not thinking about anything.' 'You were thinking about little Ruhama.' 'Who is this Ruhama?' 'And didn't I tell you about her?' said I to Rachel. 'But wasn't her name Ya'el Hayot?' asked Rachel. 'Ya'el Hayot is one thing and Ruhama is another,' I replied. 'This is little Ruhama, who is hidden like a ray of sunlight among the clouds. Father in heaven, how easy it is for girls to forget!'

I went into my room and lit the candle. I looked in the mirror to see if I was sad. But I was not sad; on the contrary, I was happy. And if you do not believe me, ask the mirror if it did not see me laughing.

At that moment I heard the thump of a wooden leg. I said to myself: Daniel Bach, our neighbor, is coming home. I will open the window and ask him what his father has written from the Land of Israel. But I was lazy, so I did not open the window and ask him about Reb Shlomo, but got into bed, put out the light, and lay down at full length. Sleep fell upon me and closed my eyes.

CHAPTER FIFTEEN

The Key That Was Lost

Yesterday I was happy as if all the world were mine; today I am sad, like one whose world is lost. What happened was that when I tried to enter the Beit Midrash I could not find the key. I said to myself: Perhaps I left it in the hotel when I was putting on my coat. So I went back to the hotel, but did not find the key. I said to myself: Perhaps I have lost it on the way. So I went about on all the roads, but did not find it.

I went to the Beit Midrash and stood before the locked door. Many thoughts passed through my mind in a short time, and this is one of them: The Beit Midrash still exists, but I am standing outside, because I have lost the key and cannot get in. What shall a man do to get in? Let him break open the door and enter.

But this door had more strength than I. No matter how hard I tried, I did not succeed in opening it. Our fathers, when they built synagogues and houses of study, used to make them with thick walls, doors, and locks. Once the doors of the Beit Midrash are locked, they can be opened only by one who has the key in his hand.

The people of the hotel saw my distress but said nothing. All the salvation of men is only a sigh, and each man needs that sigh for himself.

So far as I can see, the hotelkeeper has no reason to complain. For several days the hotel has been full, and instead of that old man who had a case in court and brought them no profit, there is a traveling salesman, a young man, who eats much and drinks much, lives and lets live.

The salesman sits in front of a glass of brandy and jokes with Babtchi, calling her *Babbete,* which means, 'Granny.' 'What will be the end of that affair?' the salesman teases. 'What affair?' asks Babtchi in surprise. 'The affair that never happened,' says the salesman. Babtchi laughs with all her might until her whole body shakes: 'And who will pay the musicians?' Says the salesman, 'This affair doesn't need musicians." Babtchi slaps his hands and says, 'Ha, ha, ha,' and blows the smoke of the cigarette in her mouth into the salesman's face. Says the salesman, 'With the same trouble the lady could have kissed me on the lips.' 'Certainly not,' says Babtchi, 'only on the mustache.' 'What a pity I haven't grown a mustache,' replies the salesman. 'Well,' says Babtchi, 'you must wait until you've grown a mustache hanging down to your feet.' The salesman laughs, 'Ha, ha, ha!' Says Babtchi, 'All this gentleman can say is ha, ha, ha!' and, putting her hands on her hips, she echoes him, 'Ha, ha, ha!' 'Babtchi, Babtchi,' cries her mother from the kitchen, 'bring me some salt.' 'Perhaps I should bring you some sweets?' Babtchi answers. 'Perhaps we should have a game of cards,' Dolik suggests to the salesman. 'What put that into your head?' says Babtchi. 'What have we left but cards?' answers Dolik. 'Cards for us and boys for you.' 'If you're thinking of this gentleman,' says Babtchi, 'you ought to know that he has a wife and children.'

In comes Lolik and finds Rachel sitting all melancholy. 'Have you heard?' he says, 'There's a rumor in the town. Yeruham . . . ' Before he can finish, Rachel's face grows pale, and she says, 'Go on.' 'Haven't you heard?' asks Lolik. 'If not, I'll tell you: Yeruham has pushed his forelock over to the right side of his forehead.'

Let us come back to our subject. The key has vanished and I cannot get into the Beit Midrash. Says Dolik, 'If you can't open the door, you bring an axe and break it in.' Says Krolka, 'Merciful God, merciful God, is it possible to do a thing like that to a house of prayer?' Dolik mocks her: 'We can't do that to one of yours, but we can to one of ours.' Krolka covers her face with her apron, crying, 'Don't listen to him, don't listen to him!'

Since the day I found the Beit Midrash locked I can find no place to go. Before I lost the key I used to go to the market-place and talk to people, or walk out to the forest, or stroll in the fields; since I have lost the key all these places have become strange to me. If I go outside, I find no satisfaction in it; if I return to the hotel, I find no satisfaction there. But I don't allow melancholy to take hold of me. I think of thousands of pathways, sometimes for a stroll and sometimes to look for the key. Finally my feet grow used to walking. My feet grow used, but not my soul. My soul weighs heavily on me and my feet carry it with difficulty. Every day I search my room; there is no place I do not look. I know that all my trouble is in vain, but I seek and seek again. Often I run to the Beit Midrash. Maybe the Almighty will perform a miracle for me and open the door. I even looked in the heaps of torn pages from the sacred books that lie in the courtyard, for when I was a young man and used to sit early and late in the Beit Midrash, I used to hide the key there, so that if anyone came before me he would find it.

One day Daniel Bach came up to me. He hunched over his wooden leg and said, 'You should do as I did. If you have lost the key, get another key made.'

That was a simple piece of advice Bach gave me, a solution that no one else had offered before he came along. And Daniel Bach went on, 'I will send you the locksmith and he will make you a new key.'

Those were hard days I spent waiting for the locksmith. Whenever anyone I did not know came into the hotel, I jumped up from my seat and ran to meet him, and when I saw that this was not the locksmith, I felt as if he had come to mock me.

If I did not know where the locksmith lived, I knew Bach's house. After all, he lived just next door; I could have gone to him to ask about the locksmith. But the reason I did not go was that I was still bothered by the Beit Midrash, for I used to circle around and examine it to see if I could find a breach through which I could enter. But the old Beit Midrash stood whole on every side, and there was no breach in it. Our fathers, when they built houses for the Torah, took great care that they should be whole on every side.

Again I thought about the books that were left in our old Beit Midrash. Only a few out of many were left there, and so long as the key was in my possession I used to go in and study them, but now that the key was lost and I could not go in, who would study them?

CHAPTER SIXTEEN

At the Graves of My Fathers

One day I was sitting at breakfast when an old woman came in, bent and wrapped up like my grandmother, may she rest in peace, at the celebration of the New Moon—only my grandmother's clothes were handsome and this one's were in rags. She came up to me, kissed my shoulder and my knee, and burst into tears.

'Who are you and why are you weeping?' I asked her. 'How should I not cry,' she replied, 'when that child died and did not live to see her son grown up.' 'Who was that child?' said I. 'Why, isn't it your mother, sir?' she replied. 'I was her governess. Such a good heart as she had you won't find anywhere in the world.' I said to her, 'Are you the Kaiserin?' She nodded her head and smiled.

I asked her to forgive me for calling her by this derogatory nickname (for there was a certain family of poor folk in our town who were quarrelsome and arrogant, and they used to be called the Kaisers, because they gave themselves airs and graces). 'Why should I be offended?' asked she. 'Everyone calls me the Kaiserin and I am not ashamed. But tell me yourself, sir, am I really a Kaiserin? Woe is me, may all the enemies of Israel have a life like mine. Now that the Kaiser is no longer Kaiser, what does it matter?' 'Are you not Elimelech's mother?' I asked. 'I am the mother of Elimelech Kaiser, who left me and went away,' she replied. 'Wouldn't it have been better if he'd taken a knife and cut my throat? Tell me yourself, where's the justice and where's the conscience? Forty years of trouble I had with him, and in the end he picked himself up and went off. All the same, it's a consolation to me that the Creator let me live to see your mother's son. I remember her when she stroked my cheeks with her little hands, her velvety hands; may I be so sure of a happy life as I'm sure I felt her stroking my cheeks. Even when she grew up she was not ashamed of me. Before every festival she used to take me into the big room in her house, open the clothes cupboard, and say, "Freide, take a dress, take a pair of shoes." And when I put on the dress a silver coin would fall out of it.'

Said I, 'Freide, if I had a dress I would give it to you; since I haven't a dress, I will give you a silver coin.' 'Who needs money? Who needs money?' said Freide. 'How many rich men we had in our town, and what happened to them? They lost their money and now they are poor. D'you think it's money I need? To buy crackers with perhaps, when I haven't the teeth to chew them? It's enough that I've lived to see your mother's son. What more do I need?' And again she kissed me on the knee and the shoulder and burst into tears.

'Don't cry, Freide,' I said to her. 'Many birds have grown their wings and flown away, and in the end come back to their nests.' 'Not a bit of it!' said Freide. 'When my son comes back I'll be lying in the ground, my eyes covered with broken bits of pottery, and I won't see him.' 'Man's destiny is death,' said I, 'and there is no expedient against death.' Freide replied, 'If only my son would close my eyes I would smile. But strange men will close my eyes, and when strange men close a dead woman's eyes, she feels pain in them, for the strange man's hand comes down without mercy, and when my son comes back and stands over my grave I won't see him, for I shall feel pain in my eyes. And if I don't see well when I'm alive— how much worse will I see after my death, after my eyes have been covered without mercy.'

'But surely you have other sons besides Elimelech,' I said. 'Four sons I had besides Elimelech,' replied Freide, 'and they were all killed—three in the war and one in the pogroms. What shall I tell you, my chick, I am like a blown-up bladder after someone has stuck a knife in it and let out the air. And now d'you want to know the end of my daughters? Oh, my pure and lovely daughters, as beautiful as kings' and emperors' daughters—their end was harder than their brothers', for their brothers died by the sword, while they died in hunger and grief. The blessed, merciful God has been crueler to me than to all the women of my town: He has killed my sons and daughters. And you say: Don't weep, Freide. And do you think I want to weep? My eyes weep by themselves, they fill with tears and weep. Even at a time when I should be glad, for I see you, my chick; even then my eyes weep. I remember you as a child sucking at the breast, when you used to play on your mother's heart, like a butterfly on a field of lilies. And I used to say to you and your mother, may she rest in peace: "This little one will be great some day." And here my prophecy has come true, and I should be glad. But what do my eyes do? They go on weeping, for it is the way of eyes to weep; they cannot control themselves, but do the bidding of the heart; and the heart, my darling, the heart is bitter.' And Freide lowered her eyes and wiped them with the hem of her coat, and wept again. And once she was weeping again she did not stop.

My hostess brought Freide a glass of tea to refresh her, and sat down and told me Freide's story. On the day when Freide rose after the mourning period for the two sons whose blood was shed at the same time, news came that another son had been killed in the war. So she and her two daughters sat down and mourned for another seven days. And where were her two remaining sons? One had been buried under a col- lapsing hill during the war, but was saved, and then was killed in the pogroms; and Elimelech was lying wounded in a hospital. One day, during the seven days' mourning, the older daughter said to the younger one, 'Our brothers are dead in battle, and we are dying of hunger. Let us go to the village; perhaps we'll find something to eat there, before we go crazy with hunger.' So they dressed themselves and went out. On the way they met a soldier. 'Where are you going, girls?' he asked. 'To look for bread,' they said. 'I haven't any bread,' said he, 'but if you want raisins I'll give you as much as you want.' And he led them to a graveyard, where he opened up a hole and took out a sack of raisins. 'Take the sack and everything in it,' he said, 'and pray for mercy for the soul of a sinner.' So they took the sack, thanked him warmly, and ran toward the town to bring it to their mother. They had not gone far before the soldier came back after them and said, 'Ungrateful girls! Not even a single kiss you've given me.' Then they realized what he wanted, so they threw down the sack and started to run away. At that moment a troop of soldiers passed by. When the soldier saw them he ran off in fear, for he was a deserter. The soldiers saw the sack and began cursing and swearing. 'The whole world is hungry,' they cried, 'and these Jews have almonds and raisins to eat.' In the end, they left the raisins and started on the girls. Before a month was out the woman had buried her two daughters, one after the other.

After Mrs. Zommer had finished telling what happened, Freide looked into my eyes and asked, 'What do you say to that event? Isn't it a fine event?' And here Freide lifted her right hand and counted with her fingers, naming each of her children who had been killed. For every name she bent one finger, except for the thumb, which she left upright. Then she raised her left hand to her eyes, rubbing her right eye with the two middle fingers, and fell silent. And I too fell silent. The blessed and merciful God was cruel to me and put no words of comfort in my mouth to console Freide.

After she had said farewell and gone away, I thought of going to the graveyard. I did not expect to find there the books that had disappeared from the Beit Midrash, but I went like any man who has happened to come to the town where his fathers are buried and goes to prostrate himself on their graves.

Our graveyard slopes upward and slopes downward, and all its slopes are full of graves that crowd in on each other. There are three that take abundantly and give abundantly: the land, the authorities, and so on. What they take away can be seen, and what they give is concealed in the graveyard: they take the living and they give the dead. Grave literally touches grave—not as in the town, where there are many places free between one house and the next. It grieves me to say it, but it is so: The men of the old Beit Midrash did right to leave the town, for the graveyard is full and there is no room for a new grave.

I walk among the graves and think of nothing at all, but the two emissaries of the heart, my two eyes, look and see. These eyes are under the control of the heart, and the heart is under the control of Him who puts to death and brings to life. Sometimes He allows us to contemplate those that are alive, and sometimes those that have died.

Those that died before the war and those that died in the war and those that died after the war lie here together, as if there were no difference between them. So long as they lived, some grieved over days gone by and some looked forward to the days to come. Now that they are dead men, the latter have abandoned their expectations and the former grieve no more.

All the powers of the eye have a limit, and a man can only see according to the range of his eyes. But even if you should cover one eye with the other, the dead would come and stand before you, and you could not help but see them completely.

Far from the other dead in the old graveyard the tabernacle of the zaddik stands out. The roof of the tabernacle has been removed, and its walls are bowed and falling. After two or three generations, not a sign of the mausoleum will remain in this heap of ruins; the generations to come will not know that a great zaddik is interred here, and he too will forget that he once filled the post of rabbi here in the town. For at the hour of his passing he promised the men of this town that he would defend them against evil—and where is his promise? Once these zaddikim have passed away and ascended on high, they pay no more heed to us; the needs of the living are trivial in the eyes of the righteous dead, and it is not worth their while to beg compassion for a trivial thing. Only think how many zaddikim have promised us that they would not rest up above until they had brought the Redeemer, but once they pass away they forget their promises; some for fear of neglecting the study of the Torah, for they cannot bear to neglect their studies in the firmament for a single hour; others because they were given the honor of expounding the Torah to the other righteous in paradise, so that none of the righteous should exert themselves too much in prayer and bring the Redeemer. One way or the other, heavy is the pain of the living.

I did not enter the zaddik's tabernacle, and I had my very good reasons; I had heard that great saints, once so many years have gone by since their passing, do not come to visit their graves. Instead, I turned to my departed relatives. First I went to the distant relatives and then to the near ones, and then to the nearest ones, so that they might inform my father and mother and keep their hearts from fainting all of a sudden. Some people refrain from visiting the graves of their father and their mother on the same day, and they are right, for when I went to my mother's grave my eyes were clear, but when I went from there to my father's grave, my eyes were blinded with tears.

I was not present at the hour of my father's passing, and I was not at his graveside when they put up his tombstone. Carved in the stone, those verses were shining white, showing no sign of the tears I shed when I composed them. Now my tears showed, but through them I could not read the verses.

Fourteen years have gone by since the day Father passed away, and still the tombstone is new. And near it, on his grave, stands a second stone, that of an old scholar, a colleague of Father's. What could the men of the town do? The dead ask for a grave and a stone, and since that old man had asked to be laid by his friend and they could find no room for his tombstone, they set it up on Father's grave. My sister used to tell me that our father often appeared to her in a dream with his hand on his heart, like one who feels oppressed and supports his heart with his hand.

When I returned from the graveyard I found Yeruham Freeman sitting on the ground repairing the road. I said to him, 'Are you repairing the road from the graveyard to the town or from the town to the graveyard?' Yeruham lifted his eyes from the ground and did not answer.

CHAPTER SEVENTEEN

Yeruham Freeman

It seems to me that no one hates me like Yeruham Freeman. Why does he hate me, when I have done him no harm? On the contrary, whenever I happen to pass him I greet him like a friend, though he answers with a mumble. I have a secret fondness for this young man. That lean body without an ounce of fat, those eyes that burn like the eyes of a sufferer from malaria, and also, if you like, his ragged, dust-colored working clothes move my heart. Every day, from sunrise to sunset, he sits in the street, pounding out gravel with his hammer or digging dirt and filling up holes to repair the streets of our town, damaged during the war. From his face you can see that he is not happy in his work, but he takes pains in the doing of it, like one who knows that there is nothing else before him. And since there is nothing else before him, he takes pains in the doing of it. I have heard that the city fathers are satisfied with his work and pay no attention to his ideas, because of which he was expelled from the Land of Israel. I am telling no tales and revealing no secrets, for everyone knows that this young man had fallen into evil ways, and before they expelled him he was imprisoned for distributing manifestoes to Arabs and Jews. In any case, since he returned here he has had nothing to do with evil things and does not mix with the other communists in the town; he has nothing to do with anyone, not even with himself. How can a man have anything to do with

himself or not have anything to do with himself? He who sings
and talks to himself has something to do with himself; he who
does not sing or talk to himself has nothing to do with himself.
It depends on whether or not he sings and talks to himself.
From sunrise to sunset Yeruham does his work in silence.
When the sun sets he loads his tools on his back, goes down to
the river, washes off the dirt, and goes back home. I do not
know what he does at home, whether he sits and reads, or
sleeps. Since I have known him I have not seen him strolling
at night, either with a girl or alone.

It is not dignified to ask one's neighbor: Why do you hate
me? If your neighbor hates you—hate him. And if you need his
help, go and make up to him, until he stops hating you. Yeruham Freeman is a simple workman, and I, thank the Lord, am
a respectable householder in Israel. Even now, when my house
is in ruins, I would not change with Yeruham. My table is set,
my bed is made, my clothes are clean, and my wife and children are fed, even though I do not grub about on the ground
and repair the roads.

A man likes to be liked by everyone; but I have given up
this desire. You can see this from the fact that the town rabbi
speaks censoriously of me because I have not gone to pay my
respects to him, and still I do not go. I am not saying that if
I go to him he will praise me, but he would show me affection.
Similarly with Zechariah Rosen. Zechariah Rosen, a merchant
in foodstuffs and one of the town's notables, has made out a
pedigree for himself back to King David. Once, when I passed
by the door of his shop, he called me in and showed me his
pedigree. I looked and saw that he claimed descent from the
great sage Rav Hai Gaon. I said to him, 'Rav Hai Gaon had
no children.' So this pedigreed fellow began to bear me a
grudge. Now if I had said to him, 'I was mistaken, I have
found in the documents of the Geniza that Rav Hai had a son
born to him in his old age,' Zechariah Rosen would immediately
change from enemy to friend. But I do not do so. Such is the
way of this man: what he can get with ease, he gives up; and
what he cannot get with ease, he runs after.

Although I wanted to be friendly with Yeruham, I did not

try to make friends with him, apart from greeting him. Once I passed by and did not greet him, because I was preoccupied with the trouble of the key and did not notice the fellow.

After I had gone on some distance, I turned my head and saw that he was stretching out his neck and looking at me between his knees. I went back to him and said, 'Listen to what I will tell you. You are acting as if you despised me, but really you wish to be my friend. Perhaps it is worth while finding out why you act like this.' 'Why? Because you were the first of all my troubles, and all the troubles that followed came through you,' replied Yeruham. 'How is that possible?' I said. 'Until I came here we did not even see each other, for I went up to the Land of Israel when you were a child, or perhaps you were not in the world at all at that time, and you say that I am the first of your troubles and the cause of all the troubles that followed.' 'That is perfectly true,' said Yeruham, 'when you left here I was not yet born.' 'You see,' said I, laughing at him, 'you have no reason to connect your affairs with me, much less to blame me for all the troubles that you say have come upon you because of me.' 'That's what you say,' said Yeruham. 'There is no reason to blame my affairs on you.' 'That is what I say, and your words support me,' said I; 'didn't you say that when I went up to the Land of Israel you were not even in existence? If so, how can you explain your words?' Said Yeruham, 'It was your departure for the Land of Israel that had these effects on me.' 'How?' I asked him, 'how, my friend? The rope the hangman used to hang the condemned man swayed a little; apparently it was not pleased with all this honor.' 'I will explain straightway,' said Yeruham. 'Explain, my friend,' said I. 'I am not an inquisitive man, but in such things I am entitled to be inquisitive. What is it, Yeruham? You are looking at me as if you had seen me in a dream.' 'When I was a child,' Yeruham replied, 'I heard many stories about you.' 'It never occurred to me that the people of my town talked about me,' said I; 'not because I am a modest fellow, but because since I shook the dust of my town from my feet I have tried to remove it from my heart. Well, what did you hear them telling about me?' 'I heard,' replied Yeruham, 'that there was a certain young man here, different from the rest of his comrades. Not better; on the contrary, in some respects worse. One day he disappeared from the town. They thought he was hiding, as usual, in the forest, but after some days had passed they asked his father, "Where is your son?" "He has gone up to the Land of Israel," the father replied.' Said I to Yeruham, 'Is there anyone here who says I did not do right in going up to the Land of Israel—or perhaps it's you who say it? I assure you I did not steal from the church and run away. I longed to go up to the Land of Israel; my father, of blessed memory, gave me money for expenses; and I went. I assure you it was clean money Father gave me. So what wrong did I do in going?' 'What wrong did you do?' cried Yeruham. 'On the contrary, you did well, for you succeeded and won a good name. But . . .' 'What do you mean by "but"?' 'But to me you did wrong,' said Yeruham; 'you did great wrong to me.' 'How did I do wrong to you?' Said Yeruham, 'Until you went up to the Land of Israel, there was nothing real about the Land in our town. You know the Zionists, young and old. All the Land of Israel means for them is something to come together about, to hold meetings and sell the shekel that makes you a member of their organization. But since the day you went up to the Land of Israel, it became something real, for one of our boys had gone to settle there. In time, when I reached years of understanding, I gave my heart to the Land of Israel, not the one of the Zionists in our town, but your Land, until the whole world was not worth so much to me as a little grain of its dust.' 'If so,' said I to Yeruham, 'surely you profited through me.' 'I thought so too,' replied Yeruham. 'That is why I was drawn after you, for you and the Land of Israel became one thing for me. I used to say to myself: I will go up to the Land of Israel and pay you a visit and tell you that I am your fellow townsman and I too have come here through you. Immediately you would take my hand in yours and look at me with affection, and I would see that I have a brother in the Land, and you would take out an orange, divide it in two, and say to me, "Take and eat." Many oranges I ate there in the Land; there were days when that was my only food; and yet I missed that piece of orange which I hoped to get from your hand.' 'And why did you not come to me?' I said to Yeruham. 'Why didn't I come to you?' said

Yeruham. 'Were you there? When I boasted to my comrades in the Land that I was going to see you, they told me, "That man has gone abroad." '

I sighed and said, 'True, very true. In those days I was living in Berlin.' 'You were living in Berlin,' said Yeruham, 'enjoying all the pleasures of the big cities, and in our hearts you had instilled the poison of the Land of Israel.' I turned on Yeruham and cried, 'Poison you call the love of the Land? I don't want to chop logic with you, but tell me, I beg of you, what was I to do, in your opinion?' Yeruham looked at me quietly and said softly, 'To die, sir, to die.'

'Are you tired of my life?' cried I. 'If your life in the Land of Israel gave you no satisfaction, my dear sir, you should have committed suicide,' replied Yeruham. 'Committed suicide?' 'Or disappeared, or changed your name, so that people might not know you were still alive, or . . .' 'Or?' '. . . or dressed yourself like an exile and gone from place to place, kissing the dust of every country, beating your breast and saying, "I am the man who drew men after me to the Land of Israel, and I was wrong. Do not follow my example." '

Said I to Yeruham, 'And was it I who persuaded others to follow me to the Land of Israel?' Yeruham replied, 'Would you like me to recite something to you, such as a song you wrote before you went up to the Land of Israel?' 'A song I wrote?' Yeruham put his feet together, raised himself to his full height before me, placed his two hands on his heart, and repeated melodiously:

'Devotion faithful unto death
I've sworn to thee by God above,
For all I have in Exile here
I'll give, Jerusalem, for thy love.'

'Be silent, man, be silent,' I said. Yeruham was not silent, but went on reciting:

'My life, my spirit, and my soul,
O Holy City, for thee I'll give—
Awake and dreaming all my joy,
My feast and Sabbath while I live.'

'Be silent, man, be silent,' I cried. Yeruham was not silent, but continued to recite:

'Though your King be gone and your people poor,
Eternal City, lofty Shrine,
The Lord has made thee all our hope,
From ancient days to the end of time.'

'If you are not silent I will leave you and go,' I said to Yeruham. He paid no heed but recited:

'And though the tomb may close me in
With all the dead beneath the ground,
In deepest pit thou art my strength,
O fortress city, world-renowned.

'I know you don't like this poem,' said Yeruham. 'Your taste has improved and you are sick of rhyming "God above" and "Jerusalem's love." But I tell you that this poem is not a good one for another reason, because it penetrates the heart and oppresses the soul.'

'When you came there and did not find me, was the Land empty?' said I to Yeruham. 'If I was not there, surely many others were there in place of me. Is the Land of Israel nothing else but me? And surely, even of the people of our town several had already settled there, and no doubt they would have given you a hearty welcome.' 'True, perfectly true,' said Yeruham. 'Several of our townsfolk had settled there.' 'You see,' said I to Yeruham, 'if I was not there, there were a thousand like me.' Yeruham smiled and said, 'A thousand like you, sir, and perhaps a thousand more. Some of them did as you; that is, they went abroad; and some of them became clerks and merchants and shopkeepers and speculators.' 'And those who went up with you, were they all workers?' I asked. 'Some of them fell sick with malaria and other diseases and died,' said Yeruham, 'and their bones were scattered in all the graveyards of the Land. And those that did not die are as good as dead. Bowing to every minor official and imploring "Be kind and merciful to me; put me, I pray you, into one of the offices, that I may eat a piece of bread."'

'And those who did not die or fall sick, where are they?'

'Where are they?' said Yeruham. 'They are scattered the world over. More than remained in the Land of Israel you can find in every one of the five continents.' 'And did you get no benefit from your stay in the Land of Israel?' 'True, perfectly true,' replied Yeruham, 'we got one great benefit from the Land, we learned the value of labor.' I held out my hands to Yeruham and said, 'And do you think that is a simple thing?' 'But labor is not simple,' answered Yeruham. And I said: 'Is that the only thing that is not simple? Is there anything simple in the world? Now let us go back to what we were speaking of at first. You condemn me because I praised the Land of Israel. Was I the first to do so? Was I the only one to do so? There is not a single generation that did not sing the praises of the Land of Israel, and I have never heard anyone reproaching them. But all the generations that lived before us found in the Land what they found in the school books; so they loved the Land and loved the books that sang its praises. But you and your comrades sought in the Land not what your forefathers sought, and not what the books tell of it, and not the Land as it is, but a Land such as you demand, and that is why the Land did not tolerate you. "A land which the Lord thy God demandeth always," say the Scriptures—not as you demand it, and not as your comrades demand it, but as the Lord your God demands it. Now I am going. You are a day laborer, Yeruham, and I do not want to keep you back. This matter we have touched on cannot be explained in a few moments, and what we have left untouched today we shall explain tomorrow.'

CHAPTER EIGHTEEN

The Virtues of Jerusalem

Since the day I arrived here I have never heard anyone mention Yeruham Freeman, except that shopkeeper from whom I bought the cloth and Dolik Zommer, my host's son, who mocked him in front of Rachel. Once I asked Daniel Bach about him and he put me off with nothing. 'That Yeruham is in charge of repairing the roads,' he said, which told me nothing new. I wonder if there is anyone in the town of whom so little is spoken as Yeruham Freeman. Just as he does not speak to people, so they do not talk about him. So I was surprised when Rachel mentioned his name.

Why did Rachel have to mention Yeruham Freeman? This needs to be explained and I do not know how to explain it, so I had best tell when she mentioned him and in what connection.

For two days I had not left my room, because I was too lazy to rise and because I had a headache. When I came out on the third day, Rachel jumped up and said, 'Yeruham Freeman asked about you.' Since I am not an inquisitive man, I did not ask her how she knew that Yeruham had asked about me, but since I have good manners I asked her how he was. And here I must add that out of one enigma there came two. First, what made Yeruham ask for me, when it seems he detests me? Second, how did his words reach her ears? And these two enigmas are nothing at all compared with the third, for when I asked Rachel how Yeruham was, she replied like one to whom all his secrets were open.

Any man may be wrong, and I more than any other man. I was wrong in thinking that Yeruham was unsociable; now I discovered that he was not. There is one person in the town, namely Rachel, who disappears from the house every day while her father is repeating the Afternoon Service, goes to Yeruham, and waits for him in his room until he returns from his work. That is why he washes in the river, so that he should come home clean.

From all that has been said, it appears that people do not mention Yeruham's name; if so, why did they suddenly speak of him? But that fact, that Rachel the innkeeper's daughter visits Yeruham, was the cause of them talking about him; from talking about her they came to talk about him.

I myself did not see Rachel going to his house. My own eyes are not capable of seeing by themselves. When I was young I used to see all I wanted to see; but when I grew a little older, my power of sight diminished and I saw only what I was shown. Now I see neither what I wish to see nor what I am

shown. So how do I know things? A rumor springs from among
the people and sometimes it reaches me. But still it is difficult
to explain what Rachel, the innkeeper's younger daughter, has
to do with Yeruham, the digger of ditches. First, because . . .
and second . . .

Why do I divide every statement into first and second?
Is it because the men of Szibucz divide their words into first
and second, or is it because I am given to two places: I live
abroad and I dream in the Land of Israel.

The Land of Israel that shows itself to me in dreams is
not the Land as it is today, but as it was years ago, when I
lived in Neveh Zedek, which means 'The Abode of Righteousness.' Today Neveh Zedek is a small suburb attached to Tel
Aviv, but in the past it was a neighborhood unto itself, the best
of them all. And little Ruhama lived there with her mother.
I do not know whether Ruhama is alive or dead, nor—if she is
alive—whether she is a violinist. In any case, her violin is dead,
for she burned it herself, to roast a little fish for a certain
young man.

Let us leave the young man who left Ruhama and return
to Ruhama. Whenever she comes to me in a dream, she comes
with her violin. Sometimes she covers her face with her violin
and calls me by name and the violin echoes her; sometimes
she plays my name with the violin and echoes it with her voice.
So long as she behaved like this I said nothing to her, but when
she began to play 'Devotion Faithful unto Death,' I rebuked
her. First, because I am tired of rhymes like 'love' and 'God
above.' And second, because I have no mind for musical
matters.

The greatness of the Land of Israel does not depend on
Neveh Zedek alone. There are places in the Land of Israel
that even in waking are like a dream. Above them all is
Jerusalem, which the Almighty sifted out from His Land,
beautiful and pure and perfect. Hence we should not be surprised at that man who lies in his bed in Szibucz and sees a
dream of Jerusalem.

A man has 248 organs and 365 sinews, corresponding to
the 613 commandments—248 positive and 365 negative—in the
Torah. Jerusalem is above them all, for it is mentioned in the

Scriptures in 614 places; so we find that Jerusalem counts for one more than man. If a man has been privileged to fulfill the commandments, he is permitted to rest in peace on his couch by night, so that he may draw strength to fulfill more commandments. If he has not been privileged and has not fulfilled commandments, he is troubled in his sleep. In any case, he is one short, the one more of Jerusalem. If he is clever, he meditates about her by day and she shows herself to him at night.

Since the day I left Jerusalem, not a day has passed when I did not think of her—not that I am clever, but because my home is there, and a man is likely to think about his home.

One night, when I was asleep in my bed, I found myself walking in the streets of Jerusalem, as a man walks when he is awake. I went into a certain bookshop. As I was going out an old man whispered to me, 'If it is books you seek, come with me.' 'Where?' I asked him. 'To my house,' said he. 'Where is your house?' I asked. 'Four cubits from here,' he said. 'Come, and you will acquire another four cubits in the Land of Israel.' I walked with him until I was tired of walking. He pointed with his hand and said to me, 'Here.' I looked in front of me but saw no sign of a house. The old man took me and brought me to a place that was like a burial vault. My limbs were numb as if they had parted from my body, and my body too seemed to have parted from me; I felt nothing but a sensation in the head, a pleasurable sensation, as if a friendly hand were stroking my head. Finally, all my being ceased, except this pleasure, which did not cease. This may seem perplexing, for surely when a man's being ceases so do his sensations, and here was utter pleasure. Still more perplexing was the fact that this very complexity gave me further pleasure. And this was a novelty, for surely the more one questions the more one is in pain. And, wonderful to relate, even this novelty gave pleasure.

The old man stooped to the ground and took out a book. I looked at it and saw that it was stamped with the seal of our old Beit Midrash. I asked if his honor came from Szibucz. He nodded his head. And although he did not give me an explicit answer, it sounded as if the name of Szibucz issued from his lips. But there was no sweetness in that name. I began to wonder whether the name was not so beautiful as I always used to think it, and perhaps I had not always thought it was beautiful, for if I had I should not have left my town. Or perhaps the name was always beautiful, and my town was beautiful, for now I had gone back there. If so, why had I left it in the beginning and gone up to the Land of Israel?

At that moment my head again began to trouble me, though not as at first, when there was a kind of pleasure in the sensation. I overcame my pain and looked again at the book and the seal that was on it, wondering how the book had reached the old man's hand, since there was an ancient ban on taking a book out of the Beit Midrash. The old man said, 'It was not I who took it out; of its own accord it made its way to me. Since the study of the Torah has been done away with in the Beit Midrash, the books make their way to us.' I looked at the old man in wonderment. What did he mean by 'to us'; surely 'to us' implies the plural, and there was no one here but him and me, and I had been following him only for a short time, so that the expression 'to us' did not apply to me. I hid my wonderment and asked, 'How much does this book cost?' He replied, 'You have not studied, my son, and all your possessions will not equal its value. But if you wish to study, the book is yours for nothing.'

I said to him, 'He who hates gifts shall live.' The old man smiled and said, 'There is no life but the Torah.' But as soon as he mentioned the word 'life' he shrank and his face was turned to dust and his voice was like the sound of a key that has gone rusty. While as for me, dear brothers, my limbs filled out and my body began to grow until I became as tall as a mountain. The vault split and I emerged. And as soon as I emerged I ran to the Beit Midrash.

CHAPTER NINETEEN

The Locksmith

I stood before the locked door, the key of which I had lost. Of all the events of the night, nothing was left me but the pain in my head. My eyes had shrunk and seemed to be strewn with salt, and because of the saltiness my eyelashes bristled. I went outdoors and looked at the passers-by. A little girl came from the slaughterer's house with a fowl in her basket. Next, a water-carrier passed with his two pitchers on his shoulders. Drops of the fowl's blood and drops of water from the full pitchers were dripping on the ground.

The air was cool, but it did not cool my head, and hunger began to torment me, for I had left the hotel that day without breakfast.

The hunger spread, conquering one limb after another, until it had conquered the whole body; but I disregarded myself and felt nothing but the sensation in my head, as if it were wrapped in a scarf that bound in the pain and kept it from escaping. I shut my eyes in pain.

Suddenly the book was revealed before me, and He that gives light to the eyes of those who wait for His word gave light to my eyes: I found there a commentary on the words of the Gemara in which the sages said: 'From then onward, the Holy One, blessed be He, speaks and Moses writes in tears.'

After that I went out into the street and found an old man with an old lock in his hand and an old key stuck in it, and locks and keys hanging on the belt around his waist. As soon as he had passed I knew that he was the locksmith and wanted to run after him, but in the meantime he had disappeared.

Daniel Bach found me standing perplexed. 'Where are your feet bound to?' said he. 'To look for the locksmith,' said I. Daniel slapped his wooden leg and said, 'Now on your way, my dear, and help us go.'

This Daniel—I do not know why he is happy. As for his livelihood, his wood was lying untouched, without a purchaser, and there was no demand for the art his wife had learned. Daniel Bach's livelihood now depended entirely on his daughter Erela, who was a teacher of Hebrew.

'Have you had a letter from your father in the Land of Israel?' I asked him. 'Yes.' 'What did your father write from the Land of Israel?' 'What did he write? He wrote that the Kohanim bless the people in the synagogue every day, and twice on days when there is an Additional Service.' 'And did he write nothing about his own affairs?' 'He wrote that he has had the privilege of praying beside the Wailing Wall and prostrating himself at Rachel's Tomb. He also wrote that the Tomb is built as a kind of synagogue, with beautiful curtains spread out there, and many candelabra hanging from the ceiling and on the walls, in which they kindle oil lamps. A great stone lies upon the Tomb; pious women measure the stone with threads, and these are well-tried specifics for finding favor with others, and so on and so forth. Father sent a thread of this kind to my daughter. Do you wish to hear any more?'

'Is he content with his way of living?' I asked. 'And is he content with his comrades?' 'As for the young comrades,' replied Daniel Bach, 'he is always singing their praises; they are all lovers of Israel, doers of good deeds, working for the settlement of the Land, speaking the Holy Tongue, providing their parents with an honorable livelihood, and giving them shelter, food, and clothing. As for the old comrades, that is, the parents of the young ones, it's the same the whole world over: they disagree about the text of the prayers, quarrel over every custom that one of them brings from his home town as if it had been handed down from Mount Sinai, and argue about such things as the prayer "And may He cause His salvation to flourish and bring His Messiah in the end." Good God above, send us the Messiah if only that we may be rid of all this.'

'And your father?' 'My father doesn't give way either. It happened once on the Sabbath eve that he was officiating in the synagogue and recited, "And the children of Israel shall keep the Sabbath." Most of the congregation banged on the tables and silenced him with a rebuke, for two Sabbaths before the opponents of the Hasidim had won a victory and decided that this paragraph should not be recited. And Father was angry all through the Sabbath. Here is the locksmith's shop.'

The shop was open, but the locksmith was not there. Where had he gone? To the house of the Gordonia pioneer group to repair the lock of the door there. I looked at the old keys that were hanging by the entrance in case I might find the key I had lost among them, but though I searched I did not find it. I said to Bach, 'Forgive me, sir, for detaining you; no doubt you find it difficult to stand on your leg.' 'If you are thinking of this wooden leg, sir,' said Mr. Bach, 'there is nothing that suits it better than to stand in one place, for then it feels like one of the trees in the forest, and perhaps it dreams that someone will make of it a couch for a king's daughter.'

We went to the Gordonia group and found the locksmith. When he saw me he smiled as if he knew me. What a wonderful thing: all the old men smile—that old man I saw last night and this locksmith as well. Most of the young men, on the contrary, were looking angry, because the communists had pulled off the lock, broken in, and soiled the pictures, and now they had to get themselves a new lock.

Although the two of them resembled each other, there was a difference between them. That old man who appeared to me last night was tall and upright, while the locksmith was small as a schoolboy, and bent, his head hanging on his chest. That old man also had a bent head, but his bending was the result of his uprightness, as one who wishes to bring his words nearer to the listener's ear bows his head and seems to be bent. Just as they were different in height, so were they different in their laughter. The laughter of that old man from Jerusalem was not truly laughter, but a smile that emerged from among the wrinkles around his mouth and vanished, and even his smile was not a smile, but the image of a smile. As for the locksmith, his laughter was true laughter, which split up into several kinds, each of them a laugh in itself, and when he laughed his body shook until one could hear the jingling of the locks and keys hanging from the belt around his waist. And even when he was not laughing aloud, a smile emerged from among the wrinkles on his face and his face shone; for he was one of the last of the Kossov Hasidim, who have learned that the world is worth rejoicing in, for so long as a man lives in this world he can acquire virtuous acts and good deeds, of which a man eats the fruits in this world and the capital remains for the next, and whoever takes these things to heart rejoices in his world, rejoices in his deeds, and lives for many a day and year. Hence the Hasidim of Kossov live for many days and years and rejoice. And if this old man's body is dry with age, there is an overplus of sap in the wrinkles of his face, which refreshes the soul and gladdens the eye.

'This is the gentleman who wishes to have a key made,' said Bach to the locksmith. The locksmith greeted me, clasping my hand joyfully, and I too rejoiced in him. First, because he would make me the key, and second, because when I was a child I used to stand at the entrance to his shop, looking at the keys and locks, for in those days I longed for a chest with a key and a lock. When, later, I gave up the idea of the chest I did not give up the idea of the key, and I would lie in bed at night thinking of it—a large, heavy key, the kind a man takes out of his pocket to open his house. I pictured this key in various shapes, but all the shapes were less important than its function and final purpose: the act of opening. Imagine it: In the center of the city stands a house, and that house has a door, like all the other houses, and on the door hangs a lock. Along comes a child from school, puts his hand in his pocket, takes out a key, pushes the key into the lock, and twists it this way and that— and immediately the whole house is open before him. What is there in that house? A table and a bed and a lamp. That is, there is nothing in the house that there is not in other houses. But that moment of the opening of the door with the key that is in the child's hand—no other moment can compare with it. So now you can imagine how wonderful was that old man, who had a hundred keys and more hanging at his shop entrance. There are hidden stores of treasure that can be opened with a sentence, as when one says, 'Open Sesame'; I was not used to seeking things that were hidden from the eye, but only things that the eye could see, and I wished to have the key to them in my possession.

There was another man in the town to whom I was drawn in my childhood. That was the collector for the Land of Israel,

and although the matter is not relevant here, I mention it because of his key. When I would hear the sound of his feet my
heart would pound. And when he would enter, and with the
key from his pocket open the collection box named after Rabbi
Meir the Wonderworker, I would stand astonished. Here was
a box into which everyone dropped coins, and this man came,
opened it, and took all the money. And no one said a word to
him; indeed, they looked at him with affection, and he would
sit and write something on a piece of paper, like a doctor
writing a prescription for a sick person, and set the writing
before Mother and say, 'May you be privileged to see the coming of the Redeemer.' I did not know who he was, this Redeemer who was spoken of in the blessing. But I knew that all
other blessings were not equal to this blessing.

The old man stood at the door of the Gordonia group's
house and examined the lock, the smile dancing in his eyes and
in the wrinkles of his face, as if he were delighted that people
were not growing lazy, but continued to make trouble for each
other, so that the blood should not congeal. I wanted to wrap
my arm around his waist and lift him up; but it was good I did
not do so, for how would I have been able to face him afterward? In short, the locksmith busied himself with his work,
scraped with a nail, and examined the lock. In the end he took
it off and made a new lock.

The man who has come to this place stands and waits. He
is well on in years and far from childhood, and still he is seeking a key. From what I have said, you understand that this
man is I, and it is I who am seeking a key, in order to open
our old Beit Midrash, for the key that was entrusted to me is
lost, and I need a new one.

When the locksmith had finished his work I said to him,
'Now will you go with me and make me the key?' He smiled
and said, 'Is the making of keys like the 145th Psalm, which we
say three times every day—"Blessed be the Lord day by day"?
Since the day I first came to act reasonably, I have not done
two tasks on one day.' 'If so,' said I, 'when will you make me
the key?' 'God willing, tomorrow,' said he. 'Tomorrow?' I cried
in surprise. He smiled and said, 'Do you believe, my son, that

tomorrow is far from today? On the contrary, tomorrow is close
and near, and this is a thing that a man should know, for if
he has not succeeded in doing something today he will do it
tomorrow.'

CHAPTER TWENTY

Our Comrades in the Diaspora

Since I have mentioned the meetinghouse, I will tell you something about it. The Gordonia group's house is actually a single
room. You go up to it by wooden steps—half stair, half ladder.
The ascent is not difficult, for after all there are only five small
steps, but the top one is shaky, and you must take care not to
be alarmed, for alarm can lead to a stumble. It seems that
these steps were not made for the house, but were brought
from elsewhere, and since they were not high enough, a plank
was added; this plank is the shaky step.

The room is longer than it is wide, and it has windows on
all four sides, but they do not let in the light, for the ruins of
the landlord's house block out the light. This house, which our
comrades have made into the group's home, is actually not a
house but an annex, built as a warehouse, for before the war
our town had become a trading center for the villages around,
and businessmen built warehouses here for their goods. After
the enemy came and laid the town in ruins and pillaged the
stores, most of the warehouses became dwellings, and the
group house is one of these. And although it has many windows, it is like a blind man who has never seen light in his life.

(Since we have set out on this figurative path, let us
continue.)

The group's house is like a blind man whose eyes have
died, but the eyes of our comrades shine with the light of the
Land of Israel, which all eyes seek to see.

There are pious men in this country who have built themselves Batei Midrashot, and they boast that when our holy
Messiah reveals himself he will come first to their Beit Mid-

rash. These young men, on the other hand, do not boast that the Messiah will come to them first; they do not mention him, but most of their thoughts are devoted to going up to the Land of Israel and cultivating the soil. I do not know which are the more worthy of love: the pious in the Diaspora who wish to trouble the Messiah to come and visit them abroad, or these young men who take the trouble to go up to the Land of Israel to prepare it for him.

These young men know what is happening in the Land of Israel in general and in detail, but they and I do not understand each other. The very words we use have different meanings. For instance, when I say 'Gordon' I mean our great poet, Yehuda Leib Gordon, while they mean Aaron David Gordon, the socialist ideologist and pioneer. My generation are men of thought, whose hands are short but whose thoughts are long, while they are men of deeds, who put doing before thinking. This Gordon of mine (that is, Yehuda Leib Gordon) was a man of thought, while their Gordon (that is, Aaron David Gordon) came along and translated thought into deeds; in other words, the one carried out what the other wrote. On the face of it, I should be glad, but I am not glad. Not because thought is more important than deed, but because . . . But this may be explained by a parable, although a not very apt one. It is like an architect who asked for stone and they gave him brick; for he intended to build a temple, while they intended to build themselves a house to live in.

I forgot that I was hungry and sat in the group's house; first, because I had promised that I would come to visit them, and second, because they had newspapers from the Land of Israel.

I read the newspapers from beginning to end. People from whom I used to keep my distance so long as I lived in the Land now became important to me when I saw their names in the newspapers. Every report about some politician who traveled to Haifa or the Valley of Jezreel moved my heart. There were men who could bore me by saying 'Good morning,' and now I sat and read their speeches.

No doubt great things are being done in the Land of Israel, but when I open the newspaper it tells me of things that are not great, for instance, about a certain man who went to Haifa or the Valley, and the like. I lay down one day's paper and pick up another day's. And what does that other day's paper do? It tells me about the same politician coming back from Haifa or the Valley! No doubt this had to be written since they had written that he went, but if they had not mentioned his going they would not have had to mention his return.

Apart from these reports there are more important ones, but the papers are in the habit of concealing the important news from me and offering the unimportant. If you are not familiar with the papers, they tell you what you do not want to know.

Most of the members of the group had assembled in honor of the new lock, and they were glad to see me sitting in their house. They had often invited me to come and lecture to them, but I had refrained from doing so. A man who cannot even listen to himself, how can he expect others to listen to him?

Until I went up to the Land of Israel I used to lecture, but since then I have made it a rule not to speak in public. I compared myself to that pious man who all his life wanted to say one prayer as it was meant to be said; when he went up to the Land of Israel he became wiser, and prayed to be able to pray even one word as it should be prayed.

'How is it possible,' they said, 'that a man comes from the Land of Israel and does not know how to make a speech?' 'For the very same reason that all the people from the Land of Israel make speeches,' said I, 'I do not. It is because of something that happened. If you wish to hear I shall tell you. The year I came to the Land of Israel, a workers' village was founded. When they laid the cornerstone they preached on the significance of the occasion. There were thirty-six speakers there who preached one after the other. Possibly each one of them expressed some new idea of his own; if not, he repeated what his colleagues had said. In the end I could not remember anything, for one came and jumbled up what the other had said, and a third came and jumbled up the words of the second.'

When the young people saw that I was not going to make

a speech, they asked me to tell them about the Land of Israel. 'My dear young people,' I said to them, 'have you ever seen a young man with his heart set on a young girl who would talk about her to someone else? If you wish, I shall tell you about the first Zion Group, which was founded when your fathers and I were young men.

'Noble and exalted was the Zionist ideal, and far from the world of action. The conquest of the communities, which Nordau demanded at the Congresses, was not needed at Szibucz, whose leaders showed no hostility to Zionism. On the contrary, some of them would come to the house of the Zion Group to read the paper or play chess, like the other Zionists in the town. Once a year we would bring a speaker. If the socialists did not come and make a disturbance, it was good; if they came and made a disturbance, it was not good. Similarly, we used to hold a Maccabee Evening on Hanukkah with speeches and recitations. Once a girl recited "Our Hope Is Not Yet Lost" by heart and the event was reported in the Hebrew papers. I know that no one has any interest in the things I am telling you, except for the man who is telling them. And much more than he is telling others of all this, he is reminding himself.'

CHAPTER ONE AND TWENTY

What This Man Tells

What this man tells:
'In the house of the Zion Group there is no change or novelty. We play chess and talk politics, and we exhaust every subject. But the subjects themselves are stale, especially for a man like me whose mind is set on the Land of Israel, and for whom anything not connected with the Land is unworthy of his attention.

'Besides the chess players and those who talk politics, there are some who tell jokes. When you hear a joke for the first time, you laugh; the second time, you smile; the third time, you shrug your shoulders; the fourth, you are bored to tears. This is something I know and perhaps you too, but those who ought to know it, namely the tellers of jokes, do not. That is why they repeat their jokes over and over and over again.

'So who makes you go to the group house? Surely you can go back to the Beit Midrash. But so long as people studied the Torah for its own sake or with an end in view, such as making a show or winning fame, you used to go into the Beit Midrash and open a book; when they stopped studying it for its own sake or with an end in view, the books changed their ways and no longer gladdened your heart. Or perhaps they did not change, but hid away their words for the time to come.

'Besides the books, you find in the Beit Midrash a few idlers sitting before an open book and talking to each other. Men's talk, it is said, is worth half as much as study, yet they talk about the rise in the price of meat and the controversies between butchers and slaughterers. I am half a vegetarian and find no interest in their chatter. What harm is there if people do not eat meat and do not slaughter living things? My vegetarianism gave great grief to my father and mother, but between ourselves, this world does not give satisfaction even to its Maker.

'In short, wherever you turn you find either boredom or weariness. Willy-nilly you return to your father's house. You find your mother cooking potatoes for the meal of the day. At that moment you imagine that September is already over; autumn is here; the rains are falling drop by drop; shadowy women are bending over, taking potatoes out of the damp and crumbling soil. A sluggish chill surrounds your heart, and you see yourself abandoned and adrift. You go into a second room and find your sisters with their friends, preparing their lessons. Seven times they have dipped their pens in the ink and still the copybook is clean. The seven wisdoms cannot be written just with the dip of a pen. It takes a great effort to put something down in writing. They chew their pens with their teeth and use them to chase away the flies. But once the pen has taken up ink, it soils their dresses and their copybooks. If a girl has soiled her dress, it can be washed, but if she has soiled her copybook, that is a misfortune, for the teacher calls a superfluous drop of ink *Zhidek*, namely, a little Jew, as a term of abuse. So they begin weeping until their voices echo from one end of the house to the other, and you cannot concentrate on even a trivial matter, such as the reason why a fly has landed on your nose. At the same time my little brother is sitting in the doorway banging with a hammer. Mother gave it to him for cracking nuts to make a cake, and when the nuts were finished he started just banging. And since it is not worth while just banging, he threatens to hit his little sister on the nose. And since she believes anything one tells her, she cries.

'Suddenly, a neighbor comes in to borrow a pot or return one. These neighbors find it difficult to stay at home, so they make the rounds of other people's houses.

'Our mother is not in the habit of visiting her neighbors, but if one of them comes in, she gives her a cordial welcome and offers her a taste of whatever she is cooking or baking. I do not begrudge the neighbors anything, but I cannot abide their exaggerations. They speak of every mouthful as if it came from the Kaiser's table.

'While this one is sitting, her husband comes in. For seven years he can do without his wife, but as soon as she comes into our house he follows to ask after her. When he comes in he takes a chair and sits and talks about what is known and what there is no need to know. At such times I feel indignant at my mother for making him welcome and listening to things she has already heard a hundred and one times. Among other things, he asks when my father will come home from the shop, as if it were an idle question. But in fact he needs my father, to borrow a little money or to have him sign a note. If so, why does he not go to see him in the shop? He has his good reasons, for in a shop a man behaves as a businessman, and my father would no doubt refuse him, while it is otherwise at home, when he comes as a friend.

'There are some who come to have my father write letters of recommendation for them to our relative in Vienna. This relative of ours is a university professor and has the title of *Hofrat*. Our townsfolk think that he is the Kaiser's counselor, and that the Kaiser does nothing without asking him first, so that in Szibucz he is regarded as a minister of state, and they pester him whenever there is any trouble. At the time when his fellows sat and busied themselves with trivial matters, he sat and read and studied; now that he has won a name in the world, all the ignoramuses in town come to ask him to do them favors. It is the way of the ignoramuses to hate wisdom and the wise. Once a man has studied and made himself a name, they come along to distract him with their petty affairs.

'My father comes home from the shop, his face sad and weary. He has had no ships wrecked at sea or cities destroyed on land, but his heart is ravaged by the cares of winning a livelihood and the pains of bringing up children. My father hoped many hopes for me, but in the end not one of them was realized; and here I am about to go up to the Land of Israel. Where is the sense of it? Since the day Szibucz was built it is unheard of that a young man should go up to the Land of Israel. And if he goes there, what will he do there? A thousand times my father has already spoken with his son, and all to no avail; now my father is silent, with a silence that is more painful than speech. His eyes that used to shine with wisdom are dimmed with sadness. My mother also is sad with the same sadness, and even sadder than my mother am I. It is not fitting for a man to tell about his sadness, especially a man who is preparing to go up to the Land of Israel.

'With his learning, his wisdom, his virtuous ways, my father could have earned a living as a rabbi in any great city, but the great merchants he used to see in his childhood, when they came before his rabbi to settle their disputes, led him astray, for he saw them behaving grandly, like wealthy men, and he tried to be like them. What he neglected, he neglected, and what he sought was not granted to him, and here he is a shopkeeper, waiting for customers. If customers come to buy, it is good; and if they do not come, it is not good.

'In short, my father should have been a rabbi, and he hoped his son would achieve what he did not. It is a virtue the Almighty has given His creatures: they wish to make right through their sons those things in which they have not succeeded. However, this is not achieved through every son. I need not go far to find proof, for I myself am an example.'

I do not know who is interested in these things, but since they weighed on me, I told them.

As I was leaving, one young man came up to me and rebuked me for making friends with Yeruham Freeman, who was a communist and an enemy of Zion. I must say that, although this young man was a Zionist and Yeruham was not, I liked Yeruham better. But even apart from this one, other people had already hinted to me that I was not doing right in talking with Yeruham Freeman in public, because he was suspected of communism and I belonged to another country, and there was danger that I would be expelled from the town.

Later on I said to myself: I was born in this town and spent most of my youth here—but an official, who was not born here and has done nothing here but enjoy the best the town can give, may come along and tell me: Go, you belong to another country and you have no permission to stay with us.

I thought of my forefathers, whose bones are interred in the town's graveyard. And I thought of my grandfather, may he rest in peace, who for forty years less one was an elder of the town, bearing his burden without asking for pay. And I remembered my uncle, may he rest in peace, who used to give wood free to the poor. I thought of my father, of blessed memory, of whom the town was proud; I thought of my other relatives who had bestowed many benefits on the townsfolk— and now the authorities, who inherited all those benefits, could come and expel me from the town. And what would I do with the key of the old Beit Midrash which the locksmith had promised to make for me? Would I give the key to Yeruham and say to him: Mr. Freeman, my brother, up till now I have looked after our old Beit Midrash; now you look after it.

CHAPTER TWO AND TWENTY

A Second Key

The locksmith kept his promise and made me a key. I took the key and said: Yesterday you were a lump of iron; the craftsman cast his eyes upon you and made you into a precious thing. Similarly, I said to myself: Yesterday you were a lump of flesh; now the Beit Midrash has been opened to you, and you have become a man. I placed the key in my pocket and said: From now on I shall watch over you, so that you may watch over me.

The Beit Midrash was just as it had been. Even the books I had studied before the key was lost were lying in the same places on the table. It looked as if they were waiting for me to come back. And I did not disappoint the books or betray their expectations. As soon as I entered the Beit Midrash I sat down and began to study.

What is the difference between the Torah I had learned before and the Torah I was learning now? Dear brothers, there is no time when man is more blessed than the time he spends in his mother's womb, for then he is taught the entire Torah, but as soon as he comes out into the air of the world, along comes an angel and strikes him on the mouth, making him forget the entire Torah. How great is the Torah that he is taught in those days—even so, there is no joy in the Torah unless one toils for it. It is like a man who has lost his key and found it.

So long as I sit and study, it is good; when I stop studying, it is not good. And if you wanted to, you could say that even while I am studying, I can feel the pain in my hands and feet and all the rest of my body. Between one key and the next, the Almighty has chilled the world and brought the winter upon us.

I have found it written in a book: You cannot change the air outside, but you can change the air inside. This was meant to refer to spiritual matters, but I interpreted it literally. I could not heat the air outside, but I could heat the air inside the Beit Midrash.

I went up to the stove and opened the door. A cold wind swept down the chimney and into the house. I said to myself: I shall put in two or three blocks of wood and kindle them; fire will at once come forth and touch the wings of the wind, and the wind will flee immediately, never to return.

I searched in the woodbin, but did not find even a chip. For many years no one had brought wood to the Beit Midrash. I remembered how, in the days gone by, when we wished to heat the stove and the wood was not sufficient, we used to take the reading desk of a householder who had avoided donating wood to the Beit Midrash, break it up, and put it in the stove. The few desks that were left in the Beit Midrash did not sense my thought. In any case, I said to them: Have no fear, I shall not touch you. On the contrary, I am glad you still exist, for I have studied the Torah on you, and inside you I used to hide the little books that made me leave off the study of the Torah. If I could burn the space inside and preserve you, I should burn the space; but since that is impossible, I shall keep my hands off you.

I explained the difficulty to the innkeeper. His wife said, 'If only we could get rid of all our troubles as easily as this one. All we have to do is go to Daniel Bach and order some wood.'

When I came to Daniel Bach's, Hanoch happened to be there, he and his horse and cart. 'Load up a cartful of wood,' Daniel said to Hanoch, 'and take it to the old Beit Midrash.'

So Hanoch took a pile of wood, put it in his cart, and persuaded his horse to start out. And he too went off with him. So the three of them, namely Hanoch, his cart, and horse, kept moving until they reached the Beit Midrash.

Hanoch's cart is small and his horse weak, and they were meant only to take haberdashery to the villages and bring back a chicken or an egg, but out of respect for Hanoch we call his cart a cart and his horse a horse.

Hanoch unloaded the wood, brought it into the Beit Midrash, and wanted to make a fire in the stove. 'Hanoch,' I said to him, 'by the time the stove heats up the horse will

catch cold. Go back to your work and I will make the fire.'
So I gave him his pay and sent him off.

Before long I had made a fire in the stove. The whole
house filled with smoke; first, because I was not accustomed
to the task, and second, because the stove had not been lit
for several years. When I was getting tired and about to despair, the stove had compassion on this man and began to
grow steadily warmer, and so did the whole Beit Midrash.
Great was the joy of that hour. I shall not exaggerate if I say
that even the walls of the Beit Midrash perspired with joy.

That day I studied for a long time, for outside it was cold
and in the Beit Midrash there was warmth. So I preferred to
sit in the Beit Midrash rather than wander about outdoors.

After the wood was finished I ordered more. Since then
Hanoch brings me a cartful of wood once every three or four
days. He is little and his horse is little and his cart is little;
these three things which are little upon the earth have to sustain a whole family. They travel about among the villages
near the town and sell haberdashery to the uncircumcised and
their women. And this is one example of the power of the
Almighty, that He provides a living for His creatures even by
way of small utensils.

Hanoch rejoices in his lot and gives joy to his horse. Before he himself eats and drinks, he feeds his animal. The
horse does not ask for bird's milk, and what he asks Hanoch
gives him. So the two of them like each other and help each
other. When Hanoch is tired the horse pulls the cart; when
the horse is tired Hanoch pulls the cart; and when the cart
is tired, both of them pull it.

'Are you making a living?' I asked Hanoch. 'Thank God,'
Hanoch replied, 'more than we deserve of Him. If we deserved
more, He would give more.' 'And don't you deserve more?' I
said to him. 'The proof is that He doesn't give more,' he replied. 'If your utensils were bigger,' said I, 'perhaps He would
give more.' 'He would give,' said Hanoch, 'but His agents
would keep what He gives for themselves.' 'Are you not satisfied with human beings either?' said I. 'I have never thought
about it,' said Hanoch. 'That means,' said I, 'that you say
things you have not thought about.' Said Hanoch, 'I do not

think about things, but whatever the blessed God puts in my
mouth I let out with my lips.'

I said to myself: Perhaps I will give Hanoch enough to
exchange his small horse and cart for a big one, so that his
income should not be so small. I hastily put my hand in my
pocket and took out a purse and said to him, 'Here is your
pay, Hanoch.' At first I wanted to give him the whole purse,
but when I had taken it out I changed my mind and gave
him a small coin. The Almighty wanted to give him the whole
purse, but the agent He chose kept His gift for himself.

This Hanoch has a weak mind, and he does not grasp
anything that is higher than his cap. Nevertheless I talk to
him about matters of the utmost significance and explain them
to him. If he does not understand, I elucidate with a parable.
But even so, he does not understand my meaning in the least,
because a man needs a little imagination for that.

'Do you know what imagination is, Hanoch?' I ask him.
'I don't know,' says he. 'If so,' I say to Hanoch, 'sit down and
I will explain it to you. Imagination is something through
which everyone in this world lives: you and I and your horse
and your cart. How can that be? Well, you go out to the village because you imagine that your income is assured there.
The same applies to your horse and the same to your cart, for
without the power of imagination the world would not go on
living. Happy is the man who uses his imagination to feed his
household, and woe to the man who uses it for vanities, like
those who present dramas and farces. Once I went into a
theater where they were showing a kind of drama. I said to
my neighbors: "I know the end of this drama from its very
beginning." And what I said was fully confirmed, because all
I had to do was mirror one thing with another. And this I did
through the power of the simple imagination, but if I had used
the higher imagination I should have been proved wrong, for
most plays are made with the simple imagination, because the
authors have not been privileged to possess the higher imagination.

'I see, Hanoch, that you do not know what theaters are,
so I will tell you. A theater is a house to which respectable
householders go. And why do they go there when they have

houses of their own? Because sometimes a man tires of his own house and goes to another house.

'That other house, the theater, is like this: People perform there who have never seen a house in their lives, but they pretend they know everything that there is in a house; so they show the householders all that there is in their own houses, and the householders are delighted and clap their hands and say: Fine, fine. Surely they should know that it is not fine, because it is not true. But there are two groups, and each believes that what is shown in the theater is true of the other. Yet there is one man who does not believe this, for that man is at home in both houses, and knows what is to be found in each of them.'

Let us leave the theaters and the plays and speak of other things. Once I told Hanoch in what year he was born, and Hanoch was surprised that I knew even this. And he did not know that from the name of a pious Jew one can tell the year of his birth. 'How so? Because you were named Hanoch after that pious man Rabbi Hanoch of Olesca, for if you had been born a year before his passing or a year after, your father would have called you after another pious man who passed away the year you were born.' Similarly I revealed to him the name of his horse. The true name of this horse, which Hanoch calls 'My right hand' and the children call 'Pharaoh's steed,' is neither 'My right hand' nor 'Pharaoh's steed,' but Henoch, for Henoch is the everyday form of the name Hanoch, and because it is not fitting to call an animal by a holy name, therefore I call him Henoch.

'Now it is worth while inquiring into the name of your cart. It is impossible to call it a chariot; first, because a chariot is usually harnessed to many horses, and second, because of the verse in *Haggai*: "And I will overthrow the chariots, and those that ride in them." You are a modest man, Hanoch; you are fit to be a shepherd. The shepherd walks beside his sheep or sits facing them and recites psalms like King David, may he rest in peace, and the whole Land of Israel is open before him, east and west, north and south. If you like, you sit by streams of water and say: "He maketh me to lie down in green pastures; He leadeth me beside the still waters." Or, if you wish, you go up to the mountains and say: "Who maketh grass to grow upon the mountains; He giveth the beast his food." Perhaps you are afraid of robber bands, but you need not be afraid. It happened once that a child went up to the heights of the mountain of Ephraim to graze his lamb. A certain Arab came, stole the child's lamb, and slaughtered it. The child began to cry. A certain shepherd came and judged the Arab according to the verdict of the Torah, which is prescribed in the section on judgments in the twenty-second chapter of the Book of Exodus. The Arab went and brought the child's father four lambs instead of one. The child's father asked the Arab, "What is this?" "I stole your son's lamb and slaughtered it," the Arab replied, "and a shepherd of your folk, of the sons of Moses, came and ordered me to make the fourfold payment." When this became known in the village, all the Jews went up to the top of the hill to the shepherd and said to him: "Master, son of Moses our Teacher, every day we are robbed, every day we are slaughtered, every day we are killed; come and guard the sheep that are led to the killing." He said to them: " 'Hide thyselves as it were for a little moment, until the indignation is past.' Wait a little until the indignation of the Almighty passes away and He gives us permission to return to the Land of Israel, and rely upon His blessed mercies that He will protect you as a shepherd his flock." '

Since the day I first met Hanoch I had not seen him rejoice so much as when he heard the story of the shepherd. And to add to his joy, I told him more things about the hills of the Land of Israel, which fill with gold at evening time, and about the valleys and gorges, whose color is like the blue of the sky, and about the sun that wraps a man around like a prayer shawl, and about the rains of the Land, which the Almighty brings down when the people of Israel do His will, and every single drop is enough to fill a mikveh. And if a little snow falls, the Almighty immediately brings out the sun and melts it. For the Land of Israel is not like the lands of the other nations, where the snow comes down without a stop and the sun hides itself and does not come out, and a man is covered and hidden by the snow and his wife and children cry and are not answered. And where is the sun? Has it no mercy on the children of Israel? In those days the sun is busy ripening the oranges in the Land of Israel and cannot visit the lands of exile.

You cannot find a better man to talk to than Hanoch. But one must be careful or one might be led to pride, for he imagines that because you are a wiseacre you are a prophet.

And it was for this that I had already rebuked him, explaining that a prophet knows nothing by himself and is only the agent of the Almighty, neither adding to nor taking away from the Almighty's message, and since the day the vision was blocked, prophecy has been taken away. And I returned to the beginning of the matter and explained to him the difference between imagination and reality. Reality is bother without bliss, and imagination is bliss without bother.

After I had explained all of this to him, I said farewell; first, so as not to weary him with words, and second, because his horse was already impatient at standing still. As he left, I told him he should bring wood to stoke the fire, for on account of our many sins we have been exiled from our Land and we cannot endure the cold.

The Frequenters of the Beit Midrash

It is to Hanoch's credit that he does his work properly. Every three or four days he brings to the Beit Midrash a cartful of chopped wood, which I lay behind the stove and arrange very neatly. Wood is all the glory of a stove, so I bow before the stove and kindle the fire in it.

The fire blazes up in the stove; the wood crackles in the fire; the resin drips from the wood and sizzles in the fire. Sometimes a maggot appears on a log and is consumed together with it. I say to the maggot, 'And in the priest's stove would you be any better off than here?' But it writhes and makes no reply. And since it does not answer I refrain from speaking further to it, not because I look down on it, but a

worm that writhes because it is being burned in the Beit Midrash is not worth speaking to.

Who let men in on the secret that a fire is being lit in the
old Beit Midrash? A bird from heaven spread the news. For
many days no one had looked at the Beit Midrash, then along
came a bird from heaven and stood on the roof and found the
chimney warm. He called his wife, his sons, and his daughters,
who came and surrounded the chimney. Their neighbors saw
and joined them. Before much time had passed, the entire
chimney was surrounded by birds.

A woman raised her eyes and said to her friend, 'Friend,
what have the birds seen that makes them gather there? Look!
There is smoke coming out of the Beit Midrash.' 'Friend,'
said her friend, 'I have heard that that Jerusalemite is keeping
the fire going in the stove, and the birds are coming to warm
themselves by the chimney.' 'Friend,' said her friend, 'I am
going to my husband to tell him.' 'Go and tell your husband,'
said her friend, 'I have no one to tell, for my husband died in
the war.' So she went and told her husband. He went into the
Beit Midrash, where he found the place warm and the stove
lit. He stretched out his hands and said, 'What a pleasure!'
When his hands and feet and the rest of his body had been
warmed, he took a book and sat down to read, until his eye-
lids were gripped by sleep and he dropped off. After a time
he awoke and said, 'Paradise, paradise!' I feel certain that in
a dream he had been shown paradise open, with the pious sitting and studying the Torah, and looking just like our Beit
Midrash.

I said to myself: What did this man lack? Only a little
warmth, a little Torah, a little Beit Midrash, a little pleasant
slumber. I am not one of those who argue with their Maker,
but at that moment I said: Master of the world, Thou who
didst create the whole universe and in whose hands the universe lies, is it difficult for Thee, if I may say so, to give a little
pleasure to Thy sorely tried and loving sons? The next day
the same man returned, and when he came in he did not run
to the stove to warm himself, but first picked up a book. The
sons of Israel are not ungrateful; if the Almighty gives them a
small part of their needs, immediately they give Him, if we

may say so, His needs; and that is not all, but they give pre-
cedence to His wants over their own needs.

An hour later another man came in. As the one behaved,
so did the other. I got up and added wood to the stove, saying to the wood: Wood, do your duty, don't hang fire, for
men take pleasure in what you do.

The two men sit side by side with books in front of them.
From their joy it can be seen that they are studying the Halacha, the law of the Torah. Since the day the Temple was laid
waste, the Holy One, blessed be He, has no foothold in His
world but the four cubits of the Halacha. Happy are you that
study the Torah, for you extend the world of the Holy One,
blessed be He, through your study.

The fire sings in the stove and the lips of those who are
studying the Torah whisper. The great hill opposite the Beit
Midrash casts shadow and longer shadow, and covers the light
of the day. As if a curtain were spread across them, the windows of the Beit Midrash gradually darken. My two guests
rise, go to the basin, wash their hands, and recite the Afternoon Service. I rise and light the lamp. One of them responds,
saying, 'Light.' 'Light for the Jews,' adds the other.

Little by little the wick consumes the kerosene and the
fire the wick. The visitors close their books and rise. They embrace the stove, kiss the mezuza on the doorpost, and slowly
leave the Beit Midrash. I lock the door and go back to the
hotel.

On the way I said to myself: If it is warm for the body
why should it be dark for the eyes? Next day, when Hanoch
brought the wood for the stove, I said to him, 'Here is some
money; bring kerosene and candles, and we will fill the lamps
with the kerosene and light two or three of the candles. Is it
not said, "Where there is Torah there is light"?'

When Hanoch came back he brought a container of kerosene and a pound of candles. 'Where is your sense, Hanoch,'
I said to him, 'that you have brought thin candles? The Gentiles, who do not need to study the Torah, can make do with
thin candles; the Jews, who do study the Torah, need big ones.
Had I been there at the hour of the Creation, I should have
asked the Holy One, blessed be He, to hang the sun, the moon,

and the stars in the Beit Midrash.' I filled the lamps with kerosene and placed two candles in the candelabrum on the
lectern. I thought many thoughts, about the sun in the firmament and the stove in our old Beit Midrash, about candles
and stars, and I said to Hanoch, 'Whatever the Holy One,
blessed be He, did in His world, He did well, and after He
had finished all His work He gave understanding to the sons
of man that they might make for themselves a kind of model
of the world on high. He had created a sun to blaze on hot
days, and He gave understanding to the sons of man to make
for themselves a stove that would warm them on cold days. He
hung the moon and the stars to give light by night, and He
gave understanding to the sons of man to make for themselves
candles and lamps that would give them light in their houses.'

Hanoch was all ears and wanted to hear more, and I too
wanted to add to the praises of the Almighty. But at that moment a man came in and interrupted me.

Let us interrupt the praise of the Almighty and consider
the deeds of His creatures. This man who came in—let us say
Levi was his name—did not take a book like Reuben and Simon, he did not extend the world of the Holy One, blessed be
He, but he embraced the stove and sighed from the bottom of
his heart. Perhaps he said: This house is warm and bright,
and my own house, where I have a sick wife and sick children,
is cold and dark.

Next morning came Judah and Issachar and Zebulun.
Judah and Issachar took books and began to study. Zebulun
stood beside the stove and did not take a book in hand and
did not extend the four cubits of the Holy One, blessed be He,
but it could be seen that he drew satisfaction from his brethren's study.

Now let us look at the doings of Dan. Not only did he
come into the Beit Midrash carrying utensils like an ignoramus, but he made use of its supplies like a boor. After warming his bones he filled his utensils with embers, so as to bring
them to his wife, who stood in the market with frozen fingers.

It did not take long before all the sons of Jacob came
along, Joseph and Benjamin, Naphtali, Gad and Asher, Jews
of our town whom I have thought fit to call by pleasant names

in keeping with their pleasant deeds, although their actual names are ugly, like Shimke, Yoshke, Veptchi, Godzhik—and other names of that sort.

My dear brothers, I wish to give you the news—if that can be considered good news—that we hold public prayers every day. And have you ever seen a place where one man of Israel finds satisfaction, where ten more men of Israel would not follow him? And when there are ten, they hold public prayers, with one of them leading. It is not my custom to lead the prayers; first, because I have adopted several practices of the Land of Israel and a version of the text that is not in use here, and I am afraid I might confuse one version with another, and second, because most of the worshippers, alas, are mourners, and they have preference in leading the prayers.

Let us take some time to speak in praise of Israel's prayers. Most of the day, people sit side by side and study the Torah. And when the time for prayer arrives, they set aside their books, wash their hands, recite the prayer of incense, light a candle on the lectern, and say Ashrei, Kaddish, and the Eighteen Benedictions, and so forth. Up till now the Holy One, blessed be He, has conversed with them through His Torah; now they converse with Him through prayer.

Sometimes a Jew comes from the market, warms his hands, bows, and says Ashrei. His voice is weak. It is difficult for the mouth that has spoken all day in the tongue of the Gentiles to utter a Hebrew word, so his speech comes out broken. And that is not all: his heart is beating like a lizard, because he has been standing in the market all day without earning his expenses but when the time has come for the afternoon prayer he has left his trading, though perhaps just when he is standing in the Beit Midrash one of the uncircumcised has come to the market and would have let him earn a copper, and he has left all his affairs and gone in to pray.

After the prayer a man does not leave the Beit Midrash without first studying a chapter of Mishna or *Ein Yaakov* or *Shulchan Aruch*. And who is not at home with Halacha or Agada reads a section of the Pentateuch or recites psalms. Sometimes a man gets up and makes some comment on the Torah or discusses the exact meaning of a verse of Scripture.

Between you and me, their remarks are not of any earthshaking importance, but they are a sign that even if the Torah has left this place, its fragrance is still in the air. Sometimes they talk about everyday matters. Although it has been said, 'In the synagogue and the Beit Midrash there should be no idle conversation,' the people are used to taking a lenient view, especially at a time when a man's heart is oppressed and he wants to distract it by talking.

I once believed that one could tell a man's experience from his conversation, but when I saw that men who had been wounded in the war talked of the distress of the pogroms and men who had been injured in the pogroms spoke of the troubles of the war, I realized that a man's experiences are one thing and his conversation another. Once I said to a man who had been wounded in the war and injured in the pogroms, 'How is it that I have never heard you mention either the war or the pogroms?' Said he, 'A man recalls his troubles after he has recovered from them, but I am still in the midst of them. And if you like I could also say that the injuries to your livelihood are worse than the injuries of war or the injuries of the pogroms—in fact, when I find a pound of grits to take home to my wife, that's a greater victory than all the victories of the Emperor.' But even when they do not mention the pogroms or the war, they do mention things that had happened to them in those days, for instance, how a man succeeded in snatching some sleep in the middle of a battle, or bringing a jug of milk to a child whose mother had been hit by a bullet while she was nursing him.

While we were sitting talking, a man came into the Beit Midrash and filled his utensils with embers. Before he left, another came and filled his utensils too. The men in the Beit Midrash flared up, crying, 'It says clearly in the *Shulchan Aruch* that it is forbidden to make common use of sacred provisions.' So they advised me to have a lock made for the stove; otherwise there would be no embers left in the Beit Midrash, for all the peddlers sitting in the market were freezing with cold and wanted to warm themselves, and if I did not lock the stove against them I might just as well invite them to come and help themselves.

'It is easy to make a lock,' I replied, 'but I am afraid I might lose the key, as I lost the key of the Beit Midrash, and I would freeze with cold. And even if I had another key made, by the time the locksmith came and made one, the cold days would be over and no one would have any need for my embers; so I would have been wicked for nothing.'

As the number of those who took embers increased, I told Hanoch to bring wood every day. When the embers in the stove diminished I added more wood. I am no longer free to pay attention to a worm consumed in the fire, because I am busy warming the men of Szibucz.

Ever since I came to years of understanding, I have hated any forms composed of different parts that do not accord with each other, especially a picture whose parts exist in reality but whose combination and conjunction exist not in reality but only in the imagination of the artist; and more especially things in which only something of the concrete image has been shifted to the abstract image—that is, when someone compares states of the soul to things of the body, as certain commentators have interpreted the verse, 'Lest ye corrupt yourselves, and make you a graven image, in the likeness of any figure.' So I was surprised to find myself beginning to make analogies and saying: There are symbolic things here—for a man from the Land of Israel has come down to bring warmth to the sons of exile.

Besides Reuben and Simon, Levi and Judah, and so forth, who sit regularly most days in the Beit Midrash, you also find Ignatz there. Ignatz does not come to warm himself—nor, needless to say, does he come to study and pray. I doubt if he is able even to recite the 'Hear, O Israel.' Ignatz was a foundling and did not study in the Hebrew school, and when he grew up he ran about the streets, until the war came and made him a soldier. When he came back from the war he became a beggar. And if he comes to the Beit Midrash, he comes to collect charity from me, for since the day we have been heating the Beit Midrash, I have been doing much sitting and little going out, so he comes here to make sure of his payment.

In my honor, Ignatz has improved his language and asks for his needs in the Holy Tongue, saying nasally 'Mu'es.' And when he stretches out his hand he does not push his face at me. Ignatz knows that I give to him even if he does not show me his disfigurement.

Since the day Dolik offered him a glass of brandy to drink through the hole in his face, which is in the place of his nose, and I rebuked Dolik, saying, 'How can a man born of a Jewish woman be so cruel?' Ignatz has taken me to his heart, and—so I have heard—he says that were he not in need he would not take money from me. Ignatz also says that even if he did not take I would give him perforce, because I am a merciful and goodhearted man who cannot bear to see my neighbor in trouble, and I give of my own accord even if I am not asked.

Ignatz is a lean, erect man with a smooth face on which nothing juts out except his mustache, which turns upward and makes the cavity of his nose a kind of pitcher. There are insignia of honor pinned to his chest, some that he won by his deeds and some that he took from his comrades who fell in the war. Before the war he used to look after horses or tout for coach passengers, and sometimes he would act as a pimp, although there was no need of it, for there were other pimps standing at the hotel doors to serve sinners who put their bodies before their souls. The people of Szibucz disagreed about him. Some said his mother was a Jewess and his father a Gentile. It happened that in a certain village near our town, forty years ago and more, there was no quorum in the synagogue, so the Jews of the village used to pray in town on the Days of Awe. One year, on the eve of the Day of Atonement, when the innkeeper and his wife went to town, they left a young girl, their relative, alone in the house, for she was sick. During the night thieves came and robbed the inn and set it on fire. One of them found the girl hiding in the garden and ravished her, and Ignatz was born of that. Others said, however, that his father and mother were both Jews, but his father was an evil man, who cast his eyes on another woman, left his wife pregnant, and ran away. When Ignatz was born it was hard for his mother to support him, so she left him at the Great Synagogue in the pile of tattered pages from the holy books in the courtyard. A childless carter saw him, picked him up and brought him home, and saw him through until the war came and Ignatz went off as a soldier. Then a grenade splinter struck him and smashed his nose, and when the war ended he came back to Szibucz, where his disfigurement gave him a head start on the other beggars. Although there are a number of beggars with deformities in our town, none of them earns as good a living as Ignatz. There is something about Ignatz's disfigurement which is not like others', for with other deformed persons, such as those without hands, by the time you have considered what this poor man will take his copper coin with, since he has no hands, you find that you forget to give it to him. The same with one who has no feet. By the time you put your hand in your pocket, you have already passed him, and he has no feet to run after you, so you put him out of your mind. It is not like that with Ignatz, who stretches out his hand and runs after you looking at you with the three holes in his face and cries, 'Pieniadze'; immediately you throw him a copper, if only so he should not look at you, especially if he says 'Mu'es,' for the Hebrew word issues from his lips like something loathsome, reverberating in the cavity of the nose he has lost.

It was all very fine of me to take up the poor man's cause against Dolik, but what I said to him, 'How can a man born of a Jewish woman treat this wretched fellow so cruelly?' did not turn out to be in my favor, for when my own turn came I saw that I was as cruel as Dolik. The first time Ignatz came to the Beit Midrash to beg charity from me, I told him to come in and warm himself. He obeyed and entered. When I was ready to go I did not find my coat. Next morning I found Ignatz dressed in my coat, and took it off him. He stared at me with his eyes and the hole in place of his nose and said to me, 'How can a man born of a Jewish woman treat his brother so cruelly and take his coat off him on a cold day like this?' So Ignatz paid me back with the same coin I had used for Dolik.

The Three Conceptions

To return to our subject. Every day we hold three services in our old Beit Midrash, and four on the Sabbath. What shall I tell first and what shall I tell last? Everyday wisdom suggests that I should first describe the six working days, on which we sustain the body; the higher wisdom suggests that I should start with the Sabbath, which sustains the soul. But since the six working days come first in the order of creation, we shall start with them.

Briefly, then, every day we hold three public services, and on Mondays and Thursdays we take out the Scroll and read the Torah. The prayer leader goes from the lectern to the Ark, takes out the Scroll, goes up with it to the pulpit, lays it on the reading desk and begins, 'May His kingdom be soon revealed and made visible unto us, and may He be gracious unto our remnant and unto the remnant of His people, the House of Israel, granting them grace, kindness, mercy, and favor . . .' and then he reads the Torah. Before returning the Scroll to the Ark he says, 'May it be His will to establish the house of our life . . . to preserve among us the wise men of Israel . . . that we may hear and receive good tidings of salvation and comfort, and that He may gather our scattered ones from the four corners of the earth. . . .' And he begs mercy 'for our brethren, the children of Israel, who are given over to trouble and captivity, whether they are on the sea or on dry land, that the All-present may have mercy upon them and bring them forth from trouble to tranquillity, from darkness to light, from subjection to redemption. . . .'

Letters have arrived from our brethren who left Szibucz —every word drenched in tears and every letter crying 'Woe!' After they left Szibucz they wandered for days on the roads and went from one place to the next, until their money was exhausted and they had to beg alms from the sons of men, who are sparing with alms but generous with abuse. At last they got on a ship and went out to sea, and the sea threatened to drown them, for this ship was rickety and unfit for the voyage; some believe that the owner intended to sink it, so as to take the insurance money and get himself a new one. (I have heard that articles written about this ship did not mention that it was full of Jews.) When the travelers escaped from the sea to dry land, the land devoured them. Every place to which they made their way cast them out as soon as they arrived. When prominent Jews made representation on their behalf to the nobles and masters of the city, they would be left alone for a day or two, and finally be sent to another city; there the same thing happened. All countries became Gehenna for them, but in Gehenna the wicked are punished on weekdays and rest on Sabbath, while these never had any rest; the wicked are taken out of Gehenna when someone gives charity in memory of their souls, but these suffered soul-destroying torments and were thrust deeper into Gehenna. Grievous were the tribulations of the war, but in the war there were enemies and friends; now the whole world has become their enemy. In the war the Emperor supplied your necessities; now the kings condemn us to hunger.

Freide the Kaiserin comes to me with a letter from her son. All those who had read out the letter to her were hard men, and they had read it in a tone of admonition, piercing her flesh, as it were, with red-hot needles. But I, says Freide, have a good heart and a gentle voice—she still remembers how I used to call her 'Feidi'—I would not be cruel to her; I would read to her her son's letter gently, not like those who read it to provoke her.

I cannot remember all of the letter—only a few lines, and they went like this: 'Not even the threat of death itself could force good tidings from me—there is only bad news to tell, for God and men have robbed me of rest and made me forget that I am a man. But alas that I am a man, for no one in the land will have mercy on me, and a dog is happier than I, for people have pity on dogs—but me they drive away. I came to a city and said: Here I shall dwell; from the fruit of my labor

I shall eat bread, whether little or much, and also send something to you, my bereaved and unfortunate mother. But they came and drove me away and said: Go. So I went to another city, and there too I found no rest. For hardly had I set foot on its soil when they cried out against me and lowered my honor to the dust and said: Be off with you—go! Thus it shall be done to a man who wants to eat a crust of bread, for from his womb his Maker made a jest of him and a derision; though he has not sinned against his God, except in worshipping Him. To what shall I compare myself, to what shall I liken myself, my forlorn mother? For I have become like the mud of the streets, which every passer-by wipes off his boots. The sun shines on me as on them, and the stars of evening twinkle, but, alas, the star of my fortune is darkened and the sun brings no healing to a man lost and unfortunate. Woe is me, Mother, that you bore me, a prey to human beasts.'

Let us leave our sorely tried brethren and hope that the Almighty will have pity on them and deliver them from trouble to tranquillity and from darkness into light, and may we receive good tidings, for the greater the evil the greater the hope. And now let us speak in praise of the Sabbath, which has been given us.

I am not one of those all of whose days are Sabbath; I say that ever since the world was created we have never had a day of rest. After the servitude in Egypt we served the golden calf and became servants to all the kings of East and West. Now we are weary of toil, and what is wrong with our seeking a day that is all Sabbath and rest?

That first Sabbath in our old Beit Midrash went like this. My hostess donated two coverings for the tables, and I bought a third for the table at which I study. I spread the cloths on the three tables and lit the two lamps and the candles, and all the people of the Beit Midrash came to pray. Between ourselves, they all came in weekday clothes, because they have no clothes for the Sabbath. But you could see a change in them. This is the change that takes place on the eve of Sabbath at dark, for man was born on Sabbath eve so that he should enter the Sabbath pure. Had he not sinned, all his days would have been Sabbath. So when the Sabbath arrives the soul remembers that first Sabbath in the Garden of Eden and changes for the better.

One of our friends, Shlomo Shamir, chanted the Welcome to the Sabbath with the melody that is customary among us. And when he pronounced the blessing 'Who spreadest over us the tabernacle of peace,' it seemed as if the Holy One, blessed be He, Himself, in person, were spreading over us His tabernacle of peace. But this peace was still that of a tabernacle, which is a temporary dwelling, but when he said, 'And the children of Israel shall keep the Sabbath,' it seemed as if we had entered into a permanent dwelling, in which was everlasting peace. And I do not exaggerate when I say that we could see with our own eyes the Holy One, blessed be He, making a covenant of peace with Israel for all eternity.

That Shlomo Shamir who led the prayers, an upholsterer by trade, knows how to read the Torah and lead the prayers. By virtue of his praying he once won a medal for valor. How? Once some Jewish soldiers were holding a service on the Days of Awe, and Shlomo led the prayers. The commander of his regiment passed by and heard him praying. 'Corporal Shamir is a brave man,' he said to his companions, and told them to give him a medal for valor.

After the service the worshippers wished each other a peaceful and pleasant Sabbath and went home quietly. I too went to my home, namely my hotel, for I live in the Land of Israel and my home is many hundreds of miles from here, and I am only a guest for the night.

I have already described my weekday table at the beginning of the book, so surely it is fitting that I tell of the Sabbath table.

On Sabbath eves, only the three of us sit together: my host, his wife, and I, because his sons and daughters come in for the meal whenever they feel like it, and they do not feel like coming just at the moment when their father is reciting the Kiddush and singing the Sabbath hymns. When there is a guest, if he is an observer of the Sabbath he eats with us and we can pronounce together the Invitation to the Grace, which is said when three observant Jews are present; if he is not,

Krolka sets him at a table by himself. On weekdays everyone is the innkeeper's master, but on Sabbath he is his own master. On weekdays, when a man's livelihood is measured out to him, he must look after his livelihood and humble himself before those on whom he depends; on Sabbath, when the Holy One, blessed be He, Himself covers the cost of the Sabbath, a man is free from the servitude of business and the yoke of others.

The hotelkeeper is not in the habit of going to synagogue on Sabbath eve, for he finds it difficult to walk because of his rheumatism; his own synagogue is far from his home and he does not go to another synagogue nearby because he does not wish to change from one holy place to another. He welcomes the Sabbath at home and waits for me before beginning the meal.

When I come in he puts his little prayer book in front of him and recites the Kiddush, his glass in his hand and the prayer book open. He is over fifty years old: for thirty years, no doubt, he has said the Kiddush on Sabbath eves, and every year has its fifty Sabbaths, so go and reckon how many times he has recited it; but still he has to hold his prayer book open during the Kiddush. First, because his heart is troubled and he is afraid he might make a mistake; and second, because a miracle happened to him through his prayer book and he was saved from death. During the war a bullet was fired at him while his prayer book was over his heart; the bullet struck the prayer book and pierced the pages until it came to the page of the Kiddush for Sabbath eve.

After cutting the bread he sings, 'All who sanctify the Sabbath day.' His voice chokes; it is not a voice but a kind of echo, like the sound that comes from wet wood as it burns. But the enthusiasm pent up in his heart makes a chant for itself, a kind of melody that stops short before it can sound out. His face is sad and his shoulders quiver, and sometimes he gropes with his hand under the table like a man seeking support. Meanwhile his wife sits opposite with her hands on her bosom, looking at him sometimes with affection and sometimes with concern. And when he reaches the verse 'Their righteousness shall shine forth like the light of the seven days,'

she rises and brings him his soup, and at the same time Krolka
comes in and brings the wife her soup. Then Krolka goes back
to the kitchen and brings me my vegetable soup. 'When I sit
like this with my husband on Sabbath eves,' says the innkeeper's wife to me, 'with our table set and the white cloth
spread on the table and candles burning, I say to myself in
wonder: Considering all the troubles that have come upon
us—for my husband was in the war and was in danger of
death at any moment—I really should not have had strength
to endure, and not only have I endured all the troubles, but
I have the happiness of welcoming the Sabbath in peace.'

As for her sons and daughters, Mrs. Zommer says that
whenever her husband, who was far away from his children
all through the war and did not have the worry of them, sees
them doing something wrong, he is angry at once. But she,
who had the worry of them all the time and saw them growing up, does not pick upon them for every little trifle. On the
contrary, she thanks God that they have come as far as they
have. Didn't they run about in the streets of Vienna for a long
time like nobody's children, refusing to accept authority? And
when they did accept her authority she was not free to look
after them, because all day she was busy working, never stopping except to bring the work to her customers, get her pay,
and buy food. Sometimes she would stand all night until morning at the door of a shop, waiting for the shopkeeper to open
up and give her her ration. When she was fortunate enough
to get it, she would prepare a meal for herself and her children, and they would eat together and be happy, and obey
her and stay at home with her. If she was not fortunate enough
to get her ration, the children would defy her and go out to
the coffeehouses to beg for their food, and she did not have
the heart to keep them at home when their stomachs were
empty.

And how was it that she came back with nothing, when
she had money and food tickets? Because the bullies would
push her aside and take their ration first, so that when her
turn came the shopkeeper would close his store and say,
'There's nothing left.' In those days men had lost their feelings; everyone robbed and stole in order to eat. Once she

stood all night in front of the shop and returned in the morning empty-handed. She got into a streetcar and wept, because
there was no food left in the house and nothing for her children to eat. An old Gentile saw her and asked, 'Why are you
so sad, madam?' She answered him that her husband had gone
to the war, leaving her all by herself with four children to
support; that she made bags and knapsacks for the soldiers,
and yesterday she had stopped work to fetch food; she had
stood all night in front of the shop, but when her turn came to
buy a man snatched away the ration card and took her share.
The old man sighed at the wickedness of men and said to her
kindly, 'Don't be so sad, madam; if he snatched the card he
did not snatch the money.' 'What is the use of the money if it
does not buy food?' she replied. 'Well said, madam,' said he,
filling his pipe, 'What is the use of money? When children are
hungry, we cannot say to them, "You are hungry, sit down and
chew the money."' As she was about to leave, he whispered
to her, 'Come with me, come with me to my house; maybe I
can give you a sack of potatoes for your money.' So she went
with him until they reached the outskirts of the town and got
on a streetcar in which they traveled until it stopped. Then
they got out and walked for as far as they walked and reached
the place that they reached. All the time the Gentile spoke to
her kindly and said such pleasant things as she had never
heard from anyone in Vienna. While they were talking he
sang the praises of his potatoes. They were good and heavy,
he said, not like the potatoes they sold in the market, which
were light as feathers. When they reached his house he asked
her, 'How much money do you have?' She told him. He filled
his pipe, puffed a while, and said, 'I'm afraid you don't have
the strength to carry all I will give you for your money.' 'Don't
be afraid, sir,' said she. 'God will give me strength for the sake
of my children, so that they should not go hungry.' 'Blessings
on your head,' said he, 'for not turning your mind away from
our God in heaven. For that I will give you a piece of cheese as
a gift.' So she gave him all her money and wanted to take the
sack. But the Gentile said to his servant or his son, 'Take the
sack and carry it to the streetcar, and don't move away before
you get it on the streetcar.' So the man took the sack and went

with her, while the old man and his wife parted from her very affectionately and said, 'Go in peace, madam, and think kindly of us.' She was sorry she had given all her money for the potatoes and left herself with only enough to pay the fare, so that she had nothing to give the fellow who had taken so much trouble for her. 'Never mind,' said he, 'never mind,' and he said farewell, wishing her pleasure in the food. After some time she reached home tired and weary, because she had stood outside all night and because the sack was heavy. But her joy gave her strength, and she rallied. She assembled her children and said to them, 'Just wait a little while, children, and I will cook you some potatoes, and while they are cooking I will give you a piece of cheese!' The children fell upon the sack and opened it with loud cries of joy. When they opened it they found a block of plaster, and under the plaster clods of earth.

My host sat as usual and said nothing. Ever since I have known him he has not uttered a single superfluous word; he does not mention the days of the war, although he was in the army from the beginning to the end. Like him, most of the people in the town who have survived the war never mention it—though their wives recall those days on every possible occasion.

I have already remarked that the innkeeper's sons and daughters do not eat at the hour of the meal. This does not mean that they make a point of not coming in for the Sabbath eve meal with their parents; sometimes they come and sometimes not. In any case, they do not come together, nor do they come to hear the Kiddush; they usually arrive in the middle of the meal and sit down to eat as on any other day.

Babtchi comes in from wherever she comes, throws down her hat and her bag, wriggles out of her coat, pats her hair with her left hand, takes a chair, sits down, and snatches up her food. Sometimes her father raises his eyes to look at her, though more than looking at her he gazes at her things, which she has scattered here and there. Then he closes his eyes again and fingers his prayer book in silence, or goes back to singing the Sabbath hymns. When Rachel comes, he shifts his chair and asks, 'Where have you been for the Kiddush? Did

you hear it or didn't you? Why don't you answer me?' Whether
she replies or not, it is not good. One way or other, he gives
her a scolding; then he puts his hand on his prayer book with
the hole in it, waits a bit, and sings his hymns.

If Dolik or Lolik comes, their father raises his eyes and
looks to see whether their heads are covered. On weekdays he
does not care if they sit bareheaded, but at the Sabbath meal
he is strict. Once Dolik forgot and did not cover his head, and
his father scolded him. 'Are you still selling hats,' said Dolik,
'that you keep trying to fit me with one?' His father rose, took
the young man's hat, put his two bent thumbs inside it, and
pushed it down angrily on his son's head, until Dolik howled
'Ouch!'

This Sabbath eve passed without a snag. The sons and
daughters did not come, and there were no guests in the
hotel. So the three of us sat together, ate and drank, and said
the grace after meals. After grace, I went out for a walk and
reached the Beit Midrash. I saw it was still lit up, and felt the
urge to go in. I took out the key, opened the door, and entered.
Not long had passed before a number of our group had come.
And you need not wonder, for in our Beit Midrash there is
light and warmth, while in their homes it is cold and dark.
True, they too have lit the Sabbath candle, but their candle is
small, and gives light only close by, leaving the rest of the
house in darkness.

When they entered, they started to praise the Sabbath, to
praise the Beit Midrash and that man who came here and
stocked the stove and lit many candles. That man was afraid
he might grow proud, for he might think he deserved all the
praise. So he lowered his head, that he might remember he is
dust of the earth, and raised his eyes, that he might ponder
in his heart that only by the will of the Almighty did he live
and only by His will were all things made, and He would
one day remove him from the earth, like a painter who removes the soot from the ceiling and covers it with plaster. At
that moment fear and trembling entered into that man's heart,
and he began to be proud of his fear of the Almighty, like the
child upon whom his father has hung his jewels. He saw that

there was no escape from immodest thoughts. What did he do? He opened a book of the Pentateuch and read. As soon as he had read two or three words of the Torah, his heart was quieted and restored to wholeness.

When the people in the Beit Midrash saw that I was in a good mood, they said to me, 'Perhaps you will tell us a word of the Torah, sir.' 'The Torah is given to all Israel,' I replied, 'and even if a man does not know how to speak, it is enough for him to begin with a word of Torah, and the Torah will tell him how to go on.' 'If so,' said they, 'perhaps you will begin.' I opened the Pentateuch and started to expound a verse from the portion of the week: 'And Jacob awakened out of his sleep. And he was afraid, and said, How awesome is this place! this is none other than the house of God.' Not like Abraham, who said, 'the Lord shall appear on a *hill*,' nor like Isaac, of whom it is said, 'And Isaac went out to meditate in the *field*,' but like Jacob who spoke of a *house*. And I expounded on these three conceptions of worship. One conception sees worship as a mountain, for man seeks high things and walks about all the time with high thoughts. The second conception sees worship as a field, for in a field you sow and reap, and there is a pleasant fragrance, as it is said, 'See, the smell of my son is as the smell of a field.' The third conception of worship, which is most dear to the Holy One, blessed be He—for Jacob our Father is described as the choicest of the Patriarchs—likens worship to a house. And He too, blessed be His Name, praises Himself by saying, 'For my house shall be called a house of prayer.' It is said in the Book of the Zohar, 'A house for Israel: a house that is to be with them, as a woman liveth with her husband in one house in joy.' For the mountain and the field are places of freedom, but a house is a guarded and respected place.

These matters may also be interpreted as referring to three eras in the annals of Israel.

In the first era, some of the sages believed that we had no need of houses and fields, for a field enslaves its owner, as it is written, 'The king is in bondage to the field.' And in the matter of houses they said, 'And who will summon up strength to build himself a house?' And if it is built, its end is to fall.

For we find it written, 'And the house fell upon the lords,' and in many scriptural passages we are told of the destruction of houses, as, 'Thou shalt build a house, and thou shalt not dwell therein,' or 'And he shall break down the house.' And there is no support for a man in a house, as it is said, 'And he went into the house, and supported his hand on the wall, and a serpent bit him.' But it is better that Israel should lift up their eyes to the hills, as David said, 'I will lift up mine eyes unto the hills,' for a hill is a high and free place, and there is no quality better than freedom, as in the case of Saul, for the main recompense he promised to the man who would kill Goliath was freedom, as it is said, 'And I will make his father's house free in Israel.'

In the second era, some of the sages spoke out against their predecessors and said: The benefits of freedom are outweighed by its disadvantages, for it leads to extinction and destruction, as it is said, 'Free among the dead, like the slain.' And similarly, we are told that when Uzziah became a leper, he 'dwelt in the house of a free one.' Rabbi Jonah the son of Jannah explains that it was called 'free' because the lepers isolated themselves there from all men. On the other hand, it is written, 'Come, my beloved, let us go forth into the field,' to till it and guard it and eat its produce, as in 'She moved him to ask of her father a field.'

The third era, and it is the last of the eras and the end of all the eras, is the era in which we are now living. And we are tired of the eras that came before, when we wandered wearily on the mountains, 'scattered on the mountains as sheep,' and we have suffered the fulfillment of the verses, 'And I shall lay thy flesh upon the mountains. . . . I shall water the land with blood, the blood that flows from you, even as high as the mountains.' Similarly with the field: 'And the hail smote every herb of the field and shattered every plant of the field.' And it is also said, 'And what they leave the beasts of the field shall eat,' and it is said, 'And all the goodliness thereof is as the flower of the field,' and 'as dung upon the open field.' But what we have to seek is 'according to the beauty of a man, to dwell in the house.' And when every house should close its doors, let us build a house of our own, so that we may dwell with Him 'as a woman liveth with her husband in one house in joy.' And it is of this that David said, 'He maketh the barren woman to keep house, and to be a joyful mother of children. Praise ye the Lord.'

It is stated in the books that the virtues of the three Patriarchs sustained Israel in the three exiles. The virtues of Abraham sustained us in the Egyptian exile, as it is said, 'For He remembered His holy promise and Abraham His servant. And He brought forth His people with joy, and His chosen with gladness.' The virtues of Isaac sustained us in the Babylonian exile, and the virtues of Jacob in this last exile of ours. Therefore we should cling most closely to the conception of Jacob, the conception of 'O house of Jacob, come ye, and let us walk in the light of the Lord.' And it was of this that Jacob said, 'So that I come again to my father's house in peace,' and of this that the rest of the verse is written, 'then shall the Lord be my God.'

From that Sabbath on, we used to come to the Beit Midrash after the meal, and I would discourse on the portion of the week, reading the Midrash and expounding it.

I made another great improvement in our old Beit Midrash. Since the beginning of the war the eternal light had been out, so I lit it in front of the tablet on the wall on which the names of the sacred communities killed in the pogroms of 1648 are engraved. Now, do the sacred martyrs need light from this world below? Surely the soul of every single righteous man who is killed by the Gentiles shines before the throne of glory, and even the seraphim cannot look upon them. But we do this in order that men should see and remember how far-reaching is the love of Israel for their Father in heaven: even when their lives are taken, they do not part from Him. And also because I have heard that it is stated in the Midrash that every single righteous man outside the Land who is killed by the Gentiles enters into the Land of Israel and does not wait until the end of days, when all those who die abroad will have to roll their way under the ground to the Land. But he who was killed for love of God enters the Land of Israel whole in body, while he who was killed through fear enters only with the limb or organ through which he died, and the rest of his limbs look out and gaze at the one that has been privileged to be interred in the Holy Land. When we light a candle for them, we help them to see the happiness of that limb and the happiness that is in store for them in the future.

On that day when I lit the eternal light for the first time, I looked at the Beit Midrash, and saw a stove burning, and an eternal light kindled, and the basin full of water, and the lamps full of kerosene, and the floor swept and clean; for once every two or three days Hanoch brings me wood for the stove and candles and a container of kerosene, and fills the basin, and on Sabbath eves he sweeps the floor and I give him wages for his trouble, sometimes generously and sometimes cordially. And here I will reveal something without shielding myself. Sometimes I take out two zlotys from my pocket, and when I see how humble he is I put one zloty back in my pocket and give him only one. If Hanoch had been clever, he would have said to me: Fix my wage, not sometimes a lot and sometimes a little. But because he is always selling haberdashery to the Gentiles, his mind is humble and he asks for nothing. And when my own heart says to me: Fix his wage and make him a beadle, so that he should not imperil his life on the roads, I put off my heart from today to tomorrow and from tomorrow to the day after.

CHAPTER FIVE AND TWENTY

In Daniel Bach's House

At the end of the Sabbath, after the benediction, I went to Daniel Bach's house to pay him for the wood. It was long since I had been so happy over the payment of a debt. First, because Daniel Bach would get money, of which he was in need; second, because the wood had given me pleasure and I wanted to thank him who had provided the wood. Although Daniel Bach and I live wall by wall, I had never been in his house before that night, except on one occasion.

This house consists of one room with a kitchen added.

You enter through the woodshed and come into the kitchen, and from there to the living room. This is the home of Mr. Bach and his wife, and Erela their daughter, and Raphael their son, who lies in bed with a torn soldier's cap on his head. At first glance he looked to me like a child; at a second glance like a young man; and at the third glance like neither a child nor a young man, but a heap of skin and flesh in which the Creator has fixed two aged eyes. Or perhaps the order was reversed: at first glance Raphael looked like a heap of skin and flesh—and so forth; but I do not remember clearly, because of the things that happened that night. Raphael has already reached the age of bar mitzvah, but his limbs are still not straight and his bones are weak, so most of the time he lies in bed. Everyone looks after him and he is loved by all. Even Erela, his sister, who boasts that she has no concern with anything that cannot be explained by reason, shows more love for her brother than her reason can explain. When I came in, Erela was sitting beside him while he fingered a picture book she had brought him. One of his hands pointed to the picture of a horseman in the book, and the other pointed to his heart, while he read, 'I am Jacob and you are Esau.' He did not notice the arrival of a guest, but his father, mother, and sister were excited at my coming and rose to welcome me with joy and cordiality.

Mr. Bach you are acquainted with; we have often had occasion to speak of him. I do not know if I have described his appearance and the other things that distinguish him from his fellows, apart from his steady companion, that is, his wooden leg. But if I have not told you before I will tell you now.

Daniel Bach is a tall man; his face is not exactly long and not exactly round, and it is surrounded by a little beard which is not exactly pointed and not exactly blunt; he seems to take care that his beard should not grow beyond the measure he has fixed for it; and in spite of his wooden leg, he is always merry. Sometimes he jests at himself and sometimes at the troubles of the times, but he never jests at others. The history of that leg has only surprises. Considering Daniel Bach's character, he was hardly the right kind of man to smuggle sac-

charin in his socks, as some women do. But Daniel Bach is not
surprised at that. First, says Daniel Bach, no one knows what
is seemly for one to do and what is not, except for the moral-
ists, who know what is permissible and what is not. (And even
then—I thought—it is doubtful whether, had they been in his
place, they would not have done the same.) Second, says
Daniel Bach, the war had taught men to do squalid deeds.
And once a man had been given leave to do such things, he
no longer distinguished between doing them for the Emperor
and doing them for himself and his livelihood. It should be
added that Daniel Bach is a lean man and his hair is chestnut
in color, with some sprinkling of grey, which makes him handsome. Not like his wife, Sara Pearl, whose hair is black and
gleaming; she is round and looks fat, although she is not really
so. Erela, on the other hand, is neither dark nor chestnut but
faded in color. As Erela is different from her father and her
mother in the color of her hair, so is she different in other
things.

Of her father I have already told you. Of her mother there
is nothing to tell. She is pleasant, quick in her movements,
kind and charitable. I heard that during the war she showed
great fortitude and courage, maintaining her household and
supporting her father-in-law and his son until they settled in
the Land of Israel. She also brought up an orphan and taught
him the Torah, and when he wanted to settle in the Land of
Israel she gave him his expenses.

This was Yeruham Freeman, whose father disappeared
when his mother conceived him and whose mother died when
she bore him. Mrs. Bach took him into her house and suckled
him with the milk of her breasts, for Yeruham was born in
the same month as Erela her daughter.

When his mother conceived him his father disappeared.
To describe the affairs of this man we must go back to the
beginning.

The beginning was like this. Once a young Lithuanian
came to our town. It was a summer day; there was not much
work in the market and the storekeepers stood outside talking
to each other. Wandering from one subject to another, the

talk turned to a Lithuanian who had come to the town and wanted to preach in the old Beit Midrash.

The rumor made no impression. The learned men were not enthusiastic about the preachers, who put the mind to sleep with parables and legends. The Hasidim were not enthusiastic about the preachers, for most of the preachers were Lithuanians, and every Lithuanian is assumed to belong to the Misnagdim, the opponents of the Hasidim. The Zionists were not enthusiastic about the preachers, because most of them at that time used to preach against Zionism on the ground that the Zionists were trying to anticipate the coming of the Messiah instead of waiting for salvation. The socialists were not enthusiastic about the preachers, and would say: The Torah and the commandments only help to dull men's minds and keep them from perceiving all the tribulations brought about by capital, and the preachers come to exhort them to observe the Torah and the commandments. Even the majority of the people were not enthusiastic about the preachers, for they were sick and tired of sermons about the seven departments of hell and that kind of thing. All that was left were a few old men and artisans, who would come to listen and doze during the sermon until the preacher finished and the beadle banged his alms box; then they would wake up and drop a copper in honor of the Torah and its preachers. And so—there was no one in the town who paid any attention to the Lithuanian.

They were still talking when along came a man carrying a book written by the newcomer, bearing numerous testimonials by great rabbis of Poland and Lithuania declaring that the author was a tremendous genius, a Sinai of learning, and a mover of mountains—and such praise would have been extraordinary even in the early generations. All these authorities wrote as one man: no praise can fully convey his greatness.

In that generation the honor of the Torah had deteriorated in our town, and there was no more respect paid to scholars because it was all paid to doctors. When the scholars saw the book and the recommendations in it, their heads were immediately lifted up. It was like the case of the king whose enemies have conquered his country and weakened his loyal support-

ers. Suddenly it is rumored that the king is returning to his
land with a host of heroes, so all his supporters summon up
strength and march out to restore him to his throne.

And why did that Lithuanian take the trouble to come
here? Wouldn't the rich Jews in Russia have jumped at him
and squandered large sums to have the privilege of getting
him for their daughters? Fine and true—except for a government decree; for when he was called up to the army he had
been found free of any blemish, and there was nothing whatever wrong with him to give the authorities an excuse for
taking a thousand pieces of silver to exempt him. So, since he
was on the government's list, he decided to go into exile, and
the leading men of the time advised him to go to Galicia,
where most of the people still had so much love for the Torah.

When evening fell, the whole town assembled in the old
Beit Midrash to hear the sermon of the young genius, but
since there was not enough room for all who came, they
brought him to the Great Synagogue. He went up and took his
place before the Holy Ark and preached with sharpness and
mastery on the Halacha, on Sifre and Sifra, Tosefta and Mechilta, the Babylonian Talmud and the Jerusalem Talmud, the
early authorities and the later authorities; and on each and
every matter he raised five or six or seven difficulties and
explained them all away with one answer. When all the objections had been answered, he went back and raised more objections about the answers. To these it seemed that there was
no answer, but again he explained them away with a single
answer. The scholars had lost their grip and could no longer
follow the connection between one matter and another, for
they already realized that not every mind could grasp the
whole give-and-take—it was so subtle. And he was like an
ever swelling fountain and a river that knows no rest.

Suddenly the voice of my father and teacher, of blessed
memory, was heard. He had already understood the character
of that young man, who was distorting the words of the Gemara and blinding the eyes of his hearers. My father and
teacher recited the text of the Gemara and showed that its
words stood fast as they were, and provoked no objections
and needed no explanations. At this, the young man shifted,

quoting the text of the Gemara as given by the great scholar
Al-Fasi, but he stumbled, for Al-Fasi had never commented
on that particular text.

Another scholar, Reb Hayim by name (this is the Reb
Hayim whom we mentioned at the beginning of the book in
connection with the divorcee's hotel), trapped the preacher
in his own words, for even if one admitted that the text of
the Gemara was as the questioner said, his explanation was
not sound, and if the explanation was not sound, then the difficulties still remained. Then my father spoke up again, and
showed that even if the text of the Gemara was as the preacher
said, the supposed difficulties were not difficult, because he
had related matters that had no relation to each other. At this,
the young man raised fresh difficulties and explained them
away in still another explanation, but once again Reb Hayim
refuted his explanations. The young man turned and referred
him to still another matter, raising other difficulties, and said,
'If you are such learned men, come forward and explain them
to me.' My father retorted and showed that the speaker had
not understood the simple meaning of the text, and therefore
the difficulties called for no explanation. And Reb Hayim
added that even so they could be explained thus and thus.
The questioner refuted Reb Hayim and offered a different
answer to the difficulties. And here he blundered in a matter
that even school children know.

Then the eyes of some learned men were opened and
they saw that the young man had twisted the text so as to
display his penetration and learning, and not to bring out
the truth of the Torah. Nevertheless, they stood there as if
intoxicated by the wine of his learning, resenting my father's
action in annihilating the words of that genius and making
him out to be a deceiver, and resenting Reb Hayim as well.
And still that young man would not quiet down and he started
his give-and-take again. Finally he shifted over to preaching
on Agada. And what did he preach? He cited, 'When He
maketh inquisition for blood, He remembereth them'—where
'maketh inquisition for blood' can also mean 'demands money,'
and 'remembereth them' can also mean 'they are male'—and
he commented: It is the nature of the male to bestow himself

upon the female; so it is with the preacher who preaches before the people to arouse their hearts to love the Torah, for
he partakes of the nature of the male, who bestows love, so
that children should be born to the Torah. But in the case of
the preacher who preaches for money, for the sake of gain, it
is the congregation that plays the part of the male, for they
are active now and he is passive, for it is they who pay him
for his preaching. And here the young man became ecstatic
and said, 'Teirinke briderlech, dear brethren, it is not to
preach for money that I have come here, but for the sake of
our sacred Torah, for it is our life and our length of days, and
even if I were given all the money in the world I would not
take it.' The Lithuanian lilt, which enfolds the heart and
warms the soul, excited the people and they all followed him.
The very fact that a young man stood before the congregation
and preached was a novelty, especially as he recited many
sections of the Gemara by heart just as a man says his daily
prayers.

When he concluded his preaching they showed him great
honor and carried him away in triumph. A certain wealthy
man sent his servant to his inn, brought his belongings to his
house, and gave him a dwelling place in keeping with his
honor. All the leading men in the town came and sat before him, and he went on with his disputations. And precisely
those doubters who had at first been skeptical of his wisdom now showed him the greatest affection. They said, 'If
he made a mistake in the Gemara, it was only because
"acuteness makes one blunder." ' In any case, they said, he
was worthy of honor, because he was marvelously learned
in the Torah. Just then, the simple folk surrounded the
house, clamoring and shouting that the rabbi should be
deposed from the seat of learning and the young genius
put in his place. And as for his being a bachelor, they wished
they had bars of gold that were worth as much—and weighed
as much—as the bride they would give to him in marriage.
And not only the simple people but some of the scholars
wanted to establish a place for him in the town, for instance by making a great yeshiva for him, so that men should
come from all countries to learn the Torah from his lips. The

town was still weary from the controversy about Reb Hayim, who had tried to get the post of Rabbi of Szibucz. (The story of Reb Hayim is a matter for itself and is not in place here.) Next day two scholars went forth to sell the book that young man had written, and everyone who could afford it bought the book, some for a crown, some for two crowns, and some for more. Meanwhile the young man sat wrapped in his tefillin, writing new interpretations to be added to the book and pronouncing disputations before his hearers, like a man who has two brains and does two things at the same time.

That rich man, who had made his house a home for this young fellow, had an only daughter, tender and sweet, pure and chaste, and he set his eye on giving her to him in marriage. He undertook to establish a great yeshiva for him, in which he would maintain at his own expense two hundred students. And so that no one should forestall him, he hurriedly made a wedding for them at once. The whole town was jealous of him, but their envy did not last long, just as the rich man's joy did not last. For all through the traditional seven days of the newlyweds' celebration, women kept coming in from the countryside crying, 'This bridegroom is my husband!' And while one was still shouting, another came and cried, 'I am his wife and he is *my* husband!' The young man was afraid that even more women would come, so he got up and ran away. The father-in-law left all his business and went to look for him, to get his daughter a divorce and not leave her tied to an absent husband all her life, for she was still a child of seventeen or eighteen. But before he could find him, she bore a son, and died. The father of the girl died, too, and they called the child, after him, Yeruham.

So Yeruham was left without a mother and without a shelter, for all his grandfather's wealth was gone. Things went so far that there was no money to hire him a wet nurse. Mrs. Bach had pity on him, so she took him and nursed him with her own milk, for Yeruham was born in the same month as her Aniela, that is, Erela. So Mrs. Bach took from the milk of Erela, that is, Aniela, and gave to Yeruham. Even in his childhood he showed strength and vigor, and drank double. That is why he is tall and handsome. For the women of today are not the

women of before the war. The women of today have not a
drop of blood in their faces or milk in their teats, but the
women before the war—Father in heaven!—when the Emperor's generals came to hold their battle exercises, and went
out to the town and saw the daughters of Israel, they would
bow down before them and say, 'Daughters of kings, we are
your servants!' But when the war came, they took the men to
be killed in battle, and the women, who looked like the daughters of kings, lost the bloom of their loveliness in the struggle
to find a piece of bread.

CHAPTER SIX AND TWENTY

The Woman and Her Children

It was during that period of the war that Mrs. Bach wandered
as far as Vienna, with her three daughters, her father-in-law,
Yeruham her father-in-law's son, and Yeruham the son of the
Lithuanian. As for her eldest son, he died on the way between
two towns and she did not know in which he was buried. Once
she sent money to each of the towns, so that if her son was
buried in one of them they should put a stone over the grave,
and they did not send back the money. After some time she
heard that both towns had been sacked and the graves in them
destroyed by the Russian artillery. And how did she earn her
living all the years she lived in Vienna? First, the government
gave forty-five crowns a month to women whose husbands
were in the army. Second, she and her two big daughters knit
gloves for soldiers and various kinds of scarves and sashes, or
sewed sacks that the troops could fill with sand and set down
in front of them to absorb the enemy's bullets. Her big daughters, as she called them, were little at that time, but by
comparison with Erela she called them big. One of them died
immediately after they came back to Szibucz, and another
died of influenza soon after her father's return.

While she was working, Mrs. Bach was free to think many
thoughts. She even got around to thinking that this war would

not come to an end so soon. True, our Emperor was waging war wisely and the Emperor of Germany was helping him, but the Russian Czar was not weak either, especially when other kings had joined him. And although the newspapers reported Austrian and German victories every day, the enemy was killing men and taking one city after another. The girls were growing up and so were the boys—Yeruham her father-in-law's son and Yeruham the son of the Lithuanian. Prices were rising, and what she and her daughters earned, as well as what the government allotted to them, was not enough to keep seven souls, namely her and her three daughters and her father-in-law and Yeruham A and Yeruham B. Other women tried to make a living in other ways. They would go around to the shops and buy food to sell at a profit, or ask for help at the 'Joint,' which would once a week distribute tins of fish and yellow and white grits from America. But she was not very good at trade or at the gates of charity. Once she gave in to the persuasions of her neighbors and went to ask for help. The official wrote down her name and address and said they would send the food to her home. So, trusting him, she made a great feast that day, and took a piece of duck and roasted it, for it was several days since she or any of her family had tasted meat. The messenger of charity came and perceived the smell of roast. He was angry and rebuked her, saying, 'It is a sin to take pity on a woman who roasts ducks when the whole world is hungry.' Then she began studying the papers to see if she could find work in keeping with her strength and honor, but by the time she would come for it others would have got there ahead of her.

In the same house where she lived there was a certain girl who was learning to become a midwife. She saw that the girl was not terribly clever, so she said: What this one can do I can do too. And it may very well be that the idea had already been awakened in her during the evacuation, for a woman had given birth on the road and had been in danger because there was no midwife to be found.

You may well say that if she could not manage with her wages while she was working, how much less so if she had to spend her time in training. But before her husband went out

to the army he had given her two thousand crowns to pay a
debt. Before she could manage to send the money the town
where the creditor lived was destroyed and all trace of him
was lost. So she hit on the idea of borrowing from his money
and learning a trade with which to make a living. Besides, she
had taken her jewels with her, and even they were worth
money. At first she used to pawn them and redeem them
over and over again, but in the end they were left in the
pawnbroker's. And here Mrs. Bach told me that she was the
granddaughter of Shifrah Puah the midwife, whose coffin was
followed by nine hundred and ninety-nine men and one
woman; Shifrah Puah her grandmother had helped to bring
them all into the world, and when she died they came to pay
her honor and accompany her to her eternal home.

One of those that Shifrah Puah her grandmother had
helped bring into the world was a distant relative of her
family called Shulkind, a very rich man and the owner of a
factory for paper products. The government used to give him
unlimited quantities of coal, because he supplied the army
with goods, and when he heard that Shifrah Puah's granddaughter was living in Vienna he sent her some coal. When
she came to thank him he asked her what she was doing. She
told him that her husband had gone to the war and she was
living with her daughters, her father-in-law, her brother-in-
law, and an orphan she had adopted, and was learning to
become a midwife. Immediately he allotted her enough to
support herself and her household, as well as to study and
train for her work. He also took her father-in-law into his
house and gave him bed and board, in return for which he
should teach Mishna to Shulkind, for Shulkind's only son had
gone out for a hike in the mountains and had fallen and been
killed, his wife—namely his son's mother—had been blinded
by her weeping, and he, the boy's father, had diverted his
attention to Torah. He also helped Erela and Yeruham the
father-in-law's son and Yeruham the Lithuanian's son to study
in a teacher-training school. Good men like him no longer exist
in the world. Had he not died he would have set them on their
feet and they would not have come to the pass they did.

That Mr. Shulkind died in this way. It happened that

once someone claimed a large sum of money from him, someone to whom he owed nothing or had already paid. The judge
ordered Shulkind to take an oath. He took a Bible, laid his
hand on it and said, 'Here let me die if I owe anything to this
man.' Before he could move from the spot he fell and died.

And why was he so good to her? Mrs. Bach said Mr. Shulkind had once told her that one night he had seen Shifrah
Puah's coffin in a dream, and all the mourners were naked and
barefoot, except for himself, who was well dressed. It seemed
reasonable that because he was rich they should give him a
place at the head of the coffin-bearers. And he himself thought
that was fitting; and indeed they did do so. They honored him
and placed him in front. But he was angry and said to himself,
'What do these people think, that they have it in their power
to give me honor? Even my janitor would not let such beggars
set foot in my house.' The dead woman's coffin shook; because
he was in the grip of his anger his hands had weakened, and
the coffin slipped. Along came a certain man and stood in his
place and said, 'It doesn't matter, sir, nothing has happened.'
And it seemed to Mr. Shulkind that this fellow was smiling,
as a man smiles to his neighbor, meaning, 'Although you have
behaved abominably, I like you.' Mr. Shulkind was angry at
this man who dared to behave as if they were equals. He
looked at him and saw that he was ragged and barefoot. He
was moved with pity for him and said to himself: After all, I
am very rich and I will lose nothing if I give this poor man
five or ten crowns—even if all the mourners for Shifrah Puah
stretch out their hands and ask for charity too. But he must
first investigate whether the man deserved charity, for im-
postors pretend to be poor and extract money from the rich.
Or perhaps he should not give them anything, but donate a
thousand crowns to a charitable society, which investigates a
poor man seven times before it gives him one copper. But if
he gave to the poor himself the entire donation would reach
them, whereas a society fritters away money on wages for officials and clerks, offices and letters, not to speak of thefts—and
not much is left for the poor. He was moved with pity for the
poor, for even the money the rich devote to them does not
reach them intact. And even though it was only a dream, Mr.

Shulkind took upon himself to pay heed to the poor, especially the exiles from his own town, who, he had heard, were wasting away with hunger.

His affairs were many, however, and his mind was not free. When he remembered the poor of his town, it was only to put them off. 'Can one man support a whole town?' he said. But he made a vow in his heart that if his fortune reached this-and-this sum he would give such-and-such for the needs of the many. When his fortune reached that sum, he was in need of money, because he was about to undertake a large contract. So he relied upon the Holy One, blessed be He, and on the charitable societies, although he did not like them: that the One should lengthen the lives of the poor and the others should support them until he could become very rich and attend to their needs himself.

He went to the supply official to receive the contract. While he was sitting and waiting he thought about his constantly growing business, and his constantly passing years, and his only son, who followed his fancy and sought all kinds of pleasures. Only yesterday his son had received the degree of doctor and today he had gone on a trip to the mountains with his friends. If he would put aside his pleasures and apply himself to his affairs, he could double his possessions and make a great name in the world. But before examining the deeds of our sons, let us examine our own deeds. After all, he too, namely old Mr. Shulkind, had left his father's affairs and gone to Vienna. If he had listened to his father he would have been a small shopkeeper and would have suffered with all the exiles of his town here—or, even worse, in the exiles' camps in Nikolsburg.

While he was sitting and thinking, he looked at the door of the official's room, which was still closed to him though he had been waiting an hour or more—which was not usual, for whenever he used to enter, the official would immediately come out to meet him and take him into his room. He pulled out his watch from his pocket and looked at it, although he did not need to, for there was a clock hanging on the wall.

As he was looking at his watch it occurred to him that perhaps it was not really made of gold, although he had bought it from an expert watchmaker and paid him the price of gold, and, after all, experts are not in the habit of deceiving. In order to put this thought out of his mind, he began thinking of other matters. Suddenly he saw that the sleeve of his coat was getting threadbare, as was common with the cloth made in wartime. He said to himself that if the official saw him he would imagine that he was a poor man, or perhaps he had already seen him and that was why he was not taking him into his room.

He pulled out his watch again and looked at it. Hardly a moment had passed since he took it out first, and how many thoughts had gone through his mind! As he put it back into his pocket, he dozed off. Or perhaps he did not doze, and he was awake when he saw this thing. What did he see? Shifrah Puah's coffin, followed by nine hundred and ninety-nine men and one woman. And that woman was his wife, the mother of his only son. This he found surprising, for she had been born in another town, not in Shifrah Puah's, so what was she doing beside the midwife's coffin? While he was thinking this, he saw that all the mourners were well dressed and each of them had a gold watch, pure gold, hanging on his clothes, while he, Mr. Shulkind, was ragged and barefoot; except for a threadbare coat he had nothing on his body.

At that moment he heard the voice of a newsboy. He awoke and bought a paper. When he looked at it he said to himself: There's nothing new, for all the Austrian and German victories in the paper are imaginary; they are meant only to prop up the people's enthusiasm and keep them from despair. So he folded the paper and gave it to someone else. While the other was sitting and reading, Mr. Shulkind felt sorry he had let the paper out of his possession without reading it to the end, for no doubt there was something in it about the hikers in the mountains. And even if there were no such news there, why shouldn't he make sure there was not, for in any case he had nothing to do. He put out his hand to ask for the return of the paper, but just then the attendant summoned him to the official's room. He went in and received the contract, and he was also entrusted with some new business, namely, making clothes out of paper.

As he left the official's room he said to himself that this new business was bigger than anything he had undertaken before. He felt angry with his son for chasing after pleasure while he had to look after the business. On his way home, Mr. Shulkind went up to a newspaper kiosk and bought a paper, but before he could read it a drizzle began to fall, so he folded up the paper and put it in his pocket.

As he reached his house he heard a scream. He went in and found his wife in a state of collapse, with a paper in her hand, screaming and weeping, 'My son, my son, my only son! Fallen on the mountains and your bones scattered!' Immediately he knew that his son had been killed on the mountains. Or perhaps he had known it already, having read it in the paper, or perhaps he glanced at the paper now and thought he had read it before.

In short, through that old man Mrs. Bach succeeded in learning to become a midwife, teaching her daughter, Yeruham A, and Yeruham B Hebrew, and having them admitted to the institute. Thus she succeeded in seeing her daughter a teacher of Hebrew; and Yeruham A, namely her father-in-law's son, and Yeruham B, namely the Lithuanian's son, earned through her their going up to the Land of Israel. And it was agreed between them, namely between Yeruham the Lithuanian's son and Aniela, that is Erela, that he would bring her there. But what do you think he did? He came back from there and began to court another girl. As he had betrayed the Land, so he betrayed his betrothed. But Erela did not betray her early ideals, and now she was teaching in the town's Hebrew school and educating pupils. If you heard children twittering in Hebrew, you could be sure it was Aniela who had taught them. Aniela is the same as Erela, for Aniela in Polish means an angel, and as the ordinary Hebrew word for angel does not apply to a woman, she called herself Erela after a word we find in the Book of Isaiah.

Besides teaching the children Hebrew, Erela has a number of other merits. Nevertheless, I do not like her; first, because of the way she articulates her speech, for she slices up her words as if with a sword, and second, because of the spectacles in front of her eyes. After every word that comes from her lips she applies her spectacles to you like a plaster to a wound. It seems to me that her father's wooden leg is as nothing compared to her spectacles. Once Rachel asked me, 'Why do you keep away from Erela, sir?' 'Because of her spectacles,' I replied. Rachel said jestingly, 'And what can a person do if his eyes are weak? But I'm sure it's only for this—that spectacles are not mentioned in the Torah.'

Since I have been living here I have not had occasion to speak to Erela except by chance. And I must say that it is no pleasure to speak to her. First, because she has seized the whole truth for herself and leaves no part for anyone else. And second, because she hangs on to every single word you utter, and from the things you have said she ascribes to you things you did not say, and argues with you about them. For instance, if you say that Reuben is a decent man, she jumps up and asks, 'Why don't you think Simon is decent?' Or if you say that a Jewish child ought to study the Bible, she jumps up and asks why you object to *Tales from the Scriptures*. 'In my opinion,' she says, 'one must not burden a child with matters that don't appeal to him; it's much better to instruct him in the *Tales from the Scriptures*.'

Between ourselves, it was a mistake to arrange the Bible stories by themselves, for this takes them out of the sphere of holiness and makes them secular. But I have never expressed my opinion on this subject in public, for if I ever began to express my opinion about everything I do not like I'd never finish.

On that occasion I was in a playful mood. I said to her, 'Would you like to hear an interesting story, madam?

'An old man and an old woman who had spent most of their days in a village among the Gentiles came to live in the city in a place of study and prayer. The old man went to the Beit Midrash, where he saw Jews sitting and studying. He sat down to listen, but understood nothing, for this was the table for great scholars, and they were discussing a difficult problem. He went and sat by another table, where they were studying Gemara. He listened attentively, but understood nothing. He went and sat by another table, where they were studying

Mishna. He listened attentively, but understood nothing. So he went and sat by the table where the children were being taught. At that moment they were studying in the Book of Samuel the story of David and Goliath and of Abigail the wife of Nabal the Carmelite. The old man listened attentively. When he came home he said to his wife, "You surely know David the author of the Psalms, don't you? Would you have believed that this David made love to another man's wife and killed a Gentile?" '

After I had told the story I felt sad, as I usually do after a jest. Why did I say that the compilers of the *Tales from the Scriptures* did wrong to arrange the stories by themselves? Because they took them out of the sphere of holiness and made them secular.

And what is holiness?

The simple meaning of the word is: a summit of the spirit that no tongue can explain. And this word was first used to denote the holiness of the Almighty, the Holiness of all holinesses, of whom it is said, 'For I am holy.'

From this summit of the spirit there emanate a number of objects, which partake of His holiness; such as Israel, of whom it is said, 'Israel is the Lord's holy portion,' for He took them to Him to be a holy people, and assigned His holiness to them, and said, 'Ye shall be holy for I am holy.' And similarly with the Tabernacle and the Temple: the Tabernacle, as it is said, 'in a holy place,' and the Temple, whose name in Hebrew testifies to its holiness. Similarly with Jerusalem, the Holy City, and the Holy Land, which have been made holy by the holiness of the Almighty and the holiness of the deeds of Israel, who are called 'a special people and a holy nation.' Similarly with special days for the nation, such as the Sabbath day, which is called the Holy Sabbath, and the Day of Atonement, which is called a Holy Day, and so with the other divine festivals. And all those things that have been said in the Torah, the Prophets, and the Writings are called the Holy Scriptures, as is said in the tractate *Sabbath*, chapter 15, 'All the Holy Scriptures must be saved from burning.' From this we learn that all these things are holy—the opposite of secular. And anyone who makes one of these things secular degrades a supreme spiritual quality, at the very time that all creatures long to become more holy and to rise higher.

CHAPTER SEVEN AND TWENTY

The Sick Child

All the while I was sitting in Bach's house, the child busied himself with his picture book and paid no attention to me. Suddenly he asked, 'Are you from the Land of Israel?' 'Yes, my dear,' I said, 'I am from the Land of Israel.' 'Were you in Jerusalem too?' he asked. 'I was in Jerusalem too,' I said. 'Did you see my uncle Yeruham?' he asked. 'No, I didn't see him,' I said. 'Why didn't you see him?' 'I just didn't happen to see him,' I said. 'Why?' 'Your uncle lived in one place and I lived in another,' I said. The child looked at me in surprise, and said, 'But don't all the Jews live together in the Land of Israel?' 'Yes, my dear,' I said, 'all the Jews live together, but even so, is it possible to see every one? There is a distance that divides one place from another, you know, and if you live in one place you do not see the person who lives in another place.' 'You don't see?' 'Certainly you don't see; every separation separates.' 'And why do I see him?' 'Whom do you see, my love?' asked the child's mother. The child laughed and said, 'I see my uncle Yeruham.' 'You see him?' said the mother in a fright. 'Yes, Mother, I see him,' said the child.

'How do you see him—in a dream?' asked the child's father. 'In a dream, and not in a dream too,' said the child. 'I always see him. Before this gentleman came in I saw my uncle Yeruham putting brown polish on his shoes.' 'Brown polish?' cried Erela in surprise. 'Yes, Erela,' said her brother, 'brown polish he put on his shoes.' Erela took off her spectacles and shined them and asked again, 'Why brown polish?' 'So that they shouldn't see the blood on them that drips from his heart.'

The child whispered to me, 'Do you know my uncle was

killed? An Arab killed him. Why did he kill him? He was a
good uncle. Once he gave me a sugar soldier riding on a sugar
horse, with a long sugar spear in his hand. The soldier was
very sweet, but I didn't eat him. I swear I didn't eat him,
though he was sweet. I only licked the horse's hoofs a little
and the spear too. And do you know my grandfather?' 'Yes,
I know your grandfather,' I said. 'He went up to Jerusalem,'
said he. Daniel stroked the child's cheek and said, 'Yes, dear,
he went up to Jerusalem.'

'And does he see my uncle Yeruham?' the child asked his
father. 'But Uncle is dead,' said his father, 'so how is it possible
to see him?' 'And if he is dead, don't you see him?' asked the
child. 'No, my love, you don't see him,' said his mother.

The child was silent for a while, and asked again: 'Why
did the Arab not die? The Arab was not a good man. After
all, he killed my uncle. What is dead? Is everyone you don't
see dead?' Said his mother, 'Some of them are dead and some
of them are alive.' 'And how do we know who is alive and who
is dead?' asked the child.

His mother sighed and said, 'Don't mention the dead, my
love.' 'Why?' 'Perhaps they will show themselves to you in a
dream.' 'If you see them will that mean they are alive, Mother?
And is Yeruham Freeman dead too?' 'Why?' 'Because I don't
see him.' 'Of course you don't see him,' said his mother. 'He
has stopped coming here.' 'Why doesn't he come here?' His
mother sighed and said, 'Because he likes it better somewhere
else.' 'What is somewhere else?' 'A place that isn't here is
somewhere else.' 'Am I not here either?' 'No, my love, no, my
darling,' said the mother, 'you are here, you are here.' 'Why
am I here and not somewhere else?' 'Because, my love, you
are a little weak,' said the mother, 'and you can't walk with
your feet.' 'Now I know.' 'What do you know, my love?' 'Why
all the places come to me.'

'What do you mean, all the places come to you?' Erela
asked her brother. 'They shift themselves and come to me,' he
replied. 'And sometimes I go to them. It's not with my feet
I go, I go to them with my self. Sometimes I fall suddenly
from a high mountain and roll over and over down to the bottom, and suddenly I find myself standing in a brook, and there

are so many fish swimming in the water, and they have no heads—only soldiers' caps. Mother, when I'm big you'll make me a soldier's knapsack and I'll go to war. Daddy, has every soldier got a wooden leg?'

The child's mother sighed and said, 'Close your eyes, my love, the time has come to sleep.' 'I'm afraid of sleeping,' said the child. 'Don't be afraid, my love, say the "Hear, O Israel." Your hands are clean, aren't they? So say: "Hear, O Israel, the Lord is our God, the Lord is One." And now say good night.' 'Good night to all the good people.' His mother kissed him and said, 'Good night, my love.'

CHAPTER EIGHT AND TWENTY

A New Face

New faces are to be seen in the Beit Midrash. Every day I come across a certain old man dressed in rags. He comes in with me and goes out with me. He sits silent, speaking with no man. It is not my way to ask: Who are you? When I shall need to know, it will be made known to me.

Except on the day I came here, and a second time when the talk turned to the later generations, I had heard no one mention the divorcee and her hotel. The people I come across have nothing to do with a hotel of that type; they do not mention it even in condemnation. But now everyone is talking about it and about the divorcee. And they also tell a story about a certain girl who came across an old man in the market. Said he to her, 'Perhaps you know if So-and-so, daughter of So-and-so, still lives here?' Said she to him, 'She is my mother.' Said he to her, 'If that is your mother, I am your father.' Immediately a rumor spread in the town that the divorcee's ex-husband had come back.

That ex-husband, Reb Hayim is his name, was a descendant of great men, a brilliant scholar and qualified for the rabbinate. I remember that when he came to live in our town everyone was talking about him and his father-in-law; about

him because of his learning, and about his father-in-law in
envy.

This father-in-law was rich in money and poor in wisdom.
He had a large dry goods store in the center of the town and
a permanent seat in the old Beit Midrash. When his daughter
reached marriageable age he heard that there was a certain
rabbi in a little town near Szibucz who had a son, a great
scholar. So he took all his money in notes and put it in a
leather wallet, went to the rabbi, and put it down in front of
him, saying, 'Rabbi, all this is stored away for the husband of
my only daughter, apart from property and chattels. Are you
willing, Rabbi, to give me your son for my daughter?' The
rabbi saw all that money and agreed to the match. The rich
man kept his promise and even more. He bought a new house,
with fine furniture and books, in which he set down his son-
in-law, engaged an attendant to attend him, hired him a seat
at the honorable eastern end of the old Beit Midrash, main-
tained him and his house generously, and even gave presents
to his father the rabbi.

So Reb Hayim used to sit and study the Torah in the
midst of wealth, and debate with the sages of the town. And
he would even find time to put down his contributions on
paper and send them to his father the rabbi and the other rabbis of the country, and they would reply with the respect due
him. Our town, which had been distinguished for rabbis to
whom questions on points of law used to be sent from all over
the country, and which at that time had no rabbi but only an
adjudicator authorized to decide minor problems of kashruth—
spoon and kettle problems—was linked once again, thanks to
Reb Hayim, through the bonds of the Torah with the other
places in Jewry.

So Reb Hayim sat and studied, while his wife carried and
delivered four daughters, and all the worry and bother of them
was on her shoulders; and she did not feel the greatness of
her husband. Or, if you like, you may say that all the honor
with which her husband was crowned did not fit her. Her
father and mother, who were proud of their son-in-law, used
to be angry with her for not trying to be worthy of him. But
she did not know what more she could do. Was it not enough

that she wore a wig that reached below her forehead and pressed upon her head like a cart wheel? Was it not enough that she was always cooking for the swarms of intermediaries who used to come from all over the country to entice him to take up a rabbinical post, waiting on them like a maidservant, and had nothing in the world except her husband's scoldings when he told her to keep the crying children quiet?

As time went on and Reb Hayim did not find a post, he began to turn his eye to the rabbinate of Szibucz. Reb Hayim used to say, 'This fellow who is performing the duties of rabbi in Szibucz is only an adjudicator and not a rabbi, so the place of rabbi is vacant; and who is fit to be rabbi if not I?' Ever since Reb Hayim's arrival, he had belittled the adjudicator. What the other permitted, he forbade, and what the other forbade, he permitted. In the end there was a quarrel between them that shook the town, and the town was divided into two parties. When the controversy spread, Reb Hayim's party met and decided to make him the rabbi. His father-in-law undertook to provide him with a livelihood all his life and exempt the town from paying a salary, and he also obligated himself to donate for the public needs, apart from what he lavished on individuals. Today, there is not a single one left in the town of all those who took part in the controversy; some have been killed in the war, others have been scattered all over the country and disappeared among all the other fallen ones. In those days they made up a third of our town. When the town was weary of the controversy, they arrived at a compromise: to make the adjudicator rabbi, and Reb Hayim the adjudicator. But Reb Hayim would not agree. He said it was not to the honor of a greater man to be the subordinate of a lesser. And so the controversy went on and on.

I had gone up to the Land of Israel before the quarrel broke out and heard only fragmentary stories that reached me there, and I was not much interested in them, for while I was in the Land of Israel I abandoned all the affairs about which they wrangled in exile, and put them out of my mind. Well, a great war spread through the town, until another war came and the whole town fled, except for a few wealthy families who bribed the enemy to leave them alone. The enemy took their money and in the end exiled them too, and Reb Hayim, the most important of them all, they took away as a prisoner. From that time on, nothing was heard of Reb Hayim until a Jew came from Russia and brought a divorce for his wife.

This Jew said that Reb Hayim had fallen ill and was afraid he might die and no one would tell his wife, so that she would be left tied to a dead man all her life. He made a certain official swear to send for a scribe; and he wrote a divorce for his wife and made the scribe swear to take it to her. In the course of time, when the war ended and the world began to return somewhat to its former state, Reb Hayim was released from captivity and went from place to place, from town to town and country to country, until after days and years he reached that woman. He came and knocked at the door, but his wife was not glad to see him, just as she had not been glad when they had married her to him. She was the daughter of an ignoramus, and while her father, who prayed in the old Beit Midrash and saw the honor that was paid to scholars, used to respect rabbis, she, who sat in the store and saw the honor paid to traders and salesmen, did not respect rabbis. Had he not sent her a divorce, or had he sent her a divorce and come back years before, she might have been reconciled to returning to him, but now that he had sent her a divorce and returned after many years, she would not be reconciled to re-marrying him, for she was already accustomed to living without a man. Not everyone is of the same opinion. Some say: What a bad woman that is, who sees him suffering and pays him no heed; and some say: What a bad man that is, who wishes to live with sinners. True, that woman has preserved her own virtue and that of her daughters, but she has certainly not preserved the virtue of the house.

Reb Hayim's coming made no impression. Most of the people of the town were new arrivals, and how should they know Reb Hayim? And those who knew him had troubles of their own and felt they could discharge all their obligations with a sigh. But when they saw him sitting in the Beit Midrash, their hearts were stirred and they cried, 'O heavens, a man who was the pride of our town, without a roof over his head!' They began inviting him to visit them, but he did not go. They brought him dishes to the Beit Midrash, but he did not accept them. They began to storm at the divorcee for not taking back her husband. 'Leave her alone,' said Reb Hayim. 'She owes me nothing.'

At first they used to wonder at Reb Hayim: a scholar, whose lips once never ceased to study, sits in silence and does not open a book. Some said that he had long since forgotten his learning through no fault of his own, or that he had achieved a new conception of the Torah and had no need of books, while some said that he was denying himself the Torah because through it he had given rise to quarreling. And how was it possible that one who had spent all his time on the Torah should sit idle without studying? But this was not the only case of its kind. There had been a previous case before the war, when a man had happened to come here who was thoroughly expert by heart in both the Talmuds, forward and backward, and no one had ever seen him holding a book, except for one volume of *The Defenders of the Faith*, which he used as a pillow for his head. There had also been a man who came to the Beit Midrash and said: 'I can reply to any question standing on one foot,' and he never opened a book either. And then there was Rabbi David, son of the great sage Zvi, who acted as a rabbi all his life, and in the end came to a place where no one knew him, and was employed as a beadle. He hid his achievements and did not reveal who he was until his passing, and when he died they engraved on his tombstone, 'Alas for the great servant whom the world has lost.'

Reb Hayim sits in our old Beit Midrash with his hands clasped. His head is bowed toward his heart, like one who wishes to sleep, but from his eyes you can see that there is no sleep in store for him. Sometimes he puts his hand to his beard and pulls it, or adjusts his hat on his head, and then clasps his hands again as in sorrow. I watch Reb Hayim, who used to set the whole town in a turmoil as if the whole town were his, until he was dislodged from his place, an exile and a wanderer, and the two pictures mingle with each other. I lower my eyes and say to myself: And now he sits here. Man's goings are of the Lord; how can a man then understand his own way?

Since the day Reb Hayim has been staying in the Beit Midrash, Hanoch's work has been easier, for Reb Hayim fills the basin with water, trims the candles, and fills the lamp with kerosene, and on Sabbath eve he sweeps the floor—everything except light the stove, which I do myself. Not because of any symbolism, for I have already said that I do not like things that are done as a kind of symbol, but because I have become used to this work and because learning together with labor is a good thing.

So I said to myself: I must pay Reb Hayim for his work, in addition to Hanoch's pay. When I wanted to pay him he pulled back his hand and shook his head from side to side, as if to say: I do not want it, I do not want it. I wished to help him in some other way. But how could I discuss it with him when he shut himself off from all talk? And if he was asked anything, he shook his head from side to side or nodded it up and down, according to his intention. These were his ways of answering yes or no.

Once I came up to him suddenly and said, 'Reb Hayim, perhaps you need something. Why are you silent all the time, sir?' He fixed his eyes on mine and looked at me for a while, and said, 'A man to whom evil things have happened had better be silent than speak, lest he say something that is not proper.'

'Read a book, sir,' said I, 'and you will distract yourself a little.' Said he, 'I have forgotten my learning.' 'Is it possible for a great scholar to forget his learning?' 'Since the day I was exiled from here,' he replied, 'I have not had a book in my hand or chanced to hear a word of the Torah.' Said I, 'Here is a book. Try, sir, and read.' Said he, 'I have already tried.' 'And was the attempt not successful?' I asked. He shook his head from side to side like a man who says: Certainly not. 'Why?' 'The eyes do not take in the letters, and the mind does not take in the matter,' said he.

From that time forth I did not bother him with words, and needless to say he did not bother to say anything to me.

Every day he came in with me and went out with me, brought water from the well to fill the basin, trimmed the candles, and filled the lamps with kerosene. When he had finished his work he sat down in the northwest corner beside the calendar on the wall, his head bowed and his hands clasped together. From his way of doing things it was clear that he was accustomed to labor. Apparently he had learned many things in the land of his captivity. I wanted to know something of what had happened to him, and therefore I told him something about the Land of Israel, thinking that perhaps his heart might be aroused and his lips opened. But his silence silenced me. We sat together in our old Beit Midrash, like two beams that support the ceiling and bear the weight of the whole building, but one beam does not speak to the other.

On the day the locksmith made me the key I decided not to let it out of my hand. When I saw Reb Hayim coming early to the Beit Midrash and leaving late, and found him every day standing and waiting for me in front of the door and sitting with me at night until I left, I wanted to give him the key, so that he should not depend on me, but he would not take it. Why? After several days I found out his reason: he was afraid he might sleep in the Beit Midrash. And where did he sleep? In the woodshed. Why not in the women's section? Because there is no women's section in our old Beit Midrash; a woman whose husband prayed in the old Beit Midrash used to pray herself in the women's section of the Great Synagogue—and no one could sleep in the Great Synagogue because of the cold.

CHAPTER NINE AND TWENTY

Winter's Cold

The great frosts for which our town is famous have arrived in full force. Awaking early one morning, we saw that the sky had darkened and the ground was frozen; the cold exuded from below and above, from valleys and gorges, mountains and hills, from the stones in the street and the clouds in the sky. A cold like this, my dear, you have never seen in your life, and I hope you may never see it. It is only in the lands of the Gentiles, on whom the Holy One, blessed be He, looks as it were with an angry eye, that such a cruel cold can grow so overpowering.

Later, toward twilight, the snow began to fall—at first little by little, in small flakes, like soft feathers, and then in great flurries, like thick wool. By the time we had returned from our evening prayers, the whole town was covered with snow, and it was still falling. In the morning all the houses were deep in snow, and still the snow kept falling. As it fell, it produced offspring like itself. At the very same moment in which it was born, it also conceived, and also gave birth to new offspring. And they too produced offspring without a stop.

The snow is beautiful to the eyes but wearisome to the body. You go out to the market and sink in the snow. You try to make your way home again but cannot find any traces of your footprints in the snow. And as you try, your blood freezes and your bones crack.

This man who came to this place is not troubled by the cold, because he has a warm coat and spends nights and days—and nights that are like days—in the Beit Midrash. When he returns to his hotel, he finds a warm stove and a warm meal and a boiling samovar. But the houses of most people in the town are full of snow and frost up to their very bedposts.

The cold rises upward. There is no bird in the heavens above nor any dog or cat on the earth below. All the birds have left for the warm countries: perhaps a pair of them are pecking at the roof of my house in Jerusalem—the house that was destroyed; perhaps they are twittering to their sisters, as they used to twitter from the roof of our old Beit Midrash.

All the roads in the town are covered with snow, and the houses are sunk in snow up to the windows. Sometimes it seems to you that the windows have sunk, and sometimes you think the ground has reached up to them. Because of the snow and frost and ice, the rags in the broken panes are covered over, and even those windows that are not broken are sealed with ice. In the past, when we were little, the winter used to trace flowers on some of the windows in the town, but now it heaps formless ice upon them. In the past, when most of the houses were heated and only a few were not, the winter was free to draw beautiful shapes; now that most of the houses are not heated, it is not free to do so.

Even our old Beit Midrash is caught in the grip of the winter. You come in, and warmth does not envelop you. You sit down, and you have no pleasure in your sitting. The wood is dwindling steadily, and Hanoch does not replace it. For three days Hanoch has not come to the Beit Midrash to bring wood. Hanoch, who used to come regularly every two or three days, has taken to other ways. I consider every stick before I put it into the stove, and I ask: Where is Hanoch and where is the wood?

A small fire burns in the stove, beguiling the eyes but not warming the body. Our stove looks like a stove in which a joker has set a burning candle to deceive people into thinking it has been lit.

What reason has Hanoch for keeping away from the Beit Midrash? Perhaps he has found a treasure in the snow and become rich, so that he need not toil any more at hauling wood. I inquired about him of the people in the Beit Midrash. Said Reuben, 'I saw him today.' Said Simon, 'Not so, but yesterday.' Said Levi, 'You say yesterday—perhaps it was the day before.' Said Judah, 'Did you see him with his cart or not with his cart?' Said Issachar, 'What difference does it make, with his cart or not with his cart?' Said Zebulun, 'It makes a great difference, for if he saw him with his cart he could not have seen him at all, for the day before yesterday was the Sabbath, so his very own words give him the lie.' Said Joseph, 'What do you think, Benjamin?' 'I think the same as you,' said Benjamin, 'but in any case it's worth finding out whether his horse was harnessed to his cart.' Said Dan, 'And what if it was?' 'If the horse was harnessed,' said Naphtali, 'that means that he has gone out on the road.' 'Is it possible a man should go out on the road in a cold like this?' said Gad. Said Asher, 'And isn't the cold of the Beit Midrash enough for us, without your having to remind us of the cold on the roads?'

I did wrong in not appointing Hanoch as a permanent

attendant. A permanent attendant does not procrastinate in bringing wood.

'Oh, Hanoch, Hanoch,' I say to him, 'why have you not brought us wood? Don't you see that the stove has cooled off and Jews are shivering because of the winter? Where is decency and where is pity? What face will you wear to meet the heavenly court at the end of your allotted span of 120 years, when you have caused pain to men of Israel?'

And since he is silent, my bitterness grows, and I say, 'You are cruel, Hanoch, and your horse Henoch is cruel, and your wagon is no better than the two of you. Jews are freezing with cold while you are strolling about for your own pleasure in the snow. Perhaps you are skating on the ice like the lords and ladies who have nothing in their lives but pleasure and enjoyment?'

All these things I did not say to Hanoch's face, for he had not come to listen to my rebukes. Where was Hanoch? This called for a thorough investigation.

Again I asked the people in the Beit Midrash, 'What could have happened to Hanoch that he has not come?' 'It seems likely,' they replied, 'that he has gone out to the countryside and stayed there because of the snow, for it is impossible to come back in snow like this. When the snow stops, Hanoch will return.' 'I am not worried about Hanoch,' said I, 'but I am worried that tomorrow we may not find wood for the stove.' 'If that is what you are worried about, sir,' said they, 'there is no reason to worry. Where there is money, there is wood, and if there is wood we will find a carrier to bring it.'

I thought that Shimke or Yoshke or Veptchi would go and bring wood. But Veptchi and Yoshke and Shimke preferred to sit by the stove. However, blessed is Reb Hayim, who went and brought the wood on his shoulder. From then on Reb Hayim would fill a sack with wood every morning and bring it to the Beit Midrash—on days when it was very cold, twice a day.

So a steady fire burns in the stove and a dozen pairs of eyes watch it to see that no one should come and take out an ember. As for myself, I do not care if a man takes an ember for his wife, but my friends disagree, saying, 'Let the fingers of the women peddlers be chilled rather than trouble an old scholar twice a day.' Daniel Bach and I tried to hire a man so as not to trouble Reb Hayim, but he asked us to leave him this good deed until Hanoch should return.

The eyes of a miser are stronger than an iron lock, for if a man comes to take an ember, twenty-four eyes assail him, and he is startled and turns back.

The snow continues to fall and the city continues to freeze, but in our old Beit Midrash it is warm, and men sit around the fire and study the Torah or talk to one another. Once or twice I said to myself: It is only right and fitting to inquire why Hanoch does not come. But, pray tell me, who will go out on a cold day to look for Hanoch?

A steady fire burns in the stove, and new men come every day to warm themselves. Some rise early and come to reserve a place beside the stove before the others arrive. I have already said that every day we say the prayers with a quorum of ten. Now—and may the devil stay far from us—I can add that we have no less than three quorums. On Sabbath eves they even bring the children in order to give them a little warmth, and the children answer 'Amen'; for apart from answering 'Amen' and reciting the 'Hear, O Israel,' they know no prayers, because there are no teachers for the children in our town, and their fathers are too busy earning a living to teach them.

I blessed myself with a deed. I bought a quart of wine and restored the ancient custom of our fathers, who would have Kiddush said on Sabbath eve in the Beit Midrash; and I let the young ones sip from the wine. The next Sabbath I took a paper bag full of sweets, and after the prayer distributed them to the children. Not to accustom them to come (and for this I have my good reasons, as it is said in the Gemara: 'Why do they not bring the fruits of Ginosar to Jerusalem? So that the pilgrims should not say: If we had made our pilgrimage only to eat the fruits of Ginosar—that would have been enough; and they would not be making the pilgrimage for its own sake'), but to give them a taste of sweet things, for they and all their families have forgotten the taste of sweetness.

CHAPTER THIRTY

On Hanoch—Who Has Gone

One day we were sitting as usual beside the stove, when the door opened with a sound of weeping and moaning and several women came into the Beit Midrash. I thought they had come to cry out at me for not allowing their men to bring them embers, but in fact they had come to cry before the Creator of the universe because of Hanoch who had not returned.

Hanoch had not returned, and his wife and children had come to tell their woes to the heavenly ear. They opened the doors of the Ark and cried, 'Hanoch, Hanoch, Father, Father!' I have forgotten to tell you that there were some Jews who were not afraid for themselves or afraid of the cold, and had gone out to look for Hanoch, but had not found him. The peasants who accompanied them said that the wolves had devoured him and no doubt his bones were hidden under the snow. But a woman's heart still hopes for mercy. So now she had come before the Blessed One with weeping and supplication and clamor, begging Him to restore her Hanoch, and her sons and daughters stood with her before the Holy Ark joining the sound of their weeping to hers.

The Scrolls of the Law stand silent in the Ark. All love and mercy and compassion are enclosed and enfolded in them. How right it would have been had the door opened suddenly and Hanoch entered alive! Dear brothers, how much good it would have done in Israel in this fallen generation of the poor in faith! Alas, the door did not open and Hanoch did not enter. Heaven forbid that the Gentiles had told the truth when they said the wolves had eaten him.

But even if a sharp sword is laid to a man's throat he should not despair of mercy. The Blessed One can still bring salvation if we know how to arouse mercy.

The rabbi of the town assembled ten honest men and
arranged for them to say verses of the psalms the first letters
of which made up the name of Hanoch. First all the verses
beginning with *Het*, then all the verses beginning with *Nun*,
then all the verses beginning with *Vav*, then all the verses beginning with *Kaf*. Then all the verses beginning with the letters of his father's name and of his mother's. Anyone who is
familiar with the various versions, editions, and printings of
the prayer book and knows that prayer books suitable for
this procedure are not to be found in our country will understand how much trouble the rabbi took.

Wrapped in their rags, ten men sat in the Great Synagogue and recited with tears and supplication, '*Haneni* . . .
Have mercy upon me, O Lord; for I am weak: O Lord, heal
me; for my bones are vexed,' in Psalm 6, and ended with the
verse '*Hanun* . . . The Lord is gracious, and full of compassion; slow to anger, and of great mercy,' in Psalm 145. Then
they rose and said a special prayer, sat down again, and said,
'*Nenateka* . . . Let us break their bands asunder,' and so forth,
and ended with '*Noten* . . . He giveth to the beast food,' and
so forth. Again they rose, said a special prayer, sat down
again, and recited. '*Vehaya* . . . And he shall be like a tree
planted by the rivers of water, that bringeth forth his fruit in
his season; his leaf also shall not wither; and whatsoever he
doeth shall prosper,' and ended with '*Vayarem* . . . He also
exalteth the horn of His people, the praise of all His saints;
even of the children of Israel, a people near unto Him. Praise
ye the Lord.' Again they rose, recited a special prayer, sat
down again, and went on until they ended with the last verse
of the Book of Psalms, '*Kol haneshama* . . . Let everything that
hath breath praise the Lord. Praise ye the Lord.' Again they
rose, said a special prayer, sat down, and recited all the verses
for the names of his father and mother. Then they rose and
said the prayer beginning 'May it be His will,' and the Kaddish, sanctifying the Name of the Lord.

I too did something: I arranged that in my Beit Midrash
they should say 'Our Father, our King' at the Morning and
Afternoon Services, verse by verse. When the rabbi heard this
he objected. 'Who is this who has come to institute new fash-

ions?' He said, 'Today he tells you: Say "Our Father, our King"; and tomorrow he will tell you: Go and play football on the Sabbath!'

I regretted that I had not gone to pay my respects to the rabbi, for if I had visited him he would not have spoken in this way. I said to myself: Let a day go by and I shall get over my regret. When a day had passed and my regret had not, I went to the rabbi to appease him.

The rabbi is near seventy, but his age is not very apparent. His face is somewhat long and his beard gold in color, and the threads of silver in it gave him the kind look of a good-tempered man. His movements are measured and his speech is gentle; he does not raise his voice too much, but adds intonation to emphasize his words. He looks well fleshed, though in fact he is lean and tall; but because he sits at ease with his arms folded over his heart, he looks well fleshed. Although he is a poor man and his stipend is small, he is dressed in satin and is careful that his clothes should be clean. I have already mentioned in the story of Reb Hayim that at the beginning the present rabbi was accepted as an adjudicator and not as rabbi, and only when the war ended and his rivals disappeared and the town dwindled was he appointed rabbi. Apart from the great controversy with Reb Hayim and the troubles of the war and the troubles of the pogroms, which are common to all, he has not been particularly affected by the sorrows of the time. His sons follow in his footsteps, if not in their learning then at least in their ways. One is a prominent worker for Agudat Israel, the orthodox party, and a bit of a scribbler in their Yiddish newspapers; a second has a kind of factory for sausages; another is a son-in-law in a rich house, and there is reason to expect that he will find a rabbinical post, for his father-in-law is on good terms on the one hand with a famous zaddik and on the other with the authorities.

It is a rule stated in the Gemara that just as it is one's duty to teach practices that will be followed, so it is one's duty not to teach practices that will not be followed. This rule the rabbi has applied to himself, and it has saved him from various kinds of difficulty. But if someone comes to ask about a point of law, he is strict; not that this is the law, but that it is fitting to be strict. The rabbi often says, 'The rules of the Torah were given to rejoice the hearts of those that learn them, and if a good deed comes to your hand, act so that your Maker should rejoice in you and be strict with yourself.' If the questioner resists him and asks, 'Is the law really so?' he says to him, 'If you know the law why do you ask me? And if you ask, it is because you do not rely on yourself, so you must rely on me.' Although his actions are measured and his speech balanced, he does not avoid idle conversation, and adorns his talk with things that put people in good humor. But he is careful not to tell two jokes one after the other, and not to tell a story that has nothing to do with what he is talking about.

When I came in he received me cordially, although it could be seen that he resented my not having come before, and he spoke to me in this wise in Aramaic: 'If I am a king (for it is said, "Who are kings? The rabbis!"), why did you not come to see me until now?' But he immediately gave me a place at his right hand, and explained that the reason he had objected to the saying of 'Our Father, our King' was that this prayer should not be recited for the troubles of an individual. Since I was silent, he thought I was annoyed because he had said, 'Today he tells you: Say "Our Father, our King," and to-morrow he will say: Go and play football on the Sabbath,' and he began discussing why it is forbidden to play football on the Sabbath. Anyone who heard him might have imagined that people did nothing else in the Land of Israel but play football every day, especially on the Sabbath. More things, too, he said in condemnation of the people of the Land of Israel, which be-cause of various preoccupations I took no notice of and did not answer. When he saw that I was silent, he changed his tone and looked at me more favorably. He raised his voice a little, not too much, adding intonation to emphasize what he was saying, and said, 'And now, sir, will you honor me by saying a blessing in my house?' Then he raised his voice above the usual and called, 'Rebetzin, bring refreshments. A Jew from the Land of Israel has come to visit us.'

A short while passed. From the kitchen I could hear foot-steps and the clattering of dishes. Although the rabbi's wife had made no reply, it was obvious that she had heard her hus-

band and was now preparing refreshments. The rabbi looked
at me affectionately and stroked his beard gently. Suddenly
he shifted his eyes from me and looked at the door, rapping
on the table with his fingers so as to hurry up his wife. I
wanted to tell him that there was no need to trouble her, for
I was neither hungry nor thirsty, but the door opened and in
came the rabbi's wife, carrying a tray with two glasses of tea
and plates full of sweetmeats, as well as some sugar and slices
of lemon. She bowed to me and said, 'Welcome!' She seemed
as old as he was, but more worn. In honor of this man who had
come to her house she wore a kind of bonnet. Her husband
looked at her approvingly, like a husband who is satisfied with
his wife, for you must know that during the war they had come
in contact with rabbis of the moderate Mizrachi party and had
seen how the world behaves.

There was a bookcase in the room. The rabbi saw that I
was looking at it and said, 'These are my books, which God
has given me. Some of them came to me by inheritance and
some I have bought with my own money. Thank God that
there is not a single book here that came to me as payment or
pledge for loans. I also have books here of the modern authors,
which my son has brought me, for the authors send him their
books so that he should mention them favorably in the papers.
I have heard that you, sir, too, have written books. I have never
looked into them. For me the books of our holy rabbis are
enough. But since we have mentioned the matter of books, I
will show you a book that I have written. Perhaps you will take
some time and look at it. I am certain that you will find pleasant things in it, based on the truth of the Torah.' He bent down
and, opening a drawer in the table, took out a kind of account
book; then he gave it to me and looked at me with affection,
waiting for me to say, 'Pure gold! Pure gold!'

While I was examining it, the door opened and in came
three men. I got up to go, but the rabbi put his right hand on
mine and said, 'On the contrary, sir. Sit down and listen to
what these Jews have to say.' Then he turned to the newcomers and said, 'Sit down, gentlemen, sit down. What have
you to say? On the contrary, speak. This Jew here is also a Jew;
on the contrary, let him hear.'

All of them began speaking in confusion. 'If you all speak at the same time,' said the rabbi, 'I cannot hear.' Then they began shouting in confusion, crying, 'Let Michael speak'— 'Let Gabriel speak'—'Let Raphael speak.' The rabbi took his beard in his hand and said, 'On the contrary, Reb Raphael, you tell me for what reason you have come.' Said Raphael, 'You ask us why we have come? The rabbi should ask us why we did not come before.' Said the rabbi, 'If you did not come to me, then there was no one to ask. Well, then, gentlemen, what have you come for?' 'We have come to you on an evil day,' said Raphael. 'Hanoch's wife won't let us be. "*Gevald*," she cries, "even the Gentiles have tried to find him, and here I live among Jews and they are doing nothing." We believe that something must be done.' 'And have I not done something?' said the rabbi. 'Have I not arranged for a quorum of ten men and assigned them what they should say? I did not, praise God, pick out the verses from the concordance; I myself, with my own hand, copied them out, with the vowels and the notes.' Said Gabriel, 'And the rabbi has accomplished nothing.' 'Be quiet, Gabriel, be quiet,' said Raphael. 'Heaven forbid that we should put words into the devil's mouth!' 'And what did I say?' said Gabriel. 'What you said should not have been said,' said Raphael, and went on: 'Prayer does a half. In any case, we believe that the rabbi should declare a fast. Perhaps the Holy One, blessed be He, will see our trouble and reveal to us where Hanoch is.' The rabbi sighed and said, 'A fast calls for repentance.' Said Michael, 'Those that are able to repent, let them repent.' The rabbi sighed and said, 'There is a man among us who is not able to repent. I have heard that that Hayim constantly visits the hotel, and it seems likely to me that he has stayed under one roof with his divorced wife without others being by.'

Said I to the rabbi, 'Perhaps you have confused the divorcee's hotel with mine.' 'The rabbi's jealousy is gone, but not his hatred,' I heard Gabriel mutter. The rabbi stroked his beard and said, 'So that you should not say that your rabbi is negligent, I hereby set you a date: if Hanoch does not return between now and the eve of the New Moon, I am prepared to declare a public fast.' So he gave them until the eve of the

New Moon. They took their leave and went, and I too went on my way.

As I was leaving, he said to me, 'Now that you know where I live, sir, come and visit me again.' I wanted to go back to him at once, like the man who came to visit a certain famous rabbi, stayed with him a few hours, and as soon as he had left went back. People said to him, 'What reason do you have to go back, after you have sat with our famous rabbi several hours?' Said he to them, 'It is said that if you have been in a place once, it is well known that you will go back to it a second time, and so that I should not need to return later, I am returning immediately.'

CHAPTER ONE AND THIRTY

Hanoch

The appointed day was approaching, but no trace of Hanoch had been found. Snow covered the land and closed the mouth of the earth. Hanoch's wife and children wandered about the town and the sound of their weeping rose to the heart of the heavens, but the heavens had forgotten mercy for men.

Again people went out to look for Hanoch; there was not a single village where they did not look. A number of Gentiles who liked Hanoch helped them, but the snow kept its secrets.

The rabbi still hesitated to declare a fast in a generation when people ate and drank on the Day of Atonement, but he agreed to ask some individuals to fast for one day, and, needless to say, he would fast with them. In the end, the men of action won their way, and the rabbi agreed against his will to declare a fast in the town. Those who were present on the occasion said that when the rabbi agreed to the fast his face was white as plaster.

On the Sabbath before the New Moon the beadle went round to all the houses of prayer in the town and declared on the rabbi's orders that if Hanoch did not return before the eve of the New Moon the entire congregation must fast on that day from morning to evening, and anyone who could not fast should redeem himself with money. This, too, the beadle announced: that all the congregation should assemble that day in the Great Synagogue an hour before the Afternoon Service, when the rabbi would preach to them.

The town scoffed, saying, 'What news is this fellow telling us? Do we eat and drink on other days? And what will the youth club do? Will they arrange a special feast as on the Day of Atonement, or just because this fast is not prescribed in the Torah will they fast too?'

When the eve of the New Moon came, the jesting ceased, and the people refrained from eating and drinking. Even visitors who happened to be in the town did not touch a mouthful.

After midday half the town assembled in the Great Synagogue. I heard that since the beginning of the war the walls of the synagogue had not seen such a large congregation; even people who do not come on the Day of Atonement came. The rabbi mounted the steps that led to the Ark, wrapped himself in his prayer shawl, and preached in trenchant terms to arouse the people and subdue their hearts to repentance, that they might be worthy to have the Almighty accept their prayers. And at the Afternoon Service the cantor took his place before the lectern and started with the prescribed prayer from Psalms and went through the entire service of the Minor Day of Atonement. Then they took out the Scroll and read from it the prescribed portion, and after the repetition by the cantor the rabbi ordered them to say 'Our Father, our King' verse by verse.

Among the congregation I found a number of people I had not seen since the day I arrived in Szibucz. Those who were close to me asked how I was, and those who stood far off nodded their heads. And you need not be surprised at this, for all those who are bitter of heart have left the town. I do not know where that man is who spoke to me with such insolence and effrontery on the Day of Atonement in the old Beit Midrash, and said that I was like one of those who would like every day to be the Day of Atonement. According to the letters his mother showed me, he has strayed to places where every day is a day of fasting and mourning, and even there they do not let him stay.

As soon as I entered the synagogue, Zechariah Rosen came up to me and began talking to me without resentment. In the course of his talk he told me how the earlier generations used to behave in every trouble and tribulation, and what psalm they used to recite. In the case of *schüler gelauf* they would say such-and-such psalms, and in other troubles they would say such-and-such psalms. There were some troubles that he had heard about from his parents, who had heard from their parents, who had heard from their parents who had lived at the time of those troubles, and there were troubles he had heard about from old men who had read of them in the old register our town used to have. That register had been burned, unfortunately—though not, as many believed, by a certain elder because he found things in it derogatory to his family; it was his son, a scholar and a distracted man, who had burned it, not on purpose but by mistake. It happened once on the eve of Passover that while clearing away the leaven he cleared away, too, all the tattered papers that had no more worth or interest, and by mistake he burned the old register together with them. It is a pity about that old register which had been burned, for it chronicled events of three hundred years and more, but you cannot condemn the inadvertent as you would the willful transgressor.

And now that Zechariah Rosen's memory had been stimulated by bygone days, he did not stop until he had told me a number of things that happened in our town. For instance, at first our old Beit Midrash was at the top of the hill and its entrance faced the bathhouse, and the tailors' synagogue was down below in the courtyard of the Great Synagogue. The less serious among our young men used to watch the women going to the baths and be led into bad thoughts; so the elders of those days had exchanged the position of the two.

And Zechariah Rosen also told me, 'I am surprised that it has not occurred to you to ask why you find a tailors' synagogue and not one of cobblers or of other trades. The reason is that once the Polish authorities oppressed the Jews; so the Jews proclaimed a ban among themselves: that no Jewish craftsman should do any work for the Poles until they had mended their ways—at that time the Poles had no craftsmen of their own. The tailors violated the ban, and the Jews refused to pray together with the transgressors, so the tailors had to make houses of prayer for themselves.' And Zechariah Rosen also told me, 'If you come to my house I will tell you some things worth hearing. As for Rav Hai, let me tell you that you and all your colleagues were not perfectly correct; I have piles and piles of proofs that I am a descendant of Rav Hai.'

While I was standing with Zechariah Rosen I saw a man looking at me. When Zechariah left me this man came up and asked how I was, and stroked my coat, as one who has a liking for me and for my clothes.

He was dressed in a thin, patched garment with a tattered collar sticking up toward his chin. His face was very lean and his eyes shining. He was bending his fingers, putting them up to his mouth to warm them with his breath, and talking to me between the blue fingers. Seeing that I did not recognize him, he smiled and said, 'Don't you recognize me, sir? You used to visit me often.' I asked him if he was the photographer.

What was there that made me ask him if he was the photographer? And what if he was the photographer? I had never had anything to do with the photographer. Again he stroked my coat and asked, 'Are you pleased with this coat I made for you?' I took his cold fingers in my hands and apologized for having been so preoccupied with Hanoch's trouble that I did not recognize him at once, and now that I had recognized him, I wondered at my failure to do so before. I asked him how his wife was.

Schuster smiled and said, 'Healthy and good, thank God, like a merry devil in the women's balcony of the synagogue. As for her lying in bed, that is first of all to spoil herself, and second so that her neighbors should come to visit her and see her bedclothes, which have come from a count's mansion— for the friendship between us I do not give his name, because he has gone down in the world, and it is no honor to a noble to speak about his decline. But I will tell you in a whisper that I did him a good turn and took them in payment for clothes

I made him. As for Hanoch, I say definitely that it's a bad business.'

The tailor sighed deeply, put his blue fingers to his mouth, and said again, 'A bad business.' I asked him if he found the fast a hardship. He twisted his lips into a kind of smile and said, 'The fast a hardship? Why should I find the fast a hardship? I am not fasting. I redeemed myself with money. I am a craftsman, full up with work, and I can't waste even an hour, and anyone who fasts can't work, especially in the cold weather, when the chill drives a man to distraction. It's a bad winter we have, and everyone wants warm clothes. Even lords and ladies, who have many clothes, want to have more made. The district governor has already sent for me, saying, "Make me two suits, and a third for ceremonial occasions, for I am invited to meet Pilsudski." I sent to tell him I was busy and could not go to him. He sent back, "If you do not make them for me I will be angry with you." I sent back, "Your honor knows that the whole town is practically naked; if I go to you that will keep me from my work, and the whole town will die of cold. Even for myself I do not find the time to make a coat. No, your honor, have pity. Jews are dying of cold." '

Here the tailor's compassion was aroused and enveloped his smile. His face grew pale and his lips began to quiver. Finally he made a downward motion with his hand and said, 'And I tell you, sir, all our trouble is in vain. Hanoch is already dead. How? Well, he follows on behind his cart, and the horse walks on in front, and the snow is falling, and Hanoch's hands get colder and colder, and all his body is cold. Still he summons up strength and goes up to his horse to see if the horse is not dead. The horse is still alive, but Hanoch is cold as a corpse. Hanoch stretches out his hands to his horse's neck and embraces him, and so they stand together. The one is cold and the other is cold, but when they stand together it seems to them that they are getting warmer, because of the power of imagination that is in every creature. Says Hanoch to his horse, "*Kindchen*, are you cold?" "No, I am not cold," says the horse to Hanoch. "I know you are cold," says Hanoch to the horse, "but you say that so as not to grieve me. I am sure your words will not be counted against you as lies. *Kindchen*, are you cold?" Before the horse can reply, the snow covers him and Hanoch. Hanoch peers from the snow and wants to get out, to reach a place where Jews live, so that he can be buried in a Jewish grave. He lifts one foot out of the snow. But what is the use of lifting one foot when you have to sink it back into the snow to take out the other foot that is sunk in the snow? But Hanoch does not think anything, for his mind is frozen and he is not capable of any thoughts in the world, but he takes out a foot and puts in a foot and bends his whole body, sometimes one way and sometimes the other, as I am showing you. But since his blood has been chilled, the body has no strength to stand, and he collapses. When he collapses he falls, and when he has fallen he cannot rise, and so he collapses and falls.' As the tailor was demonstrating Hanoch's fall, his legs collapsed, and he fell.

At the sound of his fall, many were startled and alarmed. Some moved farther off and some came closer. Cries of alarm were heard. 'Bring water, water!' 'No, vinegar, vinegar!' 'Bring a little water!' 'A man has fainted!' 'He can't lie there, you should rub him, so that his blood shouldn't freeze.' 'Who's fainted here?' 'It's the tailor from Berlin.' 'But only a minute ago I saw him talking.' 'It seems he found it too hard to fast.' 'If so we'll have to make him eat.' 'Father in heaven, what are you standing there for? Move away.'

Three or four people came forward, lifted him, and brought him to the old Beit Midrash, where they put him on a table, raised his head, sprinkled water on his face, and wet his dry lips. They took the cloth from the reading desk and a tattered prayer shawl that no one would claim and put them under his head. They wanted to bring brandy and some food. The tailor opened his eyes, looked around and said, 'There's no time, sir, I'm too busy. Why are you crowding around me? Can I clothe the whole town?' While he was talking, he dozed off again and fell asleep. His lips grew paler and paler, but his smile did not go away, as if it had frozen on his lips.

So the stricken body lay on the table in the Beit Midrash, and the pure soul ascended to beg mercy for him. It was good for the body to lie still without being vexed by the soul. And while the one was lying and the other was pleading with its

Maker, brandy was brought, and they opened his mouth and poured some into it. Reb Hayim came with a pot of black coffee in one hand and a piece of sugar in the other, and made him drink the coffee, sweetened with the sugar. Little by little the tailor returned to health to undergo fresh tribulations.

As I left, the rabbi saw me and greeted me amicably. Did I like his sermon? he asked, and what did I like about it? Finally he said that he had wanted to say more, but he saw that the congregation was weary with the fast and there were no learned men in it to understand the profundities of the Torah, so he cut it short. In the end he took my hand and said, 'Come to break your fast with me, sir, and I will tell you all I left out.'

I said to myself: If you have been in a place once, it is known that you will go back there. I will go today and I shall not have to go some other day. I asked his permission to come after the meal; I knew that he was a poor man and I did not wish to eat of a meal that is not sufficient even for the hosts themselves.

The people of the hotel were sitting at table with the guests. Krolka hurried in confusion to bring the fasters their food. Dolik and Lolik sat with their heads covered, as at the Sabbath meal, and ate as after a fast. Babtchi, too, ate her fill. Opposite her sat Rachel and looked as if she were eating.

My host sat at the head of the table and his face was sad. Because of the pain in his legs that had been troubling him all day, he had been unable to go to the synagogue to pray with the congregation. Now that the pain had gone, he sat and rubbed the sore places, either to pamper them because they were not molesting him, or to molest them because they had annoyed him all day. While he was occupied with his legs, he raised his eyes and looked at Rachel. His lips shook and he cried, 'Eat, you wicked girl, eat!' Shaken, Rachel picked up her spoon and pushed closer to the table, and her face went red as fire. When her mother saw this, she looked at her husband with surprise, and also at Rachel.

Between one course and the next, the guests talked about the day's doings. One of them, who once had studied but then had stopped, said, 'This was a fast in the true meaning of the word. For it is said in the Gemara: "Any fast which does not include the transgressors of Israel is no fast," and now some of the transgressors of Israel have fasted.' Another spoke up and said, 'As far as a fast goes, it was a fast, but what about the fasting money?' 'Fasting money? What is that?' Said the other, 'It is the payment a faster makes for what he would have laid out on his food if he had not fasted.' Someone else spoke up, 'How the Gemara begrudges the Jews any advantage, for they are not allowed to profit even from a fast.' Another spoke up, 'I undertake to pay five zlotys as fasting money. If you don't mind, Mrs. Zommer, take the money and give it to Hanoch's wife.' The whole company praised the giver, and he added, 'And if the mistress of the house thinks that the account is not correct, I will add another two or three zlotys.' By the time they had finished eating and drinking, a small sum had been collected for the benefit of that forsaken woman, Hanoch's wife.

Another spoke up and said, 'Now let us make a deal.' 'A deal? I have never heard of a deal in Szibucz.' 'Let us sell the grace after meals. Whoever gives most will lead the grace.' 'An American auction?' 'What's an American auction?' 'All those who want to buy pay in their money, and even if someone's bid was not the highest, he still has to leave as much as he specified.'

Babtchi asked, 'Can the women join in too?' 'For giving money, why not?' 'And if I win?' said Babtchi. 'You can give your father the honor,' was the reply. Said Lolik to Babtchi, 'What are you arguing about? Do you know how to say the grace?' 'Do you?' 'If I had been taught I would know.' By the time they had said grace, another sum was added to the first.

When I reached the rabbi's house I told him all that had happened. 'I will tell you something edifying,' the rabbi said. 'Once the great scholar, the author of *The Deliverances of Jacob*, was preaching on the duty of providing for a certain poor bride. After the sermon, the great scholar said, "Never has a preacher preached so persuasive a sermon as I have preached." The congregation were surprised to see a rabbi so God-fearing and distinguished in the Torah praising himself in this way. The rabbi noticed this and said, "I have persuaded

myself, and given her half her dowry." For that great scholar
was a rich man—learning and great wealth in one place. What
do you say to that, sir? Is such a power not to be envied?
Blessed is he who preaches well and practices well.'

The rabbi stroked his beard and said, 'Thank God that I
have had the privilege of arousing a number of people for the
benefit of that poor woman.'

Going from one subject to another, we came to the subject of the sages of the time.

The rabbi told me of things that had happened to him at
the great convention of the Agudat Israel in Vienna, where
some of the rabbis had objected to a legal ruling he had given
on a certain matter, and he had outargued them all, until they
admitted that the law was as he had said. While he was talking he handed me a bundle of letters that they had written
and he had written.

I glanced at the letters and remembered the words of a
certain wise man about the books of the wise men of the time.
If these authors knew what was written in their books, said he,
they too would be wise, for among their own words they cite
words from the Gemara.

'What do you say?' said the rabbi. 'Did I not outargue
them thoroughly?' 'What shall I say?' said I. 'I am from the
Land of Israel, and the scholars in the Land of Israel study
the Torah for its own sake, and it makes no difference who
outargues whom, for their only purpose is that things should
be made plain and the law should be clearly established.'
The rabbi grasped his beard angrily and said, 'And your
people are all righteous, I suppose. And those quarrels and
feuds, the slandering and the tale-bearing we hear about from
there, all these are only meant to clarify the law of the Torah?
Even the Zionists are ashamed of you.'

'It is a punishment from heaven,' said I, 'because they
opposed the kingdom of the House of David. But although
there are numerous men of strife in Jerusalem, there are more
men of peace, who deny themselves and forego the honor due
them, who study the Torah in poverty and rejoice at sufferings,
and because of their love of the Torah do not feel all the
troubles that befall them. Their actions are as goodly as their

learning, and all their deeds are sincere. And their prayers are as goodly as their actions. I will show you a congregation of pious men in Jerusalem who spend all their days in prayer, seeking nothing for their own affairs, but only that His Blessed Name be magnified in the worlds He has created. Some men are privileged to pray such a prayer once in seventy years and some once a year, but they pray in this way three times a day.' 'And what do your young men do?' said the rabbi. 'As for the young men of Israel,' I said, 'may I myself serve as expiation for their sins. They do not study like the scholars or pray like the pious men, but they plow and sow and plant, and give their lives for this Land that the Lord swore to give to our forefathers. That is why they have been privileged to have the Holy One, blessed be He, appoint them as guardians over His Land. Because they give their lives for the Land, He has entrusted the Land to them.'

The rabbi's eyes filled with tears, but he paid no heed to his tears and said, 'And what about the Sabbath?' A verse came to my mind: 'And see the good of Jerusalem all the days of thy life,' I quoted. ' "See" in the imperative. It is a man's duty to see what is good in Jerusalem, and not the evil, heaven forbid. On the Sabbath,' I said to him, 'Jews set their work aside and dress in goodly garments. He that can study, studies, and he that can read, reads, and he that can do neither strolls with his wife and children, speaking the Holy Tongue, and fulfilling in his own person the saying: "Everyone that walks four cubits in the Land of Israel and speaks the Holy Tongue is assured of life in the world to come." '

Again tears gathered in the rabbi's eyes and trickled down on his goodly beard, where they gleamed like pearls and precious stones set by the craftsman in a frame of gold. But the rabbi did not look at these pearls and precious stones, but thrust thorns into my eyes, saying things I will not repeat because of the ban on uttering slander against the Land of Israel.

I restrained my anger and answered him quietly, 'I know, sir, that your aim is Israel's welfare, but the spies in Moses' day also aimed at Israel's welfare, and what was the end of them? I should not like to sit in their company even in paradise.'

The rabbi put out his hand and laid it on my shoulder with great affection, until the warmth entered into me, and said, 'Do you know what has come into my mind? Let us go, you and I, and travel throughout the communities of the Exile to restore Israel to the good way.' 'Neither you nor I can do so,' I replied. 'Why not?' 'I, because I regard all Israel as innocent, and if it is a question of repentance, it is the Holy One, blessed be He—if I might say so—who ought to repent. As for you, sir, even if all Israel were like the ministering angels, you would not regard them as innocent.'

Midnight had come but our talk had not come to an end. Two or three times I rose to go, but the rabbi kept me back. Finally, when I took my leave, he rose and accompanied me outside.

The new moon showed clearly. The ground shone with the snow and the cold seemed to have thawed slightly. The air seemed to be changing gradually—heaven only knew whether for good or evil.

CHAPTER TWO AND THIRTY

In the Marketplace

From the day that Hanoch disappeared and Reb Hayim started to serve in his place, I have been free to my own devices, for Hanoch used to bring wood, water, and kerosene, and sweep the floor on Sabbath eves, while I used to look after the trimming of the candles and the lighting of the stove, but now Reb Hayim performs all these duties himself. He even lights the stove, because one day I was late in coming, so he came and lit it; from then onward he has been the one to light the stove.

That day I went out to the marketplace. First, because for several days I had not seen the town, and second, because the stove had been repaired and plastered, and the smell disturbed me.

The frost had weakened somewhat, and the snow had

shriveled and blackened; even in places where it had gathered in heaps it began to show cracks. The blackened snow and the cracks, although they announced that the frost was less, made me feel melancholy. The town was almost empty. The shop-keepers stood in their shops, but no customers came to buy, so not a living soul was to be seen. Perhaps a crow or a raven showed in the skies above, but on the earth below there was no one to be seen but I, who was occupied in making my way through the mud, until I reached the post office.

When I saw the post office I remembered the days of my youth, when I sat tranquilly in my father's house and poured out my thoughts in letters to friends about the idleness and the boredom and the weakening faith in the heart and the future that was wrapped in mist. The sun shone in the heavens and the gardens flourished and the trees produced fruit and the fields were full of corn and a man's livelihood was secure and a Jew could live like a human being. Nevertheless a grey sadness hung heavily over our heads and the heart was not joyful. Sometimes this sadness would luxuriate in melancholy like a maggot in an apple, and sometimes the melancholy would gnaw into it like a maggot. What did we lack at that time? Our main lack was that we did not know what we lacked. Suddenly a new light gleamed and lit up the heart. From far and near we heard that we too were like all the nations, we too had a land like all other lands, and it depended only on our own will to go up to this land and become a nation. The clever people of the time made a jest of the whole matter and showed with the clearest arguments that it was no more than an illusion. Even worse, if the nations heard that we were ambitious to become a nation, they would say: If so, what do you want here? Be off with you and go to your own country. On the surface these seemed to be sensible words, but the heart did not agree with them. In those days the mag-got ceased to gnaw at the heart, and that sadness, which was hard as iron, became a kind of gracious melancholy, like the grace of a man who has longings for something he loves. What can I add, what more can I tell? Anyone who has not experi-enced it does not understand it, and anyone who has expe-rienced it knows it by himself. Then speech was given to the dumb, and the writer's pen to the heavy of hand. The boy could not yet write two or three words correctly, and he already wrote poetry. According to reason he should have first learned language and grammar, and read the books of the poets before him; yet he did not do so, but wrote poems from his heart. And lo and behold, a miracle happened to him. A handful of words, which were not even enough to draw up a shopkeeper's bill, sufficed for the writing of a poem. It was then that I wrote my song, 'Devotion Faithful unto Death.' This was the song with which Yeruham Freeman reproached me, saying that all his troubles began with it, because he went up to the Land of Israel, with all that followed. Many years have passed and again we stand here in the marketplace of Szibucz as in the early days, when tedium devoured the heart and idleness weakened our hands.

There stands this man in Szibucz, like a stone the sculptor has wrenched from the mountain to give it a shape, but thrown aside because it was not fit to take a shape. There lies that stone in the place from which it was taken, yet it does not adhere to its place. Dust and grit cling to it, and it sprouts grass like the good earth, and the Holy One, blessed be He, brings forth the dew and brings down the rain, and the grass grows higher and higher. Really, according to reason, that stone should be content, for it has become a plot of soil in itself, which produces grass and even buds and flowers. Why then is it not joyful? Because it does not forget the hour when it lay in the sculptor's hand. Why did the craftsman not give it a shape? The craftsman is engrossed in his work and does not respond to every questioner. And even if he were ready to respond, the stone is unable to roll over and over and go to him to ask, for it is hard to move because the dust and grit cling to it. And since the stone lies in its place, it looks out over its surroundings.

Like that stone, let us, too, look. After all, we are free to look and to see.

The well of the marketplace stood as usual, pouring out water on all sides, and setting free a damp chill from itself and its two pipes, and from the damp straw in which it was wrapped. Whenever I see the ocean, or a river, or a brook, or a lake, or a spring, or a well, I like to gaze at the water. But at that moment I said to myself: If only I had a wagon, so that I could go back to the hotel and throw myself on my bed.

No wagon came to take me to the hotel, so I remained standing in the marketplace. In front of me sat a few peddler women wrapped in rags, with sacking wound around their legs and various kinds of boxes lying before them, from which rose all kinds of smells of pickled cabbage and apples that had rotted. No doubt there were goods for sale in or on these boxes. Languidly, the peddler women fixed their eyes on me and asked, without word or speech: What kind of goods are you looking for? Three or four women were walking around the marketplace with their baskets in their hands. Among them was Krolka. She did not see me, and it was good she did not, although I did not know why I should care whether she saw me or not. Finally she turned her head toward me and said, 'You here too, sir? I came out to buy something in the market, but there's nothing to buy—only pickled cabbage or rotted carrots. But what I refused yesterday I will buy today. Isn't that what they say, "The Jews despised the manna and now they eat filth"?'

The women went away. The peddlers shrank into their rags, screwed up their eyes, and closed their lips, and the marketplace was silent. The well suddenly gave tongue, its water flowed faster, and a damper chill began to rise.

One woman opened her eyes and looked at me, saying, 'Will the gentleman buy something?' I said to myself: What does this foolish woman want me to buy from her? There was Krolka, the servant at the hotel, who had inspected all the boxes and yet went away empty-handed, and this peddler woman says, 'Buy something from me.'

'Sir,' said the woman's neighbor, 'buy from her. Buy from her, sir. You'll be doing a great good deed—a house full of orphans, living orphans.' 'What shall I take it in, mother?' said I, 'I haven't a basket.' 'Buy whatever you like, sir,' said she, 'and Hanoch's wife will bring you the goods to any place you say. Isn't that so, Hanoch's wife?' Hanoch's wife nodded her head to indicate yes. Said her neighbor, 'Why don't you tell the gentleman that you will bring him his goods?' And to me she said, 'She's a sorrowful woman and she finds it hard to speak. Alas, Hanoch's wife, you want to be a peddler but you don't want to open your mouth. As I'm a true Jewess, sir, it's good stuff she has, apples and eggs. Apples you would think had just been picked from the tree.'

'What goods do you have here?' said I to Hanoch's wife. 'A dozen eggs a Gentile woman brought me from the village,' said she, 'all laid this week.' 'The gentleman can believe her,' said her neighbor. 'She doesn't tell a lie.' 'Good,' said I. 'Here is the money, and bring them to me to the old Beit Midrash.' 'I knew the gentleman had a good heart,' said her neighbor. 'Perhaps you need something else?' Said I to myself: If I do not need anything, perhaps Reb Hayim does. I said to Hanoch's wife, 'Have you something else?' 'She can bring you anything you like, sir,' said her neighbor. 'Here is the money,' said I. 'Bring me a pound of coffee, the best coffee, and three pounds of sugar.'

I went back to the Beit Midrash and waited for Hanoch's wife to bring me my purchases. When she brought them my spirits sank. How should I give Reb Hayim my goods?

After the people had left the Beit Midrash and when I was about to lock the door, I told Reb Hayim the whole story and said to him, 'As I did not refuse that woman, you will not refuse me, and will take what the woman brought.' Reb Hayim's face paled and he looked angry. 'What was I to do?' said I. 'I did not run after the chance to do a good deed. It was a matter of necessity. Now what shall I do with all these things? Perhaps I should take them to the Land of Israel and throw them into the Dead Sea?' Reb Hayim swallowed his anger and said melodiously, 'There is no need for you to trouble yourself with such things. Thank God, I am short of nothing. I saved while I was working and I have enough to keep myself for the time being, and if God spares me He will provide me with a livelihood in the future as well.' I took hold of his coat and said, 'Do me the same kindness as I did to Hanoch's wife.' He took the goods and said, 'May God bless you.' 'And you too, sir,' said I.

Reb Hayim and His Daughters

This is the place to tell something of Reb Hayim's daughters. Indeed, I should have done so at the beginning of his story, but I did not know enough about the details. Now that they have become clearer to me, I shall try to put them down.

Reb Hayim had four daughters. One of them was married to an old man in a village far away from our town, and another ran away, no one knows where. Some say she went to Russia, and some say she went to an emigrants' training farm. One stayed with her mother, but she was not always in Szibucz because from time to time she used to go to the village to help her married sister, who was burdened with sons and daughters, her own, and her husband's from his first wife, and what his first wife brought her husband from her first husband. And one of Reb Hayim's daughters, little Zippora, the youngest, did not stir from the house.

That old man who married Reb Hayim's daughter, Naphtali Zvi Hilferding was his name, had been orphaned of both father and mother in his childhood and brought up by Reb Hayim's father-in-law. When Reb Hayim came to Szibucz, the orphan became his attendant. Naphtali Zvi became fond of Reb Hayim, and Reb Hayim became so fond of Naphtali Zvi that he began to draw Naphtali Zvi closer to him, and talked to Naphtali Zvi even about matters outside the scope of an attendant. And the truth is that Reb Hayim learned a great deal from Naphtali Zvi's conversation, not only about worldly matters, but even in matters of Torah. Reb Hayim was a prodigy of learning, and like most such prodigies he used to repel people with his behavior. And when the controversy began with the adjudicator, and Reb Hayim would forbid what the other permitted and permit what the other forbade, all the scholars were antagonized by his rulings. The impression arose that he was giving rulings that were not according to the Law, and they would have liked to so clip his wings that he could not go on. What did Naphtali Zvi do? He would not leave him alone until he had written down all his reasons and arguments and submitted them to the great scholars of the day. They would reply, and whether they agreed with him or not, their answers would add to his prestige. So Naphtali Zvi would manage and guide him in other matters. Had it not been for him, Reb Hayim would have shared the fate of most prodigies, who at first studied the Torah in poverty but when they married the daughters of wealthy ignoramuses and emerged from suffering and exertion to a life of ease, soon lost interest in their studies. Thus Naphtali Zvi spent many years and did not marry, until the war came and he drifted to a certain place where he lived with a relative, a widow, whose husband had left her a shopful of goods and a houseful of children. Naphtali Zvi began to look after the orphans and busy himself with the goods. I do not know who was responsible—he, or the widow, or the Lord—but before much time had passed she married him, bore him a son and a daughter, and died.

So he was left a widower with a houseful of children, hers and theirs, and he needed a woman to look after them, as his wife had previously needed a man to look after the orphans of her first husband. Once he went to Szibucz to pray at the graves of his fathers. He visited Reb Hayim's wife to ask how she was. At that time all her daughters were still with her. He saw the eldest, who was ripe for marriage, and the little ones growing up, and the house empty—not even a worn-out copper for a dowry. He felt pity for the woman and her daughters, and he said to himself: I will engage one of them to look after my children and pay her for the service. Thus I will make things easier for the mother, and there will also be a dowry for the daughter. But he began to doubt whether this would be seemly. Was it in keeping with the honor of Reb Hayim that his daughter should be a maid, especially a maid to his own attendant? Although he would not make her work hard and would greet her with respect, nevertheless there were grounds for misgivings, for sometimes a man comes home hungry from the shop and his meal is not ready, so he scolds the maid—and thus he would spoil his good deed in one brief moment. What, then, should he do, for they needed help and he could see no other way before him? So he decided to ask the mother. As he was going to the mother, it occurred to him to speak to her about herself: that she should marry him and free herself and her daughters from the cares of a livelihood. But his heart rebuked him: Wretch! When a vessel has been put to a holy use, can it be used for a profane purpose? So he did not talk to her either about herself or about her daughter, but he began visiting her frequently. He saw Reb Hayim's eldest daughter, with whom he used to play in her childhood, at a time when the house was full of every luxury. He remembered those days when he used to carry her in his arms and she used to look into his eyes, and he would close one eye and the baby would wail, 'Oh, the eyeball has run away,' and he would open his eye again and the baby would clap her little hands in joy over the eyeball that had come back. And again, when the hair of his beard and mustache had begun to grow, she would stroke him and say, 'Grass is growing on your cheek, there's a plant growing under your nose.'

There sat that old man, who many years before had been young, with a glass of tea before him, poured out by Reb Hayim's daughter. The old man puts his hand on the glass, the steam rises from the glass, and his hands and his heart grow warmer and warmer. His lips are opened and all that was hidden in his heart rises to his tongue. And he goes on telling about days gone by, days when Reb Hayim lived honored by all, and half the town followed him and wished to appoint him rabbi. The old man looks at Reb Hayim's daughters and says, 'Days like those that have gone will never come back.' And although they have to mourn for those days, of which not the slightest trace has remained, their hearts are moved, and they want to hear more. Especially the eldest daughter, who can remember the greatness of her father when she was little, and when that old man who sits and tells the story used to dandle her on his knees, making one eyeball run away and then bringing it back.

As the old man speaks, the house grows more spacious, and its furnishings are transformed, as if the light of early days shone upon them. For many years the daughters have not sat so peacefully and at ease or heard such pleasant things as those the old man tells. While he was sitting he began thinking again: I am wealthy and my livelihood is sure, but I cannot give a dowry to Reb Hayim's daughters, for my wife's daughters from her first husband are also growing up and I must find them husbands. He began arguing with himself: I, who used to look after Reb Hayim's affairs, cannot look after my own. He took his glass, drank what was left of the tea, said the appropriate blessing, 'Creator of all lives and of their needs,' and went away.

When he returned home he was gripped by nostalgia for Reb Hayim's house. Little by little he began to put out of his mind the needs of the daughters and began to think about himself, living as he was without a wife. And it could really be said that all his life he had been without a wife. Although he had already been married and had had children from his wife, he had only married her because of the home and the livelihood she brought him, and now that she was dead he ought to look for his true mate. That was easy to say and hard to do, for his mate was twenty years younger than he, and moreover she was Reb Hayim's daughter. True, the world had changed: superior people had declined and inferiors had risen. This war had made the poor goodly and the rich ugly. If he had had it in his power, he would have crowned Reb Hayim's daughters with gold, especially his oldest daughter, who had reached her ripeness and was ready for marriage. But if he gave her his money he would be robbing the sons and daughters his wife had brought him from her first husband, as well as those she had borne for himself. And moreover, was there anyone who was fit to be that girl's husband? In any case, there was one way out of all these complications. And what was that? If he married her he would rid her of the worry of finding a dowry.

And what were the thoughts of the girl? She took after her father, who relied on Naphtali Zvi his attendant. When he visited them again, he said to her, 'I do not know if it is clear to you why I have come. And if it is clear to you, I ask you not to reply immediately. I will stay in the town two or three days. During that time consult your mother and yourself, and then give me a clear answer. Now I am going away to look after my affairs and I will bid you goodbye.'

When he returned he did not repeat what he had said, nor did she say anything to him. When her mother came in he rose and told her he had said thus-and-thus to her daughter. 'And what did you answer him?' the mother asked her daughter. She lowered her head and said, 'I do not know what to answer.' 'Yesterday,' said the mother, 'you knew, and today you have forgotten.' 'I have not forgotten,' said the daughter. 'If so,' said the mother, 'answer our friend, or perhaps I should answer in your place.' 'I will answer myself,' said the girl. The mother rose, called her other daughters, and said, 'Come and wish your sister good luck.' So they set up the bridal canopy and she went with him. Since she was weak and tender, she asked one of her sisters to live with her to help her.

I have not seen Reb Hayim's daughters, except the little one, who lives with her mother and used to come to her father to wash his linen, for the eldest was married in another town, and one daughter lives with her, and one has run away to Russia or to a training farm for emigrants. This little one, whose name is Zippora, is a silent girl; when I would ask her something she would fix her eyes on me in alarm, as one who is afraid and pleads that no one touch her. In the course of time she grew accustomed to me and would greet me with 'Shalom' in the Holy Tongue—although she did not know the Holy Tongue, and I am doubtful if she even knew how to read. I wanted to hint to her father that he should teach her to read, but I changed my mind. I said to myself: He himself does not study; why then should he teach his daughter?

About the Houses of Prayer in Our Town

Let us return to the Beit Midrash. The quorum assembles as usual, and we offer up public prayer. In the course of time, we have been joined by several shopkeepers, who come for the Morning Service so as to warm their bones before going out to their shops. It has gone so far that we hold three services, one after the other. In the course of time, even Hasidim have begun to come to our old Beit Midrash.

And here I must digress to talk about the various houses of prayer—Batei Midrashot, *shtiblech, shilechlech, kloisen,* and *kleislech*—that existed in our town.

At first all the communities from Germany, Poland and Lithuania, Bohemia and Moravia used to pray according to the Ashkenazi rite, which they received from their fathers, and their fathers from their fathers, directing their prayer toward the gate that is meant for them in heaven. And just as they all used the same rite in their prayer, so did they use special melodies, some of which were handed down at Sinai, and others received from the martyrs of Germany, who, when their enemies offered them up at the stake and they rose to heaven in the flames, uttered songs and praises in ecstasy and thanksgiving, their souls filled with ardor as they approached the Lord. They did not know that they were singing, but the voice sang by itself; and the early cantors wove this melody into the words of the prayers. And a man can still feel, when he is praying truly, that the voice sings by itself, even if he himself is not really a melodious singer. It is because of this that, wherever a Jew prays, the prayers of all Israel are uttered. And even the heavens intended their prayer to be like the prayer of Israel, as it is said, 'The heavens declare the glory of God; and the firmament showeth His handiwork.' Who is the handiwork of the Holy One, blessed be He? These are the children of Israel, of whom the Scriptures testify, 'He hath made thee, and established thee.' When the higher ones saw this, they thought in error that the days of the Messiah were near, and they revealed to the chosen individuals of that generation the secrets of prayer, the secrets of its purposes and combinations and meanings, so that these individuals should try with the power of prayer to bring nearer the End. But the time of redemption had not yet arrived for Israel in that generation; and their hearts were confused and they mistook the promise of redemption for the redemption itself. And so there were a number of men of Israel who mistakenly thought that their redemption was already here, and they abandoned the customs of their forefathers and adopted new ones, especially in their way of praying. The gates of heaven were confounded and their prayers entered in confusion, and had it not been for the Baal Shem Tov, of blessed memory, and his disciples, who knows what would have happened to us—heaven forbid?

And it was the Baal Shem Tov who replaced our rite with the rite of the exiles from Spain, descendants of the lords and nobles of the tribe of Judah. Because he saw that we were approaching the End, and the kingdom of the House of David was destined to return to its glory, he ruled that men should pray in the manner of David, peace be upon him—like a king's servants who direct their acts according to the words of the king.

When the Baal Shem Tov passed away, and his holy disciples after him, their disciples and their disciples' disciples began to differ; each sect claimed that it was following the holy Baal Shem Tov and his holy disciples, and began to alter the prayers and the melodies. Some adorned their prayers with shepherds' melodies, and said they were melodies handed down from King David, melodies that were carried into captivity among the worshippers of stars and constellations; some danced as they prayed, and clapped their hands and knocked their heads on the wall, in order to drive away strange thoughts that confused their prayers; others introduced into their prayer expressions that are entirely meaningless, and some of these are a clear interruption of prayer, like *Tatte suesser*, which means 'Sweet Father' in the Yiddish tongue. And there are reliable witnesses who testify that they heard from their fathers and grandfathers, who heard from the old men of their generation that they heard that the men of the sect used to exclaim during the reciting of the 'Hear, O Israel' '*Dawaj pozar!*' meaning 'Give fire' in Polish, which is to say, 'O blessed One, inflame my heart in Thy service.'

In our town of Szibucz there were also a number of people who followed this road, and the leaders of the generation arose and expelled them from the congregation. So they went and built a synagogue for themselves; this is the house of the Hasidim, which they call a *shtibel*, and the rest of the population call it the *Leitzim Shilechel*, the Scoffers' Synagogue.

As the zaddikim, the wonder-rabbis, multiplied, so did the numbers of the Hasidim, their followers. Some followed one zaddik and some another. Finally the Hasidim of Kossov multiplied in our town and they built a house of prayer for themselves, the Kossovite Synagogue or *Kossover Shilechel*, in King Street near the King's Well, and this is the well from which Sobieski King of Poland drank when he returned from his victorious war, and from which we draw our water for the making of matzoh.

When the Zaddik of Kossov died, his elder son took over his father's chair and the younger went to Vizhnitz, where he established his residence. The Kossovite Hasidim were thus divided into two sects: one followed the elder son and the other followed Vizhnitz. The Kossovite Hasidim in our town did not produce offspring like themselves, and their sons followed neither one zaddik nor the other. Apart from the Sephardi rite, nothing was left with the sons except the customs of the Hasidim.

As time passed, new men came to Szibucz, some of them hasidic sons-in-law who came to live with their fathers-in-law, and others simply ordinary Hasidim. These went to pray in the Kossovite prayer house, because the services there were conducted according to the Spanish rite.

There was another place of assembly for Hasidim in our town, the new Beit Midrash, so called to distinguish it from our old Beit Midrash, and there our illustrious and righteous teacher, the rabbi of the town, used to pray. Besides his greatness in the Torah, he used to devote himself to the mystic wisdom of the Kabbalah; all the princes of the Torah used to rejoice with him in his novel interpretations of the law, and seekers after salvation used to come to receive a blessing from his lips. (The illustrious author of *The Deliverances of Jacob* said of him in jest, 'Let us thank the Almighty that this illustrious scholar has left us and followed the way of Hasidism, for otherwise we would not have been able to find our bearings in the Beit Midrash; he would have overwhelmed all of us in arguments of religious law with his penetration and scholarship.') This zaddik did not beget offspring like himself, and when he died his Beit Midrash became a house of prayer for the householders, who prayed according to the Sephardi rite like their forefathers, but did not favor Hasidism like them. This is the strength of Szibucz, that it outlives the new and returns to its old ways—except for the Sephardi rite, which has already taken root.

Although Hasidism disappeared from the Beit Midrash, a number of Hasidim remained there, but they were few and insignificant, and did not lift up their heads. If anyone was found dancing or clapping his hands during the prayers, he would be silenced with a rebuke and told, 'This is a holy place and not a *kleisel*.' Once the townsfolk came to the Beit Midrash and found the bones of a goose, for the Hasidim had held a New Moon feast there during the night, and the whole Beit Midrash was in an uproar over this profanation of the Divine Name by people who turned the holy place into a tavern.

In those days the Zaddik of Ruzhin bought the estate of Potik, which is close to Szibucz, where he established the zaddik, his son, who later moved his residence to Tchortkov and became famous the world over as the Tchortkover. A number of people from Szibucz followed his leadership, and they hired a room for themselves. Some of the remnants of the Hasidim in the Beit Midrash came together and joined them. In time, the room was not enough for them and they built themselves a *klois*. This was the Tchortkovite *klois,* which had goodly men and goodly customs, for most of the worshippers were distinguished for learning, good manners, and knowledge of melody, and their prayers were sweet, not with

shouts and cries like the rest of the Hasidim, and not with
limbs frozen stiff, like the Misnagdim, their opponents, but
like the Hasidim of Ruzhin, who know before whom they
stand. And their appearance was as goodly as their prayer:
they did not have disheveled earlocks and beards and bare
necks like the Hasidim of Belz, but their earlocks were tidy,
their beards in order, and their necks covered. And their
speech was like their appearance, quiet and not noisy. They
engaged in trade and studied the Torah; on festival days they
would hold a feast in the *klois* with wine and nuts, dancing
and singing, 'Thou hast chosen us,' and so forth, and in winter,
on the Sabbath eve after the meal, they would assemble and
sit together, drinking brandy and eating chickpeas cooked
with pepper, singing, 'They that keep the Sabbath will rejoice
in Thy kingdom,' and sweetening the occasion with pleasant
tales and words of learning. When they celebrated the anniversary of the zaddik's death they would make a great feast,
with meat and wine, singing and dancing. The rest of the
people also came when they heard the sound of the rejoicing,
and looked on in surprise to see such God-fearing men dancing
so freely. While they stood watching, a Hasid would come,
take hold of one of them, draw him into the circle and dance
with him, until his heart, too, would be caught up with their
enthusiasm, and he would join the Tchortkovite Hasidim.

By no means did the whole of the *klois* follow the Tchortkover. There were certain Hasidim there who were followers
of the zaddikim of Sadagora, Husiatin, Vizhnitz, and Otonia,
and of others who did not take part in the well-known controversy. The Sadagora and Husiatin Hasidim were regarded in
the *klois* as Tchortkovites, for their zaddikim were brothers
of the Tchortkover. The Vizhnitz and the Otonia Hasidim
were regarded as inferior to these, for although the Vizhnitz
and the Otonia zaddikim were relatives of the Tchortkover,
they were not approved by Tchortkov. Still lower were the
Hasidim of the other zaddikim, who were not related to the
Zaddik of Ruzhin; they were like stepchildren in the place.
On festivals and solemn days, when everyone who was called
up for the reading of the Torah regarded it as a sacred duty
to call for blessings on the Tchortkover and all his offspring,

and his brothers the zaddikim and all their offspring, the Tchortkovites did not permit blessings to be recited for the other rabbis, for the Tchortkover is of the seed of the House of David, and if the generation were deserving, he would be King of Israel, and it is not to a king's honor that a commoner should be blessed together with him. And sometimes on the jubilation day of these other rabbis, the cantor did not refrain from reciting the Tahanun, the prayer of supplication that is not said on joyful occasions.

There was one Vizhnitz Hasid there, resolute and well-to-do, who went off with his nine sons and built a separate *klois*. This is the Vizhnitz *klois*, near the black pond behind the butcher's shop. They were joined by other Hasidim who felt like dependent strangers in the Tchortkov *klois*, as well as those the Tchortkovites did not admit because their rabbis had taken part in the well-known controversy. And here the same thing happened to them as had happened in the Tchortkov *klois*, for the Vizhnitz Hasidim ignored them as the Tchortkovites had done. So some of them returned to their former place, while some submitted to their sufferings in silence.

When the Hasidim split, it might have been thought that the congregation of the *klois* would dwindle. But in fact it did not, for some of the sons of the Tchortkovite Hasidim who had married daughters of Szibucz were in the habit of coming to pray there and, needless to say, every Tchortkovite Hasid took husbands for his daughters from the members of his own sect. They ate at their fathers-in-law's tables and had no need to earn a living, so they used to sit in the *klois* and study the Torah in peace and tranquillity. On winter nights, when they would sit each with his candle in his hand, their voices reaching the street and the golden chains on their chests reflecting the light, the neighbors would wish themselves likewise blessed, and say, 'Oh that we had sons like them.'

But the neighbors' wish was in vain; there was no one to whom the wish could apply, for the secular schools had already laid waste the Torah, and even our old Beit Midrash where the Torah was profoundly studied did not bring forth sons to the Torah. The scholars still sat there engaged in study, but it brought them no radiance, for they lacked peace of mind because their sons and sons-in-law were not students of the Torah. And why were some privileged to have sons and sons-in-law who were scholars while some were not? Because the people of our old Beit Midrash believed in all the branches of worldly wisdom, too, for they would say that Torah and worldly wisdom came down from heaven together, and anyone who is deficient in one branch of wisdom is also deficient in the Torah. So when the secular schools were opened to the Jews, they sent their sons to them, so that they should supplement the wisdom of the Torah. Once the sons had entered the schools, they did not return to the Beit Midrash, but became lawyers or doctors or pharmacists or bookkeepers, or just ordinary men without Torah or wisdom either. On the other hand, the Hasidim, who mocked at extraneous wisdom and avoided secular culture, did not send their sons to the schools, so that most of them remained with their fathers, and when Hasidism dwindled it was re-plenished from the Torah. This is what sustained it, so that it produced most of the ritual slaughterers, cantors, and teachers. And even the rabbis, slaughterers, cantors, and teachers who did not believe in Hasidism in their hearts sub-ordinated themselves to the zaddikim of the generation, for any rabbi, slaughterer, or teacher who was not subordinate to the zaddik had no hope in our community.

There was another feature of our *klois*: two or three times a year we would travel to visit our rabbi in Tchortkov. Those who have been in Tchortkov know Tchortkov, and for those who have not been there no tongue can describe it. Not only did we have the privilege of meeting that zaddik, but Hasidim from most countries met there, and we heard what was going on in the dispersion of Israel. Sometimes marriages were arranged there and new Hasidim were added to us, until we stood crowded in the *klois* for lack of place, and had it not been for the war they would have built a new house of prayer.

There was still another feature of our *klois*: from time to time visitors arrived on their way to Tchortkov or back. When a visitor came to the *klois* he would donate refresh-ments, or bring a new melody, or tell what he had seen or heard. The conversation of the travelers made even a week-day into a kind of minor festival. And sometimes the visitor would cast his eye on a young man to make a match between him and his daughter, and he would write the marriage contract and make a feast for the Hasidim.

We said above that they used to tell tales of the zaddikim, but so that you should make no mistake I will tell you that in these stories they did not mention the early zaddikim, or even the Baal Shem Tov, of blessed memory. It happened once that an old man came to our town and told a story about the Baal Shem Tov. One of our people said, 'If this had been true, it would have been mentioned in *The Book of the Praises of the Baal Shem Tov*,' and the Hasidim smiled, for they did not regard that book as authentic.

The Tchortkovite Hasidim used to talk of nothing else but the Tchortkover's fathers and his fathers' fathers, and of his brother, and of the Tchortkover himself: how the door of his room opened and how he sat on his chair and how he let his head fall back and who was present on that occasion and how he would enter the *klois* on the eve of Yom Kippur and recite the prayer 'Answer Us.' You may not think these things important, but every Tchortkovite knows that every single movement of that zaddik is designed for our benefit in this world and the next.

CHAPTER FIVE AND THIRTY

Additional Matter

In those days there shone the light of the Zaddik of Kupiczince. This zaddik did not inherit followers from his fathers, but won them for himself. He would go out from time to time to the cities and towns like the early hasidic rabbis, and wherever he went the women and the simple folk came to him, those who were not accustomed to travel to see the zaddikim, but believed in their power. Once he came to Szibucz for the Sabbath. A number of the townsfolk—even some of the well-to-do—gathered around him. Some came secretly, because they were afraid their friends might see them, but when they came they found some of their friends, who had also come in secret, for Szibucz was still regarded as a town of Misnagdim, and whoever was not called a Hasid boasted of being a Misnaged. So this zaddik came for one Sabbath and stayed for two, because of the numbers who came to him. On the two Sabbaths that he stayed in Szibucz, he presided at his table in the rabbi's Beit Midrash, and many came to him, either out of faith in the zaddikim or in order to see how zaddikim conducted themselves. This zaddik did not discourse on the Torah, for all his ways were like those of the Ruzhiner's grandsons—he behaved in royal style. When he sat at the head of the table, with the *shtreimel* set straight on his head, like the Ruzhiner's sons, and his little beard descending on his stiff collar, and rapped on the table with his fingers, humming 'Chal, chal, chal,' all the congregation were enthralled. And when he let his head drop backward and looked up, one old man, of the last of the Ruzhin Hasidim, swore that the zaddik from Kupiczince was exactly like the Ruzhiner, both in his holy appearance and in his holy movements. Before he left the town, a number of people got together and agreed to establish a *klois* in his name. Next year he came again, and now something happened that showed that this zaddik was important in the eyes of those on high and on earth. What happened was this: the Tchortkov Hasidim were indignant at him for trespassing on their territory, for Szibucz was regarded as a Tchortkover's town. And when the Rabbi of Kupiczince came to the town, the Tchortkovites did not go to welcome him. It went so far that in the same train in which the zaddik had arrived an old man, one of the leading Tchortkov Hasidim, was coming back to Szibucz, and everyone expected that he would go to the zaddik to receive his greeting. He did not do so, however, but hurried into the town so that he should not mingle with those who had come to meet the zaddik. Before he reached home he caught cold and fell ill, and everyone understood that he had been punished for not giving honor to this zaddik.

Even if this was not a prodigy, it was a lesson to those

who showed disrespect to the zaddik—even if we explain the incident by way of nature. And how by way of nature? Well, this old man was a weak fellow, and because he was running he became overheated and he sweated and caught cold. And if you like we can explain that his heart was agitated by all the honor that was being paid to one who was not his rabbi, and he fell ill through his agitation. Or, if you like, we can explain that his heart smote him, for that zaddik was of the seed of Ruzhiner and he deserved that the man should pay him honor, but in Tchortkov they had told the man that he need not do so. One way or another, the whole town became aware of the power of the rabbi from Kupiczince, and that anyone who offends his honor is punished. When I went to visit the sick man and told him what people were saying, he took my hand in his and smiled and said, 'You surely know Ephraim the idiot, the one whom they call the prophet? When he comes I give him alms. One day I did not have any small change and I sent him away with nothing. He cursed me that my windows should be broken, and before an hour had passed a heavy hail came down and broke some of the windows in my house. I said to my wife, "Did you hear the curses of that idiot?" She sighed and said, "Yes, I heard." I said to her, "If you ever run across another wonderworker, now you'll be able to recognize him right away." '

In any case, a third *klois* was built in Szibucz. This was the Kupiczince *klois,* which stands in Flourmill Street opposite the bathhouse. The Kupiczince Hasidim in our town came from the simple folk, who envied the Hasidim for whom every day was like a holy day and who treated each other with love, brotherhood, and friendship, regarding everyone who was not a Hasid as lacking in a cardinal principle of Judaism. The Kupiczince Hasidim were joined by a few intellectuals who had been Zionists at first but had not found what they wanted in the Company of Zion. So they changed their clothes and wore *shtreimels* on the Sabbath, but their heart's desire became a melancholy of their soul, for Hasidism is not acquired only by a man's desire and will, but by the preparation of the soul and the devotion of the heart. However it was, a third *klois* was established in Szibucz.

I do not remember whether the Rabbi of Kupiczince came to Szibucz a third time, and if he came whether his spirit was delighted with his Hasidim. If I were one of those who are used to piling up conjectures, I should say that once the *klois* had been established it was not worth his while to come. So long as he had no *klois* he might hope that once he had one many Hasidim would come; but now that the *klois* was established his limits were set, for if many had been inclined to follow him they would already have joined his *klois*. When a poor man has lit his little stove to cook some grits in milk, he cannot use it to roast an ox.

Thus, in short, there came to be three established hasidic prayer houses in our town, in addition to that of the Kossov Hasidim, which we have mentioned. Then the war came and destroyed them all, and all the Hasidim were scattered, some this way and some that. Some died by sword or famine, by pestilence or other plagues—heaven save us from them—while some submerged themselves in the vanities of this world in coffeehouses and card playing, except for a few individuals who withstood the troubles of the time and held firm to the faith of the sages. When the war quieted down and the roads were opened, some of these returned to the town and found it in ruins; they repaired their houses somewhat and their livelihoods somewhat and dedicated themselves to the affairs of the spirit. The Tchortkov Hasidim joined together as one man and once again made a *klois* for themselves. It was not like it had been in the beginning, but they achieved what the others did not; so all the Hasidim in the town joined up with those of Tchortkov in their house of prayer. They were almost on the point of becoming one company, all of them, and accepting authority with love, for Israel had already been tried during the days of the war and suffered one exile after another, and it was for them to realize that, so long as we have not been privileged to see the complete redemption, we must bow our heads before the powerful. But Israel has grown accustomed to the exile of Edom, and however difficult it may be, they can endure it; but they cannot endure the exile of Jacob, which is the most grievous of all exiles. So when the other Hasidim saw that there was no future for them in the Tchortkovite *klois,* they began to split away and leave, one this way and one that, and some of them came to our old Beit Midrash, although prayers were recited there according to the Ashkenazi rite.

Although prayers were recited there according to the Ashkenazi rite, these newcomers did not introduce changes in the customs of the place, nor was confusion brought into the Beit Midrash; needless to say, no one ever brought in brandy, either at a Yahrzeit of his own, to mark the anniversary of a relative's death, or at a Yahrzeit of his rabbi's. It was a strict rule in our old Beit Midrash, more than in the others, that anyone who came there to pray became like one of us. Except for the tales they told one another, you would not have known that those who now joined us were Hasidim.

These tales, some of which we have mentioned—some tell of the greatness of the zaddikim of the previous generation, and some of the zaddikim in our generation, but most of them are tales of miracles, in which the miracle is greater than the need for it and cannot be explained quite properly, except on the assumption that the zaddikim are the most beloved of the Almighty and therefore He changes the disposition of nature and transforms the order of creation in order to give pleasure to those who love Him. All of these tales start as earthly and end as spiritual, the hand of man and the hand of God acting in turn and helping one another, so that if one is afflicted by weakness the other comes to support it. And even in matters of the body the Holy One, blessed be He, performs miracles on behalf of the zaddikim, sending Elijah the Prophet to bring them a loaf of bread and bringing down a seraph to light their pipes. Oh that you could have lived to see this day, Rabbi Avigdor, you who one Sabbath eve at nightfall expelled Rabbi Uriel, the rabbi of the Hasidim, and now his disciples' disciples sit in your Beit Midrash and tell of the miracles and wonders performed by rabbis who could not hold a candle to Rabbi Uriel either in learning or in piety.

CHAPTER SIX AND THIRTY

The Letter

Since the day Reb Hayim undertook full care of the Beit Midrash, that burden has been lifted from my shoulders, so that I linger in bed, and take my time over meals, and chat with any visitor I happen to meet.

The visitors I come across in the hotel are practical men and have no inclination for idle talk, but they take time off to speak to that man who has come here, because he is from the Land of Israel, and a Jew ought to know what is going on there.

The Land of Israel has already ceased to be a matter for meetings, speeches, and banquets, and has become a matter about which most people seriously wish to know—some in time of trouble and some before the trouble comes. When another guest talks to me about the Land of Israel, if he is good at accounts he takes out pen and paper and calculates how much is the income from a house in Tel Aviv or a small farm in the countryside. Sometimes the calculation fits in well with his house and store in his own town, and if he sold them he could settle in the Land and set up a business there. But between you and me, the house and the store are mortgaged to someone else, and the stock is not worth much. So the calculator puts down his notebook and sits and wonders: What can a man do when he has no money? Because he is a poor man, must he die here like a dog? 'Tell me,' I say to him, 'why did you not go when you had the money?' The man of calculations replies with a laugh, 'When I had money I was earning a good living and I did not need to haul my bones from one place to another.'

This man who has come here is silent and does not utter a word. 'And so,' says the man of calculations, 'what can one do?' Say I, 'I don't know.' 'What do you mean, you don't know?' says the other, raising his voice in a shout. 'Because a man is poor, have you the right to lock the gates of the Land of Israel in his face? Are you making fun of me?' 'Never in my life have I made fun of any Jew,' I reply. 'And if we have to make fun, let us laugh at those that see this world of chaos as the best of worlds, and not at the Jew, who always remembers that there is another world.'

'Now I ask you,' says the other man, 'what have these young fellows done, who have no money and nothing else, that they welcome them so cordially and let them into the Land of Israel?' 'They merit this because of their labor,' say I. 'What do you mean, because of their labor?' retorts the other. 'Do you think I am sitting doing nothing? Ever since I grew up I have borne the yoke like an ox and the burden like an ass; never have I had an hour of rest.' And his toilworn face bears witness to his words.

Say I, 'And that man to whom your house and store are mortgaged—do you think he too wants to settle in the Land of Israel?' The man looks at me in surprise, thinking that I cannot put two and two together. Didn't he say that no one makes a move so long as he is earning a livelihood? 'Well,' says he, 'it seems we shall have to wait till the Messiah comes.'

Dolik breaks into our talk and says, 'Do me a favor, sir: when the Messiah comes will you recommend me to take charge of immigration certificates?'

Some people bring their complaints to me: of how much money the Zionists have taken out of the Jewish National Fund boxes in their homes, yet when they want to settle in the Land, they are not given permission. Whenever a propagandist or a lecturer or just an ordinary man from the Land of Israel came to their town, they would make great banquets for them, and when they wrote to them 'Send us certificates,' there was no response.

Some have already despaired of settling in the Land, because it is small and has little business and not everyone can make a living there, but since they happen to have met a man from the Land of Israel they wish to know what is true and what is not. They know that the truth is not as the lecturers tell and the papers write, nor is it like the defamatory reports of those who come back from there—so what is true and what is not true?

'Both these and those are words of truth,' I tell them. Say they, 'How can both things be correct, when these sing its praises and those tell its faults; these say it is a land where nothing is lacking and those say it is a land that devours its inhabitants. In the same way they speak of its people: these say they are all angels and those say they are worse than devils.' 'It is like the sun,' I replied. 'The righteous are healed by it—the wicked are consumed by it. It is the same sun: for the righteous it is healing and for the wicked it is Gehenna. So is the Land of Israel: whatever man is, that he finds in the Land.'

A man who was standing by greeted me and said, 'I ought not to have greeted you, except that I heard you came from a good family—that is why I greeted you.' Why all this anger? He had two sons, who had kept the commandments and had decent ways. They went to the Land of Israel and came back; now they had neither piety nor decent ways.

I said to myself: Another old man also had two sons, and the news came to him that their blood had been shed on one day. And Freide had two sons and their blood was shed on one day. The Holy One, blessed be He, always measures out abundantly, both for good and for evil. When He gives, He gives double, and when He takes, He takes double.

I ask that man, the father of two sons, 'Why did they come back from the Land?' He answers, 'And why did they ever go away?' So I ask, 'And why did they ever go away?' He answers, 'Why did they go away? They went to the Land to study heresy.' 'And did they learn their fill there?' 'A great question you ask,' he replies angrily. 'They even left both their tefillin and their tzitzit there. If it had not been for an old Gentile woman who lived with them there in the settlement, who used to collect the tefillin and the tallitot that the young fellows threw away and bring them to the town, they would have lain there as litter in an unclean place.'

'In every place the Gentiles have their own ways,' said I. 'Here in Szibucz the Gentiles took the tallitot and the tefillin and used them in ways I had rather not mention, and I believe the uncircumcised in your own town, sir, did the same.'

The father of two sons replied angrily, 'Whatever trouble may come, the Zionists are the first to benefit from it and draw advantage from it, to persuade the Jews to go up to the Land of Israel.' Said I, 'And do those who are not Zionists draw no benefit from the troubles?'

Let us return to our subject. Since the day Reb Hayim undertook full care of the Beit Midrash, I am free to my own devices. Sometimes I talk to a guest who happens to cross my path, and sometimes I examine my clothes and my linen, to see what should be thrown out and what should be given to a poor man.

Mrs. Zommer is a diligent and goodhearted woman. It happened once that I threw away a pair of torn socks, and found them after two days—whole and darned. Similarly with a shirt, and again with other garments. Krolka helps her; she is sorry for that man who was a guest for the night and stayed for many nights far from his wife and children, and cannot distinguish between a thing that is beyond repair and a thing that can still be repaired.

Like a seal stamped by diligent hands, so are the patches stamped on my linen and my socks, and perhaps the patches will outlast the shirt. Particularly worthy of attention is that mending in the sock. Although it is made of different threads, it makes the sock whole. Happy is he whose affairs can be repaired and have been repaired.

I have spent many words on my torn clothes, and since I do not say much about the clothes that are whole, surely I should not talk about the torn ones. But they recall to my mind the days gone by when I was a bachelor, always on the move from one room to another and from landlady to landlady. Since that time many of my affairs have changed. I married a wife, and two children were born to me; I went up to the Land of Israel, and dwelt in Jerusalem, and became a house-holder—and suddenly everything has gone back to the beginning: again I am living outside the Land, in a room in a hotel, looking after my clothes like a bachelor.

Why am I here, and my wife and children elsewhere? After our enemies had destroyed my house and left me with nothing, a great weariness entered me and my hands were too feeble to rebuild my house, which had suffered a second destruction. The first destruction was abroad, and the second in the Land of Israel; but when my house was destroyed abroad, I accepted the justice of the verdict and said: It is my punishment for choosing to live outside the Land. So I made a vow that if God was with me and restored me to the Land of Israel I should build myself a house and never leave it. Praised be the Name of the Lord, who privileged me to go up to the Land and privileged me to live in Jerusalem. I brought over my wife and children; we rented a house and bought furniture; and every day I would thank the Almighty for setting my lot among those who dwell in His city and shelter in His shadow. When I took pleasure in the air of the city, which is spiced with all good things, I used to say in surprise: If it is so in its desolation, how much more will it be in the future, when the Holy One, blessed be He, restores all the exiles and rebuilds His city. And when I used to see the young men standing among the ruins, removing the rubble and clearing away the stones that had lain there since the Destruction, building houses, planting gardens, and singing in the Holy Tongue, and birds flying, uttering their song, I was like one that dreams; for since the day Israel went into exile, all the birds of the sky had dispersed, and if a bird was seen it looked like a handful of dust or a flying clod of earth; but now at last the birds had returned to the city. The heavenly eye began to look upon us with mercy, for 'He looked down from the height of His sanctuary; from heaven did the Lord behold the earth.' Eye to eye we saw that the Almighty was looking down with favor on His Land and that a people was being created. And we already thought, in error, that the end of the exile had come and we were feasting on the years of the Messiah.

While we were living in tranquillity, the judgment struck us. The enemy raised his sword against our holy city and the cities of our God, and the houses of Israel were plundered. Jews were killed and burned and grievously tormented, and all the fruits of our toil were pillaged. 'Yet His anger has still not been appeased, and His hand—heaven forbid—is still outstretched.'

My wife and children and I emerged alive, and the sword from the desert did not strike at our persons. But my belongings were looted and my books torn up, and the house in which I thought I should live was laid desolate. 'The Lord gave and the Lord took; blessed be the Name of the Lord.'

Praised be the Name of the Lord that we emerged alive, but our household goods and my books were pillaged and torn. I, for whom every article in the Land is like a limb of the body, and every book is a part of the soul, suddenly became as one stricken in body and soul.

My wife was worse stricken than I: when the disaster fell upon us it took away all her strength, and when some began to return to their homes and rebuild the ruins, we could not do the same. Anyone who has lived through most of his life and has endured two destructions has no strength left. So she and her children went to her relatives in Germany, and I went to the town of my birth.

What I did in my town I have written in this book, and what my wife did in the home of her relatives she wrote to me in letters. From her letters it could be seen that she was not broken-hearted at living abroad; on the contrary, there was a slight measure of joy there, for she had cast off the burden of home and the trouble of guests, and was free to look after the children, to bring them up and educate them and teach them. True, the little ones longed for the Land of Israel, and at every mishap they would say: 'In Jerusalem this did not happen to us.' You may say that she too was longing for the Land a little, especially for its climate; nevertheless, she was living well abroad, for she was resting and the children were learning to recognize their family and know their origins. They were already speaking German and giving pleasure to their relatives with their accent, which sounded somewhat like Hebrew. They were also teaching their young relatives Hebrew, and it was very likely that they knew more than the *rabbiner*. Once my little girl happened to say 'Take a footstool' in Hebrew, and the *rabbiner* did not know what she meant.

A certain professor who chanced to be there said, 'Prodigious! This baby is learned in the language of the Talmud, for this word is not mentioned in Gesenius' dictionary, but it is mentioned in the dictionary of the Talmud and the Midrashim.'

I do not press my wife to return and she does not press me to return. So long as the measure of our exile is not fulfilled, we dwell abroad, she with her relatives, and I in the town of my birth, and every week we reach out to each other by letter. I write all that I can write, and she writes all that she can write.

Some of my friends in the Land also send me letters. To some I reply and to others I do not. I reply to those to whom I have nothing to say, and I do not reply to those to whom I have something to say, for since they are near to my heart, I talk to them while I talk to myself, and because there is so much to say I do not succeed in putting it on paper, so I put off my reply from day to day and week to week. But to my wife and children I write regularly, whether I have anything to tell or not. And since the day Reb Hayim took on all the burden of the Beit Midrash and I am free to my own devices, I write them even more.

The events are few and the words are many, and I add more in the margin of the letter and between the lines. I see my wife sitting by herself, turning the letter over from top to bottom and bottom to top, and screwing up her eyes to take in every single letter. And I am glad that my wife takes so much trouble with me, not like a woman who skims over her husband's letter, folds it up, and puts it away; perhaps my wife reads it again once or twice, or perhaps she reads it aloud as I read hers aloud, but her voice is more pleasant than mine.

My own letters, too, those I write to her, I am in the habit of reading aloud, and I have my own sound reason, for it is the way of the voice to hover and wander from place to place, and sometimes two places that are far away from one another are joined by the voice and combined into one, as if they were one place.

After I have written to my wife and children I say to myself: Here is the pen in my hand; I will write to the Land of Israel and ask them to send me a box of oranges. A man gets tired of eating potatoes every day, and his soul longs for a blessed fruit that rejoices the heart and the eye. Potatoes are also fit for Jews to eat, and we say a blessing over them, but oranges are more beautiful. It is not without reason that the Land of Israel was blessed with them, for the Holy One, blessed be He, plants every beautiful fruit in His garden. And what is the garden of the Holy One, blessed be He? The Land of Israel.

The orange season has come. The groves are full of fruit, hanging on their trees like little suns, their pleasant fragrance filling the land. There stand the boys and girls. If it is strength you want, there are the boys; if beauty, there are the girls. If you are a man of imagination, join the strength and the beauty together. Alas for that man who has been exiled from there.

Let us return to our subject. The groves are full of trees and the trees full of fruit. There stand the boys and girls; they pick the fruit into baskets and bring these into the packing house. There sit other girls, as fair as those we noted before, and sort the fruit. The good fruit they wrap up in tissue paper printed with Hebrew letters, and the mediocre they send out to the markets of Jerusalem and the rest of the country. There are people who feed on nothing but oranges, like the pioneers who have nothing to eat. But I, praise the Lord, have other foods as well, grown in the Land and grown abroad, and for additional enjoyment I add an orange to my meal.

I sit a little while and think: To whom shall I write. If I write to So-and-so, my friend, perhaps he will have left the Land for abroad and my letter will not reach him. The wings he made for himself to fly to the Land of Israel he has made into wheels for his feet to run abroad. Yesterday he was in the Land and today he is no longer there. Yesterday he went out of the Land to a congress and today to a conference. And if there is no congress and no conference, his body says to him: Every year you travel for the sake of duty; this year go out for your own sake—to the springs of salvation, mineral springs.

But one man there is in the Land of Israel who is not moved from his place by all the affairs of the world, neither congresses nor conferences, neither mineral springs nor the needs of the body. From the day he opened his little fruit and vegetable shop by the side of the street, he is firmly planted in his place ready to serve you, and if I write to him, my letter will find him and he will send me a box of oranges. Modest and humble is this shopkeeper, and he does not stir the world with his words. All the shopkeeper thinks of is how to sustain his house and teach his sons to read and find husbands for his daughters, and that perhaps the Almighty will help them and they will not need to stand in a shop like his, for shops are many and income is small. When Israel returned for the second time, Ezra the Scribe prescribed that there should be peddlers going around the villages; when Israel returned for the third time, they prescribed shops for themselves. In the days of Ezra, when Israel tilled the Land, they had patience to wait until the peddler should come to them; we, who have gone far away from our soil, are impatient and cannot wait; so we have set up many shops in every street and every house, in every nook and corner.

I have a special affection for this shopkeeper, for he is not like most of the shopkeepers in the Land of Israel, who ask you, after every purchase that you make, 'And what else?' They think little of you for what you have already bought. This shopkeeper has the quality of contentment; he does not try to persuade you to buy something of which you have no need, and he gives you what you need graciously. Not a month will pass before we shall eat of the oranges that this shopkeeper will send us.

CHAPTER SEVEN AND THIRTY

Oranges

The postman came and brought me a letter. For us the letter is the main thing and the bearer is secondary, but for him the letter is secondary and he is the main thing, since were it not for him Szibucz would be cut off from the world and no one would know of anything beyond its bounds.

The postman is a fleshy man and his hands and legs are

heavy. His hair is faded, and his eyes are the color of the weak beer they make in Szibucz. One end of his mustache sticks up and the other hangs down, and he has stickles growing on his chin instead of a beard. He is not like the postman of days gone by, who had a beard that was a facsimile of the Emperor Franz Josef's, and a mustache that, needless to say, used to lie on his upper lip like a hero taking his ease after victory over his enemies, for before he began to bring the people of Szibucz their letters he was one of the king's gendarmes, and the whole town was afraid of him. This postman, on the other hand, is half a peasant and half a townsman, and I doubt whether he can read the writing on the envelopes. As for one end of his mustache sticking up and the other hanging down, I blame the people of Szibucz, who are in a hurry to get their letters and leave him no time to look after his mustache.

But the pouch that hangs fiom his neck and spreads over his belly is as important as in days gone by. All the events of the time are contained in it: journals and business letters and the like. What an extraordinary thing: they took the skin off an animal that used to graze in the meadow and cry 'meh, meh,' and made it into a pouch; now that skin brings forth things that make people cry 'Woe.' However, this letter the postman has brought me is not a painful one, for it comes from the Land of Israel. I believe that even the postman was aware of this; when he handed it to me his voice was joyful.

I looked at the stamps and the Hebrew letters on them, and I said to the postman, 'I did not give you a present on your holiday; now I will give you double.' He bowed low, as far as his pouch, took the money, and said, 'Many thanks, sir.'

I said to him, 'I do not interfere in other people's business, but since this money comes from the Holy Land, it must not be used wastefully. If you are married and have children, a boy or a girl, buy them figs or dates or some other good fruit.' He put his hand on his heart, or on his pouch, and said, 'As I love God, I will buy figs and dates.' 'And I thought you would use my money to drink brandy,' said I. How strange are men's opinions; one thinks this way and one another. Or perhaps they are not strange, for in the end it turns out that they mean the same thing. 'What does the gentleman think of me?' said he. 'Since I came back from the war I have not gone into a tavern.' 'Excellent, excellent,' said I. But as I was saying so, I felt sorry: first, because I had deprived a Jewish innkeeper of trade, and second, because I had interfered in the affairs of his wife and children, when I should have been thinking of mine.

He who knows what I wrote to the Land of Israel knows what they replied. I wrote, 'Send me oranges,' and they replied, 'We have sent them.'

So this man who has come here sits and thinks to himself: One of these days the oranges are destined to find their way to Szibucz. Szibucz, which has never seen an orange since the war, suddenly receives a crateful of oranges.

I went out alone to the railway station to receive this crate, not like the first Zionists who went out to welcome the first crate of oranges from the Land of Israel, who went out joyfully, in crowds, reciting verses from the Bible. How can this man recite poetic verses when Jews are going the rounds of their brethren's groves, seeking work to keep themselves alive and being rejected in favor of the sons of Esau or Ishmael?

The station is covered in snow; facing it, the iron rails, on which the cars run, stretch out. Few persons leave Szibucz and few enter Szibucz, but the train continues to do its duty. Twice a day it leaves and comes in. Whenever it comes in, Rubberovitch the guard goes out with his rubber hand and calls melodiously, 'Szibucz.' His clothes are clean and his mustache is neat. I say to myself: Let me wait and see Rubberovitch licking his mustache when he cries 'Szibucz.' But no sooner had I a chance to see him than the bright snow dripped into my eyes and blinded them.

Between the heaps of snow stretches a chain of cars. Usually they are black, but today they are white. Above them stretches the smoke. While the smoke is making up its mind whether to rise upward or sink downward, the snow comes and covers it.

The train arrives and stops opposite the station. Half a dozen men come out with sacks in their hands, containing things with which a poor man earns his bread, such as scraps of iron and rabbit skins and the like, perhaps, too, some potatoes and carrots and cabbages and beans.

Where are the great merchants who used to come to Szibucz at this season? Wrapped in broad fur coats they would come, with the collars of their coats folded back and resting on their shoulders.

The great merchants have sold their merchandise, and have no money to buy new. True, the charity officials gave them money with which to trade, but charitable funds have no strength. They save a poor man from hunger, but they do not put him on his feet. And if they put him on his feet, they bend his back and lower his spirit, and his spirit is never restored. Just look, these men who have left the car used to be upright in stature and dressed in furs; now they are bowed and their spirits are low. Surely it is a great virtue to give charity. But it is great if one gives as a father that gives to his son, but not when one gives like a rich man who throws a copper to a pauper, for then all the evil spirits that surround a good deed rise with it.

But what should the givers of charity have done? This question is broad as the earth and deeper than the sea, and it is not in our power to answer it. But this we may say: If the benefactors of Israel had made the troubles of their brethren their own, the Holy One, blessed be He, would have helped them, and they would not have had to give and give again. But they did not make their brethren's troubles their own; they tried to salve their consciences by mere giving. Therefore their brethren remained poor, and tomorrow, if—heaven forbid—the givers themselves should be visited by trouble, the recipients of charity would be unable to help them.

And where are the traveling salesmen who used to come with a great to-do, and when the porters saw one of them looking out from the train, they would immediately hang on to the window and every porter would cry, 'Mister, let me carry your bag, I saw you first!' And the gentleman would say, 'I will give you and the other one as well,' for every salesman would bring many bags with him. Before the porters could load up with all the bags, a second salesman would appear, and a third, and a fourth. The big salesmen have nothing to do in Szibucz, because the town has dwindled and so have its needs. From time to time a traveling salesman finds his way to Szibucz and stays two or three days in a hotel, spending little and talking a great deal.

And where is the crowd of singers and musicians, men and women, who used to come in the cold days and warm the hearts of the lads with songs and music? The singers and musicians have died in the war, and others have not come in their places. Jews are entangled in troubles and wander from one exile to another, and no one seeks songs, but Rubberovitch calls, as is his way, melodiously, 'Szibucz.'

The snow comes down and the cold cuts into a man's flesh. Listless and melancholy, five or six Jews walk on, their faces toward the town. No dancing carriages have come out to meet them, or wagoners to welcome them. The wagoner knows when it is worth his while to trouble his horse, and when it is not. Not like Hanoch, who troubled Henoch for nothing, and now both of them are wandering in the world of chaos and no one knows where they are. Some say they showed themselves in a dream. And why did they not ask Hanoch where he is? Because he showed himself dead, and they were afraid to speak to a dead man.

Because I had waited for the guard to dispatch the train, I was free to my own devices. And since I was free I thought many thoughts. This was one of them: When will these Jews reach their homes, before dark or after dark? And when they reach their homes, will a glowing stove and a warm samovar be waiting for them?

And because I had started thinking, I also brought to mind their brethren, who have left Szibucz and left me the key of our old Beit Midrash. There is a special quality about this key: it is cold but the house it opens is warm. You must know that I am a Jew from the Land of Israel and I do not like the cold, so I am in the habit of recalling our old Beit Midrash, which is warm when all around is cold.

The guard dispatched the train. As the train set off with a dreadful din, snow began to cover the tracks. Still and silent, snowflakes fell on top of snowflakes, and the world grew

brighter toward evening. Anyone who is not familiar with the
ways of snow might think, mistakenly, that this brightness
will go on and on; but he does not know that today the snow
is pure and tomorrow it is black, and in the end it becomes a
morass. The rays of evening fell on the snow. But before the
snow could surround them and make them white, the rays
had darkened the snow.

I handed Rubberovitch the form I had received from the
station office. He read it and said, 'Oranges from Palestine.'
He chewed the air and read again 'Palestine.' Dear brethren,
the way this guard says 'Szibucz' with a melody, as I told you
before, is nothing compared with the melody of 'Palestine.'

I like Rubberovitch, not because of his rubber hand,
which has made him popular with the daughters of the Gentiles, who believe he is entirely made of rubber, but because
it was from his lips that I first heard the name of my town
when I returned. Today my affection for him was redoubled,
and I made him my messenger to bring me the oranges.

The oranges have come, and now they are lying in their
crate in my room, sending up a sweet fragrance, like a grove
of citrus trees in the Land of Israel. I ought to open the crate
and give an orange to Rubberovitch, who has kept his word
and not delayed the crate. But I did not open the crate and
give something from it to Rubberovitch; I compensated him
with money, for I meant all the oranges for Yeruham Freeman. First, because I owe him a piece of orange, and it is
good to give generously, and second, because I have dedicated it to him as a wedding present. On the very day I
ordered the oranges I heard that Yeruham is going to get
married, and I wanted to bring him joy on his day of rejoicing.

Yeruham Freeman ought to have married Erela Bach,
first, because he was meant for Erela, together with whom he
sucked her mother's milk, and second, because the father of
Rachel Zommer, whom people slandered by saying she followed Yeruham, could not tolerate him and would not give
her to him. However, now that days have come when a daughter rises up against her father, Rachel has followed the dictates
of her heart and is to marry Yeruham.

The Settling of the Account

We thought Mr. Zommer would turn the whole world upside down before he would let his daughter Rachel marry Yeruham, but in the end he made them a wedding. It would have been better if he had held the wedding two or three months earlier, but since he did delay it is good that he did not delay any longer.

I look at Rachel in surprise. Yesterday she was a child and today she is getting married. If you regard her as grown up, to me she is still little. Only a few days ago I spoke to her as a man speaks to a child.

I wished Rachel good fortune and, looking sideways, said to my other (he who dwells with me), 'I have already agreed with you that you should not tease me with married women. If you keep the agreement, good; if not, I will not look even at an unmarried one.' And that fool grew afraid that I might keep my word, and turned Rachel's face away from me.

And since Rachel's is turned from me, my eyes and my heart are free. So I am free to do as I wish, and I look at Rachel's husband and say to myself: Why do I like Yeruham? Is it because he lived in the Land of Israel? But then he has left the Land and speaks evil of it. Or is it because he speaks Hebrew? But then Erela and her pupils also speak Hebrew. But when you hear their language, you feel as if you had been served with mealy potatoes, in which only the worms are alive, for their language is intermingled with words that all the tasteless people have made up out of their own heads. Not so with Yeruham. When he speaks, you feel as if a man were plowing and the fragrance of the clean earth were rising all around you.

Yeruham asked me, 'Why do you not come to visit us?' 'Where?' I said. 'Where?' said he. 'What do you mean, where? To our room.' 'When?' said I. Said he, 'What do you mean, when? Any night is right.' 'Any night is right?' 'Yes—and the whole night is right.'

I took my watch out of my pocket, looked at it, and said to Yeruham, 'And what does Rachel say?' He passed his hand over his curls and said, 'My will is her will and her will is my will.' His black curls gleamed and his eyes looked at me calmly. 'You know where I am to be found,' I said to him. 'Come to me after you finish your work and I will go with you.'

After prayers Yeruham came to the yard of the Beit Midrash and waited for me behind the door. I said to myself: Let him wait until he gets cold and he will come in. Then I remembered his wife, who would be waiting for him. So I got up, put on my coat, and went with him.

Before I went I said to Reb Hayim, 'I do not know when I will come back. Will you please take the key and close the door after you?' True, I had promised the key that I would not let it out of my possession or hand it over to anyone else, but it is another matter when the hour calls.

There is a street in Szibucz that is called Synagogue Street, after the synagogue that was in that street before Chmielnicki destroyed the town. Now there is neither synagogue nor Jew in that street except for Yeruham and his wife, who have made their home there among the Gentiles.

As I entered, Rachel jumped up to meet me and affectionately pressed my hand. Yeruham bent down, opened the door of the stove, and put in a few pieces of wood. Then he rolled up his sleeves, took hold of both Rachel's hands, looked at me with one eye, and asked me, 'Perhaps we should dance a hora with her?' Rachel pulled her hands away from his, examined the table, and said, 'He hasn't even set a chair for the guest.' Yeruham took a chair and set it in front of me, while Rachel removed the cloth with which she had covered the oranges she had arranged on the table, and went and sat with her husband on the bed.

Yeruham took an orange and peeled it, in the special way of the Land of Israel. First he passed the knife around it and took off the top. Then he made six marks and folded the peel inward and put the orange in front of me whole. Rachel watched his every movement, as one who sees a fine thing and admires it.

I took the orange and recited two blessings over it: the blessing for fruit and the blessing 'Who has sustained us to this day.' Then I divided it in two, taking half for myself and giving the other half to Yeruham. Yeruham reddened and said, 'You are giving me the piece of orange that you should have given me when I went up to the Land of Israel.'

I said to him, 'Now the account is settled. From now on we turn a new leaf.' Rachel looked at her husband's face and at mine and asked, 'What kind of accounts do you have and what secrets are you hiding from me?' We explained the whole matter to her, each of us in his own way.

Rachel said to her husband, 'Now the affair is settled, you have nothing more against him.' 'Certainly Yeruham has nothing against me,' I said to her, 'but I have something against him. There is a song of mine in his possession, and I claim the song from him.'

Yeruham looked at me and said, 'What song do I have in my possession?' Said I, 'Those rhymes about God above and Jerusalem for thy love. I will not let you off until you recite them.' Yeruham examined me with both his eyes and saw that I wanted to hear them. He stood up, passed his hands over his curls, and recited the poem aloud:

> 'Devotion faithful unto death
> I've sworn to thee by God above,
> For all I have in Exile here
> I'll give, Jerusalem, for thy love.'

I said to Yeruham, 'Is that all? Surely you used to know another verse.' Yeruham went on:

> 'My life, my spirit, and my soul,
> O Holy City, for thee I'll give—
> Awake and dreaming all my joy,
> My feast and Sabbath while I live.'

'You are cutting it short,' I said to Yeruham. 'Have you

finished all your rhymes? If I am not mistaken, the poem has two more verses.'

Yeruham went on, and recited:

'Though your King be gone and your people poor,
Eternal City, lofty Shrine,
The Lord has made thee all our hope,
From ancient days to the end of time.'

And here he took both hands of Rachel and raised his voice and sang:

'And though the tomb may close me in
With all the dead beneath the ground,
In deepest pit thou art my strength,
O fortress city, world-renowned.'

I looked at my watch and said, 'The time has come to rise and go.' 'Why?' 'To have my supper.' 'Even at the hotel they will not give you olives,' said Rachel, 'so you can eat with us. Everything is ready for supper.' Yeruham fixed his eyes on me and said, 'Eat with us, eat with us. If you are afraid we will feed you pheasants in milk, you should know that I do not eat meat either.'

Rachel rose and brought bread, butter, eggs, a dish of rice, and tea. We sat and ate and drank and talked. What did we talk about and what did we not talk about? About everything that arose in the heart, about everything for which the lips found words: about the Land and its beauty, about Jews and Arabs, about the people and about their opinions, about kvutzot and about kibbutzim. What did we talk about and what did we not talk about? Rachel sat glued to her chair and listened, her face growing paler and paler. Once and twice her husband told her to go to sleep, but she did not obey.

Yeruham rose and put some pieces of wood on the stove; Rachel rose, brought us some tea, and sat down again and peeled herself an orange, taking off the top and making marks in the skin—she had taught herself to peel in the way we do in the Land of Israel. The fragrance of the orange was pleasant, and the room was tranquil and content. Behind the window and the door stretched fields of snow, but the light of the stove made us forget their terrors.

Rachel sat and ate the orange quietly, a piece at a time. For many years, neither Rachel nor anyone else in Szibucz had seen an orange, and suddenly she found herself with a crate full of them.

The sweet sun of the Land of Israel, which has concentrated itself in the oranges, shines out of Rachel's eyes. It cannot be said that Rachel is angry with Yeruham for having left the Land of Israel, for if he had not left, it would not have turned out that he should marry her. In any case, she is surprised at him.

Rachel is a clever woman and does not reveal what is in her heart. She is attached to her husband and attached to her thoughts, and does not seek to bring them together when it is better for them to be separate. So she sits and tries to put one knee on another and hear what her husband tells.

Yeruham tells about our comrades in the Land of Israel. He does not say that he is like everyone else, and even if he said so, you would not believe him. But when he tells about our comrades in the Land of Israel you might imagine that there before you sits a Jewish family man, weighing the deeds of others, cheerful, merry, and laughing. First, because Yeruham is in a good mood at this time, and second, because every person in the Land of Israel is different from his fellows—and if there is one who is not different, he is different because he is not different from everyone else.

Does Yeruham long for the Land and his comrades? One might say Yeruham has put the past out of his heart. And one might also say that a young man in the first month of his marriage has nothing but his wife. But if he could make a hole in heaven and look through there to the Land of Israel, he would watch and observe it.

Rachel sits silent, her head hunched between her shoulders. Sometimes she half closes her eyes and her eyelashes quiver, as if she wishes to grasp with them everything the eye cannot catch, and sometimes she opens her eyes and looks at her husband. Yeruham notices her eyes but pretends that he does not see; he raises his hand toward his curls, pushing them this way and that, and goes on telling. Rachel puts her hands over her heart, like the myrtle, whose leaves cover the stem. And I look on in surprise. I had always thought that Rachel's chief charm was her upright carriage, and now she shows us that even when she sits bent she is full of charm.

Let us return to our subject and listen to the words of Yeruham our comrade. Or perhaps I will tell all that I heard from Yeruham, and I hope you will be all ears.

Even in his childhood Yeruham wanted to go up to the Land of Israel, although he did not belong to the society of the Szibucz Zionists, who were older than he was. Or perhaps because he did not belong to the Zionist society he understood by himself that talk without action is worth nothing. Or perhaps a thought of this kind came to him later and he ascribed it to that time. Be that as it may, all of Yeruham's thoughts were about the Land of Israel, and it was these that made him angry all the time because the Holy One, blessed be He, was in no hurry to increase his height so that he could go up to the Land. Once and twice he ran away from his benefactors' house and they brought him back from the roadside. Finally he realized that this was not the way that would bring him to the Land of Israel and he was sad, depressed, and angry. Suddenly the war came and he was carried away to Vienna. 'And here,' said Yeruham, 'I must confess that while the whole world was sad I was happy. First, because I had reached the city of Herzl; and second, Vienna is on the way to the Land of Israel.' But he was mistaken. This war made the countries more distant from each other. Only the arrows of death united them.

Mrs. Bach has already told us what Yeruham did in Vienna: he studied Hebrew at the school with Erela and Yeruham Bach. Now let us tell what he did after the war. After the war he and Yeruham Bach went to the Land of Israel. Yeruham Bach went like a normal person, traveling by train and boat, while the other, Yeruham Freeman, did not go like all the rest, because they did not give him a passport, for his name was not correctly registered. So he took his staff and his bundle and went on foot. On he went, heel and toe, over several countries, hills and mountains, forests and lakes. Often he was in danger from violent men, who had returned from the war and were terrorizing the roads, as well as from the frontier guards, who beat and killed anyone who tried to pass without permission. By day he would hide in the forests, among the rocks, or in tunnels and caves, and at night he would lift himself from the dust and go on. Because he did not know the roads, he sometimes found himself back in the place from which he had come.

Yeruham said to me, 'You told me the story of Hanania, who found goodhearted people and went up with them; I found only one man with whom I went. It happened that once I saw a man from a distance. I was afraid he might be a murderer or a frontier guard. I wanted to hide, but I saw that he too was trying to hide. So I took my heart in my hands and went up to him. I asked him, "What are you doing here?" "And what are you looking for here?" he asked me. I told him that I was going to the Land of Israel but did not have a passport, and he told me that he was going to the Land of Israel and did not have a passport. So we went on together. After several days we reached a certain port. We found a broken-down smugglers' boat and paid them to take us to some port in the Land of Israel. So we sailed on with them over the sea without food or water. After several days they put us off near a desolate place and said, "From here onward let God help you." After several days we found another boat belonging to hashish smugglers and sailed with them to a port in the Land of Israel. When we landed, we thought the Land of Salvation had been opened to us. We kissed the soil and wanted to forget our trials. And indeed we did forget the trials of the journey because of the disturbances that were raging all over the country. Then some of our comrades, who had been privileged to arrive first, were killed. After the Land became tranquil, we went out to work.'

There was work in the Land but the employers—heaven forgive them—were not of Yeruham's kind. And here Yeruham told me many things. Those that are known to us there is no need to mention, and those that are not known to us we shall pass over in silence, so as not to arouse divine justice. Said Yeruham, 'It is not enough for a people that it has been given a land, if the land does not behave aright.' So Yeruham cast out his love from his heart and became hardened against it. He joined up with certain people and did a number of things that were not right, or perhaps he did behave aright, for if a wolf tries to devour you, you do not have to stroke its fur. Finally, the authorities came and expelled him, with some of his comrades, from the Land.

Rachel looked at her husband and suddenly her face grew alive again. All the weariness in her body left her. She sat and listened to all that Yeruham was saying. Many things Yeruham had already told her, but the main things he was telling now. Yeruham perceived what was in Rachel's heart and said, 'You shall yet hear greater things.'

'One thing I find difficult to understand,' said I to Yeruham. 'By your nature, Yeruham, you did not go up to the Land of Israel in the same way as I and my comrades of the second wave of immigration did. We of the second wave went up because of the voice in our hearts. The tales and stories we had heard in the Hebrew school; the Torah, Prophets, and Writings we had learned in our childhood; the Gemara and Midrash we had studied in our youth; and perhaps also the songs we had read—all these stirred our spirits; so we went up to the Promised Land. But you and your comrades—forgive me for saying this—you who had transgressed against all these things, why did you say that it was through me that you went up to the Land? Is a man like you inspired by rhymes about "Jerusalem my love" and "heaven above"? Give your consideration to this, my dear friend, and answer me. I do not ask you to reply at once, but in any case we ought to clear this up.'

Said Rachel, 'I thought all your accounts were already settled, but now you come along again with a new account!' Yeruham pushed his curls from right to left and said, 'Don't worry, Rachel. I can pay.' 'On the contrary, my friend,' said I, 'let us hear what you have to answer me. Or perhaps we should defer the payment to another time, for it is near midnight, and you and Rachel are tired.'

I took out my watch. Good heavens, five and a half hours I had been sitting in Yeruham and Rachel's house. I rose, put on my coat, said goodbye to them, and went off. Yeruham came after me to accompany me, but I sent him back so that his wife should not sit alone. So Yeruham went home, and I went on my way.

CHAPTER NINE AND THIRTY

In the Light of the Moon

What shall we think about now? Perhaps about Rachel and Yeruham? Yeruham and Rachel have gone to bed; let us not confuse them with our thoughts. If so, let us think about Reb Hayim, to whom I gave the key; he is no doubt sitting in the Beit Midrash counting his journeys from Szibucz to the land of his captivity and from the land of his captivity to Szibucz. Or perhaps we should think about Szibucz itself, which casts out its sons and takes them in again. If so, then even Elimelech Kaiser will return and close his mother's eyes, for if strangers close the eyes of a dead man he feels pain in his eyes, since a stranger's hand comes down without mercy. Or perhaps we should not think at all, but go back to the hotel and go to sleep. It is already midnight. The moon and the stars and the planets are evidence of this, and, if you like, so is my watch. True, the watch has stopped, but my heart tells me that it stopped at the moment when I took it out to look at it.

The moon lights up everything: the snow, and the ruined castle, and the stones that surround the castle, which the snow has covered like a flock of sheep.

The moon walked silently in the sky, lighting my path. I listened to the sound of my feet and the gurgling of the spring that welled up from the hill. This is the hill to which I used to go with my father, of blessed memory, to drink of its waters at the setting of the Sabbath in the summer, for at the setting of the Sabbath, Miriam's Well runs into all the wells in the world, and whoever succeeds in divining just that moment will have many of his wishes fulfilled.

The spring gurgled as was its way; its clear waters flowed into the washerwoman's pool, and from there to the river Stripa, which was covered with ice. The moon was full, and the snow crouched on the hill and its slopes like a flock of sheep. Meanwhile the snow seemed to disappear, and the face of the hill was covered with sheep. And that was strange, for this is not the Land of Israel, where even in winter the sheep will wander over the hills.

I heard the tinkling of a bell and saw a wagoner coming with his horse. A kind of shivering seized me, and my hair stood on end with fear, for once at this spot a wagoner came down to water his horse and slipped, and both of them fell and drowned in the river.

The wagoner approached, his head lying on the horse's neck, and came down to the stream. I took my heart in my hands and raised my eyes, and saw that it was Hanoch. I said to him, 'Hanoch, are you here?' Hanoch echoed my words and said, 'Here.' 'And is Henoch here too?' said I. The horse nodded his head, as if he were saying, 'I am here too.' 'What are you doing here?' said I to Hanoch. 'I have come to water my horse,' he replied. 'Are you not dead?' I asked him. He was silent and said nothing. I looked into his eyes and said to him, 'You ought to go to your wife; she has been weeping for you all the time. Don't you hear?' 'Hear,' replied Hanoch. 'If so,' said I, 'go back to her.' Said Hanoch, 'First I want to find rest in a Jewish grave.' 'You have gone out of your mind, Hanoch,' said I. 'You show yourself as one who is alive and yet you speak as one who is dead.' 'Dead,' replied Hanoch. 'If you are dead,' said I, 'go back to the dust.' Said Hanoch, 'And who will water my horse?' 'And is he alive?' said I. The horse neighed as if he were alive.

'Hanoch,' I said to him, 'what do you think: If I had made you a permanent attendant and given you enough wages, would what has happened have happened? The reason I ask is that there are no accidents in the world, and if this has happened to you, it means that it had to happen so, and even if I had made you a permanent attendant and given you enough wages, it would have changed nothing.'

Hanoch raised his head from the horse's neck and said,

'But we are free to choose.' 'What has free choice to do with it?' said I. 'There is free choice,' he whispered, 'for by free choice it is possible to change good to evil and vice versa.' My heart became as weak as wax.

I pulled myself together and began to speak angrily. 'That means,' said I, 'that in your opinion I am to blame for everything that has befallen you. But here you are alive, which means that nothing has happened to you. And if nothing has happened to you I am not to blame for anything. Why do you not answer me?' 'I did not hear what you said,' said Hanoch. 'You did not hear?' said I. 'It does not matter to you that I am standing in the cold when I should be lying in my bed asleep?' 'Forgive me, sir,' said Hanoch, 'I am busy looking for a grave for myself.' 'A grave?' 'It's hard lying in the snow,' replied Hanoch. I turned my eyes from him and looked at his horse and said, 'And Henoch?' 'He is looking after me, so that I should not go astray,' said Hanoch.

Henoch stood in his place, his eyes sunken, his lean ribs quivering, and his black teeth rising and falling in his mouth as if he were chewing Hanoch's words and enjoying them. Finally he lowered his head modestly, as if he were saying, 'Who am I to have been made my master's keeper?' But by the way he lowered his head it could be seen that he felt proud of himself, as if to say that, had it not been for him, his master would have gone astray.

I was irritated by the horse's deplorable modesty and wanted to say to him, 'You of the rickety backbone and the bedraggled tail, it is you who have led Hanoch into this trouble, and in the end you expect gratitude?' The horse stamped on the ground and sprinkled my face with snow water, then he put down his feet quietly and neighed in his throat. My anger rose and I wanted to strike him on the muzzle. Henoch saw that I was angry and neighed again—not a neigh of vindictiveness but a neigh of invitation to quarrel. I pretended I did not notice him and said to Hanoch, 'Between ourselves, Hanoch, it seems to me that you are in the limbo of lost souls.' Hanoch raised his two hands and looked at me, but did not answer.

I said to him, 'I have already told you that you know

nothing because you lack the power of imagination, for if you had it you would know where you are situated. Now I will ask you a simple thing which does not require the imaginative power: Which world is more beautiful, the one you have left or the one to which you have gone? Or perhaps both of them are hard, especially for him who has left one world and not entered the other. If you wish, Hanoch, I will say the Kaddish for the elevation of your soul. Why do you not answer me? Are you afraid of the rabbi, who ordered your sons not to say Kaddish and your wife not to mourn for you? What do you think about the rabbi? Did he behave well to Reb Hayim? Why do you not answer me? You are asleep. If so, I am afraid that there may happen to you a second time what happened to you the first time.'

Hanoch was sunk in sleep, and so was his horse. Only the bell on the horse's neck tinkled. The sound began to make my limbs sleepy and my eyes began to close. So I picked up my feet and went to my hotel, but before I took leave of him I reminded him of the story of the wagoner and his horse who slipped and fell into the river, and warned him to take care.

I have mentioned all this because my heart rebuked me for leaving Hanoch without protection. And here I can say that everything that happened to Hanoch did not happen because of me, and his end also proved that I was not to blame for his death. But what belongs later should not be told before. Let us return to our affairs, until the time comes that will reveal my innocence.

CHAPTER FORTY

Partnership

During the night I spent with Yeruham and Rachel, a woman came to my hotel and asked for me. If you should like to know who that woman was, she was the widow of Reb Jacob Moses, of blessed memory, and the daughter-in-law of Reb Abraham, of blessed memory. If you should like to know who

Reb Abraham was, he was the pride of our town, wealthy son of wealthy parents, scholar and son of a scholar, of distinguished lineage on his father's side, all great and sanctified scholars, as well as on the side of his father-in-law, the great scholar who wrote *The Hands of Moses,* a book that was accepted throughout the dispersions of Israel—commentaries have been written upon it; indeed, in some places it is studied by special groups, and its words are meticulously studied like the words of the early fathers. If you have heard that there were wealthy men in Szibucz, you ought to know that Reb Abraham was wealthier. And if you have heard that there were scholars in Szibucz, you ought to know that Reb Abraham was one of them. As for pedigree, there was no pedigree like his. Once we were sitting in the *klois* telling the praises of the great men of Israel. The talk turned to a famous scholar, one of the greatest of the generation, who had the same family name as Reb Abraham. I said to Reb Abraham's grandson. 'No doubt he is a relative of yours.' He motioned with his hand and said, 'We are not relatives.' And from the way he motioned with his hand we could see that we had offended the honor of his family, by describing as a relative that great scholar who did not have so noble a lineage as his.

Just as Reb Abraham's father had married him to the daughter of a great and distinguished rabbi, so did Reb Abraham marry his sons to the daughters of the great scholars of the generation, and they too gave their sons in marriage with their like. Once, on the Three Days of Circumscription, when Reb Abraham's grandson was getting married, all the relatives of the bride came to our town. When all those rabbis went out to the forest outside the town, in memory of the command 'And be ready against the third day' before the giving of the Torah in the wilderness, and stood leaning on the trees, which were in full blossom, discoursing on law and legend, we said: This is the forest our forefathers came upon when they entered Poland, where they found a tractate of the Talmud written on each tree.

Once I saw Reb Abraham. I happened to have risen early to go to school, and I saw an old man, handsome and of goodly appearance, dressed in satin, going up the steps of

the synagogue, with the satchel for his tallit and tefillin under
his arm. And it seemed to me as if he and that velvet satchel
containing his tallit and tefillin had been born together. On
one other occasion I saw him in his house. It happened that
he and my father met at a festive meal. My father expressed
a view on a point of Torah, and Reb Abraham took a different
view. Father went into the Beit Midrash, searched, and found
in the book *The Hands of Moses* proof of what he had said. So
my father sent me to Reb Abraham, and I found him sitting
in a large room, full of beautiful pictures and many mirrors
hanging on every wall, except for one wall on which there
was no mirror, but a space a cubit square, neither painted
nor decorated. 'Who are you, my son?' Reb Abraham asked.
'I am the son of the man who differed from Reb Abraham,'
I replied. 'If you will look at this book, *The Hands of Moses*,
which I have here, sir, you will see whether what my father
said was right.' He looked at it two or three moments and
said, 'Your father understood it rightly.' My spirits rose. Every
mirror reflected my image, and I saw that there were many
like me.

Reb Jacob Moses, Reb Abraham's son, and my father,
may they rest in peace, were very good friends; they used to
tell each other every new meaning they found in the Torah,
and on Sabbath they would send their sons to each other to
be examined in their studies. Even in death my father was
not parted from him, and appointed him the guardian of his
orphans, until he too died during the war.

Now that I heard his widow had come to ask for me, I
remembered the high repute of her fathers, and I was sorry
that gentle soul had taken the trouble to come to see me. So
I put on my coat and went to her house.

The house was in ruins and its head had been taken off.
A man whose head has been cut off is not alive; the same is
true of a house. And it was even hard to tell whether the
storey that still remained—the base of the body, with the large
store that had provided a livelihood for so many families—
was still standing or in ruins. Nevertheless, Sarah lived there
cramped together with her four sisters-in-law, the wives of

her husband's brothers, some of whom had been killed in the
war and some of whom had died of hunger.

Sarah looked at me in surprise. I had often been in her
husband's house when I was a child, and now my years were
as his were then. Many years had passed since then, and if
they had passed without trials she would have faced the final
day with smiles, but since they had not passed without trials,
she looked at me affectionately and sighed from the heart.
Sarah took a chair and put it in front of me. I sat down before her in silence, and she too sat in silence. I wanted to
ask about her children, but I said to myself: I will not ask,
in case—heaven forbid—they are dead. Since the war overwhelmed us you do not know whether your friend is alive,
and if he is alive whether his life is worth living. The good
years have passed when you used to ask about a man and
they would tell you: He has had a wedding in his house, he
has had a circumcision in his house, his grandson has celebrated bar mitzvah, his son-in-law is adding a third storey to
his house. Thou art righteous, O Lord, and Thy judgments
are upright. The sufferings Thou hast sent to Israel, Thou
alone knowest whether they are for good or for ill.

Four women came in one after the other: her four sisters-
in-law, who had been left widowed of their husbands. This
war has widowed the women of Israel.

A verse came to my lips: 'She has become as a widow.'
When Jeremiah saw the destruction of the First Temple, he
sat down and wrote the Book of Lamentations, and he was
not content with all the lamentations he wrote until he had
compared the congregation of Israel to a widow and said,
'She has become as a widow'—not a true widow, but like a
woman whose husband has gone overseas and intends to return to her. When we come to lament this latest destruction
we do not say enough if we say, 'She has become *as* a widow,'
but a true widow, without the word of comparison.

So this lamenter sat before the five gentle widows from
good families, whose husbands had gone away and not returned. He searched his heart for a word to say to console
them. But since the word of comparison had been taken away
he found no consolation.

Said Sarah, 'Forgive me, sir, that I have made you take this trouble. Truly there was no need to trouble. I would have come again.' I bowed my head before her and said, 'On the contrary, it is a great honor to me that I have been honored to come here. I remember this house when I used to gaze at it in humility and say, Happy the house in which learning and abundance are to be found in one place, and happy are they that dwell in it, who observe the Torah in the midst of wealth.'

Said one, 'Of all that wealth nothing is left us but one single book.' Said a second, 'And this book we wish to sell.' Said a third, 'Perhaps you will help us in this, sir.' Said a fourth, 'This book is a manuscript that has been left us by our grandfather, the illustrious author of *The Hands of Moses.*' Said I, 'Is it possible that any work by that great scholar has been left unpublished?' 'We are referring to the book *The Hands of Moses,*' said Sarah. 'But *The Hands of Moses* has already been printed several times,' said I. Said one, 'The book has been printed, but the manuscript is in our hands.' Said a second, 'And it has a special virtue for women in the hour of childbirth; I too was helped by it when my son, peace be upon him, was being born.' When she mentioned her son, she burst into tears, for he was killed in the war and his limbs were scattered, so that he could not be given a Jewish burial. 'Stop, Sarah'le, stop,' said the third. 'You have wept enough. Do not arouse the divine judgment, heaven forbid.' And she too burst into tears.

'I will explain, sir,' said one. 'It is like this. This manuscript has a special virtue, for if a woman has a hard childbirth, when it is put on her side she bears easily. And I can say that since this has been known there have been no mishaps here to women in childbirth. Be good enough, Sarah'le, bring the book.'

Sarah rose, went into another room, and returned bringing a large book, like the tractate *Sabbath* or some other large talmudic volume, and put it before me on the table. She stroked it with her hand and said, 'This is the book.' An odor of phenol and medicaments rose from the book, filling the whole house.

I opened the book and looked into it a little here and there. The writing was beautiful and clear, and the letters elegant and legible, as our forefathers used to write a hundred years ago, when they loved writing. Each letter shone from the paper, and the paper shone like a mirror. But my joy was not complete; my eyes rejoiced at the sight, but my heart did not take part in this joy.

I turned over the pages and looked into it again, here and there a little. The words were truly divine; not for nothing has the book been accepted throughout the dispersions of Israel. Nevertheless, I did not feel more in it than a man who holds an ordinary manuscript. It came into my mind that this was not the manuscript of the author. But if it was not the manuscript of that righteous man, how was it the women had been helped by it?

I turned over the pages idly, with disinterest, yet wondering what to answer the rabbis' widows who were waiting expectantly for what I had to say. Then I came to a certain place where the following was written: 'Copied from the actual sacred manuscript of our illustrious teacher, by Elyakim, surnamed Getz, a servant of the holy work.' I was surprised and astonished. Was there so much power in that amanuensis that salvation and mercy were wrought through him? Whether or not it was so, I did not know what to do. The book had been printed a number of times and was to be found in many hands, and even had it been the manuscript of the author I did not know who would buy it.

I had a shrewd idea and said, 'I am surprised at you, dear ladies. Would you take a book that our town has been privileged to own and abandon it to the outside world? And what will happen to the women who will be in need of it?' They sighed and answered, 'If the town had been in need of it, we would not have sold it for all the money in the world.' 'What do you mean by "if the town had been in need of it"? Are the women in your town like the beasts of the field who have no need of a talisman? Tomorrow you will be asked for the book and what will you answer? "We have sold the book"? Surely they will ask you, "Why have you done this thing?" as Pharaoh said to the Jewish midwives—though

Pharaoh said it because the midwives let the children live, and you, dear ladies—but let me not put words into Satan's mouth. . . . If you listen to me, even if you are offered all the silver and gold in the world you should not sell it.'

Said one, 'Pharaoh only ruled out male children, but the women in Szibucz rule out female children, too. Have you seen a cradle rocking since the day you came here?'

'Israel is not yet barren,' said I. 'I myself witnessed the marriage contract of the hotelkeeper's daughter. Surely you know Rachel, his little daughter, who married a certain young man called Yeruham Freeman, the one with the curly hair?'

It was painful to see the women's distress. The bread had vanished from the house and all their hopes lay in the money they would get from the book, and this man was telling them about some hotelkeeper's daughter who had married some young man.

'Ladies,' said I, 'who revealed to you the secret that this manuscript has this power you speak of?'

Said one, 'When the women used to come to our saintly grandfather to beg him for assistance he would push them away with the stem of the pipe in his hand, for our grandfather would say, "You want to use me for idolatry, heaven forbid. You seek salvation from the Holy One, blessed be He, and you fix your eyes on a mere mortal. If it is salvation you need, entreat the Almighty and He will save you." Once he was sitting and writing his book. A woman came and cried, "Rabbi, Rabbi, save me, for three days now my daughter is in the grip of labor pains." His pity was aroused and he said, "The new interpretations I have written today in the book will help that woman to bear in comfort." No sooner had the words left his lips than she bore a male child.'

I said to her, 'All the time that saintly man was alive, the living Torah in his mouth wrought salvation. How do you know that the same was true after his passing?' Said one, 'Have you not learned, sir, that righteous men are greater in their deaths than in their lives? Sarah'le, Sarah'le, tell the gentleman how it happened.'

Sarah sighed and said, 'When my husband, peace be upon him, was born, my mother-in-law's birthpangs were particularly painful, and they almost despaired of her. By that time her saintly father was no longer in the world. They went to prostrate themselves on his grave and could not find it, for that week a heavy snow had fallen and covered the whole of the graveyard, to the tops of the tombstones and even higher. So many mothers in childbirth had been helped by that saintly man, and now that his daughter was in great distress he was hiding himself, and his grave could not be found. So the Almighty put an idea into the midwife's mind, and she took his book and put it down beside the woman. As soon as she had put it down, immediately the woman bore her son, and that son was my husband. So everyone knew that there was a power in the book.'

'What do you think the book will fetch?' said I. Said one, 'What do we know?' Said a second, 'We ought to send it to America.' Said a third, 'Or to Rothschild.' 'I am prepared to send the book to any place you like,' said I, 'but I am not responsible for the money.' They all looked up in surprise and said, 'And would Rothschild want us to give him the book for nothing, when we are poor women?' Said one, 'I believe that if this sacred book comes into Rothschild's hands he would weigh it against gold.' Said a second, 'After all, sir, you come from the Land of Israel and you know that Rothschild has a kind heart for Jews, for if anyone comes to him he gives him a colony.' 'Rothschild has a kind heart,' said I, 'but the men who surround him are not all good. That is why I asked how much you think this manuscript is worth.' Said they, 'How much is the book worth? What do we know? How much do you think it is worth, sir?' Said I, 'There is no fixed price for books, especially for a holy book like this. If I were Rothschild I would give fifty dollars for it.' The widows' faces lit up and they said, 'Fifty dollars'; then they closed their eyes and each one whispered, 'Fifty dollars, fifty dollars!' I said to them, 'Since I am not Rothschild, how much do I have to give for the book if I buy it for myself—not for myself, but to do a good deed with it? There is a colony in Israel where there is a lying-in home, to which women come to give birth, and I had the idea of sending the book there.'

Said Sarah, 'If the book were all mine I would give it

for forty dollars, even thirty dollars, so that good deeds should be done through it.' Said her sisters-in-law, 'On condition that we are partners in the good deed.' Said I, 'If you particularly want to have a share in the good deed, I will not prevent you.'

So I gave them thirty-five dollars and said, 'In the meantime let the book stay with you, and if in thirty days you do not change your minds I will come and take it.' 'Heaven forbid that we should change our minds,' said Sarah, 'especially as we have devoted part of the money that we have taken off the price to the good deed.' 'Didn't you say, sir,' said another, 'that you would give us fifty dollars, and you gave us thirty-five? So with the money we took off the price we became partners in your good deed.' I nodded my head and said, 'In any case, I leave the book with you until I come and take it.'

Next morning Sarah came to my hotel and brought me the book. 'I heard,' said she, 'that anything that has been dedicated for the sake of the Land of Israel must not be left lying in the house.' She put the book on the table, kissed it and stroked it, and smiled at me, as one smiles to a partner, for through this book we had become partners in a good deed.

CHAPTER ONE AND FORTY

End of Winter

Hanoch's memory was buried in oblivion. Although the rabbi had forbidden his children to say the Kaddish prayer and his wife to go into mourning, there was no doubt that Hanoch was dead. I, too, was of that opinion. Since the night he had met me beside the spring, it was clear to me that he was dead.

Hanoch's wife took out a box to the marketplace and set up a stall. Her neighbors in the market did not hinder her; on the contrary, if she met with a difficult customer, they reminded him that she was at one and the same time a widow and a deserted wife, that her house was empty of bread but full of orphans, and it would be a very meritorious act to buy something from her. Even the Gentile women favored her, remembering that Hanoch her husband had been such an upright Jew; they would bring her eggs, vegetables, and honey, sometimes even a chicken, and wait until she should sell something and pay.

Her box did not attract pieces of gold, or even copper coins. In a word, Hanoch's wife did not prosper, just as the other women did not prosper; but they were accustomed to be without a livelihood, and she did not want to get accustomed. She would sit and wail and cry, or she would use an echo of her earlier weeping, which had moved all hearts but now irritated the listener. If a woman's soul has been crushed by her troubles you cannot expect her voice to be pleasant, but you do not have to stand and listen. So people would avoid her and her box, and buy elsewhere. Not only are you not filled with compassion for this wretched woman, but you feel annoyed at her for making you harden your heart.

However, her home was far from the market, so that when she sat in the marketplace the orphans were left without a meal, and when she came back she would be overcome by sleep, so that she could not manage to cook for them. When she awoke, the little ones would be sleeping and she could not sleep. She would lie on her bed and see Hanoch driving his horse forward and struggling against the snow. She would raise her voice and scream, 'Hanoch, Hanoch!' and all the neighbors would crowd into her house and ask, 'Where is he?' And she would cry, 'On my solemn oath, only a little while ago I saw him and his horse.'

At first the neighbors would pity her and try to strengthen her heart with elixirs against weakness. But when it happened a second time, they turned their eyes away from her and went away. When it happened a third time, they mocked her and said, 'Why didn't you catch the horse by his tail?' But how hard it is to catch the tail of a horse that is seen in a dream!

Once Reb Hayim and I were sitting in the Beit Midrash and there was no one there except us. I saw that he gave a sudden start, rose, then sat down again; then he rose again and came up to me, and then went back to his place. This he did several times. 'Do you want to tell me something, sir?'

I said. 'I want to ask something of you,' said he, 'but I am afraid it may be too hard for you to do.' Said I, 'Whether it is easy or hard, if it is in my power I will not fail to do it.' Reb Hayim lowered his eyes and gripped the end of the table in silence; then he raised his eyes and looked at me in silence; then he lowered his head onto his beard and said, 'If you can spare a copper, I would ask . . .' I said to him, 'If you want to give me the privilege of doing a good deed, certainly.' 'It is a favor I am asking, like the favor you did for Hanoch,' said Reb Hayim. 'It was no favor I did for Hanoch,' said I, 'I paid him for his trouble.' Said Reb Hayim, 'Perhaps you would pay me whatever you used to pay Hanoch.' 'With all my heart,' said I, 'and I'll give you even more, for Hanoch did not look after the lamps or stoke the fire, while you, sir, trim the candles and look after the lamps and stoke the fire, so your trouble is greater and you ought to receive more. But I do not know how much.' Said Reb Hayim, 'Whatever you used to pay Hanoch, you should pay me.' 'I do not know how much I used to give Hanoch,' I replied. 'I would put my hand in my pocket and give him sometimes more and sometimes less, whatever my hand brought out at the moment. If you like, I will fix your pay, so that you should not rely on a man's hand, which is sometimes open and sometimes clenched.' So I fixed his pay. Then Reb Hayim said, 'One thing more I would ask of you: please give me my pay on the fifth day of the week.' From that day forward I would give him the money for the whole week every Thursday morning.

Once I paid him for several weeks at a time, because I saw that his daughter Zippora's shoes were torn, and I said to myself: If I give him all at once he will buy shoes for her. He took the pay for the week and gave me back the rest. After some time I found out that he was giving the money to Hanoch's wife. He himself lived on the money the officers had given him for serving them when they were prisoners, as well as the money he had brought from his travels, for sometimes he had had the opportunity to do some work and earn something.

Most of the month of Adar had already gone. The snow

that had lain in heaps was shrunken, and if a little snow fell it melted while it was falling.

Reb Hayim's work was growing less. At first he would bring wood two or three times a day, but now only once, and occasionally some was left until the next day, for the cold had weakened and we did not need so much wood. As we did not need much wood, so we did not need much kerosene, for the days were beginning to draw out.

As the cold weakened and the snow shrank, the roads cleared. Men went out to their work. Those whose work was in the town went to town, and those whose work was in the villages went out to the villages.

The town took on a new appearance. The streets, which had been empty throughout the winter, filled up with people, and bargaining went on at the doors of the shops. At first glance it seemed as if Szibucz had taken up its affairs again, but at a second and truer glance, it could be seen that everyone was only standing about idly. In any case, there were more people at the streetcorners than in the Beit Midrash, for sometimes we had to wait until they came to pray, and after the prayer they would slip out without reciting psalms or studying a chapter of Mishna. Nevertheless, our old Beit Midrash was better than most of the houses of prayer in the town, for we had a quorum of ten for prayer every day, while in most of the houses of prayer there was no quorum every day, but sometimes the services were held in one and sometimes in another, according to the numbers that came and the nearness of the place. Only in the Great Synagogue were there several quorums and frequent services, and if we did not find ten men we would borrow from there and hold our service.

Most of the worshippers in the Great Synagogue were simple folk, who did not like the people of our old Beit Midrash. Why? Because in the early days, when Jews behaved with a high hand and the dignitaries used to domineer, they would make the unlearned stand beside the washbasin near the door, and not allow them to wear the fur *shtreimel* on their heads on Sabbaths and festivals, but only the broad-brimmed *spodik*, and on the Sabbath before the Ninth of Av, when scholars wore the *spodik* instead of a *shtreimel* in mourning for Jerusalem, the unlearned men were not allowed to wear even a *spodik* but only an ordinary hat, because honor was only for the learned. And although learning had vanished from the old Beit Midrash and the scholars were no better than the ignorant, the hatred of the unlearned for the scholars had not abated. Once we were about to pray and there was one lacking, so I asked one of the men in the Great Synagogue to complete the quorum. He drew himself up stiffly and said, 'That means that Moses our Teacher and eight like him cannot pray as a congregation unless you ask Zelophehad the son of Hepher to come and make up the quorum. And afterward, when you no longer need him, you come and say he is a sinner, that he was seen gathering sticks on the Sabbath day, and have him stoned to death.'

Reb Hayim swept the floor, stoked the stove, laid the cloths, and lit the candles and the lamps. We recited the Afternoon Service, welcomed in the Sabbath, and recited the Evening Service.

When the prayer leader recited the sanctification over the wine, there was no child to be found to drink it. I felt the sweets in my pocket and asked one man, 'Where is your son?' He stammered and said, 'He stayed behind with his mother.' I asked another, 'Why did you not bring your son to the Beit Midrash?' Said he, 'It's a miracle that I've brought myself. All the week long you tire yourself out on the roads; when the Sabbath comes a man wants to sit in peace.'

How beautiful were the Sabbath eves at the time when the Beit Midrash was full of Jews, and the children would surround the Ark and answer 'Amen' after the cantor; now, when the children's fathers find it a miracle that they have brought themselves to pray, how many miracles are needed to bring the children!

I felt the sweets in my pocket. The paper bags were torn and the sweets stuck to my fingers. I wiped my fingers and went home to my hotel to eat. After the meal I went back to the Beit Midrash to explain to the people the simple and the subtle of passages from the scriptural portion of the week, as I used to do on Sabbath eves. Three men had come, and were sitting beside the stove. One of them yawned and brought the others to the point of yawning, and when he stopped they yawned and brought him to the point of yawning.

I gazed at my book and cocked my ears to hear if anyone were coming. Half an hour went by, and no one came. I said to myself: And those who are sitting with me, why do they not ask me to say a word of Torah? Now, even if they ask, I will not respond. When they were silent, I said to myself: It is said that when two men sit together and discuss Torah, the Divine Presence rests among them. Whether they are many or few, one ought to speak, and even if there is only one who wishes to hear the words of the Torah, it is forbidden to withhold them from him. While I was talking to myself, they slipped away and were gone.

This man felt strange with a bellyful of Scripture verses and sayings from the sages, and no one wished to hear them. Moreover, on other Sabbaths I did not prepare anything, but whatever God put in my mouth I would speak, and for this Sabbath I had prepared many comments.

I remained alone in the Beit Midrash and gazed at the shining candles. First I said: 'You are shining in vain; but then I said: Not so, you are shining for the sake of the Sabbath. I smoothed down the clean cloth on the table and closed my book.

It was not in order that I might be popular with my fellow men that I came here, nor was it in order to sermonize on verses from the Torah. Nevertheless, these things did make my being here more pleasant, and perhaps there was also an infinitesimal feeling of pride in my heart when I used to stand and discourse in front of the congregation, but in any case not more than that of the pointer used to indicate the letters as it bends itself in the hand of the teacher.

I got up and put on my coat, but before I left I repeated to myself what I had prepared to say in public.

The portion for that week was the one beginning: 'These are the regulations of the Tabernacle,' and what I wanted to say was connected with the last verse of the portion: 'For the cloud of the Lord was upon the Tabernacle by day, and fire was on it by night, in the eyes of all the House of Israel, throughout their journeys.'

We should be precise in interpreting 'In the eyes of all the House of Israel'—do houses have eyes? And what does Rashi of blessed memory want to teach us, when he explains that the journey also includes the places where they encamped? And I went back to the verse 'And the glory of the Lord filled the Tabernacle,' for the glory of the Lord was not mingled with the cloud. Then I went back to the beginning of the portion, 'These are the regulations of the Tabernacle, the Tabernacle of Testimony.' Why was the Tabernacle mentioned twice? Because in this passage they were told that the Tabernacle was destined to be destroyed twice: the First Temple and the Second Temple. And we may ask: Was it for the Holy One, blessed be He, at this moment, when Israel had joy and gladness, to inform them of such an evil thing? But this is explained by the word that follows: 'Testimony.' It is a testimony to all the people of the world that there is forgiveness for Israel, and these are the tidings. Since the Lord poured out His wrath on the wood and the stones, but Israel remained in existence, we learn that the Tabernacle—which in Hebrew is *mishkan*—was Israel's pledge—in Hebrew *mashkon*; and this is why it is written, 'The Tabernacle of Testimony,' for it was a testimony and a pledge for Israel. And these are ancient matters. Finally I went back to the beginning and explained a number of scriptural texts about which I raised questions, and touched on a number of topical ideas which are already implied in our eternal Torah. And so I discussed the reason why the vessels were made before the Tabernacle. Although I do not go so far as to agree with the expositors who say that the vessels mentioned in the Torah allude to the virtues of the soul, I do interpret, in a manner close to theirs, that the Torah was hinting to us that we should set our virtues in order first, before entering the tent.

The candles had reached the end, but were still burning strongly. Even better were the lamps, which Reb Hayim had filled. I took the key, went out, and locked up the Beit Midrash.

And where was Reb Hayim? I heard that he had gone to Hanoch's wife, to recite the Kiddush there.

The street was empty and my heart was full. I wanted to relieve my heart, but found no companion. My shadow dragged behind me; my shadow was longer than I and broader than I, but I paid it no heed, as if it were not there.

Suddenly it occurred to me to go to the Gordonia group: first, to keep my promise, for on the day I went to look for the old locksmith to make me a key, I promised our comrades that I should come again; and second, in order to see a fellow Jew.

When I reached the house of the group, I did not find the entrance, and when I found the entrance I did not find the steps by which to go up. Later I heard that the Revisionists had dragged away the steps and thrown them into the river.

I walked around the house on all four sides, and looked at the windows, from which a little light came. I repeated various names used by Jews; perhaps I would remember one of the names of the Gordonia comrades and I would call it out so that he should come to take me up to the house. Between ourselves, even if I had called out all the names in the Torah, the Prophets, and the Writings, I should have accomplished nothing, for most of our comrades called themselves by names of their own invention, like Kuba, Luntchi, Henryk, or Yanik.

I looked at my shadow, which climbed upward and then lay flat again before me on the ground. If it had been given a mouth to speak it would have said, 'Just as you are weary, so am I weary.'

I took off my hat and wiped the sweat off my forehead. My shadow did likewise. If it had been given a mouth to speak it would have said, 'I am with you in your trouble.'

I took the two keys, the key of the Beit Midrash and the key of the hotel, and jingled them together so as to appease somewhat the boredom in my heart. What shall I tell you? I was like a man who sings songs to a heavy heart.

I began talking to myself. 'Perhaps we should leave this place.'

'Where to?' 'Wherever you want to go.' Since I did not find a place to go, I went back to my hotel.

On the way, another shadow mingled with mine, and I

saw a girl walking behind me. I began to regret having left, for if I had not, perhaps that girl would have shown me the entry to the house of the group and I would have gone in and sat down among other people—and not among shadows—and perhaps we would have had a pleasant conversation.

The girl came up and greeted me. I returned her greeting and asked, 'What are you doing in the street, miss, at such a late hour?' Erela answered, 'First, the hour is not late. And second, anyone who is going home must pass along the street.' 'If so,' said I, 'we both have the same road.' Said Erela, 'If two meet on the way, that does not mean that both have the same road.' 'And are you not going home?' said I. 'I am going home,' she replied. 'Well then,' said I, 'we do have one road, for I, too, am going home—and my hotel is next to your house.' Said Erela, 'If you are referring to the geographical aspect, sir, you are quite right, but apart from the geographical aspect, there are others, which have no relation to each other.'

I put on my hat and said, 'Father in heaven, how much does a man know what is near and what is far?' 'What do you mean: How does a man know?' said Erela. 'Whatever is near is near, and whatever is far is far.'

'Is that also something you have learned from geography?' said I, jesting. 'First,' replied Erela, 'this is something every intelligent person knows by himself. And second, anyone who studies geography no longer has any doubts as to these concepts.' 'Geography,' said I to her, 'is androgynous.'

Miss Erela turned her spectacles on me in astonishment, then she took them off and wiped them very thoroughly, then she put them back and asked me, 'On what grounds do you say so? From the grammatical point of view there is no evidence for what you say.' I bowed and said, 'I am not a conceited man, and I do not say that there is grammatical evidence for every word that comes from my lips. How is your little brother?' Said Erela, 'Why do you call him little? If you are referring to his years, he is certainly not little, and if you are thinking of his intelligence, he is greater than several people who display themselves as great.' I bowed to her and said, 'We have reached our destination, here is your house before you. If I were not afraid you might regard me as a wonderworker, I would tell you that I know what you have in your heart to say to me.' 'First,' said Erela, 'I do not believe in miracles, and second, no one knows what is in his neighbor's heart.'

I said to her, 'Look, miss, this man who stands before you knows what is in your heart and what you wish to say to me.' Said Erela, 'I'm afraid you might be proved wrong.' 'If so, I will tell you. You want to go into your house and bid me farewell.'

Said Erela, 'If so, you are mistaken. I wanted to say *au revoir.*'

So I was mistaken. I had forgotten that such a word still existed.

Miss Erela turned and went into her house, and I turned toward my hotel.

I put the key into the lock, but it did not open.

Krolka came out with a candle in her hand and said, 'What is this, sir, don't you know how to open the door?' 'I am surprised at it myself,' I replied. Krolka looked at the key in my hand and said, 'That isn't the key of our hotel.' I looked at it and saw that it was the key to the Beit Midrash. Between one thing and another I had changed the key of the hotel for the key of the Beit Midrash.

CHAPTER TWO AND FORTY

With the Sick Child

The holy Sabbath passed, but not like other Sabbaths. When the Holy One, blessed be He, wishes to chastise His creatures, He makes their Sabbaths sorrowful.

After the closing benediction, I went to Daniel Bach's house to pay for his wood. Before going in, I collected the sweets that had remained whole. I gave them to the child. He took them and arranged them in front of him in the form of a heart, and then in the form of a Shield of David. Then he took one and gave it to his mother, one to his father, then one to his sister. Finally, he took two and gave them to me.

His mother asked him, 'Why did you not give the gentleman in the same way as you gave us?' 'I don't know,' he replied. 'You don't know, my son?' said the mother in surprise. 'I'm sure you do know.' Said the child, 'First I didn't know, now I do know.' 'If so, tell us, son,' said his mother. Said the child, 'At first, I thought: Since all the candies are his, why do I have to give him any?' 'And what did you think afterward, when you did give him some?' 'Afterward,' replied the child, 'I thought perhaps he hadn't left any for himself; that's why I gave him some.' 'And why did you give each of us one and him two?' 'So that if he wanted to give, he would still have something left to give,' answered the child. 'Isn't he wise? Isn't he good?' said his mother. 'Let me kiss you, son.'

His father said to the child, 'Ask the gentleman to tell you a nice story.' The child said to me, 'If you can tell stories, so tell me what Grandpa is doing just now.' Said Erela, 'That isn't in the category of stories.' 'Well, what is it?' said the child. 'When you learn the theory of literature, you will know what is a story and what isn't a story,' said Erela. 'And if someone doesn't learn the theory of literature, doesn't he know what a story is?' said the child. 'Certainly he doesn't know,' replied Erela. 'So why don't you know how to tell stories?' said the child. 'You've learned the theory of literature, haven't you?' Said Erela, 'But I know what is a story and what isn't a story.' 'And what Grandpa is doing isn't a story?' said the child. 'No,' said Erela, 'that isn't a story.' 'And what is it?' 'That is in the category of information,' said Erela, 'so long as it is important, but if it isn't important, it's nothing at all.' 'Well,' said the child, 'let the gentleman tell me the story of nothing at all.' Erela turned her spectacles on the child and said in surprise, 'What do you mean "nothing"? If there is nothing, there isn't anything to tell.' Said the child, 'Grandpa is doing some thing, so there is something to tell. Tell me what my grandfather is doing just now, sir.'

I passed my hand over my forehead and said, 'At this moment your grandfather is sitting in a courtyard, in front of the little house—no, in front of the large house, with his head

bowed in thought, and he is saying, "Wonder of wonders, it
is not yet Passover and already it is warm in the open, just as
in the days of spring." '

'And Amnon, where is he?'

'Amnon? Who is Amnon?'

'Don't you know? Amnon is my uncle Yeruham's son.'

'Amnon,' I said to him, 'is sitting in the children's room
eating porridge with milk, and he does not leave anything in
the plate, because he is a good boy and eats everything he is
given; so the maid gives him an apple. Although oranges are
better than apples, the nurse believes that children need apples. What do you think, dear, does she do right?' 'It isn't so,'
said the child. 'What isn't so?' 'Amnon is not sitting in the
children's room,' replied the child. 'And where is he sitting?'
'You tell me.' 'Wait a moment, dear,' I said to him, 'and I will
think a little.' Said the child, 'And do you have to think?'
'And you, dear, don't you think?' 'I don't think,' said the child.
'But what then do you do?' 'I open my eyes and see,' said the
child, 'and sometimes I shut my eyes like this and see more.'
He shut his eyes and smiled. 'And what do you see?' I asked.
'First I want to know what came into your mind,' said the
child. I replied, 'I had no time to think. Now I will do the
same as you. I will shut my eyes and see what Amnon is doing.' I closed my eyes and smiled, like Raphael. Said Raphael,
'So tell me—what is Amnon doing.' Said I, 'Amnon is sitting in
Grandpa's lap, twisting his beard and saying, "Grandpa, when
I grow up, I will grow a big beard like yours." Grandpa says,
"Indeed I hope so." Then he kisses him and says, "You are
wise, son, wiser than all the lads in the settlement." ' 'And
what is my uncle Yeruham doing now?' said Raphael. I replied, 'How can I know? He is sitting high, high above the
seventh heaven, on the right hand of the Holy One, blessed
be He. You know, my son, that those who are killed for the
Land of Israel are most precious to the Almighty, and He delights in them every day, every hour, every moment.'

'And when they are sitting on God's right hand, what are
they doing?' said Raphael. 'Be still, son,' said I, 'and let me
listen. I believe they are reading the Torah before Him—the
section about the sacrifice of Isaac, for the melody is like the

melody of the Torah reading at the New Year.' The child pricked up his ears, looked up, and said, 'In fact, that's how it is.' Said Erela, 'How do you know in fact that's how it is? Have you ever been in a synagogue at the New Year and heard the reading?' Said the child, 'I've been in a synagogue and heard the reading of the Torah.' His mother looked at him in surprise: How can he say that? Since the day he was born he has not stirred from his bed. And she lowered her head in silence.

Said the child to his mother, 'Why don't you tell Erela that I was with you in the synagogue—then, at the New Year, when they brought the head of Rabbi Amnon and placed it on the lectern, and he said the *Unetaneh Tokef* prayer.' 'When was that?' asked his mother.

Said the child, 'Come, Mother, and let me whisper to you.' 'What are you saying?' cried the child's mother in surprise. 'In that year you were not even born.' 'But I was already in the world,' said the child. 'How, son, how?'

The child smiled and said, 'It was then, in that year when you fainted in the synagogue, and all the women were excited and brought you fainting drops.' Said Sara Pearl, 'That happened in the year I was pregnant with him.' 'So you see, Mother,' said Raphael, 'I was in the synagogue and saw everything. Now, Mother, tell Erela I was speaking the truth.' Tears stood in the eyes of the child's mother and she said, 'What a memory he has, God keep him.' 'It's wrong to encourage him in his fancies,' said Erela.

Daniel drummed on the table with his fingers and said, 'Arguments I hear; you started with a story and ended with an argument.'

'Daddy,' the child said, 'What is an argument?' Said Daniel, 'Erela, how can we explain it to him?' Said Erela, 'What do you mean how can we explain it? Surely it's simple: anything that people argue about is called an argument.'

The child's father smiled and said, 'You have learned Bible, son, and you remember how Abraham spoke to the Almighty about Sodom: "Perhaps there are fifty righteous men in the city; will You sweep away the righteous with the wicked?"—and so forth.' 'That isn't an argument,' said the child. 'So what is it, supplication and entreaty?' 'That's Torah,' said the child. 'For them,' said Erela, 'everything is Torah.' 'Not everything is Torah,' said the child, 'only what is written in the Torah is Torah.'

Said Daniel Bach to his wife, 'Perhaps we should have tea? What do you think about that?' 'The kettle is boiling,' said Mrs. Bach. 'I'll bring the tea right away. You'll be so kind as to drink a glass of tea, sir, won't you? I'm sorry I didn't bake a cake.' Daniel Bach smiled and said, 'My wife is of the opinion that one does not fulfill the duty of after-Sabbath supper with a cup of tea. But who told you a glass of tea calls for cakes? Was it from the Germans in Vienna you learned that?' Mrs. Bach replied, 'And without that, don't I bake you a cake?' and she blushed as she spoke.

'It is the Shavuot festival that calls for cakes,' said her husband. 'I hope to bake you a cake before then,' said Mrs. Bach. 'If you really want to, I won't stop you,' said her husband. 'Let us drink the tea before it gets cold.'

I drank and said, 'From now on, Reb Hayim's work will be easier; the spring is coming and the stove will not need wood.'

Mrs. Bach sighed and said, "Spring days are coming and winter days are going.' Said Mr. Bach, 'Even the stoves need a rest. Have you heard that Reb Hayim's son-in-law is pressing him to come and stay with him?' 'And what did Reb Hayim reply?' 'Who knows? It isn't Reb Hayim's way to tell.'

Said Erela, 'Do you think you did right, sir, to take the book from the women?' 'Which book?' 'That book whose name I forget—the one they put under the heads of silly women when they give birth.' 'Are you afraid, miss, that the town may remain without its talisman?' 'Not at all,' said Erela, 'but I am worried about this fanaticism, and because people will say that the Land of Israel needs talismans and charms and all kinds of stuff and nonsense.'

Erela's father smiled and said, 'On the contrary, Erela, it is an honor for Szibucz if people see that we too are not short of wonderworkers. And if we cannot help in the building of the Land with money, at least we help with souls.'

Said Erela, 'If I may speak before my father, I permit

myself to ask: What did Father mean by that word?' 'What word do you mean?' 'What word do I mean? If my father does not remember, I take the liberty of reminding him. What did you really mean when you spoke of "souls," that people could say that we are helping the building of the Land with souls.'

'Now that our friend has been good enough to send them that book,' replied Daniel, 'the women will not miscarry there. The result is that we are helping them with souls.' 'Father,' said Erela, 'you make me angry.' Said Mrs. Bach, 'You can't deny that the book has often done what midwives and doctors could not do.' Erela looked at her mother angrily and shrugged her shoulders, saying, 'I know there are still many people who believe in nonsense, but that it should be my fate to have my father and mother among them, that is too hard to bear.'

Her father looked at her quietly and said, 'My daughter Erela keeps to her principle that whatever is beyond our reason must not be used, even if she knows it is useful to many people, as we have seen in the virtues of the book, which has helped many women.' 'What is the use of it,' said Erela, 'helping to bear children who will believe all that nonsense?' Bach stroked his artificial leg and said, 'My daughter Erela is a rationalist. Perhaps we should drink another glass?' 'Many thanks. I believe the time has come for me to go.' 'Not at all,' said Mr. Bach, 'wait a little, sir, and let us spend some more time together. What news have you heard from the Land of Israel? For several weeks we have not had a letter from my father. Perhaps something has happened to him? Perhaps he is sick, or there have been disturbances and they have attacked Ramat Rahel? This Mufti, what is he?' 'He is an Arab.' 'And if he is an Arab,' said Mr. Bach, 'does innocent blood have to be spilled?' 'Not because he is an Arab,' I replied, 'but because the strong are always likely to attack the weak. And so long as we are few and weak, we can expect any kind of trouble.' Said Erela, 'What you are saying makes me laugh. Anyone who hears what you say might imagine that we are sitting there with folded arms, stretching out our necks to the slaughter, like our Jews in Szibucz. Anyone who reads the papers is well aware of all the heroic deeds that are being done there.'

I shook my head and said, 'I have seen more than what is written in newspapers. But what is the use of heroism that destroys its heroes? If the hero must always be engaged in warfare, in the end he is weakened and falls.' Said Erela, 'According to what you say, it follows that we should stretch out our throats and say, "Executioner, here is the neck; come, butcher me!" as our poet Bialik said so well in his poem "On the Slaughter."' 'That was not what I meant, miss,' said I. 'So what did you mean?' said she. 'I believe I am entitled to say that I understand the meaning of words. Or perhaps there is another meaning to the concept of hero, which I have not succeeded in finding in the dictionary.' 'There is no other meaning,' I replied, 'but if one may be entitled to suggest an interpretation that is not in the dictionary, I would say that a hero is the man whom everyone fears, so that no one comes to attack him.' Erela laughed and said, 'Utopia! If that is the kind of hero you are looking for, sir, you should go to the sports field. There you will find the hero you seek.' Said Mr. Bach, 'And will things go on there like this forever?'

'I have put that question to wise men,' I said, 'but their answers did not satisfy me, until a certain wise man gave me an explanation. This wise man is one whose good deeds come before his learning. At the time when most of our wise men remained abroad and preached sermons about Zionism, he went up to the Land and succeeded in doing what the organs of speech cannot do. He used to say, "Do, and expect nothing." And since he did, his deeds combined to make a substantial reality. For such is the way of deeds: if a man does one thing today and another tomorrow, in the course of time they combine into a great deed. After the Arabs had destroyed my house, leaving me without a roof to my head, he invited me into his house and gave me a bed and a table. Once he found me grieving. "Do not grieve," he said to me, "all will be well." "What good can we expect?" I said to him. "If we build, our neighbors destroy; if we plant, our neighbors uproot. See how many settlements have been laid waste in one

day, see how many families have been killed in one hour—
and you say, 'All will be well.' If good were to come out of
all this it would have come already, for our neighbors know
that we have turned the desolate wilderness into a settled
land, and they have been the first to enjoy the benefits, but in
the end they have done us all this evil. It seems to me that the
early days were better than these, and you say, 'All will be
well.' You, who said, 'Do, and expect nothing,' have suddenly
become an advocate of hope." He replied, "At first I expected
nothing, but now I expect many things, for we have already
entered into the second era." And he sat down and explained:
"There are three eras in the life of a people. In the first era,
the nation is small and weak, despised by its neighbors, who
look upon it as if it did not exist. And since it is lowly and
despised, sometimes people have pity on it and treat it kindly,
like a strong man who is kind to the weak. The second era
comes when the nation rouses itself from its lowliness and
becomes stronger and stronger. If its neighbors are wise, they
establish bonds of friendship and brotherhood with it, and
they benefit each other. If they are not wise, they hinder it at
every turn, and in the end they make war upon it. It defends
itself, and girds itself with strength and valor, because it
knows that if it falls into its enemies' hands, no one will have
mercy on it. So it does not fear the clash of shields or the
onslaught of fighters. When its neighbors see this, they make
peace with it, then they seek its friendship, and then regard
it as a nation equal to themselves. First they seek its friendship for their own advantage, then for the benefit of both,
and then they help each other. Until now we have lived in the
first era, when a nation is lowly and despised, and now we
have reached the second era, of a nation that has fortified itself and gained in strength; our children, who will come after
us, will be privileged to reach the third era, of a nation like
all the other nations. And what will come after that—no eye
has yet seen that." '

Mr. Bach stroked his neck with both hands and looked at
his sick son, who was slumbering. Then he stroked his good
leg and said, 'In the meantime, they do with us whatever a
murderer's heart may desire.'

I looked at his slumbering son and said, 'So long as we are living in the second era.' 'And when will we reach the third era?' said Mr. Bach. I got up from my chair and said, 'That depends on me and you and every man of Israel. When we go up to the Land and join our brothers, who are engaged in battle there.'

As I was going out, Mrs. Bach took me by the arm and led me to her son's bed. 'Look at him, sir,' said she, 'doesn't he look like an angel of the Lord of Hosts? When I imagine that murderers could lift their hands against a child like this, I tremble.' Said I, 'Why should the murderers come?' Said Mrs. Bach, 'But surely you want us to go to them.' 'To them?' said I, 'to whom?' 'To those murderers who killed Yeruham,' said Mrs. Bach. 'Not at all, madam,' said I. 'I want us to come to ourselves, so that the power of the murderers may be weakened.' Said Mrs. Bach, 'But then you ran away from there, sir.' I sighed and said, 'I ran away from there? And perhaps I really did run away, for anyone who leaves the Land of Israel, even for a while, is regarded as one who runs away.'

CHAPTER THREE AND FORTY

Signs of Spring

After breakfast on Sunday morning I went, as usual, to the Beit Midrash. It was a fine day and signs of spring could be seen in the land. The ice had broken; jagged pieces floated on the river; puddles of snow-water shimmered in the street and a new sun shone upon them. Bells sounded from the two Gentile houses of worship; the townsfolk, with their women, came and went. The shops were closed on the outside and the shopkeepers stood idle in the doorways, while their women stood inside and bargained with customers who had come surreptitiously to buy. Suddenly two policemen appeared—or perhaps it was one policeman who looked like two. The shopkeepers and all the other people took off their hats, bowed their heads, and smiled affectionately at the policeman. The policeman twirled his mustache and moved on. The shop-keepers clasped their hands behind their backs and looked after him until he had disappeared from sight.

Ignatz adorned himself with the decorations he had acquired in the war, some through his own deeds and some by taking from the dead. He pushed out his chest and thrust his face at the passers-by, crying, as usual, *'Pieniadze!'* meaning 'Alms!'

Yoshke, or Veptchi, or some other frequenter of the Beit Midrash, came up to me and said, 'The priest is taking a long time for his sermon today.' I felt indignant and wanted to say to him, 'I see you are more interested in the priest's sermon than in our public service, for it is several days since you came to the Beit Midrash.' But another man accosted me and said, 'The bastard gives us lots of trouble.'

I thought he was talking of Ignatz, who was rumored to be the son of a Gentile from a Jewish mother and suspected of tale-bearing to the authorities. When he saw that I did not know whom he was speaking of, he continued, 'Haven't you heard that that priest is the son of a Jewish father?' 'A Jewish father?' 'A Jewish father and a Gentile mother.' 'A fine thing,' said I. 'If it is true it may very well not be a lie. Or, contrariwise, if it is not a lie it may very well be true. But I tell you that the whole thing should have been different from the start. How? That Jew, the priest's father, should have made advances to Ignatz's mother, and that slave, Ignatz's father, should have made advances to the mother of the priest. Or perhaps you have confused the story of Ignatz with the story of the priest.' 'You make jokes, but I say we should weep,' said the man. 'Since the day the bastard came to our town we have no peace, for on every one of their feast days he incites the Gentiles against us with his sermons. Now do you believe the story is true?'

'What truth? What story?'

'The story tells of a certain lady who had a Jewish tenant farmer, a fine, handsome man. She seduced him to an act of sin, and from that sin she bore a son. She handed the child over to a nunnery and they passed him on to a monastery, and the monks taught him that religion of theirs and its ways, until he became chief of the priests in our town.' I nodded my head and said, 'If that is the way the story has been handed down to us, let us accept it.'

The man was indignant, 'I knew the priest's father after he repented,' he said. 'When I used to see him sitting in sack-cloth on the threshold of the porters' synagogue, fasting and reciting psalms, my very bones would quiver. If he had been in some other town, they would have presented their petitions to him, as they do to the rabbis of the Hasidim.'

My shoulders suddenly felt heavy. I unbuttoned my coat and went on.

For many days I had not seen Schuster and his wife. That sick woman, no one is going in to visit her. Let me go and see how she is keeping, or perhaps I had better not go, for if no one comes she forgets her sicknesses and he his exaggerations.

To go or not to go? If I find the stove lit I will go; if not, I will not go. When I came into the Beit Midrash I found Reb Hayim bent in front of the stove. I said to him, 'Have you lit the stove, sir?' Said Reb Hayim, 'I have arranged the wood and I do not know whether to set a light to it or not.' 'The winter is going,' said I, 'but the sunny days are still far off. Do you think we shall have a congregation for the After-noon Service? For the Morning Service we had to wait until a quorum gathered.' Reb Hayim spread his hands upward, as if to say that it was all in God's hands.

After Reb Hayim left I took a book to study, and remembered Schuster and his wife. I said to myself: Now the question is back at the beginning: to go or not to go? But I will fix a sign. I will open a book, and if there is a letter *lamed* at the beginning of the page, that is a sign that I should go. I opened the book and saw at the beginning of the page the word '*Lo*,' which means 'No.'

There is a *lamed* here, which means I ought to go. But this *lamed* is the beginning of the word '*Lo*'—which is meant to tell me not to go. Or perhaps, since the main thought was about the *lamed* and not about the whole word, I should follow the *lamed* and not the word as a whole. If so, that means I ought to go. *Kindchen*, it seems to me you are wasting your time.

Why are you suddenly so concerned with Schuster? Or perhaps it is not so sudden, but when you felt your coat heavy on your shoulders you thought of the man who made it. Let us leave the tailor and think of some other matter.

What shall we think about? Let us think about the adventures that happened to Reb Hayim and contemplate all those travels he made, from Szibucz to Warsaw and from Warsaw to Brisk in Lithuania, and from Brisk to Smolensk, and from Smolensk to Kazan, and from there to the places on the Volga. How wide is the world and how cramped is man's place. Now, when Reb Hayim has returned from all these places, he drags out an existence in the woodshed of our old Beit Midrash.

Does Reb Hayim intend to squander away all his days and years here? If he asked my advice I would tell him to go to his daughter, where perhaps he will gain a better end than he has here.

This book, which I opened in order to find a sign, was not suitable for study, so I closed it and took another. But it was not suitable for study either, so I closed it and took a different book. If I had taken a Gemara and studied, I would not have distracted my mind in this way. I closed the book and took out a Gemara from the bookcase. I held the Gemara in my hand and thought: What was it that man said? The father of the priest became a penitent. And in storybooks I have read that the priest himself repented.

These storybooks—are they chronicles of deeds or chronicles of the imagination? Whether the one or the other, why are there so few stories these days? Have the men of deeds disappeared or has the power of imagination diminished? Surely, wherever Jews live, they create new good deeds, which are blessed by the power of man's imagination, and receive glorification and strength from it; but where there are good deeds there is not always one who knows how to tell them. It is easier to do good deeds than to tell good stories.

What is the difference between the stories of the Hasidim

and the tales of the other great men of Israel? If you like, I may say that there is no difference: what you find in these you find in the others. But the other great men of Israel are masters of law, and are remembered for their teaching; while the Hasidim are men of deeds, and are remembered because of their deeds. And sometimes stories are ascribed to them which are already told of our early rabbis. Sometimes the name is the reason, as when an event that happened to the great Rabbi Meir of Tiktin is told of the righteous Rabbi Meir of Przemysl, and the like. But if you wish, I may say that there is a difference between them, for most tales of the great men of Israel are meant to teach the law and the commandments, morality and upright behavior, which every man can acquire; while the stories of the Hasidim are meant to enhance the glory of the zaddikim, who have been graced by heaven with the power to perform wonderful deeds, which not every man can do. The author of *Leket Yosher* wrote his book so that everyone should know how his great teacher behaved, and learn his ways in order to practice them; but when you read the stories of the Hasidim, though your soul admires them and your heart is inspired, you cannot do likewise.

Why have the Hasidim stopped coming to the old Beit Midrash? Is it because they have made peace among themselves and returned to the Tchortkovite *klois,* or have they stopped coming for the same reason as most of the other frequenters of the Beit Midrash?

I raised my eyes and looked at the great hill opposite the Beit Midrash. It was still naked, without any grass, and covered with a cold, damp darkness; tomorrow the grasses would grow on it and the sun would shine upon them. Let us close our eyes for a brief moment and stroll in another place, where the sun shines every day, and the trees blossom, and the whole land is covered with blossoms and flowers, and sheep walk between the houses, and their fleece warms your heart. Beside the sheep walks the shepherd, his satchel on his back and his flute in his mouth. Silent walk the flock, raising the dust, when suddenly a sheep stops and begins to dig in the earth, throwing himself down on the grass and bleating to his mate. And she comes to him, while the shepherd stands over them playing on his flute. Perhaps the ancestors of the shepherd were among the singers in the Temple and the songs of the Levites have survived in his flute, or perhaps his ancestors were among the destroyers of the Temple and it is the sound of the legionaries' trumpets in his mouth. What is it that oppresses my heart so much?

In the course of these musings, midday came. I put on my coat to go to my hotel.

When I came outside I heard a great noise and saw people standing around excited. I asked a child, 'What has happened here?' He looked at me startled, and did not answer. I got hold of someone and asked him, 'What has happened?' He stammered, 'Hanoch.' I found Ignatz and said to him, 'What is this excitement about?' He replied, 'Snow, sir, snow.' 'You have gone crazy,' I said to him angrily. 'What's this about snow here?' He stretched out his hand and said, 'There, there, there.' 'What are you screaming about—"There, there, there"?' said I. 'Open up your mouth and say what is there.' 'They've found Hanoch, there in the snow,' said Ignatz. 'Found Hanoch? Dead?' 'Then what?—Alive?' 'How did they find him?' 'How? . . .' But while Ignatz was trying to speak through his nose, another man came up and told me. That morning a Jew had gone out to the countryside and found Hanoch standing by his cart, embracing his horse. It seems that during the heavy snows Hanoch had frozen to death and been covered with snow, he and his horse and his cart. Now that the snow had melted, the three of them had been revealed together. It was almost certain that his horse had frozen first and, because Hanoch had tried to warm it, he had also been frozen.

Hanoch was dead and was brought to burial. The entire town walked behind his coffin. There was not a man in the town who did not come out to pay his respects to Hanoch.

With bowed heads we walked as mourners behind his coffin. After Hanoch had been forgotten by everyone, they began to tell of him again: how he had gone out on a snowy day to seek his livelihood, and how they had found him standing in the snow embracing his horse, as if he were alive. The man who found him had wanted to scold him for not letting his wife know that he was alive, but when he looked at him he saw that he was dead.

I remembered how I had told Hanoch about the martyrs from outside the Land of Israel who enter the Land immediately and do not have to wait until the dead from outside should make their way there under the ground, and how Hanoch had listened and envied them. I said to myself: Hanoch did not have the privilege of dying for the sanctification of the Divine Name, but he died for a crust of bread, so he will have to wait with all the dead from outside the Land. But I feel sure that the good angels who were created through his honest labor will ease his wanderings in this world and the next. And when our sacred Messiah comes—and may it be speedily in our days—all Israel will go out to meet him, and they will make way for the great ones, so that they should be the first to welcome the King Messiah. Then the King Messiah will say to them, 'Come, let us go to those of our brethren whom no one heeded because of their poverty.' And when the King Messiah sees Hanoch and his comrades, he will say to them, 'You needed me most; therefore I come to you first.'

CHAPTER FOUR AND FORTY

The Passover Festival

Passover was near at hand and I began to be concerned about the celebration of the festival. Really, I lacked for nothing in the hotel. My table was always properly set and my food plentiful, and no doubt I would lack nothing at the Passover as well, for the innkeeper's wife told me, 'Even though you do not eat meat, you need have no fear that you will go hungry, for I will make you tasty milk dishes such as you have never eaten in your life.' Yet a man's soul longs to sit down for the Passover with relatives and friends, especially since this is the first Passover he has spent far from his family.

But in the town where I was born I had no relatives and friends. Whoever had not died in the way of nature had died in the war; whoever had not died in the war had died from the effects of the war; and whoever had been left alive by the war had gone away to some other country. Again I stood alone, as on the first day I returned to my town. Even worse —on the day I returned I found a hotel, and now the hotel had become strange to me, for since I wished to celebrate the Passover eves in another place I forgot that I had a fixed place of my own. So far had I forgotten I had a place that I even thought of visiting the town rabbi, in the hope that he would invite me to celebrate the Seder with him. Finally it occurred to me to celebrate the Passover with Reb Hayim.

All that day this verse never left my lips: 'How good and how pleasant it is for brethren to sit together.' I would hire a woman to clear the woodshed and wash the floor; I would bring in a table and two chairs, and spread a white cloth on the table, and light many candles, and bring cushions for the festive seats, and go out to the market and buy unleavened bread and wine, and bring tasty dishes from the hotel, and Reb Hayim and I would celebrate together. 'How good and how pleasant for brothers to sit together.'

I explained the idea to Reb Hayim, but he said, 'I have already promised Hanoch's widow and orphans to celebrate with them.' 'I will celebrate with all of you,' said I. Reb Hayim looked at my clothes and said sorrowfully, 'You cannot celebrate there, sir.' 'Why not?' I asked. 'Because of the poverty,' said he. 'And am I a hater of the poor?' said I. 'No,' said he, 'but not every man can stand the poor, for their poverty has degraded them.'

I remembered several tales about men who wandered to far-off places and the Passover overtook them, and a miracle happened: some great prince, a God-fearing man who hid his good deeds from the authorities, came and invited them to celebrate the festival in his palace.

There are no miracles and wonders in these days, but if it is true that the chief of the priests in our town had a Jewish father, perhaps he observes their faith to the outward view but behaves like a pious Jew at home. Let me go to him;

perhaps he would invite me to celebrate the festival with him. While I was playing with this strange idea, the holiday came upon me and I sat down for the Passover in the hotel.

The joy of the Holy Day pervaded the entire house from the beginning of the Seder ceremony until the end. Anyone who had never seen Mr. Zommer except on that night might have been deluded into thinking that he was a joyful man. His eyes were wide open and it would be no exaggeration to say that even his eyebrows shone. On this night Mr. Zommer's eyes, which are always half closed, were open wide, and he looked at us with wholehearted affection. Rachel asked the four traditional questions, while Dolik and Lolik showed their prowess with the wineglass—and, needless to say, so did Yeruham, who drank more than any of them. Between the chapters, Mr. Zommer offered Yeruham the Haggadah and said, 'Let us hear how the Turk reads.' So Yeruham read in a Sephardi accent and a Yemenite accent, and in a strange Russian accent just as the proselytes read. When the time came to eat the afikomen at the end of the meal, it turned out that Babtchi had stolen it. Her father promised to give her a present—as is customary—and she gave the afikomen back. But then he refused to give her a piece of the afikomen unless she gave up her present. Dolik whispered to her, 'Give it up and don't eat it, for if you eat the afikomen you will be forbidden to eat or drink all night, and you will have to do without the meal with bread at the club.'

After the Seder Yeruham danced a hora, like the pioneers in the Land of Israel, and pulled his brothers-in-law and sister-in-law into the dance. Finally they took their father and mother, put them in the middle, and danced around them. Great are the festivals of the Lord, for even the triflers of this world rejoice in them.

For me the festivals of the Lord are days of meditation, especially this Passover eve, when I was far from home. I remembered days gone by, when I was a child and asked my father, of blessed memory, the four questions, and also the first year when my little son—always remembering the distinction between the living and the dead—asked me the four questions. Likewise I called to mind the Passover eves that had passed between my questions and the questions of my son, some of them years that had gone by in happiness and others that had passed without happiness. Praised be the Name of the Lord; why should a living man complain?

CHAPTER FIVE AND FORTY

In the Kaiserin's House

Many times I wanted to visit the Kaiserin, but when I remembered her the time was not right for a visit, and when the time was right for a visit I did not remember her. In the intermediate days of the Passover the two things happened to me together, and I went to see her.

Freide's house stands in Gymnasia Street near the Stripa. The war, which damaged the large houses, did not damage Freide's, and it is as whole as thirty or forty years ago, with no perceptible change apart from the change produced by many years. And as it is unaltered without, so it is unaltered within. The floor is covered with yellow plaster, and sacking is spread on the floor like a kind of carpet, and a large stove stands at the back of the house, blue with a red top. Freide's bed is near the stove. It is shaped like a kind of couch or bench: by day Freide does all her cooking on it, kneads dough and cuts noodles, and at night she takes off the board that covers it and lies down—lies but does not sleep, for in these days men cannot sleep—and sometimes she lies all night without closing an eye. And why does she not close an eye? First, because she must watch her tears, that they not soil her face. And second, because she is in the habit of watching the shadows that emerge from her household objects; this way, she feels that she is not alone. Ever since Elimelech her son went away she has been alone, and at night she wants to feel that she is not alone. 'Perhaps, my child,' she says to me, 'you say that the shadows are sins, as the children say; and I tell you that the shadows of human beings are sins, but the shadows of objects are pure, for any object is good-tempered and does human beings no harm. On the contrary, the objects are good to me, and when I tell them my troubles they do not tell me to stop chattering. You, too, my chick, are good-tempered; here I am chattering and chattering, and you sit and listen. It is because your mother's soul has entered into you. Never in her life did she scold me, and all her life she listened to my talk. But she is in the upper world, so how can I say that she has entered into you? Let me explain to you that I was not thinking of the soul itself, but of her good qualities, for a mother's qualities enter into her children, whether they are good or evil. To come back to the subject, I say that all your mother's good qualities have entered into you, her son. I said so to Zommer's wife when you sent me potatoes and matzoh and fat, and I say it again to you. And don't be annoyed with me, my chick, because I repeat myself, for because of all the sufferings I have endured I am afraid I might have forgotten, and failed to say what I wanted to say, so I say it again. A person must give praise and thanks for all that he is given, for otherwise he forgets to thank the Almighty for all the favors He does us. And when the Almighty sees that human beings are ungrateful, He turns His eyes away from them, and when, heaven forbid, He stops looking after men, they make war on each other. At the very beginning of the war I already said that all this war comes only because of the many ungrateful people in the world. Only think how many favors our Emperor, may he rest in peace, did for the Russians: when they fled from the Japanese he allowed them to encamp in his country. And he, the Russian Emperor, not only did not thank him, but made war against him. And what was his end? May the end of all the enemies of Israel be like his! Perhaps you may say that our Emperor died too. But I tell you that he died for another reason, because his days and years came to an end, and because the Jews were very troubled at the time and did not manage to beg mercy for him.

'Now let us talk about something else. I see you are looking at the window. I put some straw from the roof there, to stop the wind coming in through the holes and cracks. And as for the paper rosettes I put there, you may think I meant them for the sake of the wind, but I meant them only for beauty, for it is the way of rosettes to beautify the window. But now the winter has passed and springtime has come, so why do I not take the straw away? You should know that in our days, times have changed, and we cannot rely on the spring. Today it shows you a loving face and tomorrow it does not know you. So a person should think about his doings, and if the hour calls for it he must behave like a politician, although I do not like politics. And now I ask you not to be annoyed with me if I did not show my joy at your coming, and did not even place a chair for you, for I was so happy to see you that I forgot to tell you that I am happy. Now let me take a chair and put it before you, and you, my chick, will sit down, and we'll talk a little.'

Freide took a chair, but before she set it in front of me she sat on it herself and rubbed it with her dress. Then she stood before me, bent, as was her way, and looked at me with pleasure, every one of her wrinkles shining.

'Now,' said Freide, 'I will bring you one little cake I made from the potatoes you sent me. The cake is baked on all its sides, as the child used to like it.'

Freide brought fine little brown cakes arranged in a tin; their smell was good. This smell is not an object, not a body, and there is no substance in it at all; but when it reaches you, you are changed at once. Since the day he was exiled from his father's house, this man had not seen cakes like these; at the moment he smelled them he felt as if his youth had come back, as if he were with his mother.

I took a cake and said to Freide, 'Surely they are not made with fat?' 'Do you think,' replied Freide, 'that I deceive the world and make cakes without fat? You yourself sent me a pot of fat.' Said I, 'I don't eat meat.' 'Woe is me, my chick,' said Freide. 'If you don't eat meat, what do you eat? You're a young man, aren't you, and your bones need strengthening. You know, my dove, that anyone who doesn't eat meat, his bones rot; and you say, "I don't eat meat." On the contrary, a man must eat meat "until his lips grow tired of saying 'enough.'" I remember when I used to serve your mother, may she rest in peace, and her uncle came, her father's brother, your grandfather's brother, may he rest in peace, and your grandmother, may she rest in peace, made them milk dishes for supper, and he, may he rest in peace, said, "Milk doesn't make much sense now; if a man does not eat meat at night, how can he sleep?" And he, may he rest in peace, was a pious Jew, and did not let a superfluous word pass his lips. And if he, may he rest in peace, said so, no doubt it is so. And indeed it is so, for since the day the war came, and we cannot find a mouthful of meat for a meal, people have stopped sleeping. It is true I told you a different reason at first, but sometimes I don't sleep for one reason and sometimes for another reason, and sometimes for both reasons together. Since you don't eat anything, I wonder what I can do to gladden your heart. Perhaps you would like to see the picture of my husband, may he rest in peace. You remember Ephraim Yossel when he was an old man, but in the picture he is young, for when they took his picture he was a young man and served in the army, so he is dressed in soldier's clothes. Look at him, my chick, doesn't he look like the Emperor?'

I looked at the picture of Ephraim Yossel. This was the Ephraim Yossel whom the jesters of the town used to call Franz Josef, although they did not resemble each other. The Emperor's face was weak, like that of a man who had experienced much suffering, while Ephraim Yossel's face was like that of a man who has the whole world in his hands, for at the time he had no wife and had no cares for a livelihood. Next to him, on both sides, hung the pictures of his four sons who were killed in the war, all of them holding swords and dressed in uniform. But where was Elimelech's picture? His mother hid it behind the mirror and did not hang it up, because you do not hang up the picture of a living person and because Elimelech could not bear to see himself dressed in soldier's clothes. And why was his head wrapped in a scarf and a bunch of flowers in his hand? Because he was photographed when he was lying sick in the army hospital, and this bunch of flowers was given him by a certain lady who came to visit the casualties. 'This lady had a good heart,' Freide said, 'and although they told her that this soldier was a Jew she did not take the flowers back; on the contrary, she also gave him a dozen cigarettes and said to him that the smoke of cigarettes is sweeter than the smoke of cannons. And when she left she gave him her hand when she said goodbye, as she did to all the other soldiers, who were Gentiles. But that obstinate fellow did not kiss her hand, and I scolded him for it. And what do you think he answered me? "I am not a slave or a maidservant that I should kiss the hands of the masters." As if Ephraim Yossel his father—may he be our spokesman in heaven—was a slave; and didn't he kiss the hands of the lords and ladies?—and they used to like him—sometimes they would pat him on the shoulder affectionately. And what happened at the time of the elections the whole world knows, for a great minister, a member of parliament, kissed him on the forehead in the marketplace, and said to him, "You, tailor, you will vote for me in the elections, won't you?" And, what is most extraordinary, Elimelech is not a socialist, heaven forbid. If you don't mind, my chick, I will tell you something. When you went to the Land of Israel, or to Jerusalem—for all the troubles that have passed over me I don't remember where you went—in short, after you went there, I visited the child to console her. She said to me, "Here you are, Freide, a pair of shoes my son left behind, for he did not find room for them in his baggage; give them to Elimelech, your son." I took the shoes and ran home full of joy, because his shoes were torn. But he threw them in my face, and said, "Give them back to your lady." Of course you will understand, my chick, that I paid no attention to him and gave the shoes to his younger brother, who was also barefoot.

'Now, my chick, let us talk of other things, for I see you think this thing I have told you is not nice. And it really isn't nice, for it is not polite to kick away presents. And as for my house, which you said you thought was nice, I think it is nice too. First, because a man thinks his own house is nice, and second, because it is a gift from heaven. The wood and the stones are not a gift, for they were bought with my father's money, but the place where the house stands was given to us by the Almighty, as a man gives a gift to his friend and tells him: Take it. And how was that? In those days my father lived with his father-in-law, near this house. One Sabbath eve, in the afternoon, my father went out to bathe in the river, for on Sabbath eves in the summer Father used to bathe in the Stripa. He saw that the bank of the river had dried up. At first he was angry, because they had diverted the water where they had built a large flourmill at the side of the river. But while he was standing in the water his anger abated and his spirits rose, for it is the way of men that when wisdom enters their hearts, their anger goes away. Father said, "The bank of the river is dry and the water does not pass here; I will make me a little house." From then on, Father would examine the bank of the river and see how it was becoming firm soil, and my father was a Jew of the past generations, who, if he thought of doing a thing, did it. In short, why should I make the story any longer?—may God give you a long life, my chick— Father hired workmen, and brought beams and stones and other building materials, and started building himself a house. Some people laughed at Father and some envied him, but in any case the house was built. And when Father dedicated his house, he made a great Kiddush for all his friends, and they ate, drank, and sang hymns. So everything seemed to be good. But the best of the good started afterward, although from that best came great evil. How? Father had beams and boards left over from the building, and he wondered what he should do with these beams and boards. So he made himself a little hut for bathers. Once father made some clothes for a minister. When the minister saw the hut, he went in, took off his clothes, and went down to bathe. When he came out he gave Mother a little present. When they heard of this in the town they began coming to bathe; everyone would give a kreutzer and bathe. Finally one hut was not enough, and Father built several huts.

'So far, so good, my chick, but from now on everything went bad. When the Almighty gives a man bread, men come to wrench out his teeth. A certain lawyer, a wicked man, who profaned the Sabbath in public, Ausdauer, may his name be forgotten, built himself a house near Father's. That wicked man did not take pleasure in people's taking pleasure; he said it was not to his honor that people should go about naked near his house. So he used his tricks and they pulled down the huts. And that wicked man was not content until he had tried to have us driven off our property that the Almighty had given us, because it was not to his honor to have Father as a neighbor. He wanted to buy the house, but Father did not want to sell. From then on, not a week passed when they did not fine us, because of an eggshell that was thrown out of the house or a drop of water that was spilled in front of it. So long as Father was alive he held his own, but when Father passed away and went to his rest, and I inherited the house, I said: Either that wicked man leaves the world or we leave the house, for I am a feeble woman, my chick, and I cannot bear to be provoked; and when that wicked man reviled me I would tremble, and I could see that he and I could not live as neighbors. But Ephraim Yossel—may he be our spokesman in heaven—was a stubborn man and an angry man, and he would answer, "This pleasure, Freide, I won't give you, to leave my house because you are trembling." But Ausdauer, may his name be forgotten, was even more stubborn, and he went on tormenting us until Ephraim Yossel, may he rest in peace, agreed to sell him the house and go to America with the money. Elimelech, who is more stubborn than the whole world, dug in his heels and said, "In spite of Ausdauer we will stay here and not move." In the meantime the war came, and the Russians came and destroyed Ausdauer's house; they did not leave one stone on another. But they did not touch our house, and here it stands in its place—and more, it is finer than it was, for so long as that wicked man's house was there, it hid the sun, and now that it is destroyed it hides the sun no longer. Nevertheless, my joy is not complete, my chick. What happiness can a mother have who has been left alone, without her four sons and her two daughters, and this Elimelech, who used to shout, "We will stay here and not move," is wandering about like a man who has no home.'

Here Freide stopped and looked at me, and then started again: 'You tell me, my chick, you have read his letters, haven't you; what do you think? Is there any hope that he will come back?' 'Why should he not come back?' I said. 'That's what I say,' said Freide. 'But I am afraid he may dig in his heels as he usually does and won't want to come back, or he may come back after I am dead. And I, my chick, am not stubborn like him; I cannot dig in my heels and live until he comes back. You, my chick, you were there in Jerusalem, or in the Land of Israel, weren't you? And since everyone there knows—tell me, my chick, when will the Messiah come? Don't be afraid, my chick, I won't tell anyone else, but for myself I should like to know when the Messiah will come. You see that my house is fine and the dishes are washed and you think Freide does not need the Messiah. But I want you to know, my chick, not everything that looks nice outside is nice inside. Inside my heart, oh, my chick, everything is not so nice. So, my chick, don't be angry with me, that I want to see a little bit of pleasure.'

CHAPTER SIX AND FORTY

A New Man

As soon as I had left, a man some fifty years old came up to me. He was well dressed, his yellowish beard rounded and handsome, and all his movements were sober and deliberate. You do not see such men in Szibucz. At first sight he looked like a leader of the religious Zionist Mizrachi party who had turned up from elsewhere, but his complete self-confidence showed that he belonged to the town.

He put out his hand to greet me and said in Hebrew, 'Shalom,' but immediately greeted me again in Yiddish with 'Sholom Aleichem,' so that I should not mistake him for a Zionist. 'It is a great pleasure to make your personal acquaintance,' he said, rubbing his hands together joyfully as he spoke, and added, 'Don't you know me? If I tell you my name you will know who I am.'

In this way did Pinhas Aryeh make himself known to me. This Pinhas Aryeh was the son of the town rabbi—that son we have already mentioned, who was an important figure in the orthodox Agudat Israel and wrote in their papers. Now that the editorial office was closed for the festival period, he and his wife had come to visit his father and mother.

He immediately entered into conversation with me and told what he told. Whenever he made a statement, he started hesitantly, as if he felt doubtful, but at once added something more to reinforce the statement and tell you that this was so and there could be no question about it—like a man who is cracking a nut and hovers in the air above it with the hammer, but when he hits the nut he strikes it with all his might.

The winter cold had gone; the air was tepid, neither cold nor warm. I walked along with Pinhas Aryeh. Once he made me walk to his right, and once he made me walk to his left, and he talked without a stop. He did not notice that I was silent, or perhaps he noticed but did not care. Suddenly he put his hand on my shoulder and said, 'Surely you are one of us?' I do not know whether he really thought so, or whether he believed he was giving me pleasure by this. From then on, for all the rest of his stay in Szibucz, we used to walk together.

Spring was abroad, and the soil felt rich and soft. The skies, which had been sealed by clouds, grew clearer now; wisps of cloud embraced each other, then parted gently, as clouds do when there is peace on high. Below, too—in Szibucz, that is to say—there was a noticeable change for the better. Men were pleasant to each other and looked graciously upon this man.

Babtchi put away her leather coat and put on a new dress, like most of the girls in the town; if I am not mistaken she grew her hair longer and arranged it in a kind of coil above her neck at the back. Three or four times I met her on the street. The first time she nodded her head and greeted me, her hair dancing on her neck; the second and third times she lowered her eyes modestly. From the time I first knew Babtchi I had never seen her like this. A person's clothes change his character, and God's holy days change his clothes.

My companion watched her pass and said, 'Who is that girl walking there? Isn't she the daughter of Zommer the inn-keeper?' I nodded and went back to the subject we were talking about before. Said Pinhas Aryeh, 'He served you right,

that Yeruham, when he spurned you and came home. The
return of that pioneer is worth more than a thousand warnings
from all the God-fearing.' I lowered my head and said nothing.
'Why have you grown so sad?' asked Pinhas Aryeh. 'I remembered the story of his father,' I replied. 'Are you so grudging
and spiteful?' said he. 'What spite? What grudge?' said I.
Said Pinhas Aryeh, 'I reminded you of the act of the son who
spurned you, and you reminded me of the act of the father
who defiled the Torah, hinting that even our camp is not free
from sinners.' 'What is your camp?' I asked. 'Those who walk
in the way of the Torah,' said Pinhas Aryeh. 'You are indeed
to be envied,' said I. 'You have taken the Torah for your own,
as if you and the Torah were one.' 'Are you angry with me?'
said he. 'I am not angry, but you make me laugh,' said I. 'This
is a displeasing way you have, to pre-empt the Torah for
yourselves, as if it had been given only to you, especially as
you use the Torah for purposes that have nothing to do with
it. I do not say that we (we as opposed to you) live by the
Torah, but we want to live by it—only the vessels of our souls
are broken, and cannot hold it. The Torah is whole, but the
case in which it is kept is broken. And our longings will lead
us to accept the Torah a second time—the eternal Torah that
is never changed by the conditions of the times or the passing
of the ages. While you and your colleagues, my friend, wish
to gain power through the Torah, we wish to give the Torah
power over ourselves. And if our capability is small, our will
is great. In such matters, the will is more important than the
capability, for the will has no end, but the capability—alas—
is small and circumscribed. The will flows from the abundance
of the supreme and infinite Will, while the capability is of man
born of woman, whose days are short and full of pain. The
capability is slack, but the will is alive, and we hope it will
repair the broken vessels of our souls. Now, Reb Pinhas, I
take my leave of you.' 'Why are you in such a hurry? Perhaps
I can answer you.' 'I have no doubt you can answer me,' said
I. 'If you like, I will answer myself instead. But mere arguments accomplish nothing. Your thinking repels me from the
beginning, because you make the sacred secular. The political
affairs that interest you do not concern me, for to me the

State and its affairs are only minor servants of the Torah, and it is not for the Torah to serve them. I know, Reb Pinhas Aryeh, that I have not clarified the matter sufficiently, and to tell you the truth I have not clarified it to myself either, so silence is best. I don't believe that it is talk that will help us see this subject whole.'

'Surely you say the same things we do,' said Pinhas Aryeh. 'I say the same things, yet we disagree,' I replied. 'The reason we disagree is that you have aroused disagreement in Israel, estranging one Jew from another, for you regard anyone who does not belong to your group as if, heaven forbid, he had no share in the God of Israel.' 'And is it we who have caused the estrangement?' said Pinhas Aryeh. 'Surely it is you who have caused it, by estranging yourselves from the Torah, and thereby estranging yourselves from Israel!' 'You are a happy man,' said I, 'to have solved all doubts and grasped the truth with your own hand; grasp it firmly, or it may escape. And now that we have truly finished, I am going.' 'Where?' 'To the old Beit Midrash.' 'I am going with you,' said Pinhas Aryeh. 'I will take the key and open the door,' said I.

As soon as we entered the Beit Midrash, Pinhas Aryeh declaimed, 'How goodly are thy tents, O Jacob,' and extolled the Torah and its students, praising me for abandoning the idols of my youth and returning to the Beit Midrash. When I wanted to sit down he drew me outside. It was plain that all he had said in praise of the Torah and its students came readily to his lips from the speeches he used to deliver at meetings. Or perhaps he really loved the Torah, but since he was so busy making others love it he did not manage to study it himself. Or perhaps it was enough for him to go over that daily page of the Talmud, which perhaps he studied every day.

Although Pinhas Aryeh, the rabbi's son, was born in Szibucz, he was a new man to the town. Of the other men who grew up in Szibucz before the war, some studied the Torah because they loved it and some because they had nothing else to do, but this Pinhas Aryeh—may God save him— did not open a book, nor did I ever hear a word of commentary on the Torah from his lips. Nevertheless, he used the Torah as a keystone for his actions, whether in matters arising out of the Torah or those that had nothing to do with it.

Like his father, he loved to tell jokes, but a joke that served the father to flavor his talk served the son as a complete conversation, like a man who is frivolous and jests. Once I said to him, 'I am surprised at the way you jest and joke.' 'And I am surprised that you do not like jokes,' he answered. 'If you want to know the spirit of the people, listen to their jests.' I said, 'That is the spirit of the people in its dispersion and not in its ingathering.'

Each of us seemed strange to the other. He seemed strange to me because he loved argument, and I to him because I refrained from argument. Finally I became argumentative against my will because he credited me with ideas that had never come into my head. He seemed strange to me because he was immersed in newspapers, and I to him because I did not read them. Once I asked him where he found the time. He said he made the time because he had to read, for the sages said, 'And know what thou shalt reply to a heretic.' When he said this I knew that his enjoyment in the reading came first, and the purpose second. 'Do you also read the books they send you for review?' said I, jesting. 'I write reviews of them,' he replied, jokingly. 'What do the authors say?' I asked. 'If I praise them, what have they to say?' he answered. 'And if you disparage them?' 'Why should I pain scholars by disparaging them?'

I learned much from Pinhas Aryeh's conversation. He was acquainted with most of the pious men of the day and familiar with the leading Jews of Poland and Lithuania. All the time I was walking with him he used to tell how clever they were, and how highly regarded by the Gentile ministers, how Rabbi So-and-so had overborne a leader of the Mizrachi, and what the zaddik from So-and-so had replied to a Zionist rabbi. I would not say that his stories were gratifying, but through them I came to know what figures are popular with this generation.

Shortly before his departure I met his new wife, a tall and comely blonde, her head covered with a silken kerchief, and a single curl peeping out in memory of her beautiful hair.

Her forehead was broad and her chin narrow, like half a Shield of David slightly rounded. I heard that she was the daughter of a rich Hasid from a large city in Poland, and that she had studied in Gymnasium. Her husband boasted of her to me, saying, 'I am sure you will find her conversation pleasant.' Of all her conversation I remember only that she asked in a languid voice, 'Isn't there a café here?'

On the evening the festival ended I found Pinhas Aryeh sitting in my hotel. I thought he had come to say goodbye before leaving, and I went and sat down beside him. Then he revealed that he had come to inquire into the character of Babtchi, the innkeeper's daughter, with a view to a match. The principal, that is to say the girl, was an intelligent young woman and, as his wife told him, she was good-looking. The main thing was that his son had seen her last year and had a certain liking for her. But the prospective in-law, Babtchi's father, was something of a question mark.

I asked Pinhas Aryeh if his son was a member of Agudat Israel. He smiled. 'In any case, he is not a Zionist,' said he. 'Does he keep the commandments?' 'If he kept the commandments he would be a member of Agudat Israel,' he replied.

As he spoke he sighed. 'Let me tell you a story a friend told me,' he said. 'Once the talk between us turned on the worries of bringing up children. My friend said, "I can forgive my sons and daughters for not following the way of the Torah, but I cannot forgive them for their spitefulness. I admit," says my friend, "that a young man sometimes has to go to a theater, and I have already agreed, unwillingly, that he should go there on Sabbath eves, for then he is free from work. When he goes to the theater he shaves, so as not to look untidy. I do not inquire whether he shaves with paste or with a razor. Today, when even yeshiva students shave their beards, a man turns a blind eye on his son and does not ask whether he shaves his beard by permitted or forbidden means. But what annoys me is that, when I come back from the synagogue and chant 'Peace unto you, O ministering angels,' my son is standing there shaving. I ask him, 'Why do you have to shave in the living room and not in the bathroom?' And he, 'My sister is having a bath and I can't go in.' I say, 'A girl who is going to the opera needs to have a bath first, but what made her take a bath at the very moment when her father is going to recite the Sabbath Kiddush?' I do not suspect her, heaven forbid, of stoking the stove on the Sabbath, but I find it hard to bear."' Here a sigh broke from Pinhas Aryeh's heart, and I knew that his friend's trouble was his own.

Pinhas Aryeh returned to his town and I returned to my Beit Midrash. Again I sit and study the Torah and no one hinders me in my study. If I said that Pinhas Aryeh was a new man in Szibucz, I should add that this is truly so, for there is no one like him among those who grew up in the town. Elimelech Kaiser, for instance, keeps the commandments; though not for love—and sometimes he does so in anger, like those grumblers who serve their master because they cannot free themselves from his service. Or Daniel Bach: he believes in the Creator, although he does not keep His commandments. Because of the evil things that have befallen him, he is of the opinion that the Holy One, blessed be He, does not want to be worshipped by him. If his life had been normal he would have served God like his father and the other faithful sons of Israel. Or Nissan Zommer: he keeps the commandments of God honestly and faithfully; for him, whatever the Holy One, blessed be He, does is right. 'The precepts of the Lord are just, rejoicing the heart.' It is good for a man to put aside the cares of the hour and rise to recite the Afternoon and Evening Services. Better still is the Sabbath day, which was given for sanctity and repose; and even better are the festivals of the Lord, on which a man puts away his cares and clears them out of his heart. To sum up, whatever the Holy One, blessed be He, does is good, so long as men do not come and spoil it. How goodly were the days when the world was conducted according to God's will, until men began to offend, and made wars, and disturbed the order of the world—and their offense still continues. In his simplicity, Mr. Zommer mistakenly believes that God and man are two equal powers, acting and activating against each other, but that God is the good power, while man, on the other hand, is the evil power.

Nevertheless, we may classify Mr. Zommer among the simple servants of God who serve their Creator without affectation, although their faith is not pure. Or Hanoch, may he rest in peace, who bore the yoke like a horse and the burden like an ass, whether it was the commandments he was commanded to do by the Creator or things commanded to him by men. Or all the other sons of Szibucz, who serve their Creator, some with a broken heart and some in deep dejection. And even if they commit various offenses, they rely on His blessed mercy to turn a blind eye to their bad deeds and see their broken hearts. There are some who know not what they do, and their lack of knowledge makes them as happy as free men, because they do not examine their acts, and believe that they too come from the will of the Almighty, for if He did not will them He would not make them perform them.

Pinhas Aryeh is not like any of them. He does not grumble like Elimelech Kaiser; nor does he repudiate the commandments like Daniel Bach; nor is he humble like Hanoch, may he rest in peace; nor does he rejoice in the precepts of the Lord like Mr. Zommer. He divides the universe in his mind, not between God and men, but between man and man—that is, between those who favor Agudat Israel and those who oppose it. True, he likes to be in the company of people who have nothing to do with Agudat Israel, sometimes out of weakness and sometimes in the hope that he will influence them. He does not regard the licentiousness and heresy that have come into the world as things to be lamented, but as things that can be used to make propaganda against the Zionists. Troubles of the many and troubles of the individual, the ills of the world and the ills of the time—all can be dispelled, in his opinion, if Israel will walk in the way of the Torah. But this Torah, which Pinhas Aryeh and his faction preach—may heaven protect us—is the Torah that is preached at their meetings and in their newspapers, and we shall not go far wrong if we say that all these factions like Pinhas Aryeh's—even if their motives are for the sake of heaven—are not approved from heaven, for the Holy One, blessed be He, does not want to be employed as a means, even for the sake of a desirable end.

I have already gone on more than enough about Pinhas Aryeh, and that surely is enough.

The Passover festival has ended, spring has come. The
sun shines every day, the nights are warm and pleasant. The
earth brings forth grasses and the gardens adorn themselves
with flowers. The world has put off one appearance and put
on another. Men, too, have put off their heavy rags, and a
pleasant fragrance, like the fragrance of warm millet boiled
in honey, has begun to fill the town.

Our old Beit Midrash also has put on a new appearance.
Grasses covered the facing hills, and when I opened the window their pleasant fragrance entered my heart. But I did not
follow the fragrance. More than ever before I devoted myself
to Torah. Between one session and another I would say to
myself: Now the town forest is new again and it is worth
while going there—but I did not go, not even to the fields near
the town. I sat alone in the Beit Midrash. Of all those who
used to come to the Beit Midrash in the cold days, I alone was
left. One went after his business in the town and one went out
to his business in another town, while those who had no business preferred to walk about in the marketplace and chat with
their friends. Ever since the day after the festival there had
been no prayers in the Beit Midrash.

Reb Hayim had taken up the affairs of Hanoch's widow.
At dawn he would carry her box to the market, and at noon
he would cook a warm meal for the orphans; at the Morning
Service and the Afternoon and Evening Services he would take
them to the synagogue to say the mourners' Kaddish, and he
did not come to the Beit Midrash except on Fridays to sweep
the floor and fill the basin with water and the lamp with kerosene. I still gave him his pay every week, but at first I used
to give it on Thursday, and now I gave it on Friday. Reb
Hayim still slept in the woodshed of the Beit Midrash, and
when he entered the house he did so in silence and left in
silence, without even a brief conversation with me. I had
already grown accustomed to his not talking, and he had
grown accustomed to my not asking. I heard that he was busy

caring for Hanoch's orphans, but to his own children, who were as neglected as orphans, he paid no attention.

From my wife and children I used to receive letters every week. Once, when I opened a letter, spring flowers, which my daughter had plucked in the forest, fell out of it. I felt as if the spring were before me and wondered at all the good things I was losing. Nevertheless, I confined myself to the Beit Midrash. When I looked out I said to myself: Even if the spring multiplied a hundredfold, with each spring more beautiful than the other, I would not budge from my studies. Again I tasted the savor of that sweet solitude which I had loved all my life and which was now doubly and trebly beloved, and I felt already that I could spend all my days and years between the walls of the Beit Midrash. But when I say 'days and years' I do not mean all my days and all my years, for this man has a wife and children.

CHAPTER SEVEN AND FORTY

Among Brothers and Friends

On the first of the Three Days of Circumscription before the festival of Shavuot, two young men came to the Beit Midrash. A young man in the Beit Midrash is a novelty; all the more so two. I believe that since I returned no young man has entered the Beit Midrash. The young men came up and greeted me, and said they had come only for my sake. Why for my sake? Because in a certain village near our town there was a little group of six young men and two young women, who had abandoned the occupations of their fathers and were cultivating the soil to prepare themselves to work in the Land of Israel. They were earning a livelihood by the labor of their hands, by their work in the fields and the cowsheds with the peasants. And since they had heard that I came from the Land of Israel, they had come to ask me to stay with them for the festival.

When the young men came in, I was engrossed in study.

I said to myself: Not only are they making me neglect the Torah, but they are giving me the trouble of going to them. I looked at them like a man who is sitting on top of the world, when someone comes to tell him to undertake some sordid task.

The young men lowered their eyes and said nothing. Finally one of them—Zvi was his name—took heart and said, 'I thought that since you've come from the Land of Israel, sir, you would be glad to see young men and women working in the fields and the cowsheds for the sake of the Land.' 'My friend,' said I, 'why do you tell me tales about preparing yourselves for the Land of Israel? So did Yeruham prepare himself for the Land, and he went and stayed there for a few years. And what was the end of him? In the end he came back here, and now he decries the Land and its people.'

'If you are thinking of Yeruham Freeman, sir,' Zvi replied, 'you have reason to be angry, but there was another Yeruham, called Yeruham Bach, who was killed in guarding the Land, and I believe you have nothing against him. And if we are fated to share his end, we shall willingly accept the Almighty's decree.' I took Zvi's hand in mine, and said, 'When would you like me to come?' 'Any time,' said both of them together, 'whenever you come we shall welcome you.' Said I, 'You invited me for the festival, didn't you? Well, I shall come for the festival of Shavuot.'

On the eve of the festival, after midday, I hired a cart and set out for the village. Before I could find the comrades the whole village knew that a guest had come to the Jewish lads. Immediately some of the villagers ran on ahead to let them know, and some walked in front of the cart to show me the way.

In a farmer's house, or rather hut, the six young men and two young women had made their home. The house was half in ruins and the furniture was in pieces. In all the villages the farmers have broken-down houses, but the youthful grace of those who lived here glorified the place and its furnishings.

In honor of the festival the young men had stopped work about two hours before nightfall and I did not see them at work in the fields, but I saw the girls in the cowshed milking the cows. For many days I had not seen a cow, nor a girl either, and suddenly it came about that I saw both at the same time.

The young men introduced me to their employer, a farmer of over fifty, with hair cut straight over his forehead and a face the color of clay. The farmer looked at me with a surly face and said to the lads, 'This one is not like you.' 'What makes you say that?' said I. He pointed to my clothes and said, 'Do they have fine clothes like yours? A man who works hasn't got clothes like these.' 'Who told you I don't work?' said I. 'Perhaps you work and perhaps you don't work,' said he, scratching his forehead. 'Anyway, your work isn't work.' 'Everyone works in his own way,' I replied, 'you in your way and I in mine.' The farmer put his two hands on his knees, looked at the ground in front of him, and said, 'All right. But I say that not every way leads to some purpose.'

The young men were embarrassed to see their landlord shaming their guest, so they spoke up and explained that the work I did was of great importance and the world was in great need of it. 'All right,' said the farmer, scratching his forehead again. 'Every day people come and tell me what the world needs. But I tell you the world needs people to bring forth bread from the soil. Bread, sir, bread from the soil.'

The sun had almost set. The girls came back from the cowshed bringing the milk, went into their room and washed, and put on holiday clothes; then they set the table and lit the candles. The young men went out to the spring, washed and dressed themselves. We went into the room and welcomed the festival with prayer. A fine smell rose from the gardens and fields and vegetable plots, driving out the smell of the pigs who grunted from the nearby houses. After we had finished our prayer we recited the blessing over the wine, broke the bread, and ate what our comrades had prepared. Between one dish and the next they sang songs sweet as honey, and I told them something of the Land of Israel.

Shavuot nights are brief, and our comrades had not heard their fill of the Land before night came to an end. We said grace, rose from the table, and set out for the nearby town to pray with the congregation and hear the reading of the Torah.

We walked among the fields and gardens, vegetable patches and hedges, along crooked and winding paths. This world, which I had thought was still by night, was busy with a thousand labors. The heavens dropped down dew, the earth brought forth its grasses, and the grasses gave out fragrance. Between heaven and earth was heard the voice of the Angel of Night, saying things not every ear can hear. But the higher ear can hear, and the heavens answer that angel's voice. And down below, between our feet, played little creeping things, which the Almighty has abased to the dust, but His merciful eye watches over them even in their abasement, so that they should not be crushed. While we were walking the dawn began to break, and the town appeared out of the pure mists, which divided, then separated, then came together again as one and covered the town, until in the end town and mist were absorbed in each other, and the rooftops seemed like fringed sheets. Few are the hours of favor when this man rejoices, but this was one of them. Finally, the whole town was submerged in a white mist and all that was in the town was submerged. At that moment the cocks crowed and the birds began to twitter, to tell us that everything was in order, and that He who in His goodness continually, every day, renews the work of creation had renewed His world on that day too. At once, a new light shone, and the forest, too, which had been hidden in darkness, emerged and revealed all its trees. And every tree and branch glistened with the dew of night.

The morning of the festival had left its mark on every house; even the streets looked as if this were a special day for Israel and they need not be in a tumult as on all other days. When we entered the synagogue the congregation was in the middle of the Additional Service, and a second quorum was beginning to collect for prayer. The synagogue was adorned with branches and greenery, and its fragrance was like the fragrance of the forest.

The Kohanim went up to the pulpit and blessed the congregation with the *Shlaf-Kratzel* melody, like men who are seized by sleep and want to arouse themselves. The other worshippers, too, still had the night in their eyes. They finished their prayer and we began ours.

The cantor chanted the 'Great love' prayer with the special melody for Shavuot and dwelt upon the verse 'And to fulfill in love all the words of instruction in Thy Law.' And when he came to the verse 'Enlighten our eyes in Thy Law,' he seemed like one who wanders alone in the night and entreats the Almighty to be merciful and lighten his darkness.

More beautiful was the melody of the *Akdamut* hymn; even more beautiful was the reading of the Torah. This was a little town and the professional cantors did not reach it, so the ancient melodies were preserved and not mingled with foreign tunes. After the prayer we went out into the street. All the houses in the town were small and low, some of them actually down to the ground, and their roofs were made of straw. Some of the windows were ornamented with rosettes of green paper, in memory of the Revelation on Mount Sinai, as our forefathers used to do in honor of Shavuot.

At the doors of the houses the women stood and watched the young men, who plowed and sowed and reaped like Gentiles, but came to pray like Jews. One woman pointed at me, mentioning the Land of Israel. My comrades were delighted and said, 'Now that they have seen a man from there they will no longer say that the whole business of the Land is sheer wishful thinking.' In the big cities, where emissaries frequently come from the Land, the arrival of a man from there makes no impression; in this small town, to which no man from the Land had come before, even a man like me made an impression.

Meanwhile, a number of the townsfolk came along and invited us to say the Kiddush with them, but the two girls were furious and would not let us go, because they had prepared a fine feast in honor of the festival and wanted us to start the meal hungry, so that our enjoyment might be doubled.

Most of the townsfolk went along with us on our way to hear something about the Land of Israel. To please the old men, I told them about the Wailing Wall of the Temple, and the Cave of the Patriarchs, and the Tomb of Rachel, and the Cave of Elijah, and the Tomb of Simon the Just, and the tombs of the Great Sanhedrin and the Lesser Sanhedrin, and the Lag B'Omer celebrations at Meron, and all the other holy places. What did I tell and what did I not tell? May the Almighty not punish me if I exaggerated somewhat and went a little too far; after all, it was not for my honor that I did so, but for the honor of the Land of Israel, whose glories it is meritorious to relate even when it is in ruins—to make it beloved of Israel, that they may take to heart what they have lost and turn again in repentance.

As I was still walking and talking, an old man said to me, 'And were you in Tel Aviv as well, sir?' 'That is a great question you ask me, my old friend,' said I. 'I was in Tel Aviv before it was Tel Aviv, for this Tel Aviv was a desert of sand, a lair of foxes and jackals and night robbers. From my attic in the suburb of Neveh Zedek I used to look out on this wilderness of sand, and it did not occur to me that days would arrive when they would come and build a great city there for God and men. But suddenly Jews like you and me came and turned a desolate wilderness into a populated place, and the jackals' lair into a fine city, with some hundred thousand Jews and more. Such a city, my friends and brothers, you have never seen even in a dream. You walk about in the streets and you do not know what to wonder at first and what last: at the tall houses or the men who built them; at the wagons full of merchandise or the baby carriages in which the daughters of Israel take out their little sons; at the great sea that girds the city with its might or the flourishing gardens; at the shops full of every good thing or the signboards with their inscriptions in Hebrew. You may think that only shops selling tzitzit and tefillin have signboards in Hebrew, but I tell you that there is not a single shop in Tel Aviv that does not have a Hebrew sign over it. This Tel Aviv is like a great courtyard of the Great Synagogue, for Tel Aviv is the courtyard of Israel and Jerusalem is the Great Synagogue, for all the prayers of Israel rise from there.'

Now that I had mentioned Jerusalem I was thoroughly aroused and began to tell its praises. What did I tell and what did I not tell? Can anyone tell all the glory of Jerusalem? The city that the Holy One, blessed be He, established as His dwelling—no son of woman can proclaim all its glory.

I looked at my companions, who were gazing at me with great affection; such friendly eyes as those that were fixed on this man you have never seen even in a dream. From this you can analogize to the future: how great will the love of Israel be when they are privileged to see salvation! If at the hearing it is so great, how much more will it be at the seeing!

I looked again at my companions—first, because it is a pleasure to look at the sons of Israel, and second, because I wished to feast my eyes on the radiance of good men's faces.

One of them spoke up and said, 'Wonder of wonders: they build a city, build a city! Kings and princes destroy cities and kingdoms, but Jews come and build a city!' 'It is said in the Gemara,' I told them, 'that a man should not take leave of his fellow without quoting some word of the sages, for thus he will remember him. Now that I am taking leave of you, I will tell you something. It is said in the Gemara: a man should always dwell in a city that has been newly settled, for since it has been newly settled its sins are few. The reason I mention this is that if anyone tells you that the men of Tel Aviv are, heaven forbid, weak in obedience to the commandments, you should tell him that its sins are few.'

After I had told them this, I gave each of them my hand and took my leave affectionately, and they came after me to see me on my way. I do not remember whether we walked and talked, or whether we walked in silence. Perhaps we were silent, perhaps we talked. When the heart is full the mouth speaks, but when the soul is full a man's eyes look with affectionate sadness, and his mouth is silent.

Finally I took my leave of them and they took their leave of me. They went back to their town and we went back to the village. The earth that the Holy One, blessed be He, has given to the sons of man is full of boundaries. It is not enough that he has set a boundary between the Land of Israel and the Exile, but even this Exile is made of many exiles, and when Jews meet together, in the end they must leave each other.

Silently I walked after my comrades, meditating to myself. When I was a child I used to beseech the Holy One, blessed be He, to reveal to me the magic name by which one could go up to the Land of Israel. Something like this request I made at that moment, not for myself but for those weary of exile, weary of hoping.

Said one of our comrades, 'We should not have refused them like that; when they asked us to come in and recite the Kiddush with them, we should have gone in.' Another replied, 'On the contrary, we should have gone back to the village immediately after the service to sit down to our meal. After all, we have not had a good meal since Passover, and now, when the girls have taken the trouble to prepare a big meal, we must eat at our own table.'

And here they revealed the secret of the girls, who had prepared not one meal but two, one of milk dishes and one with meat—one for the first day of the festival and one for the second, besides a big cheesecake with butter and raisins.

The sun shone over the earth and hunger began to torment us. The young men took long strides so as to reach home quickly.

We reached the village and went into the house. The girls were quick to set the table and arrange the dishes, and each of us came and sat at his place.

One of us spoke up first and said, 'The sages were right when they fixed a short Kiddush for the festival, especially for those who have a cheesecake ready and waiting.' Another spoke up and said, 'Why are the girls taking so long?' He jumped up and went into the kitchen. When he did not return, another jumped up and went in after him. Very soon they had all got up and gone into the kitchen.

I sat alone, before the laid table. My hunger hurt. I took out a cigarette and began to smoke. In the meantime the young men came back with gloomy faces. It was clear that something bad had happened.

What had happened was this: when the girls had gone into the kitchen they had found the food cupboard open and the lock broken; no wine for Kiddush, no cake, no food at all, not even a morsel of bread was left. While we had been in the town, evil neighbors had come and taken away all that the comrades had prepared in honor of the festival.

What could be done? One of the girls went to the farmer's house to ask for something to eat, but she found his door locked. She went on to another farmer, but none of the household were at home, for that day the chief priest of Szibucz had come to a neighboring village and they had all gone to hear him preach.

The girls thought of going to the cows to get some milk, but all the cows were out to pasture, and there wasn't a drop of milk to be had. We wanted to make tea, but could not find even a pinch of tea. Those who had taken the food had taken the tea and the sugar. What could be done? They took the tea leaves that were left in the kettle from yesterday, put the kettle on the fire, and made some tea.

Close to nightfall the farmers came home and the cows returned from the meadow. The farmers' wives had pity on us and gave us what they gave. We sat and ate and drank. The meal was not large, but the joy was not small.

When the first day of the festival was ended and the eve of the second day had arrived, I said to my comrades, 'I will go to the town and bring you bread, tea and sugar, and any other food you need.' 'Heaven forbid,' they said, shocked, for they did not wish me to travel on the Holy Day. 'I belong to the Land of Israel,' I reminded them, 'and I intend to go back there, so the observance of the second day of the festival does not apply to me.' 'But what will people say?' they said.

After we had eaten, drunk, and said grace, the young men consulted and decided that two should go to the town and bring food. It took an hour to go and an hour to come back, and they spent an hour there; they brought loaves and butter, cheese and sardines, tea and sugar, a little bottle of wine, and two candles. The girls set the table and lit the candles; we recited the Kiddush over the wine and had our supper. At intervals in the meal the boys and girls sang songs sweet as honey, and I told them a little about the Land of Israel, until morning came on the second day of Shavuot.

We intended to go to town to pray with the congregation and hear the reading of the Torah, but one of the group said, 'We cannot all go, in case what happened yesterday happens again; some of us will go and some will stay at home to watch the house.' It was hard for some to give up their praying together with the congregation and the reading of the Torah, and it was hard for the others to bear the discomfort of their comrades who would remain in the village on the festival. Said I, 'You go, and I will stay here, for I belong to the Land of Israel and I have to put on the tefillin, as on a weekday, which I cannot do in public.' 'When you have come to visit us, can we leave you alone and go?' they said. 'What else do you want to do?' I said. One of them jumped up, took the festival prayer book and began to recite the prayers, and all the others took up theirs and prayed with him. They recited the festival prayers and I the prayers for weekdays. I wore my tefillin and used the ordinary prayer book, while they prayed from the festival book.

After the service, the girls set the table and we had our meal, though not with meat and fish and other festival dishes. The comrades bantered, calling the sardines fish, the bread meat, the butter compote, the cheese cake, and the tea wine, for they had brought sugar from town and we had sweetened the tea. Between courses, the boys and girls sang songs sweet as honey, and I told them a little of the Land of Israel. The farmers and their women stood in front of the window, pointing to me and saying, 'That man has been in Jerusalem and Palestine.' They think that Jerusalem and Palestine are two different places, and anyone who has been in one of them is a somebody—all the more if he has been in both. Thus we sat until evening approached and it was time for the After-noon Service. I recited the weekday prayers and they the festival prayers. Then we danced and sang, 'Thou hast chosen us from all the peoples,' until the day departed and the trees and bushes were wrapped in shadow.

Night was falling, the shadows of the trees and bushes stretched gradually toward the East. I am not a sentimental man, but at that moment I said to myself: Trees and bushes, which are inanimate objects, turn to the East, and I, who was in the East, have turned here instead. I rose and stood beside the window, looking outside. A little hedgehog was running about in the garden in front of the house, carrying some blades of grass between its prickles, for itself—and perhaps its mate—to lie on. As I stood there, looking, the moon shone into the window. We recited the Evening Service, and after the closing blessing the comrades sat down and arranged their work for the following day.

So I spent the two days of the festival and the day after with my comrades in the village. I saw them at home and outdoors, in the field and the cowshed. May the Almighty give them strength to face all the trials they bear every day and every hour, for while their fellows go idle, they stand in the sun and the wind and the rain, and when their parents scold them for leaving their shops and taking up farming, they redouble their work to win bread from the soil. I heard that all the Gentiles praised them; some of them told me that these young men flinch at no hard work, that there are some tasks which the farmers avoid but they perform out of love.

Shortly before sunset I hired a wagon to go back to town. The boys and girls accompanied me to the outskirts of the village, and one of them, called Zvi, went with me to town to buy food.

When I took my leave of them, they asked me to write down their names in a notebook, so that if we should meet in the Land of Israel I should remember them. 'Brothers,' I replied, 'I have already engraved you on my heart; I have no need of a notebook.'

This Zvi, who traveled with me, was as handsome as his name, which means 'beautiful' in Hebrew, and lovable—a handsome young man, of fine appearance, and alert and sharp. On the way he said to me, 'I will not stay here, each day I spend in exile is a pity.' 'Have you an immigration certificate?' I asked. He laughed and said, 'I myself am my own immigration certificate.' For some reason I do not know myself, I did not ask him what he meant.

The Death of Freide

When I came back to Szibucz I heard that the Kaiserin had passed away. On the second day of Shavuot, Freide had come to the synagogue for the memorial prayer and lit her candles in memory of her relatives who had died or been killed. She sat among the women muttering the lamentations and supplications by heart, because she did not know how to read. No one who saw Freide in the synagogue knew that the Angel of Death had already sharpened his knife to take her soul, but she had known it since the eve of Shavuot, and was preparing herself for her eternal home.

How did she know? Mrs. Zommer told me what Freide's neighbor told her: On the afternoon of Shavuot eve Freide was making a cheesecake and she looked for raisins to put in it, but did not find any. A soldier appeared to her and said, 'If it is raisins you want, come and I will give you some.' Remembering the story of the soldier and her daughters, she was thunderstruck. The soldier took her with him to the graveyard, where he opened a pit, took out a sackful of dust, and put her into the sack, and she knew that she was going to die. From then on, she did not stir from her house. When the second day of Shavuot came, she went to the synagogue and lit seven candles: one of tallow for the soul of her husband, who died according to the way of all flesh, and six of wax in memory of her sons and daughters. Finally, she added one candle for her own soul, to deceive the Angel of Death into thinking she was already dead, and also to have a memorial for herself, since Elimelech her son was wandering about in the world and if she died no one would remember her. When the cantor took hold of the Scroll of the Law, which was wrapped in black, and said, 'O God, full of mercy . . .' Freide lifted up her voice and cried, 'My daughters, my pure and innocent daughters, my daughters, my lovely, pious daughters.' And so she continued crying and weeping until she fainted away and they brought her home. And with the departure of the festival, her soul departed, and they buried her the next day, on the morrow of the festival. When they took off her clothes to put on her eternal garments, they found her dressed in her gravesheets, for she had already prepared herself for her eternal home.

Thus ended the life of Freide. Seventy-one years were the days of the years of Freide's life. Between her birth and her death she was married and bore five sons and two daughters. Her husband died before her and her four sons were killed in the war and the pogroms, and her two daughters died in an evil hour. No one was left but Elimelech. Only God knows where he is.

Elimelech did not come to close her eyes, and I did not follow her coffin either. I was sitting in the wagon on the road with Zvi from the pioneers' group and we were chatting pleasantly with each other at the time when the earth opened up its mouth and swallowed Freide.

The deaths of relatives and friends lead us to meditation and thought on life and death. Whether we like it or not, we remember their lives and their deaths, and thus we consider ourselves: what are we and what our lives, and on what do we spend our days and years, and with what shall we confront Him who dwells on high? Our bundles are empty and heavy. What makes their burden so heavy to carry, when they are empty? Either it is an evil spirit that plays with them, or our bodies are weakened and find it hard to carry them. Eve brought one death into the world, but we bring death upon ourselves every day and every hour through vanities and pursuit of the wind.

I sat in the hotel, and ate my food, and thought about myself, and you, and Freide, and Elimelech. And the imagination that is implanted in the heart of man envisioned Elimelech before me—hardly a moment had passed before he came and stood there. When I saw Elimelech on the Day of Atonement in the synagogue, his eyes were like the shell of a tortoise lying in the sun, and he looked at me with hatred; now there was nothing of this in his eyes, but he looked at me with great obstinacy.

I lowered my eyes and gazed at my shoes. My shoes were clean and whole. Opposite them stood Elimelech and put his two fingers on his throat and said, 'Well, what more have we to do?'

What more have we to do? That means that we have already done all that was in our power to do, and all we lack is more. What have we done and what have we not done? Many are the thoughts in a man's heart, but all his thoughts do not bring him to the point of action. If so, let us entrust ourselves to Him who does and causes to be done, and let us not ask all the time what more is to be done. Let Him do with us what He would do, for He is the Knower and He is the Doer and He is the Deed. But what can we do, when He says, 'Do'?

He says, 'Do'—and we know not what we must do. Since the day when, at the foot of Mount Sinai, we said first 'We shall do' before saying 'We shall hear,' many things have confused our hearts, and we do not know what we shall do and what we shall hear.

When I got up from the table and went to the Beit Midrash, Elimelech followed me. Often I am accompanied by Daniel Bach, or Ignatz, or someone else from Szibucz, but (it would be no exaggeration to say) this is the first time a man comes from a place several days' distance away and attaches himself to me.

I fumbled in my pocket and took out a cigarette, then fumbled in my pocket to look for a match, and lingered, to give myself time to think what I would say to Elimelech, what I would reply if he asked me whether I had performed the last kindness to his mother and walked behind her coffin, and whether I should rebuke him for not looking after his mother, for leaving her alone.

A man came up and said to me, 'If it is a match you want, here you are.' I looked at him and asked myself, 'Where has Elimelech vanished to? I wanted to tell him something, or he wanted to tell me something.'

The man took out a match, rubbed it on his sole and lit it, but by the time I put it to my mouth it had gone out. He took out a second match and said, 'Don't be like those men who, if they are offered something, turn it over in their minds until it slips from their fingers.' 'Is this a parable?' said I. 'It is the truth,' said he. 'Then He Himself, the Truth, is a parable,' said I. He put his hand on his right ear with his thumb on his Adam's apple and chanted with a chant of glory, 'And He was, and He is, and He shall be in glory.' 'You are the old cantor,' I said. 'David the beadle am I,' he said, 'who summoned the people to prayer.' 'But surely,' I said, 'I saw your tombstone in the graveyard, and if you do not believe me I will give you a sign: the picture of a hand, with a little baton in its fingers, is engraved on the tombstone, and I even still remember the rhyme on it.' 'I did not know they had put rhymes on my tombstone,' said David. 'You did not know?' 'I have not been in the graveyard.' 'And where have you been?' 'Where have I been? Rousing the sleepers to prayer; I had no time to go and lie in the grave.' 'Please, Reb David, do not be harsh with me, surely you do not mean to say that you are alive?' He looked at me and said, 'And you, are you alive?' 'What is the sense of this question?' I said. 'And what is the sense of the question you asked me?' 'Because,' I replied, 'I saw your gravestone: "Passed away the 5th day of Adar Rishon 5702," and I saw your name engraved on the tombstone. If you do not stop me I will read you the rhymes:

> "David summoned men to prayers,
> Served our folk in their affairs,
> Walked the strait and narrow way,
> Good and upright night and day.
> Heavenly prosecutor! Silence, pray." '

'Wonder of wonders,' said David. 'They even put my father's name on the tombstone,' 'Where do you see your father's name?' 'Just look at the last line,' replied David. 'It is indicated in the initials of the words.' And indeed, in Hebrew the line reads: *'Yehass alav kategor bashamayim'* — signifying *'Yakob.'* 'You are a clever fellow,' I said, 'I read the inscription and did not notice your father's name, while you noticed it though you only heard it from my lips. But that's not all. How is it, Reb David, that you use matches to make fire, when I remember that if the old men wanted to make fire, they would rub two stones together? Did you have matches in your day? Or perhaps you're not the same Reb David?' 'Who else do you think I am? Do you think I am Elimelech?' 'How do I know?' 'You don't know and you ask questions!' 'If a man asks questions, he gets a reply.' 'And if he gets a reply?' 'He adds to his knowledge.' 'Such as: when So-and-so died and what was engraved on his tombstone?' 'And is that all I know?' 'That is not all you know; you also know how to compose formulae of the same kind. Perhaps you will compose rhymes for the tombstones of Hanoch and Freide?' 'Do you think it is my duty to compose them?' 'I do not think anything. I have been given a staff in my hand to arouse the sleepers to prayer, so I arouse them and pass on.' 'And do they awake and arise?' 'It is for me to awaken them; it is not for me to check and see whether they have risen. He that is commanded to do, and does, does not turn his head back to see what others are doing. Now I take my leave of you, for I have to go, and I believe that you wanted to go too.'

'I too wanted to go, but I was delayed by Elimelech, son of the Kaiserin, my mother's nurse.' 'What are you telling me?' said Reb David, 'Elimelech lives far from here.' 'Far from here? And what is he doing?' 'Writing letters to his mother.' 'And what does he write?' 'That he wishes to return to Szibucz.' 'If so, is he likely to return?' 'If he finds the money for the journey.' 'And what else does he write?' Reb David stretched out his hand and said, 'Read.' I saw engraved on it the verse, 'And it is a time of trouble for Jacob.' I asked Reb David, 'Who was that old man who crossed my path on the day I went to make the key?' Reb David replied, 'Tell me the day he passed away and I will tell you who he was.' Reb David took his leave of me and I went into the Beit Midrash.

Ends and Realities

I returned to my Beit Midrash and my studies. I sat alone in the Beit Midrash, and no one interrupted me. Elimelech and Reb David had left. Reuben and Simon and Levi and Judah were busy earning a livelihood; they traveled about the countryside and did not come home except on Sabbath eve at dark. They could hardly take their clothes off before the Holy Day overtook them, and they welcomed the Sabbath at home or in a nearby house of prayer. This is how they earn their living: Reuben has entered into partnership with Simon, who has become an assistant to an agent for cigarette papers. This agent had a little car, shaped like a box, and Reuben, who learned to drive during the war, drives this car. They go around to the shops and taverns that sell cigarettes, and at night they sleep in the car—Reuben on the driver's seat and Simon in the box—except for the agent, who sleeps in hotels. This driver's seat is long enough for three ordinary men to sit, and if you cramp yourself and do not care about your feet hanging down outside, you can use it to sleep on, especially in the short summer nights. Levi has found himself some other way of making a living—I don't know what—while Judah goes to Lvov to bring merchandise from there and takes less pay from the shopkeepers than what they would pay for mailing. If his two hands are not sufficient, he carries the bundles on his shoulders, and if his shoulders aren't sufficient, good people come and lend him a hand. So long as the merchants of Lvov give him merchandise he takes his pay and celebrates the Sabbath; if not, he loses his outlays, as happened once when he came to buy cloth for a shopkeeper (the same one from whom I bought cloth for my coat), and the merchant would not give it to him, because the shopkeeper owed him money and had not paid.

Even Reb Hayim stays away from the Beit Midrash, except on Sabbath eves, when he sweeps the floor and fills the basin with water. And when he does come, it seems like his last coming, because his daughter and son-in-law have urged him to go and live with them. I heard that on Shavuot they visited Szibucz and Reb Hayim promised them to come.

What reason did Reb Hayim have for not going with them at once? After some time we found that he had undertaken to teach Hanoch's orphans the Kaddish and the prayers first; that was why he put off his journey.

Let us return to our affairs. I sat alone in the Beit Midrash and no one interrupted me. But if others did not interrupt me, my thoughts did. Everything I had seen and heard distracted my mind. Even things a man pays no attention to when he can see them forced themselves on me and unsettled me. For one hour I flew from one end of the world to the other; for another hour I flashed from man to man. People who had died seemed to me alive, and the living appeared to me as dead. Sometimes I saw them face to face, and sometimes I saw the tombstones on their graves.

To deliver myself from this confusion, I fixed my attention on my comrades in the countryside, with whom I had spent the festival of Shavuot. Just think: the sons of Shimke, Yoshke, Veptchi, and Godzhik have abandoned the ways of their fathers and do not wish to live on each other or on other people, but only from the hand of the Holy One, blessed be He. As for the reformation of the world, a man who reforms himself reforms the world at the same time. And even if they do not hold out, and behave like Yeruham Freeman, what they have done in the meantime combines with what others have done. It is like the soldiers of the king: one serves in the army a year, another two years, a third three—as a result the king always has an army.

I have not said all this to win approval for myself, by showing that I did my duty during the years when I worked. I know that I have done nothing yet, and here I am continuing to do things in my own way.

Every man does things in his own way; so do I in mine, in refutation of that heathen who was so insolent as to tell me that not all ways lead to a useful end.

As I have grown older, this word has grown with me. When I was a child and played with my friends, I heard people asking: And what is the end of it all? I began to write poems and people asked, mocking: After all, what is the end of it? When I went up to the Land of Israel, they said: Is this really an end for a young man to follow? And I need not say that all the time I lived there, people used to complain that they saw no end in it. Thus most of my years have passed and still I have not achieved any end.

Maimonides, of blessed memory, said in the *Guide to the Perplexed*: 'The end is the reality.' There, however, he refers to the reality of the Creator and not to ordinary reality. So the question stands as before: What is the end of this reality in which we live?

A man wastes his time a little and his thoughts waste his time a lot. It was good so long as I meditated on others, but not when I meditated on myself. When I saw this was so, I closed my book and went out for a walk, to distract my mind a little.

The day was pleasant, like the days after Shavuot, on which we do not recite the Penitential Prayer. The shopkeepers stood outside warming themselves and enjoying the new sun. Ignatz leaned on his stick, and I believe he was dozing a little, for when I passed him he did not call out either 'Pieniadze' or 'Mu'es.' The postman was on his way home, his satchel empty. He had already distributed all the letters that had come to the town. Perhaps there was a letter from Elimelech to his mother left in his satchel, or perhaps Elimelech had no mind to write. One way or the other, the postman was free to go back home, or to go into the tavern, or to dress his mustache, so that it should not hang down on one side and stand up on the other.

The air was fine, the day was pleasant. A day like this is a gift from heaven. Happy the man who does not spend it in idleness.

And praised be the Lord who put wisdom in my heart, so that I did not linger in the town, but went to the forest, where it was particularly pleasant and the air particularly fine. I know that this is not an end to pursue, but since I am not a man with an end in life, I once again did something that leads to no end.

The trees of the forest stood silent; at their feet, down there at the edge of the forest, flowed the river, the River Stripa, and it too was silent. In the past, when the entire town was inhabited, and people with an end in life lived in it, they built a mill, and the waters of the Stripa used to make the wheel go round and grind flour. Now that the city is ruined and the men with an end in life have gone, what end is there to the river and its waters? Or perhaps, after all, the river and its waters have an end, as the trees have an end, although no one cuts them down and trades in them—as Maimonides, of blessed memory, said in that passage when he was discussing reality: 'Know that there is no way to postulate an end for the whole of reality, not in our opinion . . . or according to the opinion of Aristotle.'

Many times this man has seen the forest in his town, and whenever he has seen it he has found something new. The Creator of all the world has given him the privilege of seeing what He has created in His world, and sometimes He raises him from the vegetable order and opens his eyes to see the living things that have made their homes among the trees in the forest. Though a man's eyeballs are small, the whole world is not enough for them; but sometimes a man's eyes rest on a leaf of a tree, on a lowly blade of grass in the field, on a small butterfly in the air, on a small insect, and the Holy One, blessed be He, reveals His mysteries to him.

It was good for this man that he had gone out to the forest. The forest, with its trees and branches and leaves, looked kindly upon him and sweetened his hours and moments. What was this man thinking as he lingered in the bosom of the forest? Who knows and who can remember? Perhaps he remembered the days of his youth, when he would sit there alone.

He was alone and solitary then in the forest, as he was alone in the world, for he had not yet joined himself to the world and the world had not yet joined him to itself. Since

that time he has seen the world—that world which they call
the great world, but in the end he has come back to his own
world—which they call the little world.

An unparalleled fragrance rises from the forest. What is
this grass that smells so sweet? Perhaps it is the same grass of
which the tailor's wife had spoken: if a man finds the place
where this grass grows and smells it, he returns to health.

The fragrance of that first grass was joined by the fragrance of another grass, one that grows in the forest of this
man's town, and it too was good—perhaps better than the first.
I am led on by this grass, and hear its voice, and call to it,
and feel it with my hand, and take a leaf and chew. And I
rejoice at the benefit I draw from all my senses.

After thinking of all that has been created for my enjoyment, I also thought about our old Beit Midrash. Were it not
for this old Beit Midrash, I could have remained standing in
the forest, uttering praise and thanksgiving to Him who has
such a world.

I felt in my pocket. The key was not lost. Now let us
return and see if the Beit Midrash is still there. The sun set,
and I returned to the town.

CHAPTER FIFTY

With Yeruham and Rachel

Just then Yeruham had finished his day's work and was about
to go home. He no longer ran to wash in the river, for his
home was furnished, and he even had a basin to wash in.
When he saw me, he asked me to go home with him, and I
followed along.

We walked and said nothing—I because I had come from
the forest, and he—I do not know why. Perhaps, because I
was silent, he was silent.

When we had covered half the way he stopped, arranged
the tools on his shoulder and said, 'When I went with Rachel
to visit her parents at the festival, I did not find you in the

hotel.' 'Certainly you did not find me in the hotel,' said I, 'for no one is in two places at the same time.' 'They told me you had gone to a certain village.' 'Yes, my friend,' I said, 'I went to a certain village.' 'No doubt that village has a name,' said Yeruham. 'You have guessed right, my fine fellow,' I said, 'you have guessed right.' Said Yeruham, 'That is easy to guess, and I don't know why you found it necessary to praise me for it.' 'Surely you deserve all this praise,' I replied, 'for controlling yourself, covering up your curiosity, and evading what you wish to know until I choose to tell.' 'What is there to evade?' said Yeruham. 'A man who goes to a village no doubt had to go.' 'Quite right, Yeruham,' I said, 'I had to go, and so I went. Since you know that, perhaps you know whom I found?' 'Whom you found? Gentiles and Jews.' 'And to which did I go?' 'Easy to guess: you went to the Jews.' 'Do you think I took the trouble to go to the village just to see ordinary Jews?' 'Perhaps you have friends among them,' said Yeruham. 'If I had friends among them,' I replied, 'would I have waited until now to see them?' 'Perhaps you did not know about them before,' said Yeruham, 'or perhaps . . . I'm sorry, I cannot reply to your Socratic questions.' 'You know, Yeruham, but you do not want to.' 'Why shouldn't I want to know?' 'Why shouldn't you want to reply? Tell me yourself.' 'If I knew I would not ask.' 'That means you believe that if one asks one gets a reply, for you ask and no doubt you want a reply.' 'That depends on whether you want to answer me.' 'And if I do not answer you?' 'Is it a secret from me?' 'A secret means something hidden and covered up, not something open and known. And since you know it, that means it is no secret to you. And now, my friend, let us smoke a cigarette. All the time I was in the forest I did not smoke, and you may say that I have not smoked all day. When I went to the Beit Midrash and took out a cigarette to smoke, a certain guardian came and stopped me. Later I went to the forest and forgot all about smoking. Take a cigarette, my friend, and let us send up smoke to the high heavens and their stars.' 'I don't smoke,' replied Yeruham. 'But surely I remember that you used to smoke?' 'I used to smoke and I stopped.' 'You stopped? Whatever for?' 'Because Rachel can't stand cigarette smoke.'

Rachel. For many days I had not called Rachel to mind, and
now he had reminded me of her.

'We have already reached home,' said Yeruham, 'and you
have not yet told me what village you were in, and whom
you visited. Do you want to surprise Rachel?' 'But surely
you told her.' Yeruham laughed heartily and knocked at the
door, crying, 'Rachel, Rachel, guess whom I've brought with
me.' Rachel called out from inside the house and spoke my
name.

Rachel was lying listlessly, fully dressed, on her bed. She
found it hard to bear the pains of pregnancy. How weak was
the hand she held out to me, and how strange the smile that
adorned her eyelashes; she was like a young woman who is
ashamed of her sufferings but rejoices in them.

'Was it nice there with the pioneers?' asked Rachel. 'Did
you find beautiful girls there?' 'Beautiful girls and handsome
young men as well.' 'They're handsome so long as they haven't
settled in the Land of Israel,' said Yeruham. 'When the bride
is beautiful in the eyes of the bridegroom and the bridegroom
in the eyes of the bride, they will keep their beauty all their
lives,' I answered.

Yeruham took Rachel's face in his hands and said, 'Like
us.' Rachel slapped his hands and said, 'Let me go, I have
to get up and arrange supper. The gentleman was not thinking
of us.' 'Lie still, Rachel,' said Yeruham, 'and I will get supper.'
Said Rachel, 'If you stand over me and hold my face, how
can you get supper?' 'Don't worry,' said Yeruham, 'everything
will be all right.' 'So let me go,' said Rachel. 'I'll let you go,
I'll let you go,' said Yeruham, 'if only you'll lie still.'

Yeruham took off his working clothes and put on others;
then he filled his hands with water and washed his face, and
went into the corner to arrange supper. When he got there,
he cried, 'You liar, you've already prepared everything—with
strawberries, too, and cream. If you're wasteful, Rachel, we'll
have to take all our savings out of the Anglo-Palestine.' 'What's
the Anglo-Palestine?' 'Go and teach her the A B C of the
Land of Israel,' said Yeruham. As he spoke he took down the
kerosene lamp from the wall, put it on the table, and said,
'Everything's ready for supper.' Then he bent over Rachel

and asked what she had eaten and what she wanted to eat.

The strawberries were fragrant and the cream was a pleasure to see. After three days spent in the village, where I had not eaten enough, I found this meal particularly tasty.

Yeruham plucked a strawberry out of the cream and said, 'What do you say to these strawberries? Hiding in the cream and sucking the goodness out of it. When you were in the Land of Israel didn't you long for strawberries and cream?' 'Long? What doesn't a man long for?' 'I talk about strawberries and he answers with metaphysics. Shall we drink tea or cocoa?' 'Drink a glass of sour milk,' said Rachel. 'Rachel's quite right,' said Yeruham. 'Let's drink sour milk first, then tea. If we are in exile, let us accept the burden of exile with a good grace. We have black bread here too. Faithful God and King, is there a finer food than a piece of rye bread with fresh butter? How fine this loaf is, round like a village girl and sprinkled with cumin like a charming freckle-face.' Rachel slapped his hand and said, 'Eat and don't give us these peculiar orations.'

Yeruham lifted up the loaf and smelled it. He took a knife and cut the loaf generously, spread a large piece with butter and bit into it before he had managed to spread it all, ate heartily and spread more butter on the places he had not spread at first, bit into it again, ate heartily, and urged us to eat. As he ate, he spiced his talk with phrases from the famous orators in the Land of Israel, opened his eyes wide, thumped on the table, and raised his voice, saying, 'He that is hungry ought to eat.'

Eating stimulated our appetites, and appetite stimulated our eating, until nothing was left of the loaf but a small piece, and it too disappeared down Yeruham's gullet, or the guest's.

'Now let us drink tea,' said Yeruham, 'in memory of the days when all our meals were tea and bread, or bread with tea.' He got up, brought the boiling kettle and the fragrant essence, and poured the tea. 'What shall we have to give flavor to the tea?' he said. 'The cursed ants, blast them, have nibbled away all the cake we had left from Shavuot.' He blew on the cake, chasing away the ants. When the ants had fled the cake, we saw that the cheese had shrunk and the raisins were mouldy. Yeruham shook his head in despair and said, 'A man will have to answer for every piece of food he has left uneaten.'

Rachel braced herself, got up and brought preserves made with orange peel. With all other fruits, you eat the inside and throw away the peel, but oranges are good to eat and their peel is good to eat too, so long as you candy it very well. In Rachel's praise, we must say that her confection was successful. From whom had she learned it, her mother or Krolka? Or perhaps the oranges themselves had taught her to make of their peel a food so delicate, so luxurious.

The windows were wide open, the scent of the evening dew rose from the damp soil and the trees and grasses, and a bird twittered and sang, unseen. The moon shone upon it, accompanying the chant of the bird in the moon's own way with the moon's own light. Rachel went back to her bed, while we sat and listened to the voice of the bird.

Yeruham rose, took Rachel's face in his two hands and kissed her on the lips. 'Be ashamed of yourself,' said Rachel. Yeruham closed his eyes and said, 'Behold, I am ready and prepared to be ashamed.' Rachel slapped him on the fingers and said, 'Go back to your place and sit still like a respectable person.' So Yeruham went back and sat down like a respectable person.

Rachel lay on her bed and looked at her husband and her husband's friend—at her husband because he was her husband, and at her husband's friend because he was her husband's friend.

'Tell us a little about the Land of Israel,' said Rachel to Yeruham. 'Whatever for?' said Yeruham. 'To make our guest happy,' replied Rachel. 'I'm afraid I may tell and he won't be happy,' said Yeruham. 'Why shouldn't he be happy?' 'The truth wasn't given to make us happy.'

You have never heard such a combination of opposites as Yeruham's talk. He obviously meant to disparage the Land of Israel, but its praises emerged from his disparagement. I have no intention of repeating all Yeruham said, but I will repeat some of it. For instance, he told of the great swamps that had lain rotting there in the Land of Israel for two thousand years and produced all kinds of diseases; in the end you heard that they had been healed and made into good land. Again, there were those boys and girls whose lives had been sacrificed to drain the swamps, in order to expand capital, but they had been privileged to add several villages to the Land of Israel. Perhaps it was of them that David said, inspired by the spirit of prophecy, 'And they sow the fields and plant vineyards, which yield fruits of increase.' Rachel lay on her bed, listening as she dozed and dozing as she listened.

What else did he tell that we have not yet told? Yeruham told of the gnats and mosquitoes that come in bands and cover the tents like a curtain, clinging to every man and making his hands and face look as if they were covered with scales, sucking his blood, filling him with venom and bringing malaria. When a man catches malaria, his body is weakened and he falls sick. Before he recovers from this sickness, another sickness comes and finishes him. Many have fallen sick and died, and many are as good as dead. 'Our guest knows them well.'

The guest does know them well. And for some reason I do not know, I said to Yeruham, 'If we draw up an account, we shall find that more of our dead were killed for the liberation of Poland than in draining the swamps.' 'If you find that any consolation,' said Yeruham, 'you may be consoled.' Said the guest, 'Let us be consoled, Yeruham, let us be consoled, that a group of young men has been found to give their lives for the Land of Israel.' 'For the sake of the Hebrew letters engraved on the money of the Land,' said Yeruham. 'For the sake of the Hebrew letters, and for the sake of the Land, and for the sake of the nation,' said the guest. 'So that the money of the Land of Israel should find its way into the pockets of the capitalists,' said Yeruham. 'So that the money of the Land of Israel should find its way into the pockets of the capitalists and they should spend it in the Land of Israel,' replied the guest. 'You solve the problem too lightly,' said Yeruham. 'Whether lightly or hardly, the world has not been entrusted to us and does not ask us for solutions,' replied the guest, 'but the question of ourselves—*that* may be in our power to solve.' 'In the way you follow?' 'In the way we follow, even if we make mistakes and do wrong. Mistakes and wrongs that are in our power may be put right; but we cannot put right what is not in our power.'

Yeruham banged the table angrily. Rachel was startled and aroused, and looked at us in fright. I felt sorry for her and said, 'Don't be afraid, Rachel, Yeruham wanted to wage war against the whole world and tried his strength on the table.' Yeruham laughed and said, 'Heaven help me if I argue with you.' 'If so,' said I, 'I will argue with you.' 'With verses from the Torah or sayings of the sages?' said Yeruham. I laughed and said, 'What else? With the wisdom of your wise men, whose lives are the lives of a day and whose wisdom is the wisdom of an hour?' Said Rachel to Yeruham, 'How long will you go on arguing? Perhaps you will amuse us a little.'

Like most of the lads from the kvutzot in the Land of Israel, Yeruham had been granted a double portion of humor. He stood up, folded his cap, making it like a kind of tourist's hat, and pretended to be a tourist who had come to the kvutza to photograph the pioneers. He stuck out one foot in front, bent his head to the left, fixed his eyes on a nail in the wall, and said, 'It's very fine here, very fine, but if that hill was a bit farther away from here, about ten and a half inches away, it would be much finer.' Then he lowered his head and looked at the plate, adding, 'This valley is fine, but if it moved itself a little to the right, the landscape would be quite different and much finer.'

When the Almighty made up his mind to create the Land of Israel, He did not consult a company of tourists on how He should create it. Apparently He knew full well that they would not come to dwell in it, and He created the Land according to His will. But even those for whom He created it are not content. We need not go far for the evidence: here is Yeruham Freeman—for several years he lived in the Land of Israel, and finally he left it.

Rachel asked Yeruham, 'And you and your comrades, did you give no one any reason to laugh at you?' 'We had another characteristic,' replied Yeruham, 'we loved one another. There is nothing in all the world like this love that existed between us. Only think, Rachel, lads whose parents tried to draw away customers from each other's shops live together as one, and each is happy in the happiness of his comrades. And just as he is happy in his comrade's happiness, so he is happy at every stretch of road that is built in the country, and at night they go out and dance till midnight up to high heaven and its stars.'

Rachel listened as she lay on her bed. She knew that when Yeruham danced he did not dance alone; and he did not dance with the young men among his comrades but with the young women, who worked with him on the road, for they say of them that they are beautiful as maidens and brave as youths. If at first Rachel's face looked as though all the days her husband had spent in the Land were engraved on it, now it looked as though all the nights he had spent there were engraved upon it.

Rachel turned her face away and put her hand to her heart. No one understands what the heart is. A short time before, it was happy, and now it is sad.

I rose from my chair and said, 'Time to go.'

Yeruham and Rachel were concerned with their own affairs and did not stop me, and I wanted to go because midnight was near and it is not good manners to sit all night with young people in the first year of their marriage.

When I came back to my hotel I found Mr. Zommer sitting and smoking his pipe. Midnight had already gone and still he was awake. It seemed that there was a new anxiety in his heart, and he was trying to drive it away with the tobacco in his pipe.

To give the innkeeper pleasure I told him I had come from Rachel and Yeruham's home. Mr. Zommer took his pipe out of his mouth, opened his eyes, and mumbled with his lips. It appeared that he was thinking of another difficult matter.

Between One Cigarette and Another

Once again the same commercial traveler has come to the town, and here he is, sitting in Mr. Zommer's hotel and chatting with Babtchi, but not jesting with her—and she is not laughing either. Apparently there is something between them that is beyond jesting and smutty talk.

Mr. Riegel the agent looks exhausted and he speaks in a whisper. Seven times already he has put a cigarette to his lips but has not lit it. Has he no matches, or perhaps he wants to go to the kitchen to take an ember, as the hotel-keeper does? Who can measure the spirit of man, and know what is in his heart! Babtchi sits opposite; though she sees the cigarette being crushed between his fingers she does not help by giving him a light. But she scrutinizes him with her eyes and gazes at his Adam's apple, which moves all the time, even when he is not speaking. How many sinews, my dear, are there in your Adam's apple? One, two, three? If he were a sensible man, in the habit of looking after his affairs properly, he would not forget to pass the razor over them when he shaves his beard. David Moshe, the rabbi's grandson, has no hair on his neck, although he does not shave when he comes to Szibucz, out of respect for his grandfather the rabbi, and needless to say he has no Adam's apple. Dr. Zwirn has no Adam's apple in his throat either, but he has a bald spot on his head. Or perhaps he has one, too, but you can't see it because of his double chin. On account of this double chin of his, he finds it hard to breathe, and he sleeps with his mouth open. Once when he was asleep a mouse got into his mouth. He shut his mouth and most of the mouse remained outside. Now let us imagine; if the cat came and caught the mouse by the tail, which would be better for the mouse, to stay in Zwirn's mouth, or to be eaten by the cat? Babtchi told me that whenever she sees Zwirn, it looks to her as if his mustache is made of a mouse's tail. And perhaps that is the reason why he does not attract her, although he has doubled her wages.

The commercial traveler looks at Babtchi and sees that she is not listening to what he is saying. When he discovered her for the first time she wore a leather jacket, her hair was dressed like a boy's, and she looked just like a boy; but now she is clad in a simple dress, her hair has grown, and her figure is filled out. Between winter and summer her appearance has changed. And you, my friend, said that never in your days have you seen a girl so piquant as this one. Now you must change your mind and say that this Babtchi, who is sitting before you today, is more beautiful than the Babtchi you first knew.

Lolik, Babtchi's brother, has ears and a tongue for everything. He came and sat in front of me and told me that Riegel was going to divorce his wife, but it wasn't simple, because he had children by her, and he had already given the case to a lawyer in his town, to do anything he could if only he got rid of her. If so, why does he come here? He comes to tell Babtchi. And why need Babtchi know? Lolik smiles his feminine smile and leaves me to think whatever I like. On the other hand, Mrs. Zommer told me that the commercial traveler came to Szibucz only because of that cloth merchant who had gone bankrupt and owed Riegel's master five thousand zlotys, so he had come to bring a case against him; he had put the matter in the hands of Zwirn, for whom Babtchi worked, and he was consulting Babtchi about his affairs.

Just as a man is composed of matter and spirit, so are his actions composed of matter and spirit. A commercial traveler comes to deal with matters of money and converses with Babtchi on the affairs of his spirit. In the meantime, he is between two lawyers: the one who is arranging his divorce and the one to whom he has submitted his claim against the merchant. We would not venture to intrude between two lawyers and say which is the shrewder. In any case, it seems to be easier for a man to get rid of his wife than to get his money from a shopkeeper who has gone bankrupt.

Need the shopkeeper have gone bankrupt? When I went to his shop to buy cloth for my coat, it was chock-full of merchandise, and I doubt if he has sold it all, for I have seen no one who has had a new suit made, and one can assume that all the merchandise is still where it was. But what shall the shopkeeper do with all his cloth? Should he put it under his wife's head—as she told me about Schuster's wife, who puts her cloth under her head, because she does not have a pillow for her head?

Babtchi is a sensible girl and knows how to give advice to anyone who consults her. She teaches the commercial traveler how to win Zwirn over, whom she knows like the back of her hand. About the agent's wife, whom he is about to divorce, Babtchi is silent, for when it comes to the soul's affairs, her soul is confused, because there is no peace in her soul. Sometimes the material aspect is the stronger, and sometimes the spiritual. Sometimes she says to herself: Zwirn is rich, he lives on the fat of the land and has a number of houses in the town; if he means to marry her and not to play with her, he is worth paying some attention to. And sometimes she thinks about David Moshe the rabbi's grandson, who is a handsome young man but does not earn enough, because he does not work on the Sabbath. He depends on his father, who makes up for the pay he loses on the Sabbath, for he is a cashier in a cinema—and he will always be dependent on his father, for if he should want to work on the Sabbath they will take away his position out of respect for his father, who controls the newspaper and can do harm. But then her hands, that is, Babtchi's, are not tied, and she could fill in the gap. Or perhaps Zwirn lets her work for him as long as he is pleased with her, but if she marries someone else he will dismiss her, and she will find it hard to get another post. This world is like a plain, but suddenly it rears itself up like a mountain, which is full of smaller slopes as well. What was Babtchi missing before? She was happy with her friends, and her friends were happy with her. Suddenly she and her friends know happiness no more.

Mrs. Zommer does not know what is in her daughter's heart—and even if she knew, she could not help. It would be good for her daughter to marry a rich man who earns more in one month than the whole town of Szibucz in a year. But this lawyer is a curse to the town: he sucks people's blood and devours their substance. Even when he was an assistant to Ausdauer he was notorious for his malice, and now that he is his own master he is more malicious than ever.

On the other hand, the rabbi's grandson is a fine young man, well educated and of good family, polite and courteous. He is equipped with the lore of his fathers and the lore of the world, talks Yiddish like the women's prayer book and Polish like a lady. And if you object that he makes a poor living, Mrs. Zommer says: 'In the old days, when money was money, money was not everything; all the more so in these days, when money is no longer money! He that gives life will give them a living. And as for the agent, who the gossips say is divorcing his wife for Babtchi's sake—heaven almighty, if we paid attention to every commercial traveler who makes eyes at the women wherever he goes, we would never stop.'

My host sits as usual, with his pipe in his mouth and his eyes half closed—first, because his pains have been reawakened, and second, because he wants to think about days gone by.

In days gone by, a girl would sit in her father's house and not in lawyers' offices; she would help her mother in the home, and when she was finished with her work she would read a book. When she was ripe and ready, God sent her a mate and they lived together. Actually, a lawyer's business is acceptable too, and if his father-in-law had been able to keep his word, perhaps he, Mr. Zommer, would also have become a lawyer. As for Dr. Zwirn, in whose office Babtchi works, the whole thing is not clear. What is not clear about it? If he does all kinds of doubtful things for the sake of his clients, it is only right that a lawyer should do whatever he can to win his clients' cases. But it is not right that he should do all kinds of doubtful things for his own sake, to make money out of other people's troubles. There was an old tinsmith in the town, a one-eyed man, Dr. Milch's father; Zwirn involved him in all kinds of disputes until the old man sold him his house for a song. And as for David Moshe, the rabbi's grandson, that good-for-nothing is quite out of the question. The only thing in his favor is that he is the rabbi's grandson. And then we ought to ask: One way or the other—if you respect your grandfather, why don't you follow in his footsteps? But if you don't respect him, why should anyone respect you? As for that agent, it is obvious that he is a sober and sensible man. He pays his bills generously and tips Krolka. But there is no peace between him and his wife. Perhaps he is in the right and she is not. In any case, Mr. Zommer has no intention of going into this matter, although it affects Babtchi's affairs. And if even Rachel did not obey him, it is all the more certain that Babtchi will not obey him either.

Babtchi left the agent sitting alone, for the time had come to go to her office, and since she got up suddenly and went off, the agent did not manage to ask if he might accompany her. He sits by himself and thinks about his wife and his young children. When was it he made up his mind to divorce his wife—before he came to Szibucz the first time, or after he came back? Everything goes to show that it was after he returned from Szibucz that he began to feel that he no longer loved his wife. But he says that even in the first year after their marriage he did not find her the right woman for him. If so, why did he stay with her? Because she became pregnant and he did not wish to grieve her. Before he had made up his mind, she became pregnant again, and it all went back to the beginning again, for he did not wish to grieve her by saying: I do not want you. Those who are always at home, and see their wives every day and all day, arrange things to suit themselves, but it is another matter with a commercial traveler who spends most of his time on the road: even if he makes up his mind to part with his wife, when he comes home and finds her all dressed up, and his table laid and his bed made, he forgets what he decided to do, and before he manages to reveal his intentions his wife is pregnant and he cannot grieve her.

Let us turn our attention away from the agent's heart and look at his external actions. Well, the agent took his cigarette case out of his pocket again and extracted a new cigarette. Some distance away, at another table, sits Babtchi's father, smoking his pipe. The agent says to himself: Perhaps I will get up and go to Mr. Zommer and light my cigarette from his pipe. Or perhaps I will go into the kitchen and take an ember. But if I find Mrs. Zommer there, perhaps she will start a conversation, for Mrs. Zommer is always talking, unlike her husband, who is usually silent. All other innkeepers are talkative, but this one is silent. Perhaps because he disapproves of the agent's wish to divorce the wife of his youth, and he does not know that he would spend the rest of his life with her were it not for Babtchi.

This Babtchi, may God help her, whichever way she appears, whether in a leather jacket or in a simple dress, she drives him crazy. These women are always bad. If you hate them they are bad, and if you love them they are bad. How simple it was in the winter, when you neither loved nor hated her, and she would sit and joke with you until she shook with laughter. Now that you have cast a favorable eye on her, she will not meet your eyes. If it were not for the affair of the bankrupt shopkeeper, he would take his belongings and go back to his home town.

What will happen to the shopkeeper? Zwirn is lackadaisical and does nothing. Perhaps Dolik was right when he said that he has an eye for the shopkeeper's wife? What am I to do? Should I go to the lawyer or wait for Dolik and try to find out what rumor he has heard. It is true that every conversation with Dolik costs money, because he gets me into a card game and gets money out of me. But if we put it down to business expenses, it does not matter.

The cigarette between the agent's fingers is crushed and he has already taken out another. I am afraid this one will end up like the first.

Over the Glass

Reb Hayim came and took the key, swept the floor and polished up the furnishings, and cleared away the dust with which the Beit Midrash had been filled while I was away. When I came in after him, I found the lamps full of kerosene, the basin full of fresh water, and white cloths spread on the tables; the whole hall was made ready to welcome the Sabbath in purity, and a pale greenish light completely filled the Beit Midrash, like a light that is not perceived by the eye but moves the heart.

It was good to sit by the table, or go up to the rostrum and read the weekly Scripture portion—twice in the original and once in the Aramaic translation. True, this was *Naso,* the second portion in the Book of Numbers, the longest in the Torah, but then this Sabbath eve was also a long one. He that gave the Torah is He that created the world and ordered the days, making them longer or shorter according to the order of the weekly portions.

But a man's feet want to go outside, and they justify their wish by a commandment, such as this is Sabbath eve and a man must cleanse himself in honor of the Sabbath. So this man, whose heart is tender and persuadable, obeyed his feet, especially as they justified their call with a commandment. I took the key, locked up the Beit Midrash, and went out. It was still too early to go and eat; it was already too late to go to the forest; and it was not the right time to stroll in the town, for what would people say?—'Everyone is busy preparing for the Sabbath, while that man strolls about for pleasure.'

A man came up to me, stopped me, looked at me for a little while, and said, 'Tell me, aren't you my friend So-and-so?' He put out both hands and greeted me. I returned his greeting, saying, 'You are Aaron Schutzling—what are you doing here? Don't you live in America?' 'And what are you doing here? I thought you lived there in the Land of Israel?' 'It seems,' I replied, 'that we have both been mistaken in each other.'

Aaron shook his head and said, 'Yes, my friend, both of us have been mistaken in each other. I do not live in America, and you, if we may judge from the evidence of sight, do not live in the Land of Israel. And that is not all; when I look at the two of us it seems to me that there is no America and no Land of Israel in the world, but only Szibucz—or perhaps it does not exist either, but only its name exists. Well, what is this *effendi* doing in the streets of Szibucz?' 'What am I doing here? Let me think.' 'Why think? Thoughts are tiring. Come, let us go to the bathhouse. It is Sabbath eve and they have lit the stove; we'll find a hot bath and wash in warm water and rinse in cold. Since I reached years of understanding I have found nothing better for the body than a hot bath. Of all the commandments that were given to Israel, I strictly observe this one, for every Sabbath eve I run to the baths.' 'And what about the other commandments?' 'Perhaps other people are strict about the other commandments. In any case, the Almighty will not be able to make Himself a warm coat out of all the commandments the Jews observe.' 'A strange description!' 'On the contrary, you ought to be pleased with this description, for it shows you that I believe God exists. And as for the commandments Jews observe, you and I know that they are not worth much.'

So two sons of Szibucz walk together in Szibucz, as they used to walk twenty years ago and more, before they left, one for America and the other for the Land of Israel. How old were we in those days, and what did we use to do? We were about seventeen or eighteen; I sat in the Beit Midrash, studying Talmud and Commentaries, while he was employed in the bakery, baking bread. And although we differed in our opinions, for I was a Zionist and he an anarchist, we were glad to talk to each other. Many times he used to tease me by calling me a bourgeois of the next world, because I studied the Torah and preached for Zion. And I would enrage him when I admitted part of his argument and said that there is no need for kings, since the King Messiah is destined to reign over the whole world. How many years have passed since that time! How many kings have tumbled off their thrones, and still the Son of David has not come.

The Messiah, Son of David, has not yet come and 'the Land of Israel has not yet spread into all the other lands,' but this man has come back, and he is now in Szibucz. He is like a bridegroom who went to marry a wife, only to find her sick and woebegone; so he has come back home wearing all his fine clothes, but he has no pleasure in them, for dejection has dried his bones and the clothes are too big for him. So he tries to put on his old ones, but cannot find them, for he has put them away.

'If you do not wish to go to the bathhouse,' said Schutzling, 'let us go into the hotel and drink a glass of ale in honor of this day when we have met.' I nodded and went in with him. For this I had two reasons: first, to meet my friend's wish, and second, because my conscience troubled me for spoiling the innkeeper's trade when I told the postman not to go to the hotel and drink brandy with my money.

'In the meantime,' said my friend, 'you have been in the great world.' 'And you?' 'So have I, and we have come back from there.' 'We have come back from there.' 'In the past, when we used to stroll in the streets of Szibucz, it did not enter our minds that we would visit far-off countries.' 'And when we were in the far-off countries it did not enter our minds that we would return here.' 'If it did not enter your mind that you would come back,' he replied, 'I wanted to return all the time.' Why had he been attracted to this place? Because America had not attracted him. 'And now that you have returned,' said I, 'you do not live in Szibucz.' He smiled and said, 'In this world nothing is perfect. And if you like I will tell you: it is the tragedy of my life that I do not live in Szibucz.' 'Do you love Szibucz so much?' said I. 'When a man sees that there is no place in the world that he loves, he deceives himself into thinking he loves his town. And you, do you love Szibucz?' 'I? I haven't thought about it yet.' My friend took my hand, and said, 'If so, let me tell you that all your love for the Land of Israel comes to you from Szibucz; because you love your town you love the Land of Israel.' 'How do you know that I love Szibucz?' 'Is it proof you want? If you did not love Szibucz, would you be dealing with it all your life? Would you be digging up gravestones to discover its secrets?' 'You haven't yet told me what you did in America and what you are doing today,' said I. 'What I did in America? I worked like a horse to get my bread, until with all the sweat and strain I did not manage to eat my bread. And what am I doing today? I go around to sell all kinds of useless medicines the Germans invent. Don't be sorry for me, my friend—as I am not sorry for myself. How long does a man have to live? My father, rest his soul, lived ninety years; and I will be content with fifty. And do I have to worry for my children? My father worried for me, and what use was it?' 'How many children have you?' 'How many children have I? Wait until I count them.' 'Have you gone crazy?' 'If you interrupt me I can't count.' He started counting on his fingers: 'Two that my first wife brought me from her first husband and one from her second, three daughters she bore me, and one son with the American woman, and my eldest son who was born of the dark seamstress. You remember that charming brunette; she forgave me before her death. From that son I have some satisfaction; since the day his mother died, he sends me money and clothes. And now, too, I have come with the help of his money to see if it's worth while opening a bakery here. I'm sick of my father's son having to go about as an agent for all kinds of rubbish, and he wants to take up his father's trade. But it's hopeless. You can't say that Szibucz doesn't need bread, but there isn't anyone to pay the baker.'

I asked him about his other sons and daughters. He waved his hand and said, 'Don't ask, my friend, don't ask. My youngest daughter was caught for communist activity, and her eldest sister was caught with her, though she had done no wrong; and the middle one ran away so that they shouldn't catch her, for it was she who started the business. The good times have passed when a man can say what he thinks without being punished for it. This republic is stricter than the Emperor. On the face of it, why should it care if a little high-school girl pays her respects to Lenin? Did my friends and I do any harm when we were anarchists? It's eight months now that these two children have been in prison, and I doubt whether they'll let them out in a hurry. And maybe I've made peace with the position by now, but what troubles me is my youngest son, the American woman's child. Perhaps you know of some way to save him from disaster and prevent him following in his sisters' footsteps? Perhaps I should send him to the Land of Israel? But then there, too, there is trouble and suffering, disturbances and communists.'

'The fathers have gathered wood and the sons kindle the fire,' said I. Schutzling sighed and said, 'Let us leave history to the historians and the present to the journalists, and drink another glass. What do you think of this ale? What do you drink in the Land of Israel?' 'Some drink wine, some drink soda, and some tea.' 'And don't you drink ale there?' 'There is no ale there.' 'And didn't you feel the want of it?' 'I felt other wants.' 'So even there the Land is no paradise. You haven't told me anything yet about what you did there.' 'What I did there? I haven't done anything yet.' 'You are modest, my friend.' 'I am not modest, but when a man sees that most of his life has passed and he is still at the beginning of his work, he cannot say that he has done anything. They say in the Gemara: "He who has not seen the Temple built in his days, it is as if it had been destroyed in his days." I am not thinking of the Temple, but it is a parable of all we have done in the Land of Israel.'

My friend patted me affectionately on the shoulder and said, 'It is not you that will build, just as it was not we who destroyed. What are we and who are we in this great and terrible world? Not so much as this drop of ale. What do you think of this drink? I've drunk five glasses and you've not even drunk one. Drink, my friend, drink. I'd wanted to soak my outer limbs, instead I've soaked my inner. Come here and let me kiss you. One kiss of parting, because we parted from Szibucz. And a second kiss of meeting, and then a third parting kiss, for immediately after the Sabbath I am going away. Don't say I'm drunk, but say I feel good because I have seen you. Do you remember that song the charming brunette used to sing? Let us drink to her memory and sing her song:

'In grief and pain my years have gone;
No days of joy and ease—not one.
In sorrow and nothing my life is done—
Sleep now; sleep now; sleep, my son.'

At sundown we parted. Schutzling went to his sister and
I to my hotel, to change my clothes and welcome the Sabbath
in the Great Synagogue, for there were no longer any prayers
in our old Beit Midrash.

When I came to the synagogue, the congregation had already finished the Afternoon Service, and since there were only
about two quorums it seemed as if the synagogue were empty
and still waiting for the rest of the people. Or perhaps it only
seemed so to me; for it was surely accustomed to only a score
of worshippers.

Shlomo Shamir was reciting the Welcome to the Sabbath
at the lectern, but for the Afternoon Service he went down to
the rostrum before the Ark and started with 'Bless ye the
Lord' and so forth. This is an old custom in the Great Synagogue of Szibucz, as well as in several old congregations, that
they welcome the Sabbath at the lectern, but for the Evening
Service the leader of the prayers goes down before the Ark,
for the six hymns in the Welcome to the Sabbath, as well as
'Come, my beloved,' do not belong to the original code of
prayers but are a later addition; so it was ruled that they
should be recited at the lectern, since passages that do not
belong to the early liturgy are not said before the Ark. That
is why, in our old prayer book, which was handed down in
manuscript by the early authorities on the liturgy, you do not
find either the six hymns or 'Come, my beloved,' but the
Sabbath Evening Service begins with 'Bless ye the Lord.'

Shlomo recited the prayers melodiously like the old prayer
leaders in Szibucz, who start in joy and tranquillity like the
gatekeeper who opens up the palace to the king's retinue when
they come to greet the king, and waits until they have finished
their greetings. Until the war came, Shlomo used to read the
Torah, and when the people returned to Szibucz after the war,
and could not afford to hire a cantor, he agreed to lead the

prayers without pay. Previously, before the war came, we had
two cantors in the Great Synagogue, in addition to the Reader
of the Torah. When people began to whisper that the reader
wanted to go away to America, they dismissed him, for it was
not to the honor of Szibucz that a man like that should read
the Torah in the Great Synagogue, and they appointed Shlomo
Shamir in his stead. So now he reads the Torah and recites all
the prayers if there are no others occupying the position before
the Ark. These others are new people, recently arrived from
the hamlets and villages near Szibucz, after the people of
Szibucz itself left the town, and it is they who have taken over
Szibucz and occupied all the places of honor at the eastern
end, behaving as if they owned the Great Synagogue and with
their voices making men forget the melodies handed down
from ancient generations. In a place where it was a rule that
no changes should be made either in the form of prayer, the
melodies, the structure, the number of candles, or the slightest
matter, until the coming of the Messiah, along come these
lightheaded people, who pronounce Hebrew with difficulty
and breach the fences our fathers erected. They had caused
me annoyance before, on the eve of the Day of Atonement,
and now my annoyance is redoubled.

CHAPTER THREE AND FIFTY

This Coming Generation

I returned to my hotel and sat down to eat. Mr. Riegel was
eating with us at the hotelkeeper's table, unlike the other
guests, who were not Sabbath observers and for whom Krolka
had set another table. Like a steadfast proselyte who happens
to find himself in a Jewish home for the first time, so Mr.
Riegel sat, gazing in Mr. Zommer's face with great affection,
spontaneously imitating all his movements.

After the Kiddush, Babtchi came in and sat down beside
her mother. In fact, she had already arrived before, but she

had gone to change her dress, which had been torn in an unfortunate incident that is not to be mentioned here.

Her expression was divided, as it were: one of her faces
was angry, the other was gracious. If her mother asked her
anything she replied as if from the bottom of a well. She, too,
fixed her eyes on her father's face—not like Mr. Riegel, who
gazed at him with admiration, but like a mute lamb, innocent
of sin. Her father sat as usual, his head bowed and his hands
under the table, singing the Sabbath hymns.

Between the fish and its sauce, Lolik came, followed by
Dolik, and brought news from the town. Since no one heeded
them, they smiled to themselves, one a malicious smile and
the other his feminine smile. Krolka served the table in utter
silence, took away the empty plates and brought full ones,
trimmed the candles, came in and went out, and did not utter
a sound as she came and went.

When the fingerbowl water was brought, the master of
the house raised his eyes, looked at Riegel for a while, and
knitted his eyebrows, like one who is considering a question
and does not know how to decide. He was probably wondering whether to count Riegel in for the Invitation to the Grace,
because Mr. Zommer was not in the habit of reciting the Invitation with his sons, except for Passover eves, when they
used to sit down at the table with him before the Kiddush.

After the grace, Mr. Zommer said to the agent, 'What has
Mr. Riegel to tell us?' Riegel, who was accustomed to my
host's holding his peace and not calling him by name, but
addressing him as Mr. Agent (an appellation that sets a barrier between a man and his neighbor), stammered and said,
'It is good to celebrate the Sabbath with Jews.' 'And is not
Mr. Riegel a Jew?' cried Mr. Zommer in surprise. Riegel put
his right hand on his heart and said with great enthusiasm,
'I am a Jew, Mr. Zommer, I am a Jew, but I am not the kind of
person a Jew ought to be.' 'What must a Jew do in order to
be the kind of Jew a Jew ought to be?' asked Dolik. 'What your
father does, Mr. Zommer,' replied Riegel. 'And what should a
Jewess do?' asked Lolik. 'Like Babtchi?' Babtchi stirred and
looked at him angrily. And she did not look kindly at Riegel

either. Since the day this agent came for the second time, she has not looked at him with favor. Babtchi does not hate him, but before he came for the second time she was at peace with the world and the world was at peace with her. Zwirn had doubled her pay and given her material for a dress (this was the dress he had torn on the Sabbath eve at dark), and David Moshe used to write her letters of love and salutation. She jested about it when she wished to, and when she wished to she thought about it. If Zwirn put out his lips to kiss her, she smacked him on the hand and he took it lovingly. Babtchi had never worried about this kind of thing, but suddenly the devil had got into Riegel and he was bothering her about his wives. In sober truth, Riegel had scarcely one wife, and even this one he wanted to get rid of; but in her anger Babtchi was confused and had hung two wives on him, and indeed the one who was surplus was Babtchi herself. I got up from my chair and was about to go, but Mr. Zommer said, 'Why are you getting up, sir? Sit with us and let us spend some time.'

These people have nothing to say, but when you wish to take your leave of them they say, 'Sit and let us spend some time.' Perhaps the master of the house has something to say, but he is keeping his thoughts to himself. As for Riegel, however, I doubt if he knows anything apart from bargaining over trade. Have you seen him sitting with Babtchi and crushing his cigarettes?—he deserved your pity and so did his cigarettes, but he did not deserve your wasting time with him. On the other hand, had he smoked a cigarette—which is forbidden on the Sabbath—both he and the cigarette would have felt better.

Dolik got up and went into a certain other room. When he came back he covered his mouth, to shield the smell of his cigarette.

My host fingered the tablecloth and said to his wife, 'Perhaps you would give us some of the good things you have prepared in honor of the Sabbath.' And as he spoke he smiled, like a child who has snatched the sweets before they were given him.

Mrs. Zommer hurried and brought some sweetmeats. 'And what will you give us to drink?' said Mr. Zommer. 'Perhaps soda with raspberry juice?' asked Mrs. Zommer. 'Perhaps some

real liquor?' said Mr. Zommer. 'They want to have a be-
trothal here,' said Lolik. 'Babtchi, perhaps you know who is
the bride?' 'Look in the mirror,' said Babtchi, 'and you'll
see the bride.'

Who is coming? No doubt a new guest. 'I do not take in
new guests on the Sabbath,' said the hotelkeeper. Schutzling
came in and sat down beside me.

Aaron Schutzling is not in favor with the master of the
house or the members of his family, each for his own reason.
When I realized this, I got up and went out with him.

Schutzling was depressed—perhaps because I had seen
him the worse for drink in the tavern, or perhaps because he
had left me to pay the bill, though it was he who invited me,
and a person who invites his friend to drink with him ought
to pay. 'I have taken you out of your warm nest,' said Schutzling. 'But it isn't cold outside either. Or perhaps you feel cold?
After all, you come from a warm country. What shall we do
now? Perhaps we should stroll for a while?' 'Here we are
strolling.' 'Are you angry with me?' 'Not at all, the night is
pleasant and the moon is shining—the night was made for a
stroll.' But as I was saying this, I thought: All we had to tell
we told on the Sabbath eve, and there was no need for him
to come back. Said Schutzling, 'A man's days and years are
drawn out until he pays back for all the pleasure he has had
in the world.' 'What are you referring to?' 'I was referring to
nothing else but the moon,' replied Schutzling. 'To the moon?
And what has the moon to do with it?' 'That's just it,' said
Schutzling, 'she doesn't; but this fool, Aaron, the baker's son,
believed that she still shone as in the early days when I was
a boy and the charming brunette was a young girl. When I
left the tavern, I said to myself: Let me go and see the
brunette's house. When I got there I slipped and fell into a
ditch, and almost broke my legs.' 'Do you feel pain in your
legs?' He put his hand on his heart and said, 'Here, my friend,
here I feel pain. Do you remember Knabenhut?' Schutzling
went on. 'He is dead and gone. It was through him I got to
know her at the time of the tailors' strike. Those were the
days. Days like those will never come back. You go on strike
by day, and sing and dance by night. Knabenhut did not take

part in the fun or dance with the girls, but he was not jealous of anyone who was lucky and found himself a pretty girl. During the war I found myself in Vienna and saw him standing on the bridge over the Danube, gazing at the passers-by. I wanted to pass him in silence, so as not to get him angry, as he was in the old days when I became an anarchist; after all, some said that he had betrayed me to the authorities and that I had run away to America just in time. He beckoned to me and I went up to him. "Don't come near me," he said, "I've got an infection." I stood a little distance away. He started preaching about the war and the disaster in store for us and the whole world. His voice was weak, but his words were strong and eloquent. And again I stood before him as in the early days, when he drew me out from behind the stove in my father's house and enlightened me with his speeches. Finally he whispered to me, "This generation that is coming is worse than all the generations before it. And I will tell you this too: the world is getting uglier and uglier, uglier than you and I wanted to make it." Now, my friend, we have come back to your hotel. Go in and go to sleep.' After he had gone I stood on the threshold of the hotel and looked after him. His hands, his voice were trembling . . .

'In sorrow and nothing my life is done—
Sleep now; sleep now; sleep, my son.'

It was years since I had thought of Knabenhut, though I ought to have remembered him, for there was no one in Szibucz before the war who was talked about so much, and there was never a time when he was not setting the town in a tumult, for he used to call public meetings and preach to the socialists—whom he had created and established; he organized the first tailors' strike; he called together ten thousand reapers at harvest time, and told them not to go back to work unless their wages were raised and all their demands met, for more than they depended on their masters, he said, their masters depended on them, and he kept them out three whole days until the authorities sent a regiment of gendarmes to take them back, and Knabenhut taught them that no government could coerce them. And when the gendarmes drew their

bayonets, Knabenhut held them with his speeches until their
bayonets faltered in their hands, and they were almost ready
to join their brethren, the strikers. There were some men in
Szibucz who had won a reputation in the world and at home
as well, but we did not notice them as much as we did
Knabenhut, for they added to what we knew already, but
Knabenhut came and taught us things we had never heard
before.

In the early days, when the world was founded on the
Torah, Szibucz produced rabbis, and afterward scholars. After
that it produced men of action, but they gave us no more than
the scent of action, while when Knabenhut went into public
affairs he showered us with deeds in overflowing measure.

This was the beginning of Knabenhut's doings in Szibucz.
There were wretched boys in the town, poor boys, the sons of
poor men, shop assistants and laborers, who lived like cattle,
tyrannized over day and night by their masters. When Knabenhut came along, he got them together, hired them a room and
lectured them on science and social theory, until they straightened their backs and lifted up their heads. Some of them were
devoted to him all their lives, ready to jump into fire and
water for his sake; others betrayed him, made a mockery of his
teachings, and when they reached the place where their
masters had stood and became their own masters, they behaved as their masters had behaved to them at first. Knabenhut incited his disciples against the Zionists; and during a
strike his disciples would see to it that no one stole away to
take work; but he made light of those who betrayed him, and
even when he had the opportunity he did not pay them back.

Schutzling was one of his disciples at the beginning and
was more devoted to his teacher than any of them, until Sigmund Winter came along and taught them that Knabenhut
was only a daydreamer, for he wanted to reform the world
through socialism, when there was no help for the world but
extinction.

This Sigmund Winter was the son of a doctor and one of
Knabenhut's disciples. He was distinguished from his fellows
by his black hair and his beautiful eyes, which he used to fix
on the girls. There were many stories they used to tell about

him: it was said, for instance, that he would go after a girl in the street and say to her, 'Let me look at you'—which was not customary in Szibucz, where they used to talk to girls with respect. On the other hand, he was not distinguished in his studies and would go from one high school to the other, sometimes because his teachers could not stand up to his eyes and sometimes because he could not delve deeply enough into their wisdom. There is reason to believe that he was not lacking in other qualities, which the men of Szibucz did not mention, for it was the custom in Szibucz to tell things about their great men that minimized their stature, and whenever anyone was greater than his fellows, his fellows used to say that he was not distinguished in his youth—on the contrary, that he often failed to understand points of learning known to any child, who is neither clever nor foolish. It would be no exaggeration to say that if Og, King of Bashan, had been born in our town they would have said that Rabbi Gadiel the Infant was a head taller than he. When Sigmund Winter's time came to enter the university, he went where he went and we did not know where, and we heard nothing at all of him for many years. One day a rumor spread in the town that he had been arrested in Gibraltar for an incredible act; if it had not been written in the newspapers, no one would have believed it, for he was suspected of having tried to assassinate a certain king who was passing through the country. We thought Winter's end had come, and we said it was right for it to come. Then the papers said that deputies in the Austrian parliament had protested against a foreign country throwing an Austrian citizen into prison, and—wonderful to relate— Vienna intervened and he was released. Before long, Sigmund Winter appeared. He held his head high like a prince; he had a black cape on his shoulders with its hem flowing down below his knees, and a black hat on his head tilted a little on one side, and his mustache pointing up, with a beard below like half a Shield of David, and beautiful girls of good family accompanying him, and all the ministers making way for him, because he used to walk as if the whole of Szibucz were his private estate. Before long, the papers came to Szibucz, with pictures of Kropotkin and Bakunin and Reclus, and among them the picture of Sigmund Winter. Heavens above, never had Szibucz known a young man to have his picture published abroad, especially among the world's great men. True, we did not know who Kropotkin and Bakunin and Reclus were, but we understood that they were great men, for otherwise they would not have had their pictures published in the papers. And indeed we were not wrong, for those in the know told us that the first two were princes and sons of princes, while the third, Elysée Reclus, was a university professor.

What reason did Winter have for returning to Szibucz? If it was true that he wanted to raise his hand against the King, well, there are no kings in Szibucz. After all, what harm have the kings done to him that he tries to make their lives a misery? And if he is an anarchist, what of it? People have all kinds of opinions, one more peculiar than the next, and if everyone acted on them what would the world come to?

Before long, various kinds of brochures and pamphlets were discovered, with all kinds of evil things about the commandments of the Lord and the eternal laws enunciated by the great men of all generations for the improvement of the world. On the other hand, there were good things said there about free love and the like. Before long, the town was rent with controversy; every day there were quarrels, every day people came to blows. This was not a controversy between masters and servants, or socialists and Zionists, but a controversy between socialists and their comrades. We used to think that everyone who followed Knabenhut was devoted to him forever, but in the end many turned against him and became enemies to him and their former comrades. So Knabenhut stood up and attacked them, as he had never attacked any man or faction. For who had been his rivals before? Either men who were well aware that they had a skeleton in the closet and were afraid they would be discovered, or Zionists who played with words. But here Knabenhut found rabid zealots facing him, ready to sacrifice themselves and the whole world as well. When he saw that he could not defeat them, he betrayed them to the authorities—and some say it was not he who betrayed them but one of his comrades, because in the end Knabenhut himself was punished by the authorities, as well as his opponents. Some of them fled the country and some redoubled their war against Knabenhut, while the authorities closed one eye to their actions and laughed with the other at this Knabenhut, whose disciples had seized his weapons and were sharpening them against their leader. And we too were glad. Not that our views were close to those of the anarchists—but it was like this: a man who reads the Koran is not said to have become a Turk—but anyone who reads the Gospels is suspected of being a heretic, because the one is near and the other is far.

I was not attracted by Knabenhut or his opinions, but I thought about him a great deal. A great quality is power, but greater still is the quality of renunciation. When we find both of them in one man, we admire him. These two qualities were united in Knabenhut. He showed his power in deeds, and renounced his own interests. Sometimes his means were wrong and the end was right, and sometimes his means were right and the end was wrong, but one way or the other we never heard of him seeking his own welfare. We were accustomed to men who summoned up strength to defeat their enemies and gave up a little of their own interests so that others should renounce much, but we did not see a man who gave up his own to others and for their benefit. When they tried to bribe him with a good post he would not accept it. Moreover, he abandoned philosophy and such studies, and went to study law; and he did not use it for his own selfish purposes, but served the oppressed even without pay, and borrowed money at interest to support the strikes. We were accustomed to men who squandered money for power and authority, for women or horses; Knabenhut did not chase women, or want to become a member of parliament, or seek any other kind of greatness for himself. It cannot be said that Szibucz lacked idealists, but between ourselves, how much did it cost? A man who bought a share in a Zionist bank, and took the shekel as a sign of membership, and paid a monthly contribution of twenty-five groschen to a Zionist society, was called a loyal comrade. And if he gave half a zloty for the people of Mahanayim he was called a good Zionist. But Knabenhut rented and furnished a house for his comrades, and bought books and newspapers for them, and learned to speak Yiddish so as to be able to speak to his comrades in their own language—unlike most of our leaders, who were too lazy even to learn the Hebrew alphabet.

How the World Grows Uglier

And what was the end of Knabenhut? On that Sabbath afternoon Schutzling visited me again. He had finished all his work in the town, and he was free for himself and for me. He had not done much business here, and you could even say that he had done none at all. He had just come from the pharmacist, a sickly, grumbling old Pole, who wears galoshes over his shoes summer and winter, has a woollen cloth wound around his neck, and coughs and sneezes. Schutzling said, 'The pharmacist said to me, "Once again you bring me drugs from Germany, my dear sir. The devil begot the Prussians and the Prussians begot the drugs. Do you think, my dear sir, that without these medicines the sick man cannot die? Your doctors, my dear sir, whenever they see some new kind of drug in their medical papers, immediately prescribe it for their patients, and the patients come and squawk: Give us this drug, give us this medicine. And I, my dear sir, spend money to bring them drugs. In the meantime, the Prussians have invented some other kind of medicine and the doctor prescribes the new one and the patients buy that instead of the old. Perhaps you know, my dear sir, in what way the new drug is better than the old one? I do not know and you don't know, so who knows? Now both of them are lying in my pharmacy, and even the rats don't want to touch them. Perhaps you know, my dear sir, what is the use of a pharmacy if the pharmacist does not grind the drugs, but gets them from the Prussians packed and sealed *zierlich manierlich*. If it is a question of selling, any Jewess with a shop can do it and there is no need for a scholarly man who has studied six years in high school and several years in the university." ' After Schutzling had told me of his conversation with the pharmacist, he put his arm around my neck and said, 'My dear sir, perhaps we should go out for a walk and some fresh air. A-tishoo! My nostrils are all stopped up with the smell of drugs. Well, my dear sir, pick up your feet and let us go.'

Schutzling was in a jesting mood. Every moment he would recall something the pharmacist had said to him and drag his feet as if he were wearing rubber shoes. Finally he forgot the pharmacist and went back to telling me all that was in his heart. You cannot imagine all that was in his heart. A man's mouth is small, but when it is opened it pours forth in overflowing measure.

In the course of his talk Schutzling went back to the story of Knabenhut. Although he had had many troubles on account of him, and had had to run away to America, he remembered the good Knabenhut had done him, for he had taken him from behind the stove and given him knowledge to know and understand the world, while he—namely Schutzling—had tormented him and made his life a misery, and had become an anarchist and drawn some of his comrades after him. How did anarchism come to Szibucz? Didn't the Jews love the Emperor and sing his praises, as a merciful king and lover of Jews, and pray that his years and days might be long, for so long as he was alive he defended them against every foe and enemy and accuser, and whenever any trouble overtook Jews in other countries, the people of Szibucz would say, 'How happy we are to live under the shelter of a benevolent state!' I have already said that Knabenhut had a disciple and comrade called Sigmund Winter, whom he loved very much and sent to study in the university, so that he should help him afterward in the class struggle. But Winter went and learned a different doctrine and brought it to Szibucz; he even drew away Schutzling and some of the other comrades. Then Knabenhut's disciples were divided into two factions; one remained with him and the other took up anarchism. What the anarchists did to Knabenhut we have already told, and what happened afterward we shall tell now.

After this, or perhaps before this, Knabenhut cast his eyes on a certain girl called Blume Nacht. No one knows whether he wanted to marry her or she wanted to marry him, but it is known that he married another woman, who was rich and brought him money and he went and opened a lawyer's office in Pitzyricz, near Szibucz. So he gave up socialism for a little while, because he owed twenty thousand zlotys to moneylenders, for he used to borrow money to maintain the strikers and his poor comrades, and the moneylenders pressed him to pay. They said of Knabenhut that he never managed to pay the capital, but all his life he went on paying the interest—and even that he paid from his wife's money, for he earned no more than enough for his expenses, because he did not want to appear in civil cases or money matters, which he hated, but devoted himself to criminal cases, where there is much trouble and little pay, for most poor sinners have no money to pay the lawyer's fee.

Although he had given up socialism, he was always available for any poor man injured at work whose master did not want to compensate him for pain, injury, and the rest. Likewise, if a girl was seduced by her master's son and bore a child whom he did not want to recognize, Knabenhut would take her case. In the meantime, his wife's money went and other money did not come in. In those days he went back to the love of his youth, namely philosophy, and abandoned his mistress, the study of law. As for flesh-and-blood women, he did the opposite: he abandoned his wife in favor of his mistresses. Although before he had married he had never cast his eyes upon women, he suddenly became attracted by them. And women—oh, my dear sir, a man looks for one and finds many. A Ukrainian student girl came from Switzerland to visit her sister, the doctor's wife, and Knabenhut was attracted by her; but the sister herself was drawn to Knabenhut, and—on top of that—so was her sister-in-law, the doctor's sister. Heart draws to heart and one woman draws another, and Knabenhut's heart was drawn by them all. So he left his office to his deputy, while he lay in bed reading Sophocles, or spent his time with women. So his wife took the rest of her money and went back to her father. In the meantime, the war came.

The war did not do him much good. He was not taken to serve in the army, for most of his life had passed, and later, when they took everything that walked on two legs, including old men, they exempted Knabenhut because of his sickness. Like the rest of the people who lived in Pitzyricz, he ran away at the beginning of the war to Szibucz and from Szibucz to Vienna. The little money he had taken with him was spent, and more money he did not find. His former comrades did not recognize him and he did not get new ones. He, who had set the whole country in a tumult, was abandoned in its capital. Finally, an old cynic came forward to help him. This cynic was a rich contractor, who used to make deals with ministers on the basis of 'half for me and half for you,' and Knabenhut used to denounce him in the newspapers to compel him to give an account of himself. When he heard that Knabenhut was in distress he took pity on him, or the whim took him, and he sent him money. This cynic—who, if anyone asked for a donation, would say, 'Before you came, surely you knew that I wouldn't give you anything, and just because of that I will never forgive you'—became a spendthrift where Knabenhut was concerned. Knabenhut used to take his dole and also help others. It can't be helped; a man wants to live, and so long as he lives he cannot ignore the troubles of his fellows. All that time, his benefactor did not show himself to Knabenhut. Knabenhut went to thank him, but he would not receive him. Again Knabenhut went, and again he didn't receive him. The contractor sent him a double gift by his servant. He took the money, bowed to the servant, and said, 'Today we eat and tomorrow we die.' Then he went home and locked the door. From that day on he did not leave his room, until there came that one against whom no door is locked and took him from the world—this world that is becoming even uglier than Knabenhut and his comrades wished to make it.

And what happened to Blume Nacht? What happened to Blume is a book in itself. Heaven knows when we shall write it. But now let us return to our subject.

A thousand times we have said: Let us return to our subject—but we have not returned. In the meantime, we have diverted our attention from ourselves, and we do not know which are our affairs and which are not. We started with a traveler and the key of the Beit Midrash, but we have left the traveler and the Beit Midrash and dealt with others. Let us hope for tomorrow, when Schutzling will be on his way and we shall go in and study a page of Gemara, and if the Almighty helps us we shall study it with the Commentaries.

The Face of the World

After saying my prayers at daybreak, I went into the dining room. When Krolka saw that I was up, she hurried and brought my breakfast. I thanked the Almighty for waking me at sunrise so that I could go early to the Beit Midrash after all the distractions that had kept me away so long from the Torah.

Schutzling came in and said goodbye to me. Actually, he had attended to his farewells yesterday, but his affection prompted him to repeat them on his departure.

All Schutzling's merchandise and belongings were wrapped up in an old newspaper and tied around with string, knotted and reknotted. He had not been doing much business, and the drugs he showed his customers did not take up much room. Perhaps there was even some advantage in such a bundle, for it could not be quickly opened or quickly tied; and while all that was going on, the customer would get tired and buy against his will.

I went out with Schutzling, he heading for the railway station and I for the Beit Midrash. When we reached the parting of our ways I walked on with him a few steps. These few steps led to more, and these, in turn, to even more. In this way—to cut a long story short—we reached the railway station, and there I waited with him for the train.

Old Rubberovitch came out and bowed to me; but he smiled at Schutzling and Schutzling smiled at him, for once Schutzling had come to Szibucz with a fellow agent, both of them with travel tickets for the entire year. The inspector came to examine the tickets, but they had exchanged tickets with each other. The inspector took Schutzling's ticket and found someone else's picture on it, so he put it away in his pocket and threatened to hand him over to Rubberovitch. Next, he took his colleague's ticket and saw that it also belonged to someone else, for there was another man's picture on it. So he put it away in his pocket and threatened him, as he had done to Schutzling. When they reached Szibucz he brought them before Rubberovitch and handed over the tickets. Rubberovitch looked at the pictures and their owners and did not know what the inspector wanted. Then they told him the whole story and all three of them laughed together.

When the train came, Schutzling got into the compartment and took his leave of me. But even this was not the final parting: before the train moved off he jumped down and said, 'Why should I hurry? The train leaves twice a day, but you don't find a good friend every day.'

I felt I could not leave him and go away, and even if I had left him he would not have left me. So off we both went together and returned to all the places where we had been on the Sabbath and went back over all the things we had already said—and perhaps we added a little, or perhaps we added nothing—until the time came for lunch. 'Now,' said I to Schutzling, 'let us go to the hotel for dinner.' 'What are you thinking of, my dear sir?' said Schutzling. 'Grandma will be furious if she finds out that I did not leave and went to the hotel with you. Let us go to her house and leave my baggage, and then we'll stroll all day and all night.'

So I went with him to his sister, whom Schutzling called Grandma. This Grandma—her name was Genendel—was a tall, lean old woman about seventy years old and more, censorious and pernickety. She behaved to Schutzling not like a sister but like a mother, because she had nursed him and brought him up; for his mother (this was Genendel's father's third wife) pampered herself like an old man's darling and never had time to nurse her son; but Genendel happened to give birth to a son at the same time, and so she took Schutzling, too, to herself. In fact, she and her stepmother had even mistakenly exchanged babies once. And when Schutzling's mother had a second child, Genendel also took him as her own son, and he even used to call her Mother, until he reached his years of understanding and knew his mother. Then he called his sister Grandma; to call her Sister was impossible, for a sister is usually younger than the mother, and to call her Mother was impossible, because he had a mother—so he called her Grandma.

The old woman received her younger brother with great affection, and she was affectionate to me too: first, because I was his friend, and second, because of her affection for my family, although she did not approve of me. Even in my childhood she had prophesied that I would end up with nothing, for my mother used to give me money to buy rolls and I would go and buy books. And here the old woman raised her eyebrows, looked at me, and said, 'Tell me, my friend, were these books better than Father's rolls? I doubt if they made you any cleverer. From all they say about you in the town, it's hard to see your cleverness. And it seems to me that even the Land of Israel didn't make you much wiser. Or perhaps I am wrong; by your clothes you seem to be a rich man. But I will tell you, my friend, I have seen rich men whose clothes were tattered and poor men whose clothes were fine. Now, tell me, what do they give you to eat in the hotel, real food or pages from old books? Your hostess—God forgive me for saying it—is no doubt a cheat like her father, who cheated a poor student and said he would make him a doctor, but what did he make of him?—a husband for his daughter. On the other hand, that Christian woman—what's her name?—Krolka, is a good Jewess for a Christian. Remind me, Aaron, and I will tell her to look after him. Not for his merits, but for the merits of his pious mother, peace be upon her. How many years have passed since she died and went to her eternal rest? Oh, my friend, the years have fled as if the devil had snatched them. And now, my friend, sit down and don't delay me, and I will go and prepare your lunch.'

'Genendel,' said I, 'don't trouble yourself. I am going with Aaron to eat in my hotel.' Genendel stared at me with wide-open eyes and said, 'We're not riffraff who lick the plates at hotels. My son Aaron has a home and he can eat like a respectable person. Even there, in Nikolsburg, I showed the nobles what a housewife can do. Even that doctor—may the devil make Gehenna hot for him—kept out of my way and let me behave like the mistress of the house. And when I lit the candles in honor of the Sabbath, and he came and scolded me, I stood my ground quietly as if I were in my own home, and after I had prayed for myself and my relations, I lifted up my eyes to heaven and lifted up my voice so that he should hear, and prayed for him too, that he should live to die in torment speedily with all the enemies of Zion. My friend, we do not have much pleasure in this world, but anyone who has a head on his shoulders gets himself a bit of satisfaction on the side. If you had seen him at that moment you would have kissed your fingers for joy. Now, my friend, I will go and make you a fine meal fit for the honor of your mother's son. I have heard that you don't eat meat. If I gave you meat you would eat, but there's no morsel of meat in the whole town. Tell me, my friend, if you don't eat meat what do you do with all the worms you find in your books? I thought you roasted them and ate them, but after all you don't eat meat. A fine thing—pity I haven't time to laugh a little.'

Before she came back Schutzling explained to me what had happened at Nikolsburg. At the beginning of the war, the government had seen that all the people of Galicia were streaming to Vienna, and they were afraid Vienna might be filled up with them. So they erected huts in Nikolsburg and surrounded them with barbed wire, one fence inside the other, and brought most of the refugees there. These huts were divided into rooms six feet square, with four beds in each room, two on one side and two on the other, two below and two above—and into each room they put men and women, whether close relatives or distant strangers. They did not get enough bread to eat, but on the other hand the lice got more than enough. The authorities set sentries in front of the huts, with rifles in their hands, and anyone who tried to escape was shot. This they did with great good will, for anyone who escaped cost the camp authorities money, as the government paid according to the number of souls. If a man wanted to attend to nature's demands, he had to ask for a permit from the overseer. If the overseer was in a congenial mood, he would say, 'I know you don't really need that thing; what you really want is to meet a woman there.' And he said the same

to the young women as to the young men. These overseers
were teachers who had no posts, and when they now got this
post showed that they were fit for it. A doctor was appointed
to look after the sick, a young fellow of good family from
Szibucz. If a man fell ill, the doctor would scold him
thoroughly and say, 'You're a cheat, you're perfectly healthy.'
In the end, he too fell sick and died, for diseases multiplied
and carried away good and bad. It would have been better if
he had died earlier, but even so it was a good thing, for he
did not manage to add to his wickedness.

When I had entered the house I had felt that there was
a man sitting there, though he could not be seen and his voice
was not heard. After Genendel left, he came forward and
stood before us. He looked about sixty, of medium height,
round-shouldered, with his head tilted to one side; his beard
was full and round, with more black in it than white, his
teeth coarse, yellow, and bent, his eyes grey and bashful. He
had a pen in his hand, and books and pamphlets under his arm.

He put the pen behind his ear, held out his hand and
greeted me, saying, 'My dear sir, here you are. How glad I
am to see you, especially today, which is a special day for
me!' I returned his greeting and looked at him. He lowered
his eyes and said, 'Don't you recognize me, my dear sir? You
and I were well acquainted.'

I recognized him immediately: it was Leibtche Bodenhaus. This Leibtche Bodenhaus was the husband of a woman
who sold shoes; I used to talk to him about the theory of
poetry and style. He never attracted me; in fact you might
say he bored me, but he had one good quality, or perhaps
two. First, he was twenty years older than I was, and it is a
young man's way to respect the old; second, he belonged to
another town, and since I was weary of Szibucz, anyone who
came from somewhere else seemed important to me, even if
he was not important. He was married to a woman older than
himself, who treated him with respect in front of other people,
but provoked and reviled him when no one else was present.
'If I hadn't been an old maid that no one wanted you wouldn't
have got me,' she used to say. When he wanted to run away,

she would take off his shoes, and he would sit complaining until her brother came and made peace between them. This brother of hers was a well-to-do businessman, who went in for culture, and had a large shoe store and set up a branch for them; it was next to Zommer's shop on the one side and the shop of Zwirn's father on the other—he too sold shoes—and they would compete with each other for customers.

Since the day I went up to the Land of Israel I had not heard of him or called him to mind. When I returned to Szibucz I heard talk of him, but I did not happen to see him, because he did not leave his house on account of a sore on his foot. For this sore, people said, he was indebted to his wife, who once left him barefoot, without shoes, all one winter's day, and his foot got frostbitten. But some said: Not at all, he was in perfect health and there was another reason why he did not leave his house—because he was writing a book, so as to leave some name and sign behind him, for he had no sons to preserve his memory after his death.

Leibtche Bodenhaus was a distant relative of Genendel's on his wife's side. When his wife died of one of the nine hundred and ninety-nine diseases that followed the war, and Leibtche remained without a wife, without a shield, Genendel took him into her house, gave him a bed and a table, clad and shod him, and bought him a bottle of ink and a pile of paper, so that he should sit and write his book. 'The poor fellow,' said Genendel, 'has never had any enjoyment in this world, and I hope they won't beat him in the next for his foolishness.'

Never since the day he was born has Leibtche been so soaked in delight as he is in Genendel's house, for Genendel lives on the fat of the land, since her sons send her money, some in dollars and some in marks and francs. Genendel has been fortunate in bearing nine sons, nine prosperous bakers, who make a good living and keep their mother in comfort. Before the war, Szibucz used to supply half of Europe with poultry and eggs and millet and all kinds of peas and lentils, and now it provides the world with bread. Szibucz itself has no bread, but the bakers who came from Szibucz can bake bread that does not have its like anywhere in the world.

Let us go back to Leibtche. Leibtche sits in Genendel's house and spends all his days and nights turning the Bible into rhymes. He has a double purpose in doing this: first, because the Bible is beautiful and it is a good thing to beautify it; and second, because rhymes are beautiful and fitting to beautify the Bible with. Moreover, rhymes are easy to remember, as even Schiller realized; that was why he clothed his sublime ideas in rhymes.

The day I came to Genendel's was a great day for Leibtche, for it was the day he had succeeded in completing the entire Book of Genesis in rhymes. He came and sat down before us, opened his books, and started to read. So he sat and read, until sleep overtook Schutzling and he dozed off.

'Aaron is asleep,' I said to Leibtche, 'perhaps you will stop until he wakes up?' 'Let him sleep, let him slumber,' said Leibtche: 'I don't need him, for he has already heard most of the poems, and I was not thinking of him, but of you, my dear sir, that you should hear them and set your mind to translating them into Hebrew. I am not strong in Hebrew, for in my youth it was the German language that the world thought important, so I became expert in German and am not in the habit of writing Hebrew, especially poetry, for the poet must be well versed in grammar. At first I thought of writing the poems in Hebrew, but I did not manage to write more than the first two verses. Be so good, my dear sir, as to wait a few moments until I find them and show you them.'

Schutzling awoke and said, 'And if thou canst not deliver thy friend, deliver thyself.' Then he closed his eyes and dozed off again. 'You see, my dear sir,' said Leibtche, 'the power of poetry. Even in his sleep it won't let his memory go. How many years Mr. Schutzling has not held Schiller's poems in his hand, yet he remembers them even in his sleep. I have found the rhymes I spoke of, my dear sir. With your permission, my dear sir, do please devote your attention to them.'

Leibtche did not wait for me to give my attention to his rhymes, but started reading them:

'In the beginning He created heaven and earth,
And darkness burst there—oh, how it burst!

Both Tohu and Bohu was the world before its birth,
And the spirit of God on the waters showed its worth.'

Schutzling, who was tired of feigning sleep, got up and
stretched himself. 'It's a pity Moses our Teacher didn't write
the Torah in German and put it into rhyme,' he said. 'What
an idea, Mr. Schutzling!', said Leibtche. 'Don't you know that
in Moses' time the German language did not even exist?'
'Well then,' said Schutzling, 'I am sorry it exists today.' 'What
an idea, my dear sir,' said Leibtche. 'Wasn't it in German that
Schiller wrote his sublime poems, which will endure to all
eternity, an eternal memorial to human wisdom?' But Schutzling insisted. He repeated what he had said before, and continued, 'If Moses had written the Torah in German and in
rhymes, Leibtche would not have had to take all this trouble.'
'On the contrary,' said Leibtche, 'it is a very great pleasure.'
Schutzling embraced him with all his might and said, 'But it
isn't a pleasure for us.' Leibtche looked at him in surprise and
asked, 'How can that be, Mr. Schutzling? How can a cultured
man like yourself say such a thing?' Said Schutzling, 'Show me
your copybooks, Leibtche.' Leibtche held out his copybooks
and stood by him. 'Fine handwriting,' said Schutzling, 'fine
handwriting. Go on writing, Leibtche, go on writing, it'll improve your handwriting.'

Genendel came back to set the table. While she was arranging the dishes, she asked me, 'What do you say to Leibtche's work? You're a bit of a scribbler too, aren't you?'
Leibtche replied, 'If even I, a stooped and humble man, more
worm than man, can feel a taste sweeter than honey in my
poetry, how much more must you, my dear sir.' When we sat
down to eat, Leibtche wanted to go away, because he had already eaten, and besides, he wanted to start immediately on
Exodus. But Genendel rebuked him and said, 'Wash your
hands and come to the table; your rhymes won't run away.'
So Leibtche sat down and ate, looking at me like a man whose
heart is melancholy, for he sees a cultured man wasting his
time eating and drinking when he could be listening to words
of poetry.

That day I was entirely at Schutzling's disposal. After we

had eaten and parted from Leibtche Bodenhaus, we went out for a walk. We walked and we talked until our feet were tired and our tongues were numb. Finally we stopped to rest close by Yeruham Freeman, who was busy at the time repairing a small road.

Yeruham had no respect for Schutzling and Schutzling had no liking for Yeruham, but when he came to Szibucz and met Yeruham he used to speak to him, for Schutzling is a man of words and chatter and loves anyone who lends an ear to his talk. In the course of their talk Yeruham asked Schutzling, 'How do you picture the generations to come?' 'There is an example already pictured and extant,' replied Schutzling. 'They will be one-third like Daniel Bach and one-third like Rubberovitch and one-third like Ignatz. If a trace of humanity remains in the world, they will make themselves wooden legs and rubber hands, and they will have noses like Ignatz.'

Ignatz happened to pass by at the moment. When he saw Schutzling, he recoiled and retreated. Schutzling called out to him and said, 'My dear sir, come and I will give you *pieniadze*.' Ignatz began to talk in his nasal way and said, 'It's not my fault, sir.' 'It is your fault, my dear sir,' said Schutzling, 'but I bear you no grudge, and you don't need to apologize.' Still Ignatz repeated in his nasal way, 'It's not my fault at all. It's not my fault at all.' 'What are you droning about, my dear sir,' said Schutzling. 'You have a perfect right to be at fault. Take a copper and be off with you; someone may pass in the meantime and you will lose *pieniadze*.'

When Ignatz had gone off, I asked Schutzling, 'What is the meaning of this dialogue?' 'It's a story not worth mentioning,' replied Schutzling, 'but since you want to hear it, I will tell you.' This is what happened. During the war Schutzling's little daughter fell ill and his wife went to look for a doctor. Ignatz came across her, and he took off her shoes and kept them, for at that time shoes were a valuable commodity in the market, since there was no leather to make them with. So how did that woman get back home in the snow on a stormy night? In fact she did not get back, because she was not accustomed to walking barefoot. She waddled along like a hen until they found her lying in the snow and brought her to the hospital.

'There's something else to add to the picture of the generations to come,' said Schutzling. 'In the future, all creatures will hobble with their artificial legs and gesticulate with their rubber hands and cry through their noses: "*Pieniadze, pieniadze.*"'

On Monday morning Schutzling came to my hotel again to say goodbye before he left. But, having parted with him the night before, I left the hotel before he came and went to the Beit Midrash.

CHAPTER SIX AND FIFTY

Much Idleness

On my way, a certain young man buttonholed me and started to harangue me at great length, until half the day had gone and it was time for lunch. There is no end to the things that young man said, but what he told me I have forgotten and what he did not tell I do not remember.

This young fellow knows as much about the Land of Israel as Pinhas Aryeh, the rabbi's son, does about the newspapers. The things he knows are of no consequence, but his voice makes them sound very important. Besides, he knows most of the great men of the Land face to face, for if he has never been there, he has come across them abroad at congresses and conferences. (Since the day Jerusalem was destroyed and we were exiled from our Land, exile follows at a man's heels; and even if he has the privilege of living in the Land his feet lead him abroad, for the Land of Israel is, as it were, the heart and all the other lands are the feet. When a man's heart is good, it moves his feet, and when his heart is not good, his feet move him.)

I look at my companion. His carriage is upright, his face is full and his lips thick, his shoulders are broad and his limbs brawny. I feel doubly happy to see him: first, that even in Szibucz there should be tall, strong men, and second, that he is a Zionist, and will give his strength to the Land of Israel. So I say to him, 'May you devote your strength to the Land of Israel!' and he receives my remark with a friendly look.

'When are you going to the Land?' I asked him. 'For the time being,' he replied, 'there is a great deal of work here.' 'What is this great deal of work that you have here?' 'Would you like to see?' said he. And, opening his briefcase, he straightway showed me scores of memoranda, dozens of brochures, hundreds of pamphlets, and nine hundred and ninety-nine leaflets, apart from various newspapers and monthlies. And he explained in a singsong voice that he traveled from place to place, organizing organizations and so forth.

So as not to take my leave of him too suddenly, I asked him if he was in the habit of visiting our comrades at the training farm. 'I have nothing to do with them,' said he. 'For what reason?' said I. 'There are many reasons,' said he. 'First, because they do not belong to our organization, and second . . .'

I took out my watch and looked at it, like one who is in a hurry and has no time. He saw that I was in a hurry and said, 'And when will you come to us?' 'What for?' 'To lecture to our members.' 'Are you short of lecturers?' 'All the same.' 'And what will you do?' 'I shall open the meeting, or add a few words after your talk.'

At that moment Mistress Sarah passed by. 'Forgive me,' I said to our friend, 'I must tell her something.' 'And when will you come?' 'Where?' 'To lecture.' 'You can start the meeting first,' said I, 'and while you are waiting for me go right ahead and add some remarks to follow mine.'

Mistress Sarah's modest eyes shone under her new kerchief. Great are the righteous in their deaths. Her illustrious grandfather's book had been instrumental, many years after his passing, in getting her a new kerchief.

I bowed and asked how she was. All my life I have grown up among great men and I have forgotten to bow my head to them, but when that woman appeared to me my head bowed itself. 'What have they written you from over there?' asked Mistress Sarah. 'Were they happy to get that book?' I was cunning enough not to tell her that I had not sent the book, but made up some stories out of whole cloth. For instance, I told her a tale of a pioneer and his wife who were distant from Judaism—not actually distant, for there is no one in the

Land of Israel who does evil and not good, but the distance I spoke of was in matters of the heart. When this woman's time came to give birth, her husband came and asked for the book. The supervisor of the maternity hospital, who was a clever man, at first refused, saying, 'How shall I give you the book, when the sacred author did not approve of those with impious views?' So this pioneer man undertook to discard his impious views, his wife agreed, and they gave them the book. And we may assume that they carried out what they undertook, for modern people have a way of keeping their word.

These things I told her are of no importance, for how can invented tales be of any importance? But what Mistress Sarah said was important: 'I am sure that saintly man's book will bring many hearts back to the better way.'

As I went into my hotel I said to myself: I must send off that book, so that this woman should not find out that I am a teller of fables. So I asked Krolka, 'Perhaps you have some thick paper to wrap up a parcel and some string to tie it with?' 'There is string here,' said Krolka, 'but no paper. There was a big thick sheet of paper here, but the master spread his raisins on it, which he is using to make wine for Passover.' So I got up and went to the shop to buy paper.

It was close to the hour of the Afternoon Service and the rabbi was having a stroll before prayer. He had his hands behind his back, holding his stick, which dragged along behind him. 'Have you seen my son, sir?' the rabbi asked. 'I have seen him,' I replied. 'I know that you have seen him,' said he, 'but I was thinking of spiritual seeing. What do you say, sir, is he not a great writer?' 'I have not read his writings,' I replied. 'If you do not read his articles,' said the rabbi, surprised, 'who reads them? I and people like me study Gemara. So, for whom is he writing?' 'Perhaps,' said I, 'he is writing for the ordinary folk.' 'For ordinary folk? The ordinary folk had better study *The Life of Man* or *The Shorter Code* or other books of religious law, so that they should know what is required of them. Why do you not show your face in my house?' I promised to come. 'When?' 'Tomorrow.' May God not punish me for failing to keep my word.

When I parted from the rabbi it was already dark. The

sun had set and the moon had not yet risen. In the past, the
young men and women of Szibucz used to go out to stroll at
this hour, and a special man would pass from one end of the
town to the other with a ladder on his shoulder, going from
lamp to lamp to light them; the young men would look in the
girls' faces and the girls would lower their heads; and there
was great joy in the streets of the town, because people were
fond of each other, and when they saw one another they were
happy. And indeed it was right that they should rejoice in one
another, because they were comely and their clothes were
comely. Now that the lamps are broken, and kerosene is not
very plentiful, and the man with the ladder does not come,
and the roads are in bad repair, there are no people in the
streets. I doubt if there was anyone in the street at the time
except myself and Ignatz.

When he saw me he cried in his nasal way, '*Mu'es!*' 'You
have changed your ways, Ignatz,' said I; 'you say "*Mu'es*"
before "*Pieniadze*." In fact, you do not say "*Pieniadze*" at all.'
Ignatz sighed and said, 'What is the use of my saying "*Pieniadze*" if no one gives me anything? As people say, what is the
good of knowing Polish if they do not let you in to see the
minister?'

I said to myself: This is the Ignatz who is suspected of
talebearing; let me interrogate him to see how much truth
there is in it. So I asked him, 'What is your opinion about the
people of our town?' 'They're all beggars, every one,' said
Ignatz. As he spoke, he gazed at the coin I had given him and
said, 'Believe me, sir, this is the first coin that has come my
way this week. I will go and buy some bread.' 'And who
spices your bread, the chief priest?' said I. 'Hunger,' replied
Ignatz. I wished him a good appetite and went back to my
hotel to have my supper.

Once again that old man was here, the one who once had
many fields in the villages and many houses in the town, and
had nothing left of all his wealth but debts that he was being
pressed to pay. He had already had the oath on the Bible
administered to him twice in court, and now a third oath was
being imposed on him for still another claim.

I looked up from my plate at the old man. A glass of tea

stood before him, which the mistress of the house had poured out for him in pity, and he sat blowing at the glass, although the tea had cooled. Nearby sat a man I did not know, who said to him, 'There was a certain scholar here who, when he was called upon to take the oath, would go to take the oath like a man who goes to obey a divine commandment; he would wash his hands and recite the formula: "Behold, I am ready and prepared to perform the commandment of swearing to the truth."' The old man moved his glass and said, 'He swore an honest oath, for they wanted to extract money from him which was not due, but I know that I owe money, and if I swear that I haven't any, that will be a superfluous oath, for everyone knows that I haven't any.' 'Well,' said the man, 'what will you do?' The old man spread out his hands, palms upward, and said, 'I can only rely on my Father in heaven to take my soul before that time.' The man sighed and said, 'It was a kindness the Almighty did His creatures that He gave them death.' Both of them sighed and broke into tears.

CHAPTER SEVEN AND FIFTY

Beyond the River Sambatyon

After leaving the hotel to go to the Beit Midrash, I found little Raphael lying in front of his house on his straw mattress. The sun in Szibucz does not enter a poor man's home, and if Mrs. Bach wants her child to enjoy the sun she takes him outside.

So Raphael lies in the sun and watches it with a shining face, and captures it in his hat and will not let it go, because for several months he has not seen the sun and naturally he does not want to let it go.

I tried to ignore him and pass by; first, because I wanted to go to the Beit Midrash, and second, so as not to disturb the child. But he saw me, stretched out his hand and beckoned to me. When I saw his thin fingers, with the sun shining on them, my heart was filled with pity, so I came and sat down in front of him in silence, and he too was silent.

I cannot just sit and say nothing, I said to myself. So I asked him if he felt warm. 'I am warm,' the child replied, 'are you warm too?' 'It is the same sun,' I said, 'and just as it warms the one so it warms the other; if you are warm why should I not feel warm?' 'Because you are from the Land of Israel,' the child answered, 'and the sun in the Land is twice as warm; I'm sure the whole sun here is not enough for you.' 'Men have a way of getting accustomed' said I. 'I thought anyone who had been there would feel cold here,' said Raphael. 'Why did you think so?' 'I don't know.' 'You don't know and yet you say so?' 'I know, but I don't know if you will know when I tell you.' 'Tell me, dear, tell me.' 'You tell me.' 'How can I tell you when I don't know what?' 'Then I'll ask you something else. Where is it more beautiful, there or there?' 'What do you mean, Raphael, what do you mean by "there or there"? Or perhaps you meant to ask about there or here, meaning in the Land of Israel or in Szibucz.' Said Raphael, 'Yesterday I read in a book about the River Sambatyon and the Ten Tribes and the Sons of Moses, and I ask where is it more beautiful, there or in the Land of Israel?' 'You're asking something that is clear of itself,' I replied; 'after all, the Ten Tribes and the Sons of Moses look forward all their lives to go up to the Land of Israel, and unless the Holy One, blessed be He, had not surrounded them with the River Sambatyon, wouldn't they hurry to the Land of Israel? But all week long the River Sambatyon races rapidly and casts up stones, so that no one can pass, and on the Sabbath, when it rests, they cannot cross, because they are very pious men and observe the Sabbath. And you ask where it is more beautiful! Certainly in the Land of Israel.'

'I thought,' said the child, 'that because they are not under the yoke of the Gentiles and the servitude of the nations, it is more beautiful near the Sambatyon.' 'Perfectly true,' I replied, 'they are not under the yoke of the Gentiles and the servitude of the nations, but they do not have the joy of the Land, for there is no joy of the Land but in the Land of Israel.' 'Are they really not under the yoke of the Gentiles?' said the child. 'Haven't you read that in your book?' said I. 'And aren't the Gentiles jealous of them?' 'Indeed they are jealous of them;

that is why the Gentiles go out to war against them.' 'And what do they do?' 'They fight back.' 'Like here?' 'What do you mean, like here?' 'Like what happened here in our town, when the Gentiles came and fought each other and killed each other.' I stroked his cheek and said to him, 'How can you compare the Sons of Moses our Teacher to the nations of the world? For the Sons of Moses are pure and holy, and heaven forbid that they should shed blood and defile their souls.' 'Well, then,' said Raphael, 'if people make war against them and try to kill them, what do they do? If they don't kill their enemies, their enemies will kill them.' 'They have made themselves staves of magnetic stone,' I told him, 'and when the enemy attacks them, they go out to meet them with their staves, and draw the weapons out of the enemy's hands. And when the enemy sees that he has no weapons, he turns tail and runs away. But anyone who has not managed to escape comes to the Prince of the Jews, lays his head on the doorstep of his house, and says, "My life is in your hands, my lord. Do to me as I wished to do to you." So the Prince comes out of his house, raises his hands to heaven, and says, "May the Lord witness your afflictions and restore you to better ways."'

'Where did they get these staves?' asked Raphael. 'It is a secret of the Lord for them that fear Him.' 'Have you ever seen one of them?' 'I have never seen any of them, but I have seen Gentiles who came from there, and they told me about them.' 'And have you seen one of our Jews who has been there?' 'No,' I replied. 'Why have Gentiles deserved to go there and not Jews?' asked the child. 'There are Jews who have had that privilege,' said I. 'But anyone who has found his way there does not come back. Tell me, if you were there would you want to come back here?' 'And why have the Gentiles come back from there?' 'Gentiles who cannot endure the righteousness of the Sons of Moses cannot live with them. And sometimes the Gentiles leave because they long for their own town and their own home, as in the story I told you of one of the princes of Ishmael who found his way there during the war of the Turk. You remember the story you read under the tree?' 'That prince was with the Jews of Khaibar and not with the Sons of Moses,' said Raphael. 'If so,' said I, 'I will tell you a story of a certain Arab who happened to meet the Sons of Moses. I saw this Arab in Jerusalem, and he was a great lover of the Jews; he would bow down to every single Jewish child, for every Gentile who has had the privilege of living among good and pious Jews no longer hates the people of Israel, but loves them and proclaims their righteousness to the world.' While we were talking, the child's father came up.

Daniel Bach was content, first, because he was content by nature, and second, because he had received a letter from his father. 'And what did your father write?' I asked. 'Well, he did not mention the quarrels in his congregation in Ramat Rahel, and he didn't write about the graves of the righteous men on which he prostrated himself.' 'Then what did he write about?' 'About the vineyards and the chickens and the cows, and the plantations they planted in Ramat Rahel, and how much milk each cow gives and how many eggs the chickens lay. If I did not recognize my father's handwriting, I would say the letter had been written by someone else, for what has my father to do with cattle and chickens and plantings?'

'Now I know why they disparage the Land of Israel,' said Daniel Bach. 'If this is what happens to an old man who has spent all his life in study and prayer, what can you expect of all the young men who do not study and pray?'

Sara Pearl came out. When she saw me she said, 'Where have you been, sir, all this time? Since the eve of Shavuot I believe we have not seen you.' I told her about my comrades on the farm, with whom I spent the festival, and while I was talking I felt glad I had not told Yeruham Freeman about them first, for when you talk about something a second time it does not have the same power as the first time.

Daniel Bach has already heard about those boys and girls who have gone out to work in the fields, and he is not impressed. 'If I did not know their fathers,' said Mr. Bach, 'perhaps I would be impressed by them. But since I know their parents I am not happy about the children.' However, he has no intention of spoiling my joy; anyone who wants to be happy, let him be happy.

And I am happy about them and about the time I spent with them. Let not God regard it as an offense on their part that through them I neglected the Torah for several days and have not yet returned to my studies.

'And are there children, too, who have reached the River Sambatyon?' asked Raphael. 'Didn't I tell you,' I replied, 'the story about the rabbi, author of *The Light of Life*, who had found one of the Sons of Moses on Sabbath eve at dark and put him in his pocket and forgot him there? On the Sabbath night he went into the synagogue to pray, and he heard a voice coming from his pocket and giving the response, "Amen, blessed be His Great Name."' 'That was not what I asked,' said Raphael, 'I asked if there is a child who got there.' 'Wait a moment, Raphael, and let me remember,' said I. 'You're always saying: Wait and let me remember,' said Raphael. 'First,' I replied, 'it is not proper to reply at once, because a man should first arrange his thoughts, so that they may be pleasant to his listeners. And second, it is natural for a man to forget, for exile weakens the power of memory. Now, my dear, I have remembered. There was one child in Jerusalem who reached the River Sambatyon and came back. As for how he reached there and what made him return, listen and I will tell you.

'The child's father had shoes made for his wedding day. The bridegroom asked the shoemaker if his shoes would last a long time and would not tear quickly. "You can cross the River Sambatyon in them," said the shoemaker. And the young man took these things to heart.

'After the wedding, the bridegroom told the bride what the shoemaker had said. "I can see," said she, "that you want to go to the Ten Tribes, and I know that you will go there, for this shoemaker is one of the Thirty-six Saints, and if he has said a thing it will not prove wrong." "When you bear a male child," said he, "call him Hanoch, after this Reb Hanoch the shoemaker, and when you are privileged to see the time come for him to put on the tefillin, have the tefillin prepared for him and send him out on the road, and the Holy One, blessed be He, in His mercy, will see that he reaches me." So the bridegroom rose from his bed, took his tallit and tefillin, kissed the mezuza on the doorpost, and set off on his journey. He walked and walked until he reached the River Sambatyon. When he saw the Sambatyon casting up stones to the heart of the heavens, a great terror fell upon him and he said, "How shall I cross this awesome river?" But his feet were lifted up of themselves and he crossed the river safely, and he found himself alongside the Sons of Moses.

'When the Sons of Moses saw this, they realized that he was a great saint, since he had been granted permission to reach their land, which no other man had been privileged to do, except Rabbi Meir, the author of the *Akdamut,* and the author of *The Light of Life,* and one or two other saints. They gathered around him and found him full of learning and piety; so they welcomed him and made a feast in his honor. During the feast he analyzed for them a passage from the Torah, and they recognized that his teaching was cogent, so they established a great academy for him, where he taught the Torah and did not interrupt his teaching except for prayer.

'Once, when he knelt during the thanksgiving prayer, his shoestring broke. After the prayer he remembered this, and, remembering this, remembered all that had happened to him, and that it was already thirteen years and more since he had left his wife, and if his wife had borne a son the time had come for him to fulfill the commandments. But for fear of neglecting the Torah he banished these thoughts from his heart and returned to his teaching.

'When the first day of the New Year Festival arrived, and he went out to the river to recite the Tashlich prayer, he saw a Jewish child standing on the other side. "Are you my son Hanoch?" he asked him. "Father," the child replied, "I am your son Hanoch, and I have done as you commanded Mother." Immediately the father pulled off his shoes and threw them to his child, so that he should put them on and cross the river. But the father's hands were weary from study, and the child's hands were too small, so the shoes fell into the river and did not reach the child. The child could not reach his father, and the father could not reach the child, because his shoes were lost. So they stood, one on this side of the river and one on that. "How can I help you, my son?" said the father. "It is a decree of the Holy One, blessed be He. Go back to Jerusalem and study the Torah, and when the time is ripe for the coming of the Messiah, I shall return to you with all our brethren, the

Sons of Moses and the Ten Tribes." So the child returned to his mother in Jerusalem, studied much Torah, and became a Master of the Law in Israel.'

CHAPTER EIGHT AND FIFTY

About the Unending Rains

In the past, when I used to finish the treatment of a subject of the Gemara I would go over it again, but I cannot do so today, because I have cut down my stay in the Beit Midrash and extended my walks in the fields and the forest. If it is a fine day I bathe in the river. It is natural for water to stimulate the soul and restore the body to its youth, especially when you bathe in a river in which you bathed when you were little. The water in which I bathed when I was little has already gone down to the Great Sea and been swallowed by the great fishes, but the river is still as it was in the days when I was a boy. However, when I was a boy there were many cabins standing there, and today there is not even one. In the past, when the people of our town were dressed in fine clothes, they needed a clean place to leave them in; now, when the whole town is dressed in ugly clothes, they leave them on the banks of the river.

Since I have mentioned the matter of clothes, I will mention that I had a new suit made and bought new shoes. When I went out in the street, people looked at me. Do you think they were jealous of me? Not at all: they were jealous of the people to whom I had given the old ones. Dire poverty had descended on the town. Once, when I threw away a paper cigarette pack, a respectable man fell upon it and picked it up. What for? To use it for the salt on his table.

Not every day is fine; not every day is suitable for walking or bathing in the river. There are days in Szibucz when the rain comes down without a stop, when the whole town swims in mud, and you cannot go out and cannot go in. And since it is impossible to sit all day in the hotel or the Beit Midrash and you want to see a human being, you remember that you have promised someone a visit, so you go to keep your promise.

Whom had I promised? You might ask, whom hadn't I promised. There is not a man in the town who has not invited me to visit him—not out of love for the visitor but out of sheer boredom. The town is small and its doings are few, so everyone wishes to distract himself with conversation. And since I did not know whom to visit, I visited Schuster: first, because he too was included in that promise, and second, to give some pleasure to his wife, who said that never did she find any time so welcome as the time I spent with her.

Sprintze was sitting in the big chair that Schuster had brought with him from Germany. There were two sticks lying at her feet for her to lean on when she went from bed to chair or chair to bed, for Germany had taken away her strength and dried up her legs, and but for her two sticks she would have lain there motionless as a stone. The outside door was open and on the threshold lay a copper basin, in which withered grasses were drying in the sun; Sprintze takes some for her pipe and others she uses to make a kind of tea. This tea is an elixir for the heart and a medicine for the soul, since the grasses come from the threshold of the house where she was born, and draw vitality from there, just as she herself had done. When you infuse these grasses and drink their essence, the body recovers its strength and reawakens as if it had returned to the house where it was born. 'And, my dear, although the house is in ruins and its dwellers have gone into exile,' says Sprintze, 'the grasses keep their grip and will not let go, and if you uproot them they sprout again, for it is natural for grasses, my friend, to love the source of their vitality. In this they are like human beings; only human beings abandon the source of their vitality, while grasses do not leave their place, and even if they are plucked out they sprout again and give healing to men.

'If I have not told you, my friend, sit down and let me tell you. My grandfather, may he rest in peace and speak for us in the world to come, was a porter, like his fathers and his fathers' fathers before him, and as my father, may he rest in peace, was a porter. You should know, my friend, that we come from a healthy family, who like to take hold of tools that have some substance, and not to hold the needle and stab the cloth like a flea does flesh. If I told you, my friend, about the strength and vigor of my family, you would say, "If that is so, Sprintze, why are you so sickly?" But let us not mix up one thing with another, and go back to my grandfather. Well, my friend, my grandfather, may he rest in peace, was a porter, and like all porters he would never refuse to take a glass of brandy so long as there was a copper in his pocket—and, needless to say, at times when there was not a copper in his pocket, for then he would be eaten up with anxiety, and eating calls for a drink. In those days the town was full of taverns. If he went this way he found a tavern before him, if he went the other way he found before him a tavern. In short, my friend, whichever way a man turned he would find himself turning toward a tavern, apart from the liquor shop in the middle of the town, where there were all kinds of big barrels full of brandy from which they drew liquor and gave men to drink. My grandfather, who used to live at peace with everyone, would go into this one's house and then that one's—and he did not stay away from the third either, for you must know, my friend, that he was a lively man, and never in his life was he too lazy to do something. And when he came in he would drink a glass or two, one to clear his bowels and one for enjoyment. And sometimes he would just come in and drink. Then, needless to say, before the meal and after the meal and during the meal, to steep the food in his innards, for eating without drinking is like a girl who gets pregnant, if you'll excuse me, without the ceremony of holy matrimony.

'As time went on, my grandfather started to groan from his heart: cough, cough, cough. Says my grandmother, may she rest in peace, "Ilya, perhaps you will leave the brandy alone?" He went into a rage and said to her, "What else should I drink? Perhaps grass-water like you?" "Why not?" says she. He grew angrier still at her for comparing herself to him, for he, my friend, was a big burly man and she, my friend, was as little as an ant.

'One hot summer day, on a Sabbath afternoon, my grandfather was sitting in front of his house, because he was too sick to go to the Beit Midrash and hear the rabbi's commentary on a chapter, and because he used to disturb the listeners with his cough, cough, cough. He saw a bee buzzing as it flew; he looked at it affectionately and did not drive it away, for although he was an irascible man he had a good heart. As it was buzzing and flying about he says to himself: I should like to know what this creature is looking for here. This he said once, twice, and three times. My grandfather was no expert in the conversation of bees, and that bee was no expert in the conversation of men. You might imagine that all his wishes were in vain, but I tell you, my friend, anyone who sets his mind on a certain thing will understand it in the end. And it is worth your while, my friend, to hear how this matter took shape and how my grandfather learned at last the message of what had been hidden from him.

'In short, my friend, my grandfather sits in front of his house and the bee flies over the tall grasses there and sucks from them. Says my grandfather: I should like to know what this creature is doing here and what it is sucking. So he said once, twice, and perhaps three times, for he, may he rest in peace, did not rely on reason and used to doubt whether people understood what he was saying the first time; and since he doubted others he doubted himself, so he would double every saying and treble it even when he was talking to himself. In short—why should I make the story any longer? —he said it twice and repeated it a third time. But what was the use of it all, if the bee did not know how to answer?

'Sometimes a man's reason helps him better than talking. Suddenly it came into his mind that, after all, the main purpose that bees were created for is to make honey, and it is a bee's way not to waste its time for nothing, but there is a definite purpose in every single thing it does. So, says my grandfather, what is the purpose of a bee? Surely, to make honey. Why should I draw out the story, my friend? Before long it came into grandfather's mind that the bee extracts honey from the grasses, and since bee's honey is sweet, no doubt the grasses are sweet too, and if the grasses are sweet, it follows that the tea my grandmother makes from them is sweet as well. And if it is not sweet enough, it can be sweetened with sugar as the bees do, for they buzz about the doorways of the shops and take sugar there. At that moment my grandfather was mollified and became tender as wax. And here, my friend, starts the main story. When the time came for the Sabbath evening meal, he began to groan and cough grievously. "Sprintze," says he to my grandmother, "I should like to drink something; don't you know where my bottle is?" Now, my grandmother, though she was little in body, was great in wisdom. She realized that the old man meant to take some other drink, not brandy, for the bottle he spoke of was standing in its place before his very eyes. And because she was familiar with his tempers and knew that if she told him to drink some of her tea he would get into a rage and abuse her, she was silent, then sighed and was silent again. "Sprintze," asks my grandfather, "why are you sighing so much?" Says she, "I would like to drink too, but the guests came and drank all my tea, and I haven't a drop left." "Well," says he, "if that's all, don't sigh; in a little while I'll say the blessing for the end of the Sabbath and you can cook a potful." Says she, "Is it worth while making the fire and putting on the kettle and taking all that trouble just for my own sake?" "Perhaps I should invite Elijah the Prophet to come and drink with you?" says he. Says she, "If this Elijah" (meaning my grandfather, for his name was Elijah too) "does not drink some of my tea, will Elijah the Prophet drink?" "If it's only me that's in your way," says he, "I don't mind drinking a drop or two of tea with you." In short, my friend, as soon as he had said the blessing, my grandmother got up to make the fire, and my grandfather jumped up like a boy, took the axe, and cut up some wood for her. And what more can I tell you, my friend? My grandfather drank one glass, a second, and a third, and if I weren't afraid you might think I was exaggerating, I would tell you that he did not stop there and went on to a fourth. From then on, my friend, the brandy vanished from my grandfather's house, and he did not go into drinking houses either, but sat at home and drank my grandmother's tea together with her. And if he had started when he was a young man, he would have lived a long time and still been alive today. If so, why didn't my grandmother live long, for she was in the habit of drinking tea all her life? Well, it was I that caused her death. But then I was not yet in the world when she died, so how can I say I caused her death? Well, at that time my mother, may she rest in peace, became pregnant, and she kept quarreling with Father, may he rest in peace, for he wanted the child to be called after his father's father, and she wanted it to be called after her father's father. When my grandmother heard this she said, "And if she bears a female?" She did not mean to provoke them, but wanted to prevent them quarreling. My father got angry with her, because he did not like females, and said, "If she bears a female I'll call her Sprintze, after you, Mother-in-law." Now my father was very careful never to let a lie pass his lips, and when people like that let a word pass their lips, the Powers in heaven see that it comes true. In short, my friend, why should I go on talking —cough, cough, cough—that day when I was born my grandmother was taken away from this world, so that the words of both of them could come true, she that said, "And if she bears a female," and he that said he would call her Sprintze after my grandmother.'

The rains did not stop and the mud became deeper and deeper. The hotel had no guests. Between one rain and the next, Riegel the agent came to tell Babtchi the news that he had separated from his wife. 'If so,' said Babtchi, 'it is only right to congratulate you on your good luck. So, congratulations on your good luck, sir.' 'I hope for a second piece of good luck,' said Riegel. 'If you expect a second piece of good luck, sir,' said Babtchi, 'you should go back and marry the wife you divorced.'

Riegel set out on his way, and Babtchi went on in her way, and David Moshe wrote, in his way, letters of peace and love. For each generation, its own generation of writers. The rabbi writes commentaries on the Torah, the rabbi's son writes about the love of the Torah, and the rabbi's grandson just writes about love.

Since we are talking about writing, it is worth going to visit Leibtche Bodenhaus, who is working day and night to turn the Torah into rhymes, doing what Moses never did, for in Moses' day the German language did not yet exist and they did not yet make rhymes.

A man does not always do what he is prepared to do. I set out to visit Leibtche Bodenhaus but I went in to see Zechariah Rosen—first, because his shop was nearby, and second, because he too was included in the promise, for I had promised to visit him.

His shop is long and narrow and set in a dark cellar, which he once used for rubbish. When the house was destroyed and nothing was left of it but the cellar, Zechariah Rosen opened a shop for fodder and grains. Zechariah Rosen can not only trace his descent to the illustrious Rav Hai and as far back as King David, but he is a relative of all the great men of Israel. There is no sage, no zaddik, no prince among men but Zechariah Rosen is one of his relatives. And when he mentions them, he says: Our relative the illustrious rabbi, our grandfather the zaddik, our uncle the President, leader of the Council of the Four Lands. Your soul is literally filled with joy that the golden chain still continues up to our own generation.

Since the day the controversy arose between us about Rav Hai's children, I had not been in Zechariah's shop, although he had pacified me and asked me to visit him, for I have learned that pacification sometimes leads to a new quarrel worse than the first, and I am a softhearted man and afraid of such things. On the other hand, if I did not go he would be still more annoyed, so I went to visit him.

There are few owners of horses, and still fewer gardeners. So Zechariah Rosen has time. He sits with a book in front of him, reading the testimonials printed at the beginning and the author's introduction, and picking out names from them, which he records on paper. Paper is better even than a tombstone, for if the tombstone is a large and beautiful one the Gentiles steal it and use it for their buildings, and if it is small it sinks into the ground. Paper is a different matter, for if you print a book it spreads all through the dispersions of Israel and lasts for generations.

So Zechariah Rosen sits and tells me all the glories of his father's house. Opposite him, in a corner of the shop near the wall, sits Yekutiel his son. He covers his elbows with his hands, because his coat is torn there, and his mother is dead and there is no one to patch it for him, and he has no other coat, for of all the glory of his father's house he has nothing left but the clothes on his back. Zechariah, who is an old man, pays no attention to such things; his son, being a young man, is ashamed of his torn garments.

To give the old man pleasure and show affection to the son, I said to Yekutiel, 'Have you heard what your father told us?' Yekutiel nodded his head, smiled, and said, 'Yes, I heard.' I was filled with pity for this son of a great family who had been stricken by the wheel of fortune and did not know when the wheel would revolve again and bring back his happiness, and I was grieved at the lords and nobles who had been garbed in satins and lived in palaces, while their son's son lived in a dark cellar and his clothing was torn—and perhaps his shoes were cracked too, which was why he hid his feet under the table.

So that it should not occur to him that I was looking at his shoes, I raised my eyes and looked him in the face. I said to myself: What is this smile that does not leave his lips—just a smile, or the smile of a king's son? And if he is a king's son, where is the king's daughter who awaits him? And if a king's daughter awaits him, it is certain that she does not belong to our town, for all the girls in our town have forgotten that they are kings' daughters.

I sat and thought about the daughters of my town. Rachel, my host's youngest daughter, is already married; Babtchi her sister is going to marry Dr. Zwirn, or David Moshe the rabbi's grandson, or Riegel the agent, or someone else. As for Reb Hayim's daughters, one lives with her married sister, and the other heaven only knows where. Some say she ran away to Russia and some say she lives with pioneers in some village. And the smallest one, Zippora, who washes her father's shirt, is a little butterfly, and her time has not yet come. There is one more girl, Erela Bach. Everyone who wishes her father and mother well would be glad to see her married, but she is older than Yekutiel Rosen. And even if they were both the same age, they are poor, and who will pay the matchmaker's fee?

So I sit and think about the girls in our town, those I

know and those I have heard about. Each of them will find her mate, but Yekutiel will be left without a wife or children, and the pedigree his father has discovered for him will have no heir.

Zechariah Rosen goes on talking, and in the middle he turns to a wagoner who has come to buy a bundle of hay for his horses and asks him, 'What do you want?' The customer does not like his tone, so he answers, 'I just came in to pass the time of day,' and he turns and goes away. 'Run after him and bring him back,' says Zechariah to his son. The son runs and brings back the customer, who buys the hay for his horse and pays for it. Zechariah takes the money, gives some to his son, and says, 'Buy yourself a bun.' Yekutiel takes the coin and goes out happy. I, too, am happy that the Almighty has provided a bun for this son of kings.

The rains stopped, the sun came out, the roads were getting dry, and I went out again to stroll in the fields and the forest. Sometimes I went into the Beit Midrash, but I did not stay there, only opening the door and locking it again, so that the key should not get rusty. And again I strolled as before in the fields and the forest.

One day, when I was walking in the center of the town, I passed Hanoch's house and heard the pleasant voice of a teacher with children. I stood in front of the door and saw Reb Hayim sitting on a heap of sacks with Hanoch's child in front of him. He was teaching him from the Books of Moses, his hand on the child's chin, and explaining—with chanting—each word.

Being used to finding Reb Hayim silent, I was surprised to find him talking at such length to the child and making remarks before his explanations, such as 'Raise your voice, my child, so that your father should hear you in paradise and rejoice that his son is learning the Torah of the living God. And when you have the privilege, my son, of knowing our sacred Torah, you shall have the privilege of being a good Jew, and your father will rejoice in paradise, and you too, my son, will rejoice, and our Father in heaven will also rejoice, for He has no joy except when His sons know the Torah and fulfill His commandments. Now, my son, when we have finished the chapter, let me hear if you have not forgotten the Kaddish in the meantime.'

The child kissed the book, closed it, stood up, and recited: 'Praised and sanctified be His Great Name.' 'Fine, fine,' said Reb Hayim, ' "In the world that He has created according to His will" '—and the child repeated after him, ' "According to His will." ' 'Now, my son,' said Reb Hayim, 'join all the words together. Why are you looking outside?' 'There's a man standing there,' replied the child. 'There is no one here, except for ourselves and our Father in heaven,' said Reb Hayim. 'You are tired, my son, off you go outside.'

The child went outside, while Reb Hayim took a handmill and began grinding groats. I went into the house and greeted him. Reb Hayim pointed to the heap of sacks and asked me to sit down. 'Where did you learn to grind with a mill?' I asked. 'I have ground with a bigger mill than that,' replied Reb Hayim. 'What did you grind, sir?' 'I used to grind manna for the righteous.'

A great change could be seen in Reb Hayim. Not only did he converse with me, but he jested. Finally he fell silent again. I took my leave of him and went away—first, so as not to disturb him at his work, and, second, so as not to disturb his studies.

A man is jealous of everything. I envied Reb Hayim for sitting and teaching children, for besides Hanoch's little son he also taught the other children. Of the dead one should say nothing but praise, so I hope God will not punish me for what I say, but Hanoch, may he rest in peace, did not teach his children the Torah, because he had not enough money to hire a tutor, and there were no children's tutors in the town. It is undoubtedly a privilege for Hanoch to have Reb Hayim looking after the orphans and teaching them the Torah and the mourners' Kaddish. Then I said to myself: How many boys are walking about without studying! Let me take them into the Beit Midrash and teach them a chapter from the Books of Moses.

As in a vision I saw myself sitting at the head of the table, with a group of little ones surrounding me, teaching them the

Books of Moses with Rashi's commentary, and the boys' voices in my ears bringing joy to my heart. My heart said to me, 'Do you want to settle down permanently here and not return to the Land of Israel?' I said to my heart, 'There once was a zaddik who set out for the Land. On the way he reached a certain place and saw that they knew nothing of the Torah, except the verse, "Hear, O Israel." So he stayed with them seven years and taught them Scripture and Mishna, Law and Legend, until they became scholars. At the end of the seven years he set out on his way, going on foot, because he had spent his money to buy books and had nothing left to pay for the journey. The road to the Land of Israel was infested with bands of robbers and savage beasts. A lion came and crouched before him. He got on its back and it brought him to the Land of Israel. And they called him Ben Levi—which means "Son of the Lion." '

'What have you to do with legends?' my heart said to me. 'Keep your mind on the realities.' 'I know another man in Jerusalem,' said I to my heart, 'who on the Sabbath brings the children in from the street, takes them to the Beit Midrash, recites psalms with them, and gives them sweets after each book.' I told Daniel Bach what I wanted to do. Said Daniel Bach, 'You will find sweets, but I doubt if you will find boys who want to study the Torah.'

In those days I was overcome by longing for my children— first, because it is natural for a father to long for his children, and second, because I said to myself that if they had been with me I would have taught them Torah. I wrote to my wife, and she replied, 'We had better go up to the Land of Israel.' I began thinking about it, and it was not far from what was in my heart.

My Meals Grow Meager

For some days now, things are different at the hotel. Krolka lays my table, but brings me nothing more than a light meal. Gone are the hot and nourishing dishes that give more life to those that eat them.

True, light foods are good for the body and do not burden the soul. But the trouble is that even if you eat your fill of them, you feel that something is lacking. Poland is not like the Land of Israel; there, you eat a morsel of bread with olives and tomato, and you are satisfied; here, even if you eat a gardenful of vegetables, your belly is empty. This is the curse that was called down upon the children of Israel because they said, 'We remember the cucumbers, and the melons, and the leeks, which we ate in Egypt.' The Holy One, blessed be He, said to them, 'Behold, I will exile you to the lands of the Gentiles—perhaps you will be more satisfied there.'

All this is true of breakfast. And the same is true of the midday meal. My hostess has forgotten the recipes and lore of the vegetarian physician who taught her to make all kinds of dishes. Now she makes one dish, and feeds me from it for two, even three, days. If the dish spoils, they bring me a couple of eggs and a glass of milk. Worse still: even for this light meal I have to wait. At first my hostess would apologize and say that she had not managed to prepare me a good meal because she had been busy with Rachel, but in the end she has stopped apologizing, because she has no time to talk to anyone, for she sits with Rachel every day.

A man can do without much food, but he cannot do without a little cordiality. My host sits wrapped up in his long coat, with his pipe in his mouth; sometimes he puffs smoke and sometimes he rubs his knees in silence. When I pay my bills, he counts the money silently and puts it into a leather pouch. I know he bears me no grudge—it is only the troubles with his children and the pains of his body that have left no light in his face—but what good is my knowing why he is sullen, when the heart seeks a little joy?

Since the day my hostess stopped looking after the kitchen, she has put Krolka in charge of the cooking and Babtchi in charge of the kashruth.

I did not find Babtchi particularly pleasing, and since she did not please me I did not please her. And since I did not please her, she did not feel it worth while to set a fine table for me, and she would set it as for a man who is not worth taking trouble over. Many a time I refrained from coming to the main meal of the day so that I should not have to thank her for her trouble. Another man would have gone to the tavern or the divorcee's inn, but I did not go there. So as not to go hungry, I would fill up with fruit: at first I would buy from Hanoch's wife in the market, and when Hanoch's wife had none, I bought from her neighbors.

Once I asked a certain woman, 'Why are you sitting in the market when you have nothing to sell?' 'So where should I sit,' she replied, 'in the garden of the king's palace?' When I asked another woman, she replied, 'People might put the evil eye on me and say, "That lady is sitting in the theaters"— so I sit in the market.'

The fruit that comes from the market is partly rotten and partly mouldy; you have to take pains picking out the good and throwing away the bad. Nevertheless, I used to buy from the market: first, out of habit, and second, so that Hanoch's wife should earn something. Once I came to buy and found no fruit worth eating, so I said to myself: It is natural for fruit to grow on a tree in the orchard; I will go to the orchard and take fruit from the tree.

This Gentile from whom I buy apples and pears does not frown or talk about man's end in life; he takes the money and gives me the fruit, and says, 'Enjoy the eating.' Once I came and did not find him. I asked after him and they told me he was at home. I went to his house and found him lying sick. It was then that I saw that even Gentiles can be overcome by weakness.

Since the day my meals began to grow less, I sit less in the

Beit Midrash. Whether I buy my fruit from the market or buy it from the Gentile, I am busy shopping for it and cannot spend much time in study.

So long as a man sits in the Beit Midrash he has nothing but the Torah and Israel and the Holy One, blessed be He. But as soon as he goes out, there is no Torah and the people of Israel are crushed and hard pressed, and even the Almighty Himself has, as it were, contracted Himself, and His Name is not noticed in His world.

I will leave alone all the Gentiles in my town, whether they were born in Szibucz or whether the Almighty brought them there from somewhere else, and mention only Anton Jacobowitz, alias Pan Jacobowitz, alias Antos Agopowitz, who in his youth was a pork-butcher and now in his old age is a respectable citizen, rich and with much property. His oldest son is a priest and teaches the catechism; his second is a lieutenant; and his daughters are married, one to a Polish judge and one to a noble, well-bred officer, who wears a cavalry coat. When I left Szibucz and went up to the Land of Israel, Anton was already well known in the town and popular among the people; he talked Yiddish and spiced his conversation with the Holy Tongue, and scoffed at the ignorant among us, who had neither Torah nor worldly wisdom. They told many jokes about Anton, and here is one. Once he saw a Jew, an ignoramus, on the morning of the Tish'a B'Av fast with his prayer shawl and tefillin satchel under his arm. 'Goy!' said Anton, 'Don't you know that you don't put on the tefillin at the Morning Service on Tish'a B'Av?'

When the war came and the Russians occupied Szibucz, and all the leading citizens fled, Antos was able to make friends with the officers and became the right hand of the commander, Colonel Gavrilo Vassilevitch Strachilo. They laid their hands on the property of the Jews who had fled from the fury of the oppressor and transferred the furniture and the goods to Russia. There were no Jews in the town who could challenge what he was doing, and as for the Polish and Austrian officials, who remained without food or shelter, Antos used to feed them in secret, so that if the Austrians should return they would protect him. So they took heed of his gifts and ignored his deeds.

He would supply food to the army and travel to Astrakhan to bring back dried fish for the fast days.

The children of the rich Jews, whose leftovers Antos used to lick, were no longer prominent in the town—not as in the days gone by, when most of the town was populated with Jews. Sebastian Montag, our leading citizen, died in Warsaw, on foreign soil, and his relatives could not afford to bring his coffin to Szibucz to bury him among the graves of his fathers. True, they paid him great honor in his death, for they mentioned the great deeds he had done for Poland, by virtue of which he had been elected to the Sejm, but he had not managed to go to most of the sessions: sometimes because his shoes were torn, and sometimes because he could not find a bite to eat in the morning. In Sebastian Montag's place sits a Gentile, an evil man and an enemy of Israel. His deputy is like him, and so are all the other officials. All that is left to the Jews in Szibucz is to swallow their spittle and pay taxes.

There are some people in Szibucz who envy their brethren who have gone to other places. What have their brethren found that is to be envied? They have certainly not found a golden kid carrying almonds and raisins—or even a dry crust of bread. So why should they be envied? But a man who finds things hard in his own place thinks other places are paradise, and even those who have left Szibucz write about Szibucz as if it were a paradise. Perhaps, indeed, Szibucz is really a paradise—and if not for the Jews, then for the Gentiles.

Every time Pan Jacobowitz meets me, he buttonholes me and starts a conversation. 'With you, my friend,' says Pan Jacobowitz, 'one can talk a word or two of Yiddish, for all those Jews have caught the ways of Vienna and talk half-German.' And since one can talk a word of Yiddish with me, he goes on talking. He sighs for the honor of the town, which has declined, and for the young Jews who do not know their Maker. They and their fathers, says Antos, are prepared to sell their God for a copper, but then their fathers' God was worth a copper, while to the sons He is not worth even that much.

Antos speaks Yiddish in the way they used to speak it in Szibucz before the people were exiled and took on the ways of Vienna. And he tells me of the honor of his wealth and the glory of his sons. 'My eldest,' says Antos, 'is a rabbi and presides in the yeshiva, and one son-in-law is a dayan, and scholars crowd around his door. A frequent visitor in my house is Professor Lukaciewicz. He always comes to me,' says Antos, 'on our Sabbath for the Closing Meal of the Holy Day, to eat pigs-feet with cabbage, and blood sausages, and liverwurst with us. This obstinate old man,' says Antos, 'is a great glutton, heaven help us, and as he eats—blast him—so he drinks. He drinks, blast him, heaven help us, a whole vatful of Christian wine without getting drunk.'

Besides this Lukaciewicz, another frequent visitor in Antos' house was the Russian Colonel Strachilo, who was in command in Szibucz during the occupation. After going half around the world and crossing Siberia and America he came to Szibucz. He was an old man with a bristling, erect mustache, tall, upright, and thin, and he dragged himself along leaning on his stick. Times have changed since Antos used to stand before him like a servant before his master. Now Antos is a respectable citizen, with much wealth and property, and Colonel Strachilo gets a pension from him. It is not enough to live on or to die on either, but Strachilo can't be too fussy, for whoever has the power is entitled to do as he likes. Twice a month Pan Jacobowitz's second son comes to Szibucz, to pay his respects to his father and eat whatever is cooking in his mother's pots. Whenever he comes, Colonel Strachilo and Professor Lukaciewicz and two or three other gentlemen come to show him honor, and they sit together eating and drinking and reveling, and planning how to harm the Jews. However, all credit to Antos for not taking part in their plots. 'Leave the Jews alone, poor creatures,' says he. 'They're more dead than alive; they haven't the strength to kill a flea.'

Pan Jacobowitz is perfectly right: the Jews in Szibucz are more dead than alive, and they have no strength at all. First came the war and uprooted them, and they did not take root anywhere else. Then their chattels were taken from them. Then their money was taken. Then their children were taken. Then their homes were taken. Then their livelihoods were taken. And then they were given taxes and levies, and where should the Jews get strength?

Daniel Bach hobbles along with his stick and drags along his artificial leg. For several months no one has come in to buy wood, and no woman in labor has called for his wife. And there is another trouble in his house: trouble with his daughter. True, Erela is earning enough to keep herself and help her parents, but she is a grown girl and there are no bridegrooms to be seen. We thought at first that Yeruham Freeman would marry Erela, but he went and married Rachel.

Then that shopkeeper who went bankrupt (and we had thought there was going to be a new rich man in Szibucz!) had all his trouble for nothing. Riegel the agent's lawyer, who had already helped Riegel to get rid of his wife, laid hands on the shopkeeper and got the merchandise out of the possession of the shopkeeper's wife, and I'm afraid she may go to prison.

Their shop is closed; no one enters, no one leaves. After they had taken out their merchandise in secret, the authorities came and put a clay seal on the lock, so that no one should imagine that they had closed their shop because of some celebration. Their shop is closed—though all the other shops, which are open, have no customers either. Since there are no customers, they do not bring new merchandise, and since they bring no merchandise, Yehuda has nothing to do either—this is the Yehuda who used to bring merchandise for the shopkeepers from Lvov.

Once again Riegel the agent comes and lodges at our hotel. If rumor is to be believed, he did not listen to Babtchi's advice and take his divorced wife back. And if seeing is believing, he is not sorry for it. He has little to say to Babtchi, and what he says will break no hearts. When Babtchi feels this and tries to make him talk, he pulls out his pack of cigarettes, takes a cigarette and lights it, and answers quietly, like a man whose heart is at ease, who feels no pressure. This, my friend, does not please Babtchi, like a maiden who is annoyed with the nightingale for not singing songs of love. But Mr. Riegel is not disturbed by her annoyance; he looks at his watch, as you and I do when we want to get rid of each other—I of you or you of me.

Times change and hearts change with them. For if Mr. Riegel were to behave to Babtchi as he once did, he might turn her heart to him. But Riegel is no longer concerned with turning hearts. So long as a man is married, he casts his eyes on other women; when he gets rid of his wife, he sees that it is possible to do without women.

So Riegel sits, with his glass in front of him and a cigarette case lying on the table. This case, my friend, and the matchbox, too, are of silver; his name is engraved on them and they are a gift from his master, or from himself. And they have changed his ways, for he no longer wonders whether to go to the kitchen to get an ember in order to talk with Mrs. Zommer, nor does he think of lighting his cigarette from Mr. Zommer's pipe. If we were in the habit of conjecturing, we should conjecture that at this moment he is not thinking either of Babtchi's father or of Babtchi's mother. If so, what is he thinking of? That is easy to say and hard to conjecture.

Krolka came and stood in front of Mr. Riegel, bending her head modestly and asking, as usual, in a whisper, 'Perhaps, sir, you would like a second glass?' 'Go back to your pots, Krolka,' said Babtchi, 'if Mr. Riegel wants anything I will bring it to him.' And she asked in a tender voice, 'Perhaps you would like something, Mr. Riegel? I'll bring it to you right away.' And as she spoke she fixed her eyes upon him and waited for his reply.

I did not hear what Riegel replied to Babtchi, and you, my dear sir, did not hear either, because Ignatz came in to ask the agent for alms. This Ignatz, though he has no nose, scents out anyone who comes to the town and goes to him to ask for *pieniadze*.

Mr. Zommer rose, leaning on his stick, and went to the kitchen. An hour ago he wanted to ask Krolka what Rachel was doing. It was several hours since his wife had gone to see how Rachel was, and she had not yet returned. Mr. Zommer came back and sat down, his pipe in his mouth. So Mr. Zommer sits every day and every hour from the Morning Service until the bedtime prayer.

Now let us ask how Rachel is. Perhaps Krolka knows more than she told Mr. Zommer. Krolka sighed and said, 'What shall I say and what shall I tell? The pains of pregnancy are hard on Rachel.' And since Krolka had finished all her work in the kitchen and had nothing to do, she started to tell me the things we knew, such as that everyone had thought Mr. Yeruham Freeman, Miss Rachel's husband, would marry Miss Erela Bach, that well-taught teacher, the daughter of our neighbor, Mr. Bach, from whom the Lord God had seen fit to take away one leg, and since Miss Rachel had cast her eyes on her girl friend's mate and taken him away from her, that was why the Lord God was punishing her and giving her a hard pregnancy.

Here Krolka fixed her eyes on me and asked, 'And what does an honorable gentleman like you think about it, and what do the holy books write about this kind of thing?' 'You were quite right, Krolka,' said I, 'to ask me what the holy books write about it, for if you had asked me what I think, I would not have known what to reply; for you must know, Krolka, that our reason is weak, and if we did not look in the holy books we would know nothing. As for what you asked me, I will tell you: If Yeruham had been Erela's mate, Rachel would not have been able to take him away from her, and if she took him away, it is obvious that it was proclaimed in heaven that Rachel is Yeruham's mate.' Krolka raised her two eyes to heaven and said, 'Blessed be the Almighty who teaches men wisdom.' Then she said to me, 'You have put a new soul in my heart, honorable sir.'

While we were standing there, Rachel's mother came in. She was happy and tired. All day she had been with her daughter. What had she done and what had she not done? Seven women do not do what one mother does for her daughter, and, thank the Lord, her work had been successful. But she found it hard to bear the pangs of pregnancy, did Rachel.

She found it hard to bear the pangs of pregnancy, and small wonder, for Rachel had endured many troubles. Even when she was a little girl, she had suffered from many sicknesses. She had hardly recovered from the sicknesses when the war came, and Rachel was taken from bed, still sick, and put in a sack, and carried on her mother's back in the sun and the dust of the roads. Once she fell from the sack and was cast among the thorns, where she lay without food and water, and

black hornets threatened her life. Now she is not lying among
the thorns and there are no black hornets threatening to sting
her, but she lies on a broad bed with pillows and coverlets,
and her mother feeds her with dainties and gives her milk to
drink. If you have seen a fat chicken in the market, you can
be sure it is being prepared to make gravy for Rachel; if you
have noticed that the milk in the hotel is thin, you can be sure
they have taken out all the cream for Rachel. All the money
I pay for food and lodging is spent on Rachel, for all Yeruham's earnings are not enough for more than a laborer's meal.

Yeruham does all in his power to please his mother-in-
law, but she refuses to be pleased by him. Once, Rachel was
gripped by her pains and his mother-in-law looked at him
with wrathful eyes, which clearly said: Rascal, what have
you done to my daughter? Of all Yeruham's pride, he has
nothing left but his curls, and the pride has gone out of them
too. Three or four times Yeruham came to the Beit Midrash to
tell me his woes; but he had his trouble for nothing. When I
asked him to come to the Beit Midrash he did not come; now
that he comes he does not find me. Reb Hayim said to me,
'That young fellow is wasting away with too much suspense.'

I feel sorry for Yeruham, squatting in the dust all day to
mend the roads, in winter as in summer, morning and afternoon. True, in the Land of Israel he did not build towers and
palaces either, and his work was harder than it is abroad, for
he stood up to the waist in the swamps and set his life in
danger. But in the Land of Israel what a man does leads to
some end, and if it is not for his own sake, at least it is for
others who will come after him. On the other hand, if he had
not come back from the Land he would not have found Rachel.
However, this should be said: it would have been better for
Rachel to remain without a man. Comely girls like Rachel are
comely when they are not burdened with a husband.

My other self, who lodges with me, whispered to me, 'If
it had not been for Yeruham Freeman, Rachel would have
been free, and you and I could have looked at her.' Said I to
my other, 'You are quite right, Rachel was a lovely girl.' At
once my other began to paint Rachel's face before my eyes

with all kinds of comely, alluring pictures. Said I to my other, 'A great painter is our God.' My other gritted his teeth. 'Why are you teasing me?' said I. 'It is because you ascribe my deeds to the Holy One, blessed be He,' he replied. 'It was not God who painted Rachel's face before your eyes; it was I.' Said I, 'You painted the face of Yeruham Freeman's wife, but our God painted before me the image of Rachel, the hotel-keeper's little daughter.' My other laughed and said, 'Rachel the hotelkeeper's daughter and Rachel Yeruham Freeman's wife are one and the same.' I saw how things were going, and immediately reminded him of the pact I had made with him. He began to be afraid I might change my mind and cancel the pact, so he left me alone.

CHAPTER SIXTY

In the Field

So that he should not return to the subject, I walked him off to the Beit Midrash. And so that he should not disturb me on the way, I stopped and talked to every man I met in the marketplace. And when I happened to meet Ignatz, I talked to him.

If you get accustomed to this Ignatz's droning, you can hear some sensible things from him. Once the talk turned on Hanoch and his death, and Ignatz said, 'All this hullabaloo all over the whole town on the day they found Hanoch dead in the snow—I don't know the sense of it. During the war things like that happened every day, every hour, and we didn't pay attention to them. Sometimes we found a soldier lying under his horse—he dead and the horse alive, or the horse dead and he alive. Before we could manage to separate them, we were caught by the enemy's fire and most of our fellows were blown to pieces—a hand this way and a foot that way, a man's head flying off and striking his mate's, so that both of them fell together and sank in the blood and muck.'

Let us dismiss Ignatz and go to meet Daniel Bach.

Daniel Bach hobbles along on his wooden leg, but his beard is trimmed and his face is happy. Let us go to meet him and shorten his way.

I have come to know many men in Szibucz, but I like Daniel Bach better than any, because I met him first on the day I came back to my town and because he does not weary me with futile talk that confuses the mind. Bach is not one of those who were born in Szibucz, but since he came to the town a few years before the war I look upon him as if he were a man of Szibucz; and since he was not born in Szibucz, he does does not regard himself as one of the Almighty's favored children.

When I come across Daniel Bach, I make him walk on my right, and we stroll along wherever our feet carry us. As soon as we reach the forest, he immediately turns back to the town. It is not because the road is hard and the place distant that he does not go into the forest, but I imagine that the incident in the trenches, when he looked for the tefillin and came upon one of them bound to a dead man's arm, took place in a forest, and that is why he avoids walking there.

What do we talk about and what don't we talk about? About things that one talks about, about things that a man can bend to his will, or things that make a man bend to theirs. Once the talk turned on the Land of Israel. Said Daniel Bach, 'I have every respect for old men who go up to the Land to die there, but not for those young men who go to make their lives there, for their lives are only a short cut to their deaths.' 'And here,' said I, 'do you live forever?' 'Here a man lives without a program and dies without a program,' replied Mr. Bach.

And Mr. Bach went on, 'These sanctities, the sanctity of life, and the sanctity of labor, and the sanctity of death, that you preach about, I don't know what they mean. What sanctity is there in life, or in labor, or in death? A man lives and labors and dies. Has he any choice—not to live, or not to labor, or not to die?'

And Mr. Bach went on to say, 'Those that live in sanctity do not know of it, and those who bear the name of sanctity on their lips are not aware of it. And that is not all. If a man does a thing from his heart, with conviction, what sanctity is there in the doing? That is what he was made for, that is what he wants, isn't it? And in any case I do not want to judge things I have not been appointed to judge. A man like me— it's enough for me that I keep myself alive, without bothering to judge the lives of other people.'

I remembered my comrades in the village and recalled that I had promised to go back to them. 'Come with me,' I said to him, 'and I will show you an example of Yeruham's comrades.' 'Perhaps it is worth seeing what the lads are doing there,' said Mr. Bach. 'It is many years since I stirred from the town.' So we went out to the market and bought some food, as well as some knickknacks for the two girls, hired a cart, and set off.

It was three days since the rains had stopped, and it was still damp. The ground had not hardened and the journey was easy and pleasant. The rye was standing and a pleasant fragrance rose from the fields. The horses trotted by themselves and the cart followed them. The carter sat on his perch and sang a love song about a handsome young man who went to the wars and left his beloved in the village, while Daniel and I sat back in comfort like travelers who forget their troubles in the journey.

On our way, Bach asked me if I had heard anything about Aaron Schutzling. Since Schutzling had written nothing, I had nothing to tell, and since I had nothing to tell about Schutzling we talked about other people. About whom? About those that kept all mouths busy and those whom no one remembered, until we reached the village and went out to the fields.

We found our comrades standing in the fields and loading sheaves of hay. Two of them stood on top of a wagon, while two stood on one side and two on the other, with long forks in their hands, and the boys in the wagon stood up to the waist in hay, treading it with their feet to make room for what their comrades lifted up to them. Down below, on a sheaf of hay, sat the farmer, unlit pipe in his mouth, watching the work of his laborers. The lads were busy with their work and did not notice us, while we stood watching them and their work.

When the farmer saw Bach, he took his pipe out of his mouth, tucked it into his high boots, and ran to meet us joyfully. He gripped Bach's hands and would not let them go. 'Oh, Mr. Bach, sir, if it hadn't been for you the crows would have eaten me,' he exclaimed. As he spoke, his wrinkles smoothed out, his face lost its angry expression, and something like a Jewish sadness filled his Gentile eyes. Finally he gazed at Mr. Bach's artificial leg and said, 'So this is what they have done to you, Mr. Bach, sir. And you came here with this leg of yours, and I didn't go to you even once. A man is like a pig, he squats on his dungheap and scratches himself and eats. That is the whole of man.'

So the farmer stood in front of Bach, and talked, and talked again, and showed him every kind of affection, for Daniel Bach had saved him from death, as we shall tell below —or perhaps we had better tell the story at once, in case we forget. It happened that during the war both of them were serving in the same regiment. Once the officer ordered that farmer to do such and such, but the farmer violated his orders and did the opposite, so they sentenced him to death. But Bach came along and spoke up in his defense; he said the farmer had acted as he did because he did not understand German. So they exchanged the death sentence for a lighter penalty.

After the farmer had recalled this story, he went on to say, 'All the troubles come only because people's languages are not the same. If everyone spoke the same language, they would understand each other. But people's tongues are different: the German speaks German, the Pole Polish, and the Ruthenian speaks Ruthenian. Then the Jew adds Yiddish. And now go and tell me we are brothers. How can we say we are brothers, when one of us doesn't know the other's language, and can't tell a blessing from a curse? And now the sons of the Jews come along and talk the Hebrew language, which I and even their fathers don't know. Hello, Hebrews, don't you see that you have guests? Stop your work and come to welcome your guests. That Jerusalemite from Palestine, he's come too. He's put on a new suit in your honor. Look out for him and his suit, and don't let a scrap of straw fall on it.' When the lads heard him, they jumped down and came up to us, those from the two sides of the wagon and those from the top, greeting us and waving their hands in joy. Nor did they stop rejoicing until the farmer said to them, 'You Hebrews, better stop work and get them some food, for I suppose they won't want to eat with me.'

So one of the group rushed off to the girls in the cowshed to tell them visitors had come, so that they should prepare supper, and the rest went off to change their clothes, for their master gave them permission to leave their work an hour early in honor of Mr. Bach.

The farmer took us and showed us his fields, and every man and woman who saw Bach bowed their heads in respect and asked after his health. The farmers had known him during the war, and their wives had known him after the war, for they used to buy soap from him so that their husbands should wash their hands of the blood they had shed.

In the meantime we reached our comrades, who were standing in front of the house waiting. The girls laid the table with things from the village, while I added the foodstuffs I had brought from town.

A small lamp lit up the little room, and a fine smell rose from the fields and the hay and the bread and the new cloth that was spread on the table. The boys ate with an appetite as if after a fast, and encouraged us to eat too, showing us great affection and then still more, not knowing whom to honor first and whom last—the one who had come from the Land of Israel or Mr. Bach. Said I, 'I deserve to be honored first, for I have brought you an important guest, and since you know me well as one of yourselves, you and I together will honor Mr. Bach.'

The young people thanked me for bringing them such an important guest—important for the sake of Yeruham his brother, who had been killed for the Land of Israel, as well as for his father, who lived in the Land, and for his own sake, because he had taken the trouble to visit them—unlike the other townsfolk, who scoffed at them, and even if some praised them, none took the trouble to visit them. After they had somewhat appeased their hunger and eaten all I had brought, they turned to me with great affection and asked me to tell them something from the Land of Israel. Especially pressing was Zvi—the same Zvi who had visited me a few weeks before and invited me to come here. So I did not refuse to tell them what I know and what I thought I knew. Since our comrades were well versed, in their own way, in the affairs of the Land, I did not have to explain much, and if I explained something I did so only in honor of Daniel Bach. So I sat and told my tale, until midnight came and I had not reached the end.

At that moment the kerosene came to an end, for my story was long and the lamp was small, as I said before. So we rose from the table, and that was only right, for the lads had to get up for their work at sunrise, and especially because the two girls had to get up in the middle of the night to milk the cows. While they were filling the lamp with kerosene, we went out to stroll in the fields. Our comrades went with us and continued the tale of the Land, until the talk turned on their work in the village. Daniel Bach told them in the farmer's name that he was pleased with their work—and not only that farmer, but all the farmers they had been with said they had never had such diligent workers.

The lads sighed and said, 'But what good does it do us, if then they set fire to all that we've done? Sometimes the farmer sets fire to his barn to get insurance money; and if he is not insured, his enemies come and set fire to it. And when his corn is burned, and he has not paid us our wages yet, he does not pay at all.' So, from one thing to another, we came to what happened to them on the festival of Shavuot, when their food had been stolen and they had been left without anything at all. Said Mr. Bach, 'This happened before the giving of the Torah, when they had not yet been commanded: Thou shalt not steal.'

The skies showed that midnight had passed, and the hay exhaled its sweet smell, as if it had been steeped through and perfumed by the dew, and the dew perfumed by it. The stars stood silent, one here, one there, and their light floated on the face of the firmament. Suddenly a star jumped from its place and disappeared, and mist covered its path. The night redoubled its peace, and tranquil quiet covered everything around us. Silent we returned to the house and lay down to sleep.

The lads had laid straw mattresses for us on the floor. I recited the 'Hear, O Israel,' covered myself, and said good night to Mr. Bach. But he did not answer, for he had already fallen asleep.

I too closed my eyes and said to myself: How good and pleasant it is that I have come here. In a thousand nights there is not one like this. Before I had finished praising the night, I felt a shock, as if a needle had been thrust into my face. I took out my right hand hastily to rub my cheek, and something like a needle was thrust into my hand. I took out my left hand to cover the right; it too was stabbed by the needle —or perhaps it was another needle, for it burned and stung more than the first. While I was wondering what this could be, along came a band of gnats and explained the matter.

What the gnats did above, the mice did below, squeaking and gnawing and frisking about the room. I called out to Mr. Bach, but he did not answer. I called again, but he did not answer. Is there no feeling in his flesh? Doesn't he hear the hateful, disgusting squeaking? Next morning, when I told him about it, he smiled and said, 'I know them since the days of the war, when they used to assemble in companies and battalions to gnaw the corpses, and it isn't worth wasting even an hour of sleep on them. Besides, they don't think it worth their while to tackle me, for no doubt they landed on my artificial leg first and thought I was all made of wood.'

Between the gnats and the mice came the fleas. While the mice frisked in the room and the gnats stung my face and neck, the fleas divided up the rest of my body between them. Or perhaps they went into partnership with the bugs, and what the first left the other came and took. I wanted to jump up, but I was afraid our comrades might awaken. I was sorry I had pressed them to go to sleep. If we had lengthened our talk, I should have shortened my sufferings. I raised my head and gazed at the window. Night had covered the land and there was no hope that day would dawn. All the village slept; no cock crowed, no dog cried. Meanwhile, I dozed off and slept. As soon as I fell asleep, the cock crowed, the dogs barked, and the cows moved from their shed. I heard the sound of bare feet on the floor of the other room, where the girls slept, and saw a light coming from there. 'Blessed be He that maketh the night to pass and bringeth the day,' said I. 'Soon the lads will get up and I will escape from this bed of pain.' Then sleep overcame me and I dozed off.

An hour or an hour and a half later I opened my eyes and saw that the whole room was filled with the light of day. I dressed quickly, said my prayers, and sat down with the comrades for breakfast.

I watched the faces of Daniel Bach and the boys and girls: they looked the same as the day before; there wasn't the least sign of a gnat on them. He who is easy on others, others are easy on him; he who is hard on others, others are hard on him. At that moment I made up my mind to pay no attention to fleas and gnats and bugs and mice.

When we had eaten and drunk, our comrades wanted me to stay till after the Sabbath, for on the Sabbath they were free all day and all night. Although I had made up my mind to pay no attention to the fleas and gnats, the bugs and the mice, I was afraid to stay, in case I might not stand the test.

The carter came with his cart. The farmer went out and brought Mr. Bach a bowlful of butter and a basketful of mushrooms. Before we moved off, the other farmers and their wives came and brought garlic and onions, eggs and a pair of pigeons.

Daniel Bach said goodbye to the farmer and we got onto the cart. 'Soon,' said the farmer, 'I am coming to bring your wife.' 'Is your daughter-in-law giving birth?' Daniel asked the farmer. 'Both my daughter-in-law and my wife,' said the farmer.

The comrades returned to their work and we returned to the town. The pleasant air and the wind that blew through the standing corn drove the troubles of the night out of my mind, and you needn't be surprised, for at that time I was forty-one years old, so I could endure the day even if I had not slept at night. My weary limbs began to heal, except for my skin, which was swollen from the bugs. As we neared the town, I was gripped with longing for our comrades in the village. I said to Daniel Bach, 'If I was not afraid the Gentiles would steal your treasures, I would want to go back with you to the village.' Daniel Bach was silent and made no reply. Perhaps he was thinking of the farmer and his wife and daughter-in-law, perhaps he was thinking of his brother who had been killed, or perhaps he was thinking of the gifts he was bringing to his wife. It was not every day that he brought her things like these. Finally, he turned his head to me and said, 'I find this surprising: if they are working why do they need the Land of Israel? Surely they can stay here and work and earn a living.' 'Were it not for the Land of Israel,' I replied, 'would they work so hard?' Said he, 'Whatever we talk about, you people bring in the Land of Israel.' 'Who was it brought in the Land of Israel this time—you or I?' said I. Said Daniel Bach, 'Whenever I see you, it seems to me that a strip of the Land trails along behind you, so I am reminded of the Land of Israel. In any case, the girls' parents can be pleased that they have followed the pioneers and not trailed after the communists.' 'Is that all the good you have found in our girls?' said I. 'The only good we have is not to have the worst,' he replied.

As we were sitting, the cart shook, let out a screech and stopped. The carter got off, examined the wheels, and began cursing himself and his horses and the road and all the people in the world. Finally, he straightened up and said, 'Be so kind as to get down, gentlemen. One of the wheels is broken.' 'What shall we do?' 'You do nothing,' said the carter. 'You watch the cart and horses, while I go look for a man to mend my wheel.'

'And shall we have to stand here a long time?' 'You don't need to stand,' said the carter. 'If you want, you can sit.' So the carter went off, while Daniel Bach and I sat down beside the cart, which was standing on three wheels. Half the day passed and the carter did not come back. Daniel Bach opened his bundle and said, 'Let us have lunch.' After we had eaten, we heard the sound of feet. 'There are two people coming,' said I to Daniel. 'I see four feet,' said Daniel. The carter came up, with a short, broad old man. It was the smith, who had mended the wheel and had come to get his pay.

The smith dragged along his feet slowly, and his head shook without a stop. He looked at the remains of the food and said, 'Good appetite! Is there a drop of brandy here for the throat of my mother's son?' When he heard we had no brandy, he spat into his hands and said, 'So you have eaten and not drunk?' 'And you've drunk and not eaten,' said the carter. 'I've drunk, gentlemen, I've drunk,' said the smith, 'but only one little drop.' Again he spat into his hands and said, 'To work.' An hour later, or a little less, we got back into the cart. It was almost dark when we reached the town.

CHAPTER ONE AND SIXTY

Evening

I went back to my hotel and entered my room. My throat was dry and my limbs slack, my skin was throbbing and my head felt heavy. The sun had set and the room was dark. I sat on the end of the bed and looked straight in front of me. The lamp gleamed out of the darkness. I took a match to light it, but for some reason, I do not know why, I put out the match and did not light the lamp. I took another match and lit a cigarette. And many thoughts came into my mind that are not fit to be called thoughts and do not combine to make up any matter.

Krolka knocked at the door. I was too lazy to tell her to come in. She knocked again and entered. 'I thought you had gone out, sir,' she said, 'and I came in to make your bed.' 'I am here, Krolka,' said I, 'I wanted to light the lamp and could not find a match. Perhaps you know where the matches are?' 'I'll bring you matches straightaway, sir,' said Krolka, 'or perhaps you would be so kind as to give me your matches, sir, and I will light the lamp.' I was ashamed that I had told Krolka that I had not found a match, when there was a lighted cigarette in my mouth. But I gave her no reason to doubt my truthfulness and said, 'This was the last match and my matchbox is empty. Or let us say that the box is not empty, but the matches do not catch fire. Are there no matches in the hotel? Heavens above, am I condemned to sit in darkness all night when all the lamps in the house are lit? And don't be surprised, Krolka, that I can sit here and still see all that is going on in the house. There are people, Krolka, who can see even when their eyes are closed.' 'Perhaps you will come and eat,' said Krolka. 'That is a good piece of advice you give me, Krolka,' said I, 'but what will you answer if I tell you that I am not hungry? I am not hungry at all. Perhaps you have a glass of tea? It seems to me that I am thirsty, for all day I have been standing in the sun. But I do not feel hot. In fact, I even want to get a little warmer. Well, Krolka, what were we talking about? About tea. So make me a cup of tea and I shall come straightaway.' 'Straightaway, at once, sir,' said Krolka. 'Straightaway, at once.'

Krolka went out, and I sat and thought: She said straightaway; did she mean to echo my words? No, Krolka didn't intend to echo my words or provoke me. Krolka is a good Jewess for a Christian. Where have I heard these words? And who used them? Let us sit and think.

I sat and thought, but did not remember. And it was impossible that I should find out by memory who spoke in this way, for no dictionary has yet been compiled for all the words that issue from the mouths of men.

Krolka came back and brought a lit lamp, as well as two full boxes of matches, and asked, 'Where would you like to drink your tea, sir, in your room or in the dining room?' I thought and thought and could not decide. On the one hand, how good it is to sit alone; still, one should not avoid people. True, all that day I had been with people, but if we look deeper into the matter, all those whom I had seen were an idea, and not men of flesh and blood—for instance, that farmer, who kept talking about the purpose of life, about bread, and about the soil.

'Will you take your tea in the dining room?' said Krolka. I nodded my head and said, 'I will, I will.'

Krolka is a good Jewess for a Christian; she knows what is good for you and makes it unnecessary for you to think many thoughts. For thoughts are tiring, as Schutzling my friend

said. Who asked me about Schutzling? Heaven almighty, is
there no hope of remembering who it was who called Krolka
a good Jewess for a Christian?

How quick Krolka is! In a brief while she managed to go
to the kitchen, pour me out a glass of tea, bring it into the
dining room, and come back to tell me that the tea is ready
and standing on the table. I sat down to drink. Krolka came
back again and brought me a glass of boiling milk, saying,
'Perhaps you will drink a glass of milk? Hot milk is good for
the throat and good for the nerves.'

Her voice is low and her movements restrained. Surely
Rachel is not ill, heaven forbid? Rachel is hale and hearty—so
may God always keep her in life and health.

Mr. Zommer rose, turned to face the corner and, leaning
on his stick, started to recite the Evening Service. Mrs. Zommer entered quietly and went out quietly, nodding to me as
she entered and as she went out.

I blew into my glass and said to myself: Perhaps Mrs.
Zommer wanted to tell me something, but when she saw her
husband at his prayers she went out. What did Mrs. Zommer
want to tell me, and why did she look sad? Surely Rachel is
hale and hearty.

It was many days since I had thought about the people
in the hotel—first, because nothing new had happened there,
and second, because thinking is tiring.

Thinking is tiring. Forty-one years had passed over me
and I had still not realized this; then along came Schutzling
and said it, and his words keep beating on my heart every day,
every hour, every moment.

Mr. Zommer took too long over his prayers. After he had
finished, he loosened his sash, rolled it up and put it in his
pocket, came and sat down at his table, took his pipe and
filled it, got up and went off, came back and sat down again,
screwed up his eyes and opened them again, and looked at
me as if he wanted to ask something.

I wondered where Mrs. Zommer was and why she had not
returned. I thought she wanted to tell me something. Everyone here is more silent than usual today, though it can be felt
that they want to speak.

Babtchi came in, greeted us with a nod, and offered her father a newspaper. Mr. Zommer took the paper, read the whole page that was in front of him, turned over and read on. This was a change for Mr. Zommer: he had turned over the page, though usually he does not turn it even if he is in the middle of a story. It is good for a guest when his host is a silent man. If I have no home of my own, it is good that I have found a hotel whose owner does not trouble me with talk. In any case, it would be a good thing if Mrs. Zommer came and told me what she wanted to say when she entered the dining room and found her husband at prayer.

A short time passed, and then another short time passed. Both of them combined to make a long time, and nothing at all changed in the hotel. Mr. Zommer sucked his pipe and read the paper. What was written in the paper that was so worth reading? But in any case, I bless Mr. Zommer for not stopping to tell me.

Before going to sleep I took a piece of paper, wrote on it, 'Do not wake me,' put the paper in one of my shoes and left my shoes on the threshold behind the door, so that if Krolka should come to polish my shoes she would find the notice and not waken me. This I did although I had no hope or expectation of sleeping long, and moreover I took a second piece, wrote the same words on it, and left it in my second shoe, so that if Krolka should forget the first note, the second would remind her—perhaps the Almighty would give sleep to my eyes and people would not come and waken me.

Indeed the Almighty gave me sleep, and I slept till nine, and I too gave myself sleep and slept again for another hour. After I had made up my mind to get up, I put aside the blanket and lay down, as if trying to decide whether one needed a blanket. In the meantime, I fell asleep again.

Awake or Dreaming

I do not remember whether I was awake or dreaming. But I remember that at that moment I was standing in a forest clearing, wrapped in my prayer shawl and crowned with my tefillin, when the child Raphael, Daniel Bach's son, came up with a satchel under his arm. 'Who brought you here, my son?' said I. 'Today I have become bar mitzvah,' said he, 'and I am going to the Beit Midrash.' I was overcome with pity for this pitiful child, because he was docked of both his hands and could not put on tefillin. He gazed at me with his beautiful eyes and said, 'Daddy promised to make me rubber hands.' 'Your Daddy is an honest man,' said I, 'and if he has made a promise he will keep it. Perhaps you know why your father saw fit to ask me about Schutzling?' Said Raphael, 'Daddy has gone to war and I can't ask him.'

'Between ourselves, Raphael,' I said to him, 'I suspect that your sister Erela is a communist. Doesn't she mock your father?' 'Oh, no,' said Raphael, 'she cries over him, because he can't find his arm.' I asked him, 'What does it mean, "he cannot find his arm"?' 'He lost his arm,' said Raphael. 'If so,' said I, 'where does he put on his tefillin?' 'Don't worry about that,' said Raphael, 'those for the head he puts on his head, and those for the hand he puts on someone else's arm.' 'Where does he find someone else's arm?' said I. 'He found a soldier's arm in the trench,' replied Raphael. 'Do you think he can meet his obligations with that one's arm? Isn't it written that the dead are free? When a man becomes dead, he is exempt from religious precepts, and anyone who is exempt from a precept cannot exempt anyone else.' 'I don't know,' he replied. 'You don't know,' said I, 'so why did you pretend you knew?' 'Until you asked me I knew,' replied Raphael, 'once you asked me I forgot.' 'From now on,' said I, 'I will not ask. Go, my son, go.'

'And what about you?' he said. 'I have not thought about

it yet,' I answered. 'Leave off thinking,' said he. 'And what about you?' said I. 'Don't you think?' 'If I think, I don't see,' he replied. Said I, 'And is there anything here worth seeing? Perhaps the notes I put in my shoes?' 'The postman has come and brought a lot of letters with a lot of stamps on them,' he said. 'I will go and see,' said I. Raphael looked at me: 'How can you go, when you have no shoes?' 'I have no shoes,' said I, 'do you think that Leibtche's wife has taken them off so that I should not run away?'

Along came Genendel and said, 'Shut your mouth and write your poems.' 'Do you think, Genendel, that I am Leibtche?' I said. 'If so, you are wrong, Genendel, you are wrong.' Said Leibtche, 'My dear sir, how happy I am that you have come here. Last night I saw you in a dream.' 'How did you see me?' 'Quite simply, as you appear,' said Leibtche. 'You think it is simple, but I do not think it simple,' said I. 'What was it that happened with the succah?' 'I was not to blame,' said Leibtche. 'You were to blame, my dear sir,' said I, 'but I am not angry with you.' Have you heard what this Leibtche did to me? If not, I will tell you.

Before the Festival of Tabernacles, Leibtche came to me and said, 'I will make a succah on top of yours.' 'Make it,' said I. Had I any choice to tell him, 'Don't make it'? Better if he made the succah somewhere else, or if he did not make one at all, for this Leibtche, though he turns the Torah into rhymes, does not strictly observe the religious precepts. In any case, even if he made his succah on top of mine, I did not care, for, after all, he would not sit in it. So he came and made his succah alongside mine, until both of them looked like one, but his part was bigger than mine, and more beautiful than mine. I was surprised, first, because it was impossible to tell where his succah ended and mine began, and second, . . . but I have forgotten what the second point was. Said Leibtche, 'I will cover both of them.' I relied upon him and went back to my work. On the eve of the festival, as darkness was falling, I came and saw that he had spread over the succah a sheet with holes in it, and had not covered it with branches according to the law. Said I, 'Look, that just won't do as a covering: it doesn't grow in the soil and it hasn't been picked; instead it is something fastened which can become unclean.' Leibtche looked at me with a straight face and said, 'For me—it's good enough.' I asked myself: Where shall I have my meal, when I have no properly built succah? Said my wife, 'Eat in the hotel.' 'You here?' said I. 'I have not yet bought the four species and I am afraid the shops may be shut, for this is the eve of the festival and Sabbath eve as well, and they close early. What do you think? Perhaps, since the first day of the festival falls on the Sabbath, I shall not buy the four species at all, and fulfill my obligations with the congregational citron, saving a few shillings. Times are bad and whatever we save is saved, especially as my hotel bills are heavy.'

Schutzling came up to me and smiled. Oh, how threadbare was his smile, how weary were his clothes, how crumpled was the hat on his head, the velvet hat that he had bought new in honor of the festival. I greeted him and said to myself: It is nine months since his wife has seen him, and in the meantime he has grown stunted and a kind of hump has grown on his back. And his wife is so elegant, although she has grown old before her time. I wanted to talk to him about his wife and children, but I was in a hurry to buy a citron, so I left him and ran off, thinking: Surely all the shops are closed, so what is the point of this running? It would have been better to stay with my friend. And what my heart told me, my eyes told me: the Holy Day had already started and the shops were closed. I turned and ran back to my hotel, consoling myself with the thought that my host would earn the price of a meal, at a time when he had no guests and was earning nothing.

But at that moment a group of women happened to come in, so he attended to them and paid no attention to me; he barely opened up a room for me. I went into my room and wanted to wash in honor of the festival, but I found many people there standing beside the washstand. I asked them to sit down at the writing table. When they began to do so, a number of women came and called them, so they went out. 'Now I shall wash,' I said to myself. But my host knocked at the door and said, 'The food is getting cold.' I went into the dining room and found a company of old women sitting there quietly sipping soup. 'Isn't that so, Leibtche?' I said.

Leibtche nodded his head and said, 'Yes, yes, my dear sir.' I smiled at him, but his face darkened—and not his face alone, but everything around darkened, for we had gone on talking so long that the day had passed. I got up and went into the dining room.

The dining room was empty; there was no one in it at all. Along came that one whom I know but whose name I do not know. Every day he has a different face; today he looked like a Japanese and a Tartar at the same time. Everywhere there are many like him, but here in Szibucz there is no one that resembles him in the least. He was little and he was lean; his cheeks were red and his eyes black; his mustache was black and shiny and straight, with points hanging down on both sides; and he was thirty years old, give or take a year. He twirled his mustache and stood like a man who is answering someone, and said, 'I already told you so.' Then he took a magnifying glass out of the hair on his head, looked through it, and went out. What did he mean? When had he spoken to me? When had he told me so, as he said? I sat down somewhere and closed my eyes.

Krolka came in and said, 'You are sitting in the dark, sir, I'll light the lamp for you straightaway. All day we haven't seen you, sir. Heavens above, where have you been and what have you eaten? I'll bring your supper straightaway.' I put my finger on my mouth and signaled her to be silent. Krolka crossed herself and said, 'Heavens above, I did not see that the master was standing in prayer.' After Mr. Zommer had finished the Afternoon Service, or the Evening Service, he came and sat down in his place.

My mood was middling, neither sad nor joyful. Equanimity is a great quality; it is not every day that a man achieves it.

After I had eaten and drunk I went back to my room and said to myself: I will sit and read the letters that came today. While I was sitting and reading, it came into my mind to answer the senders. So I fitted the deed to the thought and wrote letter after letter, until midnight came and I went to bed like a man who has done his duty.

I did not expect to sleep, but sleep came upon me unawares, and I slept until the day dawned and it was time to get up. Morning came; it was past nine o'clock, perhaps ten. I looked at my watch; it ticked as usual but did not show the time. Since the day I went abroad, my watch is sometimes normal and sometimes out of its mind. Not every watch can stand the air outside the Land.

To rise or not to rise? From the logical point of view, there was no need to rise, for the times were all confused, and there were no fixed hours for meals. This Babtchi, may God be kind to her, treats the guests as if every morsel she gives them were a kindness on her part. Since I was not hungry I could do without her kindnesses, and if I grew hungry, Krolka would make me a light and pleasant meal in the evening.

So I lay in bed and examined my doings. I saw that I had deceived myself, for the letters I had written were not that significant, and there wasn't that much need to write them, while the letters that remained unanswered cried out from their envelopes for a reply. From the bed to the letters that were waiting for an answer was no more than a stretch of the hand, but I had no power to stretch out a hand. So I lay in bed and wondered what I could reply and how I should make my excuses for having delayed until now. Oh, how many excuses I would have to make for having delayed my replies. After an hour or two I got out of bed and, wonderful to relate, began copying down my thoughts in writing. And if I lengthened a letter that should have been short or shortened a letter that should have been long, in the world of thought it would all be equalized. So I sat and wrote all day and part of the night. Finally, I got up from the table and went into the dining room. Then I remembered a phrase that I had struggled with the night before, namely that Krolka was a good Jewess for a Christian. I recalled that it was Genendel who had said so, and laughed at the strange combination of words. When I went into the dining room, I found Mrs. Zommer weeping and crying, 'It's all true, it's all true!'

I asked her what she was crying about, but her husband

beckoned with his hand that I should leave her alone and not ask; then he stood up and came over to me, leaning on his stick, looked at me, and said, 'Mr. Schutzling is your friend, isn't he?' I nodded my head and asked, 'Has anything happened?' Mr. Zommer replied, 'Schutzling's sister is not in good health.' Mrs. Zommer got up, wiped her eyes, and asked if I had eaten. Then she went into the kitchen and sent me my supper. She did not show herself again either that night or the next day.

CHAPTER THREE AND SIXTY

The Real Truth

Genendel sat wrapped in a woollen shawl, with a blanket on her knees. I greeted her and asked how she was. She looked at me and asked, 'Who are you?' I told her my name. 'I don't know you,' said she. 'Don't you remember, Genendel,' said I, 'that I was in your house with your brother Aaron, and you made us a big meal?' 'Yes, yes, my dear,' said Genendel, 'I remember, I remember, my dear. Take a chair and sit down in front of me. What do you say to this business?' And as she spoke she dropped her head on her breast and dozed off.

After a little while she raised her head and looked at me and asked, 'Who are you?' I told her. She nodded her head and said, 'Yes, yes, my dear, I remember. Aren't you Esther's son, aren't you? Where have you been all this time? I heard you had gone away. Wait and let me remember where you went to.' She dropped her head on her breast and dozed off.

After a little while she awoke and said, 'It seems to me that there was someone here.' 'Yes, Genendel,' said I, 'I am here.' Genendel opened her eyes and said, 'You are here. Fine, fine. Who are you, my dear? It seems to me I have already seen you. Aren't you . . . ? Wait a while and let me remember.' I told her my name again. 'Yes, yes, my dear,' said Genendel, 'I know you, don't I? Tell me, where have I seen you? What do you say to my sorrows? They take a little butterfly and wring

its neck!' And again she laid her head on her breast and closed
her eyes.

Leibtche Bodenhaus came in. Genendel awoke and said,
'You here, Aaron? Sit, son, sit. What have you to tell me,
Aaron? What did the doctor say? She will live, won't she?'
'Calm yourself, Aunt, calm yourself,' said Leibtche, 'there is a
telegram from Aaron.' 'Well, so you are here, Leibtche,' said
Genendel, 'it was good of you to come. I believe you said
something; what did you say, Leibtche? Don't be so tongue-
tied. What was the telegram you mentioned?' And as she spoke
she fixed her eyes on me and said, 'You here too? Sit down, my
dear, sit down. Perhaps you will ask Leibtche what this telegram is about. Why hasn't Aaron come?'

Leibtche took out the telegram and read, 'I have fallen
ill.' 'Who has fallen ill?' said the old woman. 'Is it Leibtche?'
'Calm yourself, Aunt,' said Leibtche. 'I am well.' 'Then why
did you say you had fallen ill?' said the old woman. 'It was
not I who had fallen ill,' said Leibtche, 'but . . .'

'Are you making a fool of me, then?' said the old woman.
'What is your wife's name? That was a woman. May God not
punish me for saying so, but I never liked her. Fool, a whole
shopful of shoes you have and you sit barefoot. Take a pair
of shoes and put them on and run away. Who is this gentleman who is sitting here with us?' Leibtche told her my name
and said, 'Don't you remember, Aunt? He was in your house,
with your brother Aaron.' The old woman looked at me kindly
and said, 'I knew your grandmother. A great woman she was.
I heard she went up to the Land of Israel.' 'It was my grandmother's mother who went up to the Land,' I told Genendel.
She nodded her head affectionately and said, 'Yes, yes, my
dear. Her mother went up to the Land of Israel. What was
her name? Milkah it was. How is she? What was the telegram
she sent us? I will tell you something that will give you
pleasure. When your grandmother saw a poor woman with a
torn dress, she would take off her cape and say, *"Was told
mir das?"* and give it to her. For that was the way respectable
ladies used to talk in those days, in antiquated language. And
what she meant was, "What do I need this for?" And how is
your mother? She's dead too. So all three of them died. And

my little butterfly died too. Everyone dies but this dry bone.'
And as she spoke, Genendel beat her heart and said, '*Was
told mir das?*' And again she laid her head on her breast and
dozed off.

I got up from my chair and said, 'What has happened
here?' 'Don't ask, my dear sir, don't ask,' said Leibtche, 'more
than my aunt knows happened here. There are things, my dear
sir, that are beyond the reach of human reason.' 'I beg of you,
Mr. Bodenhaus, tell me,' said I. 'Where is the tongue that can
tell all that has happened,' said Leibtche. 'More than we ever
knew has happened.' After a little while he beckoned to me
with his finger and I went up to him. He put his two fingers
on his mouth and said, 'My dear sir, put your ear close to
my mouth, so that the old woman should not hear.' 'Who are
all three of them?' 'My dear sir,' said Leibtche, 'have you not
heard anything? Wait a moment, if you don't mind, and I will
go and see if Aunt has wakened. Praise God, she is asleep.
There is nothing better than sleep. Since the day the news
came, she has grown old all of a sudden. Oh, my dear sir,
what are we, and what are our lives? "If the flame has caught
the cedars, what can the moss on the wall expect?" Forgive
me, my dear sir, I was not thinking of you, sir, I know how to
keep my distance. I was thinking only about myself—a worm
and not a man. Suddenly one day they take three young people
and bring them down to the grave. And I am afraid, my dear
sir, that we have not yet reached the end of it. This telegram
from Mr. Schutzling does not bode well. Read it, sir, and you
will see, but read it in a whisper, so that my aunt should not
hear. Three days ago she looked as if she were forty, and now
she is like ninety or a hundred. Hush, my dear sir, Aunt has
awakened. Don't be angry with me, my dear sir, for leaving
you and running to the old woman.'

When he came back he said, 'Now, my dear sir, she is
really asleep, and I can tell you the whole story from beginning to end. You have heard, haven't you, my dear sir, that
Mr. Schutzling has three daughters from his second wife.
"Has," I say, but I should say "had," for they are no longer
here, my dear sir, but dwelling in the shadow of the Almighty,
in the world of souls. Permit me, my dear sir, to go and see if

the old woman has not wakened. She has only heard about one that was killed, but all three have been killed, she and her two sisters. On the very same day, at the very same time, my dear sir, their blood was spilt together. How did it happen? Just as it is written in the papers. That daughter of our friend Mr. Schutzling who was not being held in prison came with her comrades to the prison keepers and bribed them with a large sum of money to let her sisters go free. But the keepers did not keep their word. They opened the gates to let them escape and told the authorities. Well, my dear sir, the moment the two sisters were about to get into the automobile where their sister was waiting, they shot at them, and they died. They were wounded and died, my dear sir. And now a telegram has come from Mr. Schutzling to say that he too is not in good health. I will go and see if Aunt is still asleep.'

Genendel awoke and said, 'Aren't you hungry, son? Sit down and eat. I have just remembered, aren't you Esther's son? How is your mother? I believe I promised you something. What do you say to our sorrows? Leibtche, Leibtche, where is Leibtche?' 'Here I am, Aunt dear,' said Leibtche, 'here I am.'

The old woman nodded and said, 'Yes, yes, Leibtche, here you are. Why haven't you brought in a chair? He is Aaron's friend, isn't he? Sit, my dear, sit. What do you think, is there any hope the child will live? Even when he was a little boy I told Aaron, "Stay away from them, my son, I don't like their Knibenkopf." What they tell, that he tried to assassinate the king, that is just a story. May God protect us from the mouth of Jacob and the hands of Esau. But what I see with my eyes is not a story. He wears a black cape. What is this dream I had? Leave me alone and I can remember.'

Leibtche was deeply moved and said, 'It was a good dream you had. A good dream you had.' 'You're a good man,' said Genendel, 'but the dream was a bad dream.' 'Good will come of it,' said Leibtche, deeply moved, 'good will come of it, Aunt.' 'Be silent!' cried the old woman. Then she lowered her head onto her breast and dozed off. 'I'm afraid she may have heard what I told you,' whispered Leibtche.

Calculations

Just as the winter here is full of snow and storms, so is the summer full of rain and wind. The sun came out in full strength and the day was glad, but suddenly the face of the sun went yellow, and the wind blew, raising the dust up to the sky. When the winds were still the heavens grew thick with clouds, the rain began to fall, and the ground was blotted out and turned into mud. Because of the rains and the winds, the clay and the mud, I shut myself up in the hotel or in the Beit Midrash.

Mrs. Zommer returned to her home and her stove, and went back to cooking tasty dishes as before: first, because such was her habit, and second, because Rachel had come to live with her.

Rachel came to live with her mother, and her mother cooked tasty dishes for her. But I did not enjoy that woman's meals, because she made them with meat for Rachel's sake. And even when they remembered to make a vegetarian meal for me, I ate without enjoyment, because of the odor of fat and meat that pervaded the house, and I used to fill up the gap with fruit.

If it was a fine day I bought my fruit from the farmer, and on a rainy day I bought it in the market and ate it in the Beit Midrash, so that the people of the hotel should not notice that I was not satisfied with their meals.

Once Reb Hayim found me sitting and eating in the Beit Midrash. 'I have bought some first fruits of the season,' I said to him, 'so that I can recite the blessing, "Who hast kept us alive to this day." Will you have some, sir?' So he sat and took some.

So that he should not suspect me of just eating for my enjoyment, for these were not really first fruits, and Reb Hayim might think that I had long since recited the blessing over them, I said to him, 'I have heard that a great and righteous man was punished in the world to come because he used to eat little fruit, and the fruits came forward and denounced him because they missed his blessing.'

Another time Reb Hayim found me trying hard to open a tin of sardines. I wanted to distract his attention from the fact that I was using the Beit Midrash for my meal, so I started to denounce all the works of technology. 'They invent all kinds of machines,' said I, 'and they have not yet invented a tin of sardines that could be opened without all this trouble.' Reb Hayim made no fuss over my using the Beit Midrash for my meals, but asked if I had some bread, for sardines must be eaten with bread.

When the rains stopped and the ground grew firm, I went out for a stroll. And as I strolled, I reached the house of Hanoch's widow. She was not at home at the time; either she was sitting in the market or going out to the villages as Hanoch used to do, only Hanoch went around with his horse and cart while she went around on foot.

Reb Hayim saw me, came out to meet me, and asked me in. When I entered he said, 'I should have offered you some fruit, but there is none here. Perhaps you will taste what I have cooked for the children?' So he brought me a plate of millet and put honey on it.

Looking like good gold, the millet filled the plate; it was covered with honey refined and pure as gold, and the fragrance rose as on the sunny days in time gone by when everything was in order and the world was joyful. For many days I had not tasted a cooked dish on a weekday, and certainly not millet with honey. But I ate with mixed feelings, because I did not know whether to pay Reb Hayim for my meal, and how much to pay. Finally I put my hand in my pocket. 'No need,' said Reb Hayim. 'Do you want, through me, to win credit for hospitality?' I said. 'I wanted to win your praise for my skill,' said he. 'Where have you learned to cook such a fine dish?' I asked him. 'Tomorrow I will cook you a finer one,' said he. 'Then even cooking you can do,' said I. 'Where did you learn it all?' 'I learned many crafts in the land where I was a prisoner,' said he, 'and this is one of them.'

From then on I happened to pass by the house of Hanoch's widow once or twice a week, and whenever I passed the
house Reb Hayim would come out to meet me and invite me
to eat with him. Sometimes he would eat with me too, and
sometimes he would not eat, but would sit before me grinding
the grits that Hanoch's widow sold in the market, or he would
sit and teach the children.

On my return I would say to myself: How much longer
shall I put up with discomfort in the hotel and have all this
trouble to get my food? True, from time to time my hostess
remembers to make me a big meal, but since the house is
filled with the odor of fat and meat, I cannot enjoy my meal.
However, such a meal generally comes suddenly, after I have
eaten my fill of fruit or bread and sardines, and I eat it on a
full stomach. And if I should rely on my hostess and not eat
elsewhere, she forgets to make me a meal. Nevertheless, this
man has no reason to complain, for if he wishes he can go back
to the Land of Israel.

For several months there have been no services in the
Beit Midrash and no one has entered, except for myself and
Reb Hayim, who comes to fill the basin and sweep the floor.
Since I calculated that the time had come for me to go back
to the Land of Israel, I made up my mind to hand over the
key to Reb Hayim. Sometimes I wanted to hand it over with
much ceremony, as I myself had received it, and sometimes
I wanted to hand it to him privately. Before I had taken any
action, I heard that Reb Hayim was going to stay with his
daughter in the village. Several times she had sent him an
invitation to stay with her; but when he did not come, she
and her husband traveled to Szibucz and made him swear to
visit them. Then Reb Hayim had given his word, and now
the time had arrived for him to go.

Once, on a Sabbath eve, when Reb Hayim came to sweep
the floor and fill the basin with water, he said to me, 'God
willing, after the Sabbath I shall go to my son-in-law.'

I should have been glad that this old scholar, who had
endured so many trials, was leaving the woodshed and going
to stay with his daughter in the village, where he would have
all his needs met without any effort; but I was not glad, for

so long as Reb Hayim was here, all the cares of the Beit Midrash were on his shoulders, and now that he was going, I
should have to bring water and sweep the floor and do all
the other things that I was not accustomed to.

I began pondering all these things, and each seemed to
me harder than the other. I could already see myself standing
by the wall and filling the pitchers with water, sweeping the
floor of the Beit Midrash, all covered with dust like Yeruham
Freeman in the streets of Szibucz.

When Reb Hayim had swept the Beit Midrash and was
about to go, I asked him where he was leaving the broom.
'Why do you ask, sir?' said he. 'If you are leaving, sir,' said I,
'who will sweep the Beit Midrash if not I?' 'And when are
you leaving, sir?' he asked. 'Where to?' said I. 'Home,' said he.
I replied, quoting the Prophet, 'For my house is a house of
prayer.' 'A man's house—that means his wife,' said he, and
then he added, 'The sooner the better.' I laughed and said,
'Are you afraid the sea will freeze?' 'Happy is he that returns
to his home while he is a man,' he replied. 'Will you stand
up for a moment,' said I. 'Look, we are both of the same
height.'

I took his hand in mine and bent my head over it, and
said, 'I had a coat made in the winter and I have no need of
it in the Land of Israel, for the Land is warm and I do not
wish to bring back with me anything superfluous. I beg of
you, Reb Hayim, do not refuse me, and take the coat.' Reb
Hayim bowed his head and went with me to the hotel. I gave
him my coat and said to him, 'How heavy this coat is. I
wonder how this man's shoulders suffered under it six months
or more.' Reb Hayim took the coat and put it on. I said to
him, 'I could not stand it in the cold days, and you wear it
on a hot day.' Said Reb Hayim, 'Honor your garment when
you do not need it, and it will honor you when you do need
it.' As he spoke, he took my hand and said, 'May the Almighty
speed your way and bring you home in peace.' 'And am I
going on a journey,' said I, 'that you have blessed me with
the traveler's blessing?' Said he, 'Go slowly, peacefully, until
you have need to hurry in sorrow.'

The peg on which my coat used to hang juts out, prominent and gleaming. So long as the coat was hanging on it, I did not see the peg; when the coat was taken away the peg was visible. And it, too—namely the coat—stands prominently before me, as if it were wrapped in itself. Heaven forbid that I should cast an envious eye at Reb Hayim for taking my coat, but that is how it is with a garment: even when it leaves a body, the body remembers it. A man is not a snake, who casts his skin, leaves it lying, and goes off. Finally, the coat disappeared and went off. Apparently it had grown accustomed to being with Reb Hayim. And it was good that it had grown accustomed to him and no longer troubled my heart, for at that time I had to have a free mind so as to count my money to see if I had enough for the journey.

This does not prove that I had it in mind to return immediately, for I had not yet found anyone to whom I could hand over the key, but I thought it was worth knowing how much money I had, as Father, of blessed memory, used to do when he would count his money before going to sleep. Not like my grandfather, may he rest in peace, who never counted his money in his life, because the sages said: 'There is no blessing except in what is hidden from the eye.' So, if a poor man approached him, he would put his hand in his pocket and give. At first he would look at the money he had brought up, to see how much that poor man was worth to the Holy One, blessed be He; when he grew older he did not look, but put his hand in his pocket and gave. He used to say, 'What have you to do with the secrets of the Merciful One?' In some respects a man is like his mother's father; in others like his own father. I am like my mother's father in that I do not look how much I give, but my grandfather did not look out of respect for the secrets of the Holy One, blessed be He, and I, out of laziness, for I am too lazy to look at money. I am like my father in that I sat down to count my money, but my father was a skilled calculator, while I am not good at calculations, and I have forgotten even the arithmetic I learned when I was a child.

How did I come to have money? If I have not told this before, I shall tell it now. When my house was destroyed the last time, and the Arabs looted my belongings, the authorities compensated me with money, but this scant sum was not enough to rebuild the house as before and buy new furniture. Besides, my wife was exhausted by our misfortunes, and she could not look after the household. So she and our children went to her relatives in Germany and I went to the town of my birth to bow down at the graves of my fathers; it was many years since I had been there, for so long as I lived in peace I found it difficult to go abroad. Since my wife and children were living with relatives, she had no need of money, so I took for my own needs all the money the authorities had given me.

It was not much money the authorities gave us, but money that comes from the Land of Israel has a special quality: what is a copper in the Land is a pound abroad, for the Land has the quality of magnanimity, and there a pound counts as a copper, while in the lands of the Gentiles, which are regarded as petty, every copper counts as a pound. This man, who had come from the Land of Israel, was therefore able to maintain himself, although he treated his money after the way of the Land of Israel, namely, with magnanimity.

I have already said above that I am not good at calculations, but I saw that I had not much money left. And so that I should not enter the Sabbath ill at ease, I stopped counting my money and left it lying until after the Sabbath.

CHAPTER FIVE AND SIXTY

Sicknesses of the Body

So long as my coat was hanging in the closet, the book *The Hands of Moses* was not to be seen; when the coat was taken away, the book was revealed.

There lay the book, and I did not know what to do with it, but I knew that it had no power, for it was not the manuscript of the saintly author, but of his amanuensis Elyakim, who was called Getz. I do not say that it was an accident that women were saved by it, but no doubt there was some other reason unknown to me. I have learned from experience that there is no accident in the world, since all events are caused by the Almighty, but men have invented this word so that we should not have to give praise and thanks to the Cause of all causes.

I picked up the book and looked at it. How comely is this writing; how comely are these letters. This is how our forefathers used to write when they wrote words of Torah, for they loved the Torah and trained their script in copying it. If most of my years had not passed, I too would train my hand according to these letters, for my script has been spoiled over many years, because I wrote in haste and was not careful with the letters. When Father, of blessed memory, started to teach me to write, he dictated to me a verse from the Torah, and then a verse from the Prophets, because there is no verse in the Torah that contains the whole alphabet including the final letters. When I knew how to write all the letters, I wrote verses from the Psalms starting with the letters of my name, such as: 'Sing unto the Lord, bless His Name . . . ,' 'And he shall be like a tree planted by the rivers of water . . . ,' 'My defense is of the Lord, which saveth the upright of heart . . . ,' 'Unto Thee, O Lord, do I lift up my soul . . . ,' 'Examine me, O Lord, and prove me . . . ,' and 'Lead me, O Lord, in Thy righteousness.' When my hand became stronger, I wrote verses that I made up myself. And still it was good, for I composed prayers and supplications, and stuck them into my prayer book to repeat after the prayers. When my hand grew more powerful, I wrote songs and poems, and it was still good, for all the songs and poems I made were made in honor of Jerusalem. When my hand became still stronger I made other songs, about a different kind of love. And when a man's heart is overflowing with trivial matters he writes in haste and is not careful about his writing. Had not most of my years now passed I should look into the book and improve my handwriting.

Most of this man's years have already passed, and if it is a question of improvement he has things that need improving more. It occurred to me to use the book to improve my children's script. I thought I would pluck out a page to send them as an example. But every generation writes its own way, and how could I impose upon them the script of bygone generations? As far as I am concerned, I think the writing of the past more beautiful. But not all that seems beautiful to me seems beautiful to others.

Time is divided into several times; into past and future and present. As far as I am concerned, all times are the same to me. What was fitting in the past is fitting in the present and fitting for the future, but in this my friends disagree with me: they say that what was fitting in the past is a burden in the present and even more in the future.

Let us leave the subject of handwriting.

The sunny days are in full force and I am shivering with cold. My blood is cold and my body chilled; if I had not given my coat to someone else I would wrap myself in it.

I sit outside, in front of the hotel, and look up. The sun is hidden among the clouds and does not look at me, because it is concerned with its travels, for it has already started to journey toward the Land of Israel.

My spirits are low. When a man comes and talks to me I bow to him, as if he were doing me a favor. And when I speak, my voice is weak. I ask myself: Did he notice that my voice was weak? And since I am engrossed in that question, I do not hear what he is saying; I become confused, and my spirits get lower still. So I wait for night, when I can go into my room and lock it against everyone.

Even on the day I came back from the village I was aware that all was not well with my body, but I paid no attention to it, until my body took me by force and shook my bones.

So again I sit all by myself and meditate, like a man who has nothing in his world but himself and his sufferings. Who was the cause of the sufferings that have befallen me? Much was due to the bad food, much to food at the wrong time, and much to hunger; finally, all the causes combined into one cause, and there befell me what befell.

I went into the pharmacy and bought drugs that people take to heal themselves of fever. When I took a pinch of quinine, I felt a pain in my heart. This heart, which I thought was strong as a rock, has suddenly become weak as wax, and in its weakness a heavy stone lies upon it and presses it down.

Every day, as soon as the stars come out, I get into bed, cover myself up, and close my eyes to sleep. Before I doze off and fall asleep, a sigh is wrenched out of my heart: what a pity for that man, who has lain down and will not get up.

So that man lies in his bed, his heart beating and beating, and this stone lies upon his heart, pressing him down. Hale and hearty he came to the town, and the whole town envied him. Now he is weaker than anyone else, and he is weaker than the night before.

One night I could not fall asleep. My spirits were low and I began picturing my own death. Perhaps my sickness was not enough to die of, but my death did not budge from before my eyes.

I lit the candle, got out of bed, sat on the chair before the table, and put both my hands on both my knees. Then I lifted my left hand and laid my head on my palm. As I sat thus, I said to myself, 'You must write a will.'

I took pen and paper and wrote how I should be treated after my passing. Because I came back from the Land of Israel, they might think that I want to be taken back there and restored to its dust, so I wrote expressly that I should be buried where I died and my bones not transferred to the Land of Israel. Because he had gone abroad, it was enough for this man to make his way to the Land with all the rest of Israel. And wouldn't it be hard to roll all the way under the ground to the Land for the resurrection? But were all the wanderings I have endured in my life easy? And does this man love his body so much that he should be concerned for it even after his death?

While I was sitting and writing, I came across the key that the elders of the Beit Midrash had entrusted to me on the Day of Atonement. I said to myself: What will happen to the key if I die? Perhaps I should instruct them in my will to put it in my hand and bury me with it, like the tailor who asked for a coffin to be made for him from the table on which he had worked, and for the measuring rule he had used to be placed in his hand, to serve as a witness that he had not taken any surplus cloth for himself; or like the scribe who ordered the pen with which he wrote the Divine Name to be placed in his hands in the grave. But they were receiving credit for what they themselves had done, because before the tools came into their hands they were ordinary tools, and only after they had come into their hands and been used were they sanctified, while that key was important from the beginning. Moreover, it was even more important before it came into my hands, for it used to open the door for students of the Torah, and what right had I to leave instructions for it to be put in my hand in the grave?

So, since I did not know what to do with the key, I dealt with the matter slyly and said: I will not mention it. And I thought about my wife and children. What shall I bequeath them before my death? What shall I ask them to do first and what last? Meanwhile the night passed and the sun began to shine. I put away the will and recited the Morning Service. Suddenly I felt as if part of my sickness had gone; I went in to have my meal, and ate with appetite; for many days I had not enjoyed a meal so much. When I had eaten and drunk I took the key and went to the Beit Midrash.

CHAPTER SIX AND SIXTY

A Great Principle of Philosophy

The rains had ended and the sun shone again. A clear light rested on the houses and the stones in the street. At every step I shook off my sickness; at every step I felt that I was reawakening. My ailments had gone, but I did not know if they would not come back. Let me enjoy today, lest I may not enjoy tomorrow.

At that moment I had no conceptual picture, spiritual or physical, of the enjoyments I sought, and if I had asked myself what enjoyment I sought, I could not have replied.

But I asked nothing, and only enjoyed all I saw. Even earthly objects, which are not designed to inspire the soul with joy, gave me satisfaction and delight.

The shopkeepers stood at the doors of their shops, as if

they were standing there for their own enjoyment. One played with the rule in his hand and one chatted with the neighboring housewife. A cat jumped from the roof of a house, stretched out all its four legs, and looked ahead suspiciously. A cart loaded with wheat passed by, with a band of children holding onto it. A woman patted her hair and looked after the cart. Lolik was walking along by the side of a lady dressed half like a man, and Ignatz was dragging along after them, droning 'Pieniadze.' The postman was coming back from his work, his empty satchel swinging back and forth. In this street even things that have no tie or connection between them mingle and combine with each other and proclaim their reality. Besides the things I have mentioned here, there were many others to be seen and perceived which I have not mentioned.

When I reached the street of the Beit Midrash, it seemed to me that the old locksmith was coming out. I followed him to greet him, and saw that it was not the locksmith. I turned in another direction. As I strolled along, I reached the divorcee's inn. Little Zippora came out, her face sad.

'Why are you sad?' I said to her. 'If it is because your father is going away, he is going to your sister, for his own good and benefit.' 'Father is not going there,' said Zippora, 'and he will not be going there soon.' 'Why?' said I. 'Hannah has written that she is coming,' said she. 'All the time she asked him to come to her, and when he is about to come, she stops him!' said I. 'Hannah is my other sister,' said Zippora, 'the one they said ran away to Russia, but she didn't run away to Russia, but has been living with a pioneers' group.' 'She was living with a pioneers' group and did not come to see her father?' said I. 'She wanted to come, but she fell ill,' said Zippora. 'If so,' said I, 'she has got better and now she is coming.' 'That's what she wrote to Father, and we don't know whether to tell Father or not.' 'What does your mother say?' I asked. 'She's hesitating, too, whether to tell him,' replied Zippora. 'What is this bundle in your hand?' I asked. 'It's a shirt we sewed for Father,' said Zippora, 'and I'm going to take it to him.' Said I, 'Your father will see you are sad and he will realize that something bad has happened, and when he asks you, you will tell him, won't you, and he will be grieved.' 'If that's so,' said Zippora, 'I'll go back home and not bring him the shirt.' 'No, it's better to bring him the shirt,' said I. 'Perhaps the gift will make him happy.' 'If that's so,' said she, 'you advise me to go to Father?' 'What advice can I give you?' said I. 'Let us rely on our Father in heaven, whose mercies are manifold. Who told you that Hannah fell sick again?' 'A young man, called Zvi, from the training farm nearby, came and brought a letter from Hannah.' 'What has Zvi to do with Hannah?' 'Mother says they are bride and groom,' said Zippora. 'Bride and groom, are they?' said I. 'Do you know Zvi?' said Zippora. 'But he said he was going up to the Land of Israel,' said I. 'First he and then she,' said Zippora. 'How is it there in the Land of Israel?' 'What a question,' said I. 'It is good there in the Land of Israel.' 'If that's so,' said she, 'why are you living here, sir? It isn't good here.' 'You are a little girl, Zippora; do you think everyone only wants what is good?' 'If a man knows what is good, why shouldn't he want what is good?' said Zippora. 'Now you are talking like a grown-up. Perhaps you have heard how Genendel is? Don't you know Genendel?' 'I know her,' said Zippora, 'but I don't know how she is.' 'I will go and see,' I told her.

But I did not go to Genendel. There are days when a man seeks his own good and shuts his eyes to other people's troubles. Before I could take to heart the virtue of visiting the sick, my heart drew me to another place: to the street of the Stripa, where a house stands in which I lived when I was a child. I had been there a thousand times; that day was the thousandth and one.

I am a son of respectable folk and I love the houses where I dwelt in my childhood. First, because a man's house is his shelter from the sun and the cold, the rain and the snow, the dust and noise of the streets; and second, because a man's house is his own domain, which he acquires in this world as a portion divided off from the world, in which no one else has any portion, nor does it make any difference whether he lives in a house of his own or has rented it from someone else. Father, of blessed memory, did not build a house for himself, and therefore we would move from house to house and dwelling to dwelling. In one of them I started to learn the Bible, in another the Gemara, and in another the *Shulchan Aruch*. Some are in ruins and some half in ruins, while of others nothing has remained but the site. But there is one house that still stands; you might even say that it is more beautiful than at first: this house is the house of the old tinsmith, which Dr. Zwirn bought from him and renovated. This war destroys with one hand and builds with the other. Before the war, no one went to Zwirn. After the war everyone began to need him, for some of those who came back from the war got hold of other people's houses, the first owners took them to court, and there was no lawyer except Zwirn. So he grew richer and richer, and bought many houses, of which this was one.

This house belonged to an old tinsmith, whom they used to call the widower, for when his first wife died in childbirth during the first year of their marriage, he did not marry again, and remained a widower all his life—which was not customary in the early days, when a man would bury a wife and marry another.

By the time we moved into his house, the tinsmith had given up his trade. He and his only son lived in the festival succah in the attic, which he had made into a kind of room, and the rest of the house he rented to Father. In this succah he lived, cooked for himself and his son, and attended to all their needs. We never heard his voice all day, except in the morning, when he would come down from the attic and say 'Good morning,' looking at us through his spectacles with great affection, and go away.

These spectacles occupied my attention a great deal, because one eyepiece was made of tin and I wanted to know why, until one of my friends explained. According to his story, once after the festival a handsome child came to him and said to him, 'Father, make me a lantern; the winter is coming and we study at night.' Now that child was not born of woman and the tinsmith did not perceive it, though he should have, as we shall see later on. Three days later the child came to take his lantern. 'Wait until I make a holder for the candle,' said the tinsmith. 'I do not need a candle,' said the child, 'Father's eye will serve me as a candle.' The child took the lantern and went away. A wind blew and the tinsmith's eye began to throb. 'What is this?' said he. 'The wind is blowing into my eye, as if it were empty.' His neighbor looked and said, 'Your eye has come out.'

I stand in this street, where I dwelt in my childhood, and I remember days gone by when I went to the cheder classes and Kuba the tinsmith's son went to the Baron Hirsch school. So long as he went to school and I to cheder we were not friends, for there was an iron barrier between the cheder children and the pupils of the school, for the first were preparing for the study of the sacred books and the others for trades or professions. When he started high school and I went to the Beit Midrash, and from there to the Zionist group, we drew closer and became friends. First, because I wanted to hear from him about Homer and Mickiewicz, and second, because he wanted to hear from me about Zionism. Where he is now, heaven only knows.

Since I had told Zippora that I was going to Genendel, I said to myself that it would not be right to deceive the child, so I left the street of the Stripa and went to Genendel.

Genendel was better, but had not recovered. She sat on a chair, all wrapped up, with a woollen blanket on her knees. Her eyes were open and her lower lip quivered incessantly. Beside her sat her brother Aaron, stroking her cheek, while she stroked his hand. It was three days since he had come to town but he had not yet gone out, so he had not come to see me. His cheeks were fallen in and his eyes sunken in their sockets. 'Only think,' said Schutzling, 'for twenty years I did not see you, and when I saw you it turned out that I should see you again. Come here, my friend, and let me kiss you.' And while he was embracing and kissing me, I was afraid, for some reason, that he might suddenly smile.

Meanwhile he looked at his sister and said, 'She has fallen asleep again. I'll tell you how it happened. That was a very strange day. Whatever I tried to do didn't succeed. I said to myself: Let me go about my business. I went into a certain office where I buy my merchandise, and my heart was sad, my friend, infinitely sad. Suddenly a shot was heard. It startled me; I got up and asked, "What sound was that I heard?" Before anyone answered, a second shot was heard, and a third. I pressed my hand to my heart and ran into the street. I met two men and asked them, "Where did those shots come from?" But they said, "We don't know." I said to myself: Why do they say they don't know?—and asked two others. Or perhaps I didn't ask them, for in a moment they had vanished. I met three men I knew and asked them. Their faces were white as chalk. They pointed to one side and said that the shots came from there. "Isn't that the direction of the prison?" "Perhaps," said they, and tried to slip away. I shouted, "Tell me who was shooting and who they were shooting at?" "It seems that there was a stray bullet," replied one of them. "Tell me what you know," I said to him. "A prisoner has escaped from prison," he stammered, "and was shot." "A man or a woman?" I asked. Their eyes streamed with tears and they nodded their heads. I went up to my office and took my hat, then I ran to the prison and found out what happened.'

The old woman awoke and said, 'Aaron, do you want to go to see your friend off? If so, go and come back right away.' I beckoned to him to sit still. 'Wait a little while,' said Genendel, 'I want to ask you something. A few years ago a Jew came from the Land of Israel and sold me some earth from the Land. If I show you the earth will you recognize whether it came from there? That Jew was the emissary of a certain society they call "Midnight," because they get up at midnight to bewail the destruction of the Temple, and he had a box full of earth from various places, arranged like a kind of pharmacy. What do you think, should I believe he brought the earth from the Land of Israel, or perhaps he took it from a rat's hole?' 'Well,' I replied, 'there is a Land of Israel, and in the Land of Israel there is earth, and that Jew you spoke of came from the Land of Israel, so why should you not believe that he brought the earth from there?' 'If I have the choice of not believing him, why should I believe him?' said Genendel. 'So why did you buy it from him?' 'That's a great question you ask,' said Genendel. 'Why did I buy? If a person knew in advance what he was doing, the world would be a real paradise.'

On my way out, I went in to speak to Leibtche Bodenhaus. His room was small and neat, with a table, a bed and a chair, a little lamp, and a picture of Moses our Teacher hanging on the wall, with two tablets in his hand inscribed with the numbers from one to ten in Roman figures and two majestic horns issuing from his head. There were two books open on the table: one the Pentateuch, and the other—not to be mentioned in the same breath—the poems of Schiller; also some blue ink, and three pens, and a little ruler, with copybooks and notebooks lying beside them, neat and clean. A room so neat and fine you could not find in the whole town.

Leibtche got up anxiously and said, rubbing his hands, 'I am so happy you have come here, my dear sir. Something I had not the courage to ask has come to me unsought. Sit down, my dear sir, sit down, and I will stand in front of you.' 'You are really living like a philosopher,' said I. 'Oh, my dear sir,' said Leibtche, 'what kind of philosopher am I if I have not yet achieved a single one of the philosophic qualities. Spinoza teaches us not to laugh, not to weep, not to be enthusiastic, but to understand—and can I say that I fulfill his teaching, except for laughing? In the other qualities, my dear sir, I am a total transgressor, and I have not been privileged to fulfill even the slightest part of them. Now, he tells us not to weep, but how should I not weep when we are surrounded by troubles, whether they come from man, from his evil instincts, or from his Creator. The same applies to enthusiasm. Is it possible not to give way to enthusiasm when I see clearly how my God above bestows His mercy upon me, on me, a lowly creature, a worm and not a man, gives me inspiration and sends me rhymes for every single verse in the Torah—besides my enthusiasm for the words of the Torah themselves, which have been handed down to us from the Deity? So how is it possible not to give way to enthusiasm? And now, my dear sir, I come to the end of the words of the sublime philosopher. He says, "but to understand"—and surely, however hard we try, we shall never understand. Let us take, for example, the verse, "God is angry every day"—is it possible to understand why He is so angry? And if we have sinned against Him, does He have to make our lives a misery and direct all His blows against us? And would it not be better if He treated us according to the philosophic principle, which means: to understand? Don't regard what I say as impudence against heaven, my dear sir.

Believe me, my dear sir, I do not have the least touch of impudence in me, or anything like it, and if you were to put your foot on my neck I would bend down low so as to give you no trouble. But what shall I do? This heart is a heart of flesh; it has not reached the heights of philosophy yet; it suffers and weeps, and sometimes it brings up ideas that are foreign to philosophy. When I sit in my room, at my table, and rhyme verse after verse, chapter after chapter, it seems to me that everything is right; when I put down my pen and put my head on my hand or my hand on my head, it seems to me that nothing in the world is right, and even the world itself, my dear sir, is not right. And how can it be right if its Creator is angry with it? Our sages, of blessed memory, have consoled us a little by saying: "And how long is His anger?— a moment." My dear sir, He is angry for a moment a day, and His creatures are angry twenty-four hours a day.

'It is not my way to mention the war. If an hour has passed without my remembering it, I feel as if a kindness has been done me. But one thing I will tell you, my dear sir. During the war I served with a certain doctor. Once they brought in a soldier, a young man, whose feet had been frozen in the trenches. Since his feet were frozen he could not move away and hide from the enemy. So he was struck by a grenade splinter, which broke his teeth and smashed his gums. His legs, my dear sir, could not be saved, for there was no more life in them, so the doctor amputated them above the knee, but he repaired his mouth. He sewed and cut and sewed and made him some kind of gums from some kind of material—I don't remember what it was. When I saw that young man, who had lost his legs and had nothing left of his face but a kind of open wound, I used to turn my face away and weep, for I was afraid I might go mad. But the doctor liked to look at him, and whenever he was not busy with the other wounded he would occupy himself with him, patching and mending his face and sticking on one strip of flesh over another. And he would mention the names of famous professors and say, "Such perfect work they have never done in their lives." Meanwhile they would bring other wounded men, and there was no room for them in his surgery. So they put the earlier group in an ambulance wagon and sent them to a certain hospital in the town. Among them was that soldier I told you of. Indeed, the doctor did not want to send him away, but his clinic was full, and every day they would bring more wounded; so the doctor tied a ticket on his neck and wrote how they should treat him, how they should feed him and what they should feed him with. And he told us to take particular care of him every hour and every moment, for he had also lost the strength of his hands and could not raise them to his mouth. We traveled at the side of the wagon, looking after the wounded and protecting them, and trying to lighten their sufferings. On the way, along came a German lieutenant. He asked us if there was room in the wagon. "The whole wagon is full of sick and wounded," we replied, "and we are taking them to the hospital in town." "I will go and see if there is no place here for a German officer," said the lieutenant. So he took the legless soldier with the shattered mouth, put him off the wagon and sat him on the ground in a lonely and desolate place. Then he came and took his place on the wagon. And now, try to understand. Surely all our efforts to understand are in vain.

'Or another example, my dear sir, an example from times of peace. But why should I sadden you, my dear sir? Sometimes I apply my mind to life and I come to the conclusion that it is not worth a man's while to live, for even if he does good and never sins, surely his very existence only brings about more evil and leads to sin, because his fellows have not reached this standard, and therefore they are compelled—both because they are evil themselves and because he is good—to do him evil. Wait for me, my dear sir, a little while; Aunt is calling me. I shall come back at once.'

CHAPTER SEVEN AND SIXTY

The Street Where I Lived in My Childhood

I did not wait for Leibtche to come back, and when he went to his aunt I went away.

I made my way to the left bank of the Stripa, where a house stands in which I lived as a child with my father and mother and my brothers and sisters. Even that morning I had intended to go there, but Zippora had come along and stopped me on the road. Although Leibtche had refrained from giving me examples of the troubles he had seen in peacetime, so as not to sadden me, I was not joyful. In these days, whether you hear about the days of the war or the days of peace, you are sad.

In days gone by, the street to which I was going was a model of tranquillity. At its beginning stood the post office, in the middle was the high school, and at the end was a convent, containing a little hospital surrounded by a large garden; between them was a row of little houses, looking out on the Stripa, and opposite the post office stood a few green benches in the shadow of acacias. It was here that the intellectuals of the town used to come to open out their newspapers and read. In the evenings boys and girls used to stroll here until nightfall, and if the occasion called for it, they would add another hour.

The benches had been taken away and the acacias cut down; most of the houses were in ruins and the intellectuals of the town were dead. What was left of all that tranquillity, except for the river, which flowed as before? This was the river in which I used to bathe, and in front of which I would light a candle on the first night of the Penitential Prayers, to give light to the souls of those who had drowned there, so that if they rose to recite the Penitential Prayers they might see the light and guard themselves against the evil spirits that tried to cling to them. But the benches had been taken away and there was no place to sit; so I went to the house where I had lived as a child.

All the other houses lined up in a row, but this one jutted out somewhat from the rest, at a little distance from the street, and you went up to it on stone steps. There was a large stone in front of the house and a kind of little garden behind it, from which something like a hill arose—and behind that was the end of the world. There, when I was a child, I had dug a little pit, like the pit of Asmodeus, King of the Demons, in the *Tractate of Divorces,* and on the slab in front of the house I would play ball with my little girl neighbors. This game was not like the boys' games, such as the overthrow of the wall of Jericho and the Battle of David and Goliath, with their parallels in the Scriptures; but it involved waving of the hands and running with the feet and beating of the heart, for when you let the ball fly in the air it becomes its own master: if it likes it rolls one way, if it likes it rolls another, and you can never be sure it will come back to you.

When did I stop playing ball with the girls? It happened that once I was running after the ball, with a little girl after me. I touched her hand with mine and blushed, so I knew that this had something of sinning in it. Then I moved away from her and played by myself. Once my teacher saw me playing and said, 'What is the sense of a boy playing ball? If you want the ball, why did you throw it away? And if you threw it away why do you run after it? Only because your evil impulse incites you to run—and if that's the case, don't listen to it.'

Did the pictures in my memory precede what I saw with my eyes, or did the sight of my eyes come before the pictures my memory drew? Whenever I see this house I remember those things.

At this moment the pictures in the soul were stronger than the sight of my eyes, and although I was standing in front of the house with my eyes open, there came before me a picture of the house as it was in days gone by, when Father and Mother, my brothers and sisters and I lived in it, we in the lower storey and the owner and his son in the festival succah in the attic. A better landlord you have never seen in your life. What a pity he did not succeed in ending his days in his own house—because of Dr. Zwirn, who took his house away for nothing. What Antos Jacobowitz had not succeeded in doing, Zwirn did.

And where was Kuba my friend, the tinsmith's son? When I went up to the Land of Israel he left high school and went to the university. If he is alive, he may be a doctor or a lawyer. Once he told me, 'When I grow up I will go to a lepers' colony and look after them.'

So I stand beside that house. All the time it was without tenants and today there is someone there. Who is this that has suddenly come to live here? Hadn't I heard that there was no one in the town who would rent this house, because Dr. Zwirn did not want to let it at a low price and there was no one to pay a high one, so the house stood empty and untenanted?

I said to myself: I will go in and see; perhaps the tenant will be courteous and show me his house. This is the house where I lived with Father and Mother and my brothers and sisters; and even if Zwirn has broken it down and rebuilt it, and changed much of it, a trace of my childhood has remained in it.

I knocked at the door, but no one opened. I knocked again, but no one opened. I looked in through the window, but saw no one, except for my shadow, and I knew it was my shadow that had deceived me before.

I went away and walked back to the end of all the houses and the end of all the ruins, till I reached the convent, which was also in ruins. Since the day I came back to Szibucz, I had not been here—and if I had, it had been at night, for if I had been here during the day I would have seen this little house with a sign hanging on the door. Most of the letters on the sign were blurred and obliterated. It seems to have been used as a target for the darts the boys throw for practice. I took my time and spelled out the letters, adding from my own knowledge what was obliterated, and I read: Dr. Jacob Milch, Physician.

A tall, lean man came out, with heavy boots like those the soldiers wear in war, and breeches of the same kind, tight-fitting up to his knees. His collar was open and his beard un-kempt. As I stood, preparing to go away, he looked at me with one eye half closed and asked, 'Aren't you So-and-so the son of So-and-so?' And immediately he stretched out his hand to greet me and called me by name again. (It was not the name I bear now, but the name they used to call me by when I was a child.) I returned his greeting and cried, 'Kuba!' It was my friend Kuba, the son of the one-eyed tinsmith. And since I did not know what to say, I asked him, 'What are you doing here?' 'What am I doing here?' replied Kuba. 'I live here. Didn't you see the sign on the door?' 'What is your sur-name?' I stammered. 'I use my mother's name,' said Kuba.

So he took me by the hand, drew me into the house, sat me down on a chair, and looked at me in utter silence, as if he had lost the power of speech. Then he passed his hand over his eyes and said, 'Why are we silent? Haven't we any-thing at all to say to each other? We used to have so much to talk about, didn't we? My new name has confused you. Father was not married according to the government's laws, and they registered me in Mother's name. So my name is Jacob Milch.' And here Kuba scratched at his unkempt beard and said, 'I heard you had come here, but on the day I heard I had to go away. Now it is three days since I came back and I'm glad you have come to see me.'

'I was strolling along the street,' said I, 'and when I got here it did not occur to me that I would find you. Besides, all the time I have been here I have not asked about you; since the war I do not ask if So-and-so is alive or not, for whomever I asked about I was told: He has already gone to his eternal rest and this was the way he died. Now that I have seen you my joy is doubled.' 'If you did not know I lived here,' said Kuba, 'how did you find me?' 'I was sick,' I replied, 'and went out for a stroll; and on my way I reached here. And another thing: since the day I returned to Szibucz I have never happened to come here before.' 'You said you were ill,' said Kuba, 'but your face contradicts you. Sit and let us chat for a while. Or perhaps I should examine you first, before your ailments disappear and I have nothing left to do.' So I enumerated all kinds of ailments—fever and sore throat and pain in the heart, all the ailments I suffered from at the time or previously.

The doctor put on a white coat, washed his hands, put a mirror on his forehead, took a small mirror in his hand, and sat me down on a chair. He too sat down, opposite me, and looked into my throat. Then he said, 'Lie down on the couch.' He examined me from top to bottom and bottom to top, thumped on my heart and my spine, told me to get up, recited the names of diseases acute and chronic, and taught me what to do for my throat and for my heart. He gave me two kinds of drugs, one against the cold and one against the pains in the heart, and did not ask me to pay, for he got them free from the pharmaceutical factories in Germany to introduce them to his patients.

As he was speaking, he looked at his watch and said, 'I must go to bring my wife. I am sorry I must leave you, but I shall not let you alone until you promise to come back tomorrow for lunch. And don't be afraid I will feed you with carrion or unclean meat; I eat neither slaughtered fowl, nor moribund birds, nor carrion, nor unclean meat.' 'Are you that vegetarian doctor who taught my hostess a thousand different kinds of vegetable dishes?' 'What good did it do,' said Kuba, 'if she still cooks meat? Didn't Mrs. Zommer tell you anything about me?' 'What was there to tell?' said I. 'When she mentioned you, she called you the vegetarian doctor, and I did not know it was you.' 'And you didn't ask about me?' 'Didn't I tell you that since the war I do not ask if So-and-so is alive or where he is. Every man I come across is an unexpected find, like Schutzling, and like you.'

Kuba looked at me and said, 'Have you heard what happened to Schutzling? I met him by chance in the train. Wasn't it enough for the guardians of the law to take one of his daughters? Why did they have to take three of them all at one time?' 'You said before that you had gone away on the day you heard of me. Where did you go to, and why did you go?' 'It was simply because a doctor, one of my friends, had fallen ill and asked me to look after his patients. And now that he is better I have come home.'

'With whom did you leave your patients?' said I. 'With

themselves and their Father in heaven,' he replied. 'Besides, there is no shortage of doctors in Szibucz. More than the patients need doctors, the doctors need patients.' But here Kuba took out his watch, screwed up his eyes regretfully, and said, 'The time has come when I must go. So you have promised to come to me tomorrow for lunch. *Servus!*'

When I told Mrs. Zommer that I was invited to lunch with Dr. Milch, she said, 'Oh, so the vegetarian doctor is in town.' Then she sighed, feeling a twinge of conscience for not having taken more pains with my food, and said, 'Tomorrow you will have a satisfying meal, sir; the vegetarian doctor is an expert cook.'

Mrs. Zommer did not appreciate the vegetarian doctor, nor did the whole town. A patient who could afford to pay a doctor would call another one; those who could not would call Dr. Milch, who would come and come again even if he was not called. And that was not all: he would give a poor Szibucz patient some of what the villagers brought him, for they were devoted to him; they used to come to be cured by him and paid him in kind—with butter and eggs, bread and vegetables and fruit. The misfortune of war and all the troubles that followed had changed many values and concepts, and had led most people to exchange their earlier views, more or less, for new ones, whether good or bad. In this there was no difference between the rest of the world and the people of Szibucz. But in regard to doctors Szibucz behaved in the same way as before the war. Szibucz was accustomed to doctors behaving as men of authority, not keeping company with everyone, but coming only to patients who paid them for their trouble. There was still an element of magic in medicine: the more a doctor kept his distance the more he was respected, and if he demanded a high fee he was described as a specialist. Dr. Milch did none of these things, but met a man and spoke to him as a friend, and if the patient was poor he would bring him the food he needed. For this people looked down on him and mocked at him behind his back. 'At first I was angry,' Kuba told me, 'but then I said to myself: If they are fools, I will not change my nature.'

Next morning I went to Kuba. There was neither servant

nor maid in his house, but his room was clean and his belongings tidy. As soon as I came in, he overwhelmed me with piles of questions—before I had managed to answer one, he asked me another. Kuba wanted to hear all at once what had happened to me in many years, and if I started to tell him he interrupted me in the middle and changed the subject. He was sad, as if all I told him was only an introduction to the main thing. What the main thing was, and what he wanted to hear from me, I do not know.

Time for lunch passed, and hunger began to torment me. I told myself that very soon he would set a full table before me and I would eat my fill; I already felt something like the pleasantness of the end of a fast, when the meal is set and prepared. Kuba was moved and excited. A thousand things he told me all at once, about our friends who had died in the war and the trees he had planted in their memory in the Herzl Forest, about a few of our friends who had been unable to endure and what they had done, about one who had become a convert, and finally had hanged himself in the privy of the church. While he was talking, Kuba jumped up and brought over a thick volume of pictures, showing himself with his friends in the high school and the university, photographed together, and at the end pictures of his teachers and professors, of the hospital where he had served and the nurses who had served with him.

'And who is this?' I asked apprehensively. Kuba bowed his head and whispered, 'This is my wife.' A tall, well built woman, blonde, with pleasant, dark blue eyes, looked out at us from the picture. I took the picture in my hand and gazed at it. Her melancholy charm gripped the heart.

Kuba bowed his head again, put the picture back in its place, and looked around him like a child who has lost his way in the forest.

I took out a cigarette and lit it. 'Since when have you been smoking?' asked Kuba in surprise. 'I don't remember you smoking. Smoking is unwholesome and bad for the health. In any case, it isn't worth smoking so close to the meal.'

He got up and brought over two glasses of milk and some dry cakes, set one glass before himself and another before

me, and said, 'Let us eat and drink.' I drank the milk but left
the cakes, so as to start the meal hungry, and waited for the
table to be set and the food to be brought. Kuba sat in his
place, one eye screwed up and the other glancing at me.
Finally he opened the closed eye as well, looked at me for
a long time and said, 'I have a grudge against you and I must
tell you. When I started university I wrote you that I wanted
to go up to the Land of Israel and asked what profession I
should choose that would be of value in the Land, and you
replied, "Study medicine." ' 'Are you annoyed with me for
advising you to study medicine?' said I. 'Not for that,' replied
Kuba, 'but because you added: "All this I have written so as
not to leave you without an answer. But if you will listen to
me, stay where you are and do not try to settle in the Land." '
'I was perfectly right,' said I. 'What is right about that?' said
Kuba. Said I, 'Anyone who wants to come to the Land comes
even if he is told not to come. And if you had truly wished
to come, you would have come.' Kuba closed one eye thought-
fully, looked at me with the other, and sat in silence.

I took his hand in mine and said, 'Yeruham Freeman is
annoyed with me because he came to the Land through me,
and you are annoyed that you did not come through me. But
what is past is past. Now tell me about your other affairs.
Didn't you tell me yesterday that you were going to bring
your wife?' 'She did not come,' said he. 'Why didn't she come?'
'Because she met her husband somewhere else. I see you don't
know what I am talking about,' continued Kuba. 'Well, I shall
explain.' 'Quite right, Kuba,' said I, 'I really do not understand what you are saying. One thing or the other: if she is
your wife, you are her husband, and if you are not her husband, she is not your wife. From what you say, on the other
hand, I gather you and her husband are two different people.'

Kuba sighed and said, 'That's how it is: my wife is not
my wife and I am not her husband.' 'If so,' said I, 'what did
you mean by saying you went to bring her?' 'Do you think
she is a rich woman and can live in a hotel?' said he. 'She has
to meet her future husband and I invited her to stay with me
to save the cost of a hotel.' 'That means you separated as
friends.' 'You say as friends,' replied Kuba, 'and I can tell you

that word is nothing to the love between us.' 'If so,' said I, 'why did you divorce her?' 'Why did I divorce her?' said Kuba. 'That is a great question you ask, and I don't know how to reply. No doubt you are hungry, I shall go and bring lunch.' He went out and came back bringing two glasses of milk. He drank one and gave me the other. 'Is this all your meal?' I asked him. 'Do you think a man must fill his stomach?' said Kuba. 'A glass of milk in the morning and a glass of milk at noon, and a piece of bread, and two or three nuts, or an apple, or a pear, are sufficient for a man's food. A man does not die of hunger but of too much eating. But if you are in the habit of pampering yourself, I will boil you an egg. Today one of the village women brought me a dozen eggs. You see, I have only been back four days and already my patients are coming back to me. Do you want your egg soft-boiled or scrambled?' 'Let us go back to what we were talking about before,' I replied. 'Meaning the reason why I divorced my wife?' 'Tell me what you are prepared to tell everyone,' said I. 'I am not prepared to tell everyone, but I am pre-pared to tell you,' said he.

Kuba's heart was full and he could not endure it. He started to tell his story. 'Are you a Kohen?' I asked. 'What has that to do with it?' he asked. 'Because the members of the priestly family are forbidden to take back their wives once they have divorced them, which is not the case with Levites and ordinary Jews,' said I. 'You're all the same,' he retorted, 'give you an inch and you want an ell. To tell you the truth, as soon as I had given her the divorce I wanted to take her back. Don't you understand a thing like that?' I smiled and said, 'What happened to you is the same as hap-pened to Hartmann.' 'Who is this Hartmann?' 'A man called Hartmann,' I replied. 'One day he gave his wife a divorce, but as they left the rabbi's house he fell in love with her again and took her back.' 'That is what happened to me,' said Kuba, 'but I had not the power to take her back. Still, she visits me and stays in my house.' 'And what will her second husband say?' I asked. 'What will he say?' said Kuba. 'He doesn't say anything.' 'And does he know everything that she is doing?' said I. 'Does he believe there is nothing at all between you?' Kuba jumped up from his chair and shouted, 'What do you think of her? There isn't a truer wife anywhere in the world. If you knew her you wouldn't ask such questions.' 'Such a wife you had and you let her go?' said I. He sighed and said, 'What is past is past, especially as she is going to marry someone else. Sit still and I will show you a letter of congratulations I wrote to her and her husband for her wedding day.'

A few days passed and I did not go to visit Kuba, because I was busy with the book *The Hands of Moses*—to send it to Jerusalem, so as to pacify the soul of Elyakim, surnamed Getz, for he had come to me in a dream and I had seen that he was angry with me. My friend Kuba had told me in my waking hours, 'I have a grudge against you,' and that clerk told me the same thing in a dream.

On my way back from the post office I turned to the left of the river and went to visit Kuba. Kuba was overwhelmed with joy to see me. He seemed to feel that he lacked something, he didn't know what; when I came to visit him he realized that it was I whom he was missing. 'I was busy,' I told him, 'and did not have time to come to see you.' 'If you had come,' he replied, 'you would not have found me.' 'Weren't you in town?' I asked. 'If you don't understand of your own accord, I shall explain,' said he. 'Did you go to visit a patient?' 'The sick went to visit the healthy,' he replied. 'Meaning?' 'Meaning: I went to my wife's wedding. Yes, my friend, yes. What was it you said: "One doesn't weep over the past"? Well, I won't weep. But this I tell you: twice I made a mistake, first, when I divorced my wife, and second, when I did not take her back.' 'There was a third mistake,' said I, 'and it was the first one: when you married her.' 'Perhaps so, perhaps not,' he replied.

Zippora

After Reb Hayim had taken his leave of me he did not go to the village to his married daughter, for his other daughter, Hannah, wrote that she was coming, and he waited for her arrival. Then Hannah fell ill again and could not come.

Once I found Reb Hayim by the well. 'Still in town, Reb Hayim?' said I. He nodded his head, as if saying: Yes, that is so. From then on, I would pass him by as if he were not there, because I realized that he did not find it pleasant to be noticed. It may be assumed that since he had said he was going, he was sorry he had not kept his word.

Once I went to the Beit Midrash and found Zippora coming out of the woodshed with a basket hanging on her arm. 'Where have you come from and where are you going, Zippora?' said I. 'I've come from visiting Father,' said Zippora. 'Father is lying sick.' 'How did your father fall sick?' said I. 'He has pains in his legs,' said Zippora. 'Your father is ill and I did not know!' said I. 'Since when has he been ill? Is it good for him to be lying in the woodshed?' 'That's what Mother thought, that it wasn't good for him to be lying there,' said Zippora, 'but what can we do? We wanted to take him over to our house and he didn't want to come.' 'How long has he been sick?' said I. 'Since Sabbath eve,' said Zippora. 'Since Sabbath eve?' 'And we didn't know,' said she. 'And what was the cause of his falling ill?' 'Opinions differ,' she answered. 'Some say he went to the rabbi to take his leave and there was a scrap of chicken lying before the door, so he slipped and fell. And some say he was standing near our house and he met a drunken Pole, and that was how he fell.' 'If so,' said I, 'I shall go to him.'

'Hannah is there, too,' said Zippora. 'Hannah there too? When did she come?' 'When did she come? An hour and a half ago.' 'I had better not go now, but later,' said I. 'Why?' 'Why?

Because Hannah is there.' 'Hannah will be glad to see you, sir,' said Zippora. 'How do you know Hannah will be glad to see me?' said I. 'As soon as she came she asked after you.' 'She asked after me? Why did she ask after me?' 'I did not ask her why she asked after you,' said Zippora. 'You did not ask her?' 'I didn't ask her.' 'And what did your father say to Hannah?' 'Father didn't say anything,' said Zippora. 'He didn't say anything? He must have said something.' 'He said, "You have been sick, daughter,"' said Zippora. 'And what did Hannah answer to that?' 'Hannah cried and said, "And now you are ill, Father dear."' 'And what did your father reply?' 'Father replied, "God will help us."' 'If so,' said I, 'there is no reason to fear his illness, for your father knows that he is regarded with favor in heaven; otherwise he would not say so. And what else did your father say to Hannah?' 'He looked at her in silence and said nothing,' said Zippora, 'or perhaps he spoke to her after I had left them.' 'If so, Zippora,' said I, 'I was right not to go to him, for I would have interrupted them. What is this basket in your hand? It is empty, isn't it?'

'Mother made some dry cakes for Father, with a little coffee, and I brought them to him,' said Zippora. 'Mother says that every day after the Morning Service Father used to refresh himself with a cake and some coffee, and all the scholars in the town used to come and ask him questions about the Torah. Sometimes they would sit with him all day and most of the night, and they would hold Afternoon and Evening Services in our house, for Father—Mother says—was as great in the Torah as two rabbis, and that was why all this happened to him. It is not good for a man to be greater than his fellows.' 'And if he is greater than his fellows, what should he do?' said I. 'He should lower himself,' she replied, 'so that they shouldn't feel it.' 'If a man lowers himself a little,' said I, 'people lower him a good deal. Is that good, Zippora?' 'But in that way people don't trouble him,' said Zippora. 'Mother told me that in those days she never had an hour's rest, for they used to come from all over to trouble him.' 'Do you think, Zippora, that your father is happier now than he was then?' said I. Zippora's eyes were filled with sadness, until my heart was touched and I wanted to weep.

'An hour has passed while we have been standing here talking,' said I. 'Perhaps I shall go in and visit your father. Where are you going, Zippora?' 'I'm going to Mother,' said she, 'she is not in good health either.' 'Your mother is ill?' 'She isn't ill and she isn't well,' said Zippora. 'We have had a hard winter. Our house is old and full of cracks, and the wind comes in. And we haven't been short of snow and ice either in our house. Once we woke up and found the legs of the bed standing in ice. Mother's heart is weak too. At first her heart was excited by Father's return, when he came back all of a sudden. By the time her heart had recovered from that, the rumor came that Hannah was going to come back. Whenever I mentioned Hannah, Mother would scold me and say, "Don't mention her name in front of me." And when I didn't mention her, Mother would mention her and say, "That girl will bring me to the grave." Suddenly Zvi came and told us that Hannah was here, here and not in Russia, here in a pioneers' group, and they had plighted their troth as bride and groom. All this came suddenly, and Mother is a weak woman; she can't stand hearing news suddenly, even if it's good news.' 'So all the burden of the house is on your shoulders, Zippora,' said I. 'How do you run the house, little housewife?' 'It would be better if it was like that,' replied Zippora. 'And isn't it like that?' 'Sometimes Mother gets out of bed and goes to market, when I have a pain in my leg because of the cold,' she replied. 'Yes, Zippora,' said I, 'I have seen that your shoes are torn.' 'Poverty is no disgrace,' said Zippora. 'Poverty is no disgrace,' said I, 'it is a misfortune.' 'There are greater misfortunes than torn shoes,' said Zippora. 'Every misfortune is a misfortune,' said I. 'Are your legs swollen, Zippora?' said I. 'My legs aren't swollen,' said Zippora, 'except the big toe on my left foot—it's a little swollen.'

'How cruel of me to make you stand,' said I, 'standing is hard on the toes.' 'I don't feel anything,' said Zippora. 'I am afraid you may have said so only to put my mind at rest for detaining you,' said I. 'I never speak like that,' said Zippora. 'What do you mean—you never speak like that? What do you mean by "like that"?' 'I never say things that aren't true,' said

Zippora. 'What did you think, Zippora? Did you think I suspected you of telling a lie? I know that you always say what
you think.' 'That's what Father told me,' said she. 'How did it
happen?' said I. 'Once,' replied Zippora, 'when Father and I
were sitting together, he said to me, "Like mother like daughter." ' 'Do you think your father was referring to the question
of telling the truth? No doubt you have noticed, Zippora, that
I talk to you as one talks to a grownup. Otherwise I would ask
you which you like better, Father or Mother.' Zippora laughed.
'Surely you know what I would answer, sir,' said she. 'What
would you answer?' Zippora laughed again. 'Both the same,'
she said.

'I have detained you again, Zippora,' said I, 'but since we
are standing talking, let me ask you something: Is Hannah
like you too? Not in the matter of telling the truth, but in
other matters.' 'Mother says Hannah is like Father,' said
Zippora. 'In what way is she like your father?' I asked. But
she was silent and did not answer.

'Who is that young fellow who passed us and greeted us?'
I asked. 'I believe I have seen him somewhere.' 'That's Yekutiel, Zechariah the fodder merchant's son,' said Zippora. I
struck myself on the forehead and said, 'But of course I know
him. I was in his father's shop once. Do you know him?' 'I
know him by sight,' said Zippora, 'but I haven't talked to him.'
'But the town isn't large, and the people are few; so how is
it you did not happen to talk to him?' 'We have no horses, so
we don't need fodder, and we have no gardens, so we don't
need seeds,' replied Zippora. 'That's why I haven't happened
to talk to him.'

'Now I will go in to your father and see how he is,' said
I. 'What do you think, Zippora? Will your father let me call
a doctor for him? You know Dr. Milch. He is my friend and
he will not ask a fee. I have heard that people mock at him;
there is an example of a man who behaves just like one of
them. You cannot please everyone. If a man behaves arro-
gantly, people envy and hate him; if he lowers himself, they
belittle him. So, what should he do? He should take the middle path. But not everyone can walk in the middle. And if even

this basket in your hand, which has no will, sometimes sways to one side and sometimes to the other, how much more so do human beings. Goodbye, Zippora, goodbye.'

CHAPTER NINE AND SIXTY

Visiting the Sick

In the shed of our old Beit Midrash, on a rickety couch with three legs, supported on stones, lay Reb Hayim, covered with the coat I had given him. Beside him sat his daughter Hannah, her shoulders bowed and her feet shifting restlessly, as if the whole of her wanted to jump forward to help the sick man, and something like a question quivering on her lips: 'Father, how can I make it easier for you?' Reb Hayim awoke and nodded his head as if he were saying: 'God will help.' Hannah fixed her melancholy eyes upon him and a spark of hope gleamed from their dark depths. And the three types of reason that exist in man—pure reason, judgment, and practical reason —joined together and immediately separated. Reb Hayim looked at her and his lashes quivered. Finally, he lowered his eyes, like a father who sees that his daughter has grown up.

Hannah rose and greeted me, pressing my hand vigorously and looking at me with great affection. As she looked her face tensed and showed a kind of doubt. Almost certainly that young man Zvi had exaggerated in singing my praises, and now that she saw me she could see nothing in me. In a little while the doubt disappeared, but so did the affection she had shown me at first, and she behaved to me as one behaves to any man who is neither angel nor demon.

'This was not how I pictured you,' said Hannah. 'And how did you picture me?' said I. 'I don't know,' said Hannah. 'Where did you hear about me?' said I. Hannah blushed and said, 'Do you think people don't hear about you?' I lowered my eyes modestly and said, 'I did not know that people spoke about me.' 'That doesn't mean that they mention you favorably,' said Hannah affectionately, and a sweet smile twinkled in her eyes. I said nothing, but looked at her.

Hannah was short and dressed in a broad, thick frock, which had been blue at first and now had faded into grey. She wore heavy sandals and no stockings. A colored kerchief, covering her head from the crown, was tied beneath her chin with a light knot. Her dress hung loose on her weary limbs. No doubt her limbs were fuller when she had the dress made, but with her illness she had lost weight, and it was now too big for her. The kerchief gave her the appearance of a married woman or a peasant girl, because the Jewish girls in our district were not in the habit of covering their heads before they were married, especially at this time, when even the married women went bareheaded. But the glow in her eyes moved the heart with its purity. This was the glow of a virgin, which is not to be seen in married women or in the daughters of the Gentiles. Her brow was broad like her father's, her mouth was slightly open, and on her tongue lay something like a long '*Nu?*' as if she were asking, 'Well, what have you to say?' Since I was silent and said nothing, she fixed her eyes on me again and said, 'Well, that's it, then. . . .'

At that moment Kuba came in. He said he had been looking for me in my hotel and had not found me; so he had gone to the Beit Midrash and found the door locked, and when he had heard a voice coming from the woodshed, he had entered. 'Well,' said Kuba, 'here you are. And what are you doing here?'

In a moment he had pulled aside the end of the coat with which Reb Hayim was covered and bent down to examine the sick man. Reb Hayim said nothing and allowed the doctor to do as he liked.

Kuba took out a slip of paper and, leaning on the wall, wrote a prescription for the patient. Then he struck himself on the forehead, exclaimed to himself, 'Fool!'—tore up the slip, and said, 'But I have all these drugs at home. I will go and bring them.'

Hannah did not know Dr. Milch, and when she saw what he was doing, there came back to her face that sign of doubt, even more clearly than at the moment she first saw me.

Kuba did not notice this and asked her all kinds of things that one does not usually ask a person immediately on first acquaintance, especially a girl. In the middle of his talk, he drew himself upright and said, 'I forgot to tell you my name; my name is Jacob Milch, Doctor Jacob Milch, physician.' Hannah bowed her head a little and gave her name.

'So you are the girl who went to Russia,' said Kuba. 'What took you there? A pair of oxen could not drag me to your Russia.' 'Have you tested the strength of oxen, sir doctor, that you are so certain they could not drag you there?' said Hannah. Kuba thrust his fingers into his unkempt beard and was about to reply. 'Miss Hannah was not in Russia,' said I, 'but in a certain pioneers' group.' Kuba's face lit up and he said, 'Well, so you were in that pioneers' group, were you? If so, why did you say you were in Russia? Is it any credit to a Jewish girl to go there? Well, so you were in a pioneers' group.'

And Kuba began to shower her with questions about every aspect of life in the group; how many members there were, what they did, when they would go up to the Land of Israel, and when she was going to go. And if she was in the group, why not in the group close to our town. And he began to praise all the comrades there. But when he came to Zvi, Hannah shrugged her shoulders. 'You don't believe me because you don't know him,' said Kuba. 'I'll take you to meet him and you'll see I haven't been exaggerating.' As he spoke he turned his head toward Reb Hayim and said, 'Reb, we ought to have a talk about Zionism, but now I shall go and bring the drugs.' Kuba pulled me by the coat and said, 'Come with me.'

When we had gone out Kuba said to me, 'That girl really pleases me. But isn't she too silent? All the time she didn't utter a word.' 'You showered her with talk,' said I, 'and did not give her a chance to speak.' 'You're right,' said Kuba, 'sometimes I talk too much. Did I really talk too much this time, too? Let us go to the pharmacy.' 'You want to go to the pharmacy?' said I. 'Didn't you say you have all the drugs at home?' 'I have some of them at home,' he replied, 'and those I haven't I shall take from the pharmacist and prepare them myself, so that it won't cost him anything. A clever girl, isn't she? What is her name? Hannah her name is. Not an ugly name.'

I followed Kuba into the pharmacy. From the way the pharmacist spoke, I saw that he had not much respect for Dr.

Milch. During the conversation, Kuba took him aside and whispered in his ear. Apparently he didn't have enough money to pay, but the pharmacist patted him on the shoulder and said courteously, 'Never mind, Doctor,' and gave him the drugs.

I asked Kuba if there was any hope that Reb Hayim would get well quickly. 'It's a slight dislocation,' said Kuba, 'nothing at all. How old is Reb Hayim? If he hadn't been an old man everything would have been all right. In any case, he won't dance at his daughter's wedding.' 'You mean at the wedding of Hannah and Zvi?' said I. 'What Zvi?' 'That young man you were praising so much.' 'Is there something between them?' asked Kuba. 'So you let me make a fool of myself and did not give me a hint? In any case, it is good that you've told me now. You know that girl really pleases me.' And as he spoke he scratched his beard. I smiled and said, 'You have already told me that.' 'What did I tell you? And if I told you, has she become uglier in the meantime? When did I tell you? I've never spoken about her. I've just seen her for the first time, haven't I. Well, so she's engaged to Zvi. I must say our fellows are handsome and they have good taste. And she is not beautiful, but she has another quality that is more than beauty. Don't you think so?' 'What quality is that?' 'I don't know what it is,' said Kuba, 'you can't see anything in her face, but there is something about her that I can't describe. I have seen many beautiful women without losing my head over them, except for my wife, or—as you insist I should say— my former wife; besides her face and her nose being beautiful, her soul is beautiful. Now let us go and mix the drugs.'

So Kuba took a kind of long bowl and a pharmacist's spoon, and ground drugs and mixed them with each other. 'Do you remember Reb Hayim in his greatness?' said he. 'The whole country was in a tumult over the controversy. Where was the sense of it? We all have the same Torah, haven't we? So why did we have to argue with each other? All the troubles of the Jews come from nothing but controversy. Sometimes I say to myself: We are no better than the Gentiles; they make war upon each other and spill visible blood, while we make controversies and spill blood that cannot be seen. Well, you

said that girl is engaged to Zvi. Good you told me. I don't
interfere in things that are none of my business. The affair of
Babtchi is in a bad state. The rabbi's grandson has found another girl, the daughter of his father's friend. The apple always ends up near its tree. So Babtchi has no one left but
Zwirn. May she please him. The swine stretches out his hoofs
and finds what suits him. Well, I've finished making up the
drugs. Now let us put them up in a packet and take them to
Reb Hayim. And if they're not *zierlich manierlich* like those
of the Prussians the pharmacist hates—and I don't like them
either—the main thing is, they will do their job. Perhaps you
are hungry? Take an apple or a pear and put it in your
pocket; I'll do the same and we'll eat on the way. I forgot to
tell you, Schutzling was asking after you.' 'When did you see
him?' 'When he was about to leave.' 'So you are Genendel's
doctor. How is she?' 'I don't know,' said Kuba. 'What do you
mean you don't know?' 'I am no doctor for patients who make
their doctors sick. I was visiting Bodenhaus.' 'Has he got a
pain in his legs too?' 'Not in his legs, but in his right thumb.
It's a pain that comes from too much writing. Writers' cramp.'
I laughed and said, 'And he told me the rhymes flew out without any trouble by the inspiration of God above. It seems the
inspiration of God above does not rest on his fingers.' 'You're
a bad man,' said Kuba. 'But I love good rhymes,' said I. 'I
have no need of poems,' said Kuba. 'I don't read them. What
do you think of Bach?' I laughed and said, 'You'd better ask
about his daughter Aniela first.' 'Why?' 'Because her name
begins with *aleph*.' By this time we had already arrived at
our destination.

Reb Hayim made light of his illness; he was sorry we
were taking so much trouble with him. But this was not the
doctor's opinion. As he left, he said to me, 'I am not worried
about his legs; it is another disturbance of his that worries me.'

CHAPTER SEVENTY

Reb Hayim's Testament

A slight dislocation in the leg had been followed by another, more serious illness, which afflicts old men as a result of much lying down. Reb Hayim accepted his pains lovingly; there was no perceptible change in him and he did not utter a groan. Every day Kuba came to change his drugs and talk with Zippora. Hannah and Zippora took turns sitting with their father, Hannah at night and Zippora by day. Sometimes Zippora would leave him, because her mother was tired out and could not stand and cook; then Zippora would have to cook for the whole family—including her father, for since the day he fell sick Reb Hayim was not fussy and ate whatever they brought him.

Once, when he and I were alone together, I asked him, 'How are you?' He whispered to me, 'God will do whatever He thinks right,' and closed his eyes.

I thought he was sleeping, and saw that he was muttering with his lips. I bent closer to him and heard him saying, 'And these are the cases in which a fowl is fit for eating: if there is a hole in the gullet or a slit . . .' When he noticed me he whispered, 'This was the halacha over which the controversy started.'

After a little while he raised his head somewhat and said, 'When a man is lying like this, he lacks nothing. He could even be content; except that man is defined as a being that moves, not as one that stands or lies. For the essence of a man's existence in the world is to acquire good deeds—and so long as he is able to walk.'

I was shocked and distressed, not because of the things he said, but because he spoke at all. Reb Hayim, who used to nod his head instead of speaking, had begun to talk at length.

In all his talk he said neither good nor ill of any human

being. That was one of the things that surprised me about
Reb Hayim: he did not mention any man in connection with
the things that had happened to him, but would open every
talk by saying, 'The Cause of all causes, in His blessed mercy,
brought it about,' and when he concluded he would say,
'Through the Cause that produces all causes, this event was
caused.' You and I, dear brethren, are also aware that everything comes from the One Master of the world, but you and
I add the deeds of human beings to His deeds, as it were, as
if He and they were partners in the matter, while Reb Hayim
did not bring in any human being as His partner.

Finally he held out to me an old, creased sheet of paper
and asked me to open it immediately after his death, before
they brought him to his last resting place. He saw that there
were tears in my eyes. He took my hand in his and said,
'The hour of my death has not yet come, but it is close, and
I ask that the terms of my testament should be carried out to
the full.'

An hour later Zippora came, followed by Kuba. The doctor examined the patient and stayed a long time. When he
left I followed him and told him that Reb Hayim had entrusted me with his will. Kuba took off his hat, shook it this
way and that, and said nothing. I was afraid to ask if he
thought Reb Hayim's death was near, and I was afraid he
might tell me of his own accord, so I went my way. Kuba put
on his hat, clasped his hands behind his back, and began walking away from me, jerking his feet in front of him. Finally he
turned his head and shouted at me, 'Why don't we see you?'
'What do you mean you don't see me?' said I. 'Don't you see
me now?' 'Because you don't come to visit me,' said Kuba.
'If I don't come to see you,' I replied, 'it is because I am taking
care of the sick man.' 'You are taking care of the sick man?'
said Kuba, 'then you can come to see me next week.' 'Next
week?' 'Servus!' My heart felt weak and a mist gathered before
my eyes. I stood there in the street and did not know where
to go. It was impossible to follow Kuba, for he had said I
should come to him next week, and this week was not yet
over. And it was impossible to go to Reb Hayim, for fear of
what he might notice in me.

That day was Sabbath eve. In the hotel they were baking and cooking and making everything ready for the Sabbath. If I am not mistaken, a new guest had arrived—or perhaps there was no guest, but I only thought there was one. Because of that guest I found it hard to stay there, and I went back to the sick man.

Vus hot ihr sich eppis in mir ungetchepit? I said suddenly in the language the people of my town speak, and I was astonished. First, because there was no one there who was following me, and second, because I thought that when I talked to myself I spoke in the Holy Tongue, and now I was speaking in the language of every day.

This man who suddenly molested me and suddenly disappeared, and appeared again all of a sudden, had a face like a butcher but a beard like an official rabbi. As I was engrossed in my thoughts, I paid him no heed. But he paid heed to me, and said, 'Are you going to see Reb Hayim?' 'How do you know I am going to see Reb Hayim?' 'Because I am going to see him too.' I said to myself: He is leading a lamb with him, so how can he go in to see Reb Hayim? He bent down, plucked a handful of grass, thrust it into the lamb's mouth, and said, 'Moses, why are you looking that way?' 'Are you talking to me?' said I. 'My name is not Moses, and I am not looking that way.' 'Moses,' he said to me, 'do you mean to tell me you are not looking that way? Now, that pigeon, which is flying there, aren't you looking at it?' 'There is no pigeon here,' I replied, 'and my name is not Moses.' 'What else then?' said he. 'Perhaps it is a bear dancing there on the rabbi's hat?' I reproached him with '*Vus hot ihr sich in mir ungetchepit?*' Said he, 'If you like, I will show you a marvel. You see this lamb? Look, I pull the rope and it disappears.' I looked this way and that and said, 'Where is the marvel you spoke of?' Said he, 'Since you believe I can do it, there is no need for me to take the trouble, but so as not to leave you empty-handed, watch me rubbing myself against the wall and saying "*Mu'es*" and you will imagine that Ignatz is here.' 'That is no marvel,' said I, 'for here is Ignatz already standing before me.' 'And I?' He struck his hat and said, 'And where am I?' 'You? Where are you?'

'Who was that man who was leading a lamb?' I asked Ignatz. Ignatz raised his head, looked at me through the three holes in his face, and said, 'There was no man here and no lamb.' 'But I saw them myself.' 'No doubt the gentleman was kind enough to imagine it,' said Ignatz. I changed the subject and said, 'It is hot today, Ignatz. I'm afraid rain will fall.' 'It's a hot day, sir,' said Ignatz. 'What is that flying over there on the roof of the Beit Midrash?' said I. 'It's a crow or a pigeon,' said Ignatz. 'If so,' said I to myself, 'that man was telling the truth.' 'What man?' 'The man with the lamb.' 'What lamb?' 'The lamb the man was leading, who is called "Moses." ' 'Moses? But who here is called Moses?' 'That's what I am asking you.' 'There are a few men called Moses in the town,' said Ignatz. 'So why did you say "I don't know"?' 'But you were asking about a particular Moses,' said Ignatz, 'and not just any Moses. *Mu'es*, sir, *mu'es*.' I gave him some money and moved on.

I went in to Reb Hayim and found Hannah sitting there dozing. She woke up, wiped her eyes, and stood up, asking me to sit. 'I am prepared to sit down,' said I, 'so that you can go home and rest a little.' 'I shall wait until Zippora comes,' said Hannah. Her father fixed his eyes upon her imploringly and said, 'Go, my daughter, go.' Hannah looked into her father's face and went out unwillingly.

'How did you pass the night?' I asked Reb Hayim. Reb Hayim bent his head toward his heart and a clear light shone from his eyes. After a little while he got out of bed and left the room. When he came back, he washed his hands and recited the benediction, 'Who created man with wisdom.' Then he got back into bed, lay down flat, and said, 'Now I am being called.'

I looked to see who was calling him. Reb Hayim noticed this and smiled.

At that moment his face shone like the flame of a candle and his eyes glowed like the sun. He washed his hands again, recited the 'Hear, O Israel,' and gave up his soul.

When the people from the Holy Burial Society came to wash his body I remembered the sheet of paper Reb Hayim had given me, and opened and read it. The will was carefully arranged in paragraphs, of which there were seven:

'a) To you, good people, I call, to you, the God-fearing men of the Holy Burial Society, who perform unselfish charity: bury me in the portion of the field where they bury the premature infants.

'b) I beseech and implore you not to set any tombstone on my grave, and if my relatives wish to make a mark on my grave let them make it of wood and write on it in simple letters, "Here lies Hayim," and add nothing more but the initials of the phrase "May his soul be bound up in the bond of everlasting life."

'c) I beseech and implore the illustrious President of the Rabbinical Court, may he live long and well, to forgive me for harassing him and offending him in public; although he surely has forgiven me of himself the humiliation I caused him, in any case I beg of him to cast out any grudge from his heart.

'd) I beseech and implore anyone to whom I have done any injury, either in body or in property, by controversy and argument—if they are alive I beg of them to pardon me with all their hearts, and if they have passed away and the place of their burial is known, I beg of merciful men, if they should happen to come across their graves, to go to beg pardon of them in my name. But they should not spend money for this purpose, as in hiring a quorum of ten men to go to their graves.

'e) I beseech and implore my daughters to show respect to their mother and not trouble her by word or hint, and I particularly beg pardon of her for all the trouble I have caused her in this world.

'f) Since no man knows his last day, therefore I charge, with the force of the charge to fulfill the commands of the dead, that, if I die and am buried on a day on which supplications are recited, no funeral orations should be delivered, and no orations be pronounced after the seven days of mourning.

'g) But I ask that a chapter of Mishna should be studied for the repose of my soul. For this purpose I leave a sum of money that I have earned by the labor of my body. And I look forward to the mercy of heaven and the mercy of men to deal graciously with my soul, studying the Mishna with the commentary, word by word, and reciting the Rabbinical Kaddish after they study, according to custom and habit. And after the Rabbinical Kaddish, they should recite Psalm 102, the prayer of the afflicted. And I am certain and confident that my virtuous daughters, long may they live, will bear me no grudge that I spend the sum of money which should have come to them as an inheritance for my own benefit and pleasure, and I hope for the mercy of heaven, for in the welfare of their father they shall fare well all their days.'

Furthermore, it was written at the end of the sheet: 'The chattels that I leave behind, such as the cooking stove, the vessel in which I boiled my coffee, my garments, such as the coat, and any other chattels that may be of any use or benefit, should be handed over as an unfettered gift to the poor and afflicted man, the honorable Yitzhak, known as Ignatz. And nothing should be altered of all the matters I prescribe this day, as if it were the charge of one at death's door, although I have written all these things being of as good health as any man. And may my words bring blessings to those who heed them.'

So Reb Hayim went to his last home and was privileged to be buried on the day he died. As we were walking behind his coffin, the rabbi bent forward and said, 'Reb Hayim was worthy to have a great funeral oration pronounced at his burial, for the funeral oration of a righteous man arouses men's hearts to penitence; but what can we do when he died on the Sabbath eve, on which no funeral orations are pronounced? Besides, he charged that there should be no oration, did he not? As a result of this, he belongs to the category of great scholars who have not been properly mourned, for according to the law it is forbidden to mourn him, and we must beg for mercy, that we should not suffer those penalties prescribed in the Gemara for a great scholar who was not properly mourned.'

After the Death of Reb Hayim

After the sealing of the grave, Zechariah Rosen took hold of me and brought me to the old graveyard, where he showed me the graves of the great men and rabbis of Szibucz, who glorified our town with their learning and revealed its merits to the world. Some of them were his relatives, some his friends' relatives, and some his wife's—she, too, was his relative, for high-bred families are in the habit of marrying into each other. As we stood there, he read out to me every single tombstone; even if there were stones on which not a single letter could be made out, Zechariah knew what was written on them. And he told me more than was written. It would be no exaggeration to say that if these things were included among the marvelous tales in *The Chain of the Kabbalah* they would be a great novelty.

When the day was over I came back to the town. I felt so weary that I did not go to synagogue, but welcomed the Sabbath in the hotel.

Mrs. Zommer lit the candles, recited the blessing with a tear in her eyes, and went to Rachel, while Mr. Zommer sat at the end of the table and recited the prayers sadly. While he was praying, Mrs. Zommer came back and stood in front of her husband, clasping her hands in anguish and urging him to shorten his prayers and go to call Sara Pearl, for there was no other midwife in the town.

Mr. Zommer took off his sash, took up his stick, and went off like a man who is going toward grief and pain, for since the day Rachel married Yeruham there had been no peace between the house of Zommer and the house of Bach. Krolka came in, went out, and came in again, opened the outside door, and went out with a candle in her hand to light the way for those who were expected.

Sara Pearl arrived and went in to Rachel. She stayed

435

with her for an hour, soothed and encouraged her, kissed her on the forehead and called her 'daughter.' Rachel clung to her, like a daughter to her mother. When Sara Pearl came in, it seemed as if the two families had made peace with one another. As she was about to go, she met Yeruham, which was a hard thing for the house of Zommer, for it reminded them of Erela's shame.

Because of Rachel's trouble, Babtchi's troubles were forgotten. Riegel had lost interest in her, and David Moses had become betrothed to another. Two or three weeks before, David Moses had written to Babtchi that she was his only love in this world and the next (he had caught his father's style); without her he had nothing to live for. Then came a newspaper giving his name together with that of his betrothed. So who was left for Babtchi? No one but Zwirn. And he began to behave to her in lordly fashion, since the desire for money had grown stronger than the desire for love, and exercised a pull on it, as a pound pulls on a copper. Sometimes Babtchi beamed at Zwirn as if his heart were still in her pocket, but he made her work like a man and stinted her wages. In this world, everything is twisted. Even the things that are deformed become still more deformed.

Babtchi sits dressed up in her best clothes. These are the clothes she has been wearing since the day she cast her eye on the rabbi's grandson. Because of them, she abandoned her old friends; in them she showed affection to Riegel; and they were bought with Zwirn's money. If Zwirn does not change his mind before the clothes wear out, Babtchi will one day put on again her leather jacket, which is crumpled and worn out; she cannot buy another, for although there are guests in the hotel, the profit on them is not enough to buy new clothes.

Because of the guests, this guest who has come to stay for a while is ignored. He still lodges in the finest room in the hotel, but no attention is paid to his food and he is not served with proper meals. The guest does not protest or complain; for no one dies of hunger, only from too much eating, as Milch said. Sometimes the guest wonders whether he should go and lodge with Kuba, who says, 'Better to live with me and not pay, than stay in the hotel and pay. Are you so fond of the smell of meat and fat, so fond of the noise and tumult, that you've stuck yourself away in the hotel?'

The guests who are to be found in the hotel every day are various: just as their affairs are not similar, so are they not the same. Of those two guests who came on the morning of the Sabbath eve, one of them is just an ordinary man who could serve as a presence at a quorum for prayer or—if you will excuse the comparison—at a game of cards; while the other has a personality, with a fine beard and a broad belly and good sense, but he has not been doing good business lately. Perhaps you have heard the story of how a certain man leased a forest from a certain lady and paid her in full for the lease, but it turned out that her husband had sold it to Pan Jacobowitz without his wife's permission. The man heard that Zommer's son was friendly with the lady and could do him a good turn, but he did not hear which son, and he understood that they were talking about Dolik, who was a shrewd and crafty fellow. So he attached himself to him and engaged him in conversation so as to make friends with him, while Lolik seemed to him to have the appearance—if you will excuse me—of a girl who had been seduced, and was not worth talking to. And when Lolik made an effort to talk to him, he replied unwillingly, like those who are so engrossed with their own interests and begrudge every word that does not pay.

At that moment Babtchi raised her head and looked at Yeruham. 'How did it turn out,' she asked her mother, 'that you gave the younger in marriage before the elder?' 'What has come into your head all of a sudden?' said her mother. 'If you couldn't do without Yeruham,' said Babtchi, 'you could have married him to me.' Yeruham raised his eyes and looked at Babtchi. Let us pray to the Cause of all causes that these eyes are not the panders of the heart.

After we had got up from the table I said to myself: If I go into my room Yeruham will come to see me, but I am tired and weary and cannot bear company. So I went outside, for walking tires the body, while idle talk tires the soul, and a man should always sacrifice his body if only he can save his soul.

Then the rain started dripping. I went into my room and

took a book by a certain author to read. Great things I did not find in it, and the little things it contained did not attract me. I stopped and looked out of the window, and it seemed as if the rain had stopped, so I got up and left my room.

Dolik came up and said, 'Are you looking to see if the rain has stopped?' (Of all the people in Szibucz, there was no one with whom I was so sparing of words as Dolik.) I nodded my head and said, 'Yes.' 'It stopped a little while ago,' said Dolik, 'and it's started to come down again.' I nodded and said, 'Yes.' 'Do you want to go out? In my opinion it is not worth your while, for you may be caught in the rain.' 'What a pity,' I said. 'If so, I will go back to my room.' 'Perhaps you will permit me to visit you in your room?' said Dolik. 'I will not detain you long.' I said to myself: Better one friend than a thousand enemies, so I said to him, 'Come in.' As he entered he said, 'Well, sir, so you live in this room. Isn't it surprising that since the day you came to live with us I have not entered your room.' I said to myself: One enemy is worse than a thousand friends. I nodded and said, 'I am surprised, too.' 'Are you tired, sir?' said Dolik. 'Yes, I am tired,' said I. 'Reb Hayim's death has made an impression on you,' said Dolik. I nodded and said nothing. Said Dolik, 'He was a saint.'

I thought to myself: Of all those who have sung Reb Hayim's praises, not one of them has used this word, which fits him so well, except this Dolik. 'You are right, Mr. Zommer,' said I, 'he was a saint.' 'All that slanderous talk that his daughter was in Russia was only a slander,' said Dolik. 'She wasn't in Russia, but in a pioneers' group. What makes such a refined girl work so hard? From the clothes she wears she doesn't seem to have made money there.' 'She is preparing herself for the Land of Israel,' said I.

'So I heard,' said Dolik, 'but what for?' 'To live a different life,' said I. 'A different life?' 'There are people who are not satisfied with this life we live here,' said I, 'and they look for a different life. Some make their lives by actions and some without actions.' 'I don't quite understand you,' said Dolik. 'How can I explain?' said I. 'Perhaps you can explain it to yourself. You said, didn't you, that Reb Hayim was a saint—which you do not say about any other man. Why? Because he

used to behave unlike other men.' Krolka came in and said,
'The gentleman who leased the forest is looking for Mr. Dolik.'
'I am busy,' said Dolik, 'and I can't come.' As soon as Krolka
left, he called her back and said, 'Tell that fat fellow that in
the meantime he can stand on his head, and if time hangs
heavy on his hands he can sing hymns. I see you are tired,
sir, so I'll go. Adieu.'

CHAPTER TWO AND SEVENTY

Between Me and Myself

On the first day of the week, after breakfast, I went to Kuba,
in order to go with him to visit Reb Hayim's family in their
mourning. On the way I said to myself: Reb Hayim has passed
away without leaving a son to recite the Kaddish for the elevation of his soul. Let me perform an act of unselfish kindness
for his sake, and study a chapter of Mishna. Immediately I
fitted the deed to the thought and went in to the Beit Midrash.

True tranquillity and peace filled the Beit Midrash, utter
tranquillity, the like of which I had not seen for many days.
The hill opposite shaded the windows and excluded the sun,
and the light of the Beit Midrash looked like light that has
been severed from the light of the universe and shines by
itself.

The lectern stood silent and the reading desk that was
on it. Opposite them stood the chest, and on it the prayer book.
For months the prayer book had not been opened, and no
prayer had risen from it, and the doors of the Ark had not
been opened, and no Scrolls of the Law had been taken out
for reading, except by the dead who come to the Beit Midrash at night. It was the same with the other books: they lay
in their cases, one here and another there, as if they were
prostrate and could not get up.

The kindness I had come to do for Reb Hayim escaped
my mind, and I picked up a Gemara. I was engrossed in my
study until noon came and the sound of the bell was heard

from the church. At this hour all the workers in the town stop their work and sit down to eat their meal. I raised my voice until the voice of the Torah overcame the voice of time.

The bell rang out again to spur the workers back to work. I, who had not stopped for a meal, continued to study, but in the morning I had studied standing, one foot on the bench and one on the floor, while now I studied sitting.

There in the hotel they had already laid the table and taken the food off the stove, and if I did not hurry my food would get cold; my hostess would be annoyed at having taken all her trouble for nothing, and perhaps Krolka would be annoyed too, because I was keeping her from washing the dishes.

A man's thoughts do not stay still. No time had passed before another thought came into my mind. Only think: a man goes out to the market, and sees two men holding onto a garment. One says: I found it; the other says: I found it; one says: It is all mine; the other says: It is all mine. If he is a lover of peace, he steps aside, so that he should not see his fellows in their anger. He goes into the Beit Midrash, opens the Gemara and finds a similar case there; so he becomes fond of them. Why? Because he has studied a page of Gemara and seen that they are spoken of in the Torah. This man is I. Though I am not well versed in the ways of the world, when I study a page of Gemara my heart fills with love and affection for even the trivial affairs of Jews, since the sages spoke of them. Great is the Torah, for it leads to love.

The day drew toward evening and the time came for the Afternoon Service. I stood up to recite a hasty prayer, so as to return immediately to my studies, but when I started 'Happy are they that dwell in Thy house,' I drew out the prayer, because it praises those who sit in the Beit Midrash.

There are some who pray quickly and say every word in haste, because they love every single word and wish to swallow it, and there are others who draw out their prayer and pronounce every word deliberately, because they love every single word and find it hard to part from it. I do not know who is more dear to me, the one who runs through his prayer or the one who draws it out. As for myself, I pronounced every

word in haste, because I loved it, and for the same reason—
that is, because of my love—I said it again. As I did in the
Afternoon Service, so I did in the Evening Service. A man
should always try to pray with the congregation, for the prayer
of many is heard, but at that time this man forgot that there
is a congregation and that there are many, but the Holy One,
blessed be He, filled, as it were, the entire universe. And this
man diminished himself until he was as nothing, so as not
to take up the room of the Divine Presence.

After finishing my prayer, I rose and lit a candle. I had
hardly fixed it in the candlestick before I was back at my
studies. If I studied aloud during the day, I raised my voice
more at night. From hour to hour the voice changed, as if it
issued from the Gemara itself. And since the voice of the
Gemara is sweet, I bent my ear to listen. The candle in my
hand was nearing its end, but I did not budge. Perhaps you
have once heard that the devotees of study used to hold a
candle between their fingers, so that if they dozed off while
studying they should scorch themselves and wake up to attend
to their studies. This man had no need for such a stratagem,
for he that learns the Torah for love neither slumbers nor
sleeps, and does not stop except to light one candle from
another and a third from the second.

Between one candle and the next I said to myself: At
this hour there is not a man in the town sitting and studying,
except myself. It was not for boasting's sake that I thought
thus, but because I rejoiced that I was preserving the world.

How many hours slipped by in this way? When I rose
from my studies and went back to the hotel, the whole town
was asleep, except for the rabbi's house. It seemed that he too
spent his nights studying the Torah. Or perhaps he was only
writing his own Torah about the Torah, so that I had preserved the world alone.

I opened the door of my hotel and went in. All the people
of the house were deep in slumber. Even from Rachel's room
nothing was to be heard. I walked on tiptoe until I reached
my room.

The lamp was lit, with the wick turned down, and it
glimmered slightly through the darkness. Next to it stood a

dish covered with a plate. Blessings on my hostess for preparing me an evening meal. I ate my fill, went to bed, and slept. It was many nights since I had had such a sweet sleep.

After taking my breakfast I went back to the Beit Midrash, and as I had done the day before so I did today, only I started at the beginning of the tractate, so as to study the Gemara in the correct order and master one tractate, instead of snatching one section here and another there.

Those were beautiful days. The three days of mourning before the Fast of Av passed and the days of consolation arrived. I felt as if the whole world were new, for I was born on the Ninth of Av, and every year, at this season, this man's heart renews itself and reawakens.

To be brief, the month of Av was at its hottest, so I did not have the trouble of keeping the stove alight. When the stove is not lit, no one comes to warm himself. All those who were accustomed to come to the Beit Midrash had gone out to seek their livelihood wherever they imagined they could find it. One was standing at the door of his shop chewing his measure, one was chewing the air, while another was going around the villages exchanging utensils for food, and would that all their trouble were not in vain.

So long as a man sits and studies, his joy is great. When he stops learning, his heart is grieved. So long as I sat and studied I was happy, but when I interrupted my learning I grieved over days gone by, when I could have sat and studied and did not do so. Like wells that are dried up, so those days and years stood before me, empty and dark. Where was my wisdom, where was my sense, how had I allowed those days and years to slip by in vain? Father in heaven, Thou allottest life to all living things and teachest man understanding— where is the understanding in the life Thou hast allotted me? 'The foolishness of man perverts his way, and his heart frets against the Lord.' The foolishness of this man has perverted his way, and instead of rebuking himself, his heart frets against the Holy One, blessed be He.

But does everything depend on a man's deeds, and are his fortunes and misfortunes caused by his actions? Does not the cause have a first Mover, so why is punishment visited on man? On this matter, the inquirers have written at great length and explained it in their own way. However, I explain it not like them, but as our sages, of blessed memory, did when they compared it to the case of a man who has two ways before him.

Let us return to our subject. 'I thought on my ways, and turned my feet unto Thy testimonies.' I regulated my thoughts with good counsel, and my feet, which had been leading me to markets and streets, fields and forests, I turned back to the Beit Midrash to study Torah.

According to my calculations, my money was enough to keep me for a month, or with economy for two. I had already been wondering what to do from now on. Was I to make my lodging in the woodshed and sleep with my hand under my head, as Reb Hayim, may he rest in peace, used to do? Besides, a man needs other things, like bread to eat and clothes to wear. Now you are clad like a gentleman, but what will you do for the morrow? A man's clothes do not last forever, and in the end you will be like that foreigner whose image you have been seeing in your imagination for several days.

Who was this foreigner? Well, one Sabbath eve at dark a man came to the hotel in our town, well dressed, with a gold chain hanging on his waistcoat, a green hat with a peacock feather on his head, and a leather satchel in his hand. He was received with great honor, because he seemed to be rich. He came in and sat down at the table and asked for a glass of tea, which was brought him. He pushed it away and said, 'I found a fly in it.' So they apologized and brought another. He made a wry face and said, 'There's a fly in the glass.' They brought him another glass, but he would not drink. When they brought him a fourth, he started to shout. 'You are giving me flies to drink.' In the morning he wrapped himself up in his prayer shawl and danced as he prayed, quite unlike the foreign Jews. People were startled and called the neighbors. There was one bully among them, who provoked him and tore his prayer shawl. 'Thief,' cried the stranger, 'you've stolen my watch.' The bully kicked him and knocked him down. People gathered from the whole street and said the man had gone crazy. A policeman came and brought him before the judge; the owners of the hotel followed and demanded their money. He looked for money to pay but could not find any. He burst into tears and said, 'They've stolen my money.' Some time later a poor man came and stood at the door of our house. I was stunned. 'Surely,' said I, 'it is that foreigner.' 'Yes,' said he, smiling, 'it is I.' Mother gave him food and drink, clothing and footwear, because he was dressed in rags and his shoes were cracked. 'Poor man,' I whispered to myself, 'what has become of you!' He smiled and said, 'Good, good.'

Let us return to our subject. My money was steadily dwindling. Every day I counted it and every day it grew less and less. 'Money, money,' I said to it, 'where have you gone? Where have you fled? Tomorrow I will want to buy clothes or shoes and you will not be there to help me.' To this my money replied, 'What are we and what is our strength?' 'When I went to buy a coat,' said I to my money, 'you did not say so; you raced to do my will.' 'In those days,' my money replied, 'we were plentiful. And the strength of the few is not as the strength of the many.' 'If so,' said I, 'what shall I do?' 'How should we know?' said my money. 'But we can give you one piece of good advice: wait a little while before you put your hand into your pocket.' 'Perhaps,' said I, jesting, 'you will be fruitful and multiply in the meantime.'

My clothes were still good and I had no need to buy new ones; my shoes, too, were whole. So that they should not get worn or torn, and I should not have to repair them, I did little walking, and when I went out I walked very soberly, so that they should last a long time.

But why should this man be afraid of a torn garment or a worn shoe? Aren't there many men of good family who go about in rags without their honesty being in any way affected? But it is in the interests of the people of our town that I should not be like one of them. In the past, when I used to engage my mind with trifles, I would ask myself: What good is it to a poor man if his neighbor is rich? If the rich man is well dressed and eats tasty dishes, does that do the poor man any good? Or what do you lose if your neighbor is as poor as you? If he were dressed in rags like you, and had nothing to eat, would that be any loss to you? Sometimes I would explain it to myself in this way: a man loves his honor as his life, so he is happy if his neighbor is rich. And sometimes I would explain it like this: it is natural for people to love beauty, so that even if the poor man does not profit from the rich man's wealth, he profits by contemplating the splendor of man. And just as he rejoices in the rich man, who adorns the world with his handsome clothes, so he is grieved at the poor man, who dims the luster of the world with his rags.

CHAPTER THREE AND SEVENTY

The Way of a Writer

I went back to my lodging and counted my money. The pounds I had brought with me had become dollars, the dollars groschen, and the groschen kreutzer. I remembered the days gone by, when my pocket was full, and thought of the days to come, when my pocket would be empty. I began valuing every coin in my possession at more than its worth, and limited my expenses to the very minimum. It came to such a pass that I wrote letters on scraps of letters that I had received. Once I wanted to write a letter to my wife and found no paper; so I took the last will and testament I had drafted when I was sick, erased what I had written, and wrote on the clean side.

I sit all by myself and see my wife straining to read the erasure. 'Don't you see what I have erased?' I say to my wife. 'I will lend you my spectacles, and you shall see.'

My wife is startled and says, 'Are you wearing spectacles? When you left the Land of Israel your eyes were good, weren't they?' 'The light of my eyes has been somewhat dimmed,' I reply. 'It is because you sit in the Beit Midrash, amid the dust of the books,' says she. 'Have you consulted doctors?' 'I am with a doctor all the time,' I reply. 'And what did the doctor tell you?' 'What did he tell me? He said to me, "Is it to study the Gemara you came here?"' 'So let us go back,' says my wife. 'And what will happen to the key?' say I. 'Leave it in the sacred Ark,' says she, 'and when the dead come to read the Torah they will take it.' 'And what about those who are not dead? What will they do?' 'In any case,' she replies, 'no one asks for the key.' 'So long as the book *The Hands of Moses* was in the town,' say I, 'no one needed the key. Now I have sent the book away, they will need the key.' 'Why has your face reddened like that?' asks my wife. 'My face has reddened? I thought it had darkened.' 'Why should it have darkened?' 'For sorrow.' 'What are you sorry for?' says my wife. 'Because I shall have to lift onto my shoulders the Ark where I left the key.' 'Do you want to load the Ark on your shoulders?' says my wife. 'Not only the Ark,' I reply, 'but the whole Beit Midrash.' Says my wife, 'The Beit Midrash will come of its own accord.' 'Do you think it will come after me?' 'And did it occur to you that it would remain alone?' 'Wait a moment,' say I to my wife, 'and I will count my money to see if I have enough for the expenses of the journey.'

My wife says to my children, 'Did you hear, children? Father is going to come back with us to the Land of Israel.' My children come up to me and embrace and kiss me and say, 'You are good, Father, you are good.' 'You be good, too,' I say to my children, 'and I will open up our old Beit Midrash for you and study Torah with you. Why have you recoiled, children? Are you afraid I will exile you out of the Land so that you should study Torah? Don't be afraid; I am going back to the Land of Israel with you, for there is no Torah like the Torah of the Land.' My children embraced me again and said, 'You are good, Father; you are good, Father.'

I look at the walls of the old Beit Midrash and say to them, 'You see, the time has come for me to go back to the Land of Israel.' The walls of the Beit Midrash stoop, as if they wish to embrace me because I am going to the Land. I say to them, 'If you wish, I will load you on my back and take you with me.' 'We are too heavy,' they reply, 'one man has not the strength to carry us on his back. But take the key and go, and when the time comes we shall follow you.' 'How do you intend to come,' say I, 'every stone by itself? No, I want you to come to the Land together. If you are ashamed to come empty-handed, I shall set my children down among you. Haven't you heard that my wife has written that she is going back to the Land with her children?'

That day a letter came from my wife, and this is what she wrote: 'You are sitting in Poland while I stay here with the children in Germany. The children are becoming accustomed to living abroad, and if we delay we shall be doubly the losers. Besides, if we are to go back, let us go back at once before the High Holidays, so that the children do not lose a year at school.'

Who has revealed to the people of my town that I am going to return to the Land of Israel? I have told no one, but the whole town comes and asks me, 'When are you going back?'

That day Yeruham Freeman asked me to wait until his wife gave birth. 'I will leave after the circumcision,' said I. Yeruham's face shone, as if he felt assured that his wife would bear a male child.

I shared in Yeruham's joy. First, that a son would be born in the town, for it was many years since a Jewish child had been born here. Second, that I had found an excuse to put off my journey, for it is not easy to uproot yourself from place to place. Yet in my heart I bore a grudge against Yeruham: not only had he left the Land, but he was delaying my return.

In those days Jerusalem stood before me, with all its environs. Once again I saw my house, as if it were still at peace, with my children playing there among the green pines whose fragrance filled the whole quarter, that sweet fragrance which flows from them until the end of the summer, when the sun rests on the trees and there is a gentle breeze, and the sky spreads out its vault of blue, and the hot earth looks up at it from among the thorns parched in the sun.

I counted my money again and shuddered; there was not enough to pay my hotel bill for the next month. Even worse, I did not have enough to pay for a place on the boat.

But I did not despair, for a certain publisher in the Land of Israel had printed several of my stories and had promised to pay my fee in full. I also had an old debt due from another publisher abroad, who had issued a few of my stories. I asked them to hurry up and pay me. The one in the Land of Israel sent no reply. No doubt he had gone abroad, for such is the way of the rich in the Land: in the cold season they go out to the hot countries, and in the hot to the cold countries. And the one abroad wrote, 'On the contrary, you owe me money. You bought so many books from me, and the cost is more than the author's fee.' What books had I bought? It is a custom among us that most readers demand that the author give them his books for nothing, and sometimes all his fee goes for the books he gives away.

Unintentionally, I have mentioned that I am a writer. Originally, the word denoted the scribe, who wrote the words of the Torah. But since everyone who engages in the craft of writing is called a writer, I am not afraid of arrogance in calling myself a writer.

I have told elsewhere the story of the poet who, when he was a child lying in his crib, was shown from heaven things no eye has ever seen. He wanted to utter poetry; a swarm of bees came and filled his mouth with honey. When he grew up and studied the Torah, he remembered all the songs and praises he wished to utter in his childhood; so he wrote them down and Israel inserted them into its prayers. And where did he get the Laments? The bees who had given him their honey stung him, and out of that pain he wrote the Laments for the Ninth of Av.

There are other poets who were not privileged in the same way as Rabbi Eleazar Hakalir, but because they were humble and modest, they regarded their misfortunes as part of the community's misfortunes and made them songs and lamentations for the House of Israel; so a man reads them as he reads a lamentation over himself.

Other poets there were who saw their own misfortunes and did not forget them, but they were very modest and made the misfortunes of the community their own, as if all the tribulations that had befallen Israel had befallen them.

Other poets there were who saw their own misfortunes and did not forget those of the community, but knew that our God is merciful and can be relied upon to reward those who suffer; so they endured their sufferings and consoled themselves with the future blessings that the Holy One, blessed be

He, is destined to bestow on Israel when it becomes His will to deliver them from their misfortunes. So they swallowed their tears and spoke in song.

We do not have the power to do like one group or the other, but we are like a child who dips his pen in the ink and writes what his master dictates. So long as his master's writing lies before him, his writing is beautiful, but when his master's writing is taken away, or when he changes it, it is not beautiful. The Holy One, blessed be He, made a covenant with all that has been created since the first six days that it should not change its function (except for the sea, which was to be split before the children of Israel), and the forms of the letters and the writing of God on the Tablets were among the things that were created in the beginning.

And here I must explain how, if I am a writer, I let the time pass without writing anything all those days I dwelt in Szibucz. Well, if something comes and knocks on my heart I send it away. When it knocks again, I say: Don't you know I hate the smell of ink? When I see that I have no escape I do my work, if only so that I shall not be pestered again. During those days I spent in my town, many things came and knocked on my heart, but when I sent them away they went off and did not come back to me.

CHAPTER FOUR AND SEVENTY

Change of Place

Let us return to our subject. I stayed in Szibucz and delayed my return to the Land of Israel because I had promised Yeruham Freeman to put off my journey until his wife should give birth. In the meantime, my money had dribbled away, although I economized in my spending and did not buy fruit from the market at a time when the whole market was full of fruit I had not tasted for many years.

I did not write my wife that I had not enough money for the cost of the journey, but continued to write about the people of my town, about Daniel Bach and Reb Hayim's orphans, about Yeruham, and about Kuba, who was inviting me to come and stay with him. From all the letters I wrote no one could have learned of my own affairs. So it is surprising that my wife sent me a ticket for the journey to the Land and money for my expenses. Or perhaps we should not be surprised, for women are likely to surprise us.

In the meantime I changed my lodging and went to stay with Kuba. On the day Kuba returned from the wedding of his divorced wife he asked me to live with him, for he found it hard to live alone, but I refused. Once I sat up with him all night, and when the dawn rose Kuba said, 'Let us eat breakfast first and then you shall go.' After we had eaten, he said, 'Lie down a little, then we shall eat lunch, and then you shall go.' When I wanted to go, he said to me, 'What are you short of here? Is it the smell of meat, or the noise in the hotel?' So he went on persuading me until I went over to live with him.

In the stories one finds in romances there are many cases in which, on the day a man comes to the end of all his money and is put out of his home, he inherits a house or a palace. Something like this happened to me with Kuba. I paid my bill to the owner of the hotel, so that I should not be ashamed when the time came for payment and I had nothing to pay with.

Kuba treated me with extraordinary hospitality. In the morning he would bring me water to wash with and a glass of clear, cold water to drink, and every day he would prepare me several meals—even with eggs, which he, as a vegetarian, did not eat himself.

In those days I did not sit much in the Beit Midrash, and I paid frequent visits to Zechariah Rosen. He was like an ever-fresh fountain and a never-ending flow of water: he talked about everything under the sun. He spoke of Szibucz, our town, and the glory of days gone by. Now the splendor of our town was gone and no one spared it a thought, for all eyes were turned to the Land of Israel; and it was still a matter for consideration whether this was right so long as the Messiah dwelt abroad, for when a king goes into exile all the great men of his country go into exile with him.

Nor did I neglect Yeruham Freeman. Whenever I met him I conversed with him. But I have already spoken of him in several places, even mentioning his handsome curls, which were all his pride, for no young man in Szibucz had the like. Now I have nothing to add about Yeruham, but I shall say something about his curls. They reminded me of the Lithuanian itinerant preachers, who let their hair grow long, and whose side-curls mingled with their hair. But this is not surprising, for his father was a Lithuanian, as we have already explained.

More than anyone else I was in the habit of visiting Daniel Bach. Sometimes Kuba would come to his house to see what his friend was doing. He would find Erela sitting with piles and piles of copybooks in front of her, correcting spelling mistakes. She did her work with rigid honesty, ferreting out and correcting every error.

As I have already said, Kuba's house stood in the same street where I lived in my childhood. According to my reckoning, I was as old as my father, of blessed memory, had been when he lived here with us. How many years have passed since then, how many sorrows have passed over our heads! When I sit alone by myself it seems to me that nothing has changed here. Once I looked in the mirror and was startled, for the image of Father's face looked out at me from the mirror, and I said to myself: What is this? Father did not use to trim his beard! And I did not realize that it was I standing in front of the mirror.

Kuba's income is scanty. A patient who has a copper in hand calls another doctor, while one who hasn't calls Kuba. Not only does he get no pay for his work, but when he has a copper in his pocket he spends it on the patient. Nevertheless, Kuba's house is full of good things. You can find there fruit and vegetables, eggs and butter, cheese and rye bread, which the peasants bring him in payment for his trouble, for the peasants have no particular fondness for rudeness in doctors, but are attracted by Dr. Milch, who treats them like a simple man. So they treat him in their own way and bring him what they eat themselves. It would be no exaggeration to say that in one corner of Kuba's house you find more than you could find in the entire Jewish market of Szibucz. And since he does not permit himself to eat eggs, he gives some to the poor and some to Mrs. Bach. So as not to rob the poor, I kept my hand off Kuba's food and bought my needs in the market. Once Kuba found me bringing something from the market, and scolded me for leaving his food to spoil and buying rotten foodstuffs from the shopkeeper.

I counted my money again, for the last time; from now on it was not worth counting, for it had shrunk to two dollars (except for the money for my traveling expenses, which I had vowed not to touch until I left). That day I stopped smoking, and Kuba praised me for it; he hated tobacco, first, because it is harmful to the body, and second, because it robs the soil, for on the ground where they grow tobacco they could have grown potatoes.

I found it hard to give up the pleasure of smoking—and harder still because a number of people were in the habit of taking a cigarette from me in the marketplace, and if I did not give them one, it was as if I were shaming them. So I went to town to buy cigarettes, so that if anyone asked me for a cigarette I should be able to give him one.

Ignatz came up to me and cried, 'Pieniadze.' The three holes in his face were repulsive, and a mocking smile seeped out from them. My anger rose and I was about to scold him, but in the end I dismissed my anger, put my hand in my pocket, brought up a dollar and gave it to him. He clutched my hand and kissed it. 'What is this, Ignatz?' said I. 'Why are you kissing my hand?' 'Because the gentleman was kind enough to give me a dollar,' he said. 'I gave you your reward,' said I, 'because you said "Pieniadze" and not "Mu'es." As you know, I come from the Land of Israel, and I cannot bear to hear the Holy Tongue used to speak of filthy lucre, so because you said "Pieniadze" and not "Mu'es" I gave you your reward. And I must tell you that I have no time to stop to talk to everyone, so I will give you a second dollar, and you must trouble me no more. From now on, even if you cry "Mu'es" all day I shall give you nothing. I am a man who is bothered enough, and I cannot waste my time on petty cash. Do you hear?' Ignatz looked at me like a deaf man who cannot hear.

I put my hand in my pocket again and gave him a second dollar.

Do you remember, my friend, the story of a certain young man who had only two coppers in his possession, so he bought a bunch of flowers with one and had his shoes shined with the other? When that happened to this man, his hands held a bunch of flowers and his shoes were shining; now his hands hold the hands of a disfigured beggar and his shoes are not shining.

After I had parted from Ignatz I said to myself: I should not have brought him to the point of weeping, for if I had given him the money little by little the poor fellow's heart would not have been so moved and he would not have wept. But the other one (namely, the devil, or the evil impulse, who does not allow me to enjoy any good deed I do) said, 'Today he weeps because you gave him all your money; tomorrow, when you have nothing to give him, he will laugh.'

CHAPTER FIVE AND SEVENTY

Preparations for the Road

Since all my money was spent, I was afraid to show myself in the street, for I felt as if everyone who met me wanted money. So I went to the Beit Midrash and sat there. I thought of all I had done and what I had not done. I thought I would study a page of Gemara—perhaps it would sweeten the passing time; but because of all my anxiety I found no satisfaction in study. I began to rail at Yeruham for holding me up because of his wife. The door opened and in came Mrs. Zommer, with another woman. She spread out her hands and said, weeping, 'I beg of you, give us the book *The Hands of Moses*—Rachel is having a difficult labor.' 'I have already sent it to the Land of Israel,' said I. 'Oh, what shall I do?' she cried, clasping her hands in anguish.

But the woman who came with Mrs. Zommer was experienced. 'What did they do before they had that book?' she said. 'And what do they do in other towns, where they do not have the book? They take the key of the Great Synagogue and put it into the woman's hands—and she gives birth.'

So they went to the synagogue to ask for the key. But they did not find it, for on that day they were administering the oath to that old man who had been required to take the oath in court, and the beadle, who had gone to bring a Scroll of the Law, had locked the synagogue and taken the key away with him.

It takes an average man a quarter of an hour to go from the synagogue to the court, but a person's thoughts speed like an arrow from a bow. Before anyone could prepare to go, the woman had an idea. 'I remember,' she said, 'once they gave a woman in her pains the key of the old Beit Midrash, and she gave birth.'

So I locked the doors of the Beit Midrash from the outside and gave her the key. Mrs. Zommer took the key and ran with all her might, as a mother runs when she is given the power to bring life and healing to her daughter, and I stood like someone who has been bereft of all he loves.

But I set aside my own desires and prayed for Rachel, for besides all the pain I felt for her, my conscience reproached me for sending away a book by which women were saved in the hour of birth. How imperfect are the kindnesses of flesh and blood! I did a favor to Mistress Sarah and her sisters-in-law, and did harm to Rachel.

As I stood there, I heard a man jeering and scoffing: 'The child does not want to come out, so as not to shame its mother, for it isn't seven months since her wedding day.'

While that one was counting days and months, the unborn child saw that it was bringing its mother into danger, so it started struggling and straining with itself. Then Rachel's mother came and put the key of our old Beit Midrash into her hand. When the child saw the key, it came out, and before much time had passed the news was heard that Rachel had borne a male child.

It was several years since a woman in Szibucz had borne either a son or a daughter. Pharaoh issued his decree only against the males, but the daughters in our town were even

more severe with themselves: they added one decree to another and bore neither males nor females. So the whole town
took notice, and one could sense a kind of joy. I went to Yeruham and offered my congratulations. He reminded me of my
promise, and I said, 'What I promised I shall fulfill.'

That day I began preparing for my journey and went to
take my leave of all those I had known in the town, whether
I knew them before I came here on this last visit or came to
know them afterward. If God had blessed them with a little
happiness, a little light in their faces, I would spin out my
story; but since they lived in sorrow and their faces were
black as kettles, why should I make the story any longer?
Poverty has many faces, but no matter which face it turns
toward you, it looks in pain and suffering. I had another cause
for regret in the house of Hanoch's wife, for I was unable to
give the orphans even a little present. I fumbled with the
buttons of my coat and thought of the sons of that teacher
in the 'Ballad of the Letters' in my book *The Bridal Canopy*,
who used to make silver buttons for his fringed garment, and
if a poor man came along he would pull off a button and give
it to him. Hanoch's orphans did not notice my regret; in fact,
they were very happy, for on that day the youngest of them
had started to recite the Kaddish by heart. All the trouble Reb
Hayim had taken had not been in vain.

On the way, I met Ignatz, but he did not cry '*Mu'es*' or
'*Pieniadze.*' Perhaps it was because he looked into my heart
and saw that the cry of '*Mu'es*' would have no effect, or because at that moment he was standing with the priest. From
the winks of that noseless fellow, it was obvious that he was
telling the priest something about me, for I noticed the priest
turning and looking at me. If his intentions were good—good;
if the contrary, may the Almighty turn it into good.

After taking leave of all my acquaintances I went to the
rabbi. He sat me down on his right hand, and rebuked me
for not showing my face to him for so many days now. I said
I had been busy. 'And is that the only reason why you did not
come to visit me?' said he. 'I come from the Land of Israel,'
I replied, 'so I find it hard to hear it disparaged, and when I
come to you, sir, you speak ill of the Land.'

The rabbi took his beard in his right hand, looked at me with affection, and said pleasantly, 'But I love you with all my soul.' 'Who am I and what am I that you should love me?' said I. 'I wish I might be found worthy to be a little grain in the dust of the Land of Israel.' 'Do I disparage the holy soil?' said the rabbi. 'I only disparage those who live on it.' 'To which of its inhabitants do you refer, sir?' said I. 'Is it to those who dedicate their lives to its soil, who revive its desolation, plow and sow, and plant life for its inhabitants? Or perhaps you refer to its guardians, who are ready to sacrifice themselves for every little piece of it, or to those who study the Torah in poverty and do not feel their sufferings, for love of the Almighty and the sacred Torah. Or perhaps to those who disregard their own honor in honoring the Divine Presence, and spend all their lives in prayer. Or perhaps you are referring, sir, to the humble people of the Land, to the carriers and porters, tailors and cobblers, carpenters and builders, plasterers and quarrymen and shoeblacks, and all the other artisans who support their families in honesty and beautify the Land with their handiwork. Once I happened to meet a tailor dressed in rags, and found that he knew all the rules and regulations of the *Arba Turim* by heart. I said to him, "You know so much and yet you put on patches." He showed me a barefoot cobbler, who knew how to quote every single source for the teachings of Maimonides, but was not fit to shine the shoes of a certain shoeblack who sat in the marketplace of Jerusalem and was capable of deciding the law on the basis of secret writings of the Zohar. And this last was only a humble pupil in the college of the porters, who were well versed in drawing out all the secrets of the Kabbalah from the Gemara. But no doubt your honor was referring to those whom the Land suckles with its milk and they impregnate it with their venom, as when a woman suckles her son, and a serpent comes and sucks with him and impregnates her with its venom. Father in heaven, if you can suffer them, we can suffer them too.' When I had finished I rose and said farewell.

The rabbi rose, took both my hands in his, and said, 'Sit down, sir, sit down, sir.' He too sat down, put his head between his hands, and said nothing. Finally he raised his head, fixed his eyes on me to tell me something, and could not find the word to say.

The rabbi's wife came in, bringing citron preserves and two glasses of tea. When her husband saw her he said, 'This gentleman is going to the Land of Israel and we shall remain here. Sweeten your tea, sir, and drink while it is hot. Take some preserves, it is citron preserves.'

So as to take my leave of the rabbi with a blessing, I drank a little, tasted a little, and finally recited the blessing, 'Who createst many living beings and their wants.' Then I asked how his son was. The rabbi rose, took a bundle of papers and laid them in front of me, saying, 'Oh, stuff and nonsense.' I rose from my chair and took my leave of them. The rabbi shook my hand and said nothing at all. Then he laid his hand on mine again and stood in silence. I took my hand out of his quietly and left. He came after me to see me on my way.

As we stood by the doorpost, he took out a zloty and said, 'I want to make you my messenger for a good deed. Give it to the first poor man you find in the Land of Israel.' 'Perhaps,' said I, 'the first one I meet will be one of those your honor is in the habit of disparaging.' The rabbi answered, ' "Thy people are all righteous: they shall inherit the Land forever." If a man has gained the privilege of dwelling in the Land of Israel, it is a sign that he is righteous.' 'Not everyone who dwells in the Land of Israel is righteous,' I replied. 'There are people among us who pretend to be righteous and denounce the truly righteous.' Said the rabbi, ' "What have you to do with the secrets of the Merciful One?" '

The Covenant

How great is the love for the Land of Israel! Because I came from there I was given the honor of being Sandak. Not the town rabbi, nor Rachel's father, but I, who am neither a great scholar nor a member of the family.

I remembered my grandfather, of blessed memory, who was the Sandak for most of the people in the town, and there was not a man in the town for whom my grandfather had acted as Sandak to whom he did not send a gift on his wedding day. It happened that a certain man had a quarrel at law with another, so they went to the rabbi and he ruled against him. So the man went and slandered the other to the authorities. The rabbi asked my grandfather to give this man the privilege of being Sandak, so that the good deed should stand him in good stead before the Almighty. There was a piece of honey cake lying in a dish from one circumcision to the next, with a bell-glass over it, and my grandfather used to give me some whenever he tested me in the Gemara and I knew my lessons. Now I sit and marvel that I have attained my grandfather's place without attaining a single one of his virtues.

Since I got up in the morning my knees had been knocking together. The soul was prepared to fulfill the commandment, but the body was afraid. Perhaps if they had circumcised the child in the Great Synagogue or the old Beit Midrash, as our fathers used to do, I would not have worried so much. First, because in the old Beit Midrash I am one of the family, and second, because Father Elijah is very punctilious and will not sit on those chairs where people have spent their time in jesting and trivialities. I said to myself: If you cannot improve the chair, improve the one who will sit on it.

The guests assembled and stood waiting for the town rabbi, who was the mohel who performed the circumcision.

Meanwhile, the door opened and in came Daniel Bach, whom the owner of the hotel had cordially invited, and who had made it up with him. Great is the power of a religious duty, for it makes peace between man and his neighbor.

Now I will tell you something more: even Erela came, that Erela who had been meant for Yeruham from the hour of her birth, but Yeruham had married Rachel, so Erela had been left without a husband. And if you do not believe me, just wait a moment and you shall see the honor they paid her, by asking her to bring in the infant.

After an hour, or perhaps less, the rabbi came. He looked graciously upon everyone and asked if everything was ready for the ceremony. He stood chatting with one and chatting with another, then he took out the circumcision knife, laid it in carbolic, washed his hands with soap and water, and said to the doctor, 'Cleanliness leads to purity.'

They wrapped up the child from the waist down to the heels with several swaddling clothes, put a cap of white silk on his head, and handed him over to Erela. Erela came into the hall, carrying the infant. All the people stood up and recited aloud, 'Blessed be he that cometh!' Erela handed over the child to Kuba and Kuba handed him over to the mohel.

The mohel held him affectionately, looked at him kindly, and chanted aloud, 'The Holy One, blessed be He, said to Abraham: Walk before me and be thou innocent.' The child looked at him and tried to hide his face in the old man's beard, because it was warm. A hair tickled his nose and he began to sneeze. The mohel handed him over to Rachel's father, who took him in his arms and laid him on the chair that had been prepared for Elijah the Prophet. As he laid him down he chanted in a quavering voice: 'This is the chair of Elijah the Prophet, of blessed memory.'

The infant thought to himself: 'Where is Father Elijah? For eight days he has not shown himself to me. Again he has flown off like a bird and is going about among the people.' He pricked up his ears and wondered whether he should be angry with Elijah for going away, or be happy that he was coming back. He wriggled in his swaddling clothes and tried to take out his hands to grasp Elijah's girdle, so as to climb up to heaven and study the Torah. And when he remembered those days in which he was surrounded by well-being and was taught the entire Torah, a smile came to his lips. He wanted to repeat what he had learned but found he had forgotten it. He opened his mouth and started to feel with his tongue. He felt the cleft on his upper lip, where the angel had struck him on the mouth and made him forget the entire Torah. With the shock, he started to cry.

As he was weeping and lamenting over the primal months which had gone by, never to return, he remembered the oath that had been administered to him at the hour when he came out into the light of the world: that he would be righteous and not wicked, and preserve his soul in purity. Dread fell upon him. He said to himself, 'I am an infant. What will become of me?' So he closed his eyes and pretended to be sleeping. It seemed to him that the day of his death had already arrived and he had nothing to fear, for he had committed no sins and his soul was still pure as on the day it had been given him from heaven. So he closed his mouth and stopped weeping, lay there quietly, and did not utter a sound.

The mohel came forward and recited, 'For Thy salvation I hope, for Thy salvation I hope. Elijah, messenger of the Covenant, behold thy infant is before thee, stand by my right hand and support me.' The infant twitched his nose and began to sniff. He said, 'If Elijah's girdle smells of light, it is a sign that my soul has returned to heaven, and if it is of leather, it is a sign that I am lying among human beings.' The mohel chanted with a trill, 'I have hope for thy salvation,' and went on with the rest of the prayer. Then he bent down, picked up the child from the chair, and said to me, 'Sit.' I wrapped myself in my tallit and sat down.

They came and put a little cushion on my knee and set a footstool at my feet. The mohel put the infant on my knees and put my right hand under the child's knees, with my thumb on the infant's legs, for so long as he has not entered the Covenant, one may fear that he might spurn the commandment.

I looked at the infant and he looked at me. Something like two sparks of blue light came from his eyes and they were covered with tears. He wrinkled his nose and puckered the skin on his forehead. At that moment the child's face changed and there was no longer any impress of what he had been engaged in before, like a man whose body is gripped by pain. I quickly put my left hand under the infant's backbone and raised him somewhat, so that his head should lie comfortably. The mohel adjusted my knees, interlocking them so that the child should not slip, for so long as he has not entered into the Covenant one may fear that he might slip away from the commandment. The mohel took the knife and said the blessing for circumcision. Yeruham then recited the blessing 'Blessed art Thou, O Lord, who has commanded us to make him enter the Covenant of Abraham our Father.' All those present answered 'Amen' and said, 'Even as he has entered into the Covenant, so may he enter into the Torah, the nuptial canopy, and good deeds.'

A glass was put into the hands of Rachel's father. He took it, screwed up his eyes, and in a tone of affection recited the blessing 'Who didst sanctify the well-beloved from the womb,' and called the child after me, to show me affection in front of Yeruham. Thus I was blessed with two privileges: first, that I sat in the same chair as Elijah, and second, that the son of our Father Abraham was called by my name. Surely it would have been better to call the child after a deceased relative, for it gives satisfaction to the dead when a living person is called by his name, but half the graveyard was full of Rachel's relatives, and they did not wish to make a choice between one and another. And the reason they did not call him after Yeruham's father was so as not to recall his shame.

After the circumcision, the rabbi took his leave and went home, for a scholar is not obliged to take part in a circumcision meal, unless there are worthy people present, as it is said in the commentary on the tractate *Passover*. But we enjoyed ourselves with honey cakes, and brandy, and sweet fish cooked with honey and raisins. We ate and drank to the health of the newly circumcised infant, and to the life of his father and mother, and the life of his grandfather and grandmother, and the lives of all those present at the circumcision meal. When everyone was glad with eating and drinking, I rose to my feet and said, 'It is a custom in Israel to give a gift to the circumcised infant, as the Holy One, blessed be He, gave the Land of Israel to Abraham our Father on the day he circumcised himself. Dear brethren, what gift can I give the child? If I give him a garment, or a hat, or socks, it is natural for the infant to grow from day to day; today my gifts will fit him, but tomorrow he will have no need of them. If I give him a silver watch, when he grows up he may become rich and buy a golden one, thus belittling my gift. But I hereby give him the key of our old Beit Midrash. It is said in the Gemara: "Synagogues and Batei Midrashot abroad are destined to be installed in the Land of Israel." Happy is he that has the key in his possession, so that he will be able to open them and enter in.'

After the handing over of the key, they brought a glass of wine and honored me by having me pronounce the grace. When I reached the fourth blessing, I remembered that I was returning to Jerusalem, and that it was still desolate. Then my mouth was closed and the springs of my eyes were opened. But I summoned up strength and completed the blessing like a man: 'Who buildeth Jerusalem in His mercy, amen,' and all the celebrants loudly and joyfully answered, 'Amen.'

CHAPTER SEVEN AND SEVENTY

How I Left My Town

After pronouncing the grace I rose from the table, took my leave of the company, and went into the room where I had been staying before I went to live with Kuba. I examined my belongings, put aside those that were fit to take with me, and left the rest for the poor.

Yeruham came in, packed up my belongings and put them on his shoulder, and went off to take them to the railway station, while I went to take my leave of Rachel and her son. Then I said farewell to my host and his wife, to Dolik and Lolik and Babtchi, and also to Krolka. Since all my money had gone I had nothing left except my traveling expenses, so I consoled her with a pretty trinket, as well as some kind words, in case she had taken more trouble with me than she was paid for. Thus I took leave of my acquaintances, of our own faith or not, and asked their pardon in case I had not treated them with sufficient respect or rebuked them when they spoke disparagingly of the Land of Israel. Finally I went to take my leave of our old Beit Midrash. Since I had handed over the key to the child I did not trouble him by asking him to lend it to me, in case he might think I did not intend to give it back, and cry—especially as it is an infant's way to take, and not to give. I stood in front of the door of the Beit Midrash and looked through the keyhole. The space of the Beit Midrash shrank within the ball of this man's eye, and a shining, clarified light shone from it.

Thus I stood for some time, until I remembered that the day was passing and the time had come to go to the station. I wiped the lock with my coat and went away.

It is half an hour's walk from the Beit Midrash to the railway station, but I took less. I did not look at the houses and the ruins as on the eve of the Day of Atonement, when I had come to the town, but I opened my nostrils wide and breathed in the odor of the town—that odor of millet boiled in honey.

At the station I found Yeruham and Kuba standing with my belongings. Kuba had been kind enough to undertake to bring my chattels from his house, so that I should be free for myself.

Besides Yeruham and Kuba there were a number of Jews there, some in Sabbath clothes and some with the skirts of their coats let down as a sign of respect and importance. Since they were standing there without sacks or any other equipment for a journey, I wondered somewhat why they had suddenly come here, but I was so busy with my own journey that I asked no questions.

Meanwhile, Daniel Bach came to take his leave of me. Indeed I had already taken my leave of him and his family an hour before, but he came on behalf of his son Raphael, for Raphael wanted his father to see that man who was going

up to the Land of Israel immediately before he left the town.
I thanked Mr. Bach for having been my guide in the town
and promised that if God privileged me to reach Jerusalem
safely, I would go and see his father, and also—for those who
are alive here are different from those who live in the after-
world—the grave of Yeruham his brother. Daniel sighed and
said, 'This is the anniversary of my brother's death.' I gazed
at Daniel Bach, who was standing on his artificial leg, which
he owed to his ignominious trade in this exile. I recalled all
the troubles that had overtaken him and, with them, his
brother who had been killed guarding the Land. Now the
father of both brothers was living in Jerusalem, where he
prayed for the repose of the soul of the son who had been
killed and no doubt also remembered the son who lived.
Surely it would have been fitting for Daniel Bach to go to the
synagogue and recite the Kaddish.

Meanwhile several other people came. Some of them I
knew and some I did not, or knew them only by sight. Szibucz
is not a large town and its inhabitants are not numerous, but
still there were people there to whom I had not happened to
talk. 'What is special about today?' I asked Daniel Bach. 'They
have come out of respect for you, sir,' he replied.

I remembered my entry into the town, unnoticed, while
now I was leaving with much ceremony. I spoke up and said,
'Listen, gentlemen, I know that it is not in my honor that you
have come here, but to give honor to the Land of Israel, because this man is going up to the Land. May it be His will
that you, too, will soon be privileged to go up to the Land.
And do you know who will accompany you? Good angels,
who stand and wait for you, will accompany you, for since
the day the Holy Temple was destroyed and Israel was dispersed among the nations, the angels have been dispersed
with them, and they stand and wait for the men of Israel, so
that they, too, may return. And do you know who will bring
you there? All the kings and princes of the earth; and, moreover, they will bring you on their shoulders as a gift to the
King Messiah, as it is said: "Behold, I will lift up mine hand
to the Gentiles, and set up my standard to the peoples; and
they shall bring thy sons in their arms, and thy daughters

shall be carried upon their shoulders. And kings shall be thy
nursing fathers, and their queens thy nursing mothers; they
shall bow down to thee with their faces toward the earth and
lick up the dust of thy feet." And until we are privileged to
see the longed-for day, may the Almighty grant you the blessing of life eternal, and may the Redeemer come to Zion speedily in our day. Amen!'

Before I came forward and spoke, Reuben and Simon,
Levi and Judah, and all the rest had started to recite the Afternoon Service as a congregation, and as I finished speaking
they finished their prayer. A voice was heard reciting the
Kaddish, and I saw Daniel Bach standing, leaning on his stick,
his voice quivering, for it was the anniversary of his brother's
death and his heart had been aroused to recite the Kaddish.
And all the congregation answered after him, 'Amen.'

The sound of the train was heard coming nearer and
nearer, puffing and blowing and whistling, till it stopped at
the station. Rubberovitch waved his cloth and cried in his
tuneful voice, 'Szibucz.'

With the train came a number of Gentiles and one Jew,
who looked like Elimelech Kaiser, and perhaps it was really
he, but he was very old and bent. Even his mother Freide,
peace be upon her, looked younger than he at the end of her
days.

All the people pushed forward, shook my hand, and took
their leave of me with love and brotherhood and friendship.
I kissed my comrade Yeruham, and Kuba, got into the carriage and stood at the window, my head facing the people
and my eyes looking into my own heart. Again Rubberovitch
waved the cloth in his hand to dispatch the train. I looked at
my brethren, the sons of my town, as they stood crowded
there looking at me. The train stirred and moved, but they
did not move. I said to myself: If they are granted the privilege of coming up to the Land of Israel, we shall see one
another again.

On the Sea

After two days I reached the port of Trieste and found my wife and children, who had arranged to come on the same day so that we should embark together on the same ship and go up together to the Land of Israel. I kissed them and said, 'Blessed be the Almighty, blessed be He, who has brought us as far as here.' 'Well,' replied my wife, 'so we are going back to the Land of Israel.' I nodded but said nothing, for my throat was choked with emotion, like a man who sees that all his hopes are coming true.

The air was pleasant, the sea was calm, and the ship moved gently. With our own eyes we saw the Land of Israel drawing steadily nearer and ourselves approaching the Land. No tongue or pen could describe our joy. The ship was full of Jews, old and young, men and women. Some were returning from the Zionist Congress and some from conferences; some from bathing resorts and some from healing spas; some from East and West and some from North and South; some from traveling in various countries and some from going around the world; some from a holiday trip and some from a pleasure trip; some from an ordinary journey and some from a journey that was ordinary; some were returning to renew their travel documents and some to start traveling again. Some of them spoke Russian or Polish, Hungarian or Rumanian, and some spoke German or Spanish, Yiddish or English; some the English of England, some the English of America, and some the English of the Land of Israel. Some of them even spoke Hebrew. Both these and those lay stretched out on deck chairs and looked at the new immigrants, who danced and sang and rejoiced.

Among the immigrants I found our comrade Zvi, from the training farm. All those days I was in the boat Zvi was happy that he had succeeded in fitting the deed to the thought and was going up to settle in the Land of Israel. He was so happy that he did not stop dancing, as if through the dance he was moving on and getting nearer to the source of his vitality. From time to time Zvi would come to see me and talk about our comrades in the Diaspora, the boys in the fields and the girls in the cowshed. They were still few, but their work was recognized, and even the peasants sang their praises. And if the farmers sometimes held up their pay, the true reward of work is work. While we were talking, Zvi asked me if I was hungry. 'What kind of question is this?' I asked, surprised. Zvi laughed and said, 'I remember the Shavuot feast, when they stole all our food and we could find nothing to eat.'

From our comrades in the village we went on to talk about the other groups in Poland, where young men and women were living to prepare themselves for work in the Land, and thus we came to speak of Hannah, the daughter of that righteous man Reb Hayim, may he rest in peace. She was still living in exile and waiting for Zvi to bring her up to the Land of Israel.

'And who gave you an immigration certificate?' I asked Zvi. He laid his hand on his heart and answered, 'I myself am my own certificate.' I thought he meant that he kept his certificate over his heart, and asked no more. But the end showed that this was not so.

Let me leave Zvi and go back to myself, and my wife and children. My wife and I also hired two deck chairs, and we sat and talked about everything that came into our heads and onto our tongues. There were many, many things to talk about—no book could contain them.

So we sat and talked about the days we had endured abroad and the days that were in store for us in the Land. There were many, many things to talk about; many books could not contain them.

'I am tired of living abroad,' said my wife. 'To all appearances, I was short of nothing, for our relatives tried to make our stay pleasant, but I missed the Land of Israel.'

'What were you short of there?' I asked the children. And since I was in a good mood I spoke up in the defense of that rabbi who did not know the Hebrew for a footstool.

'Because his mind was floating among matters of the highest import he did not pay attention to something as low as a footstool,' I said to the children. 'Children,' I said to them, 'didn't you hear that rabbi singing the praises of Israel? Didn't you hear him saying that Israel is a light to the Gentiles?' 'Father,' said my daughter, 'what are you talking about? He compared Israel to the Greeks.' 'What's wrong with comparing Israel to the Greeks?' said I. 'The Greeks were a wise and clever people, weren't they?' My daughter laughed and said, 'But then they bowed down to idols.' 'What of it?' said my son. 'They used to make dolls and play with them. You make dolls, too, don't you?' 'When I was a little child I played with dolls,' my daughter answered, 'but they did it even when they were big.' 'Praised be your good sense,' I said to my daughter. 'Now tell me what you did all the time. Did you finish all the *Tales from the Scriptures*?' 'You are laughing at me, Father,' said my daughter, 'I studied the Bible itself.'

Several people had gathered around; they stood listening to the children's conversation and praised them for their cleverness. I said to one of them, 'When a child says something clever, you should stop him before he lets slip something foolish.' So I stopped the children's conversation and talked with the people in my company about the education of the younger generation and the way they study the Bible, which makes the Holy Scriptures an everyday matter. Some said one thing and some another. I told them the story of that old man from the village who came to the Beit Midrash and heard the story of David and Goliath and the story of Bathsheba. Everyone laughed, until their laughter could be heard from one end of the ship to the other. But, as is usual with most people, they drew no moral from the story.

So we sat and talked. We talked about everything under the sun, about the great world and our little country, about summer and winter, sea and dry land. Finally I turned away from my company and turned to my children. I tested them in the Bible and made the time pass pleasantly with questions, such as: 'Where is the place where they threw Jonah into the sea?' And they replied, 'Ask the fishes and they will tell you.'

My dear friends, it would be a good thing if we could make a good ending to our story, especially as we have arrived at the good Land. But since the day we were exiled from our Land, there is no good without evil. When the ship was approaching Jaffa, Zvi jumped into the sea, because the authorities had not given him a certificate to enter the Land, and he relied on the waves to bring him to the shore. The waves were kind at that time; each wave handed him over to the next, and that one to the next again. But rocks and reefs, whose hearts are hearts of stone, struck him, and his blood flowed from their wounds. And when he escaped from the rocks and reefs, the authorities surrounded him and seized him and took him to their hospital, until he should return to health and they should return him into exile.

CHAPTER NINE AND SEVENTY

The Find

Zvi's misfortune abated my joy. After I had brought my wife and children to Jerusalem, I went to a number of men in authority to beg mercy for Zvi. Just as those rocks on which he struck were not softened, neither were the hearts of the men in authority. When I saw that this was useless, I went to the distinguished men of the day. When I saw that they were useless, I went to the leaders of the community. When I saw that they were useless I went to the public benefactors. When I saw that they were useless, I went to the lovers of charity. When I saw that they were useless, I relied on our Father in heaven.

In the meantime I stayed with my family in a certain hotel. The owners of the hotel treated me as a guest and also as a resident. At mealtimes they waited first on the guests from abroad, and when it came to paying the bill they demanded a great deal of money, as is usual with foreign guests.

It is hard to be a guest abroad, and all the more so in the

Land of Israel. So we rented a little house and bought a little
furniture. I put in the few books the marauders had left me
and sent the children to school. I set to and arranged my old
books, while my wife arranged the furniture. When I saw my
books arranged in orderly fashion in the bookcase and my
things lying in their places, I breathed a sigh of relief. For
over a year I had been wandering about in foreign lands, like
a guest for the night, and suddenly I was living in my own
house, among my belongings and my books, with my wife and
children.

Zvi's troubles overclouded my spirits. I tried to put them
out of my mind, but I could not succeed in putting them out
of my heart. In the meantime I started looking after my own
affairs and began to divert my attention from others. That is
the way of the world: people are more concerned for their
own fingernail than for someone else's whole body. Finally,
the story of Zvi slipped out of my mind entirely, and if his
name had not been mentioned in the papers among those who
were sent back abroad, I should have forgotten him.

As I sat in my own niche and enjoyed the peace of my
house I began putting out of my mind all that had happened
in Szibucz; I no longer saw before my eyes the hotel, its
owners and its guests, and the old Beit Midrash, with all those
who had come to pray and those who had not come to pray.
If I remembered them, I did so only to put them out of my
heart again, like a man who sits tranquilly in his home and
pays no attention to other men's troubles.

So I sat in the shadow of sweet tranquillity with my wife
and children—that sweet tranquillity which no man savors except when he is sitting in his own home. I occupied myself
with my affairs, and my wife with hers. One day she was
going through my pieces of luggage and laid them out in the
sun. Then she took my satchels to mend them, for through
much use the leather inside had been torn and holes had
appeared. While she was busy with the satchels she called out
to me and asked, 'What is this?' I saw she was holding a big
key that she had found in the crevices of one of the satchels.
I was stunned and astonished. It was the key of our old Beit
Midrash. But I had given it as a gift to Yeruham Freeman's

son on the day he entered into the Covenant of Abraham, so how had it made its way here? No doubt Yeruham Freeman, who had freed himself from all the commandments, was not pleased that I had made his son the guardian of the old Beit Midrash, and had hidden the key in the satchel so as to give it back to me. As I was feeling angry with Yeruham for returning me the key, my wife handed it to me and I saw that this was not the key the old locksmith had made. It was the key the elders of the old Beit Midrash had handed over to me on the Day of Atonement just before the Closing Service. A thousand times I had sought it, a thousand times I had despaired of it, a thousand times I had sought it again without finding it, and had had another key made, and now, when I had no need of one or the other, it had come back to me. How had it disappeared and how had it appeared again? No doubt one day I had left it in my satchel and it had slipped into a hole so that I could not see it, or perhaps on the day when I put on my new coat I had taken out the key from my summer clothes to put it in my winter clothes and forgotten it. How much sorrow and distress, how much trouble I would have avoided if I had had the key at the right time! But there is no argument against the past. After I had recovered somewhat from my emotions, I told the whole story to my wife, who knew nothing of it, because I had not mentioned it in my letters, for I had wanted to explain the whole matter in detail and had not managed to write before the key was lost, and once it was lost I did not mention it in my letters.

'What are you thinking of doing with the key?' said my wife, 'send it to Szibucz?' 'The one they have is superfluous,' said I, 'and you tell me to burden them with a second key!' 'Well,' said my wife, 'what will you do with it?' There came into my mouth the saying of our sages, of blessed memory: 'The synagogues and Batei Midrashot abroad are destined to be established in the Land of Israel.' And I said to myself: When they establish themselves in the Land of Israel, this man will have the key in his possession.

So I rose and put the key in a box, and hung the key of the box over my heart. I did not hang the key of the old Beit Midrash over my heart, for it was too heavy for my heart to bear; the early craftsmen used to make their keys too big and heavy for the measure of our hearts.

The key being put away in its place, I returned to my work, and whenever I remembered it, I would repeat to myself: 'The synagogues and the Batei Midrashot are destined . . . ,' and I would open my window and look outside to see if perhaps they were making their way to establish themselves in the Land of Israel. Alas, the land was desolate and silent, and the sound of the steps of the synagogues and Batei Midrashot was not heard. And still the key lies there, waiting with me for that day. However, it is made of iron and brass, and it can wait, but I, who am flesh and blood, find it hard to endure.

CHAPTER EIGHTY

The End of the Story

Let us leave the key and turn to the owner of the key. I sit in my house and do my work. People come to visit me and ask me about what I saw over there in the land of exile and I ask them about all that has happened here in the Land of Israel. As we talk, the Holy One, blessed be He, brings Szibucz before my eyes, and I close my eyes for a little while and walk among its ruins. Sometimes I stretch out my hand and wish to talk with someone from there.

After a few days I set aside all my affairs and went up to Ramat Rahel to visit Reb Shlomo Bach. I found him standing in the vegetable garden, busy hoeing. The back of his neck was sunburnt and his movements were measured, like those whose business is with the soil. I greeted him and he returned my greeting. When he recognized me, he put down his tools and sat down with me.

I told him about Daniel his son, and Sara Pearl, Daniel's wife, and Raphael and Erela, as well as about the people from our old Beit Midrash who had gone away, some to America and some elsewhere. I also told him about the other people of Szibucz, whether he asked about them or not. Thus Szibucz was privileged to be recalled in Jerusalem.

'How did you come to work in the garden?' I asked him. 'When I came to Ramat Rahel,' he replied, 'and saw that they were all engaged in settling the Land, I said to myself: Everyone is engaged in settling the Land and I am doing nothing. So I asked them to make me a teacher for the children and a cantor in our little congregation. But the old men have no need for a permanent cantor, because each of them knows how to lead the service, and the children have their own teachers and do not need this old man. When I saw that I was superfluous, I felt as if the world had darkened, so I lightened the gloom with the Torah and immersed myself in the Mishna. When I reached the tractates that deal with the religious duties that are linked to the soil of the Land of Israel, I saw that my learning was rootless. I had studied these matters abroad and found no difficulty in them, but in the Land of Israel a man's mind is renewed and he is not content with his earlier interpretations. Once I said to myself: Let me go and see what is this tree of which the sages spoke, and what is this field that is mentioned in the Mishna. When I went out, I heard the young men talking to each other, and through their words the entire subject became clear. It was not that they were referring to the Mishna, but they spoke as usual about trees and plants. I said to myself, "Wisdom cries outdoors." After that, whenever I found a difficulty in the words of the Mishna I would go to one of our comrades. If he did not know, then the gardener knew. If he did not know how to explain in our way, he explained in his own way and showed me every single thing in tangible fashion. I found out from my own experience, "Better is the sight of the eyes than the wandering of the desire." I need not say much more; the sages were right when they said, "There is no Torah like the Torah of the Land of Israel." Here I am, some seventy years old, and I was not privileged to understand the truth of the Torah until I came to the Land.'

And Reb Shlomo continued, 'Learning leads to doing. As a result of my meetings with the gardener, I was not sitting idle. When he watered the plants, I filled the vessels with water. When he dug out the thorns, I cleared them from the path. This way, I learned how to water a garden and take out the weeds and make hollows around the vines, how to plow and sow and plant. When our comrades saw this, they gave me a patch to grow vegetables, and if the Almighty grants me the privilege, I shall eat the fruits of my patch.'

And Reb Shlomo continued, 'Our young comrades are pleased with me and call me comrade, which is a title of honor and a high degree in the scale of workers. Our old comrades are not pleased with me, for since I work they think I am trying to make myself popular with the members of the kvutza. So long as I am engaged in my work, I pay no heed to what they say, but now that I have stopped working for a while I remember them.' Before I took my leave of Reb Shlomo, he showed me all the things he had planted, and brought me to the children's house, where he showed me his grandson Amnon. God grant he may be like his father and grandfather.

One more time I went up to Ramat Rahel to visit Reb Shlomo. He was standing in the middle of his patch, while the birds flew over his head and pecked at the trees. 'Is it possible that the birds should peck at the trees and the gardener does not drive them away?' said I. 'I have many joys in the Land,' Reb Shlomo replied, 'but above them all I rejoice in the birds, for they are witnesses that our redemption is at hand. We find in the Midrash: "For fifty-two years no bird was seen flying in the Land of Israel." Now that the birds have returned to this place it is a sign that Israel will return to their nests.' From the birds of heaven, Reb Shlomo went on to domestic fowl.

He took me and brought me to a place where the chickens were kept, and showed me fowl so fat that their fat had weakened their wings, and children were standing throwing them crumbs. He, too, took some scraps from his pocket and gave them to Amnon his grandson, so that he should give them to the birds. 'If you think they keep the birds for food,' said he, 'I must tell you that most of our young comrades eat no meat.' And having mentioned his comrades he immediately began to sing their praises.

A few days later Reb Shlomo came to my house to tell me the good news that Hannele his son's daughter (this was Hannah, namely Aniela, otherwise Erela) had become betrothed to a certain doctor called Jacob Milch. I congratulated Reb Shlomo, we drank to their good health, and I told him what a fine man Kuba was. 'I am certain,' I said to Reb Shlomo, 'that the couple will soon come up to the Land of Israel, and it will be a good thing for you to have relatives in the Land. Sometimes they will come to visit you, and sometimes you will go to visit them, especially on festivals, when a man wishes to sit with his family.'

So we sat for some time and talked, until evening approached and the time came for the Afternoon Service. Reb Shlomo rose and asked, 'Which side is the East?' I showed him from my window the direction of the Holy Temple. He sighed, washed his hands, and prayed. After he had completed his prayer I said to him, 'Perhaps you would leave the congregation in Ramat Rahel and pray with me.' 'There is a quorum there without me, thank God,' said Reb Shlomo.

From this the talk turned to the old men in the kvutza, who kept quarreling with each other about every little thing, for each of them believed that the Torah had been given in his town alone, and every custom that he had not seen in his town did not seem to him to be a Jewish custom at all. 'Perhaps you would like to go back,' I said to Reb Shlomo. 'Where?' 'To Szibucz,' I said. He looked at me like a deaf man who can neither hear nor speak. 'If you hurry,' I said, 'you will arrive in time for Erela's wedding. And if you wish to sit and study there I will give you the key of our old Beit Midrash.' I rose, opened the box and showed him the key, telling him the whole story. 'Here is the key before you,' I said. 'You can take the key and go back to Szibucz.' Reb Shlomo smiled and said, 'If the Almighty helps me I will sit and wait here for the footsteps of the Messiah.'

'If so,' I said to the key, 'you stay here with me.' The key was silent and gave no answer, first, because it was an inanimate thing and could not speak, and second, because the people in the Beit Midrash had already discussed that matter on the day they gave it to me.

After some time the old man took his leave of me. I went with him to see him on his way. When we reached the crossroads we parted, he going to his home and I to mine. I turned my head and saw that the birds were flying above his head. The fowl of the heavens, who had returned to the Land of Israel, were flying to accompany the old man who was returning to his nest.

I went into my house, put away the key in the box, locked the box on the outside, and hung the key over my heart. I know that no one is enthusiastic about the key of our old Beit Midrash, but I said to myself: One day our old Beit Midrash is destined to be established in the Land of Israel; better, then, for the key to be in my possession.

Here endeth the story of that man of whom we have spoken in this work that is before us, since he has returned to his home and is no longer in the category of a guest.

Nevertheless, let us tell a little more about Yeruham and Rachel. They live in peace and their son is growing up and giving pleasure to them, to his grandfather and grandmother, and also to his aunt Babtchi, who consoles herself with her sister's son. Kuba and Erela are preparing to settle in the Land of Israel, Schutzling asks me to send him an immigration certificate for his son, and Genendel asks for a handful of dust from the Land to give her contentment after her death. What Genendel wanted for her body, Leibtche Bodenhaus has done for his soul: he has sent a copy of his book to our National Library, so that he may be remembered in Jerusalem.

What else can we tell that we have not yet told? Daniel Bach strolls in the town or sits in front of his son Raphael, who lies on his bed and sees dreams the whole world over. When they have nothing to eat, they pin their hopes on those children that Sara Pearl as midwife will one day help bring into the world, those who in the future will build houses for themselves and buy beams for building and wood for their stoves.

What else can we tell? Every day letters come for me from Szibucz. Zippora has recovered and is firm on her feet. But what is the good of feet to one who has nothing to do with them? So long as her father was alive she used to go and

visit him: now he is dead, she has nowhere to go, so she sits
at home with her sister Hannah and weeps with her for Zvi,
who was sent back from the Land of Israel, and between one
time of tears and another they hope for divine mercy.

All Szibucz waits for the divine mercy, each in his own
way; trade is bad and no one earns enough for food, and if a
man earns a zloty the government comes and takes half for
taxes and half for levies. On the other hand, Antos and Zwirn
grow steadily richer, but I doubt whether that is any consolation.

There are other people in Szibucz with whom we have had
to do and of whom we have not yet written, such as Reuben
and Simon, Levi and Judah, or the tailor and his wife, or that
old man who made a key for our old Beit Midrash, or the
people of Gordonia, or all the other sons of Szibucz; but there
is a covenant made for the Land of Israel that whoever does
not settle in the Land is forgotten in the end, but everyone
who has the privilege will be remembered and written of in
the Land, as it is said (Isaiah, chapter 4), 'Everyone who is
written for life in Jerusalem.'

Now let us see what happened to that man who will live
in Jerusalem and what he did in the Land; or rather—since he
is settled in the Land and is only a tiny grain of its soil—who
will deal with a single grain when the whole Land is before
him?

The story of the guest is ended; his doings in Szibucz are
done.

Glossary

ADAR: Hebrew month; February or March.

ADDITIONAL SERVICE (*Musaf*): prayer service on the Sabbath and holidays, recited after the general Morning Prayer.

AFIKOMEN (*afikoman*): piece of matzoh eaten at the conclusion of the Seder.

AGADA: portions of the Talmud dealing with non-legal materials.

AKDAMUT: hymn recited on the Feast of Weeks (*Shavuot*) preceding the reading from the Torah.

RABBI AKIBA: leading Palestinian teacher of the second century C.E.

AL-FASI: Isaac Al-Fasi (eleventh century), author of a famous talmudic compilation.

ARBA TURIM: compendium of Jewish law by Jacob ben Asher (thirteenth-fourteenth centuries).

ASHKENAZI: pertaining to the Ashkenazim, Jews of the central European tradition, as opposed to Sephardim, Jews of the Spanish tradition, from whom they differ in ritual and in their pronunciation of Hebrew.

ASHREI ("happy"): the opening word in Psalms 84:5 and 144:15, recited in the Afternoon Prayer.

BAAL SHEM TOV ("Master of the Good Name"): founder of the hasidic movement (eighteenth century).

BEIT MIDRASH (*pl.* Batei Midrashot): House of Study, a place of learning and worship. Usually identical with the House of Prayer.

CHAJES, ZVI PEREZ (1876–1927): Chief Rabbi of Vienna, 1918–27.

CLOSING MEAL: meal preceding the fast on the Day of Atonement.

DAY OF ATONEMENT (*Yom Kippur*): the tenth of the Days of Awe, which start with the New Year's Day; a day of prayer, fasting, and forgiveness of sin.

DAYAN: member of a Jewish religious court; authority in ritual questions.

EIGHTEEN BENEDICTIONS: one of the oldest parts of the Jewish liturgy, occurring in the weekday prayer service.

EIN YAAKOV: compendium of non-legal sections from the Babylonian Talmud, by Jacob ibn Habib of Zamora (fifteenth-sixteenth centuries).

FESTIVAL OF TABERNACLES (*Sukkot*): an eight-day holiday, beginning on the fifth day after the Day of Atonement. It commemorates the wandering of the Israelites in the desert.

FOUR SPECIES: citrus (*etrog*), palm branch (*lulav*), myrtle, and willow branch, used in the prayer service on the Festival of Tabernacles.

RABBI GADIEL THE INFANT: a legendary creature of small size and great learning, known for his wondrous deeds.

GEHENNA: the Valley of Hinnom, represents the idea of Hell.

GEMARA ("completion"): part of the Talmud consisting of discussions of the Mishna. There is a distinction between the Gemara of the Babylonian Talmud and that of the Palestinian Talmud.

GENIZA: repository for Hebrew writings no longer in use; particularly applied to the one in the Ezra Synagogue in Cairo.

GUIDE TO THE PERPLEXED (*More Nevukhim*): work in religious philosophy by Moses ben Maimon (Maimonides), twelfth century.

HAGGADAH: the text of the Passover home service.

RAV HAI GAON: leading talmudic authority in Babylonia, tenth-eleventh centuries.

ELEAZAR HAKALIR: influential liturgic poet in the early Middle Ages.

HALACHA ("path"): law; portions of the Talmud dealing with legal materials and proper observance.

HANUKKAH ("dedication"): an eight-day holiday (Feast of Lights) beginning on the twenty-fifth day of Kislev (November or December), commemorating the re-dedication of the Sanctuary by the Maccabees (167 B.C.E.).

HASID (*lit.,* a pious man): a follower of Hasidism, religious movement founded by the Baal Shem Tov.

HAVDALA ("separation" of the sacred and the profane): benediction at the conclusion of the Sabbath and holidays.

KABBALAH ("tradition"): Jewish mysticism; its writings pointed to the deeper layers of religion, which it represented as the authentic "tradition" of Israel.

KADDISH: prayer recited by mourners.

KASHRUTH: dietary laws and practices.

KERITOT: talmudic tractate.

KIDDUSH ("sanctification"): benediction pronounced over wine at the commencement of the Sabbath and holidays.

KLEISEL (*pl.* kleislech): a small *klois* (see next entry).

KLOIS (*pl.* kloisen): name given from sixteenth century on in Central and Eastern Europe to a house of talmudic study, usually attached to a synagogue.

KOHEN (*pl.* Kohanim): priest, descendant of Aaron.

KVUTZA (*pl.* kvutzot): collective settlement in the Land of Israel.

LAG B'OMER: the thirty-third day of a counting of days that begins with the second day of Passover and ends with the Feast of Weeks. Festive occasions banned in this period are permitted on this day.

MAIMONIDES (Moses ben Maimon): most prominent medieval Jewish philosopher; see "Guide to the Perplexed."

MECHILTA: a midrashic work on the Book of Exodus.

MEZUZA: parchment scroll containing scriptural texts, attached to the doorpost of a Jewish home.

MIKVEH: ritual bath.

MINYAN: quorum of ten men necessary for a communal religious service.

MISHNA ("repetition"): compilation of legal teachings made by Judah Ha-Nasi about 220 C.E., which forms the basis of the Talmud.

MISNAGED (pl. Misnagdim): opponent of Hasidism.

MIZRACHI: party of religious Zionists.

MOHEL: circumciser.

NASO: a weekly portion (from the Book of Numbers).

NINTH OF AV: fast commemorating the destructions of Jerusalem.

NORDAU, MAX: author and Zionist leader (1849–1923).

PASSOVER (Pesah): eight-day holiday (in Israel, seven days) occurring in the Spring and commemorating the exodus from Egypt.

PENITENTIAL PRAYERS (Selichot): recited at night in the period preceding the Days of Awe and on the Days of Awe, except the New Year's Day.

RABBINER: German for rabbi.

RASHI: Rabbi Solomon ben Isaac, classical commentator (eleventh century) on the Bible and the Babylonian Talmud.

REB: Mister; sometimes rabbi.

REBETZIN: a rabbi's wife.

REVISIONISTS: party of activist Zionists.

SANDAK: godfather, a person chosen to hold the child during the ceremony of circumcision.

SANHEDRIN: the high council in the time of the Second Temple. Also, a talmudic tractate.

SEDER ("order"): the festive meal and home service on the first and second (in Israel, only the first) night of Passover.

SEPHARDI: pertaining to the Sephardim, descendants of the Spanish Jewish community, expelled from Spain at the end of the fifteenth century (cf. "Ashkenazi").

SHAVUOT (Feast of Weeks): a two-day holiday (in Israel, one day), seven weeks after Passover. It is a feast of first fruits and a season dedicated to the memory of the revelation on Mount Sinai.

SHILECHEL (pl. shilechlech): a small house of prayer ("shil").

SHTIBEL (pl. shtiblech): a prayer room.

SHTREIMEL: festive headgear of Eastern European Jews.

SHULCHAN ARUCH ("Arranged Table"): rabbinical code compiled by Joseph Karo, sixteenth century.

SIFRE, SIFRA: midrashic works on Leviticus and Numbers, respectively.

SUCCAH ("booth," "tabernacle"): simple shelter lived in during the holiday of Sukkot, the Feast of Tabernacles.

TAHANUN: a prayer of supplication, recited on certain weekdays.

TALLIT (pl. tallitot): prayer shawl; worn by male adults at Morning Prayer.

TASHLICH: ceremony of the "casting off" of sins on the New Year's Day.

TEFILLIN: phylacteries.

THIRTY-SIX SAINTS: perfectly just people in any given generation; their identity is unknown; their existence is necessary for the security and survival of the world.

THREE DAYS OF CIRCUMSCRIPTION: preceding the Feast of Weeks.

TISH'A B'AV (the "Ninth Day of Av"): a day of fasting in

memory of the destruction of the First Temple by the Baby-
lonians and the Second Temple by the Romans.

TOHU and BOHU: chaos; see Genesis 1:2.

TOSEFTA ("addition"): a collection of teachings of the first
two centuries C.E., related to the Mishna.

TZITZIT: fringes at the four corners of the prayer shawl.

ZADDIK ("the righteous one"): title given to the leader of a
hasidic community.

ZOHAR ("The Book of Splendor"): chief work of the earlier
Kabbalah (end of thirteenth century).

Publisher's Note

The Hebrew original of this novel appeared under the title *Oreah nata lalun* as volume VII of the first edition of Agnon's works (Schocken Publishing House, Jerusalem, 1939). The title is a phrase taken from Jeremiah 14:8. The work was reprinted several times; a definitive, revised version was issued as volume IV of the Schocken-Haaretz edition of Agnon's narratives (Jerusalem-Tel Aviv, 1953). The basic translation into English is the work of Misha Louvish. For the rendition in its present form the publisher had the cooperation of Professors Naftali C. Brandwein, Allen Mandelbaum, and Oscar Shaftel.